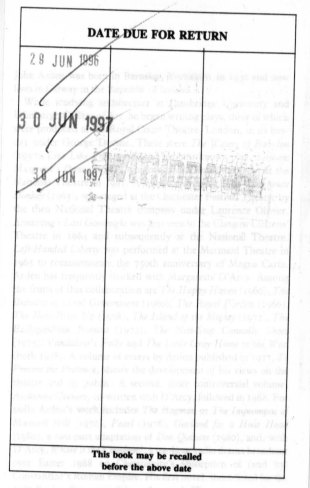

Also by John Arden

Fiction
Silence Among the Weapons – A Novel

Non-Fiction
To Present the Pretence – Essays

Plays
Serjeant Musgrave's Dance
The Waters of Babylon
Live Like Pigs
The Happy Haven
The Workhouse Donkey
Ironhand (*adapted from Goethe's*
Goetz von Berlichingen)
Left-Handed Liberty
Armstrong's Last Goodnight
Soldier, Soldier and Other Plays
Two Autobiographical Plays
Pearl

With Margaretta D'Arcy
The Business of Good Government
The Hero Rises Up
The Island of the Mighty
The Royal Pardon
The Little Gray Home in the West
The Non-Stop Connolly Show
Vandaleur's Folly
Whose is the Kingdom?
Awkward Corners – Essays

Books of Bale

A Fiction of History

JOHN ARDEN

Methuen · Minerva

1000407740

A Minerva Paperback

BOOKS OF BALE

First published in Great Britain 1988
by Methuen London
This Minerva edition published 1989
by Methuen · Mandarin
Michelin House, 81 Fulham Road, London SW3 6RB

Minerva is an imprint of the Octopus Publishing Group
Copyright © John Arden 1988

British Library Cataloguing in Publication Data

Arden, John, *1930–*
Books of Bale.
I. Title
823′.914[F]

ISBN 0-7493-9030-1

Printed in Great Britain by
Cox & Wyman Ltd, Reading, Berks.

BALE, John (1495–1563), Bishop of Ossory in Ireland, and author of a number of anti-Catholic plays, of which the greater part formed a long Miracle play, now lost. His existing works, which include Morality plays and a translation of Kirchmayer's *Pammachius*, are filled with coarse and incessant abuse of popery and priests. The most important is *Kynge Johan* (1538), which may claim to rank as the first historical drama in English literature. In its mingling of such abstract figures as Sedition, Clergy, and England, and the historical King John and Cardinal Pandolphus, the play forms a link between the medieval and the Elizabethan drama.

· *The Oxford Companion to the Theatre*

*

And he saith unto me, Seal not the sayings of the prophecy of this book: for the time is at hand.

And the spirit and the bride say: Come. And let him that heareth, say also: Come. And let him that is a-thirst, come.

(*Revelation of St John the Divine*, Chapter 22)

For Margaretta:
and for all those other artists (non-professional or professional, unsubsidised or subsidised, quiet or loud, comic or tragic, spectacular or intimate, or plain-faced un-self-conscious human) who came to join her during two full months of the teeming spring of '86 on the steps of the Arts Council in Dublin: and gave their voices and the heart of their fantasy to the open streets of the city and to the people who passed through them:
ignoring and defying the hands of Hierarchy, Coercion, Censorship, Faction, Covetousness and Avarice when they sought to grip hold upon, and make prey of, the Freedom of Art.

CONTENTS

AUTHOR'S NOTE

I have called this a 'fiction of history' because the central thread of the whole story is necessarily invented: documented history tells us most of the salient facts about John Bale, except the one that is of real interest to the novelist – whom did he marry? We know her Christian name was Dorothy, but we do not know her surname, nor where she came from, nor her age, nor her trade, nor if she had been 'spinster' or 'widow' or even (like Frau Luther) a nun. We know of two sons (at least we know Bale had two sons: it is assumed that Dorothy was their mother), we know of her ordeal before the Norwich magistrates, we know the year of her death and the location of her burial, we know she went to Ireland with her husband (but, very strangely, considering all the other details of Bale's Kilkenny experience given in his *Vocation*, not a word of how she got out of that country). And nothing else. So Dorothy, in my account, is fiction. So is Thomas Cromwell's minstrel-troupe (although his acting-company did exist, and John Bale ran it).

Lydia is fiction too (and therefore her family). There is no record of Bale having had a daughter: and no mention that any of his children were with him in Ireland. But if, in the casual machismo of sixteenth-century conventions, Bale could not be bothered to tell us whether his wife was or was not with him when the privateers kidnapped him, so equally he might not have thought a female offspring worth mention anywhere. Most of the references to his family are only incidental, used by him to illustrate some point in his polemical writings.

It is perhaps a little strong to make Bale's grand-daughter grow up to be a famous mystery-woman of literature. My excuse for this melodrama is that I needed to create some human link between Bale's theatre and that of the more celebrated Elizabethans. The artistic link is well-enough expounded by academic authorities, but that won't do for a novel. I ought to say that Anthony Munday's hand in *The Troublesome Reign of King John* is by no means accepted by all these authorities, nor is my suggestion of that play's relationship to Shakespeare's. Munday did collaborate on *Sir John Oldcastle*, he did write a pair of Robin Hood plays set in John's reign, and he is thought to have had a hand in *Sir Thomas More*. He is certainly known to have been (at least in his youth) an anti-papal government agent. It is possible I have libelled him dreadfully.

I may also have libelled Lord Wentworth, about whom history says little except to give the barest facts of his various royal appointments and tasks. But Bale did attribute to him his own conversion to Protestantism: and rumours appear to have been current among Bale's Catholic opponents that Wentworth seduced him into the re-formed camp by pandering to his lechery. Such accusations were par-for-the-course at that era, and were thrown about indiscriminately by all factions: only a fiction-writer would attach importance to them. There is a Holbein drawing of Wentworth; later made into an oil painting (now in the National Portrait Gallery) by, apparently, another hand. From the drawing, rather than the painting, I tried subjectively to deduce what might have been his character. I do not know at all whether he was friends with Sir Thomas Wyatt.

I have invented Proinsias Dubh: it seemed a good idea to counteract Bale's views on Ireland by an opinion from someone of Bale's own trade (poet rather than churchman). The more so as Irish poets were politically important at this period, although Bale did not seem concerned about them himself. There really was an Ó Dálaigh poets'-school at Finavarra in County Clare: a little obelisk marks its site today. The Smerwick massacre did take place, and became something of an obsession with Edmund Spenser. He devotes a great part of Book V of *The Faerie Queen* to a justification of the atrocity.

I have invented Konrad Spielmann. I have invented the 'Birdcage', which is rather a large invention: if there had really been such an establishment, it could hardly have been kept out of all the history-books. I took the idea of it from a TV documentary I saw recently, about a somewhat similar place in present-day Bombay; on a lengthy visit to India in 1969–70 I was very struck by the 'mediaeval' aspects of popular entertainment there, and I have consciously transferred much of its atmosphere to sixteenth-century England.

I would like to express my gratitude for the help I have had in finding things out about the background to my story. Particularly to:

Peter Happé (editor of Bale's plays), who sent me some much-needed information about the playwright's life and his marriage.

Hubert Butler of Kilkenny, who introduced me to that city and to many kind people there who were of great assistance to me.

Maurice Craig of Dublin, architectural historian, for his information about the Irish capital in Bale's period.

Jeff O'Connell of Kinvara, Co Galway, who found the essential text of Bale's *Vocation* for me in the recesses of Ireland's National University library-archives.

Mrs Mary Joyce of Corrandulla, Co Galway, for the various Irish-language words and phrases used in Book VI.

My main intention in writing *Books Of Bale* has been to attempt to reconcile two very variant notions of its hero, as obtained (1) from literary historians and (2) from historians of Ireland. On the one hand we have an important pioneer playwright of revolutionary zeal, on the other we find ourselves invited to wonder at the violent cultural colonialism of a tactless and coercive bishop. Neither set of authorities seems in general to incorporate the insights of the other (the same problem applies to comments on Spenser and Ralegh): connection is too rarely made between the achievements of English literature and the disgraces of English imperialism.

Some readers may feel I have given the Catholic cause unacceptably short shrift in my narrative. If this is so, it is because I have been trying to see the whole thing from the reformers' point of view, not necessarily the most romantic or attractive side of the question for writers. H. F. M. Prescott's splendid *The Man On A Donkey* would be a useful corrective here: I read it many years ago and kept remembering it as I wrote.

Direct quotations from the Bible are from the Wycliffe or Coverdale versions, whichever seemed most appropriate in the context.

J.A.
Co Galway, Ireland,
November 1987

CHILD AND GRANDCHILD

(1)

Rape Of Lucrece

She was born in a Christian city, Canterbury; in the reign of a Christian Queen, Elizabeth: to Christian parents who felt at last safe from the burnings and torture of the servants of Christ's Opposite. The Man of Rome, the foretold Beast, the new Nero of the Vatican, still spread his enormities wide and alive, and most observably in aggressive Spain; but from England, God be praised, their influence was all but expelled. Foreign invasion permitting, baby Lucretia could expect a life of true liberty and godly contentment. Provided she encouraged her character to be shaped by her auspicious name.

'Lucretia' was selected for her by her father. He knew what he did. He bore in mind the *Book of Genesis*, where it tells how Adam chose the names for all God's creatures and so confirmed his human dominion over them. Lucretia's mother was not asked for her agreement: it being notable, in the same book, that there was as yet no Eve when the name-giving took place. The rib-removal came later. Some of his friends asked, why a pagan name? Why, of all things, a name of *Rome*? God's elect in Canterbury should not be reminded of idols every time they called children from play. But Mr Lowlyheart rebuked their ignorance. He was proud of his Latinity, and it offered him an allegory which was Christian enough – immoveable moon-pure-chastity-to-the-point-of-death: surely Providence had here inserted into ancient legend one of those prior revelations which all sound Christian scholars should be ready to recognise? Besides, the inherited surname was itself so evocative of the Sermon on the Mount. 'Lucretia Lowlyheart': the conjuncture must make a woman thoroughly meek, clean-living, and respectful of the reputations, first of her father, and then one day (the Lord willing) of her husband. Mr Lowlyheart was sure of it, he had chosen the name himself.

He was a pedant, both by trade and personality, continuously pleased with himself for having married a bishop's daughter. His opinion of the school he kept was far higher than the actual status of the establishment itself. For it was no more than a parish school for young boys below puberty – and they were no more than the sons of moderate tradesmen. Yet it was without doubt the *best* parish school, the only one to offer full preparation for the arduous King's Grammar School. To the delight of the Vicar (and the irritation of the clergy of all the other Canterbury parishes), children came to Mr Lowlyheart from every quarter of the town. With the permission of the church-wardens he was paid a personal extra-stipendiary fee by the father of each extra-parochial child: and he told himself he deserved it. He enforced by rote into his pupils the alphabet, a limited arithmetic, a great deal of Protestant scripture, even the Latin and Greek rudiments: six days of every week year after year he whipped their little arses like wildfire. He swore he would not die until he had seen one of them Archbishop.

His own sons suffered equally, indeed more than equally, for they were available to his hand on the seventh day as well. He did not consider that the Lord's Day regulations excluded godly chastisement, which he called 'dragging the ox (or the ass) out of the pit', and reinforced with a hoarse rendering of the fourteenth chapter of *Saint Luke*. The whipping of his daughters was left to Mrs Lowlyheart, as being more decent. So was their education – until, that is to say, the year of 1591: when all of a sudden it was as though the earth had fallen open and swallowed up his entire life.

By then all his sons had superannuated themselves from his schoolroom, to the King's School, and thence to Cambridge: indeed, the eldest was already married and held a cure of souls in a village near Dover. The two elder girls were also married, to Canterbury parsons. Lucretia, alone of the brood, remained at home under her mother's care. Mr Lowlyheart had little to do with her: he was growing old and spent most of his spare time in his study among his books. He was affectionately aware of his daughter about the house, hard at work in the kitchen, the herb-garden, the sewing-closet. He assumed she was being taught all that a quiet maiden in a cathedral city needed to know, and nothing else. One day she too would have her husband found for her. He hoped it would be a clergyman; failing which, a scholar or an attorney would do. Now and then he had her repeat long portions of Holy Writ, or the Thirty-nine Articles, and she nearly always knew them very well. Mrs Lowlyheart was most competent. He thanked God that he should have chosen her.

And then: the Day came. Lucretia's sixteenth birthday. A brilliant

October morning with an ominous cold wind. Her father's gift to her was a book, a religious treatise by her grandfather – Bishop Bale, twenty-eight years dead, a strong reformer, one of the first to bring the True Word among the romanists of unreconciled Ireland. Her expression of gratitude, prompted in secret by her mother, was a rehearsed speech which pretended to be extemporary. Between morning prayer and her bowl of breakfast gruel, she curtseyed very decorously, and began: "Honoured father, my duty toward you . . .", etcetera. It was not a new idea, the small Lowlyhearts had followed this routine every year since they could first utter: but this time it was startling, even shocking, to the schoolmaster's ears. For a part of it was in Latin, and another part in Greek, and at the end she even ventured into two or three words of Hebrew. Her mother looked so proud of her, and Lucretia too looked proud – or at least it appeared she was expecting unusual praise.

For a moment her father was unable to speak. He had not had the smallest hint that these languages were being taught to her. And who had taught them, who? What strangers had been in his house, competing with his function? He made a strangulated effort, let loose a broken phrase of commendation, congratulation, he scarcely knew what, and shot out across the yard to the schoolroom with his gown half-on half-off, as though there was an alarm of fire.

All that morning he took his lessons in an uneven and virulent distraction, slapping the pupils' heads, forgetting their names, dropping his books on the table or the floor. His senior class had been set to learn the sixteenth chapter of the *Book of Numbers*, how Korah, Dathan and Abiram rebelled against Moses and Aaron, crying, "Why lift ye yourselves up then above the congregation of the Lord?" The halting repetition of this old tale of subversive folly went on and on; the boys' voices, unnerved by their master's mood, stumbled and stopped and fell out of time with one another, until Mr Lowlyheart could bear no more of it. He called up his assistant usher from the junior class to oversee the whole school for him – "Let every boy at once write out five hundred times the precept of Solomon, 'a foolish restless woman is full of words, such one as hath no knowledge' and add to it, first *Timothy* chapter two, 'I suffer not a woman to teach'. God's Host, don't look at me, sir, fill the inkhorns, sharpen the pens, lay the children to their toil!" – and he stormed back into his house, an unwonted two hours too early. His own furious oath had taken him quite aback, it was not only profane but popish. And because his conscience so reproached him for it, he immediately set about a sort of Spanish Inquisition against both wife and daughter, with frightened servants commandeered as informers and suspected accomplices.

His interrogations lasted into the small hours of the following morning. By the end of them he had established a number of appalling facts. Lucretia's docility had been no more than a mendacious mask: for two full years she had been meeting, in well-concealed seclusion, a broken-down old papist scholar, a man discharged some time ago from his employment in the King's School for incorrigible drunkenness and refusal to attend divine service. Mr Lowlyheart knew him well, or rather *had* known him. They had once had a genuine friendship. But of late he declined even to recognise him in the street, the fellow's vices were grown so apparent. And the papist had retaliated by intermittent lurchings from the door of a taproom, shouting out after Mr Lowlyheart such insults as liquor inspired in him – "Come up here, thou bald head!", "Go pickle thy rod in the dregs of Geneva", and so forth. Nevertheless, it was to this degraded ruffian that Lucretia, with her mother's connivance, and a maid-servant's overt collusion, had applied for instruction in the liberal arts, and by heaven she had paid him for it with bottles beyond counting from the Lowlyheart wine-cellar.

It was not only a matter of Greek, Latin, and a spice of Hebrew. There was poetry involved. A search of the girl's clothes-chest uncovered a piece of paper thrust in amongst her folded shifts. It was an obvious draft of an English version of the immoral Catullus, derived from the immoral Sappho, scrubbily written, erased, blotted, and re-written (it was not as though her handwriting had any excellence, which might have been some mitigation). Almost choking with nausea, Mr Lowlyheart read it, aloud for the first few words, and then his voice betrayed him and he mouthed over the page in silence:

To the vainglorious knight of the poleaxe, that his bulls'-blood ensulliment be not so far washed-off the callouses of his hot hands ere they smooth the white pelt of this heifer, thereby to commingle heat with heat and gules with her smiling argent: these ancient numbers to blow bellows under his new-fired limbeck of love.

O she (or he), such happy state is theirs, I do declare,
As Goddess' bliss (or God's) aloft in heavenly air,
That sit and see your beauteous face, and sit and swooning hearken
To your sweet sweet lips outspoken –

To laughter of your lovely voice, such music to my veins
As maketh me from top to toe ['*tetin to twat* *crossed out*] all trembling
    torture pains:
For let me but take one grace of glance and straightaway I fall
Dumb, stockstill, like a fool . . .

And then two more stanzas, illegible with emendations, except for the
half-line – 'fever is cold but sweat is hot and hot'. At the bottom a
prose colophon, bald, undeniable, incriminating:

After supper, seven o'the clock, backside of Austin Friars, we have more
than a whole hour, for he will be sound sleeping over his Seneca, she goeth
a-gossip to the hearthstone of Mrs Madge. Amorous valour, sweetheart, no
more excusings: know ye not I am today grown into a true nymph (*aetat*
16)? He that seeketh shall surely find his *tender den*.

No doubt as to the addressee: in his tumultuously working mind Mr
Lowlyheart saw an immediate picture of Sam Tenterden, butcher's
apprentice, from the slaughterhouse outside St George's Gate. He saw
other pictures as well. Like an outraged frog he leapt for his birch-rod.
His wife deserved its blows nearly as much as Lucretia: and she knew
it, and was silent, collapsed within herself at the sick thought of where
her indulgence had led. She dared not suggest the work of punishment
be left to her. She and the guilty maidservant shrank quivering out of
the room.

Lucretia was so exhausted by the hours of terrible questions that
she gave him no resistance. Also, she thought she was wicked. Only
afterwards did it occur to her that remorse was unworthy. But by then
it was too late. She had allowed him his fury: she was lucky to be still
alive. Indeed, she would not have been, save that first his arm tired
(we have said he was growing old), and next his hidden voice said
something to him, quite quietly: "Lowlyheart, had you not slept, her
loins need not have waked her thus." And then, with a sudden shame,
he took note of the angle of his codpiece. If *he* was enjoying himself,
his Saviour assuredly could not be. For the first time in his life he
accepted flagellation as a sub-division of the Sin of Lust: and upon his
own daughter . . . ? He saw himself a tyrant of incestuous frenzy, a
monstrous purple emperor from the pages of Suetonius. He saw
himself Sextus Tarquin, for oh most certainly this was a *rape*, and his
Lucretia (spread before him on her truckle-bed, face down, kirtle and
petticoats pulled upwards) was one flesh as well as one name with

Livy's heroine. The blood-flecked shattered birch-twigs fell out of his hand.

*

For a whole week he kept his study, taking no food, and drinking only an occasional cup of small beer. When he came back again, stooped and aged, into the midst of his family, he found he had no family. Lucretia had gone, and nobody knew where. Perhaps the maid had helped her to escape. Mrs Lowlyheart had beaten the maid, clumsily enough, but had got no confession. Mr Lowlyheart refused to repeat the process. "No-one shall be scourged," he said, "except, from now on, my own sinful spirit. Lucretia is not my daughter. You are not her mother. If question should be put, we no longer know her name, and therefore in no wise her whereabouts in this land." And he made no effort to find out. As he told himself it was beyond coincidence that Korah, Dathan and Abiram had been his lesson on that fateful morning: the earth had opened her mouth and swallowed them, with their houses, and all their substance. As with them, so with him.

Mrs Lowlyheart accepted, for a time, his decision. But she was unable to keep to it for ever. At last she made enquiries, very privately, and eventually with some success. It appeared that Lucretia had had a secret female friend, a few years older than herself, the married daughter of a disreputable shoemaker, John Marlowe of the parish of St Mary Bredman. This loud young woman had a bad acquaintance with stage-players and minstrel-vagabonds. Her elder brother, no longer living at home, was said to be even more closely implicated in such doings. Years before, he had attended Mr Lowlyheart's school, where his remarkable parts of learning had been sadly overshadowed by continual disobedience. It seemed clear that the shoemaker's daughter had spirited Lucretia away to London and God knows where, by introducing her to the men of an acting-company who played some nonsense in Canterbury and significantly left town the very day of the girl's disappearance. Hearing this, Mrs Lowlyheart closed her mind to the business. She did not quite share the intense moral hatred of stage-plays held by her husband, who believed all such imitation of life to be an ignoble blasphemous lie; but she knew there was no place amongst their practitioners for women, except as dependent harlots contiguous to the presentation. And, that being the case, for her also Lucretia must cease to exist.

*

Two years later, in 1593, Mr Lowlyheart died. He had turned over his school altogether to the usher, and the only book he read during the last year of his life was the Bible. He could no longer be prevailed upon to keep himself clean. Although his wife continued to tidy his house and cook his food, it cannot be said he was aware of it.

He had not been buried more than a month, when word came of another death. Young Marlowe, in a thieves'-kitchen on the Thames waterfront, stabbed in the eye by some knife-and-rope-knot bravo, the full circumstance never explained. By this time the shoemaker's son was notorious, as an atheist, or a sodomite, or a necromancer, or a papist, or a Spanish intelligencer, or a Privy Council intelligencer – there were those who said all of them at once. His murder was widely held to be a genuine Judgement. Mrs Lowlyheart made up her mind that whatever, wherever, Lucretia now was, such a Judgement must be averted from *her*. Provided it had not already come. She had dearly loved her youngest child, and still did. She had enough money to travel to London (her husband had grown quite rich from the long prosperity of his school): and she would go there and search diligently among the stage-players until she found what she needed to know. She did not tell this to any of her other children. She could not bear that they should try to prevent her.

She was only forty-six, and of strenuous body, but her decorous life in Canterbury had left her unsuited for those quarters of the capital where she would now have to move: no exaggeration to say she quailed with fear, of the people she must meet, the replies she was likely to get. But she was a bishop's daughter, and the daughter of that bishop's wife: their courage was now her courage.

She arrived, she went about, she saw pothouses and whorehouses and gaming-houses (and she would have seen much more of the tiring-houses of the public theatres, were they not all closing that summer because of the plague) – and would you believe? she was not disgusted. For whom did she meet in them, but only people? and God had made them. As for the sickness, God made that too. If He desired, she would catch it; if not, she would continue to live. It was absurd to attempt to avoid it . . . She was told that although acting-companies had gone on tour, some of their players were still about, despite the plague, preparing work for when it abated and government withdrew the ban on public gatherings.

At the Rose on the Bankside, the stage-doorkeeper refused her entrance, but she walked straight past him into the arena, erect and uncanny with the strength of her purpose – she had had a certain word from the barmaid at the tavern across the lane, a dour ironic word, of a fellow in the playhouse who handled women more than was good for them, and had been heard to talk about Canterbury, and laugh about Canterbury, many times in her bar, with a species of a young Cressida who used to bite him by the left ear.

On stools upon the stage were a number of serious men, discussing their trade and their plans for its continuance. She asked the bleating doorkeeper, was there one here by the name of Munday? Yes there was, he was a poet, and he sat among the actors, his script between his fingers, his devious face tightening with a commencement of angry passion – it seemed there was some question of cutting his lines; for the censor had objected, had accused him of writing sedition, he either did what he was told or his scenes would be given to a more amenable hand. In his own hand he twisted the script until it tore.

"Oh God," he snarled, "amenable?" He spat his consonants with dismissive arrogance: "Your god-damned little quim-lipped Stratford Shake-scene, yes?" And then he saw the lady. His manner changed at once. Mrs Lowlyheart had a strange irregular duskish beauty, despite her black clothes (perhaps even because of them), despite her haggard countenance (perhaps because of that too). And this grey-haired Munday was a man of well-seasoned forty, he could be called the right age for a woman of her age. He listened to what she told him – what she blurted out at him, indeed, careless of who else heard it. He smiled, but he did not laugh, nor did he sneer. He took her gently by the arm, and in no more than twenty minutes he had brought her confidingly to a back street behind East Cheap, a smelly region of butchers' shops and slaughter-yards. (Was Lucretia obsessed by butchers?) But the house was well-appointed, and if the windows were kept shut against the flies, it would no doubt be pleasant enough to live in . . .

A whispered word with the landlady, the brief click of coin passing: and so upstairs without announcement. In a small room, shockingly untidy, in a very large bed, which had obviously held two persons only a short time before, lay Lucretia, not quite awake but amazingly startled. Mr Munday left them together. He glided out of the house and back to the Rose, as softly as he had come. Crossing over the river, sprawling loose in the boat under the hot July sunshine, he was murmuring to himself: "So here's a salt-tipped thought . . . old bilious Bale of all people, first his slippery grand-daughter, near as slippery as myself, and now his daughter into the bargain . . . if a man can have the one, he might equally have the other . . . but tortoise, Tony, tortoise, no need for the hare just yet . . ." He lit his pipe and puffed it heavily, in case the waterman carried the plague-infection. Meanwhile Mrs Lowlyheart wept, erect, black-veiled, beside the bed. Lucretia, bending forward among the crumpled sheets, was also weeping. It was some time before either of them discovered the right words to say.

*

Mrs Lowlyheart had been christened Lydia, after that seller-of-purple who said to Saint Paul, "If ye think that I believe on the Lord, then come in to my house and abide there," and had then gone on to 'constrain' the apostle when he made, perhaps, some demur. With this in her mind, she begged, prayed, even threatened: her emotional best to *constrain* Lucretia to return with her to Canterbury. Oh yes, there were tears from the girl, renewed love for her mother, repentance for having wounded her by running away without notice, inarticulate remorse for the death of her father: but through it all she was obdurate. Canterbury was no life, London was *her* life, and she swore it was a good life. She was *not* a playhouse harlot. She was, and she could prove it, a singing-woman and an instrumentalist of already some repute, who could also when required complete a figure-of-dance without putting her fellows to shame. After only two years she was still by way of being an apprentice: but she was most honourably protected, and those who employed her had set her to work before audiences that demanded the most developed talents; why, the Aldermen of London had called for her to sing upon a day when they received the Queen . . .

Lydia was incredulous. And yet, there could be truth in it. The room was scattered with music-sheets, and instruments of music. Dancing-pumps mixed with viol-strings on shelves and stools. The clothes thrown here and there were of a quite splendid quality; they did not seem to be the gauds of a young whore, but no gentlewoman, however gallant (as far as Lydia knew about such things), would have worn them. Perhaps they were appropriate to what Lucretia referred to – and so arrogantly – as 'the business'. There were male garments as well, a costly sword hung on the wall, a pair of silver-mounted pistols, riding-boots. The 'honourable protector'? Lydia was not ready to ask.

Amidst the litter, a number of books. Apprehensively fingering their fly-leaves, Lydia did not find the godless amorism she feared: but poetry in more than one language, history, Aesop's *Fables*, the *Heptameron* of Margaret of Navarre . . . nothing, she grieved to see, about religion. She said to Lucretia, "Have you no Bible, child?"

"There might be one hereabouts, I do know there did use to be . . ." The girl rummaged for a moment, with one stocking on her leg and the other in her hand: she turned up a dusty volume in the corner of the floor, underneath a cittern and a black velvet hat with blue feathers. Lydia instantly crossed herself as though she were a papist, and then pretended she was smoothing her collar: to leave any worldly object on top of the Holy Word was to her a disastrous omen and required ancient superstition to avert it. She could not say she would have preferred there to have been no Bible at all, but . . .

She knew she ought to launch into a torrent of reproach. But Lucretia's blank refusal to respond to her first entreaties, a refusal so clearly founded upon a sense of consistent *rightness*, had brought her up all standing. So, instead, she began to talk about things that had never been mentioned between her and her daughter before. It was, to be sure, a torrent, but of a kind that neither of them expected. Mr Lowlyheart was dead, and now all this could be spoken. Lucretia, very slowly, completed her dressing, and looked at her mother wide-eyed. Deep black eyes under a black tousle of unbrushed hair, and her soft round mouth half-open. There were streaks upon her face where the tears had dried among last night's paint and powder. At one point she interrupted to ask her mother to help lace her bodice: Lydia pulled the strings for her, talking, talking, as she did so.

Apart from that, Lucretia offered neither comment nor question.

I

(*Comical*)

Lydia Remembers, Lydia Invents

And there appeared a great token in heaven. A woman clothed with the sun, and the moon under her feet, and upon her head a crown of twelve stars.
And I saw a star fall from heaven unto the earth. And to him was given the key of the bottomless pit. And he opened the bottomless pit, and there arose the smoke of a great furnace. And the sun and the air were darkened.

(Revelation of St John the Divine, Chapters 12 & 9)

(i) *Country-fashion*

That man Munday, he said he knew you, Cretia, I don't ask how long, or the nature of his knowledge. I would not believe he is a trustworthy man. But he said to me something else, he said – with the wish to flatter me – that he had read the stage-plays of my father.

You did not know Bishop Bale wrote stage-plays and acted in them? Yes, I see from your face that you do know, I suppose Munday told you. Did he tell you, however, that Bishop Bale had a wife who was what you say you are, a singing-woman, a dancing-woman, a woman of 'the business': oh yes, the sort of woman to whom a Bible might well have been the best thing to prop up a pile of rubbish?

Oh yes, I mean your grandmother who died when you were nine. And when he found her she was in no wise under an 'honourable protection'. A despised draggle-tail at a village fair, and that was all that my mother was. No, I see from your face, child, that you cannot believe it: and so Munday cannot have told you. I daresay he does not know that when my father married her, he being in those days a vow-bound romanist friar, he broke not only the law of the papist church, but the law of the king of England, if indeed he ever did correctly marry her at all. By his own lights in those days (lights a-flame since his very childhood, although they burned with the reek of old popery), he and she were wicked people: she, at all events, never repented. Many times, I do know, she wished things otherwise, but so did Judas Iscariot, and they call that 'remorse', not penitence, it was not acceptable; or so we are told in Scripture. To live thoroughly in accord with Scripture is a terrible hard practice: and even a man that becomes bishop cannot hope to do it always.

I am thinking this day, child, of what we may call 'inheritance'. Through my body I gave you my flesh and my spirit, as my mother and my father gave me mine. If your own father was right, his predestinate theology, dregs of Geneva to pickle his rod, why then, there was no help for it. Neither repentance nor remorse, good works nor faith abounding, can twist your small feet out of the trodden prints they must dance in. I now know that you are *mine*, mine alone, from my mother and father. Your brothers and sisters? What can I say but that now I recognise they are sons and daughters of Lowlyheart schoolmaster, and that's all: as they began, so will they end, Lowly-hearts to the last and no-one will reproach them. But it is Bale and Bale's woman – Mrs Dorothy, whom you scarcely remember? – they are the ones that made you.

How much of her *do* you remember? A sick old lady, aged before her natural age, bedridden in London in the house of your Uncle Paul, eating nothing but bread-and-milk, and sleeping in her roof-loft room twenty-two hours out of the twenty-four? While you, as a timorous child, that one time we came on a visit, you had quiet enforced on you all day long, even greater quiet than at home, so that 'grand-dam's quiet should not be vexed'. And why did I never tell you that such and such had been her history? Because I was a coward, Cretia, no other presentable reason. Lowlyheart schoolmaster had forbidden it. I was his young wife, I suppose half of me believed he had God's right to master me, and the rest of me was afraid of him. For all that, I now see that he too was a coward.

As a convinced devotee of Calvin's Geneva, of course he abhorred episcopacy: he ought never to have taken employment from vicar and churchwardens of an established parish, still less should he have preened himself that *my* father had been Bishop Bale. Bishop-in-retirement, certainly, with the modest status of cathedral canon, but bishop had been bishop and John Calvin would have spat in his eye. No no, Lowlyheart knew that if ever he honestly spoke his non-conformable mind he would lose his goose-and-gravy, let alone his Latin books, their ecstasy; the greater ecstasy of his birch-rod. No, no, Lowlyheart knew his true place was with the recusant drunkard that taught you your learned languages: and he had not the courage to confront it. And I think that was the deepest reason for the bloody stripes whereby he wounded you . . . but you know about *that*, let's not talk of it . . .

When I married him, with my father dead and my mother stricken silly, my brothers (as men-of-business) only wanted me off their hands into good Christian care. I had no-one to advise me. And thereupon I sold my soul. Sixteen years of age, Cretia: *your* exact age upon the day you ran away. Oh child, I do believe yours has been the better part.

*

So what was this comical bishop, who pranced upon players' platforms, even at times in a painted face? So what was this carnal wife of his, so many years his junior? And how did I, as their youngest child, grow to know their eccentricity?

To begin with, before he was bishop, I had no call to think it strange. We lived all three together in a village vicarage near Southampton: my brothers already old enough to have been bound prentice in other men's towns. Every Lord's Day in the parish church my father, an earnest parson, impoverished almost utterly, who had suffered such travail for his truth, read prayers and Scripture in solemn English (we had already a Protestant King, god-fearing Edward, God be good to him), and preached, it seemed for hours, hard profundity of argument far beyond my understanding. I remember in chief the blackness of his preaching-gown all in billows over the pulpit front, thinnest strip of white band at his neck (he refused to wear a surplice), the angry tossing of his thick dark beard when he overtook the Pope of Rome. He always overtook the Pope and uncovered his degeneracy, every Sunday, prompt as cockcrow, and quoted John's *Apocalypse* to prove his case.

But I also remember how now and again he would start to laugh, deep down below his beard, below the tide-swell of his gown: a laugh that came up slowly to his mouth, while all awaited it – widening smiles, anticipatory, throughout the congregation – and then he would stop his sermon and break joke after ploughboy's joke, sometimes upon the Pope, sometimes upon the monks and nuns, and always upon the frailties of mortal creatures and their secret sins. He would imitate the village hypocrites, the begrudging farmer, the grasping rent-collector, the ill-conditioned gossips spewing scandal and hurt at the well: oh he knew them as close as though he'd sat like a popery-priest, hearing their confession. Of course, in his young days, that is just what he had done. And therefore some of them loved him, and some of them came to hate him: but down from his pulpit he was so prodigal of his charity toward all of them (even those who still leaned to the old worship, and reviled him for having torn out the idol-images in the church) that no-one could justly condemn him as an hireling shepherd, an unworthy pastor. From the glebe-farm half our scant produce went in succour to the needy: I never heard it said he made enforcement for his tithes.

And then again, near to the end of his sermon, he would put on a quite different voice. "I see with sorrow," he would say, "so many little children who have not restrained their fidgets, and more than one that seemeth asleep. Let me awaken these small things to the love of Our Lord." And he would step down into the nave and walk amongst us, a screw of paper in his hand, full of sugar-plums or nuts: to every child a nut or sugar-plum, and then he would sit down on a low chair before the Lord's Table, and tell a story, for all the children, quite short. About Jesus, as a rule, but not always about Jesus – prophets, patriarchs, Old Testament kings: I have heard him tell tales of pirates and giants; and once he sang a song upon Robin Hood and the Great-Headed Monk (which showed, he said, how the treachery of papist churchmen led the deluded people into *banditto* violence and outlawry: we were not to delight in Robin but be saddened for his crime).

Maybe twice or thrice a year he would do a deal more than all of that: he made a play and we all acted it, in the church (or, in summertime, the churchyard). I say, we all: there were young men who had proper parts, written out on screeds of paper, which they conned till they had them by heart, and proper raiment, hats, cloaks, every colour as vivid as sunshine, glorious crowns, glittering helmets. But everyone else must do something in the play as well as the mere watching of it: we must be devils or angels or the multitude hearing Christ's Word, and as the play proceeded, so he would tell us our part – "Now," he would shout, "Angels-in-Heaven, sing up Hosannah! Sing Glory Alleluia!" And all whom he had previously marked for this chorus would leave their places at once and move around the playing-space. My mother would lead the singing – why, she sang like an angel indeed, and many times she would sing *sola*! – and my father would run alongside us, planting garlands on our heads, or pushing palm-branches into our fists, guiding our movements with his walking-cane, beating time to the music, waving the next player to come forward to make a speech. When it was needful for explication, narration, or satiric comment, he would whisk up into the pulpit, if out-of-doors onto a buttress plinth beside the church-porch, whirling his gown about him: and how he would mouth his lines!

What were these plays about? Prophets and angels, good apostles and wicked popes, good old English kings and bad old English bishops, Jesus Christ in His life on earth – I remember the fallen Lucifer, making ready to tempt Our Lord, wrapping himself in a patched and tarnished golden cope, crowning his brows with a brazen hat that had around it a triple circlet, thereby to show that popery is the greatest of satanic wiles. It is true, I was so young, I saw only the parish clerk being a funny-man wearing a bucket on his head: but later my mother told me what it was that had been meant.

Did the people like these plays? Again, excepting those who still leaned to the old worship, I am certain that they did. There was always a wide table, under the lych-gate, spread with jugs of ale: and after the play, a bagpipe, to lead to dancing on the green. Once the piper brought them dancing into the churchyard itself and thence into the porch and the nave. My father (who had withdrawn himself, briefly, to the vicarage, to change his sweated shirt) ran furious back again in his very shirt-sleeves into their midst, crying: "This is no way! No, *not* within the church: within the church was the old bad way: dear friends, you whoreson muck-rakes, we have *reformed ourselves*! To the green, if you must dance: God permitted King David to dance before the Ark, but no, He did not suffer him to kick his legs *on top* of it!" I was tired and fretful that evening, the play had gone on too long, my mother stood holding me to her breast: she was laughing and her paps shook. I stared out with such amazement to see my father wave his stick in the face of the jolly piper, in the face of the dancing countryfolk, himself so springing and leaping that it seemed he was dancing too: their delight and his distress, and by God they looked surely the same!

*

That night a curious discourse. Between dadda and mamma, as Lydia lay in her cot at the foot of their bed, fast sleeping or so they thought. It was not usual I lay in their room, you understand, we had a maid-servant and she and I would share a pallet: but I think we had come to a pass where this wench could be paid no longer and my mother perforce had sent her home to *her* mother: such exigencies of short money were constant in our house. At all events, I heard them talking.

She said: "Dance in the church or dance outside the church, do you tell me there's a difference? It all leads to the same thing. If you mislike it, you should forbid it equal-handed in both places. At all events, forbid the bagpipe. Its very shape betokens lewdness, and oh the groan of it at sunset, with the bramble-bushes hard at hand for a wicked concealment . . ." She seemed to be laughing again, refuting the severity of her words: quite otherwise with him.

He said: "I am their minister. To abate lewdness. Yet not to abate joy. I have said many times –"

"Oh you have said –"

"I have said, there is men's joy, and God's joy: and the first is not permissable unless the second be consistent with it. For certain, flesh will couple at any opportunity. But upon an open green, even with brambles, even at sunset, even under moonlight, there is some chance to be seen and heard, and therefore a shame and a deterrence. Moreover, if they sin thus in the eye of nature, it is in a sense natural. To have to hide it in a bush might yet remind them of Adam and Eve, might yet bring a sudden penitence, and lawful marriage shall be thrust into their mind, do you mark? It is, as we say, the unregenerate country-fashion; as we say, the old 'derry-down'. As you know."

"As we know." She was still laughing, and repeated 'derry-down' as though it meant more to her than a simple song-phrase. I was puzzled and listened hard.

He continued, in a voice near choking: "But in church, or in churchyard, behind tombs, even underneath God's Table, why, woman, that is not comparable. Sacred places inherit sin of the *most* unsanctified, *most* unnatural, for in them dwells the Adversary more than anywhere else, they are *his* home as well as God's, is not that what he is for . . . ? Ah you *know* what I mean. Do you think I do not know the old heat that arose in the friar-house from proximity of the so-called Host? We thought the Host not only sacred but magical-sacred at that. Such terror of its power: and therefore how terrible strong the temptation. Even a *reformed* church encloses power. Power of its sabbath-prayers. Power of ancient memories of when the Host's power was still there. You ask mockingly, is there a difference? I say fervently, there is: and huge." He choked and hummed, all phlegm in his throat and nostrils.

She said, no longer laughing, weary and dull her voice: "Twenty years ago, thirty years, nay man, more than forty. It happened in the church and it happened in the bramble-bush and even today you are not clear of it? Lord God why am I dogged by these blubberers all my life? You knew temptation of the most unsanctified, and then again a more *natural* lewdness, if that is what you call it: yet out of it came present safety, present sanctity, if that is what you call your gown-and-book, and out of it – at long remove – came little Lydia asleep at your feet . . . I suppose she *is* asleep? For if not, these are no thoughts for her ears. Silence yourself, Bale-zebub, Bull-in-the-bush, lie quiet."

Their voices now were from under the coverlet, but I thought I heard him laugh. *I* could not laugh at the strange names she called him: they were too strange altogether, I saw no reason for grown people to talk that way. I lay very very quiet until at length they were quiet. My cot being too low beneath the valence of their bed for me to more than guess at what caused – some little time later – the smacking of hard hand against soft body, and the name that *he* called *her* – 'Barbara'. Why Barbara?

Had Lowlyheart ever considered, when he married a churchman's daughter and made his life by what he thought to be strict churchman's principles, striving to chasten her flesh (and succeeding), striving to chasten *your* flesh (and failing) – had he thought, just once, that the harsh Saviour he claimed to serve had to strive with His own flesh no more than thirty years or so? For Christ died at younger age than was either my father or mother when I hearkened to them in their bed. At younger age than I am now. No more to their dealings perhaps than a fantasy of strange names and broken-off smackings, no more for me perhaps than hungry fantasy for evermore: nonetheless the body's lewdnesses do not abate with age. How *can* young Christ-made-flesh be a model for any of us, even bishops of the church, or schoolmasters of the church's parishes? I tell you your dad Lowlyheart was not only a coward but a fool.

(ii) *Why Do We Have To?*

Bale's beard had grizzled when they made him a bishop and sent him into Ireland. Ossory was his see, Kilkenny his cathedral town. He was lying ill of an ague when the letter came: he took fright, refused to go. Poor King Edward, God be good to him, he died a child, it was a child's game to choose so great a child as Bale for such a baleful preferment. Yet, in the end, he was somehow persuaded. He was too poor to bring more than one servant, Richard his clerk. He brought my mother, much in doubt whether he should or no, but, as he said, "to deny my Dorothy would be Peter's work denying Christ in the judge's kitchen-passageway: and by Christ the denial of Peter has continued to this day – bear witness, *Vaticanus Mons*, thou high-place cook-house of the great mendacity!" She had no servant, not even – or did I tell you? – a nursemaid: but she brought me. My brothers, tall young men, remained in England, and prospered at their trades. I was a baby of six, would you believe? Ah God, we were all children. My mother certainly younger than I am as I stand here: and seeing how that Munday made no scruple of his lechery toward me today, I cannot be so old even now.

As we voyaged on the ship out of Bristol, I was sickened in stomach and heart. I shed tears for my nursery-alcove at the side of the kitchen fire, my toys and my pictures (with cups of dilute pigment I had coloured-in, by mamma's help, all the doings of Noah as engraved in a printed book: the living waters of the ocean proved exceeding different from the painted waters, yes indeed). I shed tears too for my kitten I had had to leave behind at the vicarage in trust to the succeeding Parson: I feared he would not take care of her, for he had no little girl. And moreover I could not endure the horrible great waves, the violent shouting sailormen. "Oh dadda, dadda, why do we *have* to, why do we *have* to go to Ireland?" My father wrote a book afterward, wherein he said it was a call from God, the reason why we had to. But the answer he offered me on the rolling sluicing creaking ice-sheeted deck had no such simplicity: for he spoke by way of parable, which may have comprehended the notion of God's call, but also caught within itself a number of extraneous thoughts. As I think back on them, I wonder where they came from? Some hint of an ancient Fate, some cruel idol of a world before Christ (far more potent than the popery idols he had scorned in his village chancel) to which he conceived himself fettered?

At all events, it was one of his stories, thus:

About one hundred years before, or more than that maybe, there was a man Bale, or Ball, or perhaps Bull, the names have shifted. At all events, he was also a John: my father said, an ancestor. A Lollard, which is to say a Protestant after the teachings of Wycliffe, rather than of Luther or of Zwingli the Switzer (I have heard it claimed my father's own doctrine was close akin to Zwingli's). Not a clergyman, but a soldier, an archer who had fought at Agincourt, and then left the royal service because Monmouth Harry was burning Lollards. A very brave man, my father told me, but even the bravest must conceal the True Word in those days, there were so few of them that held to it anywhere. He went south and east, first to Bohemia, where for a time he found Protestants and joined in their glorious war. These were Hussites – "Hussites, you have heard the name, sweetheart, repeat it to show dadda you have learned it: Johannes Huss, the martyred saint of Prague . . . good girl." Then the troop he was with was scattered in battle and again he took himself east. Into Hungary, that land's extremity upon the borders of the horrid Turk, and again he found service and drew his bow against the Turk as valiant as any there. No questions down the far Danube as to soldiers' religion: all they craved was good men of a firm true shot, and in especial English men.

The baron whom he served was killed in battle and his troop scattered: but not all of it. The residue passed over, under their captain, to a prince-bishop of the popish church, a scarlet cardinal, who used them as his own, very fiercely against the Turk, and – grievous to tell it – against certain honest Christians as well. "Now we all know, little sweetheart Lydia, how all these cardinals are a very gruesome cyclops-breed, they will poison without conscience, and hale children of God into the fire, and chase them without conscience from one country to another – but this one was the worst of all . . . When you are older I will tell you more of the dreadful things he did. And John the archer came to believe that his serving such a gross fat behemoth (oh yes he was as fat as is that water-butt under the fore-castle there, where the shipmen get their drink) – that his serving him – do you attend me, sweetheart? – gave cause for the anger of God. God was en-angered too against the Turk, you may trust to that, but He had rather the Turk flourished than that so sore a swag-gut cardinal be the means of putting him down.

"So John the archer bethought him a purpose. He would slay and kill the Cardinal: who was, you see, well guarded against all customary attempts, so it had to be by a fashion that none could look for. And yet, for all his puzzling of it, Archer John could find no way. He did not forget his purpose: but he kept it only in the back-closet of his mind: God, he thought, would call him to it, at whatever hour the time was ripe, so let him wait . . .

"Now it happened, that after dinner, when the Cardinal must rest his horrible swollen belly in a cool and pleasant place, he would enter a

small garden in the very midst of his vast castle. All doors to the
garden locked and guarded. No windows overlooked it: except one.
And that one, so high in the wall of the great hall, who could think any
man could contrive to attain it? But upon a day John walked to his
duty, sentry-go on the uppermost leads. He was alone, and for no clear
reason, he did not follow the usual path, up the tower in the
south-west courtyard and so across the roof of the chapel: instead he
took the turret in the south-*east* courtyard, and thence turned north
along a passageway which was builded in the thick height of the side
wall of the great hall. At his elbow, as he walked, he saw a slit of a
window, giving light to the passageway from the light within the hall.
He turned his head and looked through the window – and what did he
see? but over-against him, in the opposite wall of the hall, direct in a
line but lower, the other little window, a round hole most like a flower
with four half-round petals, no more than two foot wide and with
neither glass nor shutter. He looked straight through first one opening, across the top space of the hall, and then through the other – all
indoors was deep shadow, but there beyond, the Cardinal's Garden: a
cusped tiny circle of green and gold, a fire-gleed of afternoon sunlight
hardly bearable to his eye.

"And there, therein, dead centre, in the heart of his garden, the
Cardinal strolling, straight athwart the archer's glance, fanning his
huge white face with his hat, alone at his loathsome ease, in a
green-gold glade of sin. I say there could not in all Christendom have
been two men capable of such a shot, there and then, as the Cardinal
moved! Think of it, child, two openings, the nearest hardly wider
than the barb of an arrow, and the man in the far garden moving, as I
have said! The arrow caught him straight in the folds of his throat: oh
dead he was, slain stone dead for the enhancement of God, just like
Eglon King of Moab, you recollect? in the *Book of Judges*. I tell you
not this to excite your maiden heart toward manslaughter, nor to
stiffen you in your adult days to cry blood-vengeance upon your
enemies: but to cause you to reflect upon how and why John the archer
took that passageway the day he did. He thought it was a whim or
fancy: but then afterward he knew how it must have been a Providence. Only by Providence a man might act, without plan or second
thinking, so long as he hath his purpose, all in a moment he is sent the
chance, he either taketh it or it is lost for ever. Join your hands, child,
say a prayer with me: 'Lord in Heaven, I am an ageing man, and
this Thy child is tender and fearful. Yet we go where we must go,

and Thy protection is surely upon us. Lord in Heaven, show us a sign.'"

Oh I looked all round for the sign, Cretia, so I did, I looked until my eyes turned red: but all I could see was the waves climbing higher, the icicles on the rigging, and the ship's mate beating hell out of a deckhand for some carelessness. I recall he had about a forearm's-length of tarry rope and the boy squealed when it walloped his thin shoulders, soaking wet in a torn shirt . . . Maybe my father saw something else. But I don't think so. His mind was upon his ancestor and the fortunate flying arrow. Sign enough for him in that remembrance.

(iii) *Blundering Blind*

As for Kilkenny. A well-built stone town, albeit delapidate, where the worthiest all spoke a good English: when we reached there, he discovered the depth of his task. The King (or the King's Councillors) had said, "You must make it plain that our new reformed England has its laws for the Irish just as much as for ourselves: enforce them incontinent, we know no better man!"

The hard truth of it was, which they had not troubled to tell him, it was not so much 'no better man', as no other man at all. The new laws of religion had been heard in Ireland, promulgated, read out loud, pasted up in fair black letters on every church door in the English Pale and further west, even here and there among the Ersemen of the wild bogland, wherever indeed a serjeant or a bailiff could project himself, sufficiently escorted by a troop of royal horse. And this had taken place since the year of '37, when the Parliament in Dublin had announced our eighth King Henry sole head of the Church. From '37 to '53, sixteen long years of the True Word in Ireland: and it seemed that not one single Irish soul had taken note of what it meant. Suppose I say to you, Cretia, "Every morning since you were a babe you have drunken small beer to your break-fast. But small beer," let us suppose, "is now well known to be a deadly poison: if you drink it again tomorrow, your belly-pipes will at once be corrupted and fall out into the privy in a great gush of bloody flux." You will hear me, you will think for a moment; maybe for one day, two days, you will abstain: but in the end you will but laugh and eventually revert to your common morning-draught. And if, to support my assertion, I tell you that the Spaniards and French invariably fall sick upon a mouthful of small beer, why, what will you say to me then? "Bad luck to the Spaniards and French, their brewers must be most unskilful!" And so it was with all the Irish: Erse-Irish and English-Irish. They read the placards, heaved their shoulders, and went straightway to pay their priests for a Mass, or a Confession, or a prayer for the souls in Purgatory. Whereas in England, where Bale had wrought against romanist error since long before King Henry's laws, it had been as though the people had come to him in sad affliction, pleading, "We drink small beer daily for there is naught else to quench our thirst: but behold our bowels conturb with this foul unwholesome liquor. For God's sake find us a spring of clean sweet water before we are laid in our graves!"

And as no-one in England of any authority before the year of '53 had ever spoken to Bale of Irish matters, how would the poor fool think the case of Ireland was any different? That land was pronounced 'at peace': more at peace than it had been for thirty years and more. Every thirty years they make some such pronouncement. And then do their best to give themselves the lie.

Coming to Ireland in January, and taking up his bishopric, you would think that before it was August he would have attained some understanding of the nature of the Irish peace and how by English good sense joined with Irish good heart it might yet be preserved. Perhaps he had: I was too young to follow his doings in each particular. But I do know that all through summer (if indeed it *was* summer: the rain came down and down, every thatch let in the drippings, we had pans and pisspots disposed to catch them in the very hall of the Bishop's House, when I think of Kilkenny I think first of those rotten roofs, puddles upon the floor-tiles, black clouds in a scurrying sky, wet clothes hung up continual before our smouldering fires of turf, smell of rain, smell of smoke, smell of our sodden garments . . .), I say again, all through the summer there was another smell on the driving wind. I know now it was the smell of blood, though at the time I felt only a churn of unreasoned fear. My father's face, the whisperings between him and my mother, the anxious men in soaking mantles who came by night, crowded in with him into his study, muttering and then shouting with him in everlasting private conclave: and sometimes they shook hands with him when they left, and sometimes they stormed out and he would follow them to the doorstep and roar his objurgations after them into the hopeless rain.

More than all, the way they kept me shut up in peculiar corners, and would answer me no questions. Once I was put for two whole days into a stinking stable: an uncouth strange nurse-woman sat with me, agitated, she spoke only the Erse, and sang in it, interminable miserable ditties. She fed me nasty porridge (boiled it over a reeking fire of sticks and straw, had to shovel away a heap of old horse-dung to find dry space to kindle it), while outside in the yard a young man with a hand-gun cowered under the eaves and made face he was standing sentinel. Would you not think I was being punished? I tried to ask what had been my naughtiness: but nobody would tell me. When at length my mother came to me, she pressed me to her, kissing me: "Poor Lydia, you are so afraid, but thank God you have been protected!" And she fetched me back into the house, after kissing the Ersewoman as well, stripped off my clinging clothes so be-slimed with the stable, thrust me into a tub of bubbling hot water, wrapped me up in woollen blankets, poured into me a great goblet of spiced wine with a plate of bacon-and-cabbage: and then cursed me like a boatswain when I spewed it all over her knees.

I think it must have been two-three days after that, my father (always unwittingly a clown upon horseback) came jolting his nag of a sudden into the yard – don't ask me where he'd been, I didn't know then, I don't know now – and jumped down from his awkward saddle as bold and jocular as Old King Cole. There was a change in the wind that day, the sky was new and blue, old black clouds were broken to pieces, short white tufts sweeping rapidly westward – the serving-men cast off their mantles and ran about laughing in linen shirts.

Bale called out for my mother. She had already seen him from the window, but she had been making bread, was all flour to above the elbows – not that she cared, but when there might be company she did take good pain to display herself proud, the reformed world's view of a bishop-wife (somewhere between an earl's countess and a grocer's goody, though in old-thinking Ireland none of this held any weight: she was *concubina nefaria* even to those who winked gaily at the circumstance). Therefore some delay while she spruced herself, and he fussed over his horse with his horse-boy, calling again, "What, Dorothy, where are you? Doll, Dot, I say – Dorothea, I am returned!" When she came out into the yard, with myself creeping close to her skirts, he took two strides toward her and hauled her up into his arms – she might be three inches the taller of the pair, but he twirled her around him, her feet off the ground, pushing his bearded muzzle into her drawn cheeks and the hollow of her neck.

"By God, but it is all exposed!" he roared, "I have at last the true tidings, and the devil take all rumour. Yes our poor little King *is* dead, no it is *not* Lady Jane Grey to be made Queen: *yes* it is Lady Mary, and she hath given her royal word that religion in England, and therefore, mark, in Ireland, shall still be hers alone and never the Pope's!"

So boisterous his manner of telling it, so improbable the supposed assurance from our new-chosen sovereign, even *I* was amazed, while my mother stood there frozen and her mouth worked in shock. "Lady Mary!" She spoke on a gasp. "Oh John this is catastrophe . . . ?"

All I knew of the Lady Mary was of a species of malevolent sprite, or a bad stepmother from a ballad-sheet, in her hand a magic mirror wherein she saw her own black eyes and burning death-flames in their depth. Had my father taken leave of his wits? Not that that occurred to me: but I now am persuaded that my mother did think so indeed. Remember, Cretia, not only me, but all three of us had long time been living in terror. *I* had not been told the reasons behind it: but continual rumour, death of the young King, nay *murder* of the young King, rebellion, conspiracy, treason, all these had come bounding into the inner parts of Ireland with not one word to confirm 'em, the Irish in their ignorance had adopted no end of hysterical construction. For the Irish understand no more of the English than we do of them, why else such ever-blundering bloodshed? And we, being then in Ireland, must blunder along with 'em, blind.

Now at last, my father told us, his news was authoritative. He was the first in Kilkenny to have heard it: and good God it was making him glad! From that hour I do believe my mother kept watch on my father, as we would watch a friendly dog that one day, and once only, bit hard on a caressing hand: why did it do it, and when would it happen again? Not easy to say how closely she had trusted his judgement before. These would be secrets of their bed, their Baal-bed which my small cot was too low to overlook. But I am certain her loyalty to him was undergoing crucial change. Indefinable instant of the sea-tide 'twixt flow and ebb: within a very few years oh her heart was forever broken, bread-and-milk would be all she ate, nine-tenths of her vital parts asleep till her final departure. But just then her shock displayed itself in a round broadside of scorn. She tugged him into the house, closing the door against the listening servants, demanding what the devil he meant by his foolery? I kept myself mute, underneath her flustering petticoat, little pitcher with all my ears.

He tried to calm her: with a very strange utterance – "Cah cah

cah-cah cah . . .", he was crowing at her – half a laugh, half a cry of
warning, until for downright curiosity she held her peace and let him
explain. His young man, Richard, who had been with him on his
horse-journey, was also brought into the conference. Did I say he had
made Richard a deacon, in default of any such in Kilkenny who might
be versed in the new doctrine? Reformed bishop, reformed deacon,
and every priest in the place against them: these two *contra totam
Hiberniam* slapping their hands together, making merry; either courage insensate or idiots filled with fear, that they crackled so one with
the other like thorns under a pot.

*

Still not very clear to me, the calculation he had made, or should I say
no calculation but a huge swoop of a gambler's throw? Somehow he
conceived that his knowledge of the true news put all his enemies into
his power. Or so he and Richard seemed to be saying, so urgently, to
my mother: and no less urgent her deprecation. *She* saw a papist
Queen and the death of all Protestant hopes. *He* saw a townful
of subject-nation papists who had incompetently, prematurely,
destroyed their credit with that same Queen.

I realise now by hindsight the body-politic of Kilkenny had already
gone so far as to formally acclaim in public Lady Jane as the new
monarch. Short-term against the long-term: Bale believed that he
himself was very well in credit because the acclamation of Jane had
happened in the town when he was out at his country-grange haymaking; therefore he had no part of it, therefore his discretion was bound
to be rewarded, whatever his religion. My mother, reckoning the *long*
term, could not believe such a credit could last six weeks.

"Nay, six days," she cried out in passion, "and then they will look
to it, they will say, 'Who is Bale? For all his present trimming, he
married a wife against the Pope's law, and he thinketh now to save his
bishopric? And *haymaking*? Not he. He knew that Kilkenny had
erroneously believed Jane Grey to be a secret papist, which is why they
acclaimed her: and so slily he did not tell 'em the truth of her faith
until they were fully committed. By God but he sought to *entrap* our
good Catholic Irish by absenting himself on-a-purpose!' If you can be
scheming-clever, let me tell you there are those in London can muster
up three times your subtlety. And moreover they can muster up
burning-stakes. John, I am telling you no more than what I think: I
think it is once again High Germany for you and me."

She looked in appeal to Richard. He looked at her and looked at
Bale. There was suddenly, I could sense it even from the hem of her
gown, a kind of trembling between the three of them; she put out her
hand to the young man's hand as though by her touch to win his
warmth upon her side of the argument. And he did let his finger-tips
brush against hers. But his other hand (and I had not seen this before)
was held within my father's hand: and all the warmth was between the
two men. Bale was always very warm with keen young men who
accepted his opinions and he and Richard often walked together
talking confidingly; as well, of course, their constant conference in his
study over books and papers: as well, too, their regular praying
together, now in Ireland much more frequent than it had been in our
Hampshire village. My mother withdrew her hand. She let it fall,
perhaps by accident, onto my shoulder, and she gripped me like a bird
of prey: but I did not dare whimper. This was no place for me, I knew,
yet I feared to be noticed and expelled from the uncanny tremblings I
could feel. Did I tell you we were in the bakehouse? It was a small
whitewashed room over-heated with the oven; and Bale, as he talked,
kept banging his flat hand onto a kneading-trough to give an emphasis. Little puffs of white flour rose into the air each time he did this.

He was laughing and laughing and quoting Saint Paul, *Letter to the
Romans*, chapter thirteen: "'Let every soul submit himself to the
authority of the higher powers. For there is no power but of God. The
powers that be, are ordained of God. For rulers are not to be feared for
good works.' I shall preach to them Queen Mary, the legitimacy of her
crown, and from that text. What complaint of my doctrine can they
offer against me *then*?"

Oh I know it seems impossible, now that we are all so well aware of
the persecutions of Mary's reign, that any man of forethought could
have believed she'd prove mild to her Protestant clergy, merely for a
verse from Paul upon subjects' obedience. But at that time she had
fetched home no Cardinal Pole from Italy, at that time she had
married no Philip from Spain: she *might* have become moderate.
Common sense, the constraints of power, princes *have* been known to
bridle themselves. But there appeared to my mother then, and indeed
to me now, no common sense at all about what he suggested next. He
would immediately mount a play, in Kilkenny, at the market-cross:
and he thought it should be his *God's Promises*. Wherein Christ
Scriptural, faith and grace, but by no means works and ceremonies,
doth assure the salvation of man – a Protestant re-making of all the old

Old Testament plays from Adam down as far as John Baptist. They say it had proved a most excellent play for those in England who had received the reformed doctrine. But for Ireland . . . ? Surely he knew that his sermons in Kilkenny had been gaped at uncomprehending, until scarce anyone came to hear them? Surely he knew that most of those who did hear them had left the Cathedral growling and grumbling most unchristian-like begrudgements? And he proposed now to remedy this, at a time of such confusion, by flinging his *dramatis personae* into their faces in the street?

My mother left off her open anger and tried instead a turn of irony. Very gently she asked: "*God's Promises?* Just the one play? Seven acts, a prologue, an epilogue, it lasts little more than an hour. You will add to it a sermon? Call it therefore two hours. Oh I daresay for two hours, with the help of the castle garrison, the town can be kept quiet. You wouldn't care to affix some small afterpiece to the entertainment, just in case there are a few actors not yet thoroughly torn in pieces?"

She hoped, I think, Clerk Richard even yet would understand and take her side. But he was mad for play-acting, and could think of nothing but the parts he might be given. In our village-plays it had always been him took the greatest, the most ranting; he had a voice like a gathering tempest, a big square chest, tight hamstrings, oh the true strut and splendour of Roman Roscius to embody a poet's figments in vigorous motion. And when they were Christian figments (which means not figments at all) divinity itself seemed incorporate in his frame. Proud as Chanticleer of his powers, all Richard said was, "Why not an afterpiece? The play of *The Temptation of Our Lord*, why not that? One half-hour, very brief."

My father agreed: "Why, Richard boy, why not? We'll give you the Devil to play in that one. Yes, with your brass bucket and your cope of shreds and patches. Make you a pleasant change from your Heavenly Father in *God's Promises*."

Stop. Cretia, you must be watching me just as Dorothy was watching her Bale. Lydia Lowlyheart is soft in the head, trying to make you credit I have clutched every turn of this aged conversation forty years perfect in my memory? When at the time I first heard it, it washed over me like suds of soap? True, child, true. Forgive me. Stay patient. Let me remember, let me invent . . .

Bale continued. "The people may have their dinners between one play and the other, then they won't be in any danger of confounding your two appearances . . . Second thoughts, though: the Devil as

Pope? That was very gross and comical, well-suited to an English public who have been in some fear of the Pope, knowing too well how his ministers burned men's bodies, embezzled their goods, harried them out of their own land. But in Ireland it does not seem that has quite been what they thought."

"Oh indeed, John, does it not?" A parenthesis from my mother which he entirely failed to notice.

"So, to make the Pope a laughing-stock will not, perhaps, raise laughter. The *insidious* nature of romanism would be a better emphasis? Very well, Richard, we'll have the Devil as a quiet conniving monk, as I used it first in England at the time when the monasteries beyond Humber and Mersey inspired rebellion to resist their dissolving. Or, even better, a friar of the Francis Order, for they have the most power here. But let's leave him his smoke-tub at the end, oh by all means we'll leave him that, ho ho . . . !"

She still spoke gently. "I'm quite sure Richard will remember all his lines: he has played them often enough. But who else will be in the company? You forget, as far as Kilkenny goes, these plays are brand-new. I foresee the proclamation and celebration of the new Queen must be very very soon: as you say, they dare not delay their loyal statement, not after having thrown themselves head-and-arse into Jane Grey's lap. So, how many days to find your players, how many days for them to con their parts and rehearse their action, how many days before the papists find out what Protestant raillery you have stuffed into these damned screeds of yours? My guess, you will be prevented before you even so much as begin. But even if you are not, John, who is going to be brave enough to stand out on that stage with Richard and you? Consider what kind of play they are used to in Kilkenny. Saints' plays of the old religion, more like fairy-legend than plain-faced Scripture, Virgin Marys and magic flowers . . . comical devil-romps at Halloween . . . Their actors are traditional artisans. You cannot ask for them in *your* pieces, they will say you are turning their whole souls inside-out. Oh I know they are in error, benighted foolish men, but even actors have a certain pride in the integrity of their pretence. And the whole notion of new plays, re-made to a new doctrine, in any case will be abhorrent: the Kilkenny plays are always judged by how close their action is to what was played last year and the year before that, they are not *meant* to be presentations to make people *think*. So who else will you be able to use?"

"Dear Dot, am I so rash as not to have thought of this? The young lads of Kilkenny College are ready for anything that offers a chance of gamey outburst against the complacence of the city fathers. And the schoolmaster, I know, is boldly disposed on their side, for I took his when certain priests came hectoring him for his courtship of too many fair gentlewomen. But he gave 'em news of their own loose concubines, and so stopped up their mouths!"

"What, the schoolmaster? a notorious reprobate? His pupils, all vicious bucks who drink themselves bollock-naked and roam the town every Saturday night picking fights with the native Ersemen? Jesus Christ, he *has* gone mad . . . Even to suppose that those young pups can muster the energy to learn by heart an actor's screed . . . I am married to a Tom-of-Bedlam." She collapsed upon a meal-chest and buried her face in her hands.

"Then we must let them read it. Or sing it, if need be. They have choice voices for drinking-songs, why not for the Word of God?"

"Word of God, word of Bale, through the mouths of the children of Belial . . . And he doesn't even see the contradiction."

"Let you know then where it lies, chuck: it lies in Our Lord's consorting with the publicans and sinners when the Pharisees had cast Him out! It lies in the dikes and hedgerows where He found his starveling wedding-guests to fill up His scorned table. Are you answered?"

She was sitting across the room from him, the kneading-trough between them. She spread her arms out in front of her (heedless of the floury dough on her sleeves and bosom), her head still bent onto them, and I saw the flour among her hair. Then suddenly with a great sigh, she lifted her face and nodded. "I am answered, if you like. You have but the one head: if it goes into the jaws of the dragon, then I am your woman and my flesh is dragon's meat just as much as yours. So what do you need me to do? Prepare and fit the garments, arrange as usual the music and dancing, . . . In this wild weather you'll need music from more than one instrument. There are two portative organs in the Cathedral vestry. I'll look at 'em this morning and blow away the cobwebs. I can play one of them, so you've only one other trained musician to seek. I doubt if the College has many skilled fingers for keyboards, though I'm sure you'll find plenty of drum-thumpers and doodlesack-roarers."

She rose to her feet, her red hair all unfixed and tumbling down her back (more flour to mark her fresh dress): she thrust it abruptly into its coils again, and went out of the bakehouse without a falter. I ran after her, pulling at her. My father had still not noticed me. I ran, I whinged, I plucked her gown, begging her to show me how she still loved me best of all, despite all the hard dealings of this Ireland. And of course she did show me, warm arms, warm bosom, kisses, and – from some secret cupboard – sugar-bread. Before I had finished eating it, she took me across the close into the vestry: I was to help her refurbish the organs.

How is it then, as a sick widow, and never again to get better, she lived always in my brother's wife's house, and not mine? For years before her death she was incontinent of her stools and urine, she could not walk without help because of her swollen feet, and all she ever said – as though talking in her sleep – was, "Bale was so good to me, and now they are all good to me: they put honey in my bread-and-milk, and cinnamon on Sundays." Also her eyesight failed her. Quite blind indeed by the very end. Seventy-one years old, her death's age. Queen Elizabeth is sixty already but she still jumps around like a hoyden of twelve. No, I cannot blame Lowlyheart. He was, after all, a small man, I could have mastered him, could have quashed his objections, could have kept her in Canterbury . . . could have.

Cretia, this is the truth: I could not endure to contemplate dissolution of earthly clay. Which must mean I could not believe in the carnal resurrection. Which must mean I am not Christ's daughter. Yet every week I go to church. Do you know, I am beginning to think I should have come to London sooner and put these questions to that young man Marlowe. God, how he would have scorned me. Am I right? he made a play about a German necromancer as scornful as himself, and allowed him to outface God, accepting all cold-hearted-courageous the logic of his spirit's rejection? Or did your Marlowe in his last act set the Doctor mopping and mowing, craving mercy, beshitting himself? I suppose, though, it would depend on how the player enacted it? Bale's Satan in *The Temptation* did not submit to Christ's victory with ease. He went out on a yell of triumph. The other day I found the book – where Lowlyheart had hid it, though he did not dare burn it, coward! – I looked up the speech. Did you know a threat of popery had been uttered in the Jordan wilderness, near sixteen hundred years ago? Bale makes Lucifer say:

> Though I have hindrance, it will be but for a season,
> Thy vicar at Rome I think will be my friend,
> I defy thee therefore and take thy words but as wind:
> *He* shall me worship and have the world to reward!

And he gives Jesus no direct answer to it. And the speech can, you see, be spoken in more than one way. When Richard played the part, he fell suddenly backwards snarling, down a step-ladder into a tub of smoke. But I heard Bale read it once, in Basel after we fled there, so his mood was desperate, with his angry perversity he made the lines sound as though the Devil's-pope would be high unassailable for all time evermore.

Had he played it thus in Kilkenny, they'd have taken offence, certain: but they'd also have been cheered at the revelation of his inner doubt. As it was, he offended them most, I daresay, by his stupefying appearance of having no doubt at all. They thought he was Baal, he thought he was Bull: either way, two good words for an English man who *knew* that the Irish were nothing. Oh, in order to rub it into them the more bitterly, he thrust in an additional play, *John Baptist*, to precede *The Temptation*. Full of fury against the Pharisees and Sadducees (he saw them as historic types of the Roman clergy), and also against Soldiers and Tax-Gatherers. He even wrote a few more lines to strengthen the screed *in re* the Soldiers and Tax-Gatherers. Fool enough, he was, to think that this might ingratiate his ministry with the Irish, who vex themselves like a swirl of starlings day-in day-out at the government abuses. But by the time the lines were spoken, they had no ears for them. Let me tell you.

(iv) *The Day Of The Plays*

First, I myself took part in the plays.

Yes, me, tiny as tuppence; because it was discovered, late the previous night, that the bellows of one of the portative organs were so perished it was unfit for use. I did hear Richard suggest that a man's privy hand had broken open the old leather after my mother had inspected it, but nothing was proved. Whatever the reason, another organ had to be found, and this one could not be played and bellows-blown at the same time by the same person: it needed an assistant, who but Lydia? So I must sit beside my mother, and walk beside her as she walked, pumping the bellows-lever up-and-down up-and-down. The organ was small, she carried it easily upon her hip, it was a little high up for my reach, but we practised till I got it right.

We practised in our kitchen and on our staircase, very early, before the break-fast. My father came upon us, out of his bed, his gown over his arm, his black beret stuck awry on his tufts of startled hair. He was grinding his teeth and grouching, that if they thought he would wear cope-and-mitre and carry a golden hook, then by heaven they must learn to know he was not Moses' minister but Christ's, "a Bishop Apostolic was never meant to be High Priest!" On second thoughts, he ejaculated, even a chaste white band in this town would be understood as a rag of Rome, and he angrily threw it off from his neck, calling for a rough wool scarf "with naught of the vestment about it at all!" Turning his head, he caught sight of me, under mamma's elbow, hard at work upon my pump.

"Gracious save us, you don't intend to fetch the child out upon stage with you? Suppose there should be tumult?"

"You assured me, John, you had our safety very thorough in hand. But if by any chance you have calculated wrong: don't you think she is far better within my reach than lost beyond our knowledge on the far side of hurly-burly? Also, she has my promise she will never never never be left locked in a stable again." Such strain in her voice that he offered no further objection.

*

He went off then to morning service in the Cathedral. We did not attend this, we were making ready for the procession, outside the College-house in the west end of the close. All the college-boys, marshalled by their master and by Richard: to begin with, not so naughty as I'd thought, I'd expected shameless depravity. True, some of them were late, and others set about kicking the ankles of their comrades, but my mother in a few short words put stop to *that* nonsense. They had on their attires already and looked brave and well-burnished. The musicians on parade in front of them: half-a-dozen players of the goatskin drum – they call it the 'bowrawn' and beat it with a double-knuckled bone, making a tremendous noise. My mother said, though not in the hearing of my father, that she thought it a Moorish instrument, originally appertaining to the mad dancers of Mahound. Also, a bagpipe-man, three or four screaming flageolets, and the two organs (which meant me).

To ensure good order, a squad of strong-legged Ersemen from the castle, Earl Butler of Ormond's soldiers, 'kern' and 'galloglass'. The kern were armed with darts and moved about at a swift trot in tight trews and soft brogues. Galloglass had battle-axes, pointed helmets, long leather coats. All of a very ill discipline – my mother said to Richard they were half of 'em bloody drunk already.

It was these troopers called for the music to begin, long before the prayers in the church were over. My mother said, "No no", but the other musicians were frightened, and wildly struck up a native air of violent mockery, to which the soldiers had the words: very rude words they must have been, and they shouted them out like madmen, jerking their feet, clapping their accoutrements, shaking their weapons. I have learned since, this tune was *O'Neill's March*, a burning token of Ulstermen's rebellion: to hear it in Kilkenny was a shocking thing indeed. The bad college-boys sang back at them, and one or two clods of turf were thrown. But sober men of the city train-bands came running from the church and put themselves between, before any harm was done.

And then, at a signal, the Cathedral bells began to ring, all the citizens came out of the great west door, formed a crowd on both sides of the path to give room for the procession of the Sovereign of Kilkenny (which is, as we'd say in England, the Mayor: a Mr Shea, one of the few in the town that had made friends with my father). With him were his councillors, and the justices, and grand Butler captains and gentlemen from the castle, all of them in robes-of-office, gold chains, polished staves, then the train-bands with their banners: and finally my father, at the head of the cathedral choir. Like himself, the choir-children were without surplices, very sombre in black gowns. He held his great Bible underneath his arm: he glowered about him, face all red and blotched, nostrils stretched like those of a war-horse, his beard bristling forward, his big feet stamping the gravel. It seemed there were no other clergy, and it seemed that the lay-folk were in some perturbation. My mother and Richard made a worried whispering together, they clutched hands hotly and briefly, then she grinned at me and patted my head. The bowrawns were still thundering, the church-bells clashed and rang, the organ inside the church was concluding a stately march: my father raised up his voice. "On in the name of God: to the market-cross for the Word of God!" And he led us all out of the close at a most violent striding speed.

We should have been an orderly column, but we all got mixed up on the steep path where it twisted down between the close-packed cottages through the quarter known as the Irish-town, into the bottom of main Kilkenny. It was not raining then but it had rained before and the mud was exceeding slippery. Dartmen and galloglass were shoving amongst us, hurling about their resplendent 'brackloks' – I mean the war-flags of the Irish, they whip and wave them like jugglers' baubles – they cried their oaths, laughed, ranted, as though it were a battle-rout. I saw some of them do their best to overturn a few squealing women, the college-boys were all but out-of-hand altogether, my mother set her chin, she digged her heels into the soft ground, she played a strong slow *matachin* dance-tune on her organ, a Spanish tune she used often when her spirit was en-angered: she hoped to calm the throng with it, in part she succeeded. She sang to the dance-tune loud and louder, "La la, la la-la-la, la la LAH!"

Down under the Watergate the clotted crowd began to split. The schoolmaster recalled his boys, lashing at their heads with his rod until they straightened their array. The flageolets reunited with the bowrawns. The other portative organ came back under my mother's wing: he was a very little fellow with spectacles of iron wire, who gasped that he could not play if we must keep so swift a speed. The soldiers had run on ahead, racing alongside my father (I caught glimpses of him in front of us, stalking up the Coal Market, alone in his black), while their officer stood aside, would you believe? to make water against a doorpost. I don't know what happened to the choir. As a body they were quite lost for the rest of the day.

On either side the street some scores, indeed hundreds, of very dirty people, gaping at us through matted fringes of hair. These were the poorest Irish of bog and forest, incapable of our English tongue, come to town to see the show. Bare feet, broken teeth, many of their bodies (male and female) unclothed under huge rough mantles, and their own kinfolk of the castle soldiery abused them as though they were dogs. I wonder how many amongst them had the least notion of what was toward? And if they did know, could they have cared? Indeed, I think there was a law against their being in the town at all; but of course what were laws in Ireland . . . ? I was already out of breath, my new white dress was foul with muck, one of my little shoes had come undone, and the garland of honeysuckle mamma had made for my brows had long ago fallen off. "Sweetheart, hold to your going," she encouraged me merrily, "But one more two-hundred-paces, oh there's my sturdy girl!" And I pumped and pumped again with the tears running down my face.

A mud-streaked demon of an Irish boy, I'd say ten years old, and not a stitch on him, came lunging out of the crowd. He tore at my dress, clawing it down off one shoulder nearly to the waist. Mamma, caught unaware, swung to fetch him a swipe of her fist, but the organ was in her way, she hit short and would have fallen, had not a flageolet-boy shot out his hand. I was screaming and huddling against her: just able in the swift moment to see an angry gaunt woman grab hold of the ruffian child, and slap him, slap him, slap – first this way then that, curse-words of harsh Irish like gunstones out of her mouth. She seemed to be some relative: his mother? No more, as I say, than the flash of a moment, but I had recognised her. The strange nurse who tended me when they put me in the stable.

*

Something happened just after that which I did not fully understand, as with so much of Kilkenny and its doings. My father, ahead of all, had arrived at the place where the back lane from the castle-bridge runs up into the bottom of High Street at a low angle to our left. There was a throng of people at the juncture, hiding the lane from us as we approached. Suddenly a clump of them stepped forward, up past Coal Market corner, blocking my father's path in the narrowest part of High Street. So we all came to a dead stop, and very raggedly, pressing into one another: the music failed. I could see my father remonstrate, I heard laughter, I could see a number of big galloglass, as it seemed, pushing him back. And then, a great hullooing, up out of the laneway ran two funny-men with shaven crowns; if they were priests they did not dress like priests. They had white jackets with a crossed-key *emblema* daubed on them most unskilfully, white-and-yellow striped hose, their eyes ringed with burnt cork above large red false noses from which spread black moustachios of plaited horsehair. They carried striped yellow-and-white poles: on one was perched a bishop's-mitre, gleaming gold above a cloth-of-gold cope; tied to the other was a crozier-staff, likewise golden. I had never seen such things before, I thought they looked most lovely.

Richard said: "Whatever knave had those canonicals out of the Cathedral Treasury was the same damned popery whoreson, ma'am, that split you your portative-bellows." While my father fumed at the galloglass, and our procession jammed up behind, the dart-men cleared a space through the people in front of him, deliberately ushering in a whole new band of music from out of the back lane. They had several doodlesacks, big ones (what the Irish call the war-pipes), more bowrawn-players, and, on the back of a donkey, a splendid old whitebeard hero in an Irish mantle, strumming a harp. Apart from this last, they were all dressed as wild as the first two – burnt cork, false noses, and some of them had tall pointed caps. They marched ahead of my father up into the High Street amid laughing and cheering, kicking their legs out, leaping up-and-down: up-and-down also the striped poles with their glittering burdens, in time to the music the full length of the funny-men's march. I stopped crying, began to laugh, I thought it was all good part of dadda's play. "Oh mamma, look at the funny-men!" She did look. And for certain, a grin on her face: but by no means in pleasantry. She had stopped playing her organ (not that anyone could have heard it now, the shouting was so loud), she heaved it round on its shoulder-strap to grip a stronger hold of me. "Christ's minister?" she said, "Moses' minister? Let God look out of heaven, He'd not tell one or other of us from the ministers of the Golden Calf. Oh Bale, you bloody Bale, forewarned and forearmed, and you walk us all right into it."

Let me add (as it is even now, Cretia, so strong in my mind and I still know not quite what to make of it): Richard was in stage-attire as the Heavenly Father, the schoolmaster's praefect-youth was in stage-attire as Christ the Son, and the most tall and meagre of the pupils wore the skin-coat of John Baptist. Through all the assaults and rudery, these three were suffered to pass their way unhindered: nay, the jibing multitude stood back aside from them as though in awe. And yet, as it seems to me now, how could the people not have thought them the uttermost blasphemy . . . ? I saw an old Erseman, spittle of rage upon his beard, throw filth at our bagpiper, then drop to his knees and cross himself as the school-praefect Jesus walked in front of him; and immediately after, another handful of ordure straight in the face of a boy in a Pharisee robe.

At the edges there was real fighting. I saw a tall fellow fall down through a thicket of waving fists. Somewhere behind, a smash of glass as a window was driven in. The troopers of the train-band came pushing with their bill-hooks in the opposite direction to everyone else. I could hear Mr Shea yell in Irish at the top of his voice. He appeared right on top of my mother, seized her by the elbow, without remedy he dragged her and me up the pavement, staggering and stumbling. Before I could realise how we had attained that place, we were safe behind the market-cross.

*

Kilkenny Cross is a sort of tabernacle, four gabled arches set round the central column. The Heavenly Father was to take his seat under these arches for the first play, as it were a holy statue in a church-wall niche.

(Strange, it was but a few weeks since Bale cast out all statues from the Cathedral; but then *they* could not speak plain-faced Scripture, being made of stone). To commence, however, all the players must hide themselves behind the stage, which had been builded upon trestles out into the street, level with the base of the cross. My father's sermon first. Mr Shea caught his shoulder: in his heat he still spoke his own language, remembered himself, turned angrily to English: "Nay, you'll not go on to preach, man, not now, not to preach, devil an instant of quiet will you get, I'll tell you that! Jasus, but me train-band lads are banjaxed entirely. Did you see the way the Butler soldiers are after bringing these blackguards into it? What possessed you in God's name to demand your law-n-order from the hoors in the Castle? Had you left it all to me, I'd have the street cleared in ten minutes, oh Jasus where will it end?"

He was red in the face, but my father was even redder. He turned abruptly to the Sovereign, abrupt speech, spittle flying: "The Butlers hold the Castle by grant from the Queen's Majesty; their officers are the Queen's Officers: let all these abuses be thus exposed from whence they come. What I do, I do by right and legitimate entitlement. But be easy, my homily shall not be of great length."

It was indeed of very little length. He stepped up upon the platform, opened his book, read out his text (Saint Paul to *Romans*, as he'd promised, chapter thirteen), closed his book, and bellowed against the raucous crowd: "The Apostle has thereby spoken. I repeat his word again, 'Whosoever resisteth the power, resisteth the ordinance of God.' In this street I am the power, Mr Shea is the power, and the Queen that commandeth the Castle is the power, however mutinous her mortal instruments. No further explication: it is surely abundant manifest to man, woman, child, and dog. We proceed to our enacted play."

They were all silent: unexpected, but I think now his argument was confounding them a little. Obedience to a Queen, he urged, a Queen they knew to be adamant romanist and ready, so they hoped, to drive out this heretic bishop? Surely this should be *their* argument? They held their peace, shuffling feet, muttering to one another the odd disturbed question. Mr Shea, to my mother, wiping the sweat from his broad forehead: "I'd say the play'll not trouble us much, ma'am. Being writ in English, all those 'gaelgorey' subversives" (he meant those that spoke only the Erse) "will rather the dram-shops than weary their ears with it. Jasus, they give me a sickener, telling *me* I'm no true Irishman! I'm after closing every shebeen except over the river, so we'll soon see the back of them." And indeed the roughest gangs were already moving away.

*

My father, still holding his Bible, walked three paces in a circle till his back was turned to the public. This marked his declension from preacher to player (or did he secretly think of it as *ascension*?). My mother and little Spectacles came up onto the stage behind, swinging their organs to give him music: and me, of course, me, Cretia, still a-pump, there I was. Mamma whispered to me, "Stout trouper," and ran her fingers over the keys.

The first tune was both joyful and solemn. It went on for some time, till the audience began to feel it, began to allow it to disperse their discontent. Then it was faded away, Bale turned himself again, full-face into the dragon's mouth, raised his stick into the air, and spoke as Prologue. All his own anger seemed to have fled, his voice was warm and generous:

> If profit may grow, most Christian audience,
> By knowledge of things which are but transitory
> And here for a time, of much more congruence
> Advantage may spring by the search of causes heavenly –
> As those matters are that the Gospel specify,
> Without whose knowledge no man to the Truth can fall,
> Nor ever attain to the Life Perpetual.

And so on. I learned it all at the age of thirteen, when he still hoped Queen Elizabeth's bishops would prescribe his plays for Lord's Day service in England, yes he did, he wrote letters all round, and nobody answered 'em.

I'll say this for Kilkenny, they heard his plays with a sight more courtesy than you'd give credit for. Oh, a few interruptions: there was a purple-faced drunken blacksmith at the back of the crowd who shouted intermittently, "Silken Thomas was a bloody tout for Cardinal Wolsey, so he was!", a slogan so obscure that nobody took note of it, except to laugh and call back to him: "Good man yourself, Jer-boy, God be with the work . . ." and such-like. At one point a woman near me called out, "Will you look at the little doat hanging onto the organ-pump! Holy Mary I could kiss her cheeks till I'd be swallowing her altogether!"

Upon the entry of Adam, however, deeply penitent before his Creator, there was a more serious incident. The Heavenly Father, from his arched alcove, had continued to strike awe, but when he said of Adam:

> Yea, yet must he have a greater punishment;
> Most terrible death shall bring him to his end,
> To teach him how he his Lord God shall offend –

and a crouching trembling figure crept out from behind the cross, there was a stutter of a hee-haw gasp from one side of the market-place to the other. My mother's music was not needed for this entrance, Adam had shrill flageolets in a melancholy wail, so she and I were retired from immediate view. But her eyes kept sharp open every-where: "Good God, the damned young fool, I *told* him to wear the white shift! I'll bet his lousy friends have dared him to it, look at him! Gentlemen's college for the brats of squireens indeed; more like the county Clink was his nurturing: Christ!"

For the young man was as bare as a bone, as bare as the demon-imp that tore my dress, except he had tried to gird himself with a bunch of leaves, and how I giggled when I saw how clumsy they were affixed. Between him and Heavenly Father, some five minutes of close-wrought dialogue, ending in a Latin chant to the music of the organs. Adam had to sing this kneeling, with the choir-voices from the rear of the stage. As I said, we had lost all the children of the choir, so my mother's sole voice (of such strength her sole voice) replaced them. But by this time his malicious leaves had fallen to the boards. Schoolboy bravery, well enough: but he couldn't face the exposition of his privities in broad daylight *coram populo*, the Bishop not three yards away, and God the Father glaring down at him. He had his screed in one hand, and used the other to cover himself, but not sufficient by no means, so he used the screed as well: and thereby failed on his words and sang his hymn tra-la-la-la, in the justified hope my mother's words would do for both.

I was sure she must box his ears at the end of the act: but no, she ignored him coldly. He ran away to muffle himself within a ring of sniggering comrades, while the crowd hooted and whistled to spy his stooped white hind-quarters (scored with old weals of the schoolmas-ter's rod) all a-flight into the shadow. My mother said, "Thank your mercies, child, your dad did not see fit to bring Eve into his play. For if he had, would he have looked to *me* for it, would he have told me,

'co-ordinate costume with him from whose rib you sprang'?
Foh . . . ! Stand back now, here comes Noah, bagpipe and drums for
him, and where the devil are those idiots with the emblematic
boat?"

I suppose I should be able to tell you that the insults to the Pope,
with which the plays were brimming full, raised riot among the people
again. But they didn't. The town had had its fun, the priests had made
their mockery against my father's refusal of canonical vestment; and
after that, all those who saw offence where offence was intended,
preferred to show their disgust by their absence.

Apart from Mr Shea, I think not one of the city notables had even
reached the market-cross.

So, as the day advanced, the audience fell ever smaller: after dinner
there was no more than a handful. Moreover, after dinner the sky
closed in on the Kilkenny thatches, the rain came rattling like rods of
steel, horrid cold: yet how fiercely we worked ourselves the full way
throughout those screeds, until the very final sentence – music,
singing, dancing, interminable speaking, while the scaffold grew
shiny and perilous as the back of a wave-washed whale. Three or four,
perhaps, laughed to see Richard's Satan totter over into his tub (no
smoke because of the rain), and ten or twelve cat-called their anger at
the provocation of his lines.

Then should have followed Christ comforted and fed by Angels
who sing Him a sweet Latin song in celebration of His achieved
ordeal.

*

Which Angels ought to have been the cathedral-choir.

So, as in the first play, my mother must become them all at once.
But in this case she had not learned the words. She put aside her
portative, kicked off her spongy shoes, took up a bowrawn, stepped
forward on the empty stage (Christ being under the arch), and began,
quite unexpected, entirely extempory, to dance. Little Spectacles,
quick to his instrument, saw what she did, commenced the music. She
signed to the flageolet-players, they too whistled into the tune, or
rather into her rhythm: such tune as there was, they must improvise –
which they could do, as can all Irish music. In default, then, of song to
give glory to indomitable Christ, she gave Him instead the beauty of
her body, dripping wet, her white wet skirts clapping at her legs until
she hitched up the hem into her girdle, her head-dress of honeysuckle

(she and I had been attired as a match) flattened against her forehead by the rain, her hair in rats'-tails about her neck.

I shall never forget that dance, Cretia.

Had it not been an Angel, it could have been the Daughter of Herodias (my father had a play about *her*, though I never saw it acted), it could have been her old self young, dancing for louts in East Anglian hiring-fairs. I suppose you might have called it a Spanish-like dance – oh not your papist Spain, but old Morisco, stamping and strutting, chin up, head bent back – no jingling tambourine, no castanets, only the bowrawn; and she had not the high-heeled shoes. But that was how it was.

And hardly a soul to watch her: even the few left there were beginning to drift off home. So she danced for the school-praefect Christ-boy, she danced also for Bale, for her sorrow at the foolishness of this, his forlorn hope. He watched every spring, every declination of her movement, and now he must speak the Epilogue. How much of the water on his harsh-lined cheeks was rain-water? He uttered the rhyme of general *exeunt*:

> Follow Christ alone, for He is the True Shepherd;
> The voice of strangers do never more regard.

And behold, there were no strangers to sound any voice at all. Except for him, and his Dorothy, and me. And unfortunate Deacon Richard, who had but eighteen days to live. Because they murdered him, the Irish did, even in my father's field, where the haycocks had got so wet the full harvest was intolerable delayed. For me, I daresay, Richard never had much time: though he did once carve me a little cow out of wood and painted it black with white spots. My father much admired him. The spear that stabbed him went very hard indeed into my mother's affectionate heart. In private his booming voice took on a gentleness you'd never think could go with his saturnine physiognomy, upright angularity, the hard rectitude of his handwriting when he indited my father's letters. Of my father's thoughts toward him, the nature of *that* love, all I can say, my mother mistrusted it. With young men, and my father, and her, there was an awkward silent jealousy. I sometimes saw her, as it were, *warn* him, with a curl of lip or sideways eye: and when she did he would curse himself, almost *cross* himself, as though he were still a Roman friar. There is much I do not know about him . . . Oh, Richard was betrothed; to a Southampton girl, a ship-chandler's daughter. I forget

her name – Marigold? And after his death, only a few more days, my
father, his Dorothy, and me, why, we went out of Ireland for ever.

   High Germany; and, as well, the Swiss Cantons. She had been quite
right, you see. Prognostications. She was often right.

(v) *Shaking Voices*

They say Ireland is now at peace. I don't believe one word of it. Over
the last thirty years there has been enormous war. With their religion
and our religion the war has been ten times crueller than ever it was in
the old days. And their religion is Spain's religion: we shall never be
safe from Spain. Too greatly-stretched a statement, to say it was my
father alone began this new kind of war there? All on his own, to hump
his faith, willy-nilly, like adversarial hand-baggage, off the Bristol
ship into Waterford and thence to Kilkenny?

   Who else caused the killing of Richard, but Richard's poet-bishop
master and the duty he imposed? Was he murdered because of the
hayfield (there was certainly a dispute over the bishopric farm)? Or
because of his belief, which he wielded as firm as a hay-rake? Ask an
Erseman (though you'll scarce manage the language), or ask even an
English-Irish (who you might think had the opposite opinion, but on
this point you'd be wrong), which concerns 'em deepest, the land, or
the Roman Mass? Sometimes you'll get one answer, sometimes the
other: but when the two go flush together, then you'll drink the
pouring blood. I suppose our Queen knows that.

*

The play being over, the street empty, save for the rain, we began to
gather our things to go home. My mother and Richard stood together,
dismantling a piece of scenery, the Pinnacle of the Temple whereon
Satan had tempted Christ: it was a step-ladder with battlements nailed
around it, and they had fastened it together rather too strongly. He
tugged the nails with a claw-hammer while she prevented the whole
thing falling over on top of him as he did so. She took the nails and put
them into her mouth: and then, out of the edge of her mouth, between
the nails, I heard her say a very strange thing, as though no-one else
must hear it, and her voice was shaking:

   "That is the last time I ever dance, ever. Did you think the stage was
empty, except for me? It was not. There were three of them there,

dancing along with me; two women, and one man, a shave-pate friar. Their clothes were all in rags and smouldering, charred strips of cloth swinging in the rain, I could *smell* the burnt stench off them. They caught at me as I danced and moved me hither and thither about the stage, it was *their* pattern of feet that my feet were making, not my own, no, not mine. Are you sure you did not see them? Their faces were most ghastly, skin blistered and black: and bits of white bone sticking out at the joints of their limbs. Richard, oh my love, Richard, I know their names; they were Askew and Bocher and Forest. Oh God what will I do? I know what I will *not* do: never again dance for him, nor for anyone, ever: oh this has been the last last time."

They saw me listening and at once moved apart as though nothing had been said.

*

At supper that night my mother was quite silent, whereas commonly she chattered and narrated and sharpened her tongue on the more foolish events and persons of the day. Richard (in a sympathy, I think, for he met her eyes across the table more than once) was also taciturn. This surprised me, there was surely so much to talk about: and be sure I would have talked about it, had not my father filled the silence with unending uninterruptible declamation. He was in two moods, switching from one to the other without pause or forewarning. Half of his talking-time was taken up with loud complaint that all the day had gone so ill, tumult, dissent, popery schemings against his office, the manifest treachery of the cathedral choirmaster who had, he said, deliberately removed his singing-boys from the street as soon as hostility was shown, all-of-a-piece with all Kilkenny, and what good was God's Word in a market-place where none would hear it? Yet every few minutes he swung his discourse round and began, no less loudly, to praise himself (and occasionally the rest of us) that after all the threats and provocation we had nonetheless presented our three plays start to finish without a falter, and that with not a week's preparation. The master of the College supped with us, and Bale kept nudging his elbow, breaking jokes about the whipped buttocks of young 'Adam' in *God's Promises*. This was strange, because in his other mood the miscreant boy was reviled as the main cause of the audience's early dispersal: and the schoolmaster was plainly puzzled as to what his Bishop really thought of that matter. And then, as we finished our meat, and nuts and fruit were brought in, Bale ceased to speak of the plays and began a close questioning of the schoolmaster upon the morals of his charges.

"You say you have your boys two-and-two sharing bedsteads? Danger, sir, danger: oh I know 'tis common enough for the boarding-children in our schools, it saveth expense and some say it keepeth the timorous ones from the perils of nightmare. But consider, your pupils are of an age to do the deed, don't tell me they are not, I saw the fulfilled physique of *Adam Primus Homo Nudus* this very morning, sir; hairy, *hirsutus lascivus*, a ranting roebuck, that's what *I* saw –"

Whereat my mother rose from her chair, ordered me to my bed, and went with Richard into her withdrawing-room, leaving the two older men to their snorts and expostulations. I think neither of them noticed our departure.

Worth a word, my mother's word to Richard at that step-ladder: "Oh my love", she had said. I had never heard her say it to him before. Nor, to my knowledge, in the two-and-a-half weeks succeeding, did she say it again. There is no doubt he heard it. His face was a dark pool out of which a sudden fish leapt and then submerged again. In the short time she was in Ireland she had not known any Irish face well enough to gain such a look from it. If she had, it is quite possible that Richard would have lived.

*

One more thought about Kilkenny, and that's all. Then we can send for some food. In the Kyteler house, in the back lane, just beside where the funny-men priests had lain in wait for our silly procession, there had lived a beautiful witch in the time of the Plantagenet kings, second Edward or third, she had enchanted her husbands to death, it was accused. And when her son complained that she achieved so little profit from it, she took a broom by night and swept the filth of every street down toward his threshold till it made a pile as high as the doorknocker. As she swept, she sang a song (the children of Kilkenny sing it still: in form of a game, I cannot tell you how much I was frightened by this game).

> To the house, to the house, of William my son,
> Hie all the wealth of Kilkenny town.

We'd not been in the place long, when some very beastly children – they were the brood of Mr Shea, he being my father's friend, so of course I was put to play with them – they had me in their house for supper; and then, after dark, they evaded their nurse and brought me out through the alleyways, behind the market-cross, to the house of Kyteler, all in ruin under the moonlight. Its roof was off, its windows boarded, the front door swung on the hinges. Not that anyone ever went in, it was shunned by the fearful people. The door should have been nailed, but a wild windstorm had burst the nails from the boards; bang bang bang it slammed, we could hear the flooded river roaring over its banks at the bottom of the weed-choked garden, and every other house nearby was shuttered tight against the tempest.

Oh the cruel courage of those tormenting Irish children as they dragged me inside. They lit a candle, we played 'ghosties' through the vaults, up and down the stairs. They thought it a great change from their usual game, their desperate scratching tearing game of 'the Kilkenny cats'. I bit my lips and tried to play with them. I was the Bishop's English girl, Jesus would look after me. I tried to laugh and howl just like them, if only to show I was as brave as John the Archer who beat the French at Agincourt. They blew out the candle. They scuttered for the door. I called out for them in the dark. Neither laughter nor howl nor any answer at all. I called out again.

They had left me quite alone, there in the witchcraft house, and jammed the door so I could not follow them.

In the sudden silence, when I stopped crying in order to listen – perhaps they had relented, were coming back to fetch me home? – I heard a raking noise upon the cobblestones outside: no other noise but that, no footprints, no voices, just scraping and raking, and the wail of the wind through the chinks of the building. I thought it went on for hours. So slowly, so vindictive slowly, it came on, along the street, toward the house. Each minute a little bit louder, just a tiny little bit louder: until at last it was at the door. Between me and that unearthly scraping, no more than an inch of rotten woodwork. Which is when I heard the song begin:

"To the house, to the house, of William my . . ."

Cretia, I swear to you now, it was *not* the voice of any of the Shea children. A grown woman sang the tune, in a high thin shaking crescendo: I knew then and I know today, she was two hundred years old, and yet no older than the age of my mother, between thirty years and forty. Anywhere else, had I heard such singing, I'd have said it was most beautiful, music to the glory of God, nay I'd have said it was my mother singing, who sang always in and out of the house and every night sitting beside me to make sure I went sound asleep. Anywhere else: but being there, being then, I fell on the floor in a swoon.

So Mr Shea, of course, came to find me, in generous rage at his whelps, their envenomed mischief. He took me at once in his arms up to the Bishop's House, where they gave me hot cordial to drink, and to bed for a whole week. My mother could not understand why I begged her from my bed, "Please, mamma, not to sing, not to sing, mamma, *please . . . !*"

D'you know what my father said, once he determined I was released, to an extent, from my terror? He said, "Whatever you heard, it was not Alice Kyteler the witch. Because it is apparent she was no witch, but a harshly-wronged woman who had chosen to worship God in accordance with Scripture in defiance of the popish Bishop. When he could not prove sufficient against her to convince the magnates of Ireland (she being of a family with great influence among the King's Officers), he had false confessions drawn, and sworn to under torture by her servants and their base companions, making tales of devils and familiars and bugbears for that superstitious age. There you are, you see, that is history, a clear light for clear consciences to follow even so far as the Promised Kingdom which we know will come. Pooh pooh my brave darling, to these sorcery-heresy-hunting bloodhounds who seek only the fears of the ignorant that they may practise for their own power and gain!"

He had not heard the singing. If he had, would he have said the same? To this day I assure myself, yes. In the length of time it took the archer to spy the Cardinal, string his bow, aim the arrow, shoot it, to Bishop Bale had been delivered (one day long since) the certainty of his truth. Once he had it, he had it, he would not be contradicted. Nor would he ever agree that contradictions may be of God just as much as is consistency.

CHILD AND GRANDCHILD

(2)

Foundered Affection

Poached eggs, very runny, and a bottle of uncomfortably sharp wine, having been fetched up by the landlady, Lucretia and her mother sat down to refresh their stomachs. Lucretia was still unwashed but Mrs Lowlyheart did not insist. The tray of food had put a term to her unprecedented flow of talk, and she found herself not knowing quite what to say next. Lucretia scooped at her egg with a spoon, breaking some coarse bread into the mess, pushing it about with her finger till it formed little soft hummocks of yellow and white and brown. She kept all her close attention upon this process, like a child in the gutter fiddling with mud-pies. She seemed not to be hungry.

Mrs Lowlyheart *was* hungry: she ate as though needing it to sustain herself after hours of hard work. But her eye, as she fed, flickered rapidly about the room. Between mouthfuls she offered small noises, the beginnings of sentences, which then broke off short, and made way for more bread and egg. Finally, she put down her spoon, picked up her cup, drank with gusto, twisted her features at the sourness of the wine.

"In the boat," she said, still swallowing, "in the boat that man Munday told me he admired my father more than anyone else of all the English reformers, and of all the English poets since Chaucer. He said, in our modern times it was Bale and Bale alone of the poets – of the play-making poets, he said, his own especial *bail*iwick, clever clever pun to liven his eulogy – it was Bale who stood four-square for liberty of conscience, four-square against coercion, and threw his muse into the combat, like – I think he said like Roman colour-serjeants hurling their standards before them into the enemy ranks so that all soldiers would vie to rescue the sacred *insignia*, and thereby turn the battle-tide. I replied that a muse was surely a woman, did he mean that that was how Bale had used Mrs Dorothy? If so, I said, the conceit were more ridiculous than magnificent? He smiled, was a little confused, said, no, not quite that; and then slid into a sort of reflections I thought best to ignore, upon the graces of English womanhood. He's a man who could turn the Thirty-nine Articles into a form of insidious courtship.

"I am happier without such. But perhaps, though unaware of it, he was right about the colour-serjeants. Somebody killed all the life out of my mother. And if it was not Bale, who was it? Her last years, stunned and mumbling, yes she might well have been hurled among shields and spears and tramping boots. But what did he mean, 'against coercion'? After the plays in Kilkenny, Bale roared at Mr Shea for two hours in the hall of the Bishop's House while I lay above in my loft-room bed and listened. He swore that if the train-bands and soldiers had had proper orders, and had learned how to obey 'em, they could have chopped the papist rioters into pigs'-liver stew at the first alarm, and why didn't they?

"'All I ask is that the Lord Deputy should understand the rebellious spirit here, all I ask is a strong hand, and by God I have right to ask it: I am Bishop and therefore officer of the Queen's Peace under God, I shall write to him and tell him as I have written to him already, but why hasn't he answered me? If he's out of the country, then let his co-adjutors make reply, they have little enough to do in Dublin, and soldiers enough to do it with. All I have from them is one daft word, that Ireland is at peace and will I please be so good as not to agitate it! By God but I shall be writing direct to the Queen!' Liberty of conscience? Coercion? *I* think that your Munday is more ignorant than *he* thinks. It's not for me to educate him."

Lucretia kept her head lowered, peering into the egg. Her hand went up, to adjust a strand of hair, and then stayed up, perhaps by accident, hiding her face from Lydia. "Mother, he is not *my* Munday. He has a wife and several children. It is true that for six weeks I loved him fit to die from ecstasy. It is true it was he that found me these lodgings. And found me the persons who have trained me as singing-woman. But that was above a year ago. Near upon two years, I was new in London."

"So how came your breach with him? His wife, he had concealed her, you dreamed he would wed you himself? Idiot child."

"Oh no, by no means. I knew of her at the very start, but being in a depth of trouble, I allowed him one evening to finger my face. We were alone in a wine-house snug-room, the other company had all gone home, I was weeping for my griefs, and he seemed so kind toward me that I took no thought but to kiss him. For no-one else would put an arm round me, I would allow no-one else to do it, you must believe I was determined I would *not* become a playhouse harlot, and yet I could see so little else to do, oh why did I run from Canterbury, why?"

"Why?"

"God's blood, mother, you *know* why. So he touched me, and I burnt with it. My uncertain little kiss sent my tongue into his mouth, and then his fingers on my breast, and into my placket, I tell you I was mad from anxiety, despair, foundered affection – the player that John Marlowe's daughter had given me to, that he might take me away from home, had lanced my virginity and then left me, to travel on tour beyond Worcestershire – he never even told me he was going, never even gave me a few coins to keep me eating, if only for a few days. Someone had to pay my lodging-bill, and Munday said he would."

"You mean he bought you."

"Not with his money. I was grateful: but I made clear to him, it was honestly agreed between us, it was a gift of pure friendship, nay he said a loan. That was some time before the evening I am talking of, in any case . . . His hand into my placket and mine into his codpiece. So we worked ourselves together, and such work, I can swear, can lead in to days and nights of inordinate happiness, wife and children notwithstanding, church-virtue notwithstanding, I swear it can. Oh mother, it did."

"I know little of these fornications. My own young life did not conduce . . . Maybe if *my* mother were still here . . . But you have told me, only six weeks. Surely in that there is a moral?"

"Surely. Surely indeed. Because the happiness grew out of nothing, but warmth of flesh, tears, aquavit, compassion. I do believe his compassion was as true as his aquavit was strong. But compassion from a man I did not know at all, and he gave it to a woman he did not know at all. After six weeks, I began to know him. It was sufficient. Mother, let me tell you, if Munday praises Bale, as he praised him to me, believe that Bale in all his life would never have praised Munday. All you have said to me today of my grandfather has been mere confirmation that even with his every default, he was a man that would have *hated* Munday. And hated him from good reason as a liar and a furtive practiser. I do not speak of his love-making, that was furtive and dishonest enough, but no worse than many other men's: no, but there were further matters – mother, I cannot recount them, walls have ears. I should not have said it, not even to you. This is not a safe city. Not like Canterbury. Did they not send word to Canterbury how Christopher Marlowe died?"

Lydia saw that Lucretia all of a sudden was frightened; saw how she got up from her stool and fidgeted round the room: saw how she pulled some papers out of a book, shoved them quickly into a shoe, shoved the shoe under the drapery of the bed in a series of quick movements like a conjurer's passes, had she done it or not? Short of stooping beneath the bed and reaching the shoe out to prove it, Lydia could not be certain at all that she saw what she knew she had seen. She did not know how to respond to this fear. It was beyond her county-town experience, far more awkward to enter into even than fornications in a late-night wine-house.

She said to herself, "This is just Kilkenny, just the Cantons, near as bad as the ship of Zeeland on the way to the Cantons. Then I was the child and the grown people told me nothing. Now I am old: the terror I can smell is hidden from me by this child." She tried to speak of something else, asked nervously when was he returning (meaning the man who had left his sword on the wall, his shape in Lucretia's bed).

Lucretia sat down again, there was relief in her face, the man in question could not be what frightened her. "Oh don't disturb your thoughts with him, mother. He went to Windsor and won't come back, not for a time. He says he has his duties, *noblesse oblige*. I daresay they'd be less pressing if there were no plague in London. Mother, you do know there is plague? Do you smoke a tobacco-pipe? They allege it an infallible preventive. I had my own pipe for a while, but then I found it did harm to my voice. So I damned the bloody plague and dared it to infect me. More people don't die than do."

Lydia, testily: "Wash, both your person and your clothes, sprinkle your room. Why, look at the ruff on your neck, it's as foul as a sheep's tail. And please will you take that bonnet of vanity off the top of the Blessed Word!" She flung out her hand to the Bible, grabbed it up from under hat and cittern, blew off the dust, laid it carefully on an empty shelf-space.

There were footsteps on the stairs. Lucretia looked alarmed for the briefest instant, cast her eye on the pair of pistols: then she smiled. "It's only my singing-master. He's a courteous harmless fellow, why not meet him and hear my lesson?"

II

(Pastoral)

Dorothy Dreams

And there appeared another token in heaven, and behold a great red dragon, having seven heads and ten horns and seven crowns upon his heads: and his tail drew the third part of the stars, and cast them to the earth. And the dragon stood before the woman, which was ready to be delivered: for to devour her child as soon as it were born.

And the woman fled into the wilderness, where she had a place prepared of God.

And the earth holp the woman, and the earth opened her mouth, and swallowed up the river which the dragon cast out of his mouth. And the dragon was wroth with the woman: and went and made war with the remnant of her seed.

(Revelation of St John the Divine, Chapter 12)

(i) Flight Into Egypt

The last years of the Widow Dorothy (in her son's house in London, near to St Giles' Church, Cripplegate) were spent, as Lydia said, between sleeping and sleeping, and when she woke she was still asleep. Articulate expression of thought was long gone, sight was gone, most of her hearing; which is not to say such an apparent useless slumber of the human spirit continued without dreams. Of course, they were not co-ordinated: time was dissolved in them; a series of images of what she had been, who she had been, where, of who helped to make her, and how she made herself.

She dreamed, for example, quite a lot about the Pope, sometimes with a brass bucket on his head and horns coming out over his ears, sometimes all holy and glorious with a saint's halo, a countenance of the utmost serenity, and the gentle hands of Almighty God conveying his aged body to an everlasting rest.

More often she dreamed of Bale. When she dreamed of the first time she met him, this is what she saw, in her sleep:

★

Dorothy Parsons, wretched orphan, fifteen years of age, limped slowly along the frozen road-ruts of Norfolk at the tail end of a tattered little company. Her oversize boots had great holes worn in them, she had stuffed them with straw against the winter, but the chilblains were none the less an agony. Her thin dress, striped in once-glaring red-white-and-green, was no good at all as a wind-shield, it was pressed so close against her by the gusts out of the north-east that every minute opening between warp and woof of the shoddy fabric became a stretched window-hole to let in the desperate chill: and that is to say nothing of the threadbare portions and roughly-mended three-cornered rents. To make it worse, she possessed no under-garments, except a pair of red woollen stockings that came no higher than an inch below her knees. She did have a kind of cloak: she ought not to have worn it on the road, in fact, as it was part of her stock-in-trade as a performer, being the Virgin Mary's sky-blue mantle; it was very thin material, and when she wrapped it round bosom and shoulders in a necessary double fold, it did not protect her thighs or the small of her back. Her head was tied with a kerchief of purple that had once had a gold fringe, but the wind pulled it about, and pulled her hair out of it, whipping the strands into her face. Dirty hair, it was, in original shade very fair; red, yellow, or brown, according to the way the light would strike it, though perhaps more red than anything else. But now it seemed simply mud-colour. The brass ear-rings did not enhance it. Blue misery of her clenched features overpowered all hopeful ornament to anyone who might look at her.

Not that anyone did. The road was empty, and her companions trudged in file ahead of her without any glancing behind. They were all as poorly dressed as herself. Two men, a sulky boy (or perhaps a young man; his short stature, and round hairless cunning face like a crabapple, yellow and withered, gave little clue to his exact age), and one woman: all carrying on their backs pedlar-like baskets tied with rope, all thrusting their slow footsteps forward with the help of long thick sticks. Dorothy too had her basket to carry, and its weight now and then caused her to lean on her staff with both hands and pull herself forward by main force up the more formidable slopes. The countryside was level enough, but the road was so bad it held pits and sudden stumbling-blocks that seemed absolute Alps; and they were all five so downright weary that every step was a mountain-conquest.

She was a big girl, and had she been decently fed, would even have appeared stout. Despite the ungainly posture and movement imposed upon her by the weather, by her exhaustion, she was arguably the most graceful of the party. She had better be, she thought, she was their dancer: her business to provoke some ideal of beauty among those to whom they would play that night. She only hoped there would be enough supper granted them to make it possible. Soup, bread, and a warm fire, that first; then to work. Tonight in a farmhouse perhaps; it was Twelfth Night, there should be a party somewhere, their talents would be in demand. And tomorrow, the Epiphany feast, out-of-doors on the Fair Green of Diss. Supposing they ever got there. If this cold continued, out-of-doors on the green was a horrible prospect. Perhaps sufficient money from the evening performance to allow them to buy a break-fast?

If not, then James Catgut would have to steal for them. He was good at it, as a rule, a better thief than a fiddler: and she herself had her own skill with dip-of-the-finger, though it scared her to have to use it. She also had the rudiments of another dubious skill, what her companions called the 'derry-down'. After two or three years at it, she had come to find the derry-down less frightening than tiresome, and sometimes rather comical, although there had been one or two men whose ugly demands had given her bad dreams for a long time afterwards. James Catgut, however, could be relied on to protect her from the worst of such customers. He had a sharp knife slotted at the back of his fiddle-case, and knew how to use it to create the most confusion in an adversary. He rarely needed actually to stab: the flash and flicker of his blade was so quick and alarming that men ran from him as soon as he showed it. Dorothy had a knife, or rather a pair of knives. Catgut had been teaching her some of his tricks with them, but she had applied them to her dance-routine and had never yet, thank God, required them for self-defence.

But James Catgut gave her bad dreams too. The other woman in the company was his Mrs Nelly, and Dorothy thought he was tiring of her. If so, it was possible he would come seeking compensation, his deferred reward from Dorothy for his protection and occasional tuition. He was a lean black-muzzled weasel of a man, very humorous when he chose to be, and she did not dislike him. But she did not want to anger Nelly. Nelly was as lean as her husband; lame in one leg, so she could not dance: but a passionate singer of love-ballads. Kindhearted skin-and bone, fiercely abusive in her manner, she knew all sorts of devices against the company's permanent ill-health; herbs, magic charms, particular prayers at particular shrines, poultices. She had explained to Dorothy with great care about the days of the moon and the curse of a woman's blood-flow, so that it was possible to calculate the right time and the wrong time to earn money from the derry-down. Once, when a mistake had been made, and Dorothy's curse threatened to become what more prosperous folk would call a blessing, she had given her some queer boiling drinks, built a skin-tent around her over a pit of red-hot stones in the middle of a wood, and sat her there to sweat (with cast-lead saints' images pressed between her thighs) until something happened. What did happen, said Nelly, would have been a child fit for the font, had it not come out in time.

"Mary mercy, bird, but I've left you half-dead, you ought to have told me a month ago. It was that bastard fen-man in the Waterbeach ale-stake, wasn't it? I warned you he was bad luck. You're better off by far without any of *his* puddle-water gets."

If James Catgut made Nelly into an enemy, Dorothy would have to look elsewhere for a living. In the middle of winter it would not be easy. Nelly, she thought, had indeed been a friend. She had bad dreams of Nelly hostile and Nelly's man far too friendly, she was having one now as she trudged . . .

*

Widow Dorothy in her warm bed dreamed of her own bad dreams that she had suffered when she was so young. Her wandering mind, by its own effort, shifted itself off from them: Bale was what she was to dream, Bale in the freezing weather. But there were still several miles to walk, it was getting dark, the low rolling fields were barren of all shelter. Mile after mile of them. A few naked trees on the skyline grew permanently bent over, distorted for all their lives by the unappeasable east wind. Scant black thorn-bushes and brambles in an endless double row marked out the course of the road, dipping and climbing from one shallow valley into the next: not a rooftop to be seen, nor any smudge of smoke from anyone's fire. The ruts of the road were hard ice. This dream was taking too long.

*

The town of Diss held its great fair in the warm season of the year, but upon Epiphany there was a smaller subordinate muster of trades-people there, to allow the townsfolk and neighbouring rustics to stock up their stores for the dreary months until Easter. Too much, as always, would have been eaten during the feast, larders were barer than had been planned, and in any case the goods on offer were all at reduced prices, left-overs which the travelling merchants were anxious to sell quickly and clear themselves for the coming year. Wool, cloth and livestock still cumbering the local granges could be got rid of, no less cheaply. It was not a fair for gaining wealth: more of a purge of last year's commercial incompetence, it had the atmosphere of ill-tempered loss-cutting. No place for an itinerant minstrel-troupe to visit with high expectations. If entertainers were to make money in mid-winter, it would already have been made: Christ's Nativity was all but concluded, family gatherings in hall and houseplace were now dispensing, and those who had made them laugh, made them sing and dance, incited their fireside lust with speculative artistry, had little to do but hope for maybe just a small bit of audience before sun went down and doors were shut.

A troupe without regular sponsorship had a difficulty over the Christmas, whereas those that were 'established' were normally required to spend the full twelve days upon their patron's premises; and all the neighbours invited, which meant that very few in the district would need to hire minstrels of their own. So knocking at doors and trusting to pot-luck was not a lively prospect. Streets, markets, public-houses, were of course a possibility: but then there was the problem of the law. Colleagues with patrons (and therefore official licence) were jealous of their prerogative, and might very well inform against irregular interlopers: there were penalties involved, 'rogues-and-vagabonds' was an outcast status, and Dorothy and her comrades were marked with it. It had not always been the case with them. Three years since, when she first joined them, they had had a certain standing. A letter of permission from the Sheriff of Suffolk, no less: but now all this was gone. Blame James Catgut and his woman, that time they robbed the poorbox in the church at Saxmundham. Nothing was proved, and the money was never recovered, but the suspicion had killed their licence.

They had once had a tawdry booth, and a wagon to carry its framework: the vehicle itself made them a raised stage, and the painted curtains that hung on poles at one end of it were a cramped but useful tiring-house. Now all this was gone. They must make do with whatever they could carry in their fardels, the awkward baskets that so slowed their passage as they walked. They tied their sticks together to form improvised flag-staves. They had once been a troupe of six, which meant three ten-foot poles. Now they were but five, so one pole was only half the length of the others. But they stood them in a triangle to mark out their playing-space on the green, and tied their strips of once-bright bunting to them, to stream in the cruel wind and call attention to their shivering presence.

They also called attention with their own persons. The boy Conrad (he was from Germany, God only knew how *he* got himself into this dishevelment) was strutting between the flags, blowing hunting-calls out of a bugle. He uttered cries as well, like a falconer calling a hawk: unusual high-pitched cries. He was thought to be a eunuch, poor lad; not externally – Dorothy knew, and would have preferred not to have known, that his ball-stones were where they ought to be – but somehow within his body the juices had no engendering. She herself prowled around him, in a set of feline capers, shaking her big backside and tingling a tambourine. She found it possible, in the dance, to forget just for a while the agony of chilblains.

Not easy to collect their crowd. Not, at least, if it was to be a *paying* crowd. The vendor of base-metal jewelry five yards away from their pitch outshouted them with his raucous patter, offering unheard-of bargains to exactly the sort of people they wished to attract to themselves – oafish young shepherds with impressionable girls on their arms, farmers whose wives had reproached them for inadequate Christmas presents, artisans and apprentices from the town who needed to swagger on Sundays in the churchyard among their rivals. None of these had much money to spend; by the time the show began, what little they had would already have been laid out on something solid they could take away with them.

The leader of the troupe decided it was now or never. He was a grey-haired unwholesome puffy man who called himself the 'Lowestoft Rover', having at some time followed the sea. The death of his wife, the previous year, had sickened him of his life and taken all the joy (for there had, once, been a full-hearted joy) out of his performances. She was Spanish, she never learned English, and Dorothy thought she died of despair at her error in ever leaving Cadiz on the Rover's ship. Strange, it was the very same year, 1528, that the King of England let it be known that his own Spanish wife from Aragon could die of *her* despair, and welcome . . .

The old man had named his company 'The Rover's Runagates', and dressed himself for work as a sort of mock-pirate, with tinsel-braided sea-clothes, a Barbary turban, and a battered cutlass. He bounced in between the flags, drove Dorothy and Conrad out onto the fringes with a wave of his weapon, and commenced to wheel around firing old and dirty jokes to every point of the compass. Thereby he did establish something like a circle of hearers: and he told them a long narrative about a voyage he claimed to have made where there was nothing to eat but beans, and the seamen's bowels resented it. Conrad, who could break wind at will, followed him with his breeches stretched, illustrating the story as loudly as possible. This created some laughter: and Dorothy at once ran round outside the flags, holding out her tambourine and getting a few small coins, while the next item took over the playing-space.

This was James and Nelly, singing and acting the dialogue ballad of *The Nutbrown Maid*. A simplistic piece of romantic sentiment, free from obscenity, for the Rover had noticed there were more women than men in their audience. In an outlaw's hood of lincoln-green James sang his hard life and not without pathos:

> For an outlaw this is the law, that men him take and bind,
> Without pit-ee, hangéd to be, and waver with the wind.

He taunted his girl to dare to join him:

> Yet take good heed, for ever I dread, that you could not sustain
> The thorny ways, the deep vall-ayes, the snow, the frost, the rain.

He knew about this life, and he sang what he suffered. When Nelly sang, in reply:

> For in my mind, of all mankind, I love but you alone –

and then swore she would never leave him, it was so obviously true that Dorothy felt her heart turn over. When would she ever feel such love as this that had held these two ragamuffins together through all the nasty expediencies of their trade?

Then she thought again, "James Catgut is beginning to think that Nelly is too old and worn for this song. That's because he don't watch her, like I do, when she sings. He told me that I should take her part in it next year. Up his arse-hole will I take her part! Whatever else I put my hand to, I'm not thieving my fellows' stage-business. Nelly says she has eternal pleasure from the derry-down with James Catgut. Says other women as well receive men's bodies with an equal delight, maybe when I'm as old as her I'll have learned what she's talking about . . ."

Cheerful applause for *The Nutbrown Maid*, more coppers in the tambourine: Dorothy's circulation with it became part of the next act, her solo dancing. She jigged lightly between the coin-givers, and so into the ring, emptying the money (with an insolent grace) as she glided past the Rover's knees. He sat on an upturned fardel with a red cloth spread out on his lap, watching his company, trying to enjoy his company, trying to help the people enjoy them: but his boisterous geniality collapsed every few seconds and his tired face sagged with melancholy. Dorothy's dance was athletic: her big bones had been well (and cruelly) trained. Even half-starved, she could throw somer-saults, she could dance on her hands holding her two knives by the points and jabbing their hilts into the ground to support her, while she shot her long red-stockinged legs in the air, and deftly twitched knees and thighs to hold her skirts together for ostensible decency. The Rover announced this as the *Dance of Herodias' Daughter* and it became part of a moral-allegory: he was Herod on his fardel-throne with his lap filled (or partially-filled) with jingling largesse: Catgut's fiddle provided the music, Nelly was Herodias, snuggling into the Rover's neck with libidinous kisses, and Conrad was the Vice, prancing around Dorothy and attempting (more or less in vain) to jerk down her draperies so that leering Herod could delight himself with the sight of her secret parts. Then Catgut dropped his fiddle and strode forward with a cross in his hand. He had a line or two to speak:

> John Baptist from his prison-house doth cry and he doth call
> God's vengeance upon this incest for which you go straightway to hell!

Herod said:

> I do repent, my sins are very sore,
> The daughter of my brother's wife must therefore dance no more.

But Dorothy did not stop, Conrad beat the tambourine, and her legs waved more wildly than ever. Herod said:

> My lust is too great, she danceth at my wish,
> Let her have what she craveth –

And Dorothy, swinging herself in a great leap right-side-up again, ran to Nelly, mimed a fierce whispering with her, and then shouted out:

> – *his* head, upon a dish!

The whole troupe, at that point, gave a great ululating cry, and whirled themselves into a tight group, Catgut disappeared under their clothes, and when they spread themselves out again for the tableau, there he was lying on the trodden grass with Herod's red cloth covering his head (the money having been swiftly conveyed into the Rover's pouch); and a false head of papier-maché on a plate was held out by Conrad towards Dorothy, who accepted it with what seemed to be the deepest depravity.

They had played this piece so many times that they were able to contrive the necessary sleight-of-hand at the end with some degree of precision. But they should have had their wagon-stage, they should have had their proper costumes. Catgut as the Baptist with a torn blanket thrown over his daily jacket and breeches was particularly unconvincing, and there had been a time when both Herod and Herodias wore crowns of brass, not pasteboard. All this was long gone, and the audience knew it.

James Catgut rose to his feet and offered a final prayer, identifying the allegorical meanings of the scriptural personages, Herod as 'Pride of Manstrength', Herodias as 'Worldly Desire', her Daughter as 'Carnal Temptation' and the Baptist as 'God's Truth': a few people clapped and Conrad leapt and farted to show that the Devil still held sway in an unregenerate human race. Dorothy once again threaded the crowd with the tambourine.

She was holding it out and hopefully rattling it under the runny nose of a shopkeeper with a bad cold who showed no desire to give her anything, when she heard a harsh voice behind her:

"Yes he was a wise king, Herod Antipas, until vision of loveliness overcame his brain, his addled brain overcame his conscience: and nobody, ever again, remembered his wisdom. All in a moment, wasn't it? a swift arrow to split him in the thick of his blood."

She turned to see who had spoken, but there was a huddle of yokels just at her elbow who blocked her view and tried to jostle her. One of them said, grossly enough, "Them red socks, da'rter, was a sight shorter on your wobbling shanks nor what you'd think!", and his friends guffawed. She pushed him aside, angrily, just in time to see the bustling figure of a squat broad-backed friar in a white mantle making his way through the people to a bookseller's small booth on the far side of the gimcrack-vendor. She could not see the friar's face.

*

The previous night they had performed before a bored old curate and his guests in the parsonage hall. She thought there had been a white-friar there as well, but he'd left before they finished, and she wasn't sure if it was the same. The curate was bored, and his friends were all elderly men who preferred, as a Twelfth Night treat, to drink themselves slowly stupid and ramble through lethargic prophecies of next season's wool-mart. So the Runagates had cut their programme short – a few noël-noël carols and a perfunctory (indeed skimped) dance-cum-tableau of *The Coming of the Three Wise Men*, appropriate to the date: Dorothy had been the Blessed Virgin with a doll in her arms; Nelly an Angel, a Midwife, and Saint Joseph, one after the other; while the Wise Men had oddly included a boy singing in Dutch. The Wise Men then became Herod-and-Herod's-Murderers looking for Innocents to kill, which gave an opportunity for the Rover and James Catgut to show proficiency with cutlass and stabbing-knife. It had not earned them much money, but the priest had given them supper and let them sleep on the straw in his barn.

*

Widow Dorothy moaned in her dream. She was the Mother of God, holding Baby-God. God's Father was a thin lame black-eyed woman who cursed and swore, promising hoarsely over and over again that King Herod her lover would not bloody send the Son to crucifixion, if only she could swive him sufficient; so she tumbled among the dead brown ferns with a toad-faced turbanned king, sweating over him to stir his loins, while Dorothy watched from concealment in an agony of apprehension. Hours of it, and then stillness, he was satiated, snoring easily. Until, with a heave of his swollen body, he sat up, clutched his fingers round the narrow waist of the lame woman, pulled himself from under her and tossed her out onto the pathway in an upside-down tangle of haggard thighs and scrawny teats.

"Crucify?", he slobbered, "Of course, little lords and ladies, of course we won't crucify. Instead we'll have his head on the dinner-table. Put an apple in his mouth, boy: don't you know it's a Christmas feast? D'you think I eat nothing but beans?" He reached out a fat wet hand to pull the Baby from Dorothy's breast: it had been but a dream, now it was whirlpool of nightmare. And yet she knew, as she always knew, her saviour would rescue the Saviour.

And he did.

It had all happened so many times she didn't even need to scream for him. He came bursting through the grasp of the thorns, his feet squelched in the ooze, a swirl of white gown enveloped her, she was pressed against his chest almost smothering the Baby – and all she could see was his big blotchy face, his pendulous nose, shaven crown, gleaming shaven chin protruding below heavy lips – why were his eyes closed? What did he not want to look at? Never mind, she would close hers.

He was saving her, that was all that mattered: and saving her beloved Child.

*

It was the penultimate item of the show, just before the early dusk, that brought them into so much trouble.

The Rover should never have agreed that they ate a mid-day meal in the inn at the edge of the Fair Green; they should have followed their usual practice, to break for half-an-hour and buy oddments of food at one of the cookstalls in the fair. But there were already flakes of snow on the wind, and he thought that his cold disheartened troupe might stir up their spirits just a little with a warm room and proper hot dishes. When they came to pay the bill, however, they realised they had spent nearly all they had earned all morning. It must be made up that same day, or they would have no food the next day: what to do? With misgiving, he allowed *Friar Jenkin and Barbara's Bum* to be performed just before they concluded their day's work. The final item, as always, would be the dance-battle of *King Winter and King Summer*, which varied according to the season and always went down well with country audiences: in this dreadful weather, of course, King Winter must lose the fight.

Friar Jenkin and Barbara's Bum was a Laughable Farce, of a perfectly ordinary type; being in fact about two bums, Barbara's (which was Dorothy's) and Milady Tipnostril's (Nelly's): and the Friar (Catgut at his most obnoxious) got them mixed up with lamentable consequences. It lasted perhaps twenty minutes. It was a feeble enough tale and no-one had ever laughed at it very much, but Conrad persuaded them that it presented a perfect framework for a whole new class of presentation, which might in the end, once they had thoroughly mastered it, recoup their fortunes, regain a patron, bring them absolutely back to where they deserved to belong. He talked about 'Hans Sachs, the Nuremberg Master-Singer' until Catgut admitted that it could be keen craft to have in your hood a notable foreign name, ready to reach for in tight corners; and the Rover had grudgingly, lazily, said yes, they might try it when they had time. Neither he nor James Catgut, nor either of the women, had ever heard of Hans Sachs, but 'Master-Singer' had a good sound to it, and Conrad was very persuasive.

The only trouble was, they had never properly rehearsed the new version. Conrad argued, no harm, no danger, he was playing the hero, the Bold Apprentice who rescues Barbara from the designs of the Friar: and he would insert all that was needed into the action as it went along. The meal at the inn had included hot mulled wine, and common sense had flown away on its fumes. When the Rover summoned up his last blurred objection, as they struggled from the bar-parlour into the deadly biting chill, Conrad gave him only a Dutchman's oath and a falconer's halloo. He was in truth a stubborn young fellow, his pale eyes would harden like pebbles over unexpected issues: and Dorothy knew that none of the others knew how they were going to get through the afternoon, so why not let him have his head?

Nelly then sang, and Dorothy danced, and the two of them between them did so well that nearly all the loafers left in the fair were gathered close around when the Friar Jenkin play began. Bawdy bums and brutal beatings, they rattled through the anecdote until the final thrust of the plot, the discovery by the Bold Apprentice of the Friar caught by his robe in a practicable bramble-bush, where he was laying-in-wait for Barbara. The original, as they had always played it, ended with more fisticuffs and a stewpan full of shit.

Conrad's innovation was simplicity itself. First he knocked the Friar out of the bush with a well-placed kick in the cullions, and then, as the audience made a tentative show of clapping, he pulled from his wallet a bright new printed book: "New Testament, English tongue!", he announced in his broken accent, and immediately proceeded to read from it. It was Saint Paul's condemnation to the Romans of their "hearts' lust in to uncleanness to defile their own bodies in themselves", how such behaviour changed the truth of God into a lie, worshipping and serving the creature more than the Creator. He then shoved the book into Catgut's hand and demanded, with menaces, that he read it out too. Of course Catgut could not read, and he knew that Conrad knew he couldn't: but he was brisk enough as an improviser to see what he must do. He *said* he could not read. "What, a friar, and cannot read!" roared the Bold Apprentice. "How much money for your Bible-talk have you extorted from these women under pretence of your holy learning, *ja*? You cannot read, but you can *say*. After me: say!" And so he made Friar Jenkin repeat Saint Paul quite slowly, kicking him when he dropped his voice, and altogether ending the play with a quite surprising flourish.

And moreover, Conrad was right: many people gave more money than had been given all morning. Good jokes against bad friars were liked, and audiences of an assured religious feeling were always particularly appreciative of them. Diss seemed a pious place: so why did no-one offer the Runagates supper and shelter for the night?

Conrad's version of the tale had not been a *bad* joke against *good* friars, there was no doubt of that: but something nonetheless was not quite as it ought. Catgut said it might be the book. The Rover said, "Book in a pig's turd. Scripture is Scripture, we didn't mock it, damn it: young Dutchy read it out as veritable as could be."

Catgut muttered that right minstrels never used books: their jokes should be out-of-head perfect, learned by ear and practice. These country-folk would be thinking that the Runagates had shoved themselves up above their proper status. Only clerks read out aloud: and nobody gave clerks free suppers, not if they valued their good household gear. "You can't expect 'em to invite thieves," he grumbled, "A score of words from book-print and our reputation's blown."

Conrad said nothing.

The Winter-and-Summer dance was watched by very few.

Dorothy wondered could it be something *in* the book that had so pleased the people and upset them, and all at the same time? She had never heard Saint Paul read out in English before: he sounded as priest-like as she would have expected. But 'priest-like' was in itself a worrying quality: they ought not to be meddling with it, perhaps. So many troubled tales these days about trouble with the clergy and clergy in trouble. The rumoured name of Luther came vaguely to her mind. A *German* . . . ? What *were* 'Master-Singers' . . . ? She wished they had put a few more questions to Conrad. But now it was too late: and Conrad was saying nothing.

*

Because of their mid-day indulgence, they did not dare spend at the inn again for food: although Catgut with some dip-of-the-finger among the departing fair-goers managed to secure enough unofficial money to provide himself with a leather-jack full of cider, which he generously passed round the company. The curate had made it plain they would not be welcome a second night at the parsonage; so they found a disused farm-shed of sorts standing isolated by the river's edge not far from the Fair Green, where Nelly lit a fire and cooked some oatmeal she had saved. With the onset of snow, it was not quite so cold as it had been. They went to sleep all in a lump wrapped up like a litter of piglets, snorting a thick ferment of apple out of gaping mouths and explosive guts.

An hour or so before dawn, Dorothy got up to piss. She was stooped forward outside the hut, just finishing, shivering gooseflesh under the lee of the wind, when a noise from the dark behind her shot her upright in a leap of panic. The intermittent full moon, between one hurrying snow-cloud and the next, showed her a man in white, as white as the ground all around her, staring down at her from a brambly bank between two pollard willows. He was a white-friar, she saw; his cloak clasped about him, his cowl pulled down over his white beret. The ear-flaps of the beret were tied around his chin, and altogether he gave the appearance of a greedy walking corpse, new-risen from a fresh grave. Perhaps too stout and stocky for a true ghost.

But even so, his abrupt manifestation was perfectly horrifying, and Dorothy took three steps backward, her mouth wide open but unable to scream.

"No harm, maiden, so long as you keep yourself from a plunge into the river." She checked her feet: sure enough, she was on the very brink. His words were genial, more or less: he was certainly human, but exactly how human? If his intent was as Friar Jenkin's, how to respond to it on such a blood-stopping bitter night?

It seemed he was thinking the same. He said, "True, Barbara, the friar lurketh, the *literate* friar, where the child-of-God doth uncover her person. And true I stayed to watch, for a short while permitting reprehensible distempered heat to run at rut through this cold body. Which I tell you, that I may prove to you your little breech-burning play was not short of the mark. Come: walk with me, keep warm, it is better we are not heard from the hut."

She was uneasily conscious that her skirt had got caught up behind her in her girdle. She twisted round to adjust it: he was holding a little willow-switch in his hand, and as she turned he gave her a sharp flick across her bareness. "No!" he said, and dropped the switch. "No," and he put up his other hand against her lips to cut off the cry she was making. Then he seized her by the wrist in a strong grip, too strong to be opposed, and moved her along the water's edge.

"I said to you, no harm: indeed, an active good. But I must tell it you alone, as the angel did to Saint Joseph upon the first Epiphany. When you tell the others and get them out to the land of Egypt, you don't let 'em know *I* told you. Mine hour is not yet come." He jerked on her wrist, hurting her, and dragging her round so they were face-to-face. "Tell me, that Dutch boy – Almain-Dutch or Nether-land-Dutch? – whatever he was, where did he get it? – the book, child, the Testament: heretical translation and printed abroad – did he not know it could be *death* to carry it? Are you yourself able to read the written word?"

Trembling, she answered, "A little bit, yes, the Rover taught me: but before that, my father did, before he died, that was four year since. He was a priest and very poor, but he loved me: and when my mother left him for the cheapjack out of Bletchley, he – " She was gabbling without thought, except that this strange man seemed suddenly the sort of man to whom it was possible to gabble.

He cut in: "Priest? So you will be christened, even though you are the fruit of vow-breaking. Your name?"

"Dorothy, sir, Dorothy Parsons. 'Parsons' because of – "

"Because of him. So a *parish* priest. Where?"

"Cambridge, sir: Saint Benet's. Not rightly the Parson. No more than his Curate, that's what he was, truly."

"And what year were you born?"

"I think I am fifteen."

He spoke quickly; to himself, she thought. It could hardly be to her, there was too much Latin. "*Ergo*, let's consider it, it makes it eighth Henry, *annus quintus*; *videlicet*, of Christ fifteen-hundred fourteen." And then, aloud, and quite surprised: "Why child, when you were a babe, I too was in Cambridge, Jesus College, where the friars put me, of the Order of Mount Carmel, to learn my divinity, to confound heretics, which I have done with most thoughtless diligence. I heard Mass, nay *said* Mass, many occasions in that very Benet's: yea and preached therein also. If your father was the old man I remember, he was a compassionate holy soul-priest notwithstanding his illicit woman. I did not know of her at the time. But why should I? All know about such things, saving only other priests. And we know too much to venture upon asking. Suppose one were brave enough to state openly without fear: 'Illicit women should be licit'? If so, then no more Jenkins? And how else to curb the unteachable eleventh finger where it shoots out from the root of our groin? Grubby digit, as it is, marking only the high road to the devil's gate. To say nothing of the boy-buggery, to say nothing of the filth of that . . ."

Despite the wind's knife, sweat was gleaming on his brow and his big smooth bulk of a chin dripped with it. His eyes glared out darkly, not at her, but over her shoulder, as though he searched the night for flying demons. Dorothy thought this might be the time to name her price. But somehow she felt that he had genuinely not come for any fashion of derry-down, he had a far more serious purpose. He was betraying himself, it would only be decency to stop him. She clamped her lips shut against his kiss and wried her head aside. He released her

then and crushed his hands together under his scapular, a gesture of
self-reproach:

"Forget that: forget it at once! You and your troupe, you know
where the evil lies, you make it most honest and plain in your ignorant
comedies, but they *are* ignorant and will bring you to a rigour of
chastisement, and no-one will speak in your defence: I'm damnable
certain you're not licensed by any adequate patron, no? For that
Testament, complaint has been laid. If the Justice of the Peace had not
been asleep over his flagons of Epiphany, you'd all be in the lockup
already. Shift yourselves, you shiftless runagates, be out of your hut
and out of Diss before sunrise, – " With a sudden change of tone:
"Ssh, not a sound, girl, behind the tree here, make it sharp!"

Tramping footsteps along the river-bank, lanterns, men shouting,
dogs. Dorothy saw the rotten door-plank torn away from the hut,
Nelly hauled out first, then Conrad, then the other two: their poor
baggage ripped open in the moonlight, their tinsel playing-props
scattered broad-cast until the constables found what they wanted, the
book. And then all four clustered together, driven like sheep toward
the bridge, protesting, cursing, wailing in outrage and dismay.

Someone said: "There was five, warn't there? Where's the birdy?"

Another voice: "Out on the fuck, very like. But who cares about
her? *She* won't be the reading one. It's these we've to bring in, so slap
it about: I'm perished bloody dead."

The white-friar kept Dorothy pressed close against the tree-trunk
until all was quiet. And then he let her go. He said nothing, just let her
go, commenced striding toward the bridge, after the others, and never
looked back.

*

*As the four of them sat in the stocks, stinking in their excrements, cramped in their
limbs' agony, frozen almost to the point of death, with nothing to look at but the
ducks and geese that squawked helpless on the ice of Diss Mere, she came to them
with hot water, napkins to cleanse their faces where their sometime merry
audience had pelted them with merry dirt, she brought blankets, and ointment for
their raw flogged backs; a bottle of aquavit and a kettle of soup from the inn near
the parish church and she ministered to them in their misery.*

*Corporal Work of Mercy, it was commanded of Christ, to succour all captives,
no matter what their crime. The old Curate came up the hill from his parsonage,
and gravely praised her. The white-friar who walked beside him said nothing,
but winked.*

*And yet none of this happened. It should have done: which is why, no doubt,
Widow Dorothy kept on dreaming it. She also dreamed the other story, the one*

which did happen, that she was begging her bread and desperately whoring herself, ten miles away, terrified, when the Lowestoft Rover and his people underwent the process of law.

(ii) *Terpsichore*

A long time before Dorothy and the white-friar had a further occasion to talk.

She did not forget him through those years. How could she? It was as though he was on-purpose following her about, keeping note of her hand-to-mouth life, dogging her like an implacable officer, or was it a protector, guardian-angel? Whichever it was, he scared her because he never came close, and yet he always let her know he was there and he had seen her: just a lift of the eyelid at the back of an audience, a quick hand to his ear if he passed her in the street, nod of the head through the hearth-smoke in a crowded bar-room, and then he would be gone. But the signal had been unmistakeable: 'Next time, wherever, whenever . . .'

But to begin with, she did not see him. She was at her very lowest, the winter months after the disaster of Diss, travelling in a slow zig-zag across country, tending westward and northward, Thetford, Swaffham, East Dereham, alone, relying bravely upon her new-found insolence: she had had to find it, or die.

At about Easter she came to Norwich, and no-one had prevented her. She hoped to hide herself in this busy town: she thought she succeeded. At any rate she was not accosted with any form of accusation, she heard no voice cry "heretic", felt no hand upon her shoulder. She went to see a man she knew who kept a low disorderly ale-cellar for soldiers of the castle. He offered her a job, to sing and dance while his customers drank; and once or twice, as she fulfilled this work, she thought she saw the white friar . . .

Late at night, in the back room, for selected company, she undertook to dance naked save for shoes and red stockings; the fierce erect high-heel-stamping Spanish style which the Rover's wife had tried to teach her – hysterical Juanita, or (as they'd called her) Jennet, without friends in a strange land, passing on her resentful skill the last year of her life.

But not every night, the back room. Because the Mayor and Corporation were under pressure from the Bishop to prevent such enormities, bribes had to be paid, arrangements made. "Damn that," she said. "What do I care for what you say you've to pay 'em, I'm ready both night and morning, so long as *you* pay *me*." But the work was a displeasure to her. She did not like soldiers. She was secretly most disturbed to hear about the Bishop. He was reputed a severe old man, very angry against religious deviants. The Rover's Runagates would have been brought into his diocesan court for sentence after Diss. Maybe they were not yet indicted? In which case they would still be in prison? For several weeks, she did not dare to ask.

But one night, wrapped loosely in her shawl, talking between performances to a brutal crop-haired youth who had bought her a glass of brandywine, she discovered him to be a turnkey from the Bishop's gaol. Delicately, as it were casually, she inserted her question into his rebarbative recital of the attractions of his employment (she had rather hers than his, even so). He was in the middle of an account of how a Lollard-minded weaver was being kept in such tight leg-irons that his left foot had gangrened half-way up to the knee:

"You can whiff it in the courtyard even when he's locked in his cell. O'course they *are* shit, en'they? So o'course they stink like shit: but you don't want it in your nostrils all day long to bring it home to the wife an' kidlings? Notwithstanding he still sings his hymns. He's for the bonfire at Corpus Christi, not long to go now, init? An' he won't need his leg where he's off to, so what's the odds? . . . Diss, did you say, darling? A pack o'minstrels? No, we never had *them* in. Wait a minute though, I lie. Round Christmas, wasn't that it? We was told to expect 'em. Right: an' they never came. Turned out the local bench had dropped charges. Gave 'em the stocks and the old horsewhip, but for vagabondage, none of *our* business. No, there was a white-friar, by some chance he was at the arraignment, big-headed roaring fellow, very well known, bully Bale of the Maldon house in Essex, he's a Norwich man, en'e? and the Bishop has his eye on him – trouble-maker, intellectual – well, somehow it was *him* that proved how the heretic book that was in evidence, not one of 'em could read it, that it hadn't been right-quoted in the play at all, and the previous night at the parson's house they'd all performed impeccable orthodox.

"Which o'course walloped the Parson where it hurt, well it would, wouldn't it? So *he* added his own influence, and begged 'em all off. Our clerk had been over to Diss to receive depositions. Comes back empty-handed, his ballocks froze to pistol-bullets from the weather on his ride, that's how I remember it, init? *He* made out it was all rigged, why did no-one ask 'em who gave 'em the bloody book? But in these backwards places, y'know, they all stand together: one clod-hopping cabbage-head keeps his cloak to cover another. In my view half the countryside's been subverted by the German-Dutch: stands to reason, don't it? We're that close to the seaports.

"Pity the Bishop's so old. He can't rightly keep his eye on things and look out for his proper entitlement.

"All right, then, darling, finished your drink, an't you? So where-'ud you like it? Upstairs which I've to pay for, or out in the yard where I don't? Not but what I'll not pay *you*, I'm no bloody cheat, you know . . ."

Well: they were, after all, free (oh weight off her mind!): and his name was Bale.

*

Two weeks later, she danced Spanish (but clothed) in the bar with her castanets. A white mantle in the shadows under the entry-ladder whisked out of sight up out of the house as soon as she put her eye on it: but she was sure it was him.

The next night an unusual kind of customer, who had not been there before. He watched her dance clothed; and then, in the back room, he watched her very very carefully, as though measuring her limbs for tailoring. Such a dapper little gentleman, all in black, with a gold chain, and he sipped at his drink so slowly that the landlord began to wonder should he tell him to sod off home.

*

Next night after that, a quiet night, the landlord called her over.

"No remedy", he said, "I'm paying you off. Doll Longlegs is finished and done." The name was first applied to her, pejoratively, by one of the three whores in Thetford (small and fat and jealous, they all wanted her out of town). Now she had adopted it as her business-name. She thought it rather flattering: and at least it was not filthy.

He shoved some coins at her. She tried to collect herself, but could only scream at him. He said calmly, "I'm very sorry, you've talent, I'll grieve at the lack of you. But no remedy, I've had word, clergy-word, and I don't care for it. I mean, we do have clergy here, and all sorts, as well as the soldier-boys: but there's some kinds o'clergy is queerer than others, I'd as soon not have to handle 'em, not in these times. The word I had is quite short, the Maid's Head in the Tombland, just west of the Cathedral, you're to be there at noon tomorrow, and try to get yourself up a little less grope-cunt-like, know what I mean? Here's a few extra pence to buy things with, if you don't have enough. No no, love, don't thank me, not my money and I'm glad to be rid of it. No complaints, but you're better out of here."

So he went back to his customers and left her to her dismissal. It was as though she had ceased to exist. That night she slept in a gardener's potting-shed just under the city wall.

*

'Clergy-word'? Oddly, she did not at once think of Bale. Rather she had in mind a drunken chaplain who had pestered her in the back room a week ago: but what would the likes of him have to do (either alone or with her) at the Maid's Head, the best inn in town, where archdeacons, noblemen, high-class pilgrims on the Walsingham circuit, would bring caravans of livery-servants and enough horses to equip a French war? Well: she had money now. She too would equip herself.

Mid-day, at the inn, she arrived dressed (she hoped) as decent as any old Queen of Sheba, and the porter called her 'madam' with no more than the smallest sneer. In the lords'-room, by an open window, elegant and upright in a straight-backed chair, a slender lady; all in black relieved with the whitest linen – not quite a nun's black-and-white, and certainly not funereal, she wore a multiplicity of exquisite small jewels. She would be about forty: her carved-ivory features defied defiance. She looked Dorothy up and down.

"Big," she said, "but a good carriage. We have this room alone between us for the next quarter-hour, so no indecisions, please, we speak freely but to the point. My husband says your Spanish figures, for such a lump-girl, for such a russet-head, are almost convincing: I would not believe him, but that I know his judgement and trust to it. Don't answer me: I mean to insult you, I need to see your control. From where you are, to the stairfoot, walk: I said, walk, I would inspect your back."

Wondering at herself, Dorothy walked.

"Insolent", said the lady, "every joint in your spine clicks disdain. So also my husband told me: the more so when you are stripped. However, with us, that will be finished and done with. Have you heard, in your greasy dens, of what they call 'the Italian Masque'?"

Dorothy hadn't.

"Of course not, it is new, it requires persuasive agile dancers and voices that will be *ruled*. Combined with poetic allegory, it is in great demand at the feast-givings of persons of rank. They present it themselves: but need always hired companies to give *body* to their amateur flourishings. You have lived and performed like a bitch in heat for mongrel dogs. Don't answer me, trollop, because I know you need no telling that your end will be rotten disease or a cut throat, or the whipping-post till all blood is out of you. And thereafter the hooks of hell's devils to tear you. Don't tell me you have not thought of it."

Dorothy had often thought of it. She felt a swimming through the sunshine room, a dizziness of hope, fear, resentment, and again hope.

She asked, might she sit down?

The lady said, "No: I am ruling, you will be ruled. Or if not; good-bye, good-night, and finish."

Dorothy bit her lips, bit her tongue, to keep back the angry words. Three-quarters of her urged her to plump her arse upon a bench, put feet up onto table, throw a tankard into this needle-eye face that so taunted her and reddened her cheeks. The other quarter was all hope, fighting hard to win the argument. Even as she wrought within herself, a footstep on the stair in the corner of the room: down came the dapper man who had peered and peered and sipped one cup the night before last. He did not so much as look at her, but said to his wife, "Well?"

"If she was going to go, she would have gone. I imagine she will suit us. Explain to her our purposes."

So he did. His name was Oliver, his wife was Cecilia (although, as Dorothy found out later, she had been plain Betty for her first twenty years). They were livery-dependants of the great Howard, Duke of Norfolk, licensed by him to train and administer a dance-company of nine young women, known as 'Cecilia's Muses'. Mr Oliver was a craft-master of the Beverley Minstrel's Guild, and he now lived in King's Lynn. He had already found eight dancers, and Dorothy might be the ninth, if she agreed with the conditions.

"Six months under my wife's tuition: which you'll need, which you'll need. Is it true you can sing *Jolly Rutterkin* with your legs in the air? If it is true, who taught you?"

"Lightfoot of Ely, sir, and then after that, Rover's Jennet – she was – "

"I have utterly no desire to know who she was – nor him either, your fenman-churl, good heavens! Lightfoot of Ely indeed." His voice was very tight, precise, and always soft: but it held the same steel as his wife's. "To resume: I say six months. At the end of which time, if you have not all proved capable, back into the *cloaca* the pack of you, good-bye, good-night. But if you have, and why shouldn't you? then forward – with good wages – to be extolled about the eastern parts, a complete accomplished company of nymphs: dance, music, songs of love and maybe (for great abbots' houses, bishops' halls if we are so fortunate) Polyhymnia the *sacred* muse will also be our patroness. Oh I know such names are meaningless to you; Grecian, how would you know of 'em? But six months of my careful wife and you'll dine, sup, and sleep with 'em. Well?"

They stood between her and the light, which she did not like. To consider his proposal, she thought, the best thing to do would be to turn her head sideways so they could not read her eyes. She gave them, very deliberately, the lobe of one ear to look at and the curls upon her nape. The fact was, she could scarcely believe what she had heard: yet she did not dare demonstrate her enormous great joy, lest all should come to nothing. There was still the possibility she was fetched there to be a laughing-stock. She had heard of such things, for poor girls with no protection. Her insolence was *her* protection. Despite already having called him 'sir', she would not abandon insolence just yet. After all, it had served her since Christmas, and already it was high summer.

So she replied to his final phrase. "And who the hell else am I to sleep with?"

He had not yet smiled. Now he grinned, showing very white, very even teeth. "We do not dispose of an order of nuns. Nor do we hold lease of a brothel-house. No men without my wife's permission. She will not be disposed to give it."

She said next: "The fenman-churl you wouldn't hear of: he trained me with a whip. I'm not to have that, d'you heed me? Not that, never again."

Mrs Oliver laughed, like a stick breaking. "I rule with my tongue, and you've heard it already. I rule by dismissal, and the prospect of good wages. Mr Oliver rules by his knowledge, his experience."

"Did I not tell you, I am craft-master? Of the craft of Greekish Homer, of Taillefer the Frank, of Caedmon of the English north. My discipline is a harness of honour: and it jingleth with merry bells." He drew out the last six words with a certain cold ferocity. Merriment, for Mr Oliver, would very clearly be a product of the most exact rehearsal.

"One more thing." Dorothy was determined not to be hurried. "Who told you about me? The chaplain?"

"Chaplain? What chaplain?" Oliver seemed puzzled. "Oh silly little Dorothy" (he was only about as tall as the tip of her chin), "don't you think I can't derive our needful intelligence from my brothers in the craft? Now for arrangements – " He seemed to consider she had already agreed. Perhaps she had. " – you will live for the six months in our house at Lynn. We go there horseback tomorrow. You can ride without falling? Pillion, behind me; your possessions, if you have any, on a pack-mule. And you won't ride as any Doll Longlegs: *that* name and all that gave rise to it is from now on good-bye, good-night. Your name-in-art henceforward had better be Terpsichore, we left her till the last, we left her for the tallest. When you find out who she is, make sure you live up to her."

*

Six months, then. Endurance of the unendurable; not unendurable because it degraded: but solely because it enhanced, and at such speed of achievement she thought she must surely run mad from the nervous expenditure dragged out of her body, her mind, her previous experience; out of her 'fantasy' (as the Olivers termed it), an apparently bottomless receptacle she had never before realised she had. With the other eight girls-in-training she made enemies, she made friends; she made (once) a hopeless passion of love, until Cecilia observed it and asked both her and her paramour Gillian – a small delicate-limbed elf-child from Yarmouth – which one would volunteer to say good-bye, good-night? It was Gillian that left: she had always been wanton and would not change now. She was immediately replaced by a more docile recruit, and the endless round of work continued, eighteen hours out of the twenty-four.

Most nights they were so exhausted by dance-practice, singing-practice, and the learning over and over of the words of interminable poetry (none of them could read properly, so it was all done through repetition) that they slept without dreaming. Dorothy was glad to have no dreams: though there were times her overwrought fantasy could take no rest, and then she tossed and rolled, now in the Bishop's gaol, now on a snow-swept river-bank, now in the clinging folds of a white-friar's stifling mantle.

In the daylight she forgot such things. They were allowed no holy-days: except the first hour of the morning when they all went to Mass. Mr and Mrs Oliver were insistent upon the Mass. The Duke's servants, even when professionally active on their own account, must always testify to his correct and public piety. Also, as the Duke's servants, they must all keep themselves exceedingly clean. Dorothy delighted in this. She had never known it before; and she would stand a whole half-hour in the wash-tub if she were let, sluicing and scrubbing, wringing and combing her long wet hair.

Cecilia's cruel tongue in a way caused them to despise themselves, and yet it made them proud, proudly enamoured of the work they discovered they could do. This pride gave her another dream: flowers in a green meadow, where everything was beautiful, a lovely boy like golden Apollo sang to her over his lute, a blessed virgin all in white gave suck to a winged child. Gillian would come into the dream, being the virgin, even before she and Dorothy confessed their love together. Dorothy was never sure how far her growing pride-of-achievement and Gillian were really one and the same thing. But after Gillian had been dismissed, pride-of-achievement did not decrease: the very heartbreak seemed to strengthen it.

*

At the end of the six months, Mr Oliver put them to business. They rode in gay painted wagons with his band of music, to the Duke's hall at Framlingham, for the Christmas feast. The Duke was not there, being on duty at the King's court, but many of his family were: and the younger ones required a masque. Mr Oliver had written it: he was desperate nervous for this, his first showing of his new company. He was not disappointed. Of course he and Cecilia were ferociously caustic about all the mistakes made, the carelessnesses, the minute faults in notes and dance-steps: but the Duke's household were lavish in both praise and largesse, and finally all could be said to have gone very well indeed.

After Framlingham on Nativity Eve, a round of noble and gentry houses through several counties until Lent. Abbey guest-houses also, and one or two of the bigger town halls.

It was upon the third of these visits that the white-friar recommenced his appearances.

Dorothy felt brave enough nowadays to confront Oliver directly with the question: did he know of these hauntings, and was it her or the whole company? She had not previously had a chance to see Bale in the face, unmuffled and in a good light. Now she did: and it troubled her. She found – even as she danced – she could not shut her mind to his big head, his expanse of assertive chin, and the continual frotting, writhing, twitching, of his hands clasped under his scapular. His eye, from the back of the hall, was always on her, until she put hers on him: and then at once he would dodge his head sideways.

She felt Oliver prevaricated. She asked again, "Who is he?"

He replied, "Ask Cecilia, she's the careful one," and clicked his tongue evasively. "I know so very little about the clergy and their ways: some of them are friendly to the craft, others not. If he comes to see our work, then no doubt he is invited, and those that invite him will have paid, what's wrong with that?"

She did ask Cecilia. Cecilia peeped through the curtain (they were changing costumes from one dance to the next in Norwich Guildhall, where the mayor had bespoke them for Shrove-tide), she took a quick survey of the house, and laughed. "Bale?" she said, "John Bale, they call him 'Bull-in-the-bush' because he hides after dark and pounces upon sluts. Whom he whips, I think, and not much more. Oh damn it, Russet-top, the man's notorious. If it's you he is after, for Jesus' sake keep close. Idiot, d'you not know, he could be a throat-cutter? I will *not* have this company made short of a pair of feet, not now, when our fortunes are only commencing."

When Cecilia was so rough and genial, calling to mind indeed the hidden (but known) fact that she herself once danced in just such a place as Dorothy had so recently escaped from, it meant she expected to have even more heed taken of her than usual. Dorothy decided this Bale must be very dangerous. And yet he had preserved her. The Devil looking after his own?

She spoke about him, with caution, to the other girls. Some of them had heard of him, 'Bull-in-the-bush', yes: and also 'Bale-zebub'. It appeared he was obsessed with minstrel-shows and stage-plays. He travelled the east parts preaching, very hard contorted sermons: but always he took time off to insert himself in the crowd at all manner of popular entertainments, and always he would chew his lips, frot his spatulate hands, waiting for the night-time (so the girls had it), waiting for his hiding-bush, with willow-switch and bursting loins.

During the next dance, Dorothy watched him; half-hidden, he was, behind a guildhall screen, himself at watch: sucking-in as it were the very sweat of those who must pretend to be what they were not, for the encouragement of public fantasy.

(iii) *The Maze And The Cage*

> *Widow Dorothy saw Oliver and Oliver's wife herding cattle two-by-two – as it might be Noah and Mrs Noah on the gangplank of the Ark – whips cracking in the air, their voices like ravens croaking, "One two three, one; one two three, one; one two three, one . . . !", hour after hour, day after day, while the clouds gathered dark and sultry but no rain fell.*
>
> *Did not the Lord God know, up there in His celestial oven, that she hadn't had a bath for weeks? Why, her skin blistered with heat and dust.*
>
> *She babbled to her daughter-in-law (the more-than-decent wife of her decent mercantile son), who was feeding her bread-and-milk, "For weeks they have not allowed me to have my bath, it isn't right." "That'll do, mother, swallow your slops, you are talking about you know not what. Moreover, this bodily bathing is injurious to the humours. All physicians are agreed."*

*

Rebellion by Cecilia's Muses, against the regime of the Olivers, took a year or two to develop. And when it came, it was more pathetic than militant. Sukey of Ipswich, a very gentle girl of respectable parentage, who was disliked by the others for her refinement, announced in all naïvety that she wished to become betrothed to a young man of parts who had seen her dance a score of times, and that they were thinking of immediate marriage. Mr Oliver put a stop to it: discovered the young man's father, a country squire; and discovered that paternal permission had foolishly not been considered.

In less time than anyone thought possible, the young man was off to Flanders to be buried in a wool-factor's counting-house. Disconsolate Sukey, her fantasy filled with improbable ballads, put herself into man's attire and tried to take ship at Pin Mill. The sea-captain at once saw through her disguise. He could have kidnapped her or ravished her, but fortunately he was a god-fearing man and he handed her over intact to the magistrate of the port. Good-bye, good-night, poor Sukey, back to Ipswich to her angry family: and a new apprentice-girl was speedily found from a vagabond clan in the district.

She was a mistake, nearly as wild as Yarmouth Gillian. Mr Oliver was becoming unsettled in his judgement. She ran away five weeks later, having set the whole company at odds with each other, and stolen a wide selection of their personal belongings before she went.

*

Enforcement of discipline, after these misadventures, became onerous and unpleasant. Fines, lockings-up, curtailments of artistic
opportunity, and continuous abuse from the Olivers, were now
regular procedure. The bridles no longer had merry bells, but were
seen in their starkness as restrictive ropes and straps to be broken at all
opportunity.

For Dorothy, the opportunity descended from a great height, a
Phoebus from his solar car. His name was Lord Wentworth.

He was about thirty years old, a quiet-spoken courteous man, with
an oddly innocent face, snub-nosed, bluntly trusting, like a small
boy's beloved terrier. He was manorial baron of Nettlestead in
Suffolk, just outside the town of Ipswich, earnestly making himself a
thoughtful and sound career in the king's court and army.

The Olivers brought their company to play for him at Nettlestead,
upon his eldest son's ninth birthday. An expensive but private
occasion: the only guests were family, one or two cultivated noblemen
and their ladies, some most intellectual doctors from the Cambridge colleges, and Lord Wentworth's young friend Thomas Wyatt.
Mr Wyatt was a poetical royal official currently serving as Commissioner of the Peace in Essex, which was why he was able to be
present. Under the gently represssive eye of Lady Wentworth, there
was no drunkenness at the feast, and none of the hired minstrels dared
offer any form of bawdry.

There were recitations in rhyme of the histories of King Arthur; a
group of tongue-tied farm-tenants gave a pageant of the Wentworth
ancestors and their deeds (anxiously directed by the Parson); an old
colleague of Mr Oliver's, a fat Yorkshireman with a marvellous bass
voice, sang very lengthy ballads about Saint Paul and other apostles –
one of his refrains stuck immoveably in Dorothy's mind, no doubt
because of the tune, *Clerk Sanders*, a Scots air which always made her
weep:

> Across the sea and across the sea
> Far over the sea in the ship of Rome,
> For Christ His sake I must leave my love
> And never more come sailing home.

The centre-piece of the entertainment was a *Masque of Hymen*,
including the praise of motherhood and the gallant hopes of extreme
youth. The text was composed by Wentworth and Wyatt in collabora-
tion: and Lord and Lady Wentworth and all their children took part in

it. The goddesses involved, and their attendant maidens, were played by Cecilia and the troupe. Lord Wentworth had written most of the script himself, with additional verses by Mr. Wyatt.

Despite the wholesome atmosphere of the gathering, it was clear that the poetical Wyatt had more than poetical thoughts about Oliver's nymphs. In the general dancing that succeeded the verses, he so manoeuvred himself as to be finger-to-finger with Dorothy in nearly every set. She was not inclined to repulse him: he was a light-hearted pleasant gentleman, he had (she thought) no wife with him, or other lady, to inhibit his love-making, and there was no doubt he would be a very gleaming fish for such as her to haul into the net. The question was, though: had she a net to cast? And if she had, was it good sense to use it?

After Gillian, whose sweet and wicked lips had warmed Dorothy's secret body to an awareness of derry-down she had never before suspected, she had carefully avoided all such forms of capture. Fish-nets, she understood, were not unilateral appliances: when you catch, you can be caught, by man or by woman, and God help Ipswich Sukey, *her* life must be nothing but wilderness.

There was, however, another and stronger reason for her doubt. She did not allow herself to admit it, it was foolish and demeaning, who the devil was *she* to be harbouring such presumption? But fact was fact: and indeed she was not able to take eyes from off Lord Wentworth. But impossible, in his own home, with his wife whom he loved, and a man of such great station, such obvious piety: he would no more make a mistress of a dancing-woman at his son's feast than he would – what?

"Oh God," she silently groaned, "what's wrong with Wyatt? He wants me, I don't want him, in no particular – save rank – is he inferior to Wentworth. God, his poetry is *twice* as good, don't I know so, I've just been bloody singing it – and won't *any* gentleman do, if all I want is to get clear of these damned Olivers?"

She tried to account to herself, in the most rational way, for her imaginings about Wentworth and what he would be like if she saw him without his clothes. Were his features, or were they not, if you shaved away the soft short beard, all but identical with Gillian's? Truth to tell, they were *not*: and yet, about the corner of the stubborn little mouth, the honest upthrust chin, some sort of similarity . . . Gillian's chin had been very near the same shape, but *her* mouth, *her* snub-nose, had radiated *dis*honesty so overtly, so seductively, that all of her stubbornness could surely have been no more than the blatant nerve of a born liar? Oh how she recalled the white-tawny grace of Gillian bathing in the steam of a sud-filled tub, and she fitted to it Wentworth's head and then removed his beard and then – *Gillian's* head with its sweep of dark-brown hair falling over the tender neck, how well it would suit the man's body she saw at the hall's end, so grave in the pacing dance, so narrow his ankles, so long and cool his fingers – oh . . .

And all the time the persuasive Wyatt, every conceivable classical compliment simmering from his lips, bowed and backed and stepped forward again toward her through an intricate slow pavane.

Over his shoulder she looked, once again, for Wentworth. She didn't see him: only three or four of the Cambridge professors, drinking wine at the fireside, watching the dance, determining the new theology. There among them was the white-friar. Bale-zebub with his bull's glare. When he saw that she saw him, he shoved his big snout into his cup.

And at once the dance was over.

*

Wyatt was about to say something. She half-smiled, muttered an embarrassed phrase about the heat of the hall, how her head swam, how he must excuse her – with a savage little prayer to Blessed St Uncumber, she slipped glibly through the people until she found herself alone in the garden.

The most delectable evening of an early warm summer: the sun had just gone down, leaving traces of golden flame across the sky between the tree-tops to the north-west; while the east was already blue-black and a new moon swam up into it, as many stars sparking out as Dorothy had sequins on her fragile loose masquing-gown. She thought to herself a poet would put it the other way round: call her adornments as multitudinous as the stars. But then a poet might not know they all belonged to the Olivers and must be returned to the property-hamper last thing before bed-time: whereas the stars would continue and were held to their endless circlings by no damned parchment contract in unreadable Norman-French and lawyers' oppressive Latin.

She inhaled the scent of the night-stock and wished she were dead.

In front of her was a carved sundial with impudent boys on its base, exposing to the world their as-yet harmless pricklets. She sat down on the steps, Lost Love in the company of the Loves: and (from Oliver's training) luxuriated in the allegory. Nonetheless, her sorrow was real, she *did* wish – maybe not quite death: but – just supposing Wentworth were to follow her from the hall? Could he perhaps have seen her looking at him? She was his guest (never mind the wages), she was unhappy; as a good host he might feel it his duty to console . . . But of course, he would not follow her.

Bloody Wyatt would, though. And had. This was *not* what she wanted.

"Erato?", he said, after a gentle gentlemanly pause. "Or could it perhaps be Melpomene?" She did not know how to answer: to volunteer ."Terpsichore" would sound plain daft, and might only encourage him: and in any case the Olivers had dropped these fancy muse-names a long long time ago. Gillian had laughed at them and then all the girls had laughed, until Cecilia decided it was pearls before swine.

He took her hesitation for ignorance and began (God help her) to offer a lecture upon Grecian mythology. But seeing her expression he broke off with a laugh: "Don't distress yourself; in a way I *have* come to court you, but not quite as you might think. You must realise that for three days we have been in much proximity, you and I: you cannot work upon an enacted show – at all events, not as hard as we have all worked – without being to an extent drawn in to a closeness of mutual knowledge: so what have I learned, red-head, about you? Simply this: you do not care for me, and why should you? I am a peacock."

She did not wish directly to agree with him. But as his tone was warm and friendly – "If you knew, sir, my private thought as clear as that, I am amazed you went not forth to spread your tail in front of another? All nine of us surely cannot be of the same mind?"

"Oh but I have spread my tail: as you say, there are the other eight, opportunity has not been scarce. I beg you, lady, do not sorrow for the waste of my fleeing hours."

What could he be leading to? This might go on all night and her invention in courtly wit-battle (despite all Oliver's lessons) had its limits. For God's sake she had less than three years' practice, and this conceited fellow had been at it since his childhood. But he had stopped speaking, he was looking at her with a strained expression: not so much a clever wag trying to think of his next quip, but more like – more like . . . There was something extremely sly behind the fixed smile that varnished his face: she recollected Cecilia mentioning during the rehearsals that Wyatt was a well-experienced ambassador at foreign courts. Damn him, did he think she was the treacherous French? God's name, what did he want?

Suddenly his voice was very serious indeed. "May I ask you, have you touched, even a little, in these past three days, the black unhappiness of this house?"

She was utterly nonplussed. She felt foolish. She looked foolish. She blundered in her speech. "Unhappiness? Why no – I – I have thought – I have thought that Lord Wentworth – and his family – thought that they were – "

"You have thought they are devoted. His love for his lady and hers for him, don't forget their dear children, like an altar-piece of the Nazareth carpenter-shop? He will be grateful when I tell him, unlucky gentleman: for that is the one sole picture he needs to place before the world. I myself, when little older than you are, was likewise obliged to bear myself with such miserable daily falsehood, until at length I took my courage, and then my evidence and all my shame, in front of a bench of celibate clerical judges, to split her from me complete: an adultress, oh, it was proven. Prior to that, for two long years, I had known it but could not publish it: all night, every night, bedded alone; yet every day was fair and smiling, me to her, her to me, just as you have seen it here."

"Adultress? Lady Wentworth? Lord Christ, I would never have – Jesus, but we live and learn."

"Jesus, maid, but we don't. She never played foul-bed with anyone. In her case it is much much worse. She has been told by some jack-priest (and between the holy Host and her no-less holy tongue, dear heaven, she believes it thoroughly), that *her husband is a heretic*."

"But he *can't* be . . ." If it was hard for her to credit Lady Wentworth as adultress, how much less could she accept the lord of this god-fearing house to be one of those who laid hold of Christ like a torturer, to lacerate His loving features with violent jagged pen-point till blood and black ink dripped commingled down His breast of agony? Such had been the heretic's work, as described by her father in one of his sermons: a horrible re-crucifying, almost as horrible as the things told her by the Norwich turnkey.

It appeared he stood as cautious, as non-committal, as herself. "Perhaps he is, perhaps not. But no-one has condemned him in public and he has never been privately denounced, or I think we would have heard of it. Hard to see how he could be, when the King needs him so badly. And indeed, priest or not, his fair lady would never denounce him herself. Damn my blood, she loves him bitterly. And yet, it seems, her confessor has given her certain advice, no, he has issued orders, most peremptory, listen to this: as long as suspicion remains, she must withdraw from her husband her body and yet live her life beside him, nay in the very same bed, as untouchable as a virgin nun. And by God she does it. She abhors it, but she does it: can you believe that? Oh, it's true. Because, you see, she has a greater abhorrence. She hates like very Lucifer his duties for the King."

He had dropped his voice to such a whisper that she had to lift her ear to his lips, and his hand on her shoulder pressed deep. He went on: "Insofar as the King's Majesty is putting away his own good lady . . . another one, will you note, that never played foul-bed with anybody . . . And Tom Wentworth must achieve it for him, with my help, and Tom Cranmer's help, and smokey-faced Tom Cromwell – why, every Tom-cat in England is plunged into this divorce, this annulment, whatever creature of legal casuistries it may turn out to be called – you'd think a fishmonger had strewn cod's offal all over the pavement, so many teeth and claws grabbing out for their slithery bits. Of course, *I've* been banished: to the mud-humps of Essex. They think *I* didn't grab with quite enough glee – how could I, the Lady Boleyn having carved her sweet name on my vitals, but that was before she was Caesar's, with his gold padlock to close off her cunt."

Dorothy was by now more than a little uneasy. He was forgetting to whisper. She did not know much of the meaning of 'high treason', but she had a very good notion it might sound something like this: what did they do to women found guilty of it? Burn them? Her shudder pulled her away from him, she stood up to go.

"No," he said, "Stop. I have fallen aside from my point. And *you* are in terror of secrets of state, I can see. Ah well, despite my conspiratorial manner, they are not so very, very secret. And neither is my opinion of them. The King knows it, Cromwell knows it; by Christ, Anna Boleyn knows it. And also they know that though Wyatt has a large mouth it never did them any danger. Why, at court I am *prized*, for the looseness of my humour. 'Tell it to Wyatt,' they will say, 'and before Lammastide the Bashaw of Cairo will be hearing it as new-minted news crept out to him especial through the contrivance of his spies!' Such virtue in my vice got me my ambassadorships. And when they can't use it; why then, they don't use *me*." His fleering and jeering stopped off short: he gripped her quite hard by the forearm. "To talk about spies. You spied Tom Wentworth, right through the dancing you spied him, with an eye made as wide as a windsail from all the desire you could not hide. Don't deny it. I saw it. Very well, I am here to tell you, if you want him, he is yours. Does he want you?"

Her insolence was a habit, all unwished-for she had to give way to it. "Well, does he? You seem to be his pimp. Why haven't you asked him?"

Sharp-seasoned diplomat, he refused to be insulted. "Dear Parnassus-child, of course I have. And the damfool would admit nothing. D'you know, if I were he, I'd have thrust myself at *rape* into that Madonna of his, months ago, oh I would: and let her conniving chaplain howl in his closet unheard. But you see, he is far too chivalrous. Only concomitant, far too chivalrous to nuzzle a red-haired muse-maiden for acceptable alternative. Unless an unscrupulous friend, as it might be a peacock like me, should spread his tail from him to you, hiding both of you from the moon, from the fag-end of sunset, from those naughty little knave-children making ready to water the sundial steps . . ."

Maybe he knew it, but she didn't: Wentworth had come up behind them. He was very pale in his masque-costume, purple and gold of an antique hero, a white plume in his silver helmet, bare white forearms, scarlet boots. His embarrassed reluctance contradicted his eagerness. So did hers, when she turned and saw him.

Wyatt took Dorothy's hand and laid it precisely into Wentworth's: raised his bonnet, bowed, replaced his bonnet, and withdrew backwards, as he would have gone from the royal presence. In the house beyond the terrace the music thumped for a galliard-dance. Through the blur of the lighted windows broad-shouldered silhouettes, laughing young men who tossed their partners in the air, round the hall and round it again, gathering speed, and thump thump thump . . .

*

It was absurd she should have thought he was like Gillian made male. He was near a foot taller, taller than Dorothy by a full inch.

He led her past the sundial, across a lawn, into an alley: box-hedges developing into the outer bounds of a circular maze. They entered it together, side by side, he was no longer leading her. At each division of the path he let her choose whether right or left. When she got it wrong, he said, w'th the utmost gravity, "Forfeit", took from her a piece of jewelry or a garment, and then had her take one from him, leaving them strewn on the path at the hedge-corners. It seemed not so much an amorous game as a searching-out of some hermetic mystery held concealed by the maze. Had *Wyatt* played such tricks, she would have known he had done so often enough before: but she had the strong feeling that Wentworth was creating the whole business brand-new, creating place, behaviour, atmosphere not from his own memory, or even his own desire, but from something he had studied – very like in an Italian poem-book, it was the kind of thing they had written in them, she had been told. Also, he was covertly *guiding* her to take right or wrong turning by the pressure of his hand. Did he prolong it so, in order to excel in his ecstasy? to bring her to her own proper ecstasy? or was it possible he was a Conrad, all eyes of inner fantasy and nothing as to the flesh? However, it was *his* maze, so let him make its choreography: he was at all events a less rigorous dance-master than the Olivers.

In the maze-centre, a little roundel, plot of grass six feet across, surrounding box-hedge nine feet high, the moon appeared to be poising herself directly over the entrance.

"Mary Gipsy," she said with a giggle. She was nervous and how otherwise? All her clothes, save for a green silk neck-ribbon, were gone from her: while he still wore his supposedly Greco-Roman breeches, and was stooped and graceless in getting them off. "Mary Gipsy, look at the moon."

*

The next thing she was to remember saying, and it must have been a full half-hour afterwards: "That dress of mine, and the head-tire, they've to go back to the prop-basket. Hope to God they've not got wet. You should have thought of the dew."

Well, this was the first lover, of all the men who had taken her, to have taken her at *her* longing rather than his. "*Vice versa*", she said, bragging to herself at her Latin, hoping it was appropriately enigmatical for this cultured man.

He did not answer. She looked at his face. Oh yes, certainly, 'rather than his' was true, for the tears ran down his trusting little cheeks from wide-open eyes, and all the trouble in those eyes . . . it must be his wife-business, not Dorothy, surely? And yet he had wanted, and yet he had *not* wanted. Was it God? Between him and his wife a cruel tormenting God whom both of them had made together for their own confusions, not surprising he was a blubberer. She was sure Lady Wentworth was, too. So God would be out to punish him. And therefore punish Dorothy as well. But Dorothy had always been punished. For him it was something new. She wished he would talk of it: if he were not a baron she would ask him to talk of it, she needed to know her situation, she needed to know it *now*. How *was* she to break out intimacies from a peer of the realm when he sat and shed tears in silence? In all likelihood he was about to get to his feet, collect his scattered clothes, and just go. She became brave and put her fingers' ends against his breast, and then up to his wet face: and thank God, he snuffled, and tried to smile.

"I think I must be punished for so exquisite an half-hour. But how am I to know? I repudiate the imposture of auricular confession, so there is nobody I can ask. Unless Wyatt: and the fool will laugh. You must know, this can not be continued." Yes, there it was: she had longed, she had received, and now there was no more to get. Pleasure brought no pleasure, whereas gritted teeth and legs resentfully-opened put food in her dish and rags upon her back: she should have stayed in the ale-cellar as Longlegs, all her hopes from Cecilia's Muses were as empty as her silly heart. Another minute of this and *her* eyes would be shedding, there was a trickle from the left one already. But she did not stand up, she could not: they sat facing one another over bent knees, Adam and Eve on the dark grass, an invisible applecore lying between their feet.

What *was* it she had hoped for, though? Him again? And again, maybe again and never-ending? Or simply his reward? Fish-nets had caught both ways, just as she feared they would. Loss of Gillian had been catastrophe, but the upshot had been simple: she could work at her trade with Gillian's love or she could work at it without it. And it had to be without. After all, the greedy pair of them had only been apprentices then. But now she had had (and now she had lost) the one chance to move out of her trade to an altogether new-made status: lord's mistress, fully-kept. Was not that the traditional quest-grail of the dancing-woman with eyes beyond herself? Matter-of-business, quite impersonal? She should shrug her shoulders, find another one, try again some other feast. It was the applecore was the trouble: *she* had bitten first, and she would never be rid of the taste. Status was what she should have longed for, nothing else: not *him*, no never *him*.

But he was still talking. "If I remained in England, then perhaps it would be different. But His Majesty sends me to France. Negotiation of the utmost delicacy, gain support of the French King against the Emperor: the Emperor being nephew of Queen Catherine of Aragon – I mean, of that lady who *has been* our Queen; and the Pope all confounded between them." He digressed into politics, and thence into divinity, as though forgetting she was there, for several tangled sentences, until: "Of course they should have sent Tom Wyatt, he was in France the last time. But Tom, alas, Tom, he has seen too much of the lady who is *about* to be our Queen. High treason if I told you *how* much."

She'd better make a joke of this high-treason business and bloody quickly: they'd enough grief between them without *that* kind of knife-blade to lurk behind their shadows. She stretched her naked limbs in the moonlight: "About as much as you can see of me?" A sharp twig of box-tree scratched her back and hurt her, but she managed to retain the voluptuous posture.

For him, there was no joke. He shifted his words an adequate distance from the crafty padlocked Anna. "Upon an ordinary embass-age, it would be possible for me to take you with me. Such is commonly done. But this is too important. The Emperor's spies would turn it to a scandal. My mission would be shamed. We couldn't have that."

Really, all she wanted was to be clear of the Olivers. Brought down from the heights of hope, there was no more to it than that: when she looked at it so, perhaps all was not yet lost. And perhaps it had not been God or thought of his wife that had brought his tears, but the importance of his embassage: he had – had he not? – for a moment believed he *might* take her to Paris? She endeavoured to transmute voluptuous limb-stretching into carelessness and scorn, turning her face away; let him look at her spine. It brought the right response.

"Forgive, please, dear Dorothy – oh, did you expect – ? I mean, hope for – ? I mean, you must tell me, what *did* Wyatt give promise of, on my behalf, like a Vice in a moral play? Dearest Dorothy, I have my honour."

Heavens, she'd allowed Wyatt to give promise of nothing.

Still looking away from him: "If France of all places would make me an occasion-of-shame, I'd as soon not be kept by anyone."

"Oh . . . I have said, this can not be continued. But I cannot cast you off. Gratitude – no, not gratitude – by God I am not a chafferer, throwing bargains about on a fair-green! – no, I do not mean gratitude: dearest Dorothy, I mean *love*."

Nonsense. All his love was for his wife. He was lying to her, yet she wanted to kiss him: nonsense. So she pronounced, as coldly as possible, "I'd be glad to be clear of the Olivers." (And Nelly would have shaken her and hissed into her ear, "Derry-down's to be haggled-over, *before* it happens, *always*!"). "I'd as soon not be kept. Keep myself, why can I not? Have you heard of the 'Birdcage'?"

All his love was for his wife. But for Dorothy, his honour. And thereupon he made his promises. He would pay for the re-purchase of the Olivers' contract. Pay for her to go to London, lay down rental for a room in the place called 'Birdcage', meet her bills for musical instruments, suitable clothes, a servant, and musicians when she needed to hire them. His steward would put it in hand, he'd give him orders that very night. Why, he could not have been more generous had he fetched her over to France and given her to the King there to sweeten his own King's proposals. She was so grateful (she did not despise the term, as he had), she *did* kiss him. He was nervous, he was tender, and so – at last again – was she. She paid him for his payment, crying out in her pleasure till he hushed her, they would hear in the house. She had not been wrong to long for him, even Gillian must agree upon that.

And then he left her and she realised that she would never lie with him again.

*

Not good sense to allow such delights to drop behind them such self-blame. Only one thing she need really truly blame herself for, she explained to herelf, most rationally: why to hell had she never asked him about his heresy? He had rambled on long enough about heresy in general, pointing out that despite the Pope's confoundings, despite all the other kings and emperors, England's King was no heretic, not yet at any rate, it was simply a matter of tedious church-legalities, upon which he had certainly been tedious. And all spoken knee-to-knee naked, tremor of love-making still within them, where nothing but their own two selves and their own two true beliefs should have been the hot heart of their discourse. If love cannot encompass the notion of the lovers' God, then it cannot be true love, which of course this had *not* been, had it? All his love was for his wife, with whom God no doubt was daily discourse. She must not forget that: must always bear in mind how Wentworth and Lady Wentworth were God-harried beyond endurance: she had no right to share their agony.

Upon reflection, though: he *had* said. 'The imposture of auricular confession' – yes? Now no longer enmeshed in the touch and the smell of him, she plucked in her mind at his pompous little phrase, which of course she had heard before.

Conrad in his German accent, just as pompous, just as obstinate, refusing in the exact same words to go into a church with her when she needed to tell the priest about some dirty new trick-of-the-lips that a man had had her play upon him. At the time she had thought that Conrad was wheedling to hear her confession himself, it was the sort of sideways thing he would do. Just as the priest, when she told him her story, had asked for far too much detail . . . She took damned good care, afterwards, to avoid penitential specifics. As, for instance, she told no priest just how Conrad, a day or two later, had unlaced his codpiece in broad noontide, when they were by chance alone upon a river-bank, and said, "Stroke, please, from *your* hand he will rise." Being sorry for his sadness (for always he was so inward and sad, even when he performed his fartings) she had done what he asked: and nothing rose. She suggested, perhaps, he must grow a little older, all men were not quite men at the same age, she knew that. But he hid his eyes and murmured, "How old do you think I am, *Maedchen*? *Ach*, such falsehoods the flesh tells, forget it." He ran away from her, so very fast, he was tying up his breech-strings as he bolted between the holly-trees.

But the words, nevertheless, had been precisely the same: and – now she thought of it – the English Testament, how could Conrad have afforded to buy it (unless he stole it?), and more pertinently, where did he know to find it? How strange she had never asked herself this before. But such fright and degradation from the consequence of that damned book (*heretic* book, yes, let her now be quite clear about that), what choice had she had but put it right out of her mind all these three years?

'Hans Sachs'? You could never tell, with foreigners, the degree of their education. Still less if you could not even tell their age. If a German came seeking a place in a gang of East Anglian gutter-music, then you presumed that must have been his level in his own land. He had brought to the Runagates all the right rowdy tunes and Almain clownage, the japes of Owlglass, Sausage Jack, and the like, why would any of them have asked him anything deeper? He did not encourage it.

She rose slowly from the damp grass, and wandered the maze, picking up her things from each corner, dressing herself, and thinking. She might have thought about Wentworth still, but she didn't. The man in her mind was a Norfolk weaver, one whom she had never seen, lying in chains with a black-rotten leg, singing his hymns and not stopping till they brought him to the fire.

*

On her way across the gardens to the barn where Wentworth's minstrel-guests all had their beds, she thought she saw John Bale in his white cloak standing alone beside a shrubbery. She changed her course and went round by the dovecote yard. Most of Cecilia's Muses were already asleep in the warm straw. She slipped in amongst them, and no-one questioned her.

*

The 'Birdcage' was an ambition: for all those knowledgeable young women who sang, danced, played instruments, or declaimed for a living, and hoped they would not have to offer their bodies more than they chose to. It was in the Paris Garden, on the Southwark Bankside, in the middle of an ant-heap of slums, bars, brothel-houses, said to be owned en bloc by the Bishop of Winchester in some sort of partnership with the Prior of St Mary Overy. Each separate building, however, along the Thames river-strand, was leased to its own middle-man. No-one knew for certain – although many passed on rumours – just who was the middle-man (or maybe syndicate) in receipt of the rents of the 'Birdcage'.

It was in fact as much a slum as any of the structures around it, being a series of rickety galleries, stairs, and corridors, with various-sized rooms opening off them at all levels, very dirty, very noisy, and occupying perhaps three or four ordinary house-sites with outshuts in several different directions. There was one main courtyard, just past the entrance: and then after that the visitor had to ramble into all sorts of dark smelly places before finding the room required. The hanging curtains which closed off one passageway or stair-landing after another were a vain attempt at sound-proofing put up by the sub-tenants. Some of them were mere blankets, others in the half-light looked like rich cloth of Arras with glints of gold and silver thread.

There was often a cloud of incense burning in some pot hooked up to a ceiling-beam or set on a wall-bracket: this did not give the corridors the ecclesiastical atmosphere that might have been sought.

A century earlier the whole place had been converted, from an already ancient conglomeration of farm-buildings, into what was hoped would prove a profitable inn for Canterbury pilgrims, 'at the sign of the Phoenix': but from the start it had been a failure. It was just that much too far from the south end of London Bridge, the immediate neighbourhood was too degraded (the more so since they set up the beast-baiting across the lane), and it had never been able to provide facilities for decent travellers equal to those at the Tabard or the Elephant.

When exactly it became what it now was, who could say? No doubt it had developed gradually. No-one could even be sure when people stopped calling it the Phoenix. At the start of Henry VII's reign, a Tudor portcullis-badge was painted against the burning bird on the signboard in hasty dissociation from Richard Crookback's supposed crimes; it looked like the bird's cage, a misreading that seemed appropriate to the newer uses of the house: the nickname stuck.

In 1532, when Dorothy arrived there, the sub-tenants were all women, old and young, refined and coarse, who practised their minstrel-art in their own private rooms for such clientele as they could muster. It provided them a base in London where they could work all the year round without having to join a company, travelling the shires only when they wanted to, and freeing them from the immediate need to find a patron and follow him at heel according to his arbitrary whims. If the art was now and then as much on the mattress as the mandoline, no-one complained: but if it was nothing but mattress, then the committee of sub-tenants (colloquially, the 'parliament of fowls') would demand a change of occupant. They could enforce it: they employed their bullies – but made a point of always referring to them as 'the yeomen' – and this was how the 'Birdcage' differed from the nasty stews around it. It was a crucial difference: in those places the bullies employed the women and the bawds employed the bullies. There were no bawds at the 'Birdcage'.

There was a rent-collector, who was also the house-caretaker: for legal purposes he called himself Winchester's man, but the Bishop, had he been asked, would have denied all knowledge. It is very doubtful whether there was any legal status for the establishment at all. But the truly exalted status of some of its frequenters made the question redundant. All that was needed to gain a place in the 'Birdcage' was capital: the rents were high, and contributions to the sub-tenants' internal fund (payment for the bullies, for sickness-expenses, even in some cases, pensions) were higher still, but mandatory. The women formed, in an unofficial way, their own minstrels' guild, unrecognised by the craft-masters of the regular guilds, but not unnoticed.

The premises were open for performances three evenings a week, and additionally upon special holy-days. Each woman would receive her audience in her room: often several would combine to give a joint-performance in one of the larger rooms on the ground floor. A list would be pasted up at the caretaker's lodge, showing who was doing what in which room. Gentlemen paid the caretaker a fixed fee for entry to the building (this money went to the middle-man tenant, who no doubt passed a portion on to the landlord): and then every room had its own price of admission, determined by the occupant – if you charged too much you would hear news of it, for no-one would come to you: if too little, your reputation would be blown-upon and your clientele would doubtless be rowdy.

On busy nights there was quite a crowd at the gate before it opened. When it opened, the gentlemen (they were always 'gentlemen'; and in fact most of them *were*, more or less: the prices being so high) would pour through into the courtyard and swarm up the stairs and along the galleries, jostling for admission to the most popular performers. It was a strict rule that none of them passed the lodge without depositing sword and dagger: one or two yeomen always on duty to make sure of it. Food and drink were purveyed from booths in the courtyard, and clients who wished to be comfortable would have their own servants place their orders as soon as they got in. All through the evening there was a constant traffic of bottles, glasses, and pyramids of covered dishes up and down the narrow stair-flights.

*

Dorothy's own habit, on nights when she performed, was like this.

Her experienced black-skinned maid, Belle-Savage, would be sitting at the threshold of her door when the gentlemen arrived. She would take their money, and assess their numbers, admitting them to the room and settling them in their places with a great deal of high-pitched objurgation. Belle-Savage was a known 'character', and offence was not to be taken at her manners. If it were taken (and to begin with, Dorothy had been nervous about it; until she learned the traditions of the place), then the man who took it was better off not coming there anyway. Even noblemen of the Royal Blood were not exempt from 'Birdcage' abuse if they misbehaved. *They* usually came incognito, it was said to add to the fun of the thing. Occasional ladies came as well, but – by rule of the house – always in masks.

In the room, they all sat down on cushions. Belle-Savage would pack up her money-bag, lock it away in the strong-box beside the fireplace, and take any orders for refreshment that had not yet been given. Some child or other would be screamed-for to fulfil these from downstairs. The 'Birdcage' swarmed with children at all hours: several of the women combined procreation with minstrelsy in an apparently most happy-go-lucky fashion. Meanwhile, Dorothy's musician (or musicians, the number of these hired assistants varied from night to night) would be sitting in one corner playing, until the room was filled and everybody quiet. A full room on a good night might have held thirty people: sitting so close that this man's foot would be in that man's armpit, and hatbrims would be knocking against whiskers in a most sweaty conglomeration. Food was greasily eaten from steaming dishes balanced between cluttered knees. In one corner, with a door opening directly onto it from a back corridor, Belle-Savage made certain to keep a portion of floor empty. Through this door Dorothy would make her entrance, and beyond it the back corridor served as a foetid dressing-room for herself and for all her colleagues on the same gallery of the building. It was exceedingly cramped out there and about as inconvenient as could be: but, given the dimensions of the premises, no easier arrangement was possible. Dorothy suffered badly from stage-fright: throughout her life she was to associate that narrow passageway, hot from its guttering candles, with the agonies of the damned.

When all was ready, Belle-Savage would snap together a wooden clapper, bringing the music to a halt. "Lords, ladies, expectation please, for Damosel La Haut-jambée!" (New surroundings, and a new version of an old name, specially chosen to suit them; never mind Belle-Savage's mangling of the pronunciation: the Olivers and their damned 'Terpsichore' could whistle unregarded.) Dorothy always entered at a brave rush and went firmly into her first item without any apparent recognition that anyone was there to hear her. From then on, her own personal way of killing what was left of stage-fright or of her public's diffidence. She broke out of the formality of art and greeted each person present as though he or she were a specially-invited guest. Throughout the evening she mixed public presentation with individual address in a manner quite unlike that of any other of the 'Birdcage' artists: it became popular and aroused jealousies among colleagues who could not match it with their own audiences. Some of this she had learned from Cecilia's handling of gentlemen: but a good deal of it derived from her own self-taught expediencies in the Norwich ale-cellar. She was a close laughing companion to those crowded roomfuls; and yet also a distant magic kept her (when she wanted) isolated on her square of floor-space like Saint Somebody on a reredos, as it might be twenty feet away instead of only a yard.

Her repertory was entirely English. Spanish dancing was not a practicality, not here in the 'Birdcage' where a real Spaniard rented the very next room, impossible to be competed with. But Dorothy's dances were unusual: she developed her gymnastic 'daughter-of-Herodias' style to an astonishing extreme, and her knife-play was hypnotic and genuinely dangerous. She never ever took her clothes off. Some of the 'Birdcage' women sometimes did: but it was not esteemed by their colleagues. If Haut-jambée was erotic, it was a sensuality of a supple body within carefully-designed draperies, or of verbal and musical wit which would flatter her guests to laughter at the disappointment of their lowest expectations. She found, too, she had a talent for the swift sarcastic monologue, mimicry of proud authority, what she called the 'bringing-down of mighty men from high seats.'

A quarter-hour before midnight a bell was rung from a beam in the courtyard and every performance closed. A rule of the local magistrates, written in no statute, but tacitly understood to be the condition under which the 'Birdcage' was permitted to operate, just as the magistrates were understood to be unable to operate without the tacit approval of the Bishop of Winchester's administration: the whole of these affairs being quasi-ecclesiastical, *tacit* must be understood to be ever the masterword. The yeomen-bullies made no bones about clearing the galleries with cudgels and even dogs if the gentlemen disregarded the bell after fifteen minutes' grace. Performers who wished to entertain any of their audience late at night or all night would have to play some subterfuge to keep them in their rooms: it was easily done, by arrangement with the maids and the yeomen; but any woman trying to abuse it would find herself in trouble with the committee.

(iv) *Christ-Plays*

The Widow had some difficulty in distinguishing the Nettlestead maze from the maze of crumbling woodwork and plaster and tapestry that made up the 'Birdcage'. She saw herself and Thomas Wentworth sitting on a circle of grass, clutched together, face to face, soft dark hair mixed with long red hair, their bodies livid white in the moonshine. She saw the surrounding dark green hedge: she did not see when and how it turned into a fence of bars, dusty gilt and worm-eaten, nor when the open sky above was likewise shut out with bars (but these were of wrought iron, sharp-edged, rusty). Beyond the bars, she saw suddenly a crowd of gaping people, staring at them, howling, thrusting spears and billhooks in through the gaps; until a huge great halberd-blade shot into his back, and from thence into her breast, and out at her spine. It didn't hurt; but it fixed them there: and thousands of teeth-filled faces gnashed at them from out of the dark.

The whole cage was lifted up: they hung among stars, and they heard a still small voice (which seemed to come from the brightest and yet most distant star): "Did they think they could claw My face, lacerate My loving features? Look at them, the pair of them."

*

If he had been punished for so exquisite a half-hour, she had been rewarded beyond all she had hoped or dreamed: she said this over and over after every successful performance, while she and Belle-Savage sat counting the evening's take. And then she would ask herself, how long would it last? Perhaps there *would* be punishment. Perhaps she was another Magdalene, with seven devils to be cast out of her. Through Wentworth she was rid of the first one, well and good. Yet if it was her salvation (for once, *she* had enjoyed!), to him it was something quite opposite (*he* had begun to cry). "Between his heresy and his prayerful wife, all that *I* am, all the 'Birdcage' is, must be further complication of his damnation, and mine too, and that's all: why, he won't even allow himself to confess himself to a priest."

For Dorothy, when she followed the Rover, confession was her only resource for keeping herself clean. Later, after Cecilia imposed regular hot-water baths, she found there was a difference between the washed body and the washed soul: but not too great a difference, the one reinforced the other. At the 'Birdcage' she used as many cans of boiling water as Belle-Savage could lug up the stairs for her. She also used Sir Cuthbert, an irregular chaplain who was fed and clothed by the house's sub-tenants, a boozy threadbare old goat, but he carried the Power of Peter, he could loose the soul from the bonds of sin: and his 'little nightingales', as he called them, would be safe enough in the next world so long as they remained true to their art in this one – or so she interpreted him. He said Mass in a pokey hole down one of the passages.

At times Dorothy wondered if her soul could be trusted to such a derelict. Then she would put a cloak over her glittering work-clothes and slip through the alleyways to the Priory about half-a-mile away. The Mass there, of the black-canons, was authentically solemn: but she suspected it, for other reasons. If she was their sub-tenant, and she believed that she was, then her carnal life was a financial pillarstone to their very solemnity.

She heard a sermon once, in this same St Mary Overy's, in the lay-people's chapel behind the high altar: a grave warning from a white-faced urgent canon, about the iniquities of the Bankside, the dangers incurred for local Christians who had such hell-holes on their doorstep. There was no doubt he was quite right, she *was* a Magdalene; and incorrigible, so it seemed: but where was the wandering Story-teller, the Rover of Galilee (rather than Lowestoft), to whom she could creep at dinner with an ointment-phial in hand? Not at St Mary's: the confession-priest there asked as many slimy questions as any she had ever heard, and when she temerariously asked *him* about the final destination of her rent, he bawled her out of the church.

She thought it was more honest for the 'Birdcage' women to pay meat, drink, and the occasional overcoat, directly to their old battered Cuthbert. He made no difficulty acknowledging, indeed soliciting, their gifts. It could be argued he was unduly grateful, considering the mockery they also rendered him. He was perhaps not quite as impoverished as he seemed. Some of the women were truly generous, but he managed his life so messily, poor devil.

*

Altogether there was a great deal of mockery in the place. At first sight all the women appeared serious about nothing but their work and their relationships one with the other, which were often very stormy. But Dorothy soon discovered that many clients, men of the court, men of the city, men of the church, were becoming so involved (by way of politics, business, theology) with the dragging-on of the King's divorce and its disturbing implications, that the same preoccupation spread inevitably among the women. How could it not, these men talked at night in the coney-burrow 'Birdcage' rooms far more freely than they ever would have done at home to their wives where formality and discreet servants controlled the whole tone of the house?

Sides were being taken: some of the sub-tenants, for example, were induced to sing ballads about the affair as part of their repertory. There was danger in this. The committee argued angrily whether it should not be prohibited. For a while nothing was agreed. Dorothy's own mind was fairly clear: she liked the younger men who supported Anne Boleyn, and suspected the sincerity of the old-guard when they praised Queen Spanish Catherine. Of course, she was judging only by those who came to the 'Birdcage': she never met, for example, Sir Thomas More, who was said to be a Chancellor of the utmost probity. But he was also reputed very angry against religious deviants. She remembered the Norwich Bishop, and the state of his prison: Sir Thomas More might even be as privately virtuous as a hairshirt martyr, but to Dorothy he stood chiefly for a dying weaver's putrid foot, she preferred her men-of-probity a little less contaminated.

When she heard More had lost the chancellorship, she said simply, "Serve him right." Her next neighbour was Angelina the Spaniard, a compatriot partisan of the Queen's right still to be queen – and not 'ex-queen' as Dorothy called her (with intent to provoke: Anne Boleyn was not yet crowned). Angelina commented coldly that More had not been dismissed: he had resigned as an act of conscience. If she were him, said Angelina, rather less coldly, she too would have resigned. It was a deed of *caballero* courage, so unlooked-for in an Englishman. Dorothy retorted that if that was so, then More's reputation could only gain from it, you should add to the courage some sedulous self-service as well: quite Spanish in point of fact. Angelina threw a jug of hot gravy into Dorothy's face: and Dorothy tore to pieces Angelina's mantilla, a most pretentious garment, twice as long, twice as transparent as necessary.

There followed a general mellay of the top-floor sub-tenants. Two German women came in with their fists to reinforce Dorothy, and Angelina was supported by the furious finger-nails of the Italian soprano who squalled nightly from the room at the passage-end with its 'poetical' bow-window overlooking the river. About half the 'Birdcage' women were from foreign parts: in general the northerners were for Anne, the Latins for Catherine. Most of the English looked on at this fray and laughed.

But the committee took a strict view. The combatants had had to be separated by the yeomen: and those idle louts were not supposed to be called upon for service so early in the day. They would begin to get above themselves and haunt the women's galleries at all hours, and everyone knew what *that* meant. The president of the committee had some very harsh words: she was the oldest inhabitant, Nancy of the Sarabands, who had slept with King Edward IV when he was still Duke of York, later on introducing him to Mrs Jane Shore in return for all the harvest profits from the home-farm at Windsor, a payment still honoured by the Crown. Everyone was terrified of her.

She told Dorothy and Angelina that the King's business was the King's business: let them think in decent pity of both Anna and Catalina, which one of them would they prefer to be? She demanded an answer, it was not a rhetorical question, she stabbed her sharp ebony cane on the floorboards until the two young women replied.

Dorothy spoke first: she was ashamed of herself and said so, it must be terrible for Queen Catherine, so far from her home, so elderly and stout and all her boy-children dying like that, or still-born: how could it be *her* fault? Angelina said that in all likelihood the Lady Anna would be far happier in the 'Birdcage' than at court. A king's bed was no security unless you knew how to get out of it when you needed to. Nancy smiled grimly, and clacked together her arthritic fingers till all her rings sounded out like the keys of a xylophone: "Don't talk to me about kings, you know nothing about them. *Nothing*, daughter, do you hear? But at least you admit they do not make women happy. Sometimes rich: that's another matter. At least, you both have hearts. Now have some sense into the bargain, avoid these damfool quarrels. God, we all know this is a time of ripping and tearing and scalding of innocent skin: *you are not to bring it here!* So hence and conduct yourselves, or you're out of the 'Birdcage' for good!"

On the landing they kissed each other, and (more or less) made up the dispute. But the wall between their rooms was a thin one. When they had clients in, sometimes their contrary partisanships remained audible: they avoided any mention of it if they met on the stairs.

*

It is not to say that Dorothy's success at the 'Birdcage' came upon her all at once. It was several weeks before she was well-enough settled there and with a sufficiently-known repertory to allow her to think that a full room every night might be no more than the natural merit of her talents. It is true that she worked very hard at her practising, to increase and develop those talents, but very soon she became almost

smug about them: if now and then her public showed less appreciation
than usual, it must be *their* fault, not hers. In fine weather she stepped
out about town with a belly-thrusting arrogance, Belle-Savage at her
elbow and her favourite yeoman a few paces behind, deliberately out-
facing any arrogant clergymen whom she met along the pavements.
All this time she lay with no men.

Bale she did not meet. She assumed he was about his business in the
east parts, in so far as she thought of him at all.

*

But it was not only the memory of the Bishop of Norwich that had
drawn her to the Boleyn faction. Her internal possession of the image
of Lord Wentworth was as powerful toward her opinions as though
she were a convent that owned a relic of the True Cross: she hugged
his blubberings and his long fingers, his saddened eyes and his
attempted smiles, piece by piece against her augmenting confidence,
her continuous secret doubts: he had been hers and was no longer, but
none the less she had held lease of him and his profits did not cease to
accrue. And then one day he came back from France.

Very early on a hazy August morning that promised exceptional
heat. It was the week of St Bartholomew's Fair: the Guild of Parish
Clerks was presenting its Christ-plays in Clerkenwell, in association
with the fair. Dorothy had determined to see them; and for this day,
all day, she would neither practise nor rehearse, her musicians and her
tutor could go to the fair themselves, or wherever else they chose to
ambulate: she was a free woman at her own devices and at five in the
morning she squatted and splashed and lathered herself in a very hot
barrel of bathwater.

Belle-Savage scrubbed her back with a vigour that did justice to her
name. This sharp-faced vixenish woman had come to England as a
child on a Portuguese caravel: and had developed from a benumbed
slave-captive into a sort of scorched Nelly. Dorothy thought she loved
her as once she had loved Nelly, not a warm sentimental love but a
prickly part-hostile dependence, and an intimacy of mutual self-
defence against the outside world in general, particularly its men. The
Portuguese captain, who had found Belle-Savage on the east African
sea-coast and kidnapped her, had treated her with great cruelty. She
gave him the slip in the Pool of London, going safely to ground among
sailormen's crimping-houses along the river by the Tower. And then,
for a wonder, she got out of them, far more remarkably, far more

courageously, than Dorothy out of the Norwich ale-cellar, for the black child had no-one to help her. For the last ten years she had lived at the 'Birdcage', serving one minstrel-woman after another; her knowledge of the 'business' was unfathomable: her grasp of the English tongue was erratic and very foul.

She rejoiced to scrub Dorothy, as though Dorothy in some way carried the cruelty of the caravel-captain in her skin, worry it out of her if she made her bleed for it. The more the bristles stung, the more Dorothy hissed through her teeth for the pleasure of pain, cursing beneath her breath the imbecility of old Cuthbert, the glazed corruption of the black-canons.

So early in the day visitors were not allowed, the caretaker must keep them out: but bribes, as they say, are sharper than knives. A footstep on the gallery outside Dorothy's door, a knock upon the door itself: Belle-Savage dropped brush and pumice-stone, strode to open the grille-shutter in the top panel. A quiet voice outside, Dorothy could not hear the words: but Belle-Savage's reply was outraged. 'Turd', 'swive', 'piss-drinker', 'cunny-licker', 'cullion-ulcer' and 'arse-broacher' were but a few of the decipherable rudenesses among all the flowing filth she shot out through the grille at him before banging it shut and returning to the tub. "Bella," shouted Dorothy, "you've no damn business being so vile: name-of-God, woman, I'm only having a bath. Why don't you let me know who it is?" She hung herself with a towel and padded across the floor. Something about that man's voice, surely, that it pulled her out of water like the jerk of an angler's line.

No, she was not wrong: Wentworth against the gallery-rail, leaning out over the narrow kitchen-court, looking down at some children boiling kettles for break-fast: he was trying to pretend he had not been insulted but had merely come up there to look down, it being so fine a morning.

Dorothy's first thought: whip him in, whip off her towel, and squeeze him to death. Second thought: we couldn't have that. Suppose someone notified the French? So she told him to come in and wait until she was dressed, and told Belle-Savage to give him a drink, clear the tub away, and clear away the folding bed, still shamefully laid out on the floor-square where she danced and sang. She had to carry her clothes into the back corridor. Why could she not have had the sense to make Wentworth wait on the gallery, as she would have with any other visitor?

As she dressed, or at least put on her undershift and a night-robe, he tried to talk to her through the closed door: something about her great new reputation, to which she replied with a brief yell, "Talk to my maid, I can't hear you. If you don't like her way of answering, blame yourself, you chose the hour!" When she emerged, he was still talking, about all the gentlemen whom she pleased with her art and scorned with her private person. "You do know," he was saying, "I'm not one of them. But *what* am I? A year apart, and we're both lost."

He had come full of urgent words: his reception had driven them away. He was fumbling and she let him fumble. This was her room, not his garden-maze. There was nothing now she needed from him. And he knew it too, for he spoke all at once of his own needs; to ask a favour, 'beg a boon', that was what he had come for. Upon his absurd romance-word 'boon', he even dropped on his knee like a knight in a tale. He added, "Not surprising I am timid at it. That which already you have given me is not yet repaid."

To which she answered, "Isn't it?", and looked pointedly round the room at her carpets, her silk cushions, her solid pewter utensils, the panel of tapestry on the fireplace wall of Virgin and Unicorn: and her mirror nearly long enough to see herself top-to-toe. She had even had the flaking walls between herself and her noisy neighbours wadded up with padded felt and every nail with a rosette-head. Expensive, his money, let him see how it had been used. In no more than fourteen months. Fourteen months: she had lain with no man. Would he believe her if she told him? "Let's not make a crown-piece out of a farthing." She sat among her cushions. Cool and confident, or hoping to seem so. "Did I hear you call me Dorothy? My name here is La Haut-jambeé: it's on the doorpost, why not use it?"

"'La Haut-jambeé'? The Longshanks? Or Longlegs, or something like that? I think Wyatt said 'Doll Longlegs', yes?"

"Not to *me* he didn't. Dear Christ, did he say it to you?"

"I'm afraid that he might have done. At all events someone did. Which is why I do not care to use it. However much I owe to him, I am not Tom Wyatt. You see him now and then, do you not?"

"Never again, never," she thought, "if *that's* what he knew about me already, at Nettlestead that time. Dear Christ I couldn't face him!" But aloud, she said only: "He comes to watch me, hear me sing. Yes, now and then: it's my trade. More often he does the singing himself. His own poetry, not yours."

"Does he talk about me?"

"No. For if he did, he would enter my privacy. He knows that, he's a heedful man. And I don't enter his."

She winked to Belle-Savage, who sneered, slipped out of the door, and sat down in the gallery to deter intruders. "How long have you been back from Paris?"

"Two weeks. I would have come the first day, but . . . I would have come here, of course. Except that – "

"The King's business."

"More. My wife was at Dover to meet me. She has – she has appointed a new chaplain. The previous one fell sick. Were I telling it to anyone else, I would have to say, 'Thank God'. You see, her doctrine nowadays – "

"Jesus, we live and learn. Pay yourself a fresh priest and the world turns upside-down. But let's not enter privacy. Will you believe me if I say I'm glad?"

"My dear, we should be friends. Is it possible, I may kiss you?"

"Why not? When you've told me your favour. Seeking favours can twist friendship. I'd need to know, first, whereuntil moveth your mind." She spoke so formally out of suspicion of him. This would not be quite a *personal* favour, he wore what she felt must be his ambassador's face. The King would never trust a totally simple heart, still less send such a one to France. She owed it to herself to be as careful as the King.

When he finally spoke, she was well aware that the favour he put to her was not the one he had come to ask for. "Merely to be my companion today. I am in London with no work to do, my wife has returned to Suffolk, I am to discuss affairs tomorrow with the Council: so today I am free enough to spend an hour at Bartelmy Fair, I would prefer to go with a friend. We could eat roast pork, buy things – silly ribbons, things like that. Will you come?"

"I *could* come. Because of the fair, there will be few gentlemen here before dark, the day can be all my own, as it is yours. I had meant indeed to *make* it my own. But not at the fair. I know more about fairs than I choose to remember. I will see things there that hurt me. On the other hand, the Clerkenwell plays – "

"You surely have seen such Christ-plays many times before. Erroneous theology devoid of scriptural precedent, glozing the false pretensions of Rome with pretty tales of saints' miracles, feigned relics, ridiculous purgatory-prayers. It is better to be in the market for pigs' chitterlings and bonnet-tassels than mendacious and papal indulgences. There'll be those at the fair will cheat your pocket, but all in laughter, they see you coming, we see them. Upon the fringes of the plays, however, the pardoners, the holy-bone-men, the medallion-and-scapular merchants: they are there to cheat the soul. Either go there to denounce them, scourge 'em hence as Our Lord did the temple-hucksters, or give 'em a wide berth, that's my view of it."

God, how this religion could encrust a lively spirit. His features were closed as tight as a visored helmet. She tried to explain: "I have seen the plays at Norwich upon Corpus Christi, and the same sort of thing at King's Lynn – why at Lynn I took part in them, Cecilia's Muses made an angel-choir for the Holy Virgin's Assumption. I know what they are, I know who badgers the crowds there, I know what they sell. They've done it for hundreds of years, who am I to make a riot about it? But in London they say the spectacle is more magnificent than anywhere else, except perhaps York, and I've never been to York. I couldn't attend Clerkenwell last year, I had only just arrived, I needed every hour with my instructors. This year, I am not yet by any means perfect in my art: but I can spare a day for the Parish Clerks, and I want to spare it. We can argue their theology afterwards."

"You really do desire it."

"I really do. And with you, if you will come. If not, with the Belle-Savage and my own quite critical self. Please?"

She put up her mouth to him. Her eyes smiled. She was relieved to see it melted him at once, and she took his kiss. He still had a good deal of the lover in him, even after his French embassy, even after all the household chill-and-then-warmth-again with his no-less religious wife. On the thought of his wife – "How shall I dress? I don't want to bring you scandal."

"Wear a mask and who will know you are not a great lady of court? The manners at court have changed the last year or so: Queen Catherine constrained 'em, Queen Anna makes them free. Assure yourself, you'll not be noticed, even with naked bosom."

"Assure yourself my bosom will be as modest as yours. I was thinking, rather, of my hat." It resembled a barrel-top, orange and purple, clustered with cockerel's tail-feathers. She wore it pinned so close upon one side it seemed to hang from the top of her ear. He watched her as she adjusted its exact angle in the mirror: he approved the effect, and kissed her again.

*

The Christ-plays were in a wide green field, on the edge of the north-west suburbs. It was surrounded by scaffolds for both actors and audience. They arrived late, the seats were full, and they had to take their place among the crowd in the field: she pushed and pulled forward until she brought him (reluctant) to the rim of the playing-space right opposite King Herod's scaffold. Herod had already leapt down from his high seat and was raging on the trodden grass, far more terrifically than the old Rover in this role. There was little about him to laugh at. At real peril to the audience, he swung his two-handed sword (a real sword, with jewels in its hilt) among their heads, relying on the quickness of the stage-manager's staff, ushers with white canes, to clear people out of his way. His sumptuous armour was real as well, it glittered and clanged. She had been right: these plays were truly beautiful. She had never seen anything like them for expert effect of acting, music, costume, the pre-judged movement of the men and boys.

Wentworth at her side snorted with disgust about every tenth line of the verse. She kept wishing he wouldn't, it damaged it greatly for her: being so awkwardly aware of him, she felt compelled to give thought to what the players had spoken. Impossible for her to allow the poetry just to bang itself into her, rhyme and alliteration and the piling of stanza upon stanza – she found herself splitting it in her mind even as she heard it, teasing at it, asking herself, "Do I really believe all this?" Why was she moved by what surely did seem, when she took it in with full attention, to be dangerous nonsense? Oh God, why was she moved? Why did the choice of Mary as Immaculate Bride of God bring the tears to her eyes when at the same time she knew she was not a goddess but a mortal woman and should be shown as a mortal woman, both before and after that Glorious Dove came singing toward her womb?

She had only seen the Dove from afar off as she and Wentworth broke into the outside edge of the crowd: but she had clearly heard the music that fetched It down to Mary's bower, and the tears still prickled in her eyes. "But was there really a Glorious Dove? Or was the Angel Gabriel more of a man than he looked?" She wondered (and then wondered at herself for the dreadful blasphemy), how like was the house at Nazareth to the Nettlestead garden-maze: could it have been that a nervous gentleman paid court to a foolish girl and then left her and went away (as it might be, to France), secure in the knowledge that his steward would be making arrangements with a convenient old carpenter, a man no doubt well-skilled in the putting-together of birdcages . . . ?

She shuddered at herself.

And then again, she was to wonder: "Oh God, why am I moved?" Why did Christ in the Mouth of Hell send cold fingers up her backbone, when at the same time she could not believe that all dead souls in the next world are but as prisoners in the Bishop's gaol, longing for some earthly bailsman to buy them out of their chains? Was God as Supreme Judge no better in His dealings than More as Lord Chancellor? Did He really employ demons to do the same work as that churl in Norwich? They flogged and stocked poor Nelly over a book she could not read, nor had ever seen before. This God upon that stage wore a crown of authentic gold, and His beard was a snowfall of pity. "But even so you can buy Him off: and if you can't afford to, if you try to run away, as I ran away, why then, He is so great and cruel He will catch you regardless. Bishop of Norwich couldn't catch me: but This One can, and I don't like Him."

These latter thoughts came to her at the end of the afternoon, and made her most unwilling to meet Wentworth's eye, so she turned instead to Belle-Savage. "I never asked you, Bella, I don't know why I never asked: are you baptised Christian?"

The tight black face tightened even more in an equivocal grin, spat her words into Dorothy's ear: "You mean the pouring water, criss-cross-Jesus-love-me and all bad spirits gone? Damn-my-shite they made me do it on the Portugal ship: burnt my tits with candles so I'd know what it would be, endless, past-all, all-time, if ever Jesus hear me say Jesus not biggest strongest spirit of all spirits earth-all-over. So I don't say it, do I? Up-your-cunt, do I ever say that? But you tell me, so goddam clever, how come if he is, they stuck the nails in, whipped him to pieces? So he'd know what it was like? Sound likely? Sound likely-so to me. Allright, then, pricktease, answer me this: if he know what it's like, why he do it to us? Look at it, lovely white-arse, look at it *there* –"

'There' was the final procession of damned souls thrust to hell-fire as the saved souls climbed the staircase, white-and-gold staircase, into Christ's arms and His Mother's, and His Father's (with the silver beard): while the Dove, a six-foot wingspan, hovered wonderfully at the end of the stage-crew's crane. A moment of silence, huge tableau of one hundred actors, as though carved from alabaster, the red sunset on their upturned faces. The last one to be still moving, on the greensward in front of the scaffolds, a hideous prancing Lucifer, a-crackle with fireworks from every possible bodily orifice: he sprang about among the front lines of spectators, causing children to run and cower and scream, and then back into his smoking hell, brought its great jaws down behind him, tight *shut!* and the plays were over.

*

"I would be glad," said Wentworth cautiously, as they moved away among the crowd, "I would be most grateful, if before I brought you back across river, we could pass beside Paul's. There is a preacher tonight at the Cross there who has something to say which I want very much to hear: that is, if they allow him. I know that dry divinity is not in truth a matter for a fair-day: but, well, for old friendship, your indulgence . . . ?"

"I made you see the plays which I knew you would not like. It was kind of you. Let me be kind. We'll go to St Paul's."

They walked for a while without talking. She let him hold her arm, but she was troubled by her thoughts, and she kept herself a little away from him; in feeling, that is to say. Body-to-body they were as close in the packed street as they could be.

"I won't ask you what you thought of the plays." His continued caution, which might at another time have irritated her, was oddly pleasing. "I don't want us to quarrel. But perhaps you *could* tell me: what did you think of the people who saw the plays? It seems to me, ten years ago, no, five, they would have been much more . . . much more – *joyful* . . . ?"

"You're quite right. They shuffled feet, were talking even while Lord Jesus talked. You weren't the only one to give snorts, some of them snorted more often than you did. You're quite right. But I hadn't noticed. Except you, I noticed you. How could I not? We held hands, dammit, and I felt it through your hand." She did not change her posture to him: they still walked arm-in-arm, exactly the same, but *now* she was close to him. "I ought to have noticed, I have good feel for an audience. But you're quite right. They found the day tedious, and it was making a number of them angry. They were not ready, I think, to understand *why* they were angry. Perhaps they thought simply the Parish Clerks acted not so precise as usual. Or perhaps they thought simply, it was the heat? Why, my clothes cling to me with sweat, do not yours also? It's no cooler, even now . . . Had you carried out your threat and cried denunciation, they'd still have been angry with *you*."

She was pressing him to her: she felt a creeping of sexual anticipation and ordered herself to stop it. They were going to a sermon: and it was his choice, a sermon, yes. And his wife had changed her chaplain. Nevertheless, she could not prevent her conversation turning to matters of her privacy: something in her mind had fostered a discordant itch, she had to rub the scab.

"Upon my name-feast, St Dorothy's Day, February, this year, a man came to my room when I was out in the town. One of the bullies opened the door for him and let him leave his message – which he shouldn't have, they are not supposed to use pass-keys except for alarm-of-fire or king's-officers: I was angry and kept asking him why the impertinence? He answered that the man was a foreigner and he feared it might have been important, he only did it for the best intention, so I let it go. The message was not important: being merely a basket with three apples and three roses. I thought, 'Roses in February? if this is love it is fanatic, where could he have got them from?' We are used, of course, to these small offerings, they signify no more than a quite small gallantry. But whoever sent this one had thought about my name. My father told the story, I never forget it. Dorothea was a Roman virgin on her way to her martyrdom, one Theophilus jeered at her, saying she ought to send him fruit from the Garden of Christ's Paradise, if all was as lovely there as she in her religion made claim. He is said to have wanted to love her but she had scorned him for his heathenness. So of course, after her death, an angel brought Theophilus three apples and three roses: he converted straightway to Christ, became a martyred man himself."

"I have heard the story. It is beautiful: yes. But nonsense, all these saints' tales are quite alien to true Scripture."

"So it was not you that sent them? I thought that it might have been. I thought that *you* might have thought that you and I, being the pair of us, insofar as we have been a pair, are also alien to Scripture, so therefore it might do no harm to indulge a pretty fable . . . ? Also, this foreign messenger: the bully knew not how to differ between French and Muscovite, he could not tell me, so of course I thought of France. For all I know, winter roses may be commonplace in France."

He looked at her sharply, trying to gauge the depth of her disappointment: or was she teasing him, taking it no more seriously than she would any other brief failure of some gallant to come up to expectation? She spoke as though joking: but the joke pricked him, and he walked in silence.

They had come through Newgate, and the crush in the street grew so dense she was forced a few steps behind him. She took advantage, and turned round to Belle-Savage for a quick private word. An ill-advised private word, she knew it as she spoke it, the more so after his reply about the roses. "You don't want to hear a sermon. I don't either, but I have to. Go home to the 'Birdcage', clean the room, get a neat little cold supper, plates and glasses for two, leave it on a tray: I have credit with the bar downstairs, you know the kind of wine to order. If anyone comes for me, tell 'em I'm not receiving tonight. Performance tomorrow as usual. Decent apologies to them, Bella, please, I insist, none of your damned salt!" The maid dodged away towards the river: Dorothy caught up with Wentworth, firmly wedged her arm into his.

*

The Cross outside St Paul's, on the north side of the cathedral, in the angle between choir and transept, had its own little theatre built about it. The galleries were full of citizens, with several apparent noblemen, together with their ladies; and a number of clerics. The Cross itself was an open-air pulpit under a cupola. Around its base pressed a throng of less important, but even more devoted hearers, listening to the preacher with a vivid attention that had not obtained at Clerkenwell. And yet they were just the sort whom Clerkenwell ought to have impressed, artisans, apprentices, sailors, market-women – you would not think a public holiday would give such people cause to seek out the Word of God, undiluted, undecorated. But they were here: there seemed hundreds of them.

This time it was Wentworth who pulled and pushed. He used his rank unashamedly, hectoring vergers, dropping coins into palms, waving to a very well-dressed man in a gallery as though to say, "Ah, my friend, you kept a seat for me? Very good: here I am . . ." By these devices he and Dorothy were rapidly established upon eighteen inches of narrow bench, between a fat canon and a perspiring city-wife, inconveniently behind a pillar.

The man in the pulpit had paused for an irritable moment, losing the thread of his discourse in the commotion of their late arrival.

He was John Bale.

Dorothy started, moved her head sideways so that her broad hat

and not her scarlet face was presented to him. It was bad enough
arriving late for the second time that day: but to be so late – and so
conspicuous – for the baleful white-friar was a little too much of an
omen. She made a fervent secret prayer, "Dear Lord, let him not
know who I am!" Maybe her mask was sufficient protection? Somehow, with Bale, she thought not. She gave thanks for the inconvenient
pillar.

The sermon resumed. Bale as preacher was surly, growling,
sarcastic, not entirely coherent, but undeniably effective. His sentences came tumbling over each other, with all the punctuation-
pauses in unexpected places, as though he was thinking them out
aloud and was too involved in their meaning to trouble himself to put
them together into decorous grammatical form. Most of the time he
seemed to be speaking only to those within a few feet of his pulpit, his
eyes cast down upon his notes, an implication that if others chose to
overhear him, that might be to their advantage, but if not, then – not.

She gathered that he too had been to Clerkenwell that day, and had
much the same view of the plays as Wentworth. But more ferociously
expressed. He regarded them as a mere device whereby the feigning
mass-mongers of the old dispensation could cover and cloak their
breech-burning lusts and their hunger for buggery-boys. Sodomites,
he rumbled, monks and friars and unnatural nuns, who saw in the life
of Our Lord only an opportunity to enhance their own hold over the
multitude, co-opting minstrels and poetic swaggerers into retailing
heathen legends as though they appertained to Christ's disciples,
bringing the Gospel to a level of Apuleius his *Golden Ass*, mingling
ordure of pagan Rome with the fresh-squirted defecations of Rome of
the Popes. Oh for a second Constantine who might cleanse these
horse-stalls of Augeus!

Which carried him, loosely enough, to the King's Parliament in
Westminster. He besought his audience to offer prayers – "now, dear
friends, upon your knees, supplicate now, there is no time to be
lost!" – that the Parliament Men, Lords and Commons, might, in
the ensuing session, be so guided by God's Wisdom that their
own wisdom would inspire sufficient legislation to drive the filthy
oil-of-olive palms of grasping Italian ecclesiasts out of our godly
English treasure-house once and for all.

He began to list the legislation from what appeared to be an official
document: a Bill of Appeals, a Bill of Dispensation, a Bill in Absolute
Restraint of Annates, a Bill for Submission of Clergy, a Bill of First

Fruits and Tenths, a Treason Bill; and finally, a roaring culmination (except he did not roar it, his voice dropped lower and lower, till it came out a hoarse intimidating thunder-crackle, like a storm brewing ten miles away, yet everyone heard him with the most complete clarity): the Bill of Royal Supremacy and the Bill of Succession – and by God's Grace these last two must be *sworn* to upon the Holy Word of God, God's Curse for the malingerer from so bounden an English duty. Dorothy was amazed that the people suffered this legalistic digression, which was by no means adequately explained: for example, she had no idea what Restraint of Annates could mean, or why it should be regarded as important. But her amazement was doubled when a ripple of applause came running through the homespun jackets in the yard and then along the galleries, hands clapping, cheers, abrupt cries of "English law!", "God's law for God's Englishmen!", "England's King and our old English Church!": even, "Christ came to Glastonbury before ever there was a Pope in Rome!" – the Glastonbury ejaculation from the woman beside her, her eyes popping out with enthusiasm. The fat canon, on the other hand, seemed sunk in disapproving gloom, slowly sucking and sucking at a medicinal sweetmeat.

Bale paused, to allow silence: and then continued in a different tone, a high climbing edge to his voice. "Oh yes, my friends, let us give thanks there are so many of this nation to whom the affairs of the nation are matter for such thought: it is therefore all the more strange that the great affairs of Parliament (to say naught of Convocation) are not published by the month, by the week, by the day, for wider edification of you all. Can it be possible they have forgotten – in the dusty closets and *scriptoria* of their industrious law-chambers – that there are printing-houses, there are pamphlet-sellers, there are the very ballad-singers in the street, who could make their deliberations *live*, for all the people all the time, if only the word were given?

"Nay, can they not see that these Clerkenwell plays, so sadly of the old bad guise, could, by a poet of power, be thoroughly rewritten and reformed that they might at last express true Scripture, a true English determination to abide ever by true Scripture alone! Why, how many of the parish clerks who enact them so skilfully would not rejoice to be able to utter theatric dialogue they could themselves credit even as they shouted it out? Let me tell you, more than most of them! I have talked with these excellent men. At risk of their lives they have been reading, alongside their idiot play-screeds, the Very Word in the language of England – yes, Mr Tyndale his proscribed translation – oh yes, my friends, contraband! let our souls shake in horror . . . ! And do not think, my dear friends, these clerks as they read are incapable of just comparison! Set new-laid eggs beside a rotten custard, who among you would not know which to choose? Oh the honest nose is not deceived, however dull may be the constrained and over-tutored brain . . . Notwithstanding, we are informed by mitre and crozier-staff, that to read this Word is damnable: gate of hell, pit of Acheron, the dreadful steep stairway down down to the realm of DIS!"

As he mouthed this last word, outlandishly lengthening its hissing single syllable, he looked full up, into Dorothy's face.

It was still very hot, her bum (bum of Barbara, bum of Diss) was itching beneath her in a sweat-puddle, the oppressive evening brought forth midges that flickered about her skin. Torches had been lit in the crowded corner, one of them in front of the pulpit throwing a fierce oven-light onto Bale's features from below: his wide-stretched snarling mouth seemed to be all that she could see, could he see *her* with an equal luridity?

She was sure, when he said 'Dis', it had not been part of his original text. He improvised it: as a signal to her. Otherwise, why should he slide aside from the urgency of his rhetoric, mumbling all of a sudden some pedantic gloss – "as you know, my friends, already, those of you with schooling; and for those without schooling, here is the commentary" – about how the ancients conceived of Satan as "a swart-visaged king y-clept *Dis*, being Latin-corrupt for *Deus*, corrupt insofar as God-Corrupt is Devil, and Church-corrupt is Rome – and so we return to our theme."

She would not look toward Wentworth. It was not possible that Wentworth knew about Diss, but . . . God, of course it was possible. He knew Bale. He knew Bale the very night that she, at Nettlestead, had . . . What had he and Bale not said, one to the other, concerning her? The erotic warmth, throughout her body only half-an-hour before, was now an acrid stream, curdling her with resentment head-to-foot. Her fantasy unravelled for her all sorts of conspiracies fetching her into Wentworth's garden, fetching her into the 'Birdcage', fetching her to Clerkenwell, and so at last to this place. Bale-zebub in the pulpit there had laid his trap and sprung it: it was herself, not ex-Queen Catherine nor even the Pope, who was the sole unwitting object of this public agitation, and nobody knew it but her, and John Bale; and Thomas Wentworth, let him *burn* . . . !

Bale's theme from that point on was a vast excoriation of everyone in the Church of superior station to himself, praising only the King, and Cranmer the new Archbishop – all the others, he insinuated, would sell the souls of the people for thirty silver pieces, making base adjustments with the Pope and his decayed privilege, not because they sincerely believed in the traditional transactions (which would at least have been honest), but because they somehow hoped to save their own privilege, their honours, their incomes, their social status, at the expense of eternal principle, not caring whether they enforced pauperism upon the entire nation in the process.

She did not quite follow how this related to his sub-plot (she was judging his sermon very much as she judged a play, or rather as she had found herself judging the plays that afternoon): justification that the King had now crowned his new bride with his own authority alone, a totally new authority, which nonetheless could be proven a most ancient *and traditional* power – for anyone with scope of learning to look it up and find it out.

In short, he rumbled on, Thames was no longer Thames but your antique Rubicon and the King had crossed it, oh such a brief journey, so few small coins to the waterman, from Westminster no further than over to Lambeth Palace: the annulment of the old marriage had been finally adjudged by Archbishop Cranmer – and by no Pope – and the new marriage-bonds last Whit Sunday had been knotted by Archbishop Cranmer – and by no Pope – so Rome was confounded! And yet, through the right reading of our noble English history, Rome in such context had *always* been confounded . . .

Again, he seemed to take a good deal of this knowledge for granted among his hearers, once again there was applause, this time cries of: "King John!", "Here is our new John, to defy interdict and secure his right!", "To the devil with Tom Becket, let Tom Cranmer purge his Cantuar: one-hundred-fathom deeper than mere right to adjudge marriages!", "Mere pettifogging so far, and that's all, stir up the putrefaction, I say stir it, Reverend Sir, God's help to set the shit-pot bubbling!" – and such-like academic exegesis, which came very strangely from the rougher element in the yard.

In order not to look at Wentworth, and to prove that she did not *have* to look at Bale, Dorothy had half-turned herself towards the fat canon. He was head-to-head with his next neighbour, another pouting clergyman. She heard: "I thought you told me Mr Dean had said he was taking measures. Already a score of times this gobbling fellow has passed over the mark! By heaven this is not a decent loyalty to the Crown but a frenzy of egalitarian adventure, what sort of a friar is he? and why is it permitted?"

"I don't think the Dean had thought there would be so many to hear him. We don't want a plebeian tumult."

"Nonsense, the Dean's afraid he will be seen to be taking orders *ultra vires* from the Bishop. Can we not, in defence of principle, put an end just this once to our absurd jurisdictional wrangles?"

"My dear sir, you can forget it – for here is the moment – *look* –!"

An elderly official person, of semi-clerical appearance, in a gold chain; with two beadles at his back: he had mounted the pulpit steps. The preacher took no notice of him, and continued his utterance, even though he must have known that the official was plucking from behind at his white hood to get him to stop. This went on for quite a full minute, until the pulling became too strong, Bale being almost strangled by the pressure against his throat. He broke off, and swung round: "Brother in Christ, you have a question for me?" His words were ostensibly polite: his posture had but one message, 'Here are enemies: no matter what they say, no matter what *I* say, they will never be anything else!' The official did not look at him but fixed his gaze over above him on the lower portion of the cathedral spire.

He spoke in a high reedy voice, and clearly spoke from a pre-conceived brief: "Mr Prior, you omitted to mention, when you submitted your name for tonight's pulpit, that your preaching had been inhibited by order of the Lord Bishop."

Bale smiled, a slow menacing smile, letting it travel from the official all round his congregation. "Mr Warden: the Dean of Paul's, when I handed in my name, omitted to tell *me* that the Lord Bishop and not himself was in control of his cathedral sermons." He held up his arms to everyone, in a parody-gesture of pathetic sympathy. "Dear friends, it now appears that the master of this great basilica (dedicate, as it is, to the greatest apostle) is not after all his own master: and where a bishop has spoken, who is a mere prior to stand against him? Or ex-prior, should I not say? for the Carmel-house in Maldon is no longer mine, and the brethren of the Ipswich house will not confirm my standing there – I say, who is a mere ex-prior to presume to be the instrument wherewith the Holy Spirit plays sweet music for your innermost ears? Oh I see they have brought up beadles to put Brother Bale to silence. Were there indeed a tumult, I think two would be scarce sufficient . . . ? However, there shall be no tumult. You are to pray for the Parliament Men; and pray for His Majesty: and when you have done that, pray for me. I may well be in a dungeon." His eyes still held his message: 'They will never be anything else.' But he went down the steps of the pulpit. The officers took him away: there was indeed no great tumult, although the crowd was not pleased, and they showed it as they left the yard.

*

Dorothy on his arm, neither of them saying a word, Wentworth smartly evaded a group of youths at the top of Ludgate Hill who were throwing stones and fighting with more officers. Not bothering to wait for a torch-bearer, he hurried her by back alleyways down to Puddle Dock and looked about him for a boat.

"Just one moment, where are we going?"

"I am bringing you to Bankside: surely you have work to do? You told me earlier that you did."

"Wait. I don't know. Will they put him in prison?"

"Of course they won't. He spoke for the King's policy."

"But not the Bishops'."

"The Bishops are only concerned to have no policy toward the King's policy: until they have determined one, and that's what Cranmer is for. But he has to take his time. Dr Bale and others like him remind us all that the time is short: remind Cranmer: remind the King. That's what *they* are for. There is still too much talk of accommodation with Rome."

"I was going to ask you to spend tonight with me. Or at any rate this evening. I decided I need after all do no work, and I was going to ask you. But now I don't know. Will you answer me a question: are you in fact a heretic?"

"No, I am a Christian."

"Oh God, words of God, and can anyone ever know just what any of them mean? You are not telling me lies: but all day you have not told me the truth. God, I cannot love a king's ambassador."

He stared at her, bewildered. Her images went too fast for him: what had being an ambassador to do with his love for her, if he had any? He knew that he loved his wife. He knew that tonight, if he ate supper with Dorothy, he would lie in her arms until morning. She knew that he knew this. She tore off her great hat in a rage and flapped it violently but ineffectually against his head, knocking off his neat little black velvet bonnet with all its jewels, and breaking and scattering her own plumes. "You told me you had a favour to ask. Damn your blood, you never asked it! So ask it now, you two-leggéd quicksand, and let's have no more jiggling."

In a well-ordered traditional society, singing-women do not beat hats against barons on public wharves in full sight of all the watermen hastening to tout for a fare. Nor do they use to them the language of watermen. Such things unseat foundations, delve dreadfully at firm-planted roots. But in this case, the baron was only too well aware of his own devious efforts against both roots and foundations: moreover uneasily conscious that they were the main cause of Dorothy's outrageous explosion. So he did not strike her back, nor did he walk away from her. He gathered his breath, dug his nails into his palms, squared his shoulders, and caught the eye of the first boatman to ship sculls below the steps.

"Paris Garden, two fares!" In a low tone, to her: "The complete truth, in your own room. This is no place, believe me: please." She was scared at what she had done. Her insolence should be for her advantage, not her ruin; she would sit quiet with him in the boat, and wait.

All he said, as they crossed the water, was: "Where the devil did he get that schedule of business for next session? I doubt whether even the King has it to hand at this present. Certainly it is not yet known to the Council . . ."

*

In her room, they ignored Belle-Savage's supper-tray. From opposite corners they faced one another, standing: two candlesticks half-way between them, wicks burning muggily in the humid air.

"I could not speak of this, my dear, until you had been with me where we've just been. If I am a heretic, John Bale is not: his theology is that of the King, and the King has denounced Luther. Bale may scorn what he calls mass-mongers, for he sees how they abuse their trust. But he still believes the slice of biscuit is Christ-in-flesh and I do not. These walls must be thin: who is next door?"

"Angelina is out of town, gone to the west to dance for some lords, in the hostel of the Abbot of Glastonbury. German Rotraut on the other side has warm thoughts of Luther: you are safe."

"Very good. But it's more than Luther: Luther even yet is half-hearted about the distinction between the Mass and Christ's true Eucharist. Zwingli has the only truth, and there are precious few here to understand him. I tell you this so that you see there is not much uniformity among those of us who challenge the Old Guise. And, as you know from this evening at Paul's, there is likewise little scope for fully-reasoned disputation. Upon parliament-business, yes: but making laws to re-order the temporal shape of the Church is only the beginning. And we cannot conclude it, unless we know where we need it to end. My end will be where Zwingli reached, before last year, his heroic death. Others will wish to extend no further than Luther. Others will stand still once the Pope is repudiated: overturn hierarchical order, but hold fast to its established doctrine; not logical of course, the doctrine derives from the order, lose one and the other must crumble.

"Beyond all this, there is a fourth party: overturn *all* order, hierarchical, doctrinal, social, civil, monarchical. In the Germanies the peasant-multitude ran stark mad like Wat Tyler. Men and women called Anabaptists are trying to invent what they call Christ's reasons for their own continuation of the same bloody chaos. Here in England, if we cannot find agreement between us all, our doors are wide-open for them, hordes of devils into the swept house where before there was but one. You have seen our English countryside from hedge and ditch in the foulest weather: can you tell me Wat Tyler is dead history, nothing more, as old as Arthur's Camelot and no more like to be repeated?"

"We had better sit down, I think." She felt a stab in her bladder, dreadful urgency to make water. But she could not interrupt, not now: he was at last being honest with her, informing her his full thought, therefore trusting her, perhaps even more than he trusted his changeable wife. But danger, watch out for danger: if Angelina must not hear, because a simple Angelina was threat-of-death to Baron Wentworth (and she was sure, from the tight inclining of his ear toward the partition as he spoke, that it *was* a question of death), then what could happen to Doll Longlegs, once he'd told her all his mind and made her an accomplice?

At the same time, she did not think that his views on Wat Tyler would be quite the same as hers. *He* had not had to flee in snow-time from rural constables with dancing-pumps on his feet and but a ha'penny in his purse, *he* had never found his bruised and bleeding private parts his sole defence against starvation. And yet, if she seemed hostile to his dissection of England's commonwealth, by God he had the power to put her back into all her misery. Could she trust him well enough to take the risk he would not use it? She decided to walk sideways to his argument – pisspot could wait – she murmured half of an old verse to search him out a little further.

> "When Adam delved and Eva span
> Who was then the – "

" 'Gentleman'? Quite right. We couldn't have that."

"Wat Tyler's priest, John Ball, is supposed to have made the poem." She placed her thoughts slowly, trying hard not to sound argumentative. "They say in the east parts it was Ball thought out the whole rebellion, Tyler just *did* it. I expect you'd say, then, the priest was more perilous than the soldier. They still repeat his rhymes, you know, in the places where he preached.

> John the Miller hath y-ground small small small:
> The King's Son of Heaven shall pay for all.

Oh I've heard 'em often in the ale-hovels round Colchester. Do you not fear Bale might be also a sort of Ball? He goes not so far as you in theology, you say: but dammit, a sight further in more worldly matters, oh I heard him: 'the very ballad-singers in the street,' he said, 'the excellent players of Clerkenwell, fetch *them* up to defy the pauperism that's enforced on the entire nation!' And I heard him again, years ago, getting me out to 'the land of Egypt' because my fellows had broken the law." (Ah, so Bale *had* told him: he nodded his head at 'land of Egypt', sweet Jesus, he knew all about it!) "When Joseph and Mary ran to Egypt, it was Herod's law from which they fled. So even four full years since, your Bale saw Henry as Herod?"

"Today he said he was Constantine – or could be – not consistent, I agree. A whole packload of inconsistencies about Dr Bale. You know he loves you?"

"Lusts for me: out of bushes and a deep white hood. I had hoped he would forget, I'm told he has forgotten so many of my sort: but even now my buttocks revolve in the den behind his eyes . . . and I don't know what to do about it! I think of him as a vengeful enemy, and yet I know he has been a friend. The favour you would ask, which you *still* have not told me – it hooks upon *him*, don't it? Oh God's sake let me hear it, *let me know why I am so dogged* . . . !"

She began to sob, he came across to her, put arms about her: they sat side-by-side on her cushions.

"Dear love, our poor John Bale is like those who had worshipped

Baal, halting upon both sides of the opinion at the brink of Mount Carmel, in face of the sneer of Elijah. Some think he *is* Baal: at any rate they call him so, an easy unjust joke. They edge from him in loathing because of his contortions. They cannot hear his words without thinking of his greedy tool that has thrust – so they are told – so many fleeting women and waxeth ever more tumified daily from the cauldron of his despair. He has been my friend a long time.

"I first knew him at Cambridge, when I was a gentleman-commoner with a special pattern of cap and gown to manifest thereby my rank, and he was a Jesus College theologian, already in priest's orders, meeting and disputing with Cranmer, Tyndale, Coverdale, and Latimer and Bilney and Barnes, in the upper room of the White Horse tavern, 'Little Germany' it was oft-times called by scorners, and they were frequent, far more frequent than they are now. But I went there too, he brought me there, although I was so young, to hear of Old Guise and New Guise, Luther, Melanchthon, Zwingli, the religion of Wycliffe, the religion of Huss, justification by faith or works? and how long could the Pope endure, with such intellect ranged against him? We argued, some of us, two years: others said twenty, others said no more years at all, revolution here and now, behold even in our own bright day!

"Well, Bilney is already burned: at Norwich, where you suffered. Tyndale and Coverdale live in Flanders, and if they watch not out, they will burn them in Flanders. Barnes and Latimer have survived. Though Latimer just this year is put to silence: and Barnes is still inhibited. But John Bale, sometime prophet of Baal, Carmelite friar upon Mount Carmel, holding to two sides, is not yet of one side: I tell you it is *vital* this man should determine himself! Among them all, he alone is the very 'poet of power' he cried out for in tonight's sermon: or should I say he *could* be, if only he knew what exactly he should write? As it stands, he abhors the abuses of the Rome-controlled Church: but he will not, or dare not, bring himself to question its essential identity. Is it indeed a Church? Or is it, as *I* think, fit only to be thrown over entire?

"You say he has forgotten so many of your sort, and yet, behind his eyes, your body will not vanish. Don't you understand why that is? You are his one connection with the world that he truly desires: the makers-of-art who create with both tongue and limb, the dancers with King David in front of the Ark of the Lord, the music that led Judith home from the tent of Holofernes to the gateway of Bethulia . . .

"I want him to come here, as my guest, to your room, and I want him to bring others as well: we need to re-assemble as much of the old White Horse spirit as is possible in these altered times. Laymen rather than clerics, all is so much now in the hands of laymen. We *must* obtain agreement about our new English doctrine: we *must* secure John Bale to present it to the public ear. 'To utter theatric dialogue they could themselves credit even as they shouted it out': that's technical, that means you – or someone like you – that means –"

"Are you mad? In the bloody 'Birdcage'? Are you totally out of your wits? Man, what have I done to you, you should shovel me all this danger in front of me here! Have none of you no rooms of your own?" She was shrieking and gulped her voice down, hastily, producing hiccups.

"Of course we have, but we have also servants, kinfolk, landlords and landladies, to see who is meeting and talk about it. It is not possible to come often together in any likely place without it trickling out at length to half the spies in the kingdom. Except here: because here there is no reason why all sorts of men should not assemble as regularly as they want, and no-one asks their motive because their motive is so obvious."

"Did you know this when you gave me the money?" She had drawn herself well back from his embrace till they stood again where they'd begun.

"I promised you the complete truth. Very well, let's try to tell it. When I gave you the money, I did not know why I gave it. Or rather, I thought I knew. For my honour – for my love – oh have some patience!" He was terrified she would strike him again: he had been knighted for his bravery in the French wars, and he cowered in fear of her. "Please, Dorothy, I thought I knew. But then, later, I began to wonder if occult calculation had not put my hand to your breast, my loins against your loins. All the time in Paris I condemned myself as most treacherous: and today I felt no less filthy than I did when I told my lies on behalf of the King to the liars of the King of France."

That was what *he* felt. *She* felt plain exhausted. Or would have done had her urine permitted her. "Oh go away go away go away, Wyatt pimped for *you*, and now *you* are the bawd of Bale and that's all that it comes to . . ." The pisspot was under a cloth below her music-cupboard: careless whether he saw it or not, she scrambled for it and ran, out into the back corridor. The narrow space was filled with harsh Germanic singing, Rotraut had her door open, and her colleague

Ermentruda (a fine-boned spare-fleshed silvery-blonde who always performed in men's clothes) was pulling on breeches in great haste for her next appearance. She took no notice of Dorothy's pourings, being preoccupied with her immediate work, save to nod her cropped head towards her with her malicious crooked smile. Dorothy opened a window-shutter and emptied the pot into the alley. They had to keep the shutters closed, even on such hot nights, or the men in the whorehouse opposite would watch them as they changed costumes: she was suddenly overcome with her sordid condition of life, now that she knew why she was paid for it, now that she knew what was expected . . .

It made her angry to find Wentworth had not gone. She had called him a bawd and he still stood there and wrung his bonnet between his fists. She had waved a pisspot at him and his eyes had not seen it at all. Her weariness dictated some of what she said next, but all-in-all there was much curiosity too. The more she agreed to, the more she would discover? At the moment she could not bear to have everything so half-revealed. Nothing she had heard had seemed natural to her at all: she *had* to allow these depths to be plumbed or else she'd surely break her brain.

On her knees, replacing the pot: "Notwithstanding, I am curious, woundy curious, you cadging net-maker." She stood to face him, glaring; she had never really faced him so before. At Nettlestead she had been subordinate, today she had been his equal, now she was superior, and he knew it. "If only because old John Ball, for the poor folk of East Anglia, has been very much a 'poet of power'. He was hanged for it, wasn't he? And then they cut his guts out. Notwithstanding. Bring your men here, bring your white-friar. Oh bring them whenever you want. I suppose it's as safe as anywhere. And now, I would sleep. I have dance-practice all tomorrow: I must start it three hours before you eat your goddamned break-fast."

He turned, to leave the room, and then turned again, his hand on the latch. "I should just tell you one thing. When Dr Bale was first put into the friary at Norwich, at the age of twelve, to take away his demanding belly from his parents' impoverished table, he had no choice but to go there: nobody ever claimed he was in any way *called*. And yet he was a pious boy and believed he was to live in holiness. You wouldn't think it now: he was a trusting and loveable child. He had not been there a week: the novice-master and another friar taught him to enact another trusting child, Samuel in an Old Testament play they were to perform. They brought him into the sacristy to show him the robe he would wear, and there they played a merry game with him, hoodman-blind as he changed out of his habit, rolling him on the floor until the garment was up to his armpits. And then they jammed their spouting yards into the cleft of his buttocks, who can say how many times each. And told him it was ordained of heaven for every one of the Carmel brethren, that the devil in their flesh be thus attacked and put to rout from the rear, a noble strategy first devised by the founders of the Order in the Holy Land during the Crusades. Commemoration, they said, of how David took Jerusalem, sending mighty men by stealth to climb up the dirty gutter into the hinder-parts of the city, *Kings* the second book, fourth chapter, they showed him the text: he believed them. He believed them for many months, and then, when he found out, from some other friars (who lived like Christians), what it was they had been doing to him, and how the King's law could cart them *and him* to the scaffold for it, he fell to his bed with a fever which very near killed him dead. And from which, may we say? he has never recovered.

"To bring such a man into the quiet company of a woman like yourself is not the act of a bawd, I think. It may well be an impertinence. I am sorry for it, and will not insist. Dorothy, please think about it. I love him: I love you."

He went without getting any more answer from her. She sat down and emptied the wine-bottles that Belle-Savage had left for the two of them: when she tried to eat the cold supper it rose up against her, she retched and choked, swept the platters to the floor, lay down heavily among the mess, and fell asleep.

(v) *A Hat And No Clothes*

The Widow lay deep in her pillows. Her son's wife came, to remake her bed, settle her for the night, draw back the curtain from the dormer-window to light the garret-room with moon and stars. The candle was taken away from the bedside table and replaced with a small rush-dip for night-light. It was a careful house: the dip was carefully put in a tin pan of water, in case of fire. Daughter-in-law had ready a drink of hot milk, but the Widow did not wake for it. Or was she asleep? Daughter-in-law bent over her: she was laughing, surely, among the bolsters, perhaps she was awake? "Mother, your hot milk . . . ? It will help you to rest . . ."

The old face turned into the swansdown and the old shoulders curved up into a hump. If she did wake, she would not show it. But she quivered under the

*coverlet with continuous chuckles: and daughter-in-law, after a snort of im-
patient annoyance, tip-toed out of the room. She had her own sleep to consider,
she would not hang about all night. Her husband was already in bed.*

*The Widow's dream was quite shocking, would not anyone have had to laugh?
She re-contemplated, with a wicked glee, the last communication she ever had
with Lord Wentworth.*

★

1545: she and Bale were in High Germany (having with them their
younger son) in flight and hiding from King Henry who had abruptly
put to death his diligent servant Cromwell. Smokey-faced Tom, the
killer of so many romanists, himself not roman enough for his master's
revised policy. Among the friends of Cromwell, Wentworth had
escaped disgrace. Wentworth had shown that he too could revise
himself, and (when he had to) damn-quickly: he was a man now of
maturity, a statesman of weight. He would have been a safe man to
keep on cultivating, if Bale had had the cunning. But Bale had stayed
close to Cromwell, too close, oh far too close. Committed altogether
against all hope of revision. So therefore, High Germany, and Mrs
Dorothy with him.

At just about the time she heard of appalling new dangers that
threatened their new-guise friends who had stayed in England, she
heard also that her eldest son needed her urgently in ill-omened
Norwich. He had been bound apprentice there, his parents thought
him safe: but now, in their absence, he had been forced to change
masters, and was subject to great cruelty, quite against the terms of his
original indentures. Someone had to challenge it: and in the King's
perilous law-courts. Must it be her? Put head into the dragon's
mouth? Without Bale? It was impossible that *he* could return to
England, even briefly: his name was in the book, the King's German
spies were marking his daily doings, no there was no chance that he
could make the hazardous journey, but if *she* could . . .

She sent a letter to Wentworth. An outside chance, some small
protection. Old memories: he had called her his love. Old memories:
her eldest son.

She received no answer. She made quite sure he had had her letter:
he had it and he did not answer. He lived in Nettlestead, and in
London, in great state with his changeable wife, the wife that he loved
when he swore he loved Dorothy: the wife who had revised herself
again, and yet again, and then revised *him*, just in time to save his life
when Cromwell went to the Tower.

So Dorothy travelled to England, all on her own, with no protection. She had no choice: her child's predicament had to be dealt with, at once. Her courage was rewarded. She did deal with it, and she brought him safe to Germany.

Soon after she got back, she sent a gift to Wentworth, by special messenger, an anonymous parcel, about the size of a soup-plate. It was a portrait of herself. She had had it painted, very secretly, by a good Protestant, *Meister* Lucas Cranach, who painted Luther, and Melanchthon, and other reformers, and said he wanted to paint Bale, though in fact he never did. Perhaps he was embarrassed by this picture of Bale's wife. In those days she took good care to show herself the sober helpmeet of a sober reformed clergyman who was suffering for his truth like Elijah in the *Book of Kings*. (An analogy brought up by Bale daily into their family prayers: he generously extended it to include Dorothy, whom he saw as the Widow of Zarephath, compassionate Syro-Phoenician feeding the prophet in a strange land after the brook Cherith dried up and the ravens ceased to carry him food. Across the wilderness of reformed Germany she now gave succour to her wandering Bale, for had he not in the end thrown in his hand against false Baal, and vindictive Ahab was upon his track?)

She took good care to show herself in decent clothes like a grocer's goody: to resemble an earl's countess (or a singing-woman from the 'Birdcage') would not have been strategical. But in *Meister* Lucas's studio she took off all her clothes, and then put on a feathered hat, flat and round as a barrel-head: and a heavy gold chain about her neck. Studio-properties, both of them: how could she afford such brave gear nowadays? Her living was no more than Bale's living: and he was almost a beggar, he wrote his books of church-controversy and had them printed, but the publishers paid less than nothing for them. They had to be smuggled into England, the overheads were enormous.

The artist stared at her in amazement: he said, "Gracious lady, you had not said it was *this* kind of a portrait. As we term it, an Italian-taste *Kunstwerk*; *ultramontanus*, *versteh'n Sie*? A most private little picture, for your husband's pleasure, *nicht wahr*?"

She told him only to get on with it, she wanted it very small, not much more than a miniature, she had just enough money – she counted it out on the table. She knew the title: *Venus and Cupid*, would he please paint for Cupid her elder son, John, whom she would bring to him another day, but not an *exact* portrait of him, please. She wanted him much younger.

In fact *Meister* Lucas was quite used to this sort of commission, though surprised that a woman like Dorothy should be involved. He painted a large number of such pictures for his openly Protestant customers with their well-enclosed pagan desires. He was not insincere about it: as an artist he was a divided spirit, half of him on this side of the mountains, half beyond. He was never sure whether the Virgin Mary was a mortal woman or a goddess, and if she was a goddess, was she not the Goddess of Love? In which case why was she always so heavily dressed? He told himself sometimes he was neither Jew nor Greek, but a sensual Syro-Phoenician, and if Dr Luther knew it, he'd have a fit. It is probable, had Dorothy been less discreet, and felt able to talk to him freely, she would have found they had a lot to talk about.

He posed her in a green garden, the full length of her golden body, taking a honeycomb from her naked child (who had tears on his cheeks, the bees had stung him). Her red hair was tightly swathed underneath the great hat, with some locks of it straying out in the breeze on one side. She was smiling, wicked and taunting, and her left hand caressed her belly.

So she had it sent to England, to Wentworth. She never heard whether Wentworth's wife saw it. Nor did she hear of what Wentworth said when he opened the parcel. She had sent it: and he was gone from her life. But hadn't she a nerve?

(vi) *Auricular Confession*

Dorothy was not pleased, a fortnight after her visit to Clerkenwell and Paul's Cross, to find Bale .upon her threshold, quite early in the afternoon. It was true she had told Wentworth that that evening would be convenient for his first meeting at the 'Birdcage' with his colleagues (or co-conspirators, whatever they were), and she had taken care to make sure that all was safe.

She had put up a little notice in the caretaker's lodge:

Thyss nyght hath *D'selle La Haught-jaumbaye* allreddye ben suffyct
bespoken, upon an especyall desyr off certayine gentlmenn –
her gracytude to all uther, who will awayte a next
Occasioun, and refrayne fr her door wyth alle Curtesie,

She had gone to some trouble to write it out neatly, labouring hard over the spelling, her tongue thrust forward between her lips, her

back and elbows awkwardly bent as the pen did its best to take its own
course along the paper.

Angelina was again out of town.

From politeness to Bale, but grinding her teeth, Dorothy dismissed
her cittern-teacher until the next morning. She had not expected
Wentworth to send Bale on his own, at least not this first time. But in
the end it might have been worse. The Carmelite made no pretence of
false embarrassment at entering a notorious place in broad daylight.
He had left aside his friar's habit, and was dressed modestly as a
scholar of sorts, a nondescript gown, a plain black beret to cover his
tonsure – not so much a disguise as a piece of tact. It took from him
much of his old smack of the sinister: hard now to think of him as
Bale-zebub. You might meet his like browsing in any well-kept
library. She gave him wine and spice-cakes, and waited with a pleasant
smile till he knew what he wanted to say.

It was a pity he had to start with reflections upon the Sin of Sodom.

". . . for when they let me know what was meant by that evil, I
thought the men who used it against me would have been put to some
terrible punishment. Not that I wanted them punished: in all other
respects they had been kind to me. And I still did not realise, not quite
realise, not even then, that when they hurt me so much, their story of
how the devil lived up inside my tail was utter lie from beginning to
end."

But she had agreed, had she not? to these meetings, chiefly in order
to 'plumb to the depths': and if *his* depths were to be reached, why not
as soon as late? His views upon religion, upon play-acting and
minstrel-craft, could not perhaps be disentangled from all the rest of
it; so let him talk.

"Still I hoped otherwise, that their *manner* of attack only was
wrong, that there had been some truth to the shame I felt, d'you see?
when they stripped my haunches between them. For must not shame
mean that the devil was in hiding *somewhere*, stood to reason, only
logical: ah, I was a boy for logic, two-and-two together, maketh five,
even then . . . !

"And beside, was it not the conduit for the passage of my excrements? And all knew that *they* were a secret matter, matter of shame,
even upon the farm with my parents. Keep yourself clean, they used
to say to me, 'We Bales are a cleanly family, even though poor: an
exemplar to our uncouth neighbours.'

"But no: for those two friars, there was to be no punishment.

"Some time later, I dared ask about this. I was told that the Order of Carmel was totally free of sodomy: I was only a small boy: I could easily have been mistaken. My accusing of two grown holy-men could not be taken seriously. It would ruin their lives-in-religion, discredit the house: and of course it would. But then, I asked, how was it, that when I first told what had happened, the good brethren all swore how it was horrible, unconcealable, abomination-of-desolation, crying out for the Lord God's firestorm as upon the Cities of the Plain? Had they not quoted Paul to the *Romans*, 'Also the men forsoken the kindly use of women, and men into men wroughten filthihood'?

"They replied, of course yes, so it was; were it totally proven. They had meant only to warn me that my story of the Israel soldiers going-up by the gutter was *not* to be repeated, because this was its signification: *filthihood*! And for that, the only remedy, silence. They had been lenient, I was very young, had not known what I spoke: and if ever I spoke it again, ever again, why, the firestorm upon *me*. And by that word I was more in terror than by anything else, in that but a year before I had myself seen the firestorm: over against St Peter Mancroft church, in midst of Norwich city, a young man burned to death; for possession of an English text of the Lord's Prayer, that was all. Very like had he had an Hebrew or Syriac text (as Our Saviour would doubtless have spoken it) they would equally have basted his joints. For God, from a certain date (I am not quite sure what date, maybe the death-year of St Jerome), has given utterance only in Latin – that's well-known . . .!

"And when I was put into the friary-house, those flames and that screaming came with me, I could never be rid of them. Which is why I was at first so glad the novice-master and his frolic friend had promised they would show me the quick short way to destroy the devil, and without any need for the fire. Did I tell you, while they did it, they talked Latin without cease? It was of course a rule of the Order, no other language in cloister or church, save only – of course – for the public preachings.

"The man that ordered the Norwich burning was Lord Bishop Richard Nick. Yes, Barbara, the self-same that would have burnt both you and your Runagates, had it not been for the bull-in-the-bush. I'll tell you more about him, why don't I? one of these days . . ."

★

From the next room came suddenly a loud discord of krummhorns, laughter, recriminatory protestations. Rotraut and Ermentruda were at their practice and seemed not to have agreed upon the pace of the tune they were playing. Dorothy winced: but Bale took no notice. He had his own pace, his own uncharted progress of his mind's music, and kept to it.

"When I said they had no punishment, you will understand I do not know what was said under seal-of-confession. But if penance was imposed, then in no way was it public penance. The community was not informed. I was never overtly recompensed for what I had undergone. Auricular confession: it has its uses; but, as in this case, far too often made a means to protect the harm-wreaking sinner from the consequence of his sin. Sin is against neighbour as well as against God. Repent, or not repent, your injured neighbour should know of it. Our Church, in its Old Guise, has been but scant concerned with neighbours. I see consequence triangle-wise: God, Man, man's Neighbour. Moral Theology heretofore has constructed its own triangle: God; Man: and Priest (who thereby, and falsely, becomes a sort of half-god)."

So he drew into divinity and she breathed easier, could watch him with cooler inspection, less worried than before about how far his buried lusts might be directing his discourse. He was not as old, when seen closely, as she had expected. Thirty-five, maybe forty: his heavy face less troll-like than had seemed to her at her previous strange sightings of him. A blotchy face, yes, her memory served her correctly in that. He must eat carelessly, it could be he drank to excess: but he was temperate with her wine, so perhaps he was no sponge. His hands were square-ended, strong, like a labourer's without the callouses. He planted them firm on his knees. And did not writhe them, not today: they seemed not to be struggling to be employed in some nasty action, for once, and she was glad of it. His stature short, his feet big and thrust out, his torso stocky: all told, a presentable figure, close-shaven, washed, not ill-smelling like some that frequented her room. And yet, he had not told her just why he had come this afternoon: he talked incessantly, in jerks, with no sign of a purpose. *Had* he a purpose? Or was he merely here because Wentworth had set his big feet toward her door, and he could think of no way of diverting out of such a route? But on the other hand, if Bale in the first place had set Wentworth to know Dorothy, then who was controlling whom? Let him talk: if no result, she need never repeat the ordeal.

He was back upon his old course: "Before I entered the friary, I did not even know how the deed of generation was performed. My mother had said, 'Don't bother me, child: it's been performed too often in this house, let me tell you, for *you* to be starting it. And besides, if you're a friar, you're not going to *need* to know. Outside and chop some firewood, help me boil the copper, your elder brothers want their washing done!' My father said, 'Use your eyes, boy, look at the farmyard.' To be sure, I had seen the beasts at it: dogs in the gap of the bushes, pigs in sty, once a great stallion-horse plunging a splayed mare; and always the tragical calling of cats by night as they howl out their soul in endless longsuffering, such an agony for night-time cats, and yet by day so smooth and silent, did every cat have *two* souls, dark and light, and never mixed 'em?

"But how did all this find cognation with *genus humanum*? How could I, in the image of my Maker, expect to tell a woman to splay herself like a mare so I might drive screaming into her water-flow with the pipe of *my* water-flow? Good God, not conceivable, or, if conceivable, surely most devilish: could ever my father have done it, to my mother? Could he ever? He was a rough man, but not unkindly: and moreover of modest behaviour, as so many country-churls are, no matter what their betters say of them by way of libel."

So, perhaps a year or two before he went into the friars' order, he decided in his mind that God had never intended humanity to procreate in the manner of the farmyard: no, *there must be some other way*, and a spiritual way, a mystery, a poetry, for the reproduction of the Creator's image. Dorothy felt reluctant sympathy: for as he spoke she thought of her own first dreadful 'derry-down' (Lightfoot of Ely of course, his dog-whip hanging on a hook from his cottage roof-beam to warn her of what would happen if she did not do as he told). Bale continued: he had worked out, very logically, that this remote and godly mystery would be fully explained when the gentle village priest who knew his family, and was so loved by all of them, prepared him for his Confirmation. So he put it to the priest at what seemed to be the proper time, just one day before the bishop came to lay hands on the childrens' heads. He was scared to discover that he got no proper answer: the priest was sadly flustered, muttering about purity, muttering about the need for a young boy to keep his thoughts well away from such a business, and his hand and his eye well away from the evils of his hot breech – oh if he *could* keep to that, said the priest, if only he made sure to keep to it diligently, why then, in the end, all would surely be made known. Recovering from his fluster, the priest added severely, "This very evening, boy, when you kneel at your confession, you shall humbly plead God's pardon for your very saucy question: even to have thought of asking it was a lapse into disgraceful sin. Nay, think upon it, boy, the Lord Bishop is at hand!"

Which only went to prove his worst anxieties too well-grounded; the poetry and the privy were all mixed-up together, the most holy-souled men and women could not escape the implication. Why, it lay at the very root of Christian Marriage, that most lovely of all ceremonies – he never forgot his elder sister, when he was about four years old, at church-door in her white bride-grown, her shining hair full of flowers and combed down about her shoulders, the lilies between her hands, her smile like the smile of the Mother of Jesus carved above her on the gabled porch.

So thereupon he became as he now saw, a child-heretic; he began to construct a *private doctrine of his own*, a process much accelerated in the aftermath of the friars' ravishing. Here Bale, to Dorothy's dismay, grew more and more complicated in his arguments, twisting them and straining them till she felt he needed a sharp reminder that he was in the 'Birdcage', not at college. But she held herself back: something a little human must surely be about to emerge from the abstractions, she could only wait and see. He tortuously demonstrated how this regrettable private doctrine maintained a precise division between the upper body and the lower: "God was in our head and heart, and what we saw above the girdle-line was indeed His image; but underneath, in a horrid house, between belly and arse-slot, both with man and with woman, lay the tenement of Lucifer, *he* had made those portions, all that ugly gear was *his*, and the Lord had strangely granted him a legal deed of occupancy.

"I never quite determined just why this should have been so. Except that maybe the devil, before he fell from heaven, had already had so great a share in the Creation that he was able to take away with him his rights to what he had made. Squatter's Rights, if you like: and even incarnate Christ had not been able to dispossess him, no not even Christ . . . ! And if, as they said of those two friars, it was a mortal sin to try to expel him by means of his own flesh-things, then maybe I could whip him out, burn him out, go for him there with nettles and briars? Once, oh Lord God, I took a razor to myself: but the sudden pain and blood overmastered my resolve to have an end of my flesh-things for ever."

He groaned deeply as he told her this, his voice sunk to a surging whisper, she saw tears in his eyes: and then suddenly felt tears in her own. Mary Mercy, the poor little boy, with his naked shaven head, his skin-scratching novice's gown, the bewildering chill of the Norwich cloister so far from his family house-place . . .

She put forward a tentative hand to touch him: but his own hand was in his scarf, he was pulling out a pair of spectacles to perch upon his nose, perhaps to hide his face from her. He did not see her quick gesture; and, no less quickly, she withdrew it.

He talked on, he could not stop: theoretical syllogisms mounting up through his cataract of speech till she wondered would she scream. At one point, in order to stem him, she offered him more wine. This time he seized the cup and drank it down in one big gulp, and never stopped his word-flow, while splutterings and dribblings of a perfectly good French vintage were being hiccuped all over his neck-linen. And then, with a rush, it was over. He had reached a conclusion.

"Conclusion! And I arrived at it through Augustine's refutation of the erroneous Manichees, notwithstanding I must on several points part company with the undoubted saint of Hippo. So mark this: mortal man – I call it 'man', meaning woman as well, for her desires are as his, I have heard enough confessions to be under no illusion *there* – mortal man, I say, must *use* his flesh-things: must prove they are God's not Devil's: must *not* devote them solely to but one of their two functions!"

*

He sat and looked at her. She looked at him. She had absolutely nothing to say, which was highly unprofessional. For her trade in part meant that she must sit for hours and listen to men with grievous weights upon their spirits, laying her minstrelsy aside and encouraging them to talk to her, dispensing to them little ripples of laughter and raillery to hearten them. There were many who came to the 'Birdcage' deliberately on quiet evenings for precisely such a solace: and as a rule she was well able for it. But with *this* man she was nonplussed, she even gaped like a half-wit street-doxy. He did not seem to notice. His process of thought was still on the move.

"You will wonder therefore, lady, having heard me so patiently: 'What has John Bale to say of priests and brethren under celibate vow, what indeed of nuns?' Ah to be sure you are enquiring of that." She was not, but she did not say so.

Happily, he went on to answer her supposed question without showing himself aware she had not asked it. It was an interminable reply. To preface it, he explained that the purpose of his enforced friarship had been not only to relieve the poverty of his home but to provide the Bale kinfolk, as a coherent social body, with the essential amenity of a man-in-religion – a man specially placed (through his vows and his priesthood) to talk to Heaven on their behalf, "as it were a bribed advocate, or an officer with the *pull* in a great landlord's household, a sort of Bale-delegated half-god with private access to the master's chamber."

That brought him on to the "doubtful dogma" of Intercession of Saints, which, he said, he had now come to scorn. "Is Heaven in truth no better than a nobleman's levée? Ah, pooh! unworthy fable! Oh we knew another family, as poor as ourselves, that had a cousin who was sub-steward to the Howard estates, conceive how we were jealous of *them!* So you see my friar's habit was to be our way to outpace them: and thus indeed it was. My father, he chose it for me: my mother spoke not one word against it. When I left home, she kissed me, and then she wept. I said to myself: 'Liar.'"

He pointed out, in passing, that for his family's purpose monks would have been better than friars, for monks' only function was to live shut up in cloister, making prayers all the time for those who had commissioned them, "hoping their own flesh-things would rot from a virtuous disuse (that is, were they true to their vows)." But monastic orders were expensive for a poor man's son to enter, as well as discriminatory upon grounds of social class, so his father had to find him the next best thing; which was also the far harder thing.

"For the friars, d'you see, must move in the world and not hide from it, driving their chastity, their poverty, their naked feet, down among the toiling people, by arduous example to hale them to salvation.

"Therefore temptation, under the friars' rule, must needs be redoubled. Monks meet only men and stew together with none but men. Friars meet women also. As *I* have, as you know. Yet spite of all temptation I strove always and still strive to keep the *essence* of the Carmel Rule: salvation for the people at large! And so I walk to bring it, by way of Norwich, of Ipswich, of Diss, of Nettlestead, of Paul's Cross, and wherever else. *Salvation*, to Brother Bale, being the same good word as *Reform*: I protest I am true to my vow! Not *my* fault the entire friarhood is corrupted these three hundred years. We were meant to be the friends of God's poor: alack we have become their cozeners, and live nowadays to make them a prey. Any wonder the thickheads of Diss clattered with laughter like millwheels when you showed 'em your Jenkin transfixed in the bramble-thorns, caught prisoner in midst of his rut? When I saw him, I saw myself: my Christian cloth in Christian England become a ragbag of a public jest . . ."

Then an odd switch of mood. No longer in sombre melancholy, but with a brisk sardonic throwaway: "At all events it would have been if you had not made him a Franciscan. I suppose the full white mantle was a garment beyond your resources?"

What had this to do with his doctrine as to the use of 'flesh-things'? Not that Dorothy wanted to hear much more from him on that subject: but neither did she need a repetition of his Paul's sermon. She *would* have been interested to know more about his mother: had he loved her so very greatly, he showed such a sense of betrayal? But his discourse was not to be diverted, its range of reflection was finding its own boundaries, from particular to general, and then back with a swoop to particular: "If those two upon my body had committed the Sin of Sodom, what had *I* committed in receiving their lusts? For I came to see, afterwards, that my nakedness at the time had seemed to me good sport; it had *not*, after the first few minutes, compelled me to a proper shame. And yet, will you credit, when I told it in confession, they would not accept it. They required from me account of an altogether different sin: the Bearing of False Witness, and for *that* one they fell to scourging me; until, amid my cries of pain, my useless pleas for mercy, I broke down and admitted it. So they had their *false witness*, indeed. Ah, no, it was not at all possible for me to talk to the elder brethren, not even half so freely as now I talk to you: I was dumbstruck at the whole enormity."

But one young friar, he explained, had been truly compassionate, had listened to the unhappy child's frantic ramblings, had anointed his stripes with soft hands, and – "and caused such a rising in my loins, so strangely, sweetly, at his touch, when I felt it below my back, that what could I do but believe that he too, like those others, was seeking me *contra naturam*, 'against kind' (as Wycliffe translates Saint Paul). I bit at his arm till he left me. I am sure I did him wrong: but are you surprised at it?"

So he had no-one to confide in, except hortatory, denunciatory, authoritarian intimidators: and therefore he made up his mind.

Dorothy thought sadly, "Why, he spent his whole boyhood having

to make up his mind, *and all upon his own*. For him also the flight
through the snow from the constables . . . for him also the stench of
the ale-cellar . . ."

He made up his mind, then, that in the future he would *never* confide:
no, not to anybody, but only to the Lord God.

"When I went to confession, I would number my sins mechanical,
according to form, and never never express puzzlement as to how this
or that complexity of motive and consequence could rightly be
unravelled. Which was wise of me, my confessor preferred it so, it
saved him so many heart-searchings. The difficulty came when I
attempted to talk to God. Because He did not answer. Well, of course,
He did. But how to distinguish His answer from all the other
turbulence in my spirit, hey? Hey, I am still struggling to find out the
secret of *that*! No, all upon my own it CAN NOT BE SUFFICIENT.

"I have, over the years, at last become able to talk deeply to certain
friends, young friends from whose groping fingers I need fear no
harm; insofar as I am the elder man, of – may I say? – repellent aspect,
they would not propose to *me* those sly iniquities that their fair
features might to some others give signal of. Lord Wentworth, for an
instance: a lordly man of generous intellect. Not even to him have I
shown all my detail as today I am doing, to you."

*

His hands were off his knees and she watched them in alarm, they
were once again at their beastly frotting, and his spectacles grew
misted. There were globules of sweat all over his face, he licked his
lips between his words with swift shoots of his tongue, reptilian.

"I'd suppose you'd think," he was gasping and croaking, "suppose
you'd think that with all my history I'd have come to abhor manhood,
its rapings, its cruelties, its hypocrisies, and therefrom would have
turned to use of woman for my solace? Certainly many in religion have
done this, travel the land on their friars'-circuits, insinuate with the
wives and virgins, no end of it, oh read poet Chaucer, his handling of
his Pilgrim Friar.

"Well, I do yearn for women, yes. For my vow to abstain from them
– I am deeply persuaded – has been *contra naturam*, quite as much
'against kind' as any sort of boy-buggery. But I have never been able to
converse with them, face-to-face. And today I do, today, Mistress
Barbara, here I am, I am talking to *you*! Auricular confession! Nay, is
it not most marvellous . . . ?"

To be sure, to sit and listen was a professional duty: but she saw no good reason why she should prolong it without being paid, certainly not now it grew so personal. But she must not be rough with him, for if he became rough with her she would have to call a 'Birdcage' bully to get rid of him, and what would Wentworth have to say to her then? She had, dammit, made a promise. But this Bale was all-at-once quite frightening once again to her: and she was a born bloody fool to have forgotten Cecilia's word – 'throat-cutter', was it not? Even 'whipper' was bad enough, and when she thought back upon the tale he had been telling her . . . She'd have to make some species of joke . . . Her merry laugh sounded quite unnatural in her own ears: "Face-to-face? Alas, poor gentleman, it wouldn't have been easy, when your first demand, if all is true, was that bum-cheeks rather than face-cheeks be unveiled for your dialogue? Oh God, sir, no wonder you *yearned*. What speech would have been plausible, once your slashing cane had said hello?"

An abrupt lurch of his burly body, he lumbered darkly, disturbedly, to his feet, and stood over her. Her cry for help was drowned in the violence of his first few words. Lord Christ she had judged it so wrongly. But then again, perhaps not. For he swung clear away from her to the furthest corner of the room.

"'If all is true'? It *was* true! And I swear I never *hurt* them! Not as constables would hurt them at cart's-tail: but what other way to kindle them?" Belle-Savage came running at the noise and stood amazed just inside the door, staring at Bale, who seemed not to have seen her arrival, so intense was his strangulated speech. "Yet none of them would respond, though all of them were loose-baggage, always I chose carefully, never a one of 'em that I thought would hold herself in respect, nor did *I* ever hold any respect for myself, Lord-have-mercy I lived in hell-gate, *mea culpa*, *mea culpa* . . . At Diss that time, it was the last time, and so I saved myself, because truly that night I had set out to save *you*, because you see, I had seen you dance. For Herodias' Daughter I would have whipped, but for Barbara and her scorning of the infamous Bale-Jenkin, why, maid. I thought only to save you."

Dorothy signed urgently to Belle-Savage to leave them. After a moment's hesitation, she was silently obeyed.

"But mark you," continued Bale, "I never swived them, never gave use to my tool, save its own use of itself, unfingered inside my robe, and that *did* happen. Often. Thus far my friar's vow has kept me to a sort of virtue, thus far it has kept me *in fear*." Was it then his fear that was causing him to shudder all over? She could hear the very chatter of his teeth. He told her that ever since Diss, if ever his hands had twitched for the rod, he had thrust them into a boiling kettle (they were indeed red and purple to an unusual degree), and had at once strode out searching for Dorothy, wherever she might be performing – "that the sight of you should remind me you were salvation to my sin, my sin which no confessional had been able to purge . . ."

This was too much. She would *not* be salvation, not to anyone on this earth.

But somehow she did have to bring the absurdity to an end, and without complication of her already far too complex relationship with Wentworth. If railing humour wouldn't do, would gentleness be a help? Just possible she could so manage it as to show him, first, she was not his Good Angel (didn't he realise how tyrannical such a fantasy was to her? Or did he know and not care?): and, second, that was no reason for him to think she craved his willow-switch, or his 'hot breech', or indeed any other of his quirky appurtenances. All she wished for at this moment was his absence. In the evening, in Wentworth's company (no doubt there would be other company too) – well, if Bale came in the evening, she could handle him upon a different basis. For Wentworth's sake, he *had* to come. So, let her try what she could.

She asked gently, about his shuddering, telling him she was afraid he was ill. He agreed, he had agues, had had them ever since Jesus College, "badly-built, windswept, facing the empty north, too whoreson close to the river!" She made him lie down, covered him with a quilt, and called for Belle-Savage to mull him some wine. Then, no less gently, *she* began to narrate to *him*. About the Runagates, and their various shows. She spoke quietly and quickly and never let him interrupt. Which was the easier because of his ague. She made him hear the story of another *Friar Jenkin* play (they had several, Catgut used to invent them with a facile lubricity). A real foul-bed piece, she told him, there was this girl so stonewall-chaste but only from ignorance, how did Jenkin get her to couple? how else but by boldly uncovering for her the straightness of his eleventh finger, red yearning digit where abode, he said, a very flesh-devil pulling the friar in pain behind it quick-sharp to hell-gate, only one way to rein it in, let a small pure virgin make a road for it in her lap, and so she did, for his sheer salvation: and *that* was James Catgut's fancy. Dorothy pointed to her tapestry: "See how the rearing Unicorn lays his horn in the Lady's

gentleness . . . Of course *I* played the idiot girl, Catgut had thought of
Nelly for the part, but she said she was too knowing for it, very likely
she was right? so I played it and is it not agreeable to tell you?
Confession without sanctity, it maketh withal a pungent hour: and ah
here's the wine, sip it slowly or you'll scald."

Bale tried to sit clumsily up, all muffled in quilt, coughing and
spluttering, his spectacles on their cord lost somewhere underneath
him among Dorothy's cushions; until he found them he was held
half-prostrate because the cord was tied round his neck. He fumbled,
and shook, and spoke to her in some shame.

"Don't think I am so coarse I cannot read your meaning. 'Confession without sanctity' which is in fact an enforced rape, rape of the
ear, and I am guilty: that novice-master and his friend would exult to
see me know it . . . You desire me to go." He had freed himself from
quilt and spectacle-cord, he was timid and humble, he half-stood,
half-knelt, supporting himself by the ledge of her fire-mantel. "So I
will, but first permit me. I would not be misunderstood. Please let me
tell you the chief reason I had for saving you, in Diss; I think you will
respect it. It was *not* simply Barbara's bum. And please let me tell you
what brought me to Diss in the first place. I think, for this evening's
meeting you will need to know that. I am sorry, so truly sorry, our
conversation proceeded thus. Please let me tell you."

*

"So tell," she said. She was weak as water. Must be, or surely she'd
resist this pathetic penitence?

He drank, and wiped his mouth with the end of his scarf; wiped his
livid gleaming face and forehead, shivered, sat down, and began to
speak of Bishop Richard Nick. "Bishop of Norwich: it was from *him*
and his dragonish tribunals you and your fellows had such danger.
Good order and church-conformance, he has always been mad-
zealous for them to the extremities of cruelty. He burned the young
man I told you of: and then, last year, little Tom Bilney; my oldest and
dearest friend, for whom I never felt lechery, from whom I never
feared lechery, only a deep awe for his Christ-given loving-kindness –
though his theology I could not stomach. Tom had heard things from
Martin Luther he'd have done better to keep to himself. Ricardus
Nick, and none other, made white-hot ashes out of Tom. They call
him, you know, 'Old Nick' – which is to say, the Satan-bishop – which
is to say *Ricardus Diabolus* – which is to say –"

He took a pause and a mouthful of wine, to recover himself from a fierce ague-spasm. "Because of Nick and what I knew of him, I would not, could not, leave you at risk. Why did I not warn your companions? Let us say, and say honestly, I was in fear. Five mouths speak five times wider than one. How could I trust them not to gossip? God knows they were most manifest untrustable. I myself would be at risk, accessory after the fact, were it known I had given you word. And *my* risk in that diocese? Dear God, beyond imagining. After all, I am a preaching friar. But I spoke for 'em in the justice's house, reversed his decision to remand to the bishop's court – what happened to 'em afterwards – well, they *were* a pack of vagabonds, any day they could have met with it . . ."

His sickness, for the moment, seemed to be abating. His voice became calmer. "Let us also say, and say honestly, I saw you too young, too fresh, too enkindling at your art, to allow you to be huddled with those others. Even though, for a space, you would have to endure some worse fortune. I *did* hunt you out from it as speedily as I could."

She thought about Thetford, and about the inner room, at Norwich, with her castanets. Perhaps in truth he had done all he could . . . He had mentioned her art. It might now be a good occasion to lead him on to talk more of that: if he would, she could cease to be anxious for him to go away. Also, she'd be doing her duty by Wentworth.

She had not framed her first question before he sped on with his thoughts: very soon she understood they were close enough to what she hoped from him.

"So why was I called to Diss? So cold an Epiphany, such misery for travelling, oh *of course* it was a Call. No-one would have undertaken my hard journey for a casual cause! I was spending that year at my old college in Cambridge. The Carmelites had sent me there as a youth (their one perspicacious kindness to me), to become Master of Arts in their interest; and then they had me travel abroad to their houses in France and Flanders, accomplishing further studies. Those completed, back to the Cam to qualify myself Divinity-Bachelor, and eventually Doctor, as I am now. You understand, because of my illnesses (as they called them, and *I* called them at the time – although now I should say rather my divisions of spirit, my dreadful questionings, who was I? what was I for?), because of my inability to deal with myself in cloister and on preaching-circuit, it was thought best I be reserved for a more solitary, intellectual, part: write books, issue controversy, defend the Order's purpose against the upsurge of all these heresies. I was, in short, to be Learned Champion of the Old Guise against the New, oh little did they foresee!

"My doctorate was all but attained: I had a thesis to prepare, a disputation before the senate. Every hour of every day, save when I slept, prayed, or ate, (nay even through the very acts of eating, praying, sleeping), the everlasting cross-tides of Latin dialectic broke against each other in my brain. I'm a conscientious man, I earnestly stirred them: and heavily to my own discomfort. My spirit necessarily rebelled. I would find, after shelf after shelf of theology, church history, doctrinal *minutiae*, Aristotle and Aquinas *reductio ad absurdum*, I was an-hungered for good plain English like a ditch-digger for his fireside pasty.

"And there it was beside me! One dark winter afternoon, in the dark library where I froze my bones, mine eye of an odd chance caught onto it, an inconsiderable grubby parcel lying in the shadows of a scorned and cobwebbed window-embrasure – poetry! Most strange, quite improper it should have been in that clerical bookroom at all. And also (and in these dire days, no less improper) an English Scripture, the Wycliffe text, John's *Gospel*. They were all gathered-in together among a great heap of nondescript old volumes, as though left there by a man in a hurry who never found it possible to come back and collect them. Some of the package printed, most of it manuscript, every piece in most tattered condition. As you can believe, I began at once to read: my theology went right out at window.

"Chaucer, Gower, Langland, the Scotsman Dunbar . . . and then – last of all – an entire scuffled paper-chase of small unbound fragilities; quite recent printed pamphlets, ill-made copies in several hands-of-write, single-sheet broadsides with the appearance of having been bought at street-booths in bad weather or borrowed from untidy friends, thrust hastily into pocket and then read and re-read till they began to drop to pieces: and all by the one same author! A vanished stranger's lost collection of the works of John Skelton: don't you see, it was Skelton Poet Laureate, sometime tutor to the King and *now he was Vicar of Diss!*"

"Vicar of Diss?" Dorothy knew Skelton's name but no more of him than that. From Bale's apparent excitement, he must be a poet to be honoured: was it possible that she and the Runagates had slept in his barn all unwitting, had annoyed him with their minstrel-rubbish, and despised him behind his back? At any rate it showed that all admired poets were not made after the model of Wyatt. Of course, Wentworth had asserted *John Bale* was a poet. Which would prove itself in good time, no doubt . . . She repeated, "Vicar of Diss? That old sleepyhead who –"

Foolish assumption. Bale was annoyed. "No, no, no, of course not." He snapped at her like a tetchy schoolmaster. "Sir John Clerk the Curate, in charge of the parish until Skelton returned from Westminster. But remember the year, it was 1529: he never did return. On twenty-first of June, very same day that Spanish Catherine was commanded into court at Blackfriars before Wolsey and the Pope's Commissioner to give cause why her marriage should not be made void, John Skelton died: of the sweating sickness, it was said. I had hoped above all things I would meet him that Epiphany, I did not know he was still from home. If also I'd known he had so little time, I'd immediately have gone to London. I wanted to ask him: was it true he had broke his vow? Wanted to? No, needed to: why, I was *driven*, to find out that poet. All I did find was you . . . Which was not, as you'll see, a total irrelevance. Didn't I tell you, I had been Called?"

'Was it true he had broke his vow?' She asked, of course, what vow? The vow of celibacy of course, what else had he been talking about, throughout this last half-hour? His discovery of Skelton's poems had rushed together in his mind with all the most distressing of his own preoccupations: from exhaustive reading of them he had concluded that Skelton, priest and poet, was not only a user of women (in the fashion of so many bad, and commonly ashamed, clergy), but a user of them with *pride*, nay, not so much with pride, but out of a wild conviction that by such conduct he was doing no more than fulfilling his God-given duty.

Bale had thought and thought – as he read and re-read the poems – of so many searching incidents of his university years, episodes by no means fully known to his superiors in the Carmel Order. "They did know I had taken part with my friends in the debates at the White Horse and they knew that in those days I had withstood the New Guise arguments. That was all they thought they needed to know. Brother Bale was a safe man. They had not asked me, after my travels, what I thought of the arguments *now*. Did not ask me, for example, what I thought of Thomas Cranmer, also of the Jesus College, when he married a Cambridge barmaid and told me it was better to marry than burn. He did not take priest's orders till after she died, of course: but his heart had been near-upon broken by the choice he had then to make – his career in the Church or the love of a good woman.

"Would you pay me your full attention, please!" He was more the cross pedagogue than ever, Dorothy's smothered laugh had interrupted his flow. "Of course it is hilarious when a man of parts weds in haste with a tavern-girl. 'Tee-hee I've *caught* him!' Is not that what you're thinking she cried? Let me tell you, in this case, it was absolute otherwise, I tell you they loved extremely, it hurt mine own heart to watch it: all the more bitter that I was already vow-bound and such a choice could never be for me." He showed his teeth at her, almost spiteful: "It was in fact *your father* read them the marriage-service, think of that, Damosel Parsons, before you smile again at it . . ."

He had misunderstood her. Her ironical thought had been, how convenient was the early death of young Mrs Cranmer, sad little corpse to serve as a mounting-block to Canterbury's archbishopric. But she did not say this. Instead, apologetically: "My father must have wondered, would it not have been better if *he* had done the same?" To herself, head turned aside, "Ah, Lord, I wish he had. But would it have prevented her riding the wind for Bletchley?" Bale did not hear this, but took only her first question.

"Would it not have been better if he and Cranmer could have kept both wife and priesthood?

"Which is, *mirabile dictu et credo quia impossibile*, exactly what I came to believe John Skelton had done in Diss.

"Against all regulation, against all accepted doctrine (not by any means the same thing), against all solemn oaths taken at the very altar, he had brought into his house an honest lady; his only known name for her, 'Calliope', muse of poetry, muse of *epic* poetry – but you'll know that, you were Cecilia's – and she bore him, I think, at least one child, male. Which by law should have been bastard. But he boldly maintained him legitimate: not in the poetry, that part of the story came to me only by rumour, I had to confirm it; I had to go, as you must see, to Diss.

"My reasons for these pregnant deductions?

"To start with, Skelton's courage: oh undoubted. I had years before seen his play *Magnificence*, the students of John's gave it in hall upon All Fools (Lady Margaret, our king's granddam, who founded St John's College, had been a good friend to Skelton). He wrote the play against Cardinal Wolsey when Wolsey was misleading the King into all manner of loose extravagances, as a cloak for his own ambition to corrupt himself into Peter's Chair – you'd not be old enough, I daresay, to remember that scandal? Such a fearsome soldier-hearted play, to have presented it at court (as was originally done) with the King's very person portrayed as a character in it, every phrase from the royal mouth as blazing recognizable as a lion's eyes in dark forest; that of itself argued the spirit of the poet. Because the King's part was writ more contemptuous than adulatory: and Wolsey's part, though allegorised and split into several personages, spread the Cardinal as it were upon the very floorstones, where the hall-dogs might worry him like a mutton-bone.

"This prior assessment was only augmented by what I found in the poems. *Colin Clout, Why Come Ye Not To Court?*, and a great part of a very strange piece, *Speak Parrot*, all also brandished, like a Switzer's partisan, at the same red-hatted mark. The Parrot poem gave me some difficulty, it being composed as it were in a cipher: hear you now, what d'you make of it?"

He stuck his great head forward cocked at an angle, his huge nose smelling the air, a bull's head certainly and a bull-neck under it, but the nose was a wild-boar's; and effusion of perspiration ran down into his scarf. He opened his jowl to declaim. To her amazement his voice was suddenly a high screech, staccato and peremptory. His mouth was twisted sideways, his eyes most naughtily a-squint – why of course! it was *Speak Parrot*, and Bale accordingly *spoke* parrot.

> "With my beak-e bent, and my little wanton eye,
> My feathers fresh as is the emerald green,
> About my neck a circulet like the rich ruby,
> My little legs, my feet-e both neat and clean,
> I am a minion to wait upon a queen;
> 'My proper Parrot, my little pretty fool':
> With ladies I learn, and go with them to school.

"He, Skelton, being Parrot, was therefore not responsible for the oddity of his utterance. His earlier poems against Wolsey having so vastly angered that prince, I cannot regard the precaution as in any way faint-hearted: the man had to survive, if he was still to continue writing.

"Short digression, but germane: who *taught* Parrot to Speak? 'Ladies'? He doesn't say which ladies: in terms of practical politics, I'd guess the Countess of Surrey, his she-falcon of a patroness, whose father, aspiring Buckingham, had gone to the block through Wolsey's intrigues. But I ask, was there another one: half-abstract, half-fleshly Calliope, to whom Skelton was just an instrument upon which she would play any air she fancied, so long as it was strong enough? Nay, I said something much like that of mine own self, priest-wise, Paul's Cross, did I not? Do I run into profane comparisons? Let it be . . .

"Return to Parrot. When Parrot talks, how does he talk? Listen.

> O Esebon, Esebon, to thee is come again
> Sihon, the regent *Amor-e-orum*,
> And Og, that fat hog, of Bashan, doth retain
> The crafty *coistronus Canan-e-orum!*

What d'you make of it?"

His passion was beyond bounds, he had been yelping the lines in a fury, striding the room, three paces each way until he banged up against the walls, knocking down her small furniture. She said what she had to say, no remedy: "Nothing at all, to be frank. And I don't understand the Latin bits. I suppose they *were* Latin?" As she had never been to any school (except those for her minstrel-craft: Light-foot's, little more than a bestial beast-taming corral, and the Olivers', where physique and memory were taxed to the uttermost but indepen-dent process-of-thought was not of itself instilled), she had never had a chance to see the controlled rage of the devoted scholar unsuited to teaching yet confronted by a worldly student who could not share his enormous learning-joy. In this case, a kind scholar: Bale, it was now clear, was not in her room to birch her, or even to box her ears. But she felt it was a close enough call.

He took several deep breaths and began to explain. 'Og' was Wolsey; 'Esebon' was Heshbon in the Holy Land, conquered by the Chosen People from the heathen king Sihon who had now returned and recaptured it, which naturally meant that 'Esebon' was London and 'Sihon' was either Wolsey or Wolsey's political faction: and so on through several more of Skelton's caustic close-woven stanzas. "You need a good grasp of the scriptural, mythological, historical impli-cations, of course you do, and he looked to his readers to have it: Wolsey too was no Jack Know-naught, he might well be expected to unravel it out for himself. But even if he did, he'd have had a hard toil actually to *prove* the poem seditious. Courageous enough, that poet? and most diabolic clever!"

He allowed himself one final parrot-scream:

"From Scarpary to Tartary renown therein doth spring,
With 'he said' and 'we said' – ich wot now what ich wot –
Quod magnus est dominus Judas Iscariot!"

– and declined to interpret it ("pearls before swine," she concluded),
leaving her bewildered but well-aware that the deep satisfaction she
heard in the roll of his voice was a true satisfaction of art: the
'Birdcage' had lately been bringing her many such moments.
Whatever else Bull-in-the-bush might be, he was obviously an actor of
power. Was he also the poet of power Wentworth was hoping?
Dorothy was at any rate beginning to see something of Wentworth's
intentions: for if Bale could wind himself so tight into Skelton's mind,
could uncover, so long after the immediate topicality, the intricacies
of Parrot's concealed meanings, maybe he *did* have such a mind
himself, maybe all his friar's agonies over celibacy and deeds-against-
kind had been vouchsafed him to some better end? Complexity of
poetry had to come from a complex spirit. Even Catgut when he made
his dishonest little farces, however horrid, had been impelled by his
own dishonest life, his broken love for crosspatch Nelly, his sidlings
toward Dorothy, his fear of the law's officers . . .

All over the 'Birdcage', rehearsal was going on: the stifling afternoon quivered thickly between the building's close walls, reverberat-
ing wit˙ song and instrûments, with˙ clatter of energetic feet upon
several stories of floorboards. In the next room the two German
women had now called in musicians, one of them a kettle-drummer, to
play the 'Upspring' or *Huepfauf*, a prancing bouncing dance that
shook the whole top of the house.

Dorothy said, grimly, "This place is sheer Babel-tower, I'll need
more felting on the wall. So warm today I should throw open door and
window, but how can I?"

"No, not the window, I cannot abide a draught this afternoon. But
you do your friends injustice. I think the noise is of wonder and
beauty, and fits well with the ground of our discourse.

"*Skelton's* noise was no less unstoppable, betokening always his just
pride in himself, his refusal to accept any mortal self-authorised
precepts of 'order', if he conceived they ran counter to what he knew
to be right and true. How can he have regarded the rules against
clerical marriage as in any way right and true? He was a scholar, he
must have known they were never more than only 'rules' (as opposed
to eternal principles heart-grounded in Christ Our Lord), they had

been made one time or another for some temporary reason, 'church order', 'good discipline', by mortal men made, their essential validity *nihil*. I am sure of this: because all his poetry portrays his love of women at an equal level with love of God; and moreover it was a carnal love, by no means conventional poet-dreams, nor (as they say) made 'mystic-spiritual' neither. Indeed it launched him into grave disfavour."

He began once again to quote: but this time Dorothy could listen without strain. The lines were very simple, or seeming-simple, evoking a young girl. Bale's delivery of them, quiet, fervent, appropriate, filled them with a resonance that must have come to his tongue direct from the deepest-delved silver-mine of his own forlorn imaginings.

> "My pen it is unable,
> My hand it is unstable
> My reason rude and dull
> To praise her at the full;
> Goodly mistress Jane,
> Sober, demure Diane;
> Jane this mistress hight,
> The lode star of delight,
> Dame Venus of all pleasure,
> The well of worldly treasure;
> For this most goodly flower,
> This blossom of fresh colour,
> So Jupiter me succour,
> She flourisheth new and new
> In beauty and virtue:
> *Hac claritate gemina*
> *O gloriosa femina!*"

At which point he broke off to show her how the Latin unambiguously identified the lady Jane with the Blessed Virgin, "being parodic of a well-known liturgic incantation, and so, to the orthodox, intolerable blasphemous. And as for the carnality – from the same poem, hearken!

> Whereto should I disclose
> The gartering of her hose?
> It is for to suppose
> How that she can wear
> Gorgeously her gear;

> Her fresh habiliments
> With other implements
> Like dame Flora, queen
> Of lusty summer green –

"Gartering of her hose? Whereto disclose it? How the devil should he *know* of it, this proper precise vicar, visiting the Carrow nuns to improve the ablative-absolutes of their charges? For that's where she was, young Jane, *in statu pupillari*, under care of the black-sisters at their house in the Norwich suburbs – I suppose you never went thither? Faith, I suppose not: Dolly Longlegs'd scarce be known to 'em. They are not a community notorious for worldliness, unlike some, unlike some . . . Skelton wrote, ostensible, to commiserate Jane upon the death of her tame sparrow, believe it. Let you know, he chose to travel a few hands'-breadths further than her garters.

> Her kirtle so goodly laced,
> And under that is braced
> Such pleasures that I may
> Neither write nor say;
> Yet though I write with ink,
> No man can let me think,
> For thought hath liberty,
> Thought is frank and free;
> To think a merry thought
> It cost me little nor naught."

"I see small harm in that." Dorothy gave a sniff. She resented the 'Dolly Longlegs'. "He never says he lay with her. In fact the reverse?"

"I don't think you fully measure the prim gentility of Carrow, nor the expectations of the well-seen family that put her there to await and acquire accomplishments while they looked out an appropriate husband? Certainly, in the upshot, offence was very much taken, and Skelton must apologise: which he did, in a verse addendum, and thereby made all worse. Nay, his disavowal was three parts an affirmation.

> Alas, that goodly maid,
> Why should she be afraid?
> Why should she take shame
> That her goodly name
> Honourably reported,
> Should be set and sorted
> To be matriculate
> With ladies of estate?

"As much as to say, he was sorry they were en-angered at him, but not sorry for the cause of the anger. 'Ladies of estate'? Had he compared her to historic virgins? To Clare of Assisi, perhaps; or to precellent Saint Scholastica, lady-mother of the Carrow order? Ah, to one great Virgin, yes: but (as I have said) less a comparison than an outrageous commingling of attributes. 'Ladies of estate' were nothing other than Luna, Proserpina, Diana. True, they weren't *erotic* goddesses, but nonetheless unmistakeable pagan, he had *worshipped* her as one of them, and worshipped her as Christ's Own Mary: you might say he was a pagan himself – except he wasn't, he was a POET, and saw the mythology of the Roman Church on exact the same level as the mythology of Greco-Rome, saw Ovid and *The Lives of the Saints* as all-of-a-piece. Which is pretty much the truth, I'd say, though unacceptable to the likes of Lord Bishop Richard Nick."

There was a long silence. He stared hard at Dorothy, his point apparently made. If it was, she was not sure she grasped it. He was beginning to shudder again. She broke the tension by going and calling over the gallery-rail for Belle-Savage (now down in the yard) to fetch more mulled wine from the 'Birdcage' buttery. When she turned back into the room, Bale was saying, "She was alive, lovely Jane, a live woman, and no fantasy, John Skelton saw her, talked with her, laughed with her, wept for the death of her bird, God I do believe he *touched* her: yea, he knew what woman was. What choice then but to credit the stories about his house-lady? She can have been no mere breech-burner, no sordid 'remedy' for lust intermittent, he lived with her so many years and would *not* be inhibited from her. It is said he paid fines for her to Old Nick's Archdeacon: notwithstanding he still held by her, and they could not prove him heretic. In Norwich diocese they would certainly have tried. Even though he'd been so close, at one time, to the King."

All this in a rapid low gabble, Dorothy could scarcely catch his words, she saw his energy was spent. The wine came, she gave it to him, he lay down again on her cushions, still muttering and rambling.

"'Close to the King' did not prevent him having to take Sanctuary at Westminster when Wolsey would have had his blood. Poet and priest, he knew his strength, rejoiced in it, saw with a wondrous clearness: ah Lord, that *I* could do likewise. Lord, that I could know how he did it! Three-fold juxtaposition of the two-backed greedy beast with the poetic strength of the English tongue with the blood-beat of true religion, religion out of plain Scripture; Lord, but as long as I know of him, dead though he may be, I know *I am no longer alone*."

He feebly handed her the empty cup. "Now d'you see," he said to her, hoarse, almost whimpering, "I had my reasons for going to Diss?"

"So what did you find there? And please don't tell me 'Barbara's bum'." She was, God save her, taking all his nonsense very seriously now. Something had struck at her heart.

"Naught. Old Sir John yielded nothing: how should he? He was Skelton's Curate and had been confided-in. Probably confessed-to. Decent 'Calliope' (whom I truly believe to have been John Skelton's *married wife*), was doubtless long since dead. All the parish held its tongue, afraid to be proffering scandal. Scholar's research meant nothing to the sheep-feeders of those parts. My own soul's-ease, you may imagine, meant even less. How much does it mean to *you*? Answer me not, I ought never to have put you that question. Barbara, La Haut-jambée, strutting Doll of the ungirded shanks . . . Mannerly Margery Milk-and-Ale . . ."

This last surprised her. It was the title of a song she had in her repertory: she had not known Bale knew of it. She asked him what he meant.

*

"*Mannerly Margery?* The simplicity of the name stung me, alongside of your own cognomens, so insolent they are, such children of Herodias. *Margery*'s a poem by Skelton, about another of the many women he knew, who lived, and he wrote about them: wrote very often, wrote *to* them and *for* them. Some of 'em undeniably dirty women (he'd had his years at the royal court before he took priest's orders): but not Margery. She was rural, an honest dairymaid fending off her lovers with scorn, two country clowns and a clerk. As I read the poem, she sees in the end that she cannot but love the popinjay clerk (she has after all, despite herself, yielded briefly, yea lightly, to his urgent caresses, even given him sundry small tokens – 'the best cheap flesh that ever I bought,' she sings with an irony): and thereupon he shows that he loves her too; dear goodness, he longs to *wed* her. My opinion, that clerk was Skelton."

"*My* opinion, you have it allgates incorrect. 'As you read it'? As *I* sing it, she bloody whores herself to that damnable clerk and it is *she* begs to marry *him*: the song is a harsh warning not to play the unkirtled fool in haystack and hedgerow with plausible vicious clergy." She was suddenly vicious herself, she didn't know quite why: but she knew it did her good to be able to lecture her lecturer upon the hidden context of a poem. Not that she'd had any prior inkling of its author. She had learned it from another minstrel in her usual way, and made her own mark on it in performance.

Bale might have been hurt by her tone. Just as well he wasn't, he looked so poorly. He *was* both astonished and excited by her meaning. He laughed aloud, drained his cup decisively, devoured another spice-cake. "Do I hear you say you *sing* it! Oh I've never heard it to music. Could you – ? Would you – ? You'd never *refuse*?"

So she sang for him, there and then, without accompaniment.

Why did she sing for him? To be so unprofessional, out of her hours, and charging no fee? What was worse, a maimed rendering. By rights there should have been two voices, Margery's and the Clerk's: Dorothy never presented it without young Rafey, her hurdy-gurdy player, joining in with her for the dialogue-part.

Upon the last stanza she signed to Bale to add his sick man's croak to her final refrain.

> "Gup, Christian Clout, your breath is stale,
> With mannerly Margery Milk-and-Ale.
> Gup, Christian Clout, gup, Jack of the Vale,
> With mannerly Margery Milk-and-Ale."

The Clerk has had her, to her ruin, and now turns away from her to take his careless road (according to Dorothy's interpretation, which was what she enforced upon Bale): he leaves her to the two Clowns, if they think they can console her. But she continues to scorn them as much as he does: their oafishness is no good to her at all. It ought to have been a self-reproaching bitter end to all Margery's vaunted self-will. Instead, between the two singers, the refrain's ideology foundered. Partly defeated by ague, Bale made a *totally* defeated brute of the triumphant Clerk; while Dorothy's clear music rode out so strong above him as to contradict all impression of despair.

"*Gup*," grunted Bale, breathless, in the improvised end-run of the thing. "*Gup. Gup-gup-gup!* God, I've done myself an injury. You should not have let me attempt it. But was it not majestic?"

"Majestic? Strange word to affix to a comic-song."

"But you said –"

"It's a comic-song." She decided she had had enough. In his

present state she could not of course ask him to leave: she herself would have to go, which maddened her. "By my advice you should sleep. Cover yourself with the quilt again, so. I'll leave you and visit Rotraut, I want to see is there any use I can make of that kettle-drummer of hers." She would far have preferred to sit alone for an hour or two: he had given her much to think about. "Lord Wentworth comes after supper. I'll tell Belle-Savage not to wake you till then."

Why, she knew he was a boor and a bore. Did she *have* to feel this absurd tenderness?

She bustled about, a perfunctory tidying-up of the room before she went next-door. Belle-Savage would probably not bother. She thought he had his head buried under the quilt. Ah but no! was the fool-friar wide-awake and talking *yet*?

He was, and about Wentworth. "He requires I should help him form a group of players to propagate what he calls 'True Gospel'. I said, insofar as it renounces the abuses of Papacy, well and good. And attacks the falseness of enforced vows upon the clergy, even better. But if he craves a complete new doctrine, sacramental, eschatological, after the theories of Zwingli, I am not persuaded. I said, I have made plays, many plays (of the Old Guise) for the Carmel-houses to present upon feast-days; saints'-lives plays, bible-chronicle plays (both Testaments), also allegorical-moral, and I know their uses. Let us talk of work, I said, that will examine only *the unglossed Scriptures* and find out by means of art exactly what they are saying to us. Plays, poetry, music, only to *discover*, I said: not yet, I said, to dogmatise. We have had too much of dogma. Make free, I said, the ancient spirit of England, who is now as a widow-woman cruelly misused in her bereavement, bound hand-and-foot to litigious worldly clergy who distort the terms of her legacy, embezzling every bequest, eating up the very house over her head, every time she seeketh justice she is caught in a trap of statutes; and none, I said, can cut her out of it . . ."

She thought it best to ignore him: he seemed to be growing delirious. She was sure of it when his words suddenly jerked and skidded, right back to his buggering friars.

"That novice-master, you know, he was never given the young boys into his charge again, at least I am glad of that. But I thought often, did they refuse to proceed further against him because they had known of his wickedness already? Nay, worse, because they had *shared* it, he had procured for them, yes? Investigation of *him*, then all of it would have been known? They were to be sure suspicious-speedy in sending me off to Cambridge, mark you that, mark you that. Nay, lady, do you suppose – ?"

She supposed nothing. She went straight to Rotraut.

(vii) *Nelly Dead*
After all this, what could she do but sit down with Rotraut and her wiry friend, and accept the drink they put before her. The drumming and dancing was over, the musicians were drinking too: and they all discussed future work in some heat. Ermentruda, a very sharp woman, did not want to lose the kettle-man, even part-time, to Dorothy just yet, and they all had to haggle, with plump big-busted Rotraut pouring out Rhine-wine at every retort.

*

Belle-Savage came in to tell Dorothy there were two men at her door, arrived one-after-the-other like a dunning creditor with attendant bailiff; while the shave-head on her floor was up and swaggering, acting already as though he were host to this pair of whoresons. Was she to take their money, or what?

"No no, these are not to pay. Not with money, Godsake, but I hope one day with something. I'll go to them the back way: and Bella, guard the gallery."

The house was already filling with gentlemen, it was best they should see nothing at her room tonight out of the ordinary. In the back corridor she dipped a cloth in a bowl of water and sluiced her head. She was horribly, unexpectedly, drunk. The Germans didn't care, they had no performance tonight: they laughed to see her stagger. But she *did* care. This was important. She had entered into something from which no way out, or at least she could see none. God, she couldn't even see the door-latch.

In her room: Wentworth, an ambassador-face. Bale, arrogant, expansive, well-refreshed from his sleep. And a small clerkly young man with a pallid face, almost-white eyeballs, and a fatuous wispy apology for a blonde chin-beard. She did not think, surely? she had seen him before; but he leered at her, familiar, as though he was a long-lost half-brother. God in heaven, it was Conrad!

"God in heaven," she said, "Conrad!"

Bale crowed triumphantly. His arm was about the young man's soft shoulder. "Hah! You never thought! We have retained for you a strong surprise! Young Conrad and myself are already old companions in the work of the new-found light, no longer need he blow his wind for the roar of a thoughtless mob."

She had known it all the time. "Why, I've known it all the time, oh Conrad my love and my flower: all the time you were a scrip-scripture-smugglerer, of course you were, auriculate-confession, boy; go give me a big big hug."

He submitted: but dubiously, most startled by Dorothy's manner. Obviously he had been given a different account of her. "Gracious lady, did you not hear? I am not now a *Kraut*-eating clown, nor have been, for long time. I cannot act too easily in distinguished English plays, by reason of the language: although I make some expert shift, do I not, *Bruder* Johann?"

Bale grinned at him, paternally: and said, "Hah, we delved for talent."

"In principle, however – " (oh certainly Conrad was matured) – "in principle however I can serve as director-of-stage and coadjutor of poet and robe-maker: from the great help I have been given by this kindness of brother John I have acquired most elevating experience in three-four years. It was told to me: you also. But here – in this 'Birds'-cage'? It is not quite a brothel-house, but –"

Dorothy's boozy levity was gone all at once. "It's not at all a brothel-house and if you think it is you're a damned little *Dummkopf*. I'll thank you to give my work the respect I'd be glad to give yours. If you don't believe me, ask my lord. My lord, I am not drunk, I must request you to inform him so."

Wentworth was very dry. "The lady is not drunk, *Meinherr*, so let us proceed to business." He shot the bolt on her gallery door. "Practicality. Shall we talk ways and means? I take it that spitfire blackamoor is at her post outside?"

*

For the next hour, a most earnest and intelligent discussion, between the three men, as to how, when, where, a new acting company could be set up for the promulgation of a scriptural and socially-effective reformed Christian drama.

Dorothy spoke once, near the beginning. She said, "Why am I here? I do not enact plays. I do not know at all whether or not I am concerned for reformation of anything, or at least to the extent of spending my hours upon it: you will reform, I'll receive, if I like what you give me, I'll be glad. But *will* I like it? I want – oh I'll tell you what *I* want. I want all this whole damned world to be upside-down, inside-out, and made again into Paradise garden. Can you do it? Can the King? Can I? I don't believe it."

They looked at her. They were deep in argument about financial backing, about patronage, she had interrupted quite out of due order. Wentworth smiled. "Paradise garden," he said slowly, "can only be re-planted when Christ has been rediscovered. We study our charts for the voyage, Dorothy, and you as much as anyone can help us set a course. Admitting, as you do admit, that you would hope for the same fair haven. Don't think I have not found out what songs you have sung in this house. 'Bringing down the mighty men'? You sang for it: now we do it. And we are not only to talk about plays. But that comes first as it is more expensive. We will not keep you waiting too long."

She felt patronised and had half a mind to return to Rotràut, at once. But immediately she was ashamed to be in drink and foolish-frivolous. These men were despising her in her very own room. It must not be allowed. She sat up (she had been sprawling across six cushions) and made herself look wise. Ermentruda's canny face was the face for this occasion.

She listened, and said no more.

Wentworth was to provide the essential nobleman's protection; and to pay – with contributions from a number of like-minded magnates and sympathetic churchmen, most of them cautiously anonymous, but he knew who they would be. One name was so anonymous it virtually shrieked itself through every sentence of their talk: Thomas Cromwell, the King's high-climbing 'projector', without whom clearly nothing could be accomplished. They looked as wise as Dorothy (or as Ermentruda) when they talked of *him*: a look she had seen on many gentlemen's countenances, whenever this name was mentioned. Respect? Fear? Envy? This evening, confidence, too.

Bale made difficulty when Wentworth said 'the King's Church'. "Not to detract from his lawful Majesty, but surely the 'Church of All the English' is what we mean?" The King as its Head would be in position of *trust*, he must not be seen as in any sense a *priestly idol*, a *romish vicar*, a *proprietor*. Wentworth said, or muttered, "Treason laws. Let's not be misunderstood . . ." Bale replied, yes, but if they could get clearance for a correct turn of phrase? (By implication, from Cromwell.)

Bale was to write the plays: Conrad to act as manager of external contacts where neither Bale nor Wentworth could penetrate. He had sold his forbidden books to many communities of reformed souls who were, as yet, not ready to declare themselves. These plays (and their playing-places) would be designed to bring them to daylight. "I have," he averred, "ear to the roots of your grass. *I* talk to those, *you* to your high assistance, Lambeth Palace *undsoweiter* and so we combine effort –". Bale and Wentworth clicked their tongues at him. Cranmer no more than Cromwell to be named even in private, no, not yet!

Dorothy felt angry. It seemed she was the 'in private' and she resented it. It was her room.

Bale had much to say about the atrophy of art in England: the best players in the world, he thought, the most potent poets, yet all they could show was old discredited matter within excellence of form.

"Bear in mind, the very name 'New Guise' in plays and poetry heretofore hath been given only to Vices and Devilkins: from today forward, the Great Rehabilitation!" Let them take the extant form, he urged them, take the audiences' expectations that went with the form, and then – "upside-down, inside-out" – "Paradise garden, as milady saith, revealed beneath the last year's compost-heap!" But actors to bring their skills to such startling new material – how to be found? "Three-quarters of them; no ideas upon religion at all, save for blankest superstition: they'll hang themselves with saints' medallions under their raiment to guard against losing their lines, they'll cross their breasts with patter-and-mutter of *Ave Maria* before making their entry upon stage, they'll pay for hired Masses to ensure success with a notable audience, they'll –"

"We couldn't have that," said Wentworth.

Conrad tried to insist that all recruits for the company should first make satisfactory answer to a catechism of faith. "No," snapped Bale at once: "Assuredly *not*! Inquisitorial, and thus unacceptable romanism. And who's to approve the answer: you? me? my lord? Or do you intend their views, or even my play-text, be sent to one in Germany, or the Swiss Cantons, for an *imprimatur*?"

"We couldn't have that."

"*Bruder* Johann, *ach Brüder, seh'n Sie nicht dass –*?"

"English, please." Wentworth was irritated.

Conrad tried again. "I am saying to you, brother John, if only you can listen: it is not just for *one* to adjudicate these things, but the *community collective* of *Jesu-Christus reformatus*, as according to words of Scripture –".

Bale slapped his hand on the table: "No!" He was sweating again, he swabbed his scarf all over his face and his vast tonsure. "The community collective, if it exists in England, which I doubt, will deliver adjudication after, not before, it has witnessed and heard our play! Which is why, to make start, I propose for our first subject, not an immediate scripture-piece, which will only confuse where there is already such confusion of doctrine: but a taut examination of the history of the Church in England; King John, his strife with Rome. For there we have a common ground with all who shall hear us. Highly traditional subject, an earthly ruler torn in his spirit between his good voices and his bad ones, Skelton Laureate my exemplar, *Magnificence*. King Magnificence gains good counsel from Felicity and Measure, Perseverance, Circumspection, and so forth: and is assailed by Counterfeit-Countenance, Crafty Conveyance, Cloakéd Collusion, Folly. To rule his kingdom, he learns at last to accept the good, cast out the bad. But not before he first yieldeth space to the bad and suffereth grievous consequence. His kingdom-by-allegory: his own soul – and also the realm of England. Every stage-player well-knoweth how such a play should be done, every audience can tell the shape of it from its very commencement.

"Now: suppose we give our king the name of a true history-king, John Plantagenet, who so unjustly became a byword for tyrannical refusal of English liberty when in truth he sought only the truest liberty of all, a free soul for all his people in the freedom of God's Blessed Word! Skelton's knaves were understood to be aimed at the power of Wolsey: ours shall define the Pope and his institutions. Our king shall be seen, first, as history's John; second, as England's Henry; and third, as an Everyman preyed upon by dark priest-workings. Also by common vices, such as afflict all human souls.

"I am thinking already of a number of names – Sedition, Dissimulation, Usurpéd Power, Private Wealth. Madam, that Herod-play in Diss? Herod, Herodias, her Daughter, and John Baptist was also Pride of Manstrength, Worldly Desire, Carnal Temptation and – and Repentance?"

"God's Truth," corrected Dorothy coldly: but she was pleased he had been courteous enough to refer himself to her twice. Perhaps she did have some use here. Bale's notions were in fact vivid. She could already see his play. But what had she to do with plays? That rubbishy Herod-piece was no more than a dance, it held no true stage-argument. And the *Friar Jenkin*s were scrummages in drunken bar-rooms, burst breeches, tossed-up skirts. Never once a full-formed acted play.

"It should have been Repentance. They had no coherent thought, those Runagates . . . But the double names, historical, allegorical, *there* is a concept, yes? Sedition disguised as Langton, Archbishop, who levied war upon John; and then again disguised as a Monk, to conspire against John's life – and by 'Monk' we show *monasticism!* – full history of religious orders: inclusive conspectus of how they got their lands and houses by deliberate sleight-of-hand, eliciting royal charters and perverting the benefactions, to live and work on English soil as occult agents of *Vaticanus Mons!* And all this in the one *persona!* You see the device, you follow through the complexity –?"

Wentworth and Conrad were snatched into his babbling enthusiasm: it seemed then and there the play might be made before midnight. As they all three shouted out their notions all-at-once, and the sounds of the evening's minstrelcraft from all the other women's rooms merged in a clashing cacophany, Dorothy's fantasy began to work, very oddly began to work, she felt the multiple echoes throughout the old buildings must inevitably centre upon this one small room of hers, the heart of the house, she thought, condensing and distilling all the music, movement, desire, satisfaction and frustration that filled up the 'Birdcage' like blood in a mobile body.

If God with a silent thunderbolt, down her chimney this very moment, were to strike all three of them dead, would not every artist top-to-bottom of the house fall immediately close-padlocked silent? Were she God, she would do it, just to see would it work . . . No, she must *not* giggle. Conrad was making a point.

Conrad was a damned fanatic. Anything Bale wanted to do would be better done without him; she had already concluded this after only an hour of him. He was remonstrating: "I think you speak too much, over too much, about *peril* to your actors if they are not well-taken with their new guise of play-style. Of course there is always peril when old tyrannies are to be *totgeschlagen*, down-struck, *kaput!* It is not courageous, *Bruder*, to think of it always –"

Wentworth, as knight-at-arms, took umbrage at what might be a reflection on his own courage, but he kept his temper. "*Meinherr*, the question is, not how far we may *dare* to advance our project, but how far will our project gain if we are so foolish as to exceed the ascertainable bounds of safety. I assure you, if we commence by arousing tumult, it will be so much good work laid waste, and that, sir, is our Alpha and Omega."

"Good *men* laid waste," put in Bale. "We will only begin to succeed if we can be seen to be actively supporting the King and his ministers. It may well be, in the end, that we meet in confrontation; government shall say, 'Stop'; and ourselves and our audience, 'Go on!' But that end cannot be reached if our beginnings are thought seditious. I say 'seditious', not 'heretical': our understanding of the theology in our work must come from acute questioning, and we must indeed *dare* to question, take facts (as with King John), hold 'em up to the light, search them without fear of popish intransigence; Godsake, keep our arrow for the one proper target or we'll all be in the mucky ditch!"

Dorothy was not sure where Bale stood exactly. On the one hand he seemed to think Conrad would go too far too fast, on the other he was clearly going about to set out too fast himself, rendering himself unable to overtake his own footsteps. It looked as though Wentworth was becoming nervous. For he said, firmly, to close this part of the discussion: "Usurpéd false religion has made enough martyrs in England these late years. I have not called this meeting to enrol any more such names." No, but to enrol Bale in the army of the New Guise, she thought: who is already pushing through to the vaunt-guard, his gun not even loaded! She did not know where this left *her*. Bale was wild, Wentworth was cunning, Conrad was stark mad: listen to him now!

"It is not justice to sneer at martyrs. Their good crown is *unendlich*, everlasting, we can *not*, must *not* withhold it!"

Dorothy sprang to her feet with such abrupt aggression he fell back as if she had hit him. "Nor did you withhold it, Conrad, from the old Rover and his silly crew when you slid into the prop-basket a death-dealing book and none of us knew what it meant! My God, when I think of what might have happened!"

He recovered himself and his eyes were ice. "What did happen, gracious lady, happened to me and to those others. Not to you. Where were you? Two days and a night, mid-winter, in the stocks, one hundred lashes upon naked backs, you know the woman Eleanor died of it? Not then, but a month later, no doubt as to the reason. Her man Catgut, rat of the drains, became an informer for the Archdeacon, introducing himself into other minstrel-troupes to seek evidence of further heresy, *mein Gott* but *he* was no martyr. I think the Rover went back to sea, best place for him, no-one had laughed at his jests many a

long year. Perhaps not quite to sea. I met him on the quay at
Lowestoft, he called himself night-watchman, I had to bribe him so I
could bring through a chest of Tyndale Bible-texts. But oh yes, there
was martyrdom. For me, for her, perhaps in a way for the old man.
Our Lord shall call the ignorant as well as the schooled. I myself,
gracious lady, have all these four years given thanks, given glory, for
my suffering then. I rejoice that I did what I did."

Dorothy stared in dumb misery and shock. "I did not know that
Nelly died," she muttered, and then sat. "You Lutheran bastard,"
she said. No-one else spoke. This was not what had been expected.
She said, "I must revenge her." She thought: first by killing Conrad.
Then she thought again. "Keep your arrow for your own proper
target."

She said, "I agree with Prior Bale. We must dare but we must not be
foolish. If we are to work, our work must have *use*. If I am to revenge, I
need to fulfil that revenge. What happened at Diss fulfilled nothing,
had no use for anyone, except of course for Conrad's glory. I look to
Mr Bale and to my lord to ensure it does not happen again. Otherwise,
my room: it will not be available. Nor will be my services. *If*, that is to
say, my services are in demand. Are they?"

*

She spoke to them as cold and cutting as Cecilia had once spoken to
her: without realising it she had absorbed Cecilia's very voice and
stored it for this moment. There was a long silence.

Conrad sulked: he had been insulted. Bale, deeply troubled, was
upon the verge of tears. Wentworth cleared his throat, smoothed his
moustache, began a very formal speech.

"*Confessio fidei*: that we may all know the reasons for my presence
here, and no misunderstanding. I believe that Jesus Christ, being
made man, crucified, risen, liveth in heaven and on earth amongst us
all to this day (by virtue of His Holy Spirit) that He may bring us to
His Kingdom with no less simplicity, no less rational action, than that
which He pursued through His thirty-three years of childhood,
growth, manhood. He wore carpenter-clothes, or maybe hedge-
preacher clothes; His feet blistered when he walked in sandals; you
could kiss Him or eat with Him, if you had the nerve, and many did.
Sometimes His earthly friends drank too much and He loved them,
sometimes they whored themselves, and He loved them even better.
He gave them bread and wine and said, 'This is ME,' and no vestured

priest took the supper from His hands to pass it amongst them. Simon Peter had a wife: He did not tell him to put her away. Simon Peter had a sword, and He did *not* approve its use, nay He set palm upon the wound it made and healed the officer's ear. This is the Christ I seek, and I hope that we all seek. Revenge, we do not require."

Again, silence. Bale snuffled, licking the tears from the edge of his mouth as they trickled unstoppably. Conrad seemed to be counting the beat of a dancer's music that floated up from a room downstairs. Dorothy said, "I drink, and I have whored: good, I am most fit to be a citizen of this Kingdom. But then, I say I long for a sharp-edged weapon and you tell me you don't need me. I am all at-a-blow *un*fit, not by any action but by speculation about action, and that from a sore-rended heart. Inconsistency? Packload? Remember the phrase?

"Forget my motive, watch my deed: sure, my lord, in the upshot, deed will re-shape motive. Have trust in your own Christ. His choice of friends and lovers – to begin with – was much at random. So let yours be. *Confessio fidei*: they killed her with their power, so therefore their power must die."

"Not with peace but with sword, *also komm'ich*." Conrad held his ice-eyes askant, and Wentworth could not hear him properly, the German accent was so thick: "*Confessio fidei*." Wentworth did not deign to ask him to repeat himself.

Bale was growling. "From hedges and ditches, He brought 'em in to his marriage-feast. When did He send seven devils out of Magdalene? Before or after she called him 'Saviour'? Work for every hand, a talent for every pouch. God knows, *my* pouch hath holes in it yet. And that which is put in it, I am still tempted in fear to bury. *Confessio fidei*: my Christ hath a darkened face, through my labour may the light soon shine . . . Gentle Barbara, you ask, are your services in demand? I tell you, yes, and here is how. Not wise to encompass you among the enactors of stage-plays; for no good reason, except that it is never done. A company of men-players is acceptable everywhere, but set a woman amongst 'em, all will think the plays are to be rubbed up against like bitches' rumps, not *heard* with intellectual rigour. But we also plan a minstrel-troupe, of a quite new complexion, to sing and dance and jest in honour of Lord Jesus. Or, more exactly, in honour of Lord Jesus made new for the liberty of England's Christians. Women as minstrels are as customary as men in plays; again for no good reason, but that is how it is done. The Olivers of Lynn showed you what can be accomplished, in manner of sobriety and secular grace, howbeit in accordance with naught but the Old Guise faith. Not all things Italianate are as degraded as their Church there, though the corrupters in that land wreak havoc. But not to go so far as Italy: in the Low Countries I have seen what are termed the Rhetoric-shows, moral fables and pageants, and women upon their stages; their presence was chaste and lovely. Can you order such a company with us?"

"Why not?" Her mind was decided, her experience all of a sudden seemed to flower at the idea. "But am I to leave the 'Birdcage'? It is not very chaste, but without question it's the heart of my art. Moreover I earn from it. You say you want no martyrs: gold and silver is not so tedious to me that I would throw it away cheerfully. Well?"

Wentworth grinned, a merry little grin, infected by her renewed irony: he loved her ironical, even though he was timorous of the places where her irony led. "Why, of course you don't leave the 'Birdcage'. How else would we use your room? We have to hold this meeting again and again until all is made perfect, also to rehearse our work, also to debate other matters, for which – I fear, Dorothy, you must be excluded: certain persons of high estate who dare not come hither with any external witness to their dealings. Will you trust me that those dealings shall in no wise incriminate you? Will you trust me that we serve the King, but because of the King's enemies we must serve him under the cloak? For instance, upon next Tuesday, I would be grateful if your door were made open to our hand, and then for two hours, three hours, we were entirely alone here. Can you let us in and slip out, so – ?" He gestured to the entry into her back-corridor.

"Oh yes, I can go to Rotraut. I can either sit and listen there, or take my part in pleasing her gentlemen; if Ermentruda does not mind. In any case, if we talk of minstrel-troupes, those two should be included. They are both of 'em sturdy Luther-wenches, and brave; although so far in England they have kept their opinions quite quiet. May I speak to them of it?"

It was time for them all to go home. It was agreed that Prior Bale should meet Dorothy elsewhere during the week to discuss ways and means for the minstrel-troupe. "Two can come together outside the 'Birdcage' without attracting notice. It is three or more that causeth talk."

*

Left alone, she lay on her cushions and spoke to dead Nelly.

When Bale crept softly in again, she had nothing to say to him, but: "Am I wrong to say prayers for her soul? Would I be wrong to pay for a Mass? Very well, I will be wrong. I'll give the money to old Cuthbert tomorrow and I don't care a damn what you tell me." The tears were all sticky on her cheeks: his were now dry.

He seemed ashamed of himself, however, mumbling something about it's being only the *abuse* of the doctrine of Purgatory to which he was opposed, at any rate until such time as he was vouchsafed a further clearness . . . His voice died away. He was shivering again. She could not think why he had returned, Belle-Savage should have kept him out; where *was* the neglectful creature? Carousing with her cronies in the yard's alcoves, she supposed. Belle-Savage drank, she must be corrected. She saw Bale staring fixedly at her Virgin-and-Unicorn, after fidgeting all over the room. Then it came to her what he was about.

"Jesus, we live and learn . . ." she groaned. "After all that has been said . . . You want me to quench your devil that grows into a finger-post, lay the unicorn into the lap of my pure virginity. And by Christ you are abashed to ask for it, you come and hope it will all fall natural. Well, it won't. Neither with you nor – nor any other, not any more. Have you not heard, in this place, I lie with no men?"

She spoke with a bold hypocrisy. She spoke truth, but truth was a lie; because of course she had lain with *women*, at least with one woman, and often. She and Rotraut had been so warm together, from the very first day they found themselves in adjoining rooms, more companionship than lust – ah no, she could not deny lust. How many times? Leave it at 'often'. Although Satan's own hooks would not bring her to tell Friar Bale, she had confessed it each week to Sir Cuthbert; he had made little of it. "Love," he'd croon, "sweet love among sweet hearts, be glad for it, my child; you ask, was it sin? When sweetness is soured, then we have sin and we *know it*. If you think there has been sourness, say Our Lady's Rosary, twenty times? one hundred? She won't count. Oh, and if your charity *could* see its way to a very small bottle of that sweet little wine they call 'rob-davey' . . . ?"

And then Ermentruda had come back from Germany, Ermentruda was Rotraut's friend for all of five years: end of 'often'. The whole thing had been a sort of roly-poly recapitulation, recollection, of

Gillian; though not quite the same needle-joy, and not the tearing sorrow. All told, a generous happiness, and at the finish her displacement had been kind and unspoken, no quarrel. It did not tear her . . . not too much.

Bloody Bale was bloody torn. "But I was the one that worked a magic miracle, found apples and roses in winter, grown under a great man's glazing: I had not thought it could be done, and I had to give his gardener, oh God I know not *how* much!"

If this revelation was meant to delight her, it failed utterly. "And you looked for no reward: and now you come seeking one. Can you not see I want nothing but to be left on my own with my grief? Take your ague-fits out of here." He neither went nor spoke. Something else would have to be said, so she said it. "I wonder you have had no thought of the venereal pox? Every woman of any sense in a place like this is stark terrified of it. So am I. Some of 'em say it's a judgement of God, but I don't believe that. There's no more whorage in the world than ever has been, why should God commence His judgements now? For all agree the killing pox is only these few years entered amongst us. Add to which, it shall putrefy reformed Christians just as much as the unregenerate, which would cross His divine plan for making pure His religion, no? Some of 'em say, too, that the only way for a man to cure it is to wipe off its rot from himself by entering a clean woman, and then another and another. There are those of that opinion come here, Christ help us! Derry-down to end *all* derry-down. No man into *me* for as long as I'm in this work."

She meant it, every word: how was it she had not thought of this, though, a fortnight ago, when she ordered Belle-Savage to lay supper for herself and Wentworth? And Wentworth new-come-over from gaudy infected France! She put the frightening thought aside. "It don't hinder my trade, I'm not alone here in making such a rule – celibate rule: but *my* rule, not the Pope's. Practicality, not virtue. The music I am paid for is well worth the money I charge, without any addition of mustard. Ask downstairs for Alison of Chichester – she was my maid's last employer – I met her the day I arrived here to take over the room from her. She was infected, she had to leave, the committee had found out. Act of treachery to all of us not to have told the committee herself. But why revile her? She was as white as the whites of her desolate eyes for what had befallen. We took a collection of money to help her on her way, but . . ."

He was choking, whether with anger or remorse: just very possibly, with the effort to explain that she had entirely mistaken him. After a moment, his congested face shot out one or two words – "How dare – dare – dare you – " and then, all in a lump: "how *dare* you presume that I might be poxed: I told you (and should *never* have done) that my celibate vow has been *kept*! Desire, desire, yes, but *never* fulfilment: and all I thought to do now, all I thought to mean, was – was – was –". He smothered himself into silence.

Dorothy glowered at him, dead Nelly and dead Alison wide alive in her mind, and she hated him for bringing Alison back into her remembrance just now. The news of Nelly on its own had been heavier than she thought she could cope with.

"Roses," she said and he quailed at the contempt in her voice. "*I saw* the deathly rose-flower broken out upon Alison's face: curdling her skin between nostrils and lip, damn you I *saw* it and I don't forget. Gelded Conrad, I suppose, was the foreign messenger you sent with your pimp-basket. Well?"

But by then Bale was out of the room. He had to be, anyway, the bell was ringing to clear the house.

Left alone once again, she lay once again on the cushions: but her consciousness of Nelly's presence had been stamped into darkness by Bale's intrusive feet. Instead, she thought she had with her, fluttering just beyond her corner of vision, in and out of the shadows at the back of the candle, a very soft little whey-faced ghost, not daring to make itself known lest Dorothy prove as stern as the committee. Begging, did it seem, for some old 'Birdcage' music, as a sign of the house's forgiveness . . . ?

Dorothy took up her cittern (of which she was not fully sure, her lessons had but lately begun), and gave herself a tremulous note. She felt a sudden sharp trickle of cold all down her spine. In a small voice, and with no drama, she sang this new ballad – since midsummer it had been going the rounds:

> "As I walked out in the gardens of Bankside
> As I walked out by the Bankside one day
> I saw a young maiden in a boat on the water
> All wrapped in white linen as cold as the clay.
>
> "'O had he but warned me before he disordered me,
> Had he but warned me of it in time,
> I could have got pills and salts of white mercury
> But now I'm cut down in the height of my prime.

> "'O send for young minstrels to dance with my coffin,
> With hautboys and flamboys and the cry of their song.
> Let one of them carry a bunch of red roses:
> I'm a poor singing-woman and I know I've done wrong.'"

If the song had not been made about Alison, then Alison's life had been made for the song. By the time the last stanza was concluded, Alison's furtive pleadings were no longer in Dorothy's room. "Roses," said Dorothy, "red roses and *God Damn*."

★

Bale could have told her before he went – perhaps it *was* to tell her, that brought him back; and his confusion at her weeping had muddled his errand: or perhaps not? – he was staying at Lord Wentworth's house in the Strand, and therefore (if she and he were to work together) the connection would be a simple one. He was now confirmed Prior of the Ipswich Carmelites, through Wentworth's local influence: but for the time being he was an absentee prior, his work for the New Guise in the capital was too important to be abandoned, even for a short while.

As it was, she so frightened him that he did not come again to the 'Birdcage' and his next approach to her was made by his old method, dogging and flitting about her as she carried on her daily life. She made no approach to him: when they needed her she would be ready, let them initiate, she had had her say. The next Tuesday she opened her door to some serious men who looked straight through her, even Wentworth did: she understood and went to Rotraut, leaving them to occupy her room in privacy. Bale had not been one of them.

★

Shortly after she took to her bed, Widow Dorothy dreamed – just the one time – of the pox. She saw it as an army of creatures, two legs, four legs, six and even ten, galloping widdershins round and round a bright meadow under a horrible blotched sun, bluey-green smears on the pulsing brazen disc. Each creature was in some way a deformity of itself, although in itself each creature was deformed. Dragons' heads, serpents' scales, rams' hoofs, dogs' teeth, monstrous cows' udders dragging the ground, pelts and the roots of feathers thick with carbuncles, rotted with pus – and each creature carried a rider, a naked human being, young and beautiful, black or white, male or female, their hair streaming in the wind, their limbs stretched out with apparent joy at the freedom and speed of their course. In the centre of the race-track, for that was what it was, lay a black stagnant pool covered all over with floating weed: in and amongst the weed more

slim naked bodies swam, splashed, leapt like dolphins. From the middle of the
pool stood up a fountain, the shape of a unicorn's horn: but it did not spout, it
trickled, and the trickle was shiny with putrescence.
This dream of the Widow's was not repeated.

(viii) *The Two-Backed Beast*
On the weekend after the Tuesday the whole city was awakened by a
frenzy of church bells: Queen Anne had passed through child-bed safe
and sound: a tiny new-born new-guise princess had been held up and
smacked by the midwife and she had roared like her father's daughter.
Elizabeth! – And why wasn't she a son? Had all this coil-and-toil,
between King, Pope, lawyers, and bishops, been after all for nothing?
Queen Catherine had had a daughter. What could Elizabeth do for the
English that Catherine's Mary could not? Irrelevant and treasonable
question. Anna was fertile, she was young, she enkindled the King,
the nation's prayers would yet be answered.

The nation, at the same time, was counting its impertinent fingers.
The baby was born in September, nine months back from September
brought you to December but the wedding had been in June: and the
nation said 'oh-ho'. An announcement from Court: there had in fact
been an earlier wedding, held in secret for the soundest political
reasons, in January; and the child was a month premature. The nation
said, 'oh-ho-*ho* . . . ?', and continued to go to church. Parliament
continued with huge tiers of legislation, and Thomas Wyatt came to
the 'Birdcage' so abominably drunk that Dorothy had to have him
thrown out.

*

She was shopping for professional finery among the goldsmiths in
Cheapside, a hot thunderous day, her temper was bad, she was
harassed more than usually by touting apprentices trying to pull her
and push her to their masters' shops: Belle-Savage kept them away
with her fists and so did Dorothy's yeoman, but the little bastards
were incorrigible. She saw Bale again – for the third time in two days –
and her annoyance increased. He was in his friar's habit, taking
a drink of water from the conduit in the middle of the busy
street. She tried to avoid him. He moved quickly and blocked her
way.

"St Mary-le-Bow, a few doors along. We can sit inside a church and they'll all think I am hearing your sins. Not that I *want* to hear them. True or not so true, I know too much of them already."

His jocularity was gross. "No more than I've heard of yours," she snapped, and still tried to avoid him.

"'Practicality, not virtue' – that's no way to speak to a priest! Some would say your vow's reason was even worse than the reason whereby Jenkin seduced the dim-witted village chastity." Was he drunk? Perhaps he pretended to be: clergymen-in-wine were two-a-penny these days on the street, there were so many difficulties hemming their lives, whatever their opinions of public affairs. And it made a useful excuse for friar to accost painted woman. She did have to talk to the man: yes, she'd go to the church. She sent Belle-Savage and the yeoman home with her purchases.

Before they reached the porch, he suddenly stopped, causing awkward disruption among hurrying passers-by, provoking comments – "Watch where you're stepping to," "Out of the way, shave-head," "Catch your whores by night, why can't you?", and so forth. He took no notice: but fixed her with his eye and blurted, "If I had known that he would tell you your Nelly was dead, I would never have had him brought. *I* did not know of it: you'd have thought he would have told *me*."

They found a bench in a side-chapel. It was very dark. A bunch of candles in front of the chapel's image, that was all. Who was the saint? Pale-skinned Sebastian, filled up with arrows. He reminded her, slightly, of Wentworth. And Wentworth was just like Gillian. No: she must listen to Bale.

"Concerning the minstrel-troupe: all goes ahead." And, briefly, highly business-like, he explained to her the arrangements. She thought they were of good sense, and told him so. She had some suggestions of her own. She could have had this talk with any man in the business, of vigorous good sense. It did not seem to be Bale at all. Then suddenly it was. "I'll save the rest for another occasion, I have notions yet to be pursued. Listen, please, I returned to your room that night for more than one reason. I'll tell you the chief of 'em. I had more to say about John Skelton. I felt I had betrayed you by not giving you the full story. I felt I did not know how to deal with the full story. I have thought a good deal about it, since.

"After I came to Diss, Epiphany, and found no evidences, I let the matter drop. For a year, I was working instead upon scriptural intuitions in several earlier of our poets – William Langland, his *Piers*

Ploughman, his wrath against clerical exorbitance – query, was Langland a Lollard . . . ?

"I did not come to talk of Langland. What I have to say grew out of Langland, that's all. Thus. In my search for manuscripts, I sent letters far and wide, and told my correspondents I would buy or borrow anything of any of the English poets, all grist to my general mill. A man let me have sight of a piece of John Skelton I had not heard of before. It was printed, '28, the year before he died, by God, his last known work: *A Replication Against Certain Young Scholars Abjured Of Late*. And dedicate, would you believe, to Cardinal Wolsey! In the most demeaning servile terms, only a very few years after Skelton had had to hide himself in Westminster Sanctuary from the fury of that same Cardinal, having so boldly declared himself a proud enemy of the pomps of Rome!

"And if this were not enough, who were the scholars whom he vilified in his final poem? God help me, I should have told you, shabby hypocrisy to have concealed it. One of them was Thomas Bilney, yes, my Cambridge friend.

"For Bilney and another were condemned for alleged heresy and enforced against their wills to repudiate their teachings. It was yet a few years more before Bilney summoned the courage to go so gallantly to his death. But Skelton, the one man whom I thought as gallant as Bilney, Skelton saw Bilney humiliate in the white shirt of public penance: where the Cardinal had been too merciful to order stake and fire and torture, it was Skelton instead who scorched him with cruel poetry, hotter than flames. Oh I know not what to think. There may have been some mitigation. Skelton was old and ill, he had won his battle against Wolsey, had been allowed out of Sanctuary without prosecution, maybe he thought Bilney was a kind of savage Anabaptist, who can tell . . . ? I can quote you a few lines:

> I say, thou mad March hare,
> I wonder how ye dare –
> Wot ye what ye said
> Of Mary, mother and maid?
> With bawdry at her ye brayed:
> With bawdy words unmeet
> Your tongues were too fleet;
> Your sermon was not sweet;
> Ye were nothing discreet;
> Ye were in a drunken heat –

and a great deal more of the same."

"What had Bilney said about the Mother of God?"

"That it was idolatry to offer prayers to Her images."

"Is it?"

"I am not sure. Such a view would appear the extreme of crudest blasphemy, so therefore I am cautious. But Tom Bilney had good arguments. I can swear it was an honest opinion. I never knew a more conscientious man. The accusation of bawdry is ridiculous. Bilney was most decent *in toto*, far more so than I can be."

"Which is not to say much. May I tell you what I think?"

"For God's sake, do."

"The lady in Skelton's parsonage – Calliope?"

"Yes."

"The parson's bawdy 'breech-burner'."

"No! I *told* you. If all is true, he idolised her, he – ah: I follow your thought. An attack upon the doctrines of the Blessed Virgin was an attack upon Skelton himself, his own poetry, his own true-love (who would, by-the-by, have been long in her grave by then), and of course, in his great age, he came furiously to her defence! Ah yes, he was a good old poet: ah yes, he misunderstood; but Christ's Wounds, he had courage, and all those that knew him truly would have known what he meant! Impossible to tell you how much you have relieved my spirit. Skelton's Calliope was his Queen of Heaven, he knew in his conscience she had been his God-made wife: he defied Rome by defending Rome against unfortunate Bilney. Tragical. Blind eyes: blind eyes on both sides . . .

"A fierce skilful shot with his last arrow, and he hit the wrong target, yes. Which is why we must take such care with my lord and young Conrad and the progress of our present schemes. We said, save it for another occasion, but until then, brood over this. A strange tale, and it's quite true, and I tell it to myself often.

"Upon a time, four generations since, there was a man of my blood, Bale. A mercenary soldier, a rapacious dead-shot archer, he travelled the world for bloody plunder, and became a captain for some prelate in Transylvania, have you heard of it? He brought with him his camp-harlot, a Polack woman, of no good character. One day in the castle he looked through a little slit-window: directly opposite, lower down, another small window, as round as a rose. And through both of these windows, he saw into a secret garden and there, upon the grass, rolled his Polack with his master the prelate: a splayed mare – or rather

heifer – he came in behind like a *bull*. The bowman could see no more
of her than the propped archway of her legs, but he recognised her
coloured stockings, Cracovian work, no-one else in the castle wore
anything like them. There could not in all Christendom have been two
men capable of such a shot, there and then, as the prelate steered his
cow! All in a moment that archer was sent his chance, he either took it
or lost it for ever! He saw his master making booty of a woman who
was his own booty, his heart was filled with hate, and he let fly his
arrow incontinent, oh yes it killed the prelate. Right into the midst of
his fat loin. But the man Bale was so hard a bowman, it went into the
woman as well, he had skewered them both together; both of them
dead at once.

"Which was not what he had intended: I tell you he loved his
woman, all he wanted was to get her again into his bed . . . The whole
tale is abominable sordid. But, you know, Our Lord Jesus made an
unjust steward an exemplar for all good Christians, so why should I
not take *my* moral, my precept of caution, from a bloodthirsty
war-butcher? Yes . . ."

*

His eye wavered away from hers as he thought about the meaning of
his story, he tapped the fingers of one hand into the palm of the other
and sucked-in through his teeth. Was he bringing the interview to an
end? She shifted her posture to imply that was what she would prefer,
but got no response from him. He was looking out from the dark
chapel into the chancel: the chancel was not so dark, nor was it bright,
the sun outside was hidden by a lower of heavy cloud. And the east
window through which it should have shone (some hours yet before
noon) was obscured by a great reredos. A verger was lighting candles
on the high altar, Mass must be about to begin there: each flame, as it
straightened itself and burned upward in a strong flare, fetched out
another facet of the painted and carved design.

She could see the Lady Mary, high up in the centre. All around her
the Sorrows of Her Blessed Condition: she wept for Her Son, stripped
and crucified; helped lift Him from His cross; sat supporting Him
next the tomb, a sagging corpse across Her knees. Her chief image
nursed Him as a child: and there, for a portion, She had had joy.

Bale whispered: "Gold-work glistering, blue and white and candle-
yellow, red blood on the wan flesh, the shine of varnished tear-drops
. . . consider it, long-legged lady, consider what we are seeing.

Suppose, this storm-threatening morning, that you were a new-come stranger, into London from outside Christendom, as it were that blackface maid of yours: but shall we say, not Africa. India rather? And one such as I to lead you in here, and show you *that*: what would you think?"

He gave her no time to find an answer but went straight on with his own. "I think you might think, you had seen her before. In her home among the spice-trees, where they call her by the name of Kali. I have read that name in books of the Portugals' voyages: it signifieth the goddess of both birth and destruction, who is delivered of her child, feeds him at her dug, and then causes his torture and death. For would it not seem that *she* has created all that murder, that pain, all around her? And now she presides over it, as calm as she is cruel, with her next sacrificial babe in her arms? Ah, she weeps to see the murdering: but they are tears of an enticing crocodile, open her sweet mouth, you would see the sharpened teeth. Turn your head and see another of her children, whom ruthless she has filled with arrows. No doubt after lying with him, running her fingers'-ends thrilling all a-down his bare body. How far is this nightmare congruent with the Christ-life that Lord Wentworth so lovelily gave word to, the other evening in your room? Hey, can you answer me? No, you keep your mouth shut. Are you afraid I will spy your teeth?

"And yet they place it here, in a main church of this Christian city. Not only into Sebastian have her arrows gone this morning. One of them into *me*: and what am I to do with it? Pluck it out and shoot it back? Of course, of course, yes. But oh God, what is my mark, what *is* my proper target? Am I Bilney? Am I Skelton? Yes, I *did* want the two-backed beast when I crept into your room. Am I damned? Are *you* damnation?"

Thereupon this queer prior surged forward through the church. Right up against the chancel-screen, at its north end, pressed into the corner made by a pillar-base, he knelt heavily like a bulging sack, clutched his face into his hands and began to pray in an incessant hum that could be heard all the way down the nave. Dorothy slipped out of the building, just as the priests and acolytes came in for the Mass. Her cheeks were wet with the spittle of Bale's close whispering: and the gathering congregation stared curiously at her. Bale was praying before the very images he had just described as 'nightmare'. Would it be possible, *at all* possible, to accomplish craft-and-art with such a grotesque being? But she wanted to do it: and if the minstrel-troupe were truly a project independent from the acting-company, she might be able to do it without too much confusion from his confusions. But he must *not* be allowed to talk of her as his damnation. A few days ago he had said 'salvation': and that must be prevented, too. She was just a *colleague*, and she wanted to work . . . Him and his two-backed beast. Faugh.

Idol-worship? The Virgin Mary? Very possibly, yes. That reredos was indeed all pain, and unending pain, continuing without remission, if one judged by the images: and if one judged by the world to be seen all about us. It was true, the Lady did appear to *preside*. The complete excuse for living torturers, whether king's or pope's. How could they help it, it was ordained? They must learn that the death of Nelly had *not* been inevitable: they were there to be called to account. Let her work, then, and do the calling.

*

She went to Nettlestead for Christmas Twelve-days, attended by Belle Savage and a yeoman. Lord and Lady Wentworth had called together minstrels, as was customary, for the length of the feast. It was not openly stated, but those they chose were those whom Dorothy was to organise for further promulgation of the Reformed New Guise of England.

All the Yule entertainment was founded upon this assumption.

The fat man from Yorkshire was there (his town was Doncaster, a small place but important as gateway to the north parts): with a whole new range of scriptural ballads. Rotraut was there, upon Dorothy's recommendation. She knew a number of Lutheran songs, for which Ermentruda and herself had supplied English translations, clumsy line-for-line versions: Dorothy had to speak them in-between the lines of singing, but it was better than nothing. Some songs were by Luther himself, and one of them by Hans Sachs (yes, he was no invention: this 'master-singer' did indeed exist. Dorothy felt rather foolish). Ermentruda came for one day only, she had other professional visits for the remainder of the feast: she and Rotraut made a viciously hilarious dance-drama out of some old Rhineland tale of the boatman lured to wreck by Lorelei on her rock. Lorelei was the romish harlot as described in *Revelation* (a *fat* harlot, Rotraut); and from strutting Ermentruda, as a blindly conceited young boatman wielding an anchor, she sustained unmentionable damage. Lady Wentworth was graciously pleased to smile: everyone else shook with guffaws. The

Nettlestead party was not quite all sober piety this time: emotions began to run out of control. The New Guise, now so much more open, was exciting people's nerves.

Altogether there were about a dozen like-minded minstrels. They were to form a pool of talent, from which small groups or individuals could be made available to travel at any time to wherever there was a public need for them. It was a pity, thought Dorothy, that Conrad had to be one: but he seemed to be obligatory. He had refused to be thought of as a '*Kraut*-eating clown' but in fact that was what he still was, and very adept at it. He no longer farted (much), and his Owlglass was now a determined partisan rather than the anarchic outrage of all high-living high-thinking hypocrites of any religion or none: but the new direction seemed to suit him, and offstage he was almost reasonable.

He had obtained a number of play-scripts (by Sachs and other Almain masters) and was at work turning these into English. Wentworth himself helped to make the English presentable, but Bale was to polish the final versions. Bale already had a Latin draft of a new German play by a man called Kirchmayer. It was called *Pammachius*, or (very roughly) *Bloody Battler Against Us Everywhere*. It would show how the popes had called upon Satan to help them wrest control from the old Roman emperors, and had thereafter been subject to the Infernal Will. Bale, said Conrad, would make an English version: but he was anxious to finish *King John* first.

Bale himself was not at Nettlestead. He was spending some of the Twelve Days at the Earl of Oxford's London house, presenting actors in a pair of short plays, one upon the King's marriages, the other an explication of the gradual corrupting of God's Word through the historical distortion of the powers of the Roman Bishopric. Dorothy understood that these were fairly cautious pieces, going no further in their views than current legislation implied. Conrad sneered they would "much ingratiate us with government, for that, it now seems, is what we must do." But then he shrugged and laughed. "*Ach so*: we are of a comradeship, *ja*? Ducks new-stepping out of their ducks'-pond, to walk in a good line, none must walk faster than other, or else the line is to-broke, in sunder, no more unity. *Ist besser, vielleicht?*"

A second reason for Bale's absence. He'd had to go straight to Ipswich, to investigate a network of buggery and general breech-burning among his friars. A dossier had been sent him (with covering-letter of great distress) by the novice-master: it seemed as though every day in the Carmelite house some new enormity was being uncovered. He came once out to Nettlestead to hold conference about it with Wentworth, but did not take time off to speak to Dorothy. Conrad said Wentworth had said that all this detective-work was making Bale so unpopular with the Ipswich brethren that he might have to go soon to some other friary elsewhere. The house at Doncaster was at present without a prior, perhaps that would be a suitable appointment: anyway, Lord Wentworth would initiate some approaches. The Yorkshire minstrel had told him that the Old Guise in the north was exceeding strong: some fresh thought would be desirable there.

On the whole, a successful, productive, progressive Yuletide.

*

If the Widow dreamed only once of the pox, she never dreamed about her reprehensible behaviour the week after those twelve days. It was as though, as soon as it happened, she put it so firmly out of her mind that even in her last disintegration it could not be drawn back again from the shadows to which she had banished it. Wentworth, in her final mind, was the sharer of her golden cage, the recipient of her naked portrait, no further allusion swam up through the depths.

There was nothing left in her dreams to suggest the full seven days and nights she and he spent, alone, in an untenanted fort in Essex, on the edge of the coastal mudflats.

Part of his property, this fort, miles away from all habitation except some hovels where smugglers left their gear and a few poor peasants came in calm weather to catch fish from coracles. Lady Wentworth thought her man was on his travels, making circuit of political associates before the deep winter set in. Rotraut thought (and let it be known back at the 'Birdcage') that Dorothy was in Cambridge, fulfilling engagements agreed upon with some of the academic doctors who had attended the Nettlestead Christmas.

It was cold enough in the fort: they had very little food, they made huge fires out of driftwood and spent hour after hour under fur rugs on the stone floor, practically in the hearth, the floor softened for them by a thick layer of soldiers' palliasses which must have been mouldering there since the year of Bosworth.

She did nothing all that week: but break and break her vow. She forgot all Nelly's calendar teaching, she forgot the venereal pox, and she could give herself no reason for it. It was not as though she was drunk.

But in a way, of course, drunk is just what she had been. Throughout the Christmas feast she had poured into herself a most sharp stinging wine (or aquavitae, rather than wine), a fermentation compounded of newly-achieved new-guise artistry, the heat of gratified audiences, the intimacy between herself and her colleagues and Wentworth; and the awareness they all felt of the unprecedented freedom of heart and freedom of life that was now the great end of all their efforts, where before they had done no better than earn a living. So much more leaping-vital, these argumentative rehearsals, these performances, these late suppers after performance, than ever before in her experience.

And add to all that, tensing her flesh and keeping it tense until the very end of the feast-tide, the warm sweet existence of Rotraut, with whom she had been working so much more closely than at any time in the 'Birdcage' rooms: she had not succumbed again to Rotraut's body, even though the German dumpling had showed most apparently that her favours were available (except for the night of Ermentruda's visit, which went without saying). Rotraut's soft round hands had been constantly caressing her, Rotraut's bubbling laughter had teased at her, mockingly tempting her, both by daylight and firelit dusk: and Dorothy had left her alone.

Perhaps, as culmination of such a crowded space of tight excitement, Wentworth was inevitable. By an odd chance, on the final morning, Dorothy met him, alone in his maze. She was walking there, hooded and furred already for her journey back to London, her footsteps crisp on the frosty grass. Why was she there? She could not have answered honestly to such a question, had it been put to her by a Judgement-day Archangel. Why was he there? Why should he not be? it was his maze. She went down on her knees to him, astonishingly, as though begging a boon. Her hands reached round behind him, her finger-nails dug into his buttocks, with her teeth she plucked unfastened the silver-tagged laces of his trunk-hose. Neither of them said a word.

Nor did they speak even several hours later: when they found themselves, as much to their mutual alarm as arousal, on horseback, at a hand-gallop along iron-hard perilous roads, in the clinging estuary mist that hid from them (and hid them from) the mournful margins of the Essex coast.

So they swived one another in his ice-palace fort until they were sore (certainly she was, she did not ask about him): and then, at week's end, their strange taciturn parting, he to his wife, she to the city: "Shall we be friends ever?" she asked. "Oh, yes," he replied, "always friends. Why not?" "I cannot tell you why not. I think friends might have had more to talk of." "We did not talk, Dorothy: we were." "Were is not are, my lord. God go with you." "And with you."

They were at a fork in the road: his way led to the right, hers to the left, and the hoof-beats of their horses rang out loud and then faded simultaneously like the two parts of a song at command of the choir-master's hand. The only audience to the diminuendo was a broken-toothed old woman who had watched them from over the rim of her cottage half-door, mumbling to herself with a slow curiosity.

At the next village Dorothy was to meet, by appointment, Belle-Savage and her travelling-yeoman: they would be waiting for her outside the inn. It was none of their business what she had been up to, and in any case she paid them more than handsomely for their discretion.

The Widow's dreams were not paid, but they kept her own old secret from her

with quite as much eyelid-drooping loyalty as ever maid or bully had mustered:
she knew her dreams, she knew her servants, they knew her.

(ix) *The Pilgrims' Road*

At the 'Birdcage' once again, in her cushion-littered hot little room, she felt utterly diminished: and very, very angry. She looked at herself in her mirror and said, "This is *not* a face to be proud of. Can I ever trust its statements again? Ever trust these long bones, these treacherous limb-joints?" After a few days of the bitterest internal reproach, she began her life again as before, bland self-assurance, bare-faced self-perjury: none of it had happened.

Early in Lent, she realised most definitely she was impregnate with Wentworth's child. She refused to tell herself it was his, she refused to go to him for any assistance, she told herself only about the Virgin Mary and her own uncontrollable speculations the day of the Clerkenwell plays. (Bale's speculations in St Mary-le-bow were *not* part of her fantasies.) No doubt she could have laid a claim upon Wentworth, discreetly, submissively, these things were often done, noblemen's bastards were as common as parsons' by-blows – in the 'Birdcage', a great deal commoner – and much better endowed. She could have asked Belle-Savage, or some other experienced 'Birdcage' woman, to help her quell the child before it lived. But she bore in mind Nelly and the sweat-tent and the saints'-images: poor Nelly, her thin legs clenched in the stocks and blood all over her back, seemed to sit at night in the corner of the room when all the gentlemen were gone, saying to her, "No. Not this one. No."

So she left all such courses alone, and continued with her work. By the time she grew too unwieldy to perform any more, whoever had sent to her the Archangel Gabriel would have made whatever arrangements He thought necessary. She had acted outside her own control, despite all her resolution: very well, then that's how it was. Something was *intended*, somewhere: she must be patient and wait to find out.

When Wentworth came to see her, as he did now and then, she talked business and looked straight past him if he seemed to be approaching her privacy.

Bale never came: he *had* gone to Doncaster, and was in trouble already with the Archbishop of York. Once again his preaching had surged beyond his official licence – Conrad was surely wrong, there could have been no 'ingratiation' – and she understood from

Wentworth that Cromwell's protection had had to be invoked. She supposed the gadfly Carmelite would soon be coming south again. The north parts were obviously very old-guise indeed.

*

It must not be thought her seven days' lecherous aberration and its consequence made her incapable of business. She did not moon and mope, and her performances were as pungent as ever, even more so. With a harsh nervous edge to her singing that had not been there before. She gave her Bankside audiences political-religious items which would have scared her (and them) over the hilltops a year or two before. And she became much more wary of her neighbour Angelina.

In truth, the events of the time would make anyone wary. The division in the city between king's friends and pope's friends was becoming a weeping red wound; secret informers were everywhere: far too many people were going mysteriously to gaol. Growing courage, growing cowardice, as a result; and not all gaolings were mysterious.

Sir Thomas More, for example, had flatly refused to give sworn assent to the new oath of Royal Supremacy over the Church, and so had the Bishop of Rochester. Both were in prison, shortly to be executed, the word ran. Also the greater part of an entire London monastery, brethren of the Clerkenwell Charterhouse, reputed extremely austere, were publicly recalcitrant: their arrest too was expected any day.

An ecstatic nun from Canterbury, who had seen visions of the Blessed Virgin, was hanged at Tyburn with her clerical sponsors: not because she saw the Virgin, but because the Virgin used Her appearances to make treasonable remarks about the King and the new Queen, and the nun was foolish enough to repeat them. Dorothy wondered, would the King have the Virgin Herself hanged, if he were able to put an informer on Her trail . . . Herod very nearly did, in an age no less murky than this one, except that an angel gave warning. But had not 'Herod', after all, ended up being bribed by bible-smugglers . . . ?

Dreams, truths, play-poems, visions. Dorothy had visions of Nelly. Now that her baby was to be as fatherless as Jesus, she was not inclined to believe that the nun was either cynical or deluded, as the prosecutors made out. But, if the visions were true, then surely the King was marching to hell-gate: and all artistic work in support of his policy must needs be on the same doomed journey?

Not necessarily so. Angelina was the nun's impassioned defender. With such an advocate, the nun's cause, whatever the truth of the visions, could not be the only good cause: its opponents had most clear justification. Angelina called the nun 'the holy Maid', even after the execution; her room next to Dorothy's filled up with newly-bought Madonna cult-images at the rate of about two a day: it also filled up with some disturbing and sinister visitors, whose appearance and habits confirmed Dorothy very firmly in her adherence to the New Guise. Men who whispered from behind their cloaks and brought their own bodyguard with them, posting him, hand-on-hidden-knife, in the gallery as they talked (despite the house's prohibition of weapons): swarthy-faced foreigners; or, where they were English, very bad English with very bad hats, more appropriate to the thieves' stew-houses down the lane. Moreover Angelina's sense of security was inadequate: these fellows came at all hours with a dangerous but secret arrogance.

Dorothy too, of course, had her secret men to her room; but they were effectively secret, and, she thought, truly religious. Angelina's were more like paid agents of possibly religious people whose right hand knew not the deeds of the left. Angelina was fanatical, rancorous, stupid: when she talked of 'the holy Maid' you'd think she meant the Virgin Herself, not Her message-girl. Conrad was a fanatic, yes and a foreigner. He and the Spaniard were well-matched for callous sincerity. But he *did* seek a muddled freedom from out the midst of this quickset of cruelty, somehow. Angelina and her clients moved only to plant more thorns.

She could not make up her mind, ought she to tell Wentworth? Become a spy upon spies? Ignorantly embroil herself in intrigues with no foreseeable ending? Moreover their *beginning* would certainly be highly ambiguous. For all she knew, Angelina and herself might well turn out to be acting unwittingly for the same ultimate master. Who could say who he was? Was Tyburn Tree within his gift? The nun had reached the gallows with terrifying suddenness. Her entrails were not torn out, she was strangled to death only, but Dorothy did not care to follow her: nor did she wish to send Angelina there. Start tale-bearing to king's counsellors – or to the confidential advisers of king's counsellors, which is what Wentworth was – you wrap your arms around catastrophe.

Let the likes of More and Bishop Fisher lose their lives, if they were bent on it. They had been high enough in the world to learn and accept the occupational risks. *And* they were used to condemning others. Singing-women were not strong enough to play such games. In particular, not pregnant singing-women.

So long as Angelina gave no sign of knowing about Dorothy's visitors, Dorothy would keep a blind eye toward Angelina. If Conrad and some farouche Iberian were one night to swap hack-and-stab upon the 'Birdcage' stairs, total innocence was her best defence. But of course, she was far from innocent: they had racks in the Tower, by God they could *pull* it out of her and kill her child in the process. What *was* she to do?

★

She went and had a word with old Nancy. Or rather, she slid in to Nancy's densely-decorated, dimly-lit, unbearably stuffy room (along an obscure passage somewhere out at the back of the building), quietly squatted down on a rich heap of furs and velvets, and waited to be spoken to.

Nancy was holding court, from her brocaded bed, propped up on bolsters, a yellow-white ancient face half-hidden beneath a lace cap, once-beautiful slender fingers crooked together on her breast playing painfully in the folds of her deep ermine muff. Three or four 'Birdcage' women were crouched around the bed. One of them held a lute, and strummed very low-toned chords to keep time to Nancy's singing. She no longer sang for general gentlemen, only for her few most especial old friends and maybe the occasional young one; and now and then for the more tender of the girls.

When Dorothy entered, she was in the middle of *Go, Heart Hurt With Adversity* – a song of her youth, of the days when two roses fought for the crown, when knights-at-arms were only just beginning to make their politics in secret chambers instead of under banners, among crested helms, on the stricken field.

> "Farewell my joy and welcome pain
> Till I see my lady again . . ."

When she saw Dorothy, she broke off, on the prolonged first syllable of 'lady'. The lutanist stopped too. Nancy then deliberately sang the whole couplet without accompaniment, and took a deep breath, wheezing with the effort. Her voice was still most clear and sweet, though very very faint. She smiled abruptly at Dorothy and hooded her sharp green eyes.

"Give me *Chevy Chase*," she said to the girl with the lute. "Lady Mary but it moves my heart more than the sound of a trumpet. So many young men lay down on that field and died, and what was it for? Why, for nothing, the King of Scots is still in Scotland, the King of England still in England: and either of them at any time ready to fight it all over again. Play."

Dorothy felt there was going to be a message for her in the choice of song. She was sure of it when she heard the choice of stanzas. *Chevy Chase* was a terrible long ballad, old Nancy would never sing all of it, but you would have expected her to start at the beginning . . . She didn't.

> "Last night I dreamed a dreary dream
> Beyond the Isle of Skye:
> I saw a dead man win a fight
> And that dead man was I.
>
> 'Oh bury me by the bramble bush
> That grows on yonder moor,
> And never let my brave men know
> That a kindly Scot lies there.

"So they buried him, he was Earl Douglas, and his soldiers won the fight. When Percy wanted to yield, the man who had laid hold of him showed him the bush, but it wouldn't do, oh no not at all, Northumberland lords were proud."

She caught her breath again, and again started off, jumping a score of verses, drawing out the slow melancholy air till it seemed she would never finish.

> "I will not yield to a bramble bush
> Nor will I yield to a briar:
> But I would yield to the Earl Douglas
> Or Montgomery, if he were here.

"Do we ask, who was Montgomery? Nobody had thought of him until that moment. He came lurching out of the brambles: and behold he was in charge. And the song-ballad was over. Except, when the minstrels sang it, they had to end it with a prayer: that's what they call the Old Religion. We don't grieve for it, we don't forget it: we lived our lives for it, and it's broken up. Try to put it together again, and you'll break up the whole world. Dear children, do you not realise, *Humpty Dumpty* is a true tale?"

She was neither chuckling nor weeping, but both were in her voice. Dorothy thought for an instant the old lady showed her dotage: but she knew at once she was wrong. The green eyes flashed again.

"Play, daughter, one more wheel of the tune, the minstrel's prayer.

> Jesu Christ, our bales abate
> And to the bliss us bring.
> This was the Hunting of the Cheviot,
> God send us all good ending."

And then she fell silent, ceased to look at Dorothy, gave a slight nod and a sway of one hand toward the lute-girl; who understood her without need for words and commenced at once to play a dancing-tune, a Castilian tune, high-stomached and tragic. Always the same ancient saraband craved by Nancy of the Sarabands, whenever her thoughts were uneasy.

It was obvious to Dorothy that no more 'advice' would be given to her that day. She had not even had an opportunity to state her problem. But this was the way it had been with Nancy for most of the past year. She had become a sort of oracle: sometimes you could un-ravel her riddles, sometimes not. She always seemed to know far more about you than you could rationally expect her to know. She was indeed three-parts of a witch: and all the 'Birdcage' was well aware of it.

It went without saying, a benevolent witch, more of a fairy-lady in truth: but there were some very odd stories. A careless maid had once walked into her room without knocking at a time when she was not available to visitors, and had seen her naked as a needle, in front of her mirror, leaning on her cane, peering at the reflection of her withered and sagging body. But the image in the mirror was a radiant young girl "with breasts like cherries and all that golden hair right down to the backs of her knees." The maid had had the sense, so it was said, immediately to put up her hand in front of her eyes: she counted twelve and took it away again, and there was Nancy snoring in bed, in her night-gown and shawls, a silk drapery hung over the looking-glass, and no indication that she had not been asleep for hours.

So these riddles, today's riddles, riddles made on purpose for Dorothy: how to read them? *Bales* in the song meant 'injuries', to be abated by Jesu Christ (but if Jesu Christ was the Christ of Humpty Dumpty, broken up, irreparable, it followed He could abate nothing). *Bales* must also mean *John* Bale, injurious John, ir-repairable John. But why, unless the riddle identified the man with the cause? For were not Dorothy's problems the entire problem of the new-guise cause? Why did not the song point to Wentworth, her original new-guise lover? Or to Conrad? Or even to Rotraut, who had once bloodied Angelina's nose in defence of Boleyn against More?

Surely it must be thus: Nancy saw John Bale as more crucial than all of them, God knew why. Saw him as a potential injury that could not be mended; unless by his *own* Christ-Jesu, scriptural, new-guise, undreamed-of by the long-dead maker of the *Chevy Chase* song-ballad: in which case, he *could* be mended, could even be the reverse of *Bale. Bliss* . . . ?

Nancy had sung 'bramble-bush' where for certain the poem had 'bracken-bush'. Whatever rumours of Bale in the 'Birdcage' might have filtered through to the old woman, surely quite impossible any bramble-bush could have been part of the tale?

Nancy had said of a man in the song (a man lurching out of brambles), "behold he was in charge."

If indeed she meant Bale, then God help! What warning! And yet such a sweetness about the way she'd said those words, Dorothy must believe she'd intended them for *hope*. When Nancy gave *warnings* she was as grim as a portcullis.

Riddles.

*

Her father, on his death-bed, she remembered, had talked in riddles. All his parish-curate dogmatism seemed to have flown away from him with the ebbing of his strength, the onset of the griping pains that first took all use of his stomach and finally of his life.

She pictured to herself the smelly little lodging they lived in, the attic-storey above a cookshop, in a narrow passage that led crookedly from the Cambridge market-place, round the back of St Michael's church, and so across the main street down through a warren of scholars' hostels and monastic outbuildings towards the river. Drunken students were quarrelling in the lane, and the reek of black-pudding came up through the floorboards. The walls of the room were unpainted dung-plaster, broken patches here and there showing the wattles behind. A rudimentary crucifix the only orna-ment, and at the bed's head a blue canvas cloth daubed with an outline of a Virgin-and-Child in white.

She was eleven years old, overgrown and gawky. She looked after
her father all by herself, except sometimes the squalid woman who
swilled-down the tables in the cookshop would come with a bowl of
soup, or an offer to boil some laundry in her copper.

Dorothy's mother had left five years before, and the old man had
been ailing ever since. Now his superior, Parson Eustace of St Benet's,
had been in, brisk and craftsman-like, to give him the Last Rites,
bullying as usual: and had then gone, saying to her off-handed, "If
you need me again, you know the vicarage . . ." He always pretended
that Dorothy was some sort of servant-girl. To recognise his Curate's
daughter would imply altogether too much.

Her father seemed to be sleeping, so she took down one of his books
and tried to practise her reading. It was his English book (the other
three were Latin, ecclesiastical). It had some saints' legends, and a bit
of *The Canterbury Tales*; a few pages of ballads, not all of them
complete, and enough of Malory's *Arthur* to make her want to know
how it had begun and what happened at the end. Lancelot and
Guenever were in love and had caused a dreadful war, and then the
ragged pages fell away into a vortex of battles and mutual hatred. It
was not a proper volume at all, of course; the bookseller in St
Edward's Passage had had a fire in his shop, had salvaged these
portions of print, bound them together, and offered them to the
Curate for a very small sum. He had bought them for Dorothy, and
had done his poor best to improvise the missing parts by memory or
invention.

She was puzzling over a blurred woodcut of the Wife of Bath,
wondering for the hundredth time how she could travel on an English
road if her horse was really so much taller than the trees through which
she passed, when her father stirred and began to speak. A low croak
from the bed: she could barely distinguish the words.

"I was just now talking to your mother. Not her fault she went to
Bletchley – she craved me tell you – I was talking to her. She came in.
I'm not sure but she was in the bed. Not still here, is she?" His mind
was no longer in balance.

"No sir, nobody's here. Sir Eustace an hour ago, you told him your
confession." She always called her father 'sir'. He loved her very
much, but he knew he was not allowed her; so he kept her, and made
her keep, at a little distance, in case he remembered how truly much he
loved, and forgot to be penitent.

"Sir Eustace? Confession? No I didn't. I told it to your mother, she being in Bletchley. She had to go there, you see, because it is so fair a golden city, all y-builded upon an hill: there are golden vanes a-top of the steeples that King Arthur put there in olden time. Not at all like unto this flat Cambridge. She had such need for the joys of Bletchley. How could I withhold them from her? And now she hath told me wondrous things.

"As, for an instance, when there are three within a garden, and two are driven out, she that remaineth hath the apple-tree all to herself . . . And to whom she giveth the fruit thereof, that one shall be angel or devil, because there is none else to share her Paradise, angels and devils made it atween them, who can say which is which? Do not Michael and Lucifer have exact the same appearance, two soldiers in the late roses-war, one for York, one for Lancaster . . . ?

"And where was God when they made the garden? Aloft, aloft, dear little Dorothy, awaiting the cool of the day, that He might walk among the rose-briars and take His pleasure. His mortal friends have been driven out in their breeches of green leaves, so He hath no-one any more to walk with, save only the maid with the apples. She is not the one He made from a rib-bone, that one has been driven to Bletchley: no, this is another, she was there before He was, against all hazard her fruit is good . . .

"What do you read? *Are* you reading? What? I cannot hear you."

"It is the Wife of Bath, engraven, sir."

"Ah yes, upon the Pilgrims' Road. We are all upon that road. You sit and you know not that you walk. I lie here bed-rid, and I *do* know. You shall discover. Your mother was the Wife of Bath, gap-toothed and laughing always. Her legs were very long, almost longer than the horse's. I cannot see the picture now, but I hold it behind mine eyes. If she stretched them from the stirrup, they caught in the tops of thorn-trees, alas how sore her feet were wounded. Natheless, she travelled that road."

And so, after his last confession, his orthodox clerical mind drifted uncatchably out of balance, and away he went – where?

Three days later, the cookshop proprietor, not knowing what else to do with her – he had no need of an extra servant, and St Benet's priest had shown no interest – sold her to Lightfoot of Ely for three shillings and fourpence.

*

Dorothy said nothing to Nancy, but bent over and kissed her softly on one cheek, a kiss of respect and gratitude: and so back to her own room. Here she pondered: concealed messages, from Nancy's song, from Bale's sermon at Paul's Cross, were they in truth supplied to her, as she thought, or was her fantasy so arrogant that she created them out of nothing and made herself believe them? Perhaps the Nun of Kent had been on the cliff's-edge of madness? God, but it had been great cruelty to hang her . . . She must set herself to work and forbid all these antic dreams. Forbid them, forbid.

*

She supposed that her baby would be born in early October. By July, as she told Rotraut, it was "dancing Herodias' Daughter" in her womb: should it be a boy she would call him John – head-on-a-dish came to mind, which some would have thought an unlucky premonition. But when she had danced for John Baptist's head at Diss, another John had seen her, approved her as a *vision of loveliness*, and saved her from the constables. At all events, she thoroughly refused to admit that any *Thomas* had a right to name her child.

Nelly gave her to understand that John would indeed be a very good name . . . and then, to her relief (but also to her disappointment), Nelly ceased to sit in her room. Perhaps this was because Dorothy had so firmly assured her that revenge was well under way, and of course in that room she must have seen and heard the preparations.

Thomas Wentworth, about this time, paid a visit, unaccompanied. His first for several months. He had been travelling (a genuine journey for political reasons). He was both lordly and diffident. He had not known she was pregnant. As soon as he saw her shape he was about to say something, but she turned upon him such a frozen face that he stammered and fell silent. She said, "No, don't go. I am performing tonight, maybe for a week or two longer, then I finish for this season. You should stay for the show, there are new songs. No new dances: but I am thinking of some. Also I have been thinking of making masques, for the New-Guise troupe, in addition to our straightforward minstrelcraft."

There had been spring and summer engagements for the troupe, in houses where people knew what to expect and had shown themselves ready to applaud it. Conrad had been highly satisfied. So far, no difficulties with legal authorities, church or crown (if indeed, these days, one could discern a difference). But the masques were a harder matter, she needed a chorus of young people, and had not been able to recruit them conveniently. She explained the problems to Wentworth: between them, they reached solutions.

"I think, though, my lord –" (her tone to him was fully formal) – "it should wait until next year. Unless, by Christmas, it will be possible for me to return to an active work, and gather together something for the feast, perhaps at Nettlestead?"

He winced. "Nettlestead . . . Not this year. Not practicable at Nettlestead this year." Of course not. Lady Wentworth was with child, too, which was well known: to be born, as was well-known, toward November. He did not mention this, nor did she, nor did either of them mention child-birth at all. But he did start to say – "Oh Dorothy, do you not understand that I am –".

Interrupting him, a Cecilia-voice: "Very well, you say 'not practicable'. Perhaps the Earl of Oxford's place?"

He chewed his lip, and fell-in, awkwardly enough, with her line of talk: yes, he agreed, milord of Oxford, he would write to him, or better still, speak to him personally. Letters might go astray, and could breed *misunderstanding*, if read by the *wrong people* . . . "I should tell you, Dorothy, these affairs are becoming far less simple than they seemed: ramifications unpredictable, elaborations of the queerest consequence; walk anywhere, and you trip . . .

"Consider, for example, the Irish interventions."

She had heard nothing about Ireland, and was not very interested. All she knew of the place was the poor impression given her by a pathetic row that had blown up one night between two of her gentlemen. A captain-of-horse, with a very curious accent, had been addressed as 'Paddy-Teague' by a young sprig from the Inns of Court.

This was evidently an insult, he responded with a sharp one-two, kick-in-the-gut and fist-to-the-jaw: she called up bullies to get rid of the pair of them. But before he was expelled, the soldier had time to expostulate that he was as English as any man present, God-damn-their-souls, only that his father, being born in Northampton, was after following the colours to Limerick against the King's Irish Rebels, and why should he not? 'twas his duty: and if he himself was born in Limerick and reared there, sure-to-God he wasn't going to take from any blagyaird of a Londonman a word the likes of *Paddy-Teague*, when he'd split the windpipe of a wild O'Cooney in Athlone castle-garth, so he had, for putting the name of *Sassenach* on him – and what kind of place was this anyway, where they con*fis*-cated a soldier's sword at behest of a clatther of screech-owls?

Despite her apathy toward the subject, Wentworth explained it at length.

A young nobleman, 'Silken Thomas' Fitzgerald, had raised armed rebellion in Dublin, because his father, Earl of Kildare – in prison in London – was rumoured to have been executed. Irish revolts were no novelty: but this one was bloodier than most. The Archbishop of Dublin had been murdered by the rebels.

Wentworth said the King had hoped for that prelate to introduce the new ecclesiastical legislation, little by little, into the colony, but now all was spoiled. "So much is unhandily troublesome, but susceptible of draconian cure. Now, for the elaboration . . ." Silken Thomas had agents in Europe, conferring with France and the Emperor: could one or both of them assist his insurrection? It seemed probable the Emperor might. Papal Excommunication of the King of England was rumoured: if it took place, an international crusade could theoretically be levied – and Irish rebels would include themselves in it.

Which meant the Butlers as well as the Fitzgeralds, the native Ersemen as well as the Butlers; and a Franco-German-Spanish-Italian army could set foot on the beaches of Cork –

Dorothy was impatient: "We couldn't have that, of course. But why should we? What's an excommunication, it should make any difference? I was told once I ought to be excommunicate on account of my trade (Rotraut and Ermentruda *were* – which is why they became Luthers): but, whatever about Germany, if I need a priest here, I can find one. And when did any of these kings last make a war, just because the Pope told him to? No: you invent bogies."

Wentworth was offended. He pointed out he was a man of diplomatic experience, much called-upon for advice in this area: all possibilities, however remote, must be contemplated by His Majesty's Council. He looked once again at Dorothy's jutting belly, opened his mouth, shut it, sighed, and concluded his visit by telling her that a masque at Easter would be better than Yule, and Oxford more disposed to be its host if given that much more time. Otherwise, far too many imponderables. He did not stay for her performance that night: nor did she see him again for a long while.

(x) *I Spy My Mark*

John Bale came to London from the north parts in December. On Christmas Eve he swept into the 'Birdcage', for the first time in that building letting himself be seen in his friar's habit and white mantle.

He found Dorothy on a stool at her fireside, suckling her little son, with Belle-Savage hanging napkins out to dry along the chimney-piece. He pulled off his mantle and swirled it onto the floor, a supernumerary hearth-rug. As he did so, he declaimed: "All in a moment, through two windows, I spy my mark, fly my arrow! I'd pluck the habit over my head as well, but before womankind it would not be seemly. So instead, I obliterate it thus."

He had dumped a canvas valise inside the door: now he dragged it open, and drew out of it a thick coat of yellow bordered with russet, an array of brass buttons down its front. He thrust his arms into it and fastened it incongruously over his robe. He tossed his white beret into a corner.

"Damosels, expectation!" he cried. "Where there was tonsure: the burgeoning locks of freedom – Samson yet shall live!" Some slight fuzz indeed, putting forth on his pate, although it looked as though he would be naturally more than half bald. Dorothy noticed he had retained one small shaven area in the middle of the back of his head: the size of a secular priest's tonsure. He laughed: "Hah! I've been naked-topped so long, the hairs have not learned how to grow. Cover them up," he said, "they are at present little more than a blemish. A furtive frightened whisper of liberation, it does not deserve audience." He found a flat red cap in his valise, and put it on at an outlandish tilt. It had a small feather in it, like the bonnet of an apprentice on Boxing Day. Heaven only knew what he thought he looked like, and Dorothy laughed and laughed. Belle-Savage joined in, and the baby began to crow. He turned toward the mirror, saw the effect, sat on his bum on the floor with a bounce, laughing and laughing too, until they all must stop for breath. Dorothy had never before heard him vent such honest merriment.

"Very well," she said, "we've laughed. Now tell me what it means."

"What d'you suppose it means, except that I am no longer friar?"

"But of course you are a friar. You took an unbreakable vow."

"So did you: and look what we have."

She had finished feeding the baby, and was holding him out for

Belle-Savage to take while she fastened up her bodice: but Bale got in first and gathered him into his arms. "Look what we have," he said. "But mark you, I don't ask how."

"Bugger-nothing to ask *about*, if you squeedge him tight as that, man!" Belle-Savage, very jealous, grabbed the child back and laid him on Bale's cloak to change his wet swaddlings. There were squalls and wails, which covered over Dorothy's confusion.

"To be frank with you, Barbara, I do know what I am not. What I *am* is less easy to encompass. If they say I am a friar, I deny it. They will contradict me, but they are ignorant. Cloister-vows are an imposition, in my case fraudulently got when I was not of age to comprehend 'em. I have blown 'em away – poof! My priest's vows, however: perhaps a different thing. There was episcopal ordination, and bishops have laid hands since the very first apostles, upon whom Our Lord laid *His* hands. In those days, no papacy pretended, Saint Peter was one among equals. He had a wife too: and he was bishop. I can justify these arguments with letter-of-text and footnote, I can write them at such length that we'd work our way through three popes' lifetimes before they were all collated by that beehive of canon-lawyers, *parasiti Vaticanenses*, and in the end rejected by them. For assuredly they would be, though Canterbury might tell a different tale. I've a tale about *him* – hah! But let it wait.

"We discuss Christianity: and I have not even asked. I have held him on my lap without even thinking of it: shameful. But *if* I am still priest, and despite my fool's raiment, I must put the question: is this innocent knave a Child-of-Christ?"

His jocularity had vanished, giving place to a grave kindness, quite new, Dorothy thought, from him to her – except once, at Diss, when he had said, had he not? – 'No harm', 'an active good', 'the angel to St Joseph upon the first Epiphany'. She replied, "Sir Cuthbert baptised him. Rotraut was god-mother.'

He frowned. There was something about Rotraut and Ermentruda he did not quite like. As well there might be. '*Contra naturam*': could he recognise its signs in women? "At least," in an undertone, "it was not your heathen woman." Belle-Savage could not have heard: but Dorothy was annoyed. "My maid is no heathen: and I asked her, but she refused."

"Presumptuous. Why?"

"She said she would not be responsible for anyone's Christianity in a land where all Christians were killing each other for Christ."

Belle-Savage did hear that, nodded her head, swore filthily.

"Conrad is the godfather," added Dorothy.

"Conrad? That's no good. I doubt if he believes in baptism. When I talked to him some time ago he was so deep into the Almain sectarians, heaven knows what he believes." He cleared his throat and looked sheepish. "If need be, I too will stand godfather: a reinforcement. D'you hear that, young –" He was addressing the baby, now in his cradle, quietly gurgling. "– young what?"

Dorothy tried to be matter-of-fact: "We called him John."

Bale flushed all over, and shifted his great head in a rapid sideways motion as though shaking the blood down again. "Ah . . .", he said, dropping his glance to between his knees. "Ah. John. Yes. The Forerunner, and also the Beloved Disciple. Thereby he will have two saints, to pray to if you pray to saints. That's what my mother told *me*. I do not pray to saints. My arrow is flown." He shifted his head some more. "Lord Wentworth at last compelled my understanding from the third *Book of Kings*: between two sides of opinion I stand at halt no longer, I am come down from Carmel Hill! He and I have argued greatly, but all is at last made known." This was very ambiguous. Dorothy had hoped that Wentworth would not be mentioned. And what did 'all' mean? Religious matters only, or . . . ? She successfully forbade herself to recollect the coastal fort.

"So there be no mistakes," he proceeded now very academic-like, ticking off his points on his fingers. "I am convinced beyond all backsliding of these following religious truths. First, the King is empowered (as God's consecrate chief English man) to administer the Church in England, whereas the Bishop of Rome has never been so empowered.

"Second, if all authority from Rome was at all time unauthorised, all doctrine derivative from such authority must therefore go by the board.

"Third!" – his voice rose, a leap of hoarse excitement out of all decorum with a normal social intercourse: "The unauthorised authority was never the mere error of fallible Man but *ab origino* Satanic! I say to you, woman, the entire Roman Papacy, the church-order it has produced, is unassailably *of the Devil*, always has been, always shall . . . !"

He did not pause to see the effect of his huge doctrine upon Dorothy (which was abrupt: *of the Devil* was far more than just tumbling Humpty Dumpty, king's-horses and king's-men were now jumping in great boots on his fragments), instead, he skidded his discourse into a widely expanding area of justification and illustration, commencing with the Roman emperors and the Council of Nicaea.

"*Tempore Constantini Imperatoris* – now mark: at that council, there was no Bishop of Rome even present, so little was his supremacy then suspected." But the council itself was on all hands deemed authoritative, had it not provided (to the lasting satisfaction of both Old Guise and New), the fulfilled Christian Creed? If authoritative, then the Holy Spirit must have been present at its deliberations. But the origin of the papacy could legitimately be traced to the council and to the emperor who had convened it. Bale inferred he would postpone consideration of the anomaly for a few minutes, it would be desirable for Dorothy first to understand the traditions of Christ available to God's English, before he proceeded to elucidate *imperial* misdoings, from which we in this island had a most providential means of dialectical escape.

She was, confusedly, glad to hear it. A wild thought had flashed through her brain that perhaps Bale was about to convert her to the enormities of Saracen Mahound, and she glanced sideways in some alarm toward Belle-Savage and the baby. Her son was surely properly christened, Bale had asked about that – oh God he did not mean that such a baptism was *of the Devil?* But then Bale had mentioned Wentworth, who (whatever else about him) had neither turned Turk nor grown into mad Anabaptism: and moreover Bale had sneered at the vagaries of Conrad. Maybe this new idea of a totally infernal Church was not quite as insane as it sounded. She had better listen and attempt to understand.

So she was told how in Britain, immediately after the Resurrection, and following the well-attested visit here of Joseph of Arimathea (Bale attested it, at scholarly length), a Christian practice had developed independent of what was later to evolve from Rome and eventually subsume the whole community of faith. It was based upon the existing spiritualities of the Druids, so spiritual indeed that they must have been vouchsafed a Prior Revelation, akin to that experienced by the prophets of old Israel. Hence, among other benefits, a native British monastic system from the earliest times, which did *not* exclude chaste wedlock for devotees of the religious life. "Not that such is relevant to monkery nowadays, which goeth all awry without remedy, after the precepts of Roman Benedict. No: history must ever move. We cannot return to the Druids. Nowadays we need, before all things, a schooled and practicable parish clergy!" – (and with wives: *sine qua non*).

Bale explained the sort of doctrines in which such a clergy ought to be schooled.

"Here at last Lord Wentworth has brought me to a great clearness. I shall not weary you with detail –".

He went into growing detail, accumulating, from Wentworth's views, from Zwingli's, with side-blows at Luther, apologies towards Melanchthon, until he finally rejected Transubstantiate Eucharist, Purgatory, and Auricular Confession (which he had once, Dorothy remembered, described as having its uses), declared Faith to be greater than Works; and the Papacy ("*ab origino*") to be responsible for all such errors by its deliberate malicious policy, making priests instead of ministers, and masters out of ordinate servants. She sat still and listened. His theology went largely beyond her: but the mind that had arrived at the theology was not beyond her, not quite, she might even, one of these days, begin to understand it. Never in all her life so great a puzzle as this man. She tried (as she had often tried) to think of him twenty-six years ago, a violated child. Not easy to imagine: but she could do it. His lips would have pressed in, just so, as they did now: obstinate, and desperate anxious.

"How did I reach these things – I mean how, prior to Wentworth's final correlation of them into my mind – did I attain that state wherefrom talk with him could prove so crucial? Bear in mind, I was friar, not monk."

He pointed out how the friars had originally been established to *reform* the existing order; nay, if need be, to overturn it. In Wycliffe's day a great part of the enlightened Lollardry had come from the friars. Bale had discovered, at university, some small survival of this tradition among even the corrupted Carmelites; and thereupon he had built to attain his own clearness.

He had, he said, thought for a long time that the Church would reform itself, that the Almain-Dutchmen (although most honest) were nonetheless erroneous, in that heedlessly they split the good unity of Christendom. Now at last he comprehended that his timorous opinion had been utterly untenable.

Wentworth had been easing him, nay thrusting him, in this direction for many years: but in the upshot (Bale conceded) it was not quite Wentworth but a quasi-miraculous Revelatory Personal Experience that had fixed his final mind – yet with vigour he affirmed the Mighty

Insight could never have come had Wentworth not prepared the ground for it. "His diligence, his analytical powers, his noble patience, his warmth and sympathy man-to-man . . . Ah! and *then* – it was as though an eagle had descended upon me and snatched me suddenly skyward, my little ankles are still kicking in the empty air!"

She must laugh: his great feet, attached to great knobbed ankles, were set firmly upon her floor like the bases of monument-columns.

"No, I am not ridiculous. Dazed, yes, but not absurd." She straightened her face.

The Insight had laid hold on him as he wrestled in his study with the arguments of *King John*. Needing a break from the work, he had turned to another play, Kirchmayer's *Pammachius* that Conrad had sent him. For the first time Bale read it with care. To begin with, he could not accept the German author's implicit assumption that Nicaea was a Satanic council. Yet surely there had been something very wrong with that colloquy . . . ? It *had* allowed the emperors a power within the Church, which they misused, almost immediately, to set up the popes in Rome. "Sheer laziness, in point of fact, they thought they were saving themselves great trouble from doctrinal discordance." But if the Holy Spirit had been present in the Council, this imprudent development could not have developed, could it?

"So are we to conclude that the Holy Spirit was *not* then present, and all good consequence of the Council must needs have been accidental? Or worse, that there were *no* good consequence, but only illusion thereof?

"Unendurable, incredible, a faith-shaking damnable logic – *unless* . . .

"*Unless* Christ Himself had known it would be so, and had given His Church forewarning . . . ?"

So why had not the Church been forewarned? Obviously, because the significant Word was made dark, and deliberately, to tempt Satan to the surface, and thus cause him and his work in the end to be recognised and ruined (no matter how many years hence). Such a forewarning must be infallible, so therefore it was written down in some book of the Canonical Scripture: and what darker book than John's *Apocalypse*?

As soon as he understood this, with his own play and Kirchmayer's still open on his desk, Bale had hunted Saint John's messages through chapter after chapter; he read and he read, and he prayed as he read – he was hours at it, he told Dorothy, the full length of a stormy night – groaning and declaiming, keeping all the house awake in his Doncaster lodging (for the friars in that town had by now refused him access to their premises).

Dorothy imagined him: she could not possibly laugh again, she bit blood from her lip trying not to.

"It was as though I myself stood helpless upon the Isle of Patmos, heard the Trumpets, saw the Horsemen, watched the Breaking of the terrible Seals – until at last, at the very last – lo! but mine eyes were opened.

"I was turning the pages yet again and again, putting together all congruences of the vision; and as I crouched there I heard a voice, '*Habet!*' it said, as though the very creak of the book's binding spoke to me: '*Habet*,' 'he's got it,' and so I had."

In a sort of ecstasy he outlined (or rather, sang) his discovery. Extremely complex and mystical argument, cabbalistically justified, it turned upon the appalling deduction that the seventh head of the Great Beast was nothing other than the Papal Throne.

"Our Lord Jesus Christ, through John Son of Thunder, sings in my mouth; and dances, from this moment, in the pen between my fingers!"

Dorothy was really interested. Also ashamed, that her interest should be proving so inexpressibly minstrel-foolish: she did her best to concentrate upon the grimness of the portentous heads and of the scarlet Whore that rode behind them, but she could not restrain herself from trivial speculation – when Rotraut and Ermentruda placed this same Whore on a rock in the Rhine, had they too been seized by an eagle? They *must* have been, look at Germany, what better place in Christendom for the seventh head to receive its death-throes, of course the poor Whore lived there. Great pity, though, that Dorothy never heard her two friends at it, in their frenzies all night like Bale at Doncaster: perhaps these mystical things came easier to women . . .?

No! – she must forget this, she had to *listen* to him for heaven's sake – already he had moved to a new topic, his rant abated, each point once again ticked off briskly on his fingers.

"But now; as to my present state, its tangled legalities.

"It is clear – I am mortal sure of it – that government shortly will abolish all monks, nuns, friars, collegiate canons, in the realm." He showed her how King and counsellors would assume into their power every general good of the monasteries – hospitality, care of the sick, alms-giving, education, preservation of priceless books – and devote them to the general good of the entire Christian nation! A project of great public beneficence, long overdue, calculated to make England the envy of the enlightened world – and speedily to be advanced by the imminent abandonment of the cheating pretensions of Purgatory.

"What possible use will religious houses have, once prayers are no longer needed for the souls of dead patrons? Lord Wentworth, for example, hereditary lay-patron of the Ipswich grey-friars, will immediately convert the assets into a stipend-fund for new clergymen – preachers of reform in his villages, dwellers with their families among the families of his estates. Admirable!"

But all this, as yet, was by no means achieved.

"We cannot be rid of every monk-house in half-an-hour. Nor can we be sure that everyone in Parliament will be ready to repudiate Purgatory – certainly not every cleric – nay conceivably not even the King . . ."

As he said 'King' he remembered what must have slipped his mind in the concentration of his reasoning: Belle-Savage was still in the room. She was rocking John's cradle, crooning in her African language. Dorothy thought that Christian origins would not enthral her: but it was unwise to talk about kings in quite such an open manner, the most trustworthy friends could be tortured to talk. She saw Bale's hesitation, and whispered: "Into Rotraut's room. She is my Lutheran and more incriminate than either you or I: we shall be safe with her."

*

Rotraut was in bed, very slubbered with half-finished sleep. Ermentruda was not there. Bale refused *aquavitae*, as did Dorothy (she thought it would not be the best ingredient for her breast-milk), but some Rhine-wine was pointed out to them. Bale continued his explanation. Rotraut, having opened her eyes extremely wide at his appearance, pulled herself up on her messy pillows and listened attentively.

"I say, it is not everyone in this land who rejects Purgatory: and therefore some other reason for dissolution of monasteries will have to be adduced for public acceptance. In fact, a pair of reasons, both of them excellent.

"One: the monks are too rich, embezzling the people's wealth and misusing it. Accumulated lands and moneys cannot serve to advance the alleged function of purgatory-prayer, even to those who accept its validity.

"Two: they are morally corrupt. And from experience, do I not know it!

"But to establish these reasons there has to be open accounting made, a just king cannot condemn at large upon unproven individual assertions: so examination must be made into monkish lives, commissioners must be sent out. Don't you see, it will take years. In the meantime, I am a vow-breaker, a runaway, a renegade, in danger of the bishops' courts: I cannot proclaim my liberty to all-and-sundry as I have shown it to you. I cannot call myself a secular clergyman and go asking for a benefice. I cannot look for a place in a Cambridge college, the monks are still all-pervasive there. I have no other choice but to wait for events in patience, and sullenly confine myself to the writing and presentation of plays. In poverty, confine myself; and also perhaps in fear and peril . . . But this ridiculous buttercup coat – from our acting-company wardrobe – is not so daft, what d'you think? Under Wentworth's protection, I might even find a living as an honest stage-play craftsman. Howbeit . . . howbeit . . . my fellow-players will still think of me as a friar.

"They will watch me from sideways eyes, to espy every moment of my life: wondering, what does he do, this man that was under vow? Does he rut himself wholesale through the bawdy-houses of the land, or will he now keep as chaste as he once swore to be, being made eunuch by so many years of friary-house enforcement? I shall be as it were continuously, unrelievedly, alone on the actors' platform, with only my rehearsed part to keep me company, my terrible stage-fright, my subterranean apprehension that there is nobody behind the booth-curtain to answer the cue when I give it them.

"Gracious lady –" he turned toward Rotraut, and bowed as he spoke to her: "You are my witness. As a free man and an English clergyman, I am asking Mrs Dorothy, will she have me as a husband? As the father of her son? I know she loves you, *Jungfrau* Rotraut. I am asking you to let her go – if she is willing – into a man's love no deeper than yours, but perhaps in these fearful days, a little more efficacious, more protective. I am asking."

*

He crossed his hands on his chest, bowed again, to both of them, and sat down slowly, palms on knees, waiting stolidly for an answer. He remembered his new hat, and whipped it off, a comical clumsy afterthought.

Dorothy had sometimes speculated that some man might one day ask for her in marriage: she never guessed the question would be made through a third party in her presence. Maybe she should have had the aquavit: she would certainly have some Rhine-wine; and she poured herself a glass, shaking not a little, wondering if she was about to giggle. Like a fool, she poured another glass, and offered it to Bale. He looked at her without moving, an unreadable blank stare, and his hands remained on his breast. In an attempt to preserve normality, no doubt, Rotraut put out *her* hand.

"*Rheinwein, Liebchen, ja ja, ganz gut um Gottes Willen, trinken wir schnell – pros't.*"

"*Prosit!*" gobbled Dorothy, and the two women looked wildly at one another as they drank. Rotraut had to sit up to take the glass: then she suddenly felt her negligent array might be compromising the situation. She slid quickly down into the bedclothes, spilling some of the wine. She lay huddled there, only eyes and nose visible, and one bare arm holding the glass. In a strange little voice, half-muffled by the sheets, she said: "*Ach, Liebchen* Dorothea, what have you been telling him about myself and yourself? Why need he ask *me*? *Sakrament*, you are not 'Truda!"

It was clearly hopeless now to pretend she was not undressed: she jerked herself up again, spilling the glass again, forceful and direct. "Of course, if you will marry him, how can I forbid it? 'Birdcage' women make many marriages; despised yet admired, then all-at-once we are honoured wives, born again quite new into *Buergerhaus und Schloss* – perhaps not *Schloss*, but oftentimes *Buergerhaus*, sometimes, it has been known. But today, with this *Mensch*, now? 'Protection', does he imply? He will give it? How can he? *Lieber Gott*, is he not runaway? Himself in danger? Has he not said? *Ach* Longlegs, you would be mad to take him. *Doktor* Martin's new *Frau* Luther, she had been nun, which was much worse danger, but think, *Kindchen*, think, they had already their protection, Prince of Saxony was defending them, so much a greater man than any Wentworth: I tell you, less than the King is *no* protection in this England. Now you to tell me: what do you think the King will think?"

They looked at Bale. He was pressing his lips in, sucking them, gnawing them between his teeth. He took his time, and they waited for him. Speaking low down in his throat: "Without doubt, if the

King knew, he would take it very hard. I daresay he would first ask, 'Who is this little friar, who assumes it upon himself to predict and perhaps compel our royal policy toward all friars?' Which is why, of course, he must *not* know."

"God's Christ," Dorothy burst out, "You mean to keep it secret? She's quite right, I *would* be mad, and you twice as mad as me!"

"No," said Bale, "No. Look at it another way. If you and I were to lodge together, without marriage, you'd be my breech-burner, none would condemn *you*, or not much: they would say it was your trade; singing-woman, what else do such wenches do? And condemning *me* they would only say, part-and-parcel of his defection from friary-vows, it does not make it worse, maybe even mitigates, the poor man could not conquer his lust. Which would be convenient if lust was what concerned us."

"And lust does not concern you?" Rotraut snorted a broken laugh into her wine.

Bale took her sarcasm quite seriously: "No, I do not believe so. If Mrs Dorothy accepted me, I *know* it would not be for lust. It would be, as I have said, because she has a child and no father for it: *that* is where the protection is needed, and even if we were in danger, we could both of us provide for her son's safety, he would become twice as safe, whatever our own trouble. As for myself: to leave the order is nothing, mere delinquency, and many do it. The fat ballad-man from Doncaster was once a Franciscan, I think, and who cares? Such unthinking runaways are like Friar Tuck in Sherwood, they disappear among the people: unless perhaps one day some bishop decides to make examples of them, and sends his summoner. Therefore if Bale throws away his discredited cowl, he must do it as Bale, Doctor of Divinity, Prior, a man who has thought it right and good to do, according to his principles, his dignity, his new-attained theology: Christian marriage for Bale is the *sine-qua-non* by which he finds liberty outside the corrupted cloister. Lust is not relevant. I would impose no right of ownership over my wife's body: would live virgin, if she wished it. Or not, if she decided othergates."

He turned directly to Dorothy: "For you, peace of mind in regard to the child's upbringing. For me, peace of conscience, in that I would live as I should always have lived; a man with a church-fast woman, between him and her their own privacy, to mingle flesh if it seemeth good to them, but all that to depend upon whatever growth-of-love God's liturgy can stimulate. I believe it is equal benefit, one pound against sixteen ounces. We have had a strange history together, over several years, it has hurt us both: let us sanctify it? What do you say?"

She could at first say nothing, how could she? The whole proposition was ridiculous. But Rotraut had *her* view: "Child's upbringing? In the 'Birdcage' is all the protection your sweet babe shall need. From *all* of us, we are your friends. Think of it, and tell him: no."

Dorothy thought of all Bale's logic, only a few minutes since, in her own room: Wycliffe, Zwingli, Luther, Druids, Nicaean Council, and above all, *Apocalypse*, oh so logical – "No logic at all. Godsake, Mr Bale, and you from Jesus College: however could you justify such an argument to your professor? I'll give it you in short: to prove your principles you must take a wife, or the muck-minded people will sneer and accuse you of unconquered lust. *But*, if you do, the King will rage. So therefore you must hide your principles at the same time that you prove 'em, to let the King think your lust is all. Oh what is the point of being known as high-principled Bale, if no-one must know it? Give me more Rhenish, and take some yourself, it might possibly clear your brain."

"Dear Haut-jambée, *Dorothy* –! I never said that *no-one* must know it. I confound your own argument, thus: Lord God, He will know it. His minister, who will clasp our hands before the Lord God's supper-table, he too will know. For the season, that will be sufficient. Because you and I will also know; our consciences will be clear, even though we must live virtuous under pretence of living otherwise, as did the first Christians when Rome's emperors made persecution. It is not an unprecedented subterfuge. And be assured, the time will come when we will show ourselves true-wedded to all the wondering world, and son John will be then no bastard. I repeat, son John: his future life, his pride in his parents. I am his father."

At that point he did take wine, as though to toast his suppositional paternity. He was a boor and a bore, she had long ago decided so. But tears were in his eyes when he spoke of 'son John'. And inside Bale's unshapely frame, with its tormenting finger-post, its twisted longings that confused brain with groin and prayer with poetry, there was a deep heart of *love* and she was only now beginning to see how deep. Her own tears began to prickle: was it the Rhenish, or was it just sorrow for Bale, that he made himself such a monkey in public?

Then in behind her thoughts came a sour little catchpoll of unworthy suggestion, feeling her collar when she least expected it, as constables always do. Had Wentworth put Bale up to it? To conceal from his noble self his fatherhood of son John, as she concealed it from *herself*? If so, it was infamous. But it had to be examined.

"Did Lord Wentworth put you up to this?"

He was astonished, and – she thought – unaffectedly so. "Lord Wentworth? Why ever should he?"

If he did not know, she could not tell him. Perhaps indeed he did not know.

"Lord Wentworth has said nothing to me," he said. "Not about you, that is. He does agree that religion of the New Guise shall encourage a married clergy: but we spoke about it in general terms, never specific: never into the privacy of me and you, or of anyone else. I do not even know that he knows about your child. Did you tell him?"

"I did not. But when you say you are my baby's father, do you never wonder who his blood-father in truth might be?"

"Oh, Dorothy, of course I wondered. You told me once you made a vow, and of course you did not keep it; practicality, not virtue, was it not? So I concluded that you found it practical to take a man. You didn't take me. But whomever you did take had no further purpose than the deed: it could have been anyone, your trade is promiscuous, I do not, and will not, enquire. All I say of it, is this: your love-choice was *not* practical. Beyond the deed, there must be a purpose, and today I am offering one . . . I could have wished that the man had been me. But I do not hate him. He was one that takes life more lightly than I can: happier, surely. Let him roam."

She said to herself, "He must suspect Wentworth. Did he not hover that night upon the fringe of the Nettlestead maze? He suspects: he keeps his counsel. I know: I keep my counsel. Let's be private, it's much better."

So she shrugged herself out of the grasp of the catchpoll. But still she had not answered Bale. Now she made up her mind. As he had proposed, not to her, but to Rotraut, so through Rotraut should the answer be passed . . . oh: he knew that she and Rotraut were – that they had been – that they had *done*. How *could* he know? And why did he take it so calmly?

He so abhorred it when men went with men, did he think women's vices more pardonable? Or did he perhaps not realise that, by his standards, it *was* vice? Did he assume that there was no carnality, just words of excessive sentiment? Not possible: he had heard confessions, all sorts of them, for years. Maybe it secretly pleased him to meditate upon two women joined hotly in one bed. But no, not possible either:

such pleasure would force him forward to unbridled denunciation. In all likelihood, he believed that all women were so insatiably lustful, it made little final difference what they did. If God was to pardon them, it would be simply for being Eve's daughters, their strange nature such that there was nothing *contra naturam*. He lived for men, and among men: he strove almost in vain to find women fellow-humans. And *that* was why he needed this marriage. She, Dorothy, was to be his landfall on a brand-new Columbus-island, and she did not like the idea, not one little bit.

She would not tell him so. Find a reason to save both faces: it would be a true reason, too.

"Very well, Rotey, I am telling the gentleman: no. For this very good reason. I cannot live with anyone, whatever his principles, if he does not make it clear to me: which is he, priest or poet? I think Dr Bale is still undecided. But *I* am aware that he is both, and it won't do . . . Sir, you'll rend yourself in pieces, to establish which part to learn first, and which is the chief part in the play. And all those in the house, if you are able to find a house to stage your dangerous interlude, all those will be rent likewise."

She said this very finally: and he saw that it was so. Rotraut, now finished with her wine and on to the aquavit, leaned forward from the bed, pulled Bale by the wrist, caught his face down to hers, and kissed him. He averted his eyes from her breasts and so out of the room heavily. Dorothy ran after him, to steer him into her own door: she did not want him to leave her in such gloom. Good God, was she getting to *like* him?

He made a muddle of picking up his friar's cowled cloak. He said, in a kind of madness: "I can't wear *this!* And yet how to cover my rome-rag raiment below my belt? How?"

So she found him, from her wardrobe-alcove, an old pair of swaggery soldier's breeches, asymmetrical in the German style, which Ermentruda had lent her for a dance she used to do. He allowed himself to be put to change in the back corridor, and came out again in the breeches, the yellow coat and hat, with his Carmelite habit over his arm. Belle-Savage clapped her hands: and lodged the baby into his grasp for a kiss. (Dorothy had prompted her, while Bale was behind the door.) He was still very sad. But he took Dorothy's hand, and held it for an instant to his thick wet lips, as wet as a beast's muzzle. Then he left.

★

Next day, Christmas Day, Ermentruda and Rotraut played an engagement at the Earl of Oxford's and returned in the evening to the 'Birdcage' to make their own feast with Dorothy and son John. The three women got riotous drunk, Dorothy explaining, "Just this once, it won't kill the baby, and I *was* at Midnight Mass." Ermentruda told a story she had recently heard. It concerned the Archbishop of Canterbury. Perhaps the same story that Bale was about to tell the previous day. It appeared that Thomas Cranmer, a year or two back, on the King's business in Germany, had married a second wife, although he was a priest, although he was only a priest because his first wife had died so young. Then he heard he was to be Archbishop. And he dared not admit to her existence. So what did he do with her? Leave her in Germany?

"How could he? He must ride her every night, he could not stop, all his fury of the New Guise gone into his man-stones; *hoppla, schoene* Longlegs, *hoppla!* I think, with all things new, we make such trouble for our cunny-holes – I wonder, did we know what we did, when we told the priests, 'no more of your orders!'? See the end of this *Maerchen*, then? He put her into a trunk with holes bored in the lid, and carried her home behind him, in the luggage-boot of his carriage, in the hold of the Hamburg ship! And now she lives secret in his Lambeth here, and goes into the trunk again every time that one knocks upon his door . . . ! Dorothea, you must have *Lieder* made of it, and sing them broadly – *ach*, not to mock good Cranmer, but the laws that oppress him, *natuerlich . . . ! Natuerlich.*"

They all three thanked their intoxicated stars they were not wedded to irregular pastors.

"With *unser* Luther, a great trouble," said Rotraut, "He chose his virgin nun – and he a virgin monk? So how could they know what to do? And who would tell them?"

(xi) *The End Of The 'Birdcage'*

For another half-year Dorothy remained at the 'Birdcage'. Eight years now since the King first decided that he would slough his old wife like a snake-skin, and public apprehension grew continually with the growth of those years: where would it end? 'Worse was it never': trials, gaolings, disgracings, executions, informations laid, and no apparent conclusion to be looked for. Bale sent to Dorothy some sheets of a poem with the general catch-phrase for a refrain, and a covering note to say he thought it was an old one of Skelton's: would she care to use it in her repertory? She did, with topical additions; and often rolled it over on her tongue when ever more gruesome news came into the house with the evening's gentlemen.

> To thee, Lord, I make my moan,
> For thou mayst help us every one:
> Alas, the people is so woe-begone,
> Worse was it never!
>
> We have exiled verity.
> God is neither dead nor sick;
> He *may* amend all yet . . .

But –

> After better I hope ever,
> For worse was it never.

And yet many did not seem to fear. They exulted, either in their strength for the Old Guise, or their fervour for the New. Dorothy could not believe that any of this exultation was free of a hidden trembling. Hers was not, even when she stiffened herself with thought of Nelly: trembling Wentworth kept himself clear of all save foreign affairs, and the Irish complication; which must have seemed safer to him. He never came to the 'Birdcage' now: although some of his quiet associates did, still using her room once a fortnight or so, which was not very convenient, now she had the baby there. But she had promised and she kept to the arrangement.

She rarely saw Bale. He had accepted her decision: and that was that. He sent her little presents for John, a woollen ball for him to throw out of his cradle, or a rattle, or a shapeless rag-doll. Also a German wood-block alphabet, each letter of devotional significance, $A = Antichristus$ (the Pope), $B = Boanerges$ (Saints James and John, arms full of translated Scripture), $C = Christus$ $Redivivus$ (patting Luther on the head), etcetera – absurdly inappropriate for a child of four months. He sent back the military breeches, but too late. Ermentruda found out that Dorothy had let him wear them and took very great offence. This was unfortunate: not being on speaking-terms with Ermentruda meant an embarrassment with Rotraut too, and Dorothy had not so many friends now in the 'Birdcage' that she could afford to lose them. The New-Guise minstrel-troupe had caused unpleasant rumours in the unquiet times, and many of the women avoided her.

But there were those who helped her rear the baby, and the older children of the house were diligent and kind-hearted in looking after him.

Very soon she was back at her work: but here again she had quarrels. Not with Ermentruda, always highly professional, if cold and distant, but with Conrad, who was becoming quirky, authoritarian, sulking at every decision that was not his own.

In April old Nancy died. King Henry sent a grand court-gentleman to represent him at the funeral in St Mary Overy. Intimidated, the black-canons agreed to a full choral Requiem Mass. As she listened to the anthems, Dorothy could not help thinking about a poem-of-elegy for King Edward IV that Nancy had once chanted to her, with great sadness in her voice. She thought it would have fitted very well at the funeral, and would have been good for the court-gentleman to hear, had the canons had it in their service-book.

> *Miseremini mei*, ye that be my friends!
> This world hath conform-ed me, down-e to fall.
> How may I endure, when that everything ends?
> What cre-ature is born to be etern-al?
> Now there is now more but 'Pray for me all'.
> Thus say I, Edward, that late was your king,
> And twenty-two years ruled this imperi-al,
> Some unto pleasure, and some to no liking.

'Some to no liking'. In May King Henry's governance hanged and gutted the Charterhouse monks, in June it beheaded the Bishop of Rochester, in July Sir Thomas More.

In August it closed down the 'Birdcage'.

*

Not, on the surface, a very dreadful occasion: no sudden brutality of swearing and beating in a midnight raid, not at all a simulacrum of what happened at Diss six-and-a-half years earlier: but it was none the less calamitous.

Bale had broken his custom and paid Dorothy a private visit, two days before; and he told her it would happen. Or rather, he hinted: but he did not hint the exact date, so the warning was of small use to her or to the others when she passed it along. He had given the impression they would all be safe for another three months: perfectly honestly; he had not been told the full truth.

His informant was Secretary Cromwell, to whom he was now, he said, close. He implied that the Bishop of Winchester and Cromwell

were at odds about religious policy, that Cromwell thought a number
of Winchester's intrigues were commencing from his disreputable
Bankside properties (Dorothy had said not a word about Angelina,
but Bale seemed well aware of her), and Winchester thought Cromwell's agents were infiltrating far too freely in the general London
underworld. Add to which, the new celebrity of the New-Guise
minstrel-troupe had upset the regular Minstrels' Guild, and the
'Birdcage' had always been an eyesore to the Bankside bawds: two
quite powerful groups to come together against it. So two powerful
men, Secretary and Bishop, decided – in mutual suspicion – to come
together themselves. They would put an embargo on the premises:
and the public would be told that government was raising the moral
tone, licensed debauchery being an outworn symptom of corrupt
papal pretensions. But it would be done under form of law, and there
would be nothing too sudden.

But it was sudden. The women were all visited by a sheriff's officer
with a handful of writs. They must be off the ground by sunrise the
very next morning, or they would be adjudged in Contempt of Court.
He did not make it clear *which* court: and those smart enough to ask
him were bluntly referred to the papers he had issued. Latin, Law-
French, so crabbedly written that no-one could make sense of them.
But the officer had behind him a small squad of armed men with
the king's rose on their jackets, in the face of which all argument must
fail. A red-and-white rose, to symbolise national harmony after the
York-and-Lancaster wars.

So where did they all go, once their home was barred to them? Some
of them went as petitioners to the houses of their regular gentlemen,
hoping for protection, patronage, subsidies: and a few of them found
what they sought. Some of them went on the road, either alone or with
troupes. Some of them ended up in the brothel-houses nearby, from
which they had once been overjoyed to escape.

Angelina went to prison.

Dorothy did not know about Angelina until a while later. On the
morning of the eviction all the women were gathered in the main
courtyard and at the gate, in considerable tumult – weeping here and
there, but for the most part an angry tumult. The yeomen, anxious to
earn their last 'Birdcage' pence, before they too were absorbed into the
district and became simple bullies again, were carrying furniture and
ornaments and musical instruments from the rooms, creating to-do
about finding street-porters, handcarts, boats.

It was still dark, which made everything more difficult. Then, suddenly, through the crowd, came Bale.

He was angry and anxious: he sprang to gather Dorothy and her party together in a flurry of bother, demanding of her, "Where will you go? Where will you go?"

"With Rotraut and 'Truda, until –" (for Ermentruda, dreadful emergency had made immediate reconciliation: she was a woman of a fine loyalty).

"Until when? Where are *they* going? *Jungfrau*, where will you go?"

Rotraut answered distractedly, "With *unser* Longlegs, where else? We have sent to that fool Conrad but he has not yet come –"

"But where to?" snapped Dorothy back at her, "Where the hell to?" John, in Belle-Savage's arms, was roaring for the breast and this was no time to give it him.

Bale took control: "With me, with me, you cannot stop here, not at all, not safe at all, not to stop here – come!" He hustled, barked, worried at them like a sheepdog, hastening them out of the building: most of their baggage came after on a cart. As they pushed and scrambled toward the river-stage (Bale was in such inexplicable hurry), Dorothy turned her head and saw the sheriff's officer and his men invading the courtyard, a great many men, three times as many as on the previous day.

Bale had a pair of boats waiting: they were loaded precariously, and put out toward the north bank weighed down to the rowlocks. Once afloat, she asked him again, "Where?" He replied, "To my house. I have a house, or I rent most of a house, in the fields behind Convent Garden, it's very quiet, we'll land at Strand Lane; after that, it's not so far. We'll talk about everything later. I had no notion this would happen, not so soon, not like this."

*

His house proved to be a decrepit farm-cottage (the attached farm with its scatter of outbuildings was no longer in business) hard by a narrow thoroughfare, tall hedges almost meeting over a deep morass of trodden cow-dung: Drury Lane, straggling away from the town's end. An area of shanties and little hen-runs, with a doubtful population of old-fashioned rustics, vagabonds, beggars, impoverished squatters; and a decayed untenanted gentry-house behind high demesne walls.

The cottage was far from comfortable, but not intolerable, given the circumstances. Bale shared it with the original farmer, a very old man in his second childhood, who kept a leaky lean-to for himself, and sat outside on the doorstep all day in a stupor, looking at the mud in the yard. There was a rakish cur-dog to keep out strangers, and the first thing Bale did was to introduce him to Dorothy and the others. The creature's aspect was forbidding, nor was he reassured by Bale's nervous reassurances. Desirable to give his shreds-and-patches small aggressions a wide berth.

In the bare house-place they all sat down to a breakfast of last night's rabbit-stew, heated up over a fire of gathered sticks. Sea-coal was not often available here: the carters refused to bog their wheels in the lane. Bale said grace, ponderously, in Latin (Cambridge scholarship overwhelming his dislike of romish ritual). Short silence while they took their first mouthfuls.

Dorothy asked: "What will happen to the 'Birdcage'?"

"Oh, now that it is closed and morals preserved, some pimp will raise the money from a group of city aldermen, and fill it up with his whores. He'll have to wait a few months, I daresay: for the look of the thing. But government will not object, they will have it well within their own control, and Winchester and the black-canons can easily find some form of words to distance themselves from the lease."

Then he told them about Angelina. "She will have been taken quietly in the street after she left this morning. They did not want witnesses to the arrest. In particular, the Bishop of Winchester must not find out about it just yet . . . No no, you *cannot* visit her: and no-one will be told which gaol she is in. I know she is your colleague, even though you had broils, but things are far past any point where 'Birdcage' colleagues necessarily hold their fortunes in common, or need any longer compassionate one with the other. She has been active for the opposite party: if you make connection with her, you will be deemed to have two faces, her party to play against ours. Oh they'll let you in to that lock-up, but you'll never get out. They do not intend to bring her to public trial. She is there to give them names, of all of her friends: the Emperor's agents, in intrigue with the Princess Mary, she knows scores of names. If she don't give the names, they'll put names to her from their own list and keep her at it till she agrees she knows 'em, and signs papers to incriminate. I would think she won't refuse. In all likelihood, no need of the rack.

"Why could you not have told us about her months ago? You *must* have seen what she was up to?

"When she's given them what they require, they'll probably flog her and ship her to Spain: she'll have fulfilled her purpose. God, you're white in the face. Well you might be, all three of you. Let me tell you, only last night I had a most urgent warning: Winchester's men were to lift *you*, in exact the same way, but to his Clink, his diocesan gaol, for exact the same reason; only opposite, *vice versa*, you understand. In your case there would be heresy-charges to cover any illegal detention. Your maids would have been included." (Ermentruda and Rotraut had a young London girl with them, Sally.) "Why d'you think I was in such great haste? Had to get you all over the river, out of Winchester jurisdiction. I don't think the Bishop of London will be prepared to act for him, I don't think so: I hope not.

"It's a good thing I am friends with Cromwell. Did you know, by-the-by, he is taking the acting-company out of Wentworth's hands altogether? Wentworth bears himself far smaller than heretofore: it has been put to him, his doctrine is a little too extreme for the present exigencies of government. Too extreme, that is to say, from a man of his rank. They won't inhibit *my* doctrine, I am small enough already to be lost without trace if the King wishes to curb Cromwell. But he won't, not just yet. So for the time, I am safe; and therefore, you are safe. No, Winchester won't dare proceed against you now. Cromwell will be having a quiet word with Cranmer, and Cranmer will pass it on."

"Safe?" burst out Dorothy, "safe for what? Where? Is the minstrel-troupe disbanded, or has Cromwell prigged that as well? Dip-of-the-finger: what in hell has been going on? Devil's shit-pot and we all seethe together!" She was cold as a stone with shock, although the kitchen was oppressively warm.

"Yes, he has prigged it: *adopted* it, a better word. Did I not make that clear? And its work will be just as it was. As for where . . . do you have money?"

They all had money, they had brought it out in purses strapped under their clothes: and a small weight of jewels as well.

Bale picked at a rabbit-bone. His manner was so matter-of-fact that Dorothy knew it was a mask: the man was in a turmoil underneath. He threw the bone among the rushes before he had half-finished the meat on it, and pulled his hand away angrily as the dog came for a quick snap. "With your 'Birdcage' closed, you'll have difficulty earning at the same rate you're used to. From the minstrel-troupe, some moneys, of course. But now that all is as it is, the name of New-Guise will cling to all your work, not easy to make engagements in households of the old tendencies. Maybe already it is not easy? Rabbit-stew'll be your staple for some time to come.

"Is it beyond your endurance? So withdraw, now, from the minstrel-troupe: extend yourselves on your own, make noise as loud as possible that religion is *not* your interest. Never has been, never will be. You choose to dissociate. A possible course of action." He looked bleakly around the table, shook his head. "Whether the likes of gallstone Winchester will believe you is a different matter. And if he does not, I don't think Cromwell will trouble to protect you. He protects only his partisans. Without him behind me, I'd be powerless to assist."

"This Winchester," said Rotraut slowly, thinking it out, "*his* name will be expected, by the torturers, from Angelina?"

"*Christus-Kreuz,*" Ermentruda was weeping: "the poor woman."

Bale ignored her and answered Rotraut. "Not for use, not just yet. But whatever they find she knows against him, they will keep upon file. Winchester is not overtly papalist. He helped Cranmer frame a case for annulment of the Catherine-marriage. His devotional doctrine, however, is not changed from what it always was. Scripture in English, for example: he would still persuade the King it merits priestly burning. He abhors priestly matrimony. And moreover, he's a cunning bastard. We'll not see the end of him for a very long time. He will compass all methods to see the end of *us.*"

Dorothy said, "You've given us a 'course of action' and at once you withdraw the donation. Is that all? No other gift? Very well, we must starve. I should be glad of it. The scourged blood of Catgut's Nelly is *begging* me to be glad of it 'Continue, continue,' it squeaks and mutters – squeaks and mutters – squeaks . . ." These last words, themselves in a mutter.

He shoved his plate aside: he had eaten hardly any of the food. He crumbled a lump of bread in his fingers till it all fell away onto the table-top. He edged from his stool and so toward the door, a discreetly inconspicuous motion, as though going out to relieve himself without breaking up the party: but on the threshold he paused, twitched his head in a vague gesture: "Dorothy, please . . . ?" And then left the house. Wondering, she followed him. Rotraut put her arm round Ermentruda and sat close.

*

Outside in the yard, Bale was standing in a channel of rainwater, the weather had turned bad while they were eating. Dorothy would not go to him: she stayed under the overhang of the thatch. So he came to her.

"There *is* another course. I put it to you without the other two, because if *you* do not accept it, it is useless for them. My first thought was, of course, we are largely at work together, making plays, making minstrelsy, for the same cause: so why not all of you stay together here in this house, it is large enough, and we share our money, share our danger, share whatever protection is vouchsafed? It seemed so simple.

"But you see, I must not act until I am certain that Lord God will approve my action. All night I have bent my knees to Him. And into my heart His Word penetrated, in the very last hour of darkness, oh for once *I did receive answer!* To begin with, He said to me: 'My servant John, you are my minister. You have sins upon your soul, in especial the Sin of Lechery. You cannot seek shrift any more from pretending priests, you must account yourself to Me alone. Will you take into your house three women of a certain life, two of whom you know to be intimate *contra naturam* one with the other; and the third, perhaps, also?'

"Well, they are, are they not? I was in their 'Birdcage' room; well, *Jungfrau* Rotraut's room, but the Ermentruda used it more than she used her own, and that bed was well wide enough for two, there were clothes of two women on the hooks – oh I have eyes. And look at them now –" Through the cottage-door ajar, the Germans could be seen in their embrace, sitting as still as church-images at the table.

"No: please –" he changed his tone from denunciation to entreaty: "Do not go! you have nowhere to go to, I have not told you everything – *please!*" (Dorothy, beginning to move, halted again, and watched him warily.) "I say, first God told me that. I beseeched Him immediate; there were times, I suggested humbly, when His over-nice examination of the doings of others contravened His own Son's charity." (How he was troubled by recollection of this prayer: it must have taken him by surprise, even as he made it.) "'Yes,' God said to me, 'yes, the carnality of these women is nothing but kindly. *Against kind*, but exceeding kindly. What about *yours*?', He said: and I knew what He meant. He meant that if I lived with you, there would be no bound to the lust that would torment me. However great my resolution. He meant that I would become a ravaged lurking stumbling-block not only to myself and my hopes of heaven, but – by dint of scandal in the hands of enemies, Winchester and a hundred others – to the entire way of reformation in this land, until even Cromwell must repudiate me.

> Wee-willy-winkie runs through the town
> Thrusting like a pole-axe through the gap of his gown . . .

do you think I was not aware of this full truth of the Lord's warning?"

Dorothy now saw this drift. She could not bear to keep pace with him, he approached his thought so dreadfully slowly. "You'll marry me," she said, voice quavering between scorn and sympathy. "You'll make a bargain to have your lechery confined in God's Law to me, and then there is no sin, and your house will be *my* house, and I can never break away from you without myself committing a sin, and 'Truda and Rotraut can go to – go to *Dis* if they want, which is where you think they are already, so what's the odds?"

He was determined not to be injured. He kept his words very level. "No. They will stay here. Here by right, as your guests, and I will not allow myself to probe into their privacy. But I would ask you to caution them, for their own sakes, and all of our sakes, the likes of Winchester must never be ignored from now on, we are in danger. As for my lechery, as I told you in Rotraut's room upon the former day, if you will not subscribe to it, I shall not constrain. Solemn promise: I shall not.

"It is probable I repel you. But so long as you seemed available to give yourself to – to other men –" (the way he said it, she now knew beyond all doubt that he knew who was John's father) "– how could I help hoping you could as easily be mine also? As a clergyman's church-sworn wife you would no more offer me dreams that I might suddenly come to violate you – oh I have had such wicked dreams – than if you were Tom Cranmer's wife."

It took her a moment to work out the moral contortion of this: when she perceived it, she wrinkled her nose in disgust. But disgust with a sort of laugh: it was so hard to take him seriously. But one of his phrases, surely, was in need of expansion. "'Church-sworn'? In what church? You may not do it, it's against the law. I never thought of this, the last time you asked me. What possible clergyman would dare – ?"

"Cranmer would dare. He secretly married Lady Anne to the King, and his own secret wife – mind you, you must not talk of *her*, I ought not to have told you, not even the King has been officially informed, and none of the other bishops know – for heaven's sake keep it from your frivolous German girls, they'll blab it all over the town. Oh I think he would dare, I hope he might, or failing him, his chaplain – rival bishops cannot search and find out what goes on in the Lambeth Palace chapel – it might be done, exceeding careful . . .

"And then consider, your baby John, his loving father at last. Ah but you can't persuade yourself, would *you* have a loving husband? Six years, Dorothy Longlegs, six, I have blundered and blustered around you: I said at the first, 'no harm' – has there been any harm?"

"No, in honesty, no. Not harm, but grievous embarrassment. And Jesus, but *that* won't stop . . . This time I do not ask Rotraut, I ask Nelly. She was always wise. Of no morals, but with a close-contriving cunning mind: she knew so much, and was so ignorant. I'll ask her. I think she'll answer in less than a minute." All of a sudden, Dorothy was gay: she felt free as a flying arrow.

*

Their marriage took place a week later: the Archbishop's chaplain made it. Cranmer himself, 'exceeding careful', took good care not to be at home that day. Did she worry any more, was it priest or poet she wed? That now seemed less important. Above all, he was a man-on-the-run – whether or not he had Cromwell's protection (in which she did not trust at all: very likely, were she assured she could rely on it absolutely, she would have loathed the very idea). Being on the run, however, no better place for them to live than Drury Lane. Perhaps, at end of all, the Reformed Way might turn out to be the prevailing way. Her guess, so far at any rate, had done better than Angelina's.

God be kind to Angelina. Nelly had been treated no worse.

(xii) *Dorothy's Bride-Bed*

The Widow no longer distinguished Nelly from Angelina. She never dreamed of her marriage without dreaming also of a demonic Flagellation. There was Bale and herself, hand-in-hand before the hesitant chaplain (he was far from convinced his Archbishop was right to set him to this duty), there was the altar behind the chaplain: behind the altar, as living reredos, two men in leather jackets whipped gleefully at the Sacred Body – it was not Christ, but a writhing woman whom they had roped up to the Pillar; and Pilate-Cromwell-Winchester-Norwich sat at one side and washed his hands.

This fantasy blurred itself always into its next stage: herself brought to bed, Bale's bed, by Ermentruda and Rotraut, Sally and Belle-Savage in attendance, her little John as Cupid flying on wires above them. Cecilia's Muses, for so they were costumed, making a masque to the same music that had been used for the birthday-treat of Lord Wentworth's son. The bed was huge, bigger than would have been plausible for the King at Hampton Court: Bale lay in it, watched and waited for the handmaidens to despoil her of her bridal gown. But should it not have been the bridegroom brought to the bed of the bride?

While they did this, singing, she saw Pilate through an archway beyond the bed's head, leading her who had been scourged, and saying (or was it Cupid saying?): "Ecce femina."

*

In fact, her first bride-bedding was neither so stately nor so secret-horrible. In fact it was 'quite daft', as she told herself the morning afterwards.

For a month she and Bale did not sleep together: she made her mind up, she would refrain from him, because she could not make up her mind whether or no she had any desire for him. Her brain said, no she hadn't, he *did* repel her, always had. Her fantasy, her curiosity, were telling her something else, but she had to be certain what. So she, with Belle-Savage and John, took the loft-room above the house-place end; the Germans and their girl used the least ruinous of the farm's outhouses; and Bale slept on the floor of the house-place, warmed by the hearth-stone, *that* much was due to him in lieu.

On the thirtieth night her fantasy overcame her. She could hear him groaning below, in disordered wrack of half-slumber; his indigestion or his loneliness, or both, caused him such unease every night, and she always heard. Like that princess in the legend who must kiss a frog to make it a man, she lay and thought of the possibilities of his blotched body, his loving and lunging spirit: and then she could think of it no more. She rolled quietly from her bed, pulled on a pair of slippers, went down the loft-ladder with all precautions against its creaking. She was sure that Belle-Savage was asleep, but she was wrong. The black woman's wedge-face peered out between blankets to watch her go, two white eyes sardonic in the dark.

Bale did not wake when she moved in beside him. When he found her in the morning with her hand between his thighs, he could not know whether she had loved him in his sleep or not: nor would she tell him. She was his *succuba*, she said: if he liked it not, let him exorcise.

From then on, every night, in the one bed, a mattress of rushes on the house-place flagstones, they were husband-and-wife at last. When he discovered from her there were gentle ways as well as fierce to play the two-backed-beast, he played it without abhorring himself, began to learn a species of mercy toward both him and her, began to give thanks for his theological prescience: flesh-things indeed were for his use, and his Lord God was pleased that he should use them. Then she had to tame him from his barbarous self-gratulation. But she admitted it, his flesh was exciting to her, she honestly admitted that.

It was also productive. By the year's end she was pregnant again. Her second son was born. Bale insisted that they call him Paul. He was starting to identify himself with that apostle, for no very good reason, except that both men changed their doctrine after long rebellion against the ox-goad, and both had a dreadful hard time of it.

Many days were spent with the minstrels or the players, rehearsing in the tumble-down barn, or – in fine weather – the yard; and performing wherever young Conrad or some other could find them an audience.

Bale, at home, read and wrote, wrote and read. He dressed always as a scholar, shabby-genteel, but most respectable: his Drury Lane neighbours called him 'the sexton': and none of them seemed to know he was a clergyman. He accumulated expensive books and would very soon beggar himself. The money fetched by Dorothy from the 'Birdcage' was all too rapidly spent.

She did not find it easy to have her hot baths in the cottage. There was no adequate copper, and the well was a long way off, too far to walk comfortably with a succession of heavy buckets.

(xii) *Cur-dog*

Neither did Widow Dorothy ever dream of her marriage without dreaming also of the cur-dog of Drury Lane, how it howled. They were not good friends, she and he (he could not truly be termed an 'it', so very much a Bale-dog he was; she used to call him 'Bliss' as contrary to his nature, but he never answered to any name save 'Jack-priest', once given him by the senile cottager).

The pair of them, woman and dog, wandered round in front of this tall castle: her two children toddling after her, tripping over and falling and crying along the edge of the moat. She looked up at the walls and held out her arms, and her hair blew in the wind: she seemed to be all in rags, her old red-white-and-green rags from the fenland roads. The dog raced round in circles, looking up wry-necked at the walls as well; and howling: now and then chasing the children, baring his dire teeth at Dorothy's legs, making a rush for the moat and recoiling from the leap in a sudden loss of his spiteful courage.

High above raised drawbridge, lowered portcullis, blankly shut gate, sat Bale in King's robes, upon the barbican platform with its battlements and pinnacle-statues of heraldic beasts rampant. He was staring out over the land, his eyes far beyond Dorothy, his ears listening to a music that had nothing to do with her locked-out plight. And then he did seem to see her, for he pointed his sceptre toward her, and spoke. "Sweet Bathsheba, take your bath," he said, "There is the fountain under that tree: it is clear fresh water of Jordan, having flowed hither between the banks of Thames."

The dog howled and howled: from the inside of the castle came a surge of men running the length of the battlements. Their leader was a small pale whirlwind of a fellow screaming war-oaths in German: and he flung himself on Bale, and all his fierce men with him. They tore off his royal adornments, they were trying to rip his testicles with the curved pruning-knives they pulled from their belts, until in the frenzy of struggle they all fell out of sight, down behind the parapet. The last thing she saw of Bale was his raging head (still with its crown on, knocked slantwise over one ear): it reared up desperate from the ruck.

In wordless agony he pled for her help, just as she, a few minutes since, had been appealing for his. But moat and walls remained impassable: and the dog howled.

(3)

Christ's Daughter, Or Diana's?

Lydia stayed with Lucretia for several days: the man of the Windsor duties was for the time well out of the way (she asked no questions), the lodging – when cleaned up – was as commodious as could be expected in so over-crowded a city; and at the end of the week Lucretia was to perform at a betrothal party given in a gentleman's country house, out beyond Highgate. There were few such opportunities for musicians' professional services during the plague-summer, but Muswell Hill on the northern heights was deemed safe enough. The danger, that guests or artists going up there from town might bring the infection with them, had been overlooked: but then, with serious families, the need for good music would naturally outweigh such niggling fears. The clear air was bound to *disperse the miasma*, it was held.

Lucretia wanted her mother to see her at work. She arranged for Lydia to be in the gallery of the hall among the family domestics and the better class of tenants. Of course Lydia had often enough attended festivities in the homes of Lowlyheart's Canterbury associates, and they had not always been made dull by Genevan rigidity. But those affairs were never on such a scale, nor had she ever been encouraged to take much note of the hired entertainers: now there was a real interest, a new interest – despite her reservations – a diverting one, she entered into it whole-heartedly.

First, what delight to listen to this music, the music of London with all possible innovations new-brought-in from France, Italy, even inimical Spain. And the dancing that it served, the family-masque, the sumptuous costumes, the unbelievable dexterity of the two hired dancers who bounded and sprang like fireflies! Lydia had some memory (stirred by her talk with Lucretia) of her own mother once telling of a birthday-masque in olden time in some great East Anglian house. This is how it had been, beautiful! And just so had Dorothy played her part in it.

Secondly, she was introduced to her daughter's fellow-performers, male and female. To her surprise, she found them not only friendly but of sweet and pleasing manners. Of course, they were not gentry (so their refinement lacked arrogance), and neither were they of the learned clerical caste she had been taught to revere in Canterbury (so they laughed and joked with a freedom that enlivened, she found, far more than it disturbed).

Altogether, she was better reconciled to Lucretia's new life than she had been able conceivably to admit less than a week ago. She understood, too, without having much knowledge of it, that Lucretia's quality among the other musicians was very well regarded, and justifiably well regarded. The child had had a solo song, which she accompanied on her own cittern, and the hall-full of revelling guests had sat as still as Christmas midnight to hear it. Some of them even weeping at its tenderness. Lydia had wept without shame. And yet the matter of the song, she thought, had hinted at adultery? So strange, at a young gentlewoman's troth-making? But indeed, there was no Geneva on Muswell Hill.

*

Two further reservations, prolonged beyond the week.

Lucretia's men, and she dared not ask further: she had heard (and deduced) enough already. The girl, and this was clear, continued sinful; regretting only the sin's discomforts, not the sin itself. There seemed no remedy, except to cut herself off from her once more, or to remain silent. So therefore silence, at least for the present.

And then, Lucretia's fear. The papers she had hidden, the curious words concerning Munday. Lydia did ask about this, several times. Her worried importunity extracted only an idle tale of a colleague's debts, and the need to hold some bonds for him until sheriff's officers were off his track: Lydia did not believe a word of it. But if her child was so well grown as to fend for herself and thrive among the artists of London, then no doubt she was able to cope – or to find friends to help her cope – with whatever associated entanglements her fending and thriving had pulled around her. Even if she were not, she did not need a mother of total inexperience to bungle matters on her behalf.

Since Lucretia ran from home, Lydia had so closed herself in upon her fruitless anxieties for her, that this visit and its discoveries acted now like a declaration (from Sovereign and Parliament) of total religious indulgence: it was as though the Old Guise – superstitious forms, coercive priestcraft – had once again given way to the free reading of God's free Scripture made new in the people's own language. And this time no restriction of doctrine: all could believe as they needed. Lydia was made free: of herself and of her chains of sin. She remembered all she had forgotten, and therefore at last her daughter was hers again. Which meant she must not continue to live with her, even though she yearned so greatly to live at least *near* her.

She must sell the Canterbury house and make a home in London. But not with her brothers. They had succeeded to the worst parts of their father and had nothing of their mother: and Lowlyheart had been *their* idea. During her short stay in the city she had knocked at neither of their doors.

She hired horses from the livery-stable for herself and her maid. With an honest groom as an escort she took the Old Kent Road at far greater speed than might be thought seemly for a middle-aged widowed goodwife. She did not know what she would do: but nothing would be the same again.

*

But then there was delay. To sell the house was none too easy, the usher who had succeeded Lowlyheart as master of the school put in a claim for the dwelling, he said it was an integral part of the educational premises and went to the courts to prove it. The title was indeed unclear: and the whole matter sank without trace for two or three years into a midden-heap of parchment where festering lawyer-maggots battened and bred out of all control. And her other children, sons and daughters, stuck in their greedy hands to compound the mixter-maxter even further.

She had no choice but to stay fixed under the disputed roof, or at any rate to keep servants there. She could not afford to do that and spend time in London as well. So she wrote often to Lucretia, and quite often had letters in return. Now and then she went up to town for limited and inconvenient visits. At least, she remained in touch: and nothing very terrible appeared to be happening.

Except to herself. She could not stop thinking about Anthony Munday. The man, she was quite sure, had positively admired her: his insidious behaviour could have meant nothing else. He had villainously seduced Lucretia, and Lucretia despised his character: and Lydia ought to have hated him. So why did she keep brooding on the wicked and nonsensical proposition that a poet of pitying heart could not (under the circumstances) have resisted her daughter at that time – *she* had not been able to resist Lucretia's stricken beauty when she entered the East Cheap room – and that therefore he cannot have been so very much to blame?

Some most unexpected maggots, and by no means legal ones, swarmed in Lydia's own secret midden-heap: she was obliquely aware of them, her throat retched at the thought of them, and when she tried to pray for God's Grace to drive them away, she could only bring up those strange unholy words she had spoken to Lucretia, "Which must mean I am not Christ's daughter".

If not Christ's, then whose? Diana's, of the Ephesians? that she should dream of a man's long arms, when those arms had stretched already to catch the windfall fruit of her womb?

She had enough Calvin-Geneva in her to yield herself despairing to predestinate evil if she once let it run. But surely a dream was but a dream: no reason to believe she would ever meet him again, she had no idea where he lived, and she could certainly abstain from any attempt to find out.

Ah, but she knew where he worked.

And having once accepted that the playhouses were no sin, she found herself drawn to them every time she came to London.

III

(Historical)

A Word from Til

> *And there came out of the smoke locusts upon the earth; and unto them was given power as the scorpions of the earth have power. And it was said unto them, that they should not hurt the grass of the earth; neither any green thing; neither any tree; but only those men which have not the seal in their foreheads, and to them was commanded, that they should not kill them, but that they should be vexed five months, and their pain was as the pain that cometh of a scorpion, when he hath stong a man. And in those days shall men seek death, and shall not find it.*
>
> (Revelation of St John the Divine, Chapter 9)

Towards the end of the year 1547 a letter was sent to the city of Strassburg, addressed to a certain divine, who had been Lutheran but was now reported at odds with his church-leaders upon the Doctrine of the Eucharist and upon matters of ecclesiastical discipline.

The writer of the letter was Konrad Spielmann, otherwise known as Conradus Joculator, *pamphleteer and independent Protestant agitator, born in the Siegenwald, educated at Wittenberg, at one time exiled to England (where people called him 'Dutch Conrad'; and were, on the whole, ignorant of his history). Now he lived in Marburg and issued a regular newsletter under the name of his old stage-character, 'Til Eulenspiegel' – in English, Owlglass.*

Konrad had never met the Strassburg pastor in the flesh, but had been sending him the pseudonymous newsletter for a year or two. A degree of concealment was desirable in Germany at this time: the population being politically and confessionally polarised. Correspondence had to be protected from police-searches, whether imperial, hierarchical, or appertaining to the self-governing principalities (Catholic or Protestant): you never knew who would be reading what.

There were in fact two letters to Strassburg. The first was very brief.

*　　*　　*

[Written in Latin.]

Esteemed Rev. Dr von G –

This is to recommend, to your hospitality in Christ Scriptural, the Rev. Dr Johannes Baleus, late of Cantabrigia, an exile, who is at this present in your city and may shortly call upon you. He is in hopes of the favour of the new young King of England (Eduardus), and has, I understand, already been promised a benefice. Be so kind, worshipful *Herr Doktor*, to speed him on his way with as little discommodity as possible. He travels with his wife, *Frau* Dorothea: she is great with child, and will need a most sedulous attention lest she miscarry upon the road. Even-so the mother of Our Lord proceeded with her blessed Burden to the census of Bethlehem. Pray Heaven there will be found for *Frau* Dorothea a safer harbour than that supplied (by unbelieving Jews) to her sacred precursor: pray Heaven there shall be Room At The Inn.

> In the uncurtailed hope of a
> New Resurrection for Christendom,
> I remain with all respect and
> duty –
>
> Cs. Jr.

*

The second was much longer, indeed it resembled an edition of the newsletter rather than a private message, albeit a more personal edition than was usual even for Konrad. His public commentaries were always quite scurrilously personal, also highly egocentric. As 'Til' he seemed unable to write upon any subject whatever without prefacing his account with a long straggle of comminatory ejaculations despising the current state of Germany and the Germans. Of course, as a rule, the state of Germany was the main matter of his discourse, and his readers were prepared for any amount of solipsism before they got into the meat of the argument – it was a sort of 'trade mark' of the newsletters, and there were many to appreciate it. But sometimes Konrad's mannerisms were not thought appropriate. A number of his subscribers were beginning to wonder if he might not be going off his head.

* * *

[Written in Platt-Deutsch of the Siegenwald, with odd words and phrases in Hoch-Deutsch.]

A WORD FROM TIL: READ! MEMORISE! BURN!

(By the same messenger that brings you the other one: only, that was to be carried in his wallet, and this one will be sewn into the saddle of his horse.)

*

(i) Contradictio Anglicana, *Generally And Particularly Expounded by Til*

Is it true that Strassburg, since the Emperor's defeat of the Lutherans at Muehlberg Battle, is now to be so purged by the victors that it will become a romanist city? If so, you and many others will be seeking your safety elsewhere: and Til is particularly anxious that Dr Bale be not left entirely to stir for himself in the confusion. Not that Til likes the man: Til does not like him at all.

But it is vital for events in England that all the Protestant English who fled from the late Henry Bluebeard be got back there as soon as possible, to ensure at least a modicum of pressure upon their new small king and to keep him safe from Scylla-headed venom-fanged papalizers[1] (*exempli gratia:* Gardiner, Winchester Bishop; Bonner, London Bishop). Also to keep him safe from political chameleons (*Cantuar* Cranmer, and his kind) – who are not, in Til's opinion, the strongest conceivable adult guardians for a child-monarch in such a year of brute transition.

Gardiner, we hear, has been put into prison *pro tem:* perhaps also Bonner? If so, good, good, good . . . but they may let them out and they *must* be countered at court!

Has Til great hopes for the English?

* .

To whom or what are Til's hopes (or fears) any longer relevant?

There was a time when Til thought that Our Luther – *der grosser Herr Doktor Martinus,* deceased – would first bring all the Germanies to Christ Scriptural, and thence the French, the English, even Italy and Spain. *Ecclesia Reformata* would grow from within itself, seeded and manured from Salem-Wittenberg, casting its pollen *via* the wings of evangelist-angels as far as Rome itself. Was the hope of a Reformed Pope so entirely idiotic?

Yes it was.

[1] When I say *papalizers*, or the like, call to your mind that such men have all sworn to their King's religious supremacy. True papists, acknowledging Rome openly, are hard to be found. But between professedly anti-papal reformers and sincere Protestants, a great gulf. All it needs is a papist sovereign (Mary? She *could* become Queen . . .): the English ruling caste would revert in a week.

T. Eul.

Dr Martinus became in the end his own pope, Dr Martinus controlled his own territories under the rule of his own princes, Dr Martinus controlled his own clergy, his own laity, his own forms of prayer – but when he found that his own peasants *refused* his control, refused to accept his denunciation of their rebellion against landlords and serf-masters, why then he had his gallows (oh yes he could control *them!*), his wheels-of-torture, iron cages, burning-stakes, without respite hard at work all over the lands, so thoroughly to restore his newly-infallible Word!

And now we have this Treaty, subsequent to the slaughter of Muehlberg: Emperor won, but Emperor doesn't win, because Lutherans, though defeated, are not *conquered*. Therefore: make partition! One half of the map for Luther's people, one half for Rome's.

Germans, do what you are told in your own designated area the way you are told it, or you die.

Ecclesia Reformata Indivisa Universalis? – *Quatsch! Dreck*, draff, rubbish, nonsense! Shiteheap!

PROPOSITION THAT REFORM IS POSSIBLE IN BUT ONE HALF-NATION IS *DECEIT-OF-ANTICHRISTUS!*

Saith Til.

*

But Luther, will you say, from your incorrigible kind heart (and this Englishman Bale, who is coming to your door, has already said it), was nonetheless a *patriarch?* And a poet of great majesty – his Bible in German, his hymns, will survive him for all time? The man was the Teuton Homer fixing Christ into the German language as the old blind bard fixed the Olympian false-gods into the Greek, and little children will learn his texts generation upon generation?

Til will tell you what Luther's fixed.

Oppression in the name of liberty, obedience in the name of compromise, extremism in the name of moderation.

And what happened to the TONGUE OF FIRE that came upon the Apostles, *united*, at Pentecost?

When Our Luther nailed his writ to the Wittenberg church-door, he too had a Tongue of Fire. Did he snuff it out himself? Or did God?

*

Forgive Til's digressive hysteria: but today he is living in perhaps the very worst time of all his life, when he watches the bitter reaping of the crops he helped to sow, and discovers there is nothing there to eat.

*

Til is supposed to be explaining England, to help you know what to do with this Bale.

In England there was no Tongue of Fire, at any stage.

There were a few Christians of the New Guise (English New Guise, Lollards rather than Luthers), a few Christians of the determined Old Guise, and very many Christians whose only religion was to do what their neighbours did and never to be seen doing different.

Also in England a selfish spectacular king who wanted a new wife.

So he got one and the Church had to reform itself to let him do it.

Dear brethren-in-Christ, a *spiritual decision!* Til prefers to call it *Contradictio Anglicana:* and at first, being in England himself, begging and farting for an English living, Til embraced it, yes he did!

Til was a pauper knave as well as a fool in those days, and eventually, as you'd expect, both his poverty and his foolery led him sorely into disillusion. He learned to *beware of hope.* Therefore he says, there is no more hope for England than for Germany, except this: because there was never any Tongue of Fire in that land, we do not need to look for one, therefore disappointment, disillusion, must surely be less.

Therefore we can *encourage:* we can send them Dr Bale.

You might even care to go there yourself? Cranmer is out and scouting for scholarly Germans, we are informed; the English universities having failed to stock his Church with a sufficiency of literate reform . . .

Do you ask, was England *ever* through-and-through Christian, even of the popish complexion? No, Til supposes not. Although Bale will maintain his land was always and more anciently more Christian than anyone else's; save only for Galilee, I daresay.

But Bale is a patriot fanatic: a poet in the English tongue as Luther was in ours. For him a Tongue of Fire is facility in the broke-back metre of the old alliterative verse (though usually without alliteration) and clumping rural rhymes clapped on at the end of each line. His saints, as far as I can gather, are any old poets whom he can falsely present as proto-Protestants – a Langland, a Skelton, you won't have encountered them. In short, he is an insular pragmatist, and we must use him as we find him.

He hates all the Gardiner papalizers . . .

*

He has been in the Germanies since 1540, and has published much in English from a number of what were then our freer cities. Lately, from this Marburg, he issued a pamphlet about Anne Askew, English martyr; he has also written about Sir John Oldcastle, English martyr of the old Lollard times: and a plethora of would-be theoretical doctrinal dissertations. His play from our own Kirchmayer, *Pammachius*, which Til helped him to assemble from the author's foul-papers, was presented at Cambridge, in Bale's enforced absence, some two years ago. Gardiner Bishop of Winchester was driven wildwood mad by this presentation, all plays on religious themes having been banned in '43 by royal edict from Bluebeard and his gang – all those men rich from monk-robbing but nonetheless tenacious in their hatred of Christ Scriptural, they persecuted papist and true Protestant with an equal equanimity, and therefore needed plays about nothing but light loves, arse-fartings (but meaningless ones), and mild ethical argument that must always stop short of enquiring 'whose ethics? God's or men's? Do we seek worldly advantage by them or eternal salvation?'

How can there be serious plays that are *not* upon religion, one way or the other? Again, *Contradictio Anglicana*: an Englishman of developed intellectual theory is your one-eyed man in the blind men's kingdom. Splendidly unique: and impossibly unreliable.

Til has said all this to Bale, one time or another, without any dialectical success. An example: Til pointed out to him that the Anna-Boleyn marriage was a typical example of ultra-English expediency. Bale denied it, angrily claiming that it was just as much a matter of theological principle as any of the Wittenberg decisions. "How dare you so sneer and insinuate!" he yelped. "'Convenient bed-solace for insatiate great men' indeed! What about Luther and his permission for the *Landgraf* Philip's bigamy, hey?"

Til at that time (it was hard upon Bale's arrival here in Germany) had long ceased to be reverent towards Luther, but chose to pretend otherwise, not being too sure of Bale's own position after the lapse of years. Til felt called upon to observe that there had indeed been an issue of principle – an issue of Natural Law – in the case of this *Landgraf* of Hesse.

"Oh yes and we damn well know what it was!" Oh festering malice on the part of John Bale! *Of course* we both knew what it was. Til felt deeply wounded at the tendentious illustration. For the *Landgraf* was afflicted with a third palpable testicle, medically impossible for one wife to suffice him, Luther's permission was therapeutic, logical, fundamentally ethical. And Bale was compelled to agree.

"Then tell me, Dr Bale, of the logics, the therapeutics, the ethics, of Boleyn and her delicious breech? If the Pope had given permission, then the King would have taken permission, and there'd be no New Guise in England at all! And for sure with any other Pope there would indeed have been permission: historical coincidence that the Emperor (Aragon Catherine's nephew) had the Pope in his pocket at that time . . ."

undsoweiter, undsoweiter . . .

Til analysed.

"Yet do not think," continued Til, destroying his own case the better to enrage Bale (malice can work two ways), "do not think neither that the *Landgraf*'s sad matter was devoid of political expedience." Til drew a map of Germany, showing Hesse in danger of being sucked into the Emperor's orbit: ha! the loyalty of its prince to Luther's cause had need to be secured somehow.

Sauce for goose, sauce for gander. By now the entangled Bale could not distinguish north from south. Til triumphed:

"Raspberry fart, ha! ha! *Confuto te, Domine!*" Bale broke away then from serious dispute and relieved his disturbance, by breaking into the breaking of jokes, about the abundance, or lack, of testicular potence, how one man will contrast with another, *undsoweiter*: he well knew this was not a theme that moved *Til* to much laughter.

*

With his Wycliffist theories, his Cranmerist praxis, his pseudo-Zwinglian *idealismus*, this Bale who invokes your friendship, your house-warmth, must assuredly puzzle you greatly: so therefore, good *Herr Doktor*, let conscientious Til (in all critical cognency) sketch out his strange English life for you, insofar as it has come under Til's observation.

Forget 'Til' for the rest of this paper. Til is I, I am I, I am 'Dutch Conrad' that dwelt in exile, to play Eulenspiegel, to play Jack Sausage (which is what the English call our Hanswurst-fool when he dirties himself for their applause); and also to convey my Bible-boxes. I sat in the stocks, I was a scourged martyr: and that was the self-same day I first set eyes upon John Bale . . .

*

Konrad's letter from this point recapitulated most of what has already been told. His view of Bale's wedding and all that led up to it was very much

*(and unpleasantly) his own view. He claimed that Bale's pursuit of
Dorothy was as King Henry's lust for Anne Boleyn, her consent for bed
being withheld until he would guarantee marriage. And that this sordid
'cunt-extortion' (Konrad's phrase) was chief if not sole incentive for Bale to
adopt Protestant doctrine. Konrad affected to excuse the circumstances,
suggesting that there might be a hidden divine purpose in such 'swiftly-
tugging priapisms' – they were physical phenomena of a kind he himself
could only guess at, but which the more fortunate von G– might possibly
recognise as common enough among well-built men in their prime of life.
Nevertheless, he added, the Strassburg doctor need not be too apprehensive
about Frau Bale. In decorous company she would surely conduct herself
with due attention to place and time – she had been among the German
decencies long enough to know what was required. Unless, that is to say, she
were to be crossed. In which case . . .*

(ii) Contradictio In Rure (*Between Suffolkland And The Westfields Of* Londinium)

– in which case, keep very clear of the full reach of her arm, which is a
long one and trained among carrion-crows in that 'Birdcage'
aforementioned. I have known her years and years and would not trust
her an inch. If she was not pregnant, I would say, 'watch her in
Strassburg': her ageing husband has a good lumpy forehead for horns.
When she was scarce more than a child she was at my forlorn codpiece
always.

How far is she at heart a convinced Protestant? Even a Cranmerist?
God knows. I say it deliberately: He has protected her so far – or
Someone has. Do I hint at the Adversary, '*der alt boese Feind*', to quote
our late Martinus? Hard to say. I have no proofs. As a singing-woman
for our cause she accomplished so much artistry: and yet it always
seemed to me her artistry meant more to her than the cause. Can
Christ's dominion really be strengthened by a woman dancing on her
hands . . . ?

And if her artistry is not from Christ, then – from Whom? And how
should this apply to the artistry of her husband's words? Are words in
a stage-play of a different moral quality from those in a devotional
pamphlet? God knows.

No: I cannot believe *Frau* Dorothea is thoroughly washed in
Jordan. But this I must say of her: she is *stout*. A stoutness preserved
by who knows how much internal strain and effort, not visible to the

outside glance: but watch her at her dancing-practice, see the enormous daily pain she deliberately lets surge through her body every time she reaches out to some new striding movement or posture (surely she will not be dancing and leaping in your house: but keep an eye on her, she will try to slip away unnoticed to supple her limbs, even when bearing this child). By stout, I mean stout-hearted, not thick-fleshed, of course, all her dancing has inhibited that. Nonetheless, when she eats, she *devours*: you will see.

However obtuse her husband, she has always contrived to be at whichever of his elbows needed a prop, has heaved him up to vertical (if only for a short time) and put immediate halt to his totterings and waverings. For the man is a mess, *ein Dreckkerl*, and looks it. He will take some getting-used-to, if you expect a solemn divine. Everywhere he goes, he blunders, as though by choice. He was in Marburg with me. I warned him about the war, the unstable situation, but no: he *must* go to Strassburg because a notable bookseller had advertised an auction, and now he will be trapped there.

You will wonder why he comes to your table unshaven, a bleary-eyed old-English-sheepdog: he is not trying to insult you on purpose. Someone wrote to him that his friend Cranmer was so stricken with grief for the death of the eighth Henry that he swore he would never shave again. Did not Giuliano de' Medici, called Pope Clement, swear the same when the Emperor's troops sacked Rome? It does not seem to me a very Protestant thing to do. But then, I say again, what is an English Protestant? A creed as though scratched on a wet road surface in the middle of a downpour, yet they pride themselves upon it, perched out there, as they are, on the very fringe of the Christian world. (I except Ireland, no more Christian than the Tartar steppes of Russ: I except the Americas, mere continuation of Portugal and Spain, popish.)

Anyway, Bale thought he should follow Cranmer's example, although his wearisome exile is owed solely to the king he laments. Unfortunately his bristles are of slow and uneven growth, and it will take years before he can co-ordinate them into an authoritative ornament for his chin-heavy discoloured face. My own beard reached its miserable peak when I was near thirty: one day I found I could actually *count* its hairs: so from then on I have shaved . . . He is never very clean these days, and his nose is far too big and red. His wife has an enchanting nose. I say this deliberately. But do not let yourself be *rapt* by it, nor by the fact that she washes herself all day long.

Impossible to see how such a pair can be compatible, unless – as I have hinted – they have entered some most murky contract. Concerning which, I make no jokes: at Wittenberg I attended the manic lectures of a certain reclusive professor, on the Cabbalist sources of Albigensian error (his only assistant then being a snuffling shuffling library-spider called Wagner): of late years, however, this Dr Faust has introduced to the world a new amanuensis; Helen of Troy, if you will believe it! Between his claims for her powers and common-room rumour as to how he obtained her and what he and mysterious others do with her after dark, one can only draw the direst conclusions. He purports to be a Lutheran. We live and learn.

*

I have brought Bale's strange history to 1536, when Cromwell began to dissolve monasteries: and an illegally-married friar became that much safer. With only a small amount of intrigue and backstairs inducement, he secured a secular benefice, to be Curate at Thorndon in Suffolkland, a village of the Duke of Suffolk, King Henry's idle brother-in-law. Suffolk would give such positions to anyone, if Cromwell recommended it: a comfortable lord who knew who held the power.

There was no manor-house at Thorndon: a dismal straggling place, where the Duke's local bailiff attended to all the affairs of the estate from his farm in the parish – it would have been ridiculous to call him the Squire. The nearest magnate was Sir Humphrey Wingfield, a short ride away from the village. He was a bullying enclosing landlord who held his fields on a lease from the Duke, and drove many to penury.

The district should have been prosperous – it had been, not so long before – but the enclosures were brought in everywhere, with ominous results. Where crops had been grown in the long-accustomed tenants' portions, now only the speculators' sheep were pastured, and the poor cultivators had no choice beyond starvation, or going on the road to beg and threaten, or rising in rebellion to repeat that Peasants' War we knew in our own lands twenty years ago. This third choice they have not yet taken. I always told them they would have to – although I could not recommend it there and then, bearing in mind what happened here. But: when they *shall* successfully rise, it can only be in the name of Christ Scriptural, correctly defined. I told them the German failure was largely due to the inability of the peasant leaders to understand that 'correctly'. It means they all have to be as well-indoctrinated in the New Religion as are their enemies in the old philosophy of 'every man in his due degree': if they are *not* fanatical, then fanatical hatred will win, there is enough and to spare of it in the highest places of state and church. When the wild horsemen of Mahomet conquered all the middle-orient in less than a generation, they knew this far better than any Roman or Persian opposed to them: so it must be with us.

But I do not think that Thorndon will be the *locus* of revolt.

Remember I knew these regions as long ago as '28: even in those days all we could earn at Thorndon for two full hours of the Rover's Runagates was a platter of soggy bread and nettle soup from some kind old woman – they were not only poor, but sullen with it. They were also superstitious, desperately clinging to all old ceremonies, in so far as their priest could drag pence from them to pay for his conjurings. The enclosures had near killed the village: the Duke trusted to his bailiff, and the bailiff was a great keeper of sheep.

*

When Bale received the curacy, he found the Parson absent most of the time – it was not his only parish. The parsonage, as it were abandoned, was falling into ruin, and that was where Bale would lodge. All the thatch was tumbled in on the windward side. I came with him to oversee the place, we were working at the time upon a series of John Baptist plays, expressive of regeneration through the Water of Life, true Repentance by confession direct to the ear of God and thereby Grace and good conduct immediately consequent (and resulting from such Grace): I had constant dispute with Bale, I could not see how he could reconcile his new theology and the old in the manner that he pretended. Such a working of his troubled spirit, each scene that he wrote, he tore up again, furiously complaining that every time he had the theoretical divinity correctly synopsised, his 'living English' (oh how he clung to it!) would shift his meaning from what it ought to be, and before he knew what had happened, all his Scripture was distorted in the interests of dramatic vigour.

I told him, "You tell me what it is you need to say, I will write it in German – or *you* write it, if you insist, in Latin, you are adept at Latin, but beware of popery-phrases – and thence into English: thus your English language will be servant and not master."

To which he answered, English thought was the only conceivable thought for a true Englishman's doctrine, and therefore he must fight with its words until he bowed them to his will. Pastor and poet, in fact, locked in unending struggle, internecine, suicidal.

All this, you are to imagine, in the bug-ridden Thorndon ale-house, the Black Horse: we must seek our dire shelter there while thatcher and carpenter did their worst with the leaking parsonage. Bale was horrified by his first sight of the church, one of the ugliest I have found in a part of England where in general they used to build with great beauty and uprightness, albeit in a mistaken faith. It is a loutish barn of flint, with no aisles, and ramshackle furnishing. A squat square tower devoid of pinnacles sits over the porch all out of shape, as I have seen poor Bale (when costive) hunched and groaning upon his close-stool. From the churchyard (thistles, nettles, docks) the village runs off slightly downhill to the west – a wide unco-ordinated street, or enlongated green (except that it is mostly mud) nearly a mile from end to end. The cottages are widely spaced on both sides of this dreary strip, little clumps of underbrush thrusting up between them. If they were clumps of trees, there might be some dignity to the expanse: but when they were trees, the peasants chopped them down for fuel, and keep on chopping, so they never grow. I say 'cottages', but they are in truth hovels, built (as so often in east England) by sticking posts in the earth and tilting them to meet at the top, sliding a ridge-pole over them where they cross, and thatching from apex to ground-level.

By the calendar still summer, but it was already autumn, a bad year's darkening: and this was the long-hoped-for preferment for a scholar who believed himself so useful to Cromwell, Cranmer, Wentworth and all the others of the King's forward faction? I said to him: "It is banishment."

He swore at me with the foulest oaths, said, "No, we are close to London, this *is* the best they can do for me, how *dare* you break my spirit! Look here," he said, "If I can prove the Gospel brought to life in the sagging minds of Thorndon, I can prove it alive anywhere: no despair! Pray to God, boy, pray! and remember St Paul, how he went from Damascus first to the desert regions of hopeless Arabia, and after that to Antioch, and only after Antioch did he venture upon Jerusalem – even then he must go forth to benighted cities beyond the bounds, Ephesus, Corinth, Thessalonica. And unto Rome he came only as a prisoner in bonds. No cause for complaint, no cause at all, boy, we must not be sinful-proud!"

★

He had with him the new Bible, Coverdale's improvement of Tyndale, now ordered by the King to be placed and read in every church. In Thorndon only the bailiff could read, and *he* thought God's Word was expressly written in Latin – in English it could not be trusted and probably was not true. The Parson on his few visits (chiefly to collect his tithes) took fright at the responsibility. So Bale plunged himself into it, and read and read aloud, all hours, after every Mass. (More or less a Luther Mass: if pressed he might have said he held the Elements *con-sub* and not *trans-sub*. He hoped and prayed that none would press him.)

The people stood with open mouths. They comprehended nothing. He should have read less of St Paul and more of the Gospels, plain tales, Christ's compassion for the sick and sinful. I told him, he was not consistent: his plays were rough vernacular, there was much of the same in Scripture, he should keep to it and stay clear of abstract thought: Thorndon was neither Cambridge nor Paul's Cross. He angrily rebuffed me: *I* was not consistent, he alleged: *I* was the abstractionist, if *I* had my way his plays would be all Paul and no Christ, and put together in High German and Latin!

Mainly he was afraid lest too vivid a bible-Christ would resemble the sermons he was trained to give as a young friar, what he called his 'mountebank medicine-preachings' for Peter's Pence and the sale of Indulgences – very much like that Tetzel who so stung our Luther when our Luther was young and surprising. Little by little, however, Bale began to learn his trade as a peasants' pastor. I say 'little by little' – those days at Thorndon were such misery, they seemed to drag till the crack of doom – sober fact, it was no more than a matter of weeks before he discovered the proper style. And when he discovered it – but first I must digress to write of his private affairs.

I was with him in Thorndon for four months. At the end of which time he said to me, "There is no more work now I can conveniently do on these plays. Go back to London, Conrad, and start the company rehearsing *King John*: I promised it to Lord Cromwell if possible before the end of Christmas-tide and there is much to be done with it. If I can steal a few days I will join you there in early December and shape ends where you have rough-hewn. In any case, I cannot tolerate any more of your good advice. You have altogether confounded me and I no longer know whether I come or go. This parish does not require the complexities of German argument: we need only a plain-faced Christ, the Man of Love, the God of Salvation, who assumed our guilt upon Him that we might all-at-once come into His Kingdom! And I beg you, boy –" (I could not abide his always calling me 'boy': did he not realise I was thirty-two? How old was Alexander when he took up the Grecian crown; how old our Lord, indeed, when He first fetched staff and scrip out onto the itinerant hills?) "I beg you, boy," he snarled at me, "do not open your teeth and inform me that Christ as Second Adam assuming our human guilt is a far more complex concept than can be embraced in so short a phrase. I am not anxious to hear the words 'elect' or 'predestinate' either – I accept their importance, but *not* their immediate relevance. Had Dorothy been here she'd have called halt to this ludicrous theorising – weeks ago, she would have called it – Lord God give me peace of mind . . ."

*

You see, he might have just possibly brought his wife into Thorndon as his 'housekeeper', his 'breech-burner', his 'remedy', although the Parson was bothered about such things and in his nervous way would certainly have made trouble. But by now Bale had two children, boys, one of six months, the other already two years (they are in Strassburg with him: you will see). For the new Curate to arrive as a family man, having (as was known) been heretofore a vow-bound friar, would have caused a greater scandal than any of his friends in government were ready to cope with at that time. And then, even supposing his marriage to be proclaimed, men would ask, what was its date? They would count their fingers and discover his elder son conceived – and born – before it took place. They would no doubt ask "Where?". And the answer must be, the 'Birdcage' . . . ! He had tumbled his Dorothea in a high-class London *lupanar*, and thereafter it had taken her three-quarters of a year to compel him to his promise of wedlock.

What could they say, either of them, to such a revelation?

For myself, I was never sure why Bale should have been so positive the child was his own. Those 'Birdcage' women were anyone's, provided 'anyone' was able to pay for their jewelries and luxurious *Krimskrams*. I was not: and had I had sufficient money, I would not have spent it *there*. Although, no doubt, had I so chosen, I could have found and enjoyed from one of the inmates some form of solace well-enough suited to my bodily lack: when loins will not serve a man, eyes and ears and tongue are often tuned to a high pitch of salacity, but I won't speculate . . .

Lacking, then, a wife at Thorndon, he turned more and more to me, keeping me most damnably hard at work. Nor did he pay me. I had to act as though I were appointed his parish-clerk, but I was supposed to be there as a member of the acting-company and living on the wages I drew for that purpose.

There were quiet evenings. We relinquished the Black Horse as soon as we possibly could, and camped out in the half-repaired parsonage. It was, for Bale, no worse than the shanty he had been inhabiting among the finger-dippers of Drury Lane: whereas *my* London lodgings were very precisely kept; small, but you might say finical in their neatness (my landlord had been a gentleman-usher in a dowager's household). The contrast was obscene, and so was the loneliness. After dark we lit one candle and talked interminably. I have given you some samples. But then there were silences, in the half-dark, perhaps whole hours of silence, during which neither one of us offered to go to bed, in case – yes, in case the other were to construe it as an invitation. This being the first time I had ever been alone with Bale for any lengthy period, his drawing towards young men, and then withdrawing, the courting by word, then almost-but-not-quite by touch, was utterly new to me. I ought to have suspected it, but hadn't. Even so, was I really to believe it? He had surged after his Dorothea for maybe six years, and having caught her, he'd filled her womb, already, twice. Which could prove suspicion either way, both yes and no. I was horribly frightened.

Almost as frightened as I was when *she*, in the Runagate days, cornered me on a river-bank and searched me for my absent manhood.

Oh and he was frightened too. He began to freeze toward me, to abuse me with vicious word-whips. To digress in his sermon on Sundays into ferocious uncoverings of the abominable deeds of the Sodomites. I suppose in his secret heart he tended even more toward antinomian Anabaptism than I did. (Later on, I must explain to you some of my tendencies. They are most relevant to my explication of Bale.)

Had he offered me the employment of parish-clerk, do you know I do believe I would have accepted? It would somehow have arranged our companionship upon a level that could be discussed and understood. As it was, being in his house for an indefinite time, only for 'consultations', with my complete work awaiting me with the players in London, this was anomalous, it was a mutilation, it created *pain*, as (they say) a soldier who loses his foot in battle will feel pain therein years after, rheumatism in his wooden leg. But when he *sent* me to

London, to rehearse his pretentious play, I felt he said "Behind me, Satan!": and I hated him.

The advice of La Haut-jambée would have been welcomed in Thorndon. *My* opinions were intolerable.

★

Where was she, all this while? In that hen-house in Drury Lane, still companioned with Rotraut and the other one: I am sorry to say they were impoverished.

They could no longer pay for their maids, so they sent them back to Southwark to find *successful* courtesans to titivate. They continued their minstrelsy (we worked now and then together) but Cromwell was less concerned with it than he was with the regular stage-plays: he felt it appealed chiefly to the leisured magnates in their great halls, of a class which he needed no longer to try to convert. They were not intellectual, and he had them now clenched to his purse-belt, as the monasteries one-by-one fell vacant of occupants, and the monks' lands and goods came into his gift. The plays were for the *serious* English, which to Cromwell (and Bale) meant the scholarly clergy and the responsible city-artisans. Calvin gains his men from such ranks, perhaps it was a correct judgement.

But income for Bale's wife had fallen, she was reduced to taking-in washing, while the two Germans, I suspect, took-in certain men as well. Dorothea always claimed she had no part in this, and that it did not happen in the house with her. If it did happen, she'd say, it must have been in the city, in some candle-less hole-and-corner, and they told her nothing about it. Do you believe? When you see her, think of it, imagine how many lies such a woman can tell you and never unsmooth her face . . .

There can be no doubt, though, it was hardship for her to feed and clothe her children. I was at the cottage upon occasions, bringing moneys, small enough, from her husband. Had she liked me better, I might have stayed longer and been able to enquire more carefully into her circumstances. She always sent the same message back to Bale: "We eat and we sing, and you preach. So far, no cause for distress. Conrad has seen me: he will tell you how I am." Cold messages, would you not think? And implying some ironical distrust of myself? And what would *I* say, to Bale? I hinted that she was in want, and he abused me for mocking his difficulties, where could he go, what could he do, did I not know he was doing his best? I gather his acceptance of the curacy had been cause of disaffection between them.

So I changed my tack and suggested that after all she now seemed to live more easily. He abused me again, angrily asking had Wentworth or another been giving her things, how could a man turn his back on a beautiful wife and allow these libertine lords to creep and creep around – why was I not more watchful of her visitors? His bad conscience and jealousy sickened me: and then there was another potential difficulty, a brother of Bale's turned up.

(iii) Verba Seditiosa (*Thorndon*)

This brother was a corn-factor established in Stowmarket whom he had not seen for decades. He had made money over the years: he had come to think that Bale was something of a disgrace to the family, having gone to be a friar and a successful friar at that – Divinity Doctor, Prior of Ipswich – and yet being so queer-reputed among the towns of east England – 'Bull-in-the-bush', he had heard of that – the quarrels with bishops and other friars, he had heard of those – the acting-company prancings and rantings, he had heard of them – and now, this blank refusal to wear the tonsure any longer!

He knew nothing about the wife, but he meant that his younger kinsman should not rag-tag and trudge as a country curate, if *he* could help it.

He erupted one day into the parsonage as Bale and I sat at our papers. No heartfelt fraternal kisses or even handshakes, but a brusque flinging down of his mission upon the table.

"I've seen Bill and I've seen Andy, and Ned had a letter wrote which he had sent from the old home and Molly and Kate set their marks to it, so you see it's all the family: and we want a straight answer, 'bor. Are you what they call a heretic?"

"Of course I'm not. How would the Bishop have ever let me come here if that was what he thought of me?"

"I don't know what the Bishop thought, 'bor. Bishops have been deceived before now, I can tell you. You were sent into the white-friars to make prayers for us, and for Mam and Dad, and Grandad and everyone. In my view you've gone back on a right solemn family trust. Dad and Mam had to stint theirselves to pay your premium to that Carmel-house: if you don't remember it, *we* do. You should have treated us with fairity, and you've not."

"Oh come on, Simon, come on, I reckon I have. I reckon it's been more nor fairity, I reckon its been an overplus."

He spoke as I had not heard him speak: one boor to another. Later on he learned to bring this accent into his preaching – later on? The very next Sunday. His Divinity Doctorate flew away like swallows in winter: he was quick enough to take a point – when proffered to him by an Englishman. Not so free in acceptance of a German opinion . . .

"Would you set yourself down, Simon, 'bor, and pay some heed to what I'm telling you. I have never forgot, never, the duty of my prayers for you. It's just a question of what prayers, when and how, and who they go to. Now, where's the best judge of it? A Cambridge College, or a Stowmarket grain-warehouse? I put it to you straight, Simon, where?"

"Folk are talking. You weren't paid-for to take last rites to labourers' widows: you weren't paid-for to slop around in a dirty den the like o'this, sucking-up to bloody sheep-herders so they'll give you your Easter offerings, meanwhile you live on gruel and shame the name of Bale. Dammit, Jack, look at your cassock, it's got holes in it that rats could run through!"

"Aye, folk are talking . . . They'll always talk and now I know what it is they're talking about. The corn-business, none too prosperous, on account of the sheep, isn't it? And you think that being in Thorndon I'm boozing-chums with all them cormorants as cram theirselves with ruined tillage-acres? Why, you must ha' gone whey-brained to imagine your own brother in that like o' company! D'you reckon if I was, I'd be supping nought but gruel? Godsake, man, have some sense. Wait for the Rector, when he comes, and talk to *him* about bloody sheep-herders: you'll find *him* a sucker-up, all right, a sight nearer your mark, but not me, 'bor, not me."

"Your hand on that?"

"Done."

They shook hands across the table, or, rather, struck hands, as men do in a country fair when sealing a bargain over a sale of pigs.

"Right, Jack, I'm glad to hear it: Bale's word's his bond as always? To get back, though, to this heresy-business . . . Folk are talking."

"Of course they're talking. And so they should. Lord God didn't make 'em dumb. These days there's a lot to talk about. For an instance, the north parts. You've heard of the rebellion there?" I'll tell you more of that shortly. It was a most menacing insurrection and had only just broken out.

"Bloody monks in fear for their treasures? I'm not surprised, but I don't like to hear of solid farming folk in support of them. But what's that to do wi' Suffolk, Jack? If we rebel in Suffolk it won't be to help no monks. Against enclosures, that's *our* cause, God keep us from having to take it."

"Aye, God keep. But there *are* monks, and gentry, and sheep-herders very like, as might rebel in Suffolk to give aid to the north parts. Whereat the King's ministers want a very close eye kept upon Suffolk. Close eye and a sharp ear. If I tell you in all confidence that a mere curate with holes in his cassock would not be here, were it not that milord Cromwell and sundry others has thought it best that this very place was the very place they needed him – if I tell you that, Simkin, you'll understand, won't you, how my doctrine can't be but approved in the highest circles? You do accept that the King's Grace has the right to adjudge folks' doctrine?"

"Oh o'course I'd trust the King ever before any o'these bishops, that's for certain. And it's now made law: and we all give thanks. But if what you hint to me, 'bor, is the way we want to look at it – why –"

He was highly impressed, I could see, by the notion that his brother was a well-commended royal spy. He had dropped his noisy voice (he was a roarer, this elder Bale, even louder than the young one), and tilted his cap down over his eyes to receive official secrets in an appropriate posture.

"– why, then, I say no more. I'll tell the family to say no more. And my hand upon it, Jack. Done?"

"Done."

"All I ask is, you be careful. There's murderous men about. These sheep-herders wouldn't scruple to spear you with your own dung-fork if they thought you was onto them."

He got up to leave; his mission was concluded, no nonsense, he was back to his warehouse. He had an afterthought.

"Oh, one thing about these monks and that. It's the small houses they're getting rid of this year, right? And then next year or so, the big ones. What about the friars? Are they to be treated all the same as the monks and nuns?"

"I reckon, in due time."

"Which means that even if you'd stayed, like, in the Carmel, you'd very soon be having the King's boot up your backend, and we'd lose the premium any-road?"

"I reckon: soon or late."

The brother seemed relieved. But not totally satisfied. "I daresay, if you do your work well for the King here in Suffolk, he'd not be averse to subscribing you some gratuity . . . ? Bear in mind that premium, Jack. The family could do with it, if the friars have no more use. I'll calculate the interest as must ha' mounted by now. But only if the King should choose to make it worth your while."

"I'll not forget the family, 'bor."

"And don't you go thinking, 'bor, once them Carmels are shut up, that you're free to take your turn among the women, north and south. I'd say a vow was a vow for life, dooms-bad luck to ignore it: you're still held to it, right? Don't shame the name of Bale, Jack, and we'll back you through and through."

*

The northern rebellion, in Lincolnland, Yorkshireland, and Lancasterland, was disturbing Bale most severely. He may have mendaciously played a game of official secrets to satisfy his rural brother, but nonetheless he did fear spreading consequences all over England. The talk in Thorndon was highly seditious – I heard it myself.

True, 'folk will always talk', but the bailiff's wife, a significant symptom, was outrageous and direct. Moreover, she encouraged others. She disliked Bale intensely. And she was angry and frightened when her husband was suddenly called upon to press soldiers from the Thorndon clodhoppers and bring them north to the Duke of Suffolk, who was in Lincoln to put down revolt.

One day she had planted herself, gossiping very raucously, in the middle of Thorndon street with a clutch of other women, all wives of the bailiff's faction who depended on his favours to scrape any odd job of work. Bale came down from the church and splashed past them in the October mist, tipping his beret with a frown: he knew what they thought of him. He did not expect respect, but he would not, at this stage, refuse to give it: they were, after all, parishioners.

Mrs Kirk raised her voice a notch higher: "Them in the north as has risen are all the good Christian men of England: what they do is for the common weal: and my man sent against 'em, God speed him, he knows what to do! By God, 'bor, but he knows where the stronger part is, and he'll hold wi'that: you don't think he'll bide at head o' the Duke's muster till he's forced to kill and slay his fellow-English!"

"It's not our Duke is calling musters," screamed another scrawny ignorance. "It's that Crumble does all the harm. Why, my man knew when Crumble was the Cardinal's crawling office-jack wi'scarce a good gown to his shoulders!"

And old Mrs Page, a most spiteful body, walked straight in front of Bale, with, "There's sheep-herders drive our good men off of the land, and dirty Crumble Pen-and-ink drives 'em into the muster and so into the wars, pull-devil pull-baker till all poor souls are dead and murdered!" Mrs Page disliked the Bailiff Kirks as much as she did Bale: she had her views on the Curate's doctrine. "There's one thing about the northern men: they'll bring back to us the old learning. Never good luck in England since Latin prayer went out of window! How can the likes of an old woman like me be expected to learn all this English!"

Bale had begun saying *Paternoster* and *Credo* not only in English but in the rawest Suffolk English, and this attack on his demotic principles cut him very deeply. But he walked straight away from them as though he had heard nothing. Later, he said to me, "Things were spoken which, if reported, could lead to whipping-posts and worse. 'Dirty-Crumble-Pen-and-ink' might well be a burning-matter in the present state of affairs. Lord Cromwell is leaping suspicious at any word from any quarter, and kennel-barked jests of an old distempered bitch against his own name are not going to make him *laugh* . . . But flog Mother Page? Flog half the village? Am I their pastor or their catchpoll? No: but I'll write it down. I may need it, in my own defence. I'll write it and I'll keep it safe. When soldiers are on the move, all breeds of espials follow after them. Chances are that ill-got bailiff may well report *me* for the very things his wife has said . . ."

*

Kirk and his levies came home from Lincoln in short order: they had not seen any fighting, and the rebels had been suppressed within ten days. There was more insurrection, and lasting much longer, in the other northern lands, but the Duke of Suffolk not being employed against it, his muster was soon disbanded. When Kirk heard how his wife had been addressing the world in his absence, he immediately took steps, as Bale had feared, to safeguard his position.

His chance was given him in November, when the 'King's Book' arrived at Thorndon. This was a new statement of the approved doctrine of the English Church, in ten articles, delivered to the Rector by a royal commissioner. My dear friend, do I need to project for you a full analysis? You must by now have had sufficient indication of the kind of hodge-podge and unprincipled compromise, neither fish nor fowl, which Cranmer and his quasi-Protestants were confecting together all through these years. Looked at with the pages held to the right and the eye to the left, you would think it to be broadly 'Lutheran': shift it across and read it with the opposite eye, you saw at once it was old-style roman. All the bishops had agreed to it, including Winchester: which tells you something.

The Rector of Thorndon came to his parish, and handed the book to Bale. "This has to be preached upon, Sir John – I mean, I should say, *Doctor* Bale, not accustomed, these high academic honours, my own curate, ha h'm – yes, preached upon: peremptory, from London. You're from London, you claim to understand what's going on in their minds up there: read it over and make what you can of it . . ." I looked into the book: I told Bale, *opportunity!* Confront (*coram populo*, in public, brazen-faced, no diffident half-measures!) the government's base retreat from all that had been said and done since the Catherine-marriage was first denounced. Compel Cromwell, either to left or right, like Elijah, to take a stand.

That was the day he sent me to London.

I cannot tell in detail how Bale did preach on the book. I have no doubt he confounded its romanism and its reformism into a thoroughly non-revolutionary crypto-Lollardish neo-Zwinglian hugger-mugger, to be mis-taken and mis-applied by hearers of all shades of opinion. Opinionated he himself would decidedly have been, in his weirdly positive yet imprecise way, denying Purgatory but affirming the Mass, denying Roman canonisation but giving Thomas Aquinas his saintly title (how on earth he thought Aquinas's elaborate intellectual structures would mean anything to Thorndon I simply do not know: but once a schoolman always a schoolman!), and equivocating about Confession until apparently the people thought he meant that *he* was the only man to go to, while all other priests were drunken rascals. He also had much to say about 'spiritual whoredoms' – meaning, no doubt, romishness; but somehow he contrived to suggest that the wives of the parish were whores!

At least, that was the interpretation that Mrs Kirk rejoiced to make.

By the time she had spread it about, everyone else was sure they had all heard the same thing. I know what his trouble was, of course: he had nailed his doctrine to the flagpost, that the King as Head of the Church must be obeyed in all things (reference, Paul to the *Romans*, his favourite quotation). But if the 'King's Book' contained items that showed the King's doctrine to be untenable – why, what could he do but twist and twine until he'd fought his way through it all? (Ha, even Bale at last must recognise *Contradictio Anglicana* . . . !) Unhappily he was not able to resolve his contortions before he mounted the altar-steps – Thorndon did not run to a pulpit. So the whole congregation had to hear not only what he had to say but also what he thought about before he decided to say it. But he *did* say, and all heard him, that "nothing should be held infallible, unless it is plainly expressed in the sacred Scripture of God." Elijah from Carmel upon the New Carmel! He said it.

Kirk had been busy. He had received forewarning that the Ten Articles were to be preached upon. He did not trust himself to detect heresy or treason all by himself unaided: he sent word to Sir Humphrey Wingfield, who abandoned his own church and rode over to Thorndon for his morning devotions, moustachios at point; and his estate-clerk beside his elbow, holding a significant notebook.

(iv) *Til Sees* Captivus Regis: Rex Ipse *Sees Til*

A week after Christmas, I was at Drury Lane, having high words with *Frau* Dorothea, children bawling fit to burst, the dog barking and snapping and chasing itself, wet washing all over the house-place. In comes a dirty boy with a desperate scrap of paper: a message from Greenwich Palace, only delivered upon promise of an enormous bribe to the Chief Porter, saying that Bale was in the guardroom there, held on charges by his bishop, he had been there nearly a month, without money, hardly fed at all, and beaten-up every day by papistical ruffians of the palace-guard who had been told he was an Anabaptist.

Her immediate thought was to go to Greenwich and plead for him – "The Court is at Greenwich, Lord Wentworth will be with the Court, he owes me this deliverance, I will plead with him to bring me to Cromwell – to Cranmer – I will –"

I said, quite quietly, "Who are you?" And at that she stopped dead short – she had already cloak and pattens on to fling herself direct upon the road – let me tell you she is not stupid, she saw at once what I meant. How could a heretical priest be saved by the tears of his – *wife* . . . ? Not only *persona non grata*: she was absolutely *persona non*.

And Wentworth would know all about it anyway. As Bale's sometime patron, as a neighbouring landowner, and in the absence of the

Duke of Suffolk, he would have to be told: in all likelihood he would
be made responsible for drawing the indictment. Heresy trials and
civil trials were all intermingled now in Henry's new theocracy, there
would probably be charges of treason if the preliminary hearings
revealed too much.

"Revealed too much? Too much of what, Conrad? What do you
know that you haven't told me, damn you!"

Objectively, I knew nothing. "It is only that his enemies in that
village have begrudged the forced recruitment to put down the north
rebellion, and so they'll be as frightened as he is; and so they will go to
great men in the Church, of the papalizing faction, and inadvertently
frighten *them*. For needful to them all that they show how a German
Lutheran is more dangerous even than a romanist. This bishop they
have complained to, he is at one with Winchester Gardiner, *nein*? I
warned your Bale often he pressed Luther and stupid Zwingli too far
forward in so surly a parish, I warned him –"

"Oh shut your arrant throat before I fill it with your teeth. What
God's-devil-dressed-as-angel made him ever take the curacy? It could
not have been the stipend, the stipend is pauper's-nothing, and all of
the fool's house-repairs have to be paid out of it first –"

"Left only with his play-writing, poor lady, he could not live. But
agreed, it was not wise, it was –"

"His wisdom is for *me* to question, me alone, and I speak to myself,
not to you. But if they secure great men, we shall have to do the same.
Lord Wentworth of a surety will –"

I would like to know why she kept harping upon Wentworth. He
had nothing now to do with either minstrel or stage-play work. I had
been in the same room as himself and Dorothea on earlier occasions,
and he had never struck me as a man in any way ready to assist her:
certainly not in an emergency. He was filled with surface piety and
looked straight down his silly snub nose at singing-women and other
menials. He always treated *me* as though I had accosted him from a
doorway and begged a farthing for a glass of ale. Our work of
propaganda was for him a crude necessity, only to be encouraged while
he had political use for it; and then, finish. I tried to explain, if he was
told to prosecute Bale, he would do it.

It was less than a year since Anna Boleyn died for adulteries.
Thomas Wyatt had been in prison as one of her alleged lovers; he had
in the end escaped with his life, but very narrowly: and Wentworth
was his friend. Wentworth was also one of those that sat in judgement

on Lady Anna. And now here was this Longlegs who wanted me to go
and see him, even wanted me to go to Cromwell! Be damned if I would
trust myself just then within two miles of either.

Yet something must be done, for if they burned Bale, all those who
had worked with him in whatever capacity, theatrical, ecclesiastical,
even in his academical researches, would at once come under suspicion. I would have fled across the sea: but I was totally without
funds. I had only just rendered account of the minstrel-troupe
earnings to Cromwell's purser, all the money I had in my pocket was a
few pence of my own miserable wage. I must have half-spoken
something of this: because Dorothea at once leapt at my face: "You
were yesterday with Cromwell's purser! And you do not dare to go
today! Jesus, we live and learn: sweet Jesus, the martyr of Diss . . ."

Did I tell you I was never able to withstand that woman's
scorn?

*

I had just enough money to pay Bale's promised bribe to the Chief
Porter at Greenwich gatehouse, and to offer a fee on my own account.
He looked at me oddly. "If you say you want to *see* him, 'sir' . . . I
daresay it can be fixed . . . Just wait here a moment, please. I'll have to
have a word with my partner . . . Thank you very much, 'sir'."
(Another fee: I had not thought my wallet was quite so deep.) "I'll
make sure, 'sir', that he knows it came from *you*."

He sauntered off into the back room of his lodge. I tried not to be
noticed by a cavalcade of noblemen and high-pitched ladies who came
clattering past the sentinels on the river-wharf, and in under the arch,
swathed in furs, their horse-hoofs striking sparks out of the frosted
paving-stones. One of them was Wentworth. He *did* notice me, as I
hung about, blue with cold, like an innkeeper's ostler. But he did not
draw rein or offer to speak.

The porter returned and beckoned me in. "If they ask who's been to
see him, I shall have to say *you* was; a young Dutchman, I shall have to
say . . . D'you think, now, that'll do him much good, in his present
circumstance, 'sir'?" This one really *was* the last penny. In the hope
he would not say 'Dutchman'. But however much I gave him, he
would say what best suited his interest. He led me through two rooms,
obstructed by lounging guardsmen, to a corner turret of the great
gatehouse, toward his 'partner' at an inner door (a strong grill of
wrought iron, half-way up the turret stair).

This man searched me, quite roughly: and then I must go up with him. A short twist of the stair-spiral, until we came through a trapdoor into an octagonal brick-walled room shaped like the inside of a bottle, slits for light above head-height, leaking damp down every wall-surface. Bale huddled in one corner. The place was filthy, sparse wet straw loosely strewn among the years-old muck on the flagged floor. Freezing cold. My hand against the wall felt ice where the damp was spreading. The cold did not diminish the smell: and there he sat, and wrote, his piece of paper held on his knee with a shaking hand, for he had neither stool nor table.

He was appallingly unkempt, his face covered with bruises, shuddering all over, clearly as ill as he could be. I could not see whether they had even given him a blanket. As soon as I entered, he started up to greet me, but forgot the short chain that held his ankle to a floor-staple, and very nearly pitched forward onto his face. The warder laughed.

"A foreign gent to talk to you, vicar. I'd hoped he might ha'brought you that second lot o'cash you owe me; bugger me, though, not a penny. No more messages, then, and no hot breakfast: and just be sure he speaks King's English, none of your fucking Dutch. D'you hear that, Rutterkin, I'll be *listening*!" No 'sir' now, not even ironical: and a hard punch into my kidneys as he pushed me forward. I fell onto my knees in the ooze and stayed there. The less I moved about, the better. Orders must have gone out, no private interviews with this prisoner.

Bale did not seem to care, one way or the other, all he could think of was his long list of immediate demands. He brushed aside my attempted consolations – "Never mind that, you haven't got long: you must tell me at once, what have you done, what are you going to do, who have you seen?"

I thought he would have asked how his wife was: but she had obviously got his message, and no doubt he did not wish the warders to hear too much about her. I had hoped to start off with a few words of her good health, thus postponing his direct questions. When I found I could not, I floundered. He thrust several sheets of illegible scrawled paper into my hand: "See, here is to Lord Wentworth, here is to Lord Privy Seal –" (Cromwell) – "here is to my brother. You see my conditions, how can I write with decency? Copy them all out afresh before you deliver them, and do it at once, boy, d'you hear? They would not give me paper until yesterday, and then with no pens, and the ink was frozen, I'd to melt it with my spittle, I'd to *pay* for a pen this morning, I've worn it half-away already – pay? no, but *promise* to pay, you must see them reimbursed or God knows what they'll do to me –" The warder laughed. Bale ignored him.

"So copy them, clean sheets, they go to great men. My brother will have to show his to a parson or parish clerk, I can't think he is literate. Oh, and this one here, this is for Mr Leland, if you can find him, he'll be out upon his journeyings, even in midwinter. Find out where he's gone, send it after him: copy it first, clean sheets."

Without pausing to let me ask who was Mr Leland (or any other essential question), he began at great speed to expound a *précis* of what he had been writing.

In fact, he was not quite so much the victim of a united hostile village as you might think. He had compiled long lists, in his most academic manner, full of 'to wits' and '*videlicets*' and 'as-afore-mentioneds', of people in and near Thorndon who would speak in his support, and I realised that after I left the parish he had taken pains to make some allies. His brother was to get to horse and immediately ride round these individuals and secure their *affidavits*. I expressed a certain doubt, but he brushed it aside. "Simon Bale is a *Bale*! Our good name before anything: thank the Lord he came to see me! And of course he's a man of energy, or how else could he have thrived in Stowmarket? When I last saw him years ago he was hedging and ditching for the Squire's home-farm at Cove near Dunwich: in his own way he has risen even faster than myself."

I had to laugh in that disgusting cell, to hear his pride; but he cut me short again. "What I have said to Lord Wentworth: he *must* demand the right to examine me himself. So far I am only questioned by those of the Bishop's opinion. Sir Humphrey Wingfield was at me for four hours. He cannot refuse Wentworth's co-adjudication: a neighbour-ing landowner who outranks him so greatly – he *cannot* refuse. And I have let my lord know that he should follow up the Duke of Suffolk. This Bailiff Kirk, when with the army in Lincoln, did he make any motions of ill-discipline or disaffection? Where the wife speaks at home, the husband abroad may well have let slip the rhyme to her refrain. I have heard the mustered levies were not in good behaviour, which is why the Duke sent them south again: he had offered them to the Duke of Norfolk for further service in Yorkshire, but they were refused as a pack of skrimshankers. Tell Wentworth, tell him today; I am *convinced* he must be at Court! God, that Wingfield, boot-and-saddle, with all we can find out, we will throw him over the wall . . . !"

And so on, for about a quarter-hour. When the warder rudely told us the interview was at an end, and hurried me down the stair again, I could still hear Bale through the chinks in the trapdoor, calling after me –

"– and d'ye hear, boy, don't forget – *item*: check my notes on the King's Articles of Religion – they confiscated my budget of notes, insist they let you see them! – *item*: tell my brother to make sharp enquiry as to how Kirk kept proportions of the Duke's rents for his own pockets – he did, you know – I know it, I am *sure* it can be proved – !"

We passed the grill, it slammed, I could hear no more. As I was going through the guardrooms into the open air, my handful of papers was suddenly snatched from my grasp by the Chief Porter. "Oh no, 'sir', not these: you're not taking these out with you, fuck that for a fool's-day game, 'sir'."

"Then what is to be done with them?" I faltered. There was a dreadful menace about the man's mixture of insolent politeness and abrupt foul-mouth. A male version of Dorothea. Had Bale seen the similarity?

"What's to be done? Oh very probably, 'sir', they'll be packaged for me lord the bishop and hung on a nail in his privy – OUT!"

I obeyed him, and stood again, stunned and fatuous, on the cobblestones under the arch. How to dare go back into the lodge and ask permission from such brutes to pass into the palace and fruitlessly wait upon Wentworth? They had taken all I had in bribes, I had nothing for a boat back to the city, I would have to walk. How to dare face that woman, on fire before her children with alarm and rage for her husband's safety? Maybe I should wait. Maybe Wentworth or one of his people would come out on the wharf and see me.

As for Cromwell . . . ? I preferred to think as little about Cromwell as I possibly could. The blood congealed at his very name. It was said around town that anyone could see him at any time, without formality, so long as the business was important. But if he decided that this business was *not* important, if for his own good reasons he had made up his mind that a Lutheran in prison was what the kingdom needed just at present, then my approaching him would only give him cause to gaol *two* Lutherans and advantageously double his bet. In any case, where *was* Cromwell? He rarely haunted the Court's festivities. He was probably spending Christmas at his house in Broad Street. So there was nothing here-and-now I could do in regard to him. Good.

*

It occurred to me Bale had been in that dolorous tower over almost the whole of Christmas, and he never thought fit to complain of it. He complained of the state of his pen, his frozen ink, but chiefly he complained of me, that I did not immediately comprehend his full torrent of instructions. Even in extremity his main preoccupation was his furious zeal for words, not so much for the good he would get of them as for the harm they would do his enemies. Did he think he was a martyr? In a year's time, if he got free, he would cry his ordeal in prayerful triumph from the steeples of England: but just now humble submission to his sufferings-in-Christ could not be further from his mind. Maybe his self-analogy with Paul of Tarsus had a truth? *He* must have written like a madman in his Roman guardroom. Witness some four-score pages in the last part of the New Testament.

An inconsiderable rat-faced man, a sort of subfusc attorney's clerk, came sidelong out of the courtyard, and placed himself quietly next to me, as I moved my feet once more to give place to cantering horses. When they were gone through, he said, "He passed you letters, I suppose? And they took them from you in the lodge?"

I looked at him in surprise, not knowing how to receive him. Friend or provocative-agent? He nodded to show he understood my dilemma, and slipped into the lodge. I could just hear his last words to the porter, as the latter, respectful, disconcerted, made haste to hand over the papers: "Never mind what you were told. You are now told quite different. If you are told to go to the moon, you'll be there with your dog and lantern. That's what you're paid for. Be alert."

"Now," he said to me, taking me by the elbow, "we'll bring these to where they ought to be. Inconspicuous, please, about the courtyards: a couple of clerks, that's all we are, upon tedious non-Yuletide business." I must have been gaping a little: how should I not?

For from a filigree gilded porch underneath an oriel window the King and his new Queen Jane were emerging arm-in-arm, gorgeously cloaked and hooded against the smack of the outdoor cold. With them billowed a glistering cloud of padded, slashed, and jewelled courtiers; fur-stoled tippeted clerics; pages; ladies-in-waiting: fretful footmen at the trot guarding them, guiding them, making sure they could not lose themselves in one hundred feet of cobbled yard, making sure they were not *annoyed* . . . He was, as you must have heard, a big man. His bigness increased by the bulk of his layers of clothes. Also by his ability to cause all about him to cringe. It had not been so when he was a youth, they say: in those days he had been a boy among noisy boys; and when he enjoyed himself, he had genuinely wished all others to love life with him.

Times were changing, because he had changed them: and because they were changing, he had changed. He gripped his wife as though she were his prisoner, assured that he had caught the last one available to him, and she was never going from him, never. I saw her face, puffy and anxious, trying to smile her delight at his holy-day boyishness. She did not seem an intelligent woman. But she was not, I am sure, fool enough to forget how the free gaiety of her predecessor had been noted by silent informers, enquired into, carefully analysed in dark little offices, and finally made affidavits of, a pretext for the headsman's sword . . .

I was always surprised when I heard Henry laugh. I would have expected a lion-roar, or a harsh wolfhound bark in the manner of John Bale (you'll hear those barks often enough in Strassburg: he laughs for the anger he arouses both in himself and in everyone else). But this king had a voice like a girl. A small round mouth in a wide slab of a bearded face, and a small note piping out of it. All his swaggering was kept for our *eyes*: while we watched it, our brains were unable to connect it with what came into our ears. Hence, I believe, half the terror he inspired – he looked like Herod raging, but his sound was the tree-snake of Eden.

I had seen him before, of course, but never at such close range. He almost fell over my foot. The entire party at high speed swept on across the court and in at another arch, the great hall, where the trumpeters were already proclaiming dinner. My guide had whipped me back into the corner of a buttress, we doffed caps and crooked our knees. "They allowed you too long in the gate-house," he said crossly. "This yard should have been empty. The chamberlains have observed us and will no doubt make a difficulty: but they *must* learn that the palace contains work as well as pleasure. It cannot always be done in the back-kitchen-passageways."

(v) Til *In Terrore*
Nonetheless it was precisely into a back-kitchen-passageway that we

eventually threaded ourselves, among waiters and cooks and steam and off-duty trumpeters and minstrels awaiting their call (I recognised some of them), and the usual crowd of inexplicable hangers-on, poor relations of serving-men looking for perquisite left-overs, ragged boys looking for a paid hour or two at the dish-washing, hopeless petitioners offering money to have letters dropped into the King's plate. Between the entrance to the kitchen itself and the flight of steps that led up into the hall was a small door with a man sitting in front of it, as faded-dismal as the one who had brought me there. He opened up for us without speaking or rising from his stool: we squeezed past him, and up a stairway, spiral as in the gatehouse, and no less narrow and dark. At the top, another small door. The rat-faced man tapped at it, and in we went, quietly.

Of course, I had had some dealings with Cromwell. Unavoidable: I was his minstrel and the organiser of his acting-company. But always at his house, where he met his people *en levée*, officially affable; not pompous, but not familiar. I had never been with him alone, my instructions as a rule arriving through his purser who was simply – a purser. Now, in his private office, he sat and ate his dinner: and the sound of the King's dinner – shouting, laughter, music, the bustle of servants, the continuous bang of the ever-swinging service-doors – came floating up to a small window. I did not get to look through it, but it must have given into the upper reaches of the hall.

He spread himself heavily behind a table which was loaded with piles of documents, all very neatly ordered, with coloured tags pinned to their edges. A small space was cleared in front of him, and upon it was a tray with a dish of plum-pudding and half a glass of wine. He ate, in small mouthfuls, carefully, as if in doubt of his digestion, all through the time I was with him. When he finished the pudding, he went on to another dish with sugared fruit in it, which he took from a side-table. He kept wiping his tight mouth with a napkin between bites. The rat-faced man stayed in the room, but so unobtrusively he might not have been there at all.

There was honestly nothing in Cromwell's manner to make me frightened: my fear was due solely to what I knew of him. I tried to tell myself that he too was a cringer in front of the King. Not easy to believe, but perfectly true. The higher they were, the lower they grovelled, all of them: and yet the King was less intelligent than most of them, that was known. For certain, less intelligent than this one.

Rat-face had given him the letters, and he shuffled them in one hand while he managed his spoon with the other.

"Lord Wentworth? Yes, I would imagine his lordship will be concerned. He will know some of these Suffolk people. Does he know Wingfield? Do *you* know whether he knows Wingfield, *Meinherr* Conrad?"

"Sir-lord, I cannot say."

"Do you know Wingfield yourself? Have you been there – Thorney? Thorndon? Have you?"

"*Jawohl*, sir-lord, yes. I have met Sir Humphrey."

"Knowledgeable or stupid? I don't mean about farming, or fox-hunting. Theology. Well?" He spoke quietly, deliberately, with deliberate significant pauses, some of them very long, and always with an unsmoothable rasp at the back of his words as though he had grown a thorn in his throat.

"He is, lord, *ein guter Junker*, a country gentleman, English, who approves what he has always known."

"Would he wait for a bishop to *tell* him what he's always known?"

"If the bishop was already known to him as an approver of traditional things."

"Yes? Yes, this one is. Not quite so sharp as my lord of Winchester, but sharp enough, sharp. By letter-of-law he is going to burn our unhappy Dr Bale. By letter-of-law we can't stop him. The complaint from Wingfield was presented in proper form; our playwright, as curate, is under discipline to his bishop: and the bishop is determining him heretic. If you've been at Thorndon, he'll probably burn you too. On the other hand: the bailiff. Wingfield has incorporated him as witness-in-support of the charge. Bale believes he can be discredited. He says, 'the Duke of Suffolk': suggests the Duke may tell me that the bailiff was mutinous when in the north. Such a view being founded upon the bailiff's wife's comments – have you read the wife's comments?" He pushed Bale's paper over to me.

"'The wife of William Kirk, bailiff of the said Thorndon,'" he was quoting from the paper from memory, a very rapid memory indeed (he had only had it on his desk for two minutes), "'she said that the good Christian men of England were in the north and they were risen for the common wealth, concluding thus: "My husband is now gone into the north, God speed him. By God he will hold with the stronger part."'" If we have a chance to connect *that* with Sir Humphrey

Wingfield . . . ? By letter-of-law it won't excuse Bale. His arguments on the King's Articles were *not* what was intended. But if we can connect bailiff, and bailiff's wife, and Wingfield, *and* the Bishop . . . connect them, *Meinherr*, into what could be seen as an East Anglian cabal to give succour and support to the terrorism of the northern rebels . . . ? A regrettably tenuous evidence: but it does present a chance that letter-of-law on the matter of heresy might not in the end be pressed.

"Did you yourself ever hear this Mrs Kirk?"

So far I was holding my dignity and he was permitting me to hold it ('*Meinherr* . . .'). It seemed he was trying to save us. I cast my eye down the paper. I noticed that Bale, despite the length and detail of his depositions, had taken care not to mention Mrs Page's choice epithet – 'Dirty Crumble Pen-and-ink'. This was strange. I would have thought it was his trumping-card.

No, not so strange: Cromwell would have asked why did not Bale immediately have her arrested, he would suspect Bale of some sympathy with her views, he would want to know what other names people in Thorndon, in London, at the 'Birdcage', everywhere, what names they *all* had for him, he would never leave it alone and in the end he would leave *us* to the mercy of Bale's bishop.

Even as I considered these daunting possibilities, something happened with his Christmas pudding. He found a silver sixpence in it. Had he been a greedy eater, he would probably have swallowed it. His mind was very far from dinner, just then. Slowly, most reflectively, he put fingers in his mouth, and very slowly took out the coin, very slowly he turned it between finger and thumb, holding it up to the candle-light to see it properly.

"Dominick, look at this: I have gained the good-luck piece."

The rat-faced man was sardonic: he and his master had an intimacy. "I am glad to see *someone* loves you, m'lord."

"Indeed." He gave a tight smile. "And why not? It is Yule, the customs are jovial." He moistened finger and thumb with his tongue and rubbed the coin carefully to remove all remains of pudding. He placed it beside his plate on a napkin, and looked at it. "*Meinherr* Conrad, you didn't answer me. I said, did you hear these village women?"

"I did hear them once, lord; this account seems exact."

"Dr Bale has gone to a great trouble to answer Wingfield's objections to his sermon, point by point. In a heresy-trial such arguments are useless. You either accept the given doctrine or you don't, and it is obvious Bale didn't. What's this about whores? Nobody told him to preach about whores. He's not in the white-friars now. I put him into Thorndon to let the county know that all the friars are finished: but as secular clergy they are perfectly serviceable so long as they tell the people that the King's Articles are mandatory; he rules the Church by God's command. More importantly, by Act of Parliament. Why in God's name couldn't Bale simply have said so? Not a bishop in the realm could have faulted him in that: except old Fisher, the traitor of Rochester, out of the grave talking through the red red hole that used to be his neck."

He allowed himself a brief chuckle and quenched it with a sip of wine. His eye fell on the sixpence. He meditated for a moment. "Dominick, whoever loves me, they ought not to have access to Privy Seal's privy dish. It need not have been a *love*-token."

"We can establish the name of the cook, m'lord, have him put to the question."

"Have him put under surveillance. Discover his acquaintance. If it turn out he knows anyone on lists D or G, then we have a *prima facie* of conspiracy: in which case the question *would* be appropriate. Not otherwise, it is Yule."

The rat-faced man wrote a memorandum on a tablet from his wallet. Cromwell looked at me again and resumed: "I sometimes wonder, does Dr Bale have any idea at all what's been happening in England these last half-dozen years. Look at these."

He ran his fingers down a heap of documents, found the tag he sought, and pulled out a huge thick folder. "Letters, addressed to me, personally to me: asking for this, that, the other, from all the dissolved monasteries. Here's a man wants to buy a set of brocaded vestments to turn them into wall-hangings. Here's another one finds a shed full of farm-implements in a priory-grange and begs me for a pair of scythe-blades, *gratis*; unused, he says, he's cut his thumb on them. Here's a woman smelling emeralds on one of the nuns' monstrances, and gulping at me for a bright new necklace. And here, my friend – " He held up several sheets of closely-written paper. " – here, my friend, is my friend John Bale, with annotated lists of monks' libraries in seven cloisters, and asking my assurance that some worthy Cambridge College – Jesus, understood – will be granted them, also *gratis*, for the preservation of English letters. Good God, does he think I am a charitable educationalist? If Cambridge can pay, Cambridge can have.

If not: then the bookbinders, the grocers, the soap-sellers, they'll all buy paper and parchment at good market price – and good market price is what this kingdom needs. The exchequer is depleted, I have told him one hundred times. The only purpose of all this –"

He waved both arms out over his piled desk. "– is to help the King to fill it. *Meinherr*: you see my meaning? I am wondering is Bale fit to hold any sort of cure-of-souls, in a Church quite incapable of lenient laughter at his stultiloquy, a Church which did not even laugh when Thomas More made his last quiet searching joke." More had asked, as he climbed the scaffold, for someone to give him a hand up, but he would find his own way down easily enough. I had not thought Cromwell would have appreciated that. But he was chuckling again, and almost choked on a candied gooseberry.

"No no, *Meinherr* Conrad: our friend is a fool and we might as well let him burn. It will keep some bishops loyal. With things as they are, in the north, we need all the loyalty we can get. On the other hand, he is my playwright. I think his plays ponderous and their verse often doggerel. But their matter is much to the point, they are my only poetical outbreak, vicarious, but mine: I would not have it interrupted. Besides, if *you* burn too, we shall have no-one to blow wind at the Pope. Is it known, about his 'Birdcage' woman?"

I was too worried by the implication of his gruesome frivolity to answer straight away. He was weighing Bale's usefulness against the usefulness of old-fashioned bishops as though both pans of the scales had feathers in, or little heaps of dust. One puff and they were empty. Should he puff to the right, or the left? I hesitated. He shook his head. "If *I* had known, at the time Thorndon curacy fell vacant, I should certainly have looked elsewhere. It appears they can still keep secrets in Lambeth. Dominick, make a note –" The tablets were out again. "No more secrets in Lambeth. Put a man in: the chaplain's office. That fellow we have there is no good. What department is he?"

"The Archbishop's robing-room, m'lord."

"Ridiculous. I don't want to know about moths. If he has to be a menial, why not the porter's lodge? At least he would see who comes in and who goes out. Attend to it. I thought I asked about Madam La Haut-jambée. Well?"

My attention had wandered. I was thinking out why he spoke of his spies in my hearing. Of course, it must be to let me know he was ubiquitous: but suppose I warned the Archbishop? Well, the

Archbishop would then know the ubiquity of Privy Seal. He said
"Well?" again, angrily.

"She has never been to Thorndon, lord. And I think he never
speaks of her."

"He'd better not. If I can save him, he must put her in a box.
Cranmer did: *he* can. And then post her oversea. His stink is already
sniffed, thanks to the nostrils of Squire Wingfield. We want no
woman-sweat augmenting the aroma. And she does sweat, I've seen
her streaming, armpits and groin in that Herodias dance of hers, to
soak her filmy costume till it clingeth to her a second skin." The thorn
in his throat now seemed an entire whinbush. He shuffled the letters
some more. "So: Mr Leland? You can copy this one, Dominick, and
let Leland have it. I believe he's gone to Bath. A plea from *him* would
come most handy. He can send it straight to me and I'll show it to the
King. The King is foolish-fond of Mr Leland just at present. You
know who he is, *Meinherr*? Royal Antiquary, no less, travelling the
country to write a vast book and tell the world how wonderful is
England – history, tradition, piety, and a Solomonic wealth of
architecture. So long as Mr Leland shows England more wonderful
than France, the King will hear no wrong of him, and therefore no
wrong of his friends. He's a far more useful friend to Bale than any of
your *virtuoso* Wentworths. Let me see, *Meinherr* Conrad, how useful
are *you*?"

His narrow eyes, dark currants from his own Yuletide pudding,
between creases of rolled pastry, were looking straight into *my* eyes.
His hefty square head hunched forward, and the collar of his gown
climbed up behind it. I had seen Bale in such a posture, but with him it
meant introspection. This man, however, projected *outwards*. Detect-
ing treasons through an entire nation. He virtually whispered his final
sentences.

"If Bale's wife goes oversea, maybe *you* should accompany her. Our
modest revolution is not yet quite ready for the enthusiasm of the
Almain-Dutch. Essential at the moment we consolidate tradition. Be
warned, there is a fat Yorkshireman in the minstrel-troupe has better
songs than you have. He is pious, you are satirical. If they couldn't
laugh at More, they'll not laugh at anything. Tradition and piety,
that's the playbill, from now on. And obedience, of course. Your
Owlglass arse is obedient to you, sir: but not, I suspect, necessarily to
me. So be warned, and move your haunches. Tomorrow, would be
best. But not until you've written to the excellent Bale brother. A

Stowmarket cornfactor, the very heart of English oak. Oh yes, we'll save the Curate. Off you go."

(vi) *Til* In Ignominia

I walked down the stair, through the turmoil of the kitchen-entry, attempting to understand just what had taken place. By the time I was out in the yard, under gathering river-mist night, where the torch-bearers' flames by hall-porch and gatehouse fizzled in the icy vapour, I had it all clear.

Bale would be delivered, but a price must be paid to his bishop. *I* was the price, effectively banished from England under no form of law: and so was Dorothea. And so were her babies. And so – I must conclude – was whatever joy-of-heart Bale's wife-bed had brought him, a quality I could not estimate.

The man Dominick caught up with me and nudged me gently against the wall, half-way to the gate. "He said 'tomorrow'. A figure of speech. You have this *King John* as yet still under rehearsal. You have engagements for his minstrel-troupe. He does not mean you should not complete them. To withdraw his entertainment-budget in the middle of Christmas Twelve-days would seem too abrupt, a concession, even surrender: my Lord Privy Seal Cromwell does not concede. However, by the next tide of festivity, I mean Shrove, there will be no more minstrel-troupe. By Shrove you will have left us. Call at the purser for outstanding wages: no doubt also a gratuity. Damosel Longlegs as well . . . Do you know what it was that clinched him to intervene on behalf of Dr Bale? In his letter to Privy Seal, your sometime white-friar wrote: 'I shall apply with my uttermost power from henceforth to serve God and my Prince with more soberness.' Recognition, do you see? of what our policy requires. And the first time we have heard it from Bale. Let's hear it from you too. Poetic self-judgement just as much as ecclesiastical."

"Do you mean, I am to *modify* his text of *King John*?"

Rat-grin in the rat-face. "Do you think he would stand for that? It is his master's-piece, his only child: Doll Longlegs' brats could be anyone's, in comparison, would you not say? When he wrote the word 'soberness' I dare hazard he meant only in preaching. But Privy Seal will take it further. So what to be done?" He said it again, "What to be done?" and eyed me sideways.

I had awful prevision: Bale out of his prison, distorted with anger,

trembling with ague, sitting at my dress-rehearsal, hearing line after
line cut or mutilated, or simply muted in the delivery: actors torn
between author and director-of-the-stage: messages to the Palace, to
Broad Street, to Lambeth, *ultimata*, disaster. Rat-face spoke further:
"Privy Seal has some hope the King's Grace will condescend to hear
this moral history. Twelfth Night feast, a play about his royal
predecessor, what stage-plot more appropriate? But not if there are
passages in it of too specific a doctrinal nature, Almain-Dutch or
Switzer: you'll know what we mean."

*

I looked down at my feet, cracked the ice in a shining gutter with a
stamp of my heel: and uttered without watching his face. Almost
without opening my mouth. "There would be no difficulty, were he to
remain, in – in the gatehouse, until – after the presentation."

If a cock crew that night in any of the Greenwich barnyards, I did
not hear it. The music from the King's great hall was altogether too
loud. Dominick withdrew.

*

At the gatehouse, a porter, signalling me. Not the same man I had
dealt with before. He indicated a door under the arch, the opposite
side from his lodge. Alarmed, but unable to ignore the instruction
(there were four halberdiers within their weapons'-length of my
head), I went in. Lord Wentworth – all sables-fur and gold chains –
was leaning against the mantel of a small fireplace where three or four
bits of sea-coal burned sootily. The room was some sort of accounts
office, desk, pigeon-holes, wall-charts. No-one else in it, no candle, so
it was hard to make out his features: the firelight was insufficient.

"*Meinherr* Conrad, I saw you today. Not convenient then to show
that I saw you. Not really convenient now. You have been with – with
my Lord Privy Seal?" He used to call him Tom. Smokey-faced Tom, I
heard him call him once. I nodded. "Yes? I had hoped so. I let his man
know you were here. Have you a hint for me?"

"A hint, sir-lord?" What *was* he talking about?

He was angry I did not understand him at once. With reluctance he
said what a nobleman of his importance should never have to say to a
clown. "Ah, what does it matter . . . ? Am I to prosecute Bale, or
defend him? His friend or his enemy, which? You *must* have been
given some clue."

"Defence, lord, I am almost certain. He accepted Dr Bale's letters. It is yet possible, I think, no prosecution."

"You 'think'? You are 'almost certain'? You can define it no further than that?"

"Lord, the Privy Seal is not quite a direct gentleman. I do not dare convey a directness where there was none."

He had to make the best of this. He knew it would be true. With Cromwell nothing was said, ever, that could not later be denied. Even his final promise – "Oh yes, we'll save the Curate" – could be turned to mean all sorts of things – for example, save him from hell by burning him at the stake.

"Then in that case, it will be safe for me to relieve his confinement? I want you to tell his – tell Mrs Dorothy, I want you to tell her, will you please let her know –" I cannot say why he was so embarrassed by this message: perhaps he felt he should have been to see her long before, to inform her of Bale's arrest. But if I were a lordship, if I defaulted thus in such a small obligation to one who had been (but was no longer) under my patronage, I would carry it with a haughty sneer – chivalry to singing-women was surely of a limited priority. She had, however, said, "He owes me this deliverance," a remark unexplained. I have asked her about it since. But she gave me no answer. Her privacy has always been totally impregnable. The message, when he got it out, was straightforward enough. To let her know he would ensure a more comfortable cell, and pay all the outstanding gaol-keeper's fees: no more chains, proper food, pen-and-paper unrestricted, and if Dorothea herself wanted to visit –

"Lord, I doubt that that would be – lord, I *know* it to be not possible." I had to tell him then all the 'boxes', the 'oversea'.

He said, "Oh God": and sat down in the accountant's chair. In that position the fire was full upon his face. He was a man in an agony: I could not look at him. At last he spoke slowly, thinking out his course. "This is not the way it should be done. For yourself, I see no alternative. As he saith, Almain-Dutch, you *are* a foreign man, you bring an agitation, when observed from – from a certain perspective. With rebellions in the land, the balance of sedition, the placing of this disadvantage against that, it is no doubt better for you, and for the cause, that you go. If my Lord Privy Seal does not pay you sufficient, you may call upon *my* resources. Consider it closed. But, for her . . . if she stay in London beyond Shrove, they will hunt her. Nettlestead? No no: not Nettlestead, we couldn't have that . . . The coastal fort is

still ungarrisoned. Dare I offer, dare she accept, once again the cold
shelter of the fort . . . ?"

*

His voice had sunk to a self-communing murmur, I was not sure
whether he meant me to hear, so I looked straight at the fire and stood
still. He startled me by a jerk of movement, dragging his chair round,
stooping, poking viciously at the coals.

He dropped the poker with a clang and shot to his feet. "Tell her I
will send to her. Tell her, I suggest, the fort. Tell her, if she agrees: it
will be done upon her own conditions. Not mine: hers. Make sure she
understands that. Tell her, I am a great man, at elbow of the King, in
one way much greater than when I first met her." Remember, please,
this Wentworth was first-cousin to Jane Seymour the new Queen. He,
more than anyone in Greenwich Palace those days, should have been
able to ride high and rough-shod. But: "In another way," he said,
"less than one-quarter the size. Tell her, there is – shrinking. All our
bodies are too small, and our clothes are much too large. So large that
we can turn ourselves within the one pair of trunkhose, front-to-back,
and no-one notices. Not a wrinkle upon the cloth."

He stopped himself, aware that a plain (if allusive) message had
drifted into pointless allegory, and was in any case none of my
business. He ordered me out of Greenwich without further courtesy.
It would have been thoughtful of him, had he offered me my
boat-fare: but he did not. I made bold to ask for it. The coins were into
my hand in the one movement with his departure from the room. He
would have no more to do with me: unless I failed to carry his message,
and then he would follow me like a wolfhound and tear me. I could see
it in the set of his teeth: very dog-like, that lord's physiognomy.

(vii) *Preservatio*

As I presented it to her: I had been first to see Wentworth at
Greenwich, that being my commission; he had referred me to
Cromwell, and Bale had been visited as a consequence of these lords'
concern. The whole affair was a sad error of incompetent administration: confusion between departments of Church and of State. But
documents were, alas, on file, and Bale's release must now depend
upon the speed of cunctative bureaucracy. It could not be guaranteed

he would be out before *King John* was staged. But Cromwell was most earnest that he *would* do his best.

She put her arms round me, bit her lip, refused to weep. She did not say very much. When she asked me, was it possible – any hope – ? did I possibly think – ?, I knew she meant to ask, 'Could she visit him?', and was afraid of an answer. We had had all this before. I began to lose patience. Her gratitude for my treachery was causing me a most unusual embarrassment: I passed wind, it was *involuntary*! Another minute, it would be diarrhoea.

But she said, "God, you were brave, Conrad, going into that place today! I had not thought you could have done it. When *you* were taken, at Diss, I ran and ran and ran . . ."

I gave her Wentworth's message, following my version of the reason for Cromwell's *ultimatum* which had caused it. My most arid revolutionist gusto: in order to placate their reactionary papalist elements, the time-serving feudalists in government had brought pressure upon Cromwell to appear to betray the progressive cause he claimed to espouse: a temporary expedient which would ultimately inevitably serve for a knife in his own back. But as a *buergerliche Novus Homo*, only tolerated for the deftness of his financial manipulations on behalf of the ruling caste, he had no solid political base to withstand these occult attempts . . . so, for me, Germany. Scapegoat Til. Scapegoat La Haut-jambée . . . ?

I'd burst into it, with some harshness. She foresaw what I would say. Until I said 'fort'. At that, she gave one great shudder, head to foot, goose like a Roman omen-bird over her grave: and then nothing. Her privacy was impregnable.

She plucked her elder son from under the table, where he was making a house out of his wooden alphabet-blocks within a house made of a blanket spread over the table and hanging down to the floor-rushes; she plunged him into her bosom as she walked up and down. Half-buried between her breasts, he gave little moans of protest, till I feared she was holding him so tight he would smother. The room was warm – she had piled the fire with spitting logs – she was bare-footed, her skirts had been kilted up for some dancing-practice before I arrived: and she paced up and down, up and down, for ages she kept on pacing, like the King's leopardess in London Tower. I think she forgot I was there. She was talking to the child, but her words were incoherent. At last, she halted, and saw me, as though she had not expected me in the house at all.

"Ah: Conrad? You said . . . ? Fort? You said, he would send to me. But before he does, he wants an answer. So that he will know what to send? I have it right, have I not? Sweet Jesus, it must be midnight. Why isn't this child in bed?" Her son had gone to sleep in her grasp. She laid him very carefully into his bed-box in the corner, and then stooped over the cradle beside it to see that the younger one had not been woken.

"'Truda and Rotraut are both in bed, they don't like the cold weather. In the Rover's days we were much colder. Weren't we, Conrad? Much. One night at Bury St Edmunds I thought I would truly die. Conrad, listen to me. Go to Wentworth, or send to him, it doesn't matter which. The word is 'Yes': and my condition? He did say, upon my condition? My condition is that Bale is a free man before I go. My condition is that he agrees. You understand me: *Bale agrees*. Birds have nests, foxes have dens, the Daughter of Woman has nowhere. All I want is to lay my head: all my life they have been taking all of the pillow-stones for themselves."

*

You will remember I told you I had earlier criticized Bale for his refusal to face the Historic Necessity of Confrontation with the Illusory Reformism of this government? Such always was the gist of my debates with him, at least I hope it was. It is probable you will be thinking that here and now was confrontation: and what was I doing about it? Surely, you will think, if the papists in the north were in arms to reverse the revolutionary gains, then this must be the time to assert those gains so solidly that they would not only be preserved but extended?

Ah . . . such a perspective does not take into account the prevalent condition of England. The English were more frightened, indeed *are* more frightened, of irreconcilable civil war than of any other social phenomenon. Change their Church or keep it, for the greater part they remain equable, and go to sermons of either extremity with at most shrugs and grunts of a moderate disconcertion (I speak of the generality: there are of course determined forces in defined interest-pockets of the population). But once you appear to threaten them with any repetition of the roses-quarrel of the last century (even though it was not a *total* quarrel, being élitist, dynastic, confined largely to the ruling families, their territorial militia, and hired bands of mercenaries), the English people will at once come together, instinctively, to reinforce the power of the crown, the only watchword will be 'loyalty', the only enemy will be dissidence – and they do not care an Owlglass burp whether that dissidence (objectively) be reactionary or progressive.

Experto crede, I speak what I know: if the King, defying the Pope, must send out soldiers in defence of his defiance, the nation at large will also defy the Pope: but *only insofar* as the limits of such defiance are set by the King-and-Council and made apparent through regional sheriffs by promulgation of Acts of Parliament. In other words, public support will be available not so much for augmentation of the struggle with Rome as for the defensive *preservation of the limits the King has set*. In other words, for Bale in prison, for Conradus Joculator attempting to maintain the integrity of Bale's play, for Conradus facing deportation, for Bale's wife facing the legally-unrecognisable nature of her marriage – no more friends in England than you could number on one hand's fingers.

I trust this brief analysis will elucidate for you my compelling reservations *in re* the ostensible possibility of my adopting a resistant stance – an *individualist* resistant stance – toward the cultural-doctrinal-political-personal crisis of January 1537. My decisions, I hold, were justified both tactically and strategically. In any case, we are still alive – me, Bale, La Haut-jambée – and surely that is the *sine qua non*?

*

I will deal first with the *King John* production. Bale, *mirabile dictu*, was still in custody, although indeed with improved conditions. The play was given, on Twelfth Night, at Cromwell's house in Broad Street. Interestingly, not in the house itself: he lived in a rented property belonging to the Austin Friars, but it had no hall large enough to accommodate King and Court for a formal festivity, so the evening's proceedings were moved across the garden to the friary-hall itself. The brethren were naturally invited.

They knew that their tenant was actively in process of securing their dissolution (it took place the following year and he pulled down their buildings to erect himself a small palace): they also knew the play had hard things to say about religious orders – as you can imagine, their response to it was *mixed*. However, it was a show: they did not pay for it themselves, they had all been promised secular benefices, school-masterships, hospital wardenships, and the like, provided they disbanded their community without undue fuss, and the presence of King and Queen was an excellent opportunity for them to show their 'loyalty' – which they did, with appreciative warmth.

Bale's play, given in full, would have lasted perhaps between two and three hours. King Henry would never have sat after dinner for so great a time to watch a single play on *any* subject. His entertainments were commonly long-drawn-out: but always full of varied items, none of which was to continue more than forty minutes.

I once took part in an expansive programme upon his coronation-anniversary at Hampton Court. Myself, Rotraut and Ermentruda danced the *Huepfauf* and fooled and sang for maybe twelve minutes: and were incontinently signalled-off by the Master of the Revels to give place to a team of jugglers, who in turn must curtail their act in favour of two Turkish wrestlers. After the wrestlers came a comedy – not by Bale's people, but John Heywood's (our chief playwright-rival, a crypto-papist who on the whole kept very clear of heavily-contentious subject-matter). The King was fond of Heywood's work, but on this occasion something went wrong.

In the middle of an absurd argument between a Water-miller who wanted wet weather and a wind-miller who wanted gales, Henry Bluebeard began to yawn. When a Gentlewoman and a Washerwoman came disputing about sunshine, he shifted in his seat. And finally – as the God-of-the-Weather launched into a series of truisms (all people have need of the sort of weather they severally need)[1] – he was heard to remark that a wet day was a wet day, there was nothing we could do about it except wait for it to clear up, and although he knew his good English folk loved to talk about nothing else, an hour-and-a-quarter upon this subject at that hour of night was seventy-five minutes too long – "Give me some light!" he called, "Away!" And the interrupted actors received not one third of their contracted fee.

So the reduction of *King John* to less than half its original length was circumstantially unavoidable, and not even Bale could have made any serious objection. As to which parts of the script were cut: well, I knew my duty. 'Loyalty', 'more soberness', 'obedience to the King's Articles'. We had to strike out, in great haste, such lines as these (dialogue between King John and his advisers) –

---

[1] Maybe Heywood meant to hint to the King, "We all have need of the sort of *religion* we severally need"? But if so, he pusillanimously eschewed direct statement, and the meliorist-reactionary point of his play was lost.

T. Eul.

CLERGY:
If you continue, you will Holy Church confound.
KING JOHN:
Nay, no Holy Church, nor faithful congregation,
But an heap of adders of Antichrist's generation.
CIVIL ORDER:
It pitieth me much that you are to them so hard.
KING JOHN:
It pitieth me more that *you* them so much regard.
They destroy men's souls with damnable superstition . . .

(*etcetera*)

– 'superstition' might be taken to mean the sort of semi-papal doctrine in the Articles which had already caused Bale so much grief, and we could not suffer the risk; while to attribute 'Holy Church' (unqualified) to the engendering of Antichrist would have been lunatic under the present circumstances. On the other hand, there was no problem one-third-way down the same page where King John asserts his authority:

KING JOHN:
Arise, Clergy, arise, and ever be obedient,
And, as God commandeth you, take us for your governor.
CLERGY:
By the grace of God, the Pope shall be my ruler.
KING JOHN:
What say ye, Clergy? *Who* is your governor?
CLERGY:
Ha, did I stumble? I said – my *prince* is my ruler.

But all this chopping and changing took ages (some lines had to be half-cut, half-kept, losing both rhythm and rhyme): I had been forced to sit up all night messing with it, scrubbing out ink-blots, nearly in tears before morning. And then the actors had to relearn it, and *they* were in tears too. So finally all came on stage with their scripts thrust humiliatingly into their sleeves in case they lost their words – and some of them *did* lose them, and had to *read* them willy-nilly. Which was villainously unprofessional, but thank God, the King laughed at it: being comfortably under the egocentric assumption that as he himself was most accurately (and flatteringly) portrayed by the first-player, the company must be made nervous by the thought of *lèse-majesté*, and of that he was delighted to absolve them. Indeed, no sooner had the first-player effected his entrance, in his second role,

Imperial Majesty (as King John his appearance was non-committal, a crowned emblem from a pack of cards), than the genial monarch called out aloud to Cromwell, "By the Mass, Privy Seal – !" ('*by the Mass*,' yes. No wonder his Articles were as they were.) "This fellow should be sent to Holbein's workshop straightway to give him his lesson in how to paint our face, ha?"

Of course we ought to have had a prompter, and it ought to have been me. But because Bale was in prison, I had to take his parts (reading them *in toto* from off the script). I was well-enough able for Clergy, and for Usurpéd Power (*alias* the Pope), giving my best qualities, respectively, of servile-weakness-developing-into-reformed-strength, and brute arrogance. The difficulty was Widow England, who, without her head-tire and with her dress concealed under a vast scholar's gown, was also Baleus Prolocutor introducing the play (*Conradus* Prolocutor, and most of the lines cut – 'Antichrist', again!). The Widow was the only female role, though not a young one, and Bale would have played it with an urgent sort of fish-wife vitality. I shaved my feeble beard and did my best: but I cannot say my German-accented English was in any way helpful to the part. Suppressed sniggers from the audience all the way through: Good Queen Jane dared to make a joke to her husband – "'Widow Dutchland', I'd have thought, dear heart; if he had not told us different!" But the King snapped his fingers at her to shut her up – yes, *he* knew better than to laugh at his England. I thanked him with an impertinent Eulenspiegel curtsey, and then wished to God I hadn't: I was not playing a clown-role (luckily I had the presence of mind to omit the fart). Neither Hal nor Jenny took offence, as it happened; but I found myself shaking with terror for the rest of the performance.

Bale's imprisonment, too, had unsettled the company. I told them that without doubt he'd be out by the end of the week, *earlier if the play went well*, which might have been too nerve-racking an incentive.

Our much-wronged *Jungfrau*, the scornful Longlegs, had organised the music. I'd expected she would not be there for the performance, but there she damned well *was*, will you believe? – as though she had no trouble in all the world beyond ordering the musicians into their places, furnishing them with their proper scores, darting her arm out to give them their cues – oh yes, and herself joining in with her cittern for one of the pieces. She was most angry-vainglorious right through the evening: and I think she had her suspicions about those cuts in the text. She swore at me filthily once, when I was changing my costume back-stage: for the rest of the time she ignored me.

Yet I think, may I say? that the presentation was a success. A bonus upon our wages, and – at the end – a commendation from the royal lips: "John Plantagenet was unlucky, in that he had no good poets to maintain him, all those of his day that writ of him were monks of mischief. Thank you, gentlemen, you have shown us such is not the case with us!" Then, swiftly turning upon his host's landlords, the friars, behind him: "*Is* it, Father Prior? No, not in Broad Street, never in Broad Street. Be sure that you keep it so."

*

Bale was released two days later. I was agreeably relieved to find he made little of the dismemberment of the play. Indeed he would not at first talk of it, preferring instead to evade all serious problems of church, state, cultural matters and personal conflicts by fossicking on about something that seemed to me to be of no conceivable consequence at all. (This conversation took place in my room in Aldgate – he had been at his Drury Lane establishment for two days and a night – between him and his wife there *must* have been heart-rendings: but nothing whatever of it to me. I'd once thought I had his confidence.)

His obsessive narration dealt only with a visit he had made, just before his arrest, to a village called Eye, nearly half-way between Thorndon and Diss. Here he had found the elder sister of the woman he termed 'John Skelton's Calliope', "very old, very blind, disinclined to tell me too much, because, as she said rudely, it was none of my business: her sister had shamed the family by being honoured by a naughty poet. I asked her, how 'shamed'? for one knows that in these rural places the more ignorant regard a priest's woman as having lifted the household status by such a connection, and this household was clearly very poor, very ignorant. She answered that the shame was – in her own words – 'on account it was a *honour*: she went and she said they was wedded man-and-wife, and that babe o'theirs was *honourable* being a child of the Garland of Laurel, which I dunno and none of us knew what devilment she could a' meant. Being true for all time that no priest-man's ever a *married* man, whatever he do with his flesh-thing. In nature 'tis not possible, so what could she a' meant, 'bor, but there was witchcraft-spells to it, summat o'that? Allgates, poor Margery's dead, and the babe's growed up otherwheres, and *I'm* to die soon, likely, and that's all I'm going to tell you.' She was an ugly old hag: but when young, I think not. Very like the sister too would have had somewhat of beauty. Pride of soul she surely had. I stumbled on her, strange, wasn't looking for her at all, I was searching out Kirk's delinquencies in Eye, as it happened: but somebody happened to mention her. I went to see her. That was it. Mannerly Margery Milk-and-Ale, ha."

Relief or resentment that he didn't care to talk of *King John*? But even so, he had to talk of it, I could not let it rest. I forced him to hear me explain what I'd been forced to do, cut the script, change the sequences, how was I to know at the last moment the King would be there –?

He slammed his hand on the table, as if to say, 'finish with it!' Then, with a sour smile, as though he half-forgave (half-forgiving less than half the truth): "As far as I'm concerned, *King John* has not yet been staged. What His Majesty heard was – was some improvised nonsense got together by harassed players in the absence of an author: we forget about it, we look forward to our first presentation. I'm told Cranmer has hopes of a showing at Lambeth one of these days. His sermons are long enough – no reason why he should not endure a play of an equal duration. For the Archbishop: complete text: entire meaning: no fudging of veracious history!"

Had his wife told him she'd had her suspicions of me? I think not. She must have feared lest she drive him mad.

And it did happen, the full play – in two parts, over two days – not in Lambeth but at Canterbury, and not for another two years. I myself was not there, but Bale informs me that Cranmer was delighted by the doctrine, the scholarship, the dramatic power, the strength of language, the excellence of all the players. Bale informs me it made his name. Caused all men of taste to forget Heywood absolutely. Caused many in the business to enquire why English history was not used more often as an inspiration for the playwright's art.

Caused at least one eminent foreign poet to send him a profound letter: David Lindsay of the Mount, chief herald to the King of Scotland, upon an ambassadorial visit, had been to Canterbury on purpose to see the play – he wrote comparing Bale to the Roman Ennius, stating that out of the fountain of this epoch-making work the mature tide of English drama would assuredly be seen to flood. He praised in particular the learned courage of the playwright – who –

– did skulk nocht frae sic peril whilk ane mair timid hairt micht peradventure haf dreidit: nae consequence, politic nor doctrinaire, of your stark theime did we see shifit-frae or left fallow like ane disregardit glebe. Forbye, for your guid carlish rage against enormities of the Kirk, ye wad remeidless be brent in Scotland!

Cranmer had gone to much trouble to provide that sort of audience. It did wonders for Bale's conceit.

But he still is not Hans Sachs. And Kirchmayer can outmatch him any day. English drama, in my opinion, will remain just as it is, a vigorous but incurably provincial offshoot of our *Hocheuropa* school of letters: cultural equivalent of its concomitant religion and politics. *Experto crede. King John* was much improved by being cut in London to forty minutes.

(viii) Contradictio Contra Naturam

By this time you will have come to a certain conclusion about Dorothea and 'the fort'? That Wentworth was offering to hide her, if she agreed to become his mistress? Of course, yes: the only wonder was, he had not had her before. Extraordinary she should have been caught by a ruffled old barn-owl like John Bale, while ignoring for so many years so desirable a baron (a hateful baron, yes: but his well-paid-for trim body was very long and strong, his smile upon rare occasions *captivating*). At all events, the disparity was now most appropriately redressed.

After Bale came to see me, he spent a week more in Drury Lane, and then went back to Thorndon, leaving her to await whatever Wentworth laid ready for her. I assume he had, during this time, 'agreed', as she had specified. The exact nature of his agreement can only be speculated upon: I made a few deductions from what the Rotraut told me, about a month later.

For Rotraut and Ermentruda, some time towards the commencement of February, received their own message from Lord Privy Seal: they too, they heard, were no longer needed by 'traditional' England, they too must be off and out back to Germany before Shrove. Rotraut came to see me to consult about the journey, she thought we might all three travel together, and even work together, once we got happily to what she so excitedly called "*das schoene Vaterland, ach Gott, Konrad-Heimat . . . !*" I concluded that their gratuity was a great deal more adequate than the one I had been awarded, as she spoke with animation about setting up a '*Musik-und-Tanzsaal*' in Rostock or Luebeck or somewhere else along the Baltic coast, not at all a district that held any attraction for me. I think she had been consorting with the Hansa mariners in London river during her days of indigence: she came from those parts, anyway.

But she made it very clear that her deportation was no hardship; anything, she said, rather than remain in London in such a time of fear and suspicion. Ermentruda and herself had only come to England to make money: and all they needed to leave England was enough money to render it worthwhile. I cannot say why Cromwell's office should have treated them so handsomely. I was soon to find out that these matters in that office were very carefully calculated. Perhaps one or both of them had slept with some great man, had come to know a little too much about him, and it seemed easier to pay them off rather than to intimidate. Speculation: she did not tell me.

But intimidation had come first. She *did* tell me about that, how, after Bale had gone back to Thorndon, the Drury Lane farmhouse was beset with night-time lurkers; their dog had been mysteriously poisoned; they had had threatening messages nailed to the gatepost, warning them, all three, that informers were at work after them, heresy, treason, misprision of clergy-crime, concubinage *contra naturam*: everything about them seemed to be known to somebody and they daily expected the constables with a search-warrant.[1] They burned letters – they hid scripts – they buried a few pieces of jewelry because they were the gifts of Protestant admirers (not that they had many jewels left unpawned) – and they terrified one another with their terrors. Rotraut would have left at once, but Ermentruda said no, the stricken Longlegs was their friend, they could not, must not, abandon her before she heard from Wentworth. So they stayed on: and all three of them quarrelled mercilessly; love, apprehension, resentment, fouling their tempers like offal dropped into a well.

When she talked about Bale and his wife, Rotraut was oddly evasive, seeming to want to confide in me, but not desiring to tell me too much. I think there was some deep personal difficulty between herself and Dorothea, because Rotraut was usually a ruthless gossip, even in regard to her friends. She must have made promise not to reveal; but could not prevent herself from a *degree* of revelation, the more so as we talked of Germany, in German: *'Heimat'* loosened her tongue.

---

[1] Was there evidence against them? In English courts, who needs evidence? Their 'own unaided statements' would at once have convicted.

                                                                    T. Eul.

This much I learned. The day Bale returned from prison, pale, sick, all disordered, and his wife told him what I had said to her about the 'fort', he fell onto her bed under the loft-ladder and wept for a full three hours. Ermentruda, at length, was fetched in from her out-house room (Rotraut not being at home) by little John coming crying in fear across the yard – "Mamma fighting him, pulling him, I don't like it, he's got *teeth* – !" She found Dorothea dragging furiously at Bale's body, while he lay rolled up in a tight ball among the bed-clothes, clutching his hands into the mattress, biting at her to make her let go, dreadful noises out of his unshaven face as of cats in a roof-ridge brawl; and Paul, the baby, tossing in his cradle and screaming like an unwatched whistle-kettle. The Ermentruda stood no nonsense, she threw a water-bucket over the pair of them.

But ten minutes later Bale was up and threatening self-murder with a carving-knife. Dorothea could deal with *that*: she had learned knives well, from the Catgut man. But their best earthenware bowl got broken in the struggle and half-a-gallon of fresh milk ran all over the flagstones. Dorothea swore, if the bastard wanted death, she would kill her own self and welcome. Presumably he blamed her for demanding from him their rash marriage, whereas she blamed him that she had not spent these years as Wentworth's established mistress with lap-dogs and her black woman in silk and a fat steward with a silver collar. To go to Wentworth now (in flight from Cromwell, bishops, whipping-posts, burning-stake even), was a very different business, hole-and-corner, always frightened, no chance at all for her to strut the town bare-bosomed, belly out and jewels gleaming: by Christ, but she had wasted her life. And what about the children?

Rotraut came into the house just then, just in time to see Bale packed up the ladder into the loft, and Dorothea scrambling after him. As he went, he groaned some words, the first coherent ones either German had heard him utter: "I am *not* Paul of Tarsus, neither Saul nor Paul, but *Joseph*." Did the Rotraut know what he meant? I am persuaded she did, but she's a buttocky sly stubborn Pomeranian, and when she talked to me she had of course been at my schnapps; she lowered her eyelids and pretended she had understood nothing.

I did however arrive at a tentative theory. Joseph in *Genesis*-book had gone to gaol: charged with rape of Potiphar's wife. But she had framed him, had she not? for his refusal to lie with her. Was it possible that such a means had been employed by Dorothea to get Bale into the marriage?

I mentioned earlier, 'cunt-extortion': if this theory was correct, I must add to it 'police-extortion', and of course at such a juncture it would be most vivid to his recollection, with the foul odours of Greenwich tower not yet cleansed from the creases of his body. I dared not put it to Rotraut, because she was growing most objectionable and would have refrained from no abuse of me in defence of her friend. 'Her friend': that struck off another train of thought.

If Rotraut lay with men it was for money and not pleasure. Could it also be that Bale had no true zest for a normal fornication? Had he commenced to frequent Dorothea as a cloak for his other, more dangerous desires – desires toward Wentworth perhaps, certainly toward me, toward the various boys who played women's roles in the acting-company? If so, she had called his bluff with most dreadful finality.

I was not sure that any of these theories were consistent one with another. I only record them here to show the difficulty of recording *anything* about so gargoylish a man as Bale, so sphinx-like a woman as La Haut-jambée. We can but look at them as they appear to us, shrug our shoulders, write what we see, and that's it.

The night following, and the day after, Bale stayed in the loft and all was silent. In the evening, he visited me, and rambled about Skelton. Turning the old woman's 'witchcraft-spells' over in his mind, he returned to Drury Lane, fetched Dorothy into the loft with him, and there they remained quite alone, without even the children, for as many days and nights as he was in London. I asked the Rotraut what did they do there? Did they couple? She said oh no, had they been at that game the floor-joists would have rattled, it was that kind of house: she and Ermentruda had been much in the room downstairs and they never heard a thing. She supposed they *talked*.

Dorothea came down at regular intervals to feed the children. Otherwise she left them – quite careless – with the Germans, who were angry at her, you may be sure, but could get no sense out of her. She would not speak to them. Once, and only once, as she sat and gave suck, she cried aloud, suddenly: "God's curse, is this love, true love as in the Lancelot-books? That he is always where he should *not* be: and I am his *fish*, that's all I am – dragged in the trawl-net through sand and rock and barnacle." And then she laughed and could not stop. I guessed she was talking about Wentworth. "Was she?", said Rotraut with a hiccup. "Mistake to tell you anything, Konrad. Go to hell, you unballocked arse-farter."

I made up my mind I would travel to Germany by myself. Women who lie with women ought in theory to make good *Kameradschaft* with men who can lie with nobody: but the theory is ill-conceived. *Experto crede*.

Then she started telling me all in a drunken rush how Wentworth had sent for his mistress, sent two mounted grooms with a spare riding-horse, and a pack-mule with panniers for the little children, and off they all went to the Pool to embark upon a river-barge for somewhere. As they trotted down the steep lane toward the Strand, Bale came all undressed out of the cottage to yell a farewell message – "He has said it is his reparation, and after this he can do no more! So be it, in the name of God! God send him no more need to make any more amends . . . !" Dorothea did not turn her head.

But how can he have been there? The Rotraut told me he had gone to Thorndon, leaving all three women to intimidation? I pressed her, she evaded. And then, with more schnapps, came the truth, or part of it. Bale had intended to remain at Drury Lane until Dorothea was safely away. But on the seventh night of his stay there he came down from the loft to go outside for a necessary purpose: he heard his wife in the Germans' outbuilding, sobbing and sobbing. He went in to see: she was feeding no child (both babies were asleep already) but lying on a bed with Rotraut in her arms and one hand stretched out to clutch Ermentruda's hand as though she would be pulled from drowning. "It was nothing," said Rotraut, "Well, perhaps not so very much of nothing, perhaps something, *ach vielleicht*, but so little a tender thing he could not have seen, yet he made up his mind it was: *contra naturam*, his worst fears. So *natuerlich* he would have no more of her, he hired horse for his parish that very night and rode all in the dark to get there." *Then* came the weeks of fear: and then, again, Bale. He could not indeed leave her, he had to be there when Wentworth sent; he *was* there: and Dorothea refused to talk to him. He waited in that cottage, shunned by the three of them, three days until the grooms arrived, and shouted farewell as I have said.

As soon as she had gone, once more he was off to Thorndon, once more he was resident curate, writing plays, writing books, preaching, praying, and dourly triumphing over those who had had him gaoled. But his superiors worked hard to be rid of him: can you blame them?

(ix) Contradictio *Wife-And-No-Wife:* Incognito-Et-Cognito, *Twice*

I had made ready for my voyage: a summons came from Broad Street. The man who sent for me was Dominick. He had orders for me. I was to wait. I would soon be going to Germany: but not until certain commissions were prepared by Lord Privy Seal which he wished me – no, commanded me – to execute once I got there. It was implied that my gratuity might well be increased. If I ignored the instruction, it was also implied, there would be no gratuity, there might indeed be a gaol-cell. I was, in short, to serve as a Cromwell-agent on the continent, furthering his intrigues (well-concealed from the official diplomatists) among a number of great men and small men whose Protestant leanings appeared useful to English policy. The King, I gathered, had not been told of his Privy Seal's initiative. And I was to live in Broad Street, secure and secluded, until the day of my departure, so that he would not find out. I felt immensely important. Also worried: I did not like this hiding from the King. A faint echo of rattling gallows-ropes came blown upon the winter wind.

These arrangements prevented me hearing anything more just then about the Bale-business.

Mind you, I was not displeased to take a hand in bringing the Lutheran states and the English together. Ah, I do admit to inconsistency, before you accuse me of it. I was ideologically opposed to Lutheran states, *per se*, of course: but they were there in being, an objective fact. So let us use them. All the King wanted to do – and do as a great king, upon an equality with other great kings, none of your *Landgraf, Pfalzgraf, Markgraf* nonentities – was to play off France and the Emperor one against the other, just as he had always done. He was obsessed, moreover, by the treachery of his kinsman, Reginald Pole, an English cardinal-in-exile, a man easily encouraged, who had inspired himself with the Yorkshireland rebellion, and was stirring all southern Europe for a crusade to reclaim England for the Pope. Henry could not see how much more easily all this could be withstood by help of strong Protestant allies. But then, he was no Protestant: only an outcast Catholic, driving his inflamed huge feet through a wilderness of his own laying-waste.

*

After Easter, then, I left for Hamburg, fulfilled my first commission tiresomely slowly but without danger, and returned several months later by way of the Low Countries. I had to report to Broad Street for fresh instructions: it was emphasised that my short stay in England prior to my next assignment was *not to be known*. So I must at all costs avoid Harwich, where the Antwerp ship put in, because I would certainly be noted there by several clandestine agents, English and foreign, who had attached themselves to the port-authorities.

With discreet venality, Cromwell's office had arranged beforehand for a river-barge to meet the ship by night, close to the Essex coast, where we were standing-off to await the tide. The morning was foggy and therefore safe: my barge brought me into Hamford Water, a lagoon of mud-flats and half-tide islands, just inland of the Naze. A man from Colchester was supposed to be ready on the causeway with a horse: but he had not arrived. All my baggage was a *Rueckensack*, so I slung it on my shoulders and ill-temperedly began to walk. I could have waited for him: but I ran great risk of being held and questioned by coastguards. I must get myself away from the sea as soon as I could. Fear of invasion was constant at that time, from the French, from the Empire, from both: no stranger along the shores but was thought to be some sort of spy. And I was some sort of spy: I could not afford to be caught.

At the first village (Thorpe-le-Soken, I have since heard it is called), a meagre place, almost as mean as Thorndon, I decided to be bold, and to present myself as a Netherlands pedlar with a sales-circuit in those parts, making my way back to Zeebrugge to replenish merchandise; I had lost my road to Harwich in the fog. I went into the ale-stake to make a plausible enquiry: and I found myself face-to-face with La Haut-jambée.

She was serving at the bar. Bare legs into clogs, a greasy apron, an old red shawl, her hair caught up with a grimy kerchief as though she had pulled herself out of bed only six minutes ago, dressed herself in two minutes, broken-fast in one: and all unwashed for weeks. At her worst days in Drury Lane she appeared far less utilitarian. At her worst days in Drury Lane she never forgot to wash.

*

There were some peasants in the room, drenching their throats by way of mid-morning refreshment. I must not recognise Dorothea before they were gone: nor, I understood, would she greet me. We were both illegal residents. So I asked for a drink in my poorest English, and requested the Harwich road. She shrugged her shoulders and referred me, without speaking, to the peasants: who laboriously conveyed that I was a stupid Dutchman, didn't all the world know where Harwich was? and that I was to turn sharp right at Beaumont and then right again at Great Oakley but *not* turn left at Little Oakley, mind that: not *left*. They drained their mugs, shouldered their spades, and went out.

I said: "Is this the 'fort'?"

She said: "It's not. The fort is full of soldiers, put there by the King. Don't you know we're expecting war?"

As I leaned on the bar I saw her elder child was clinging to her skirt, coarsely clothed in linsey-woolsey, but I would say well-enough fed. "Mamma, mamma, Uncle Conrad!" She told him shortly he was mistaken, I was not an uncle but a stranger, and would he go into the yard and play. He whinged that there was fog, he was feared of the boggart-man that lived in the fog; and he stayed where he was.

"Little pitchers," I said. I could see, through the door behind her, the baby in a wheeled playing-pen: I hoped he would not trundle himself toward me, also giving evidence of knowledge of my face or voice.

She did not ask what I was doing. I expect she guessed the general shape of it. It did not appear that the shape of her guesses pleased her. "I think you'd best be on your road." She was talking as she had talked when I first knew her, east-England boor-speech; disguised in voice as well as raiment.

A man came into the bar from the back of the house, the landlord, hefting an ale-keg. He tumbled it onto the counter, and worked his strained arms about with a groan. Another group of peasants entered at that moment. Dorothea took their orders, while the landlord bent over his keg to knock the tap in. He kept his eyes on me as much as upon the job. I thought they were surprisingly bright eyes, expressionless, but they missed nothing.

"Uncle Conrad," bleated that brat again.

There was an awful silence.

"Ah," said the landlord, filling mugs from the new keg for the peasants, "you're a stranger. Lost your road?"

"Harwich," she answered for me, as she passed the mugs along the bar.

"Ah," said the landlord, and straightened up.

"I know him," she stated. She had to: he knew that she knew me. He had very sharp, bright eyes. "Years since. His name's Conrad, he's a Flemisher. Pedlar and that. Zeebrugge." Then she turned to me and fixed me: a 'think-hard-before-you-speak' face, about as friendly as a side of bacon. "Mr Conrad, this man's my husband. His name's Joe. Shake his hand. You didn't know, when we last met, your old friend Mary'd be spoused into the ale-trade: but it's a good house, quiet, and I'm content with it."

She turned again and went out, bringing the child with her. She shut the door of the back room: I heard her humming rhymes to the baby inside, and rattling the beads on its playing-pen.

★

This was all very difficult. Because of the peasants, I realised, nothing other could be said. But how much did the landlord know? Was *he* under the impression she was a 'Mary'? Had he really married her? It was possible: Bale's marriage being against the law, she might not have committed bigamy. I shook his hand, as instructed. He had a firm grip, and held it a long time, sizing me up. He was about sixty years old, with cropped grey hair, and grey stubble round a strong mouth. If the child knew me, then 'Mary' and I must have 'last met' quite recently.

I offered, "Your wife, she's a good woman. She has not too much talk."

"No, mister: she don't. Work, but not talk. Best of all, that sort, for a widower-man. She'll last me out, and longer. I'd say though, as I'd last *her*, for as long as ever she needs. She won't have no fears wi'me. And them young lads needs fathering. Even in such a backwards place. Best of all, for lorn young lads, a backwards place, maybe."

He said all this very carefully, as though anxious I should take note of it. I finished my drink and made to go. He had one more thing to say.

"Queer, though. I mean the names. Joseph and Mary. There was jokes made. Land of Egypt and all that. But we take no heed. Your road to the sea-quays: straight to Beaumont, turn sharp right."

I had intended to wait in the bar on the chance that my horseman came through – after this village I could not be sure he would be on the same road as me. But thus dismissed, I had to leave.

★

She had come out quietly through the back of the ale-house, and was waiting for me at the end of the street, half-hidden behind some hawthorns. She put her hand out to my arm, to hold me an ell's length from her. She had run, she panted a little.

"If you see Bale – if you see him –"

"I won't."

"Damn your Dutch confidence, I said 'if'. You might: and you'll need words. You're to tell him Joe Brewer is Wentworth's man: and well-chosen. I'm surprised you didn't know him. You've travelled these parts before, haven't you? You might well have sold him a Bible one time. Did he say anything about Egypt?"

"Yes, he did, as so happened."

"Tell Bale. He'll know why. There's more than one of 'em in the world beyond him."

"More than one of what?"

"Josephs," she said, and ran off into the fog, back along between the cottages. I could hear her clogs go, click-clack, for a while after I lost her to sight. Joseph. I had had the wrong Testament; although Egypt was in both stories. But I still did not entirely understand. I mean, not understand the exact facts and circumstances. Bale himself, to an *extent*, I understood: and still do. Dorothea is an uncracked nut. I have often asked her since, to explain more to me about Joe Brewer: but she never would. I was not to see her again, until I met her with Bale in Germany, four or five years afterwards.

*

One final recollection of my conversation with Rotraut. I asked her: when Dorothea went off with the Wentworth servants, and Bale was left with herself and Ermentruda, had he had anything to say to either of them before he departed for Thorndon?

She peered at me woozily, the schnapps was working strong.

"Had he'd anything to say, to her, me, both-of-us, for neither of us had spoken to him three days, didn't I say so? *Lieber Konrad*, he has so much to say, always, that man: and that day, *ach ja*, but he could not say it. He got himself some words, *ja*: 'The man that is without sin, let him throw first stone.' That's what he said, and he said it again, and so again. Would you not think he was telling us, 'wicked women, you are forgiven'? For he said it to *us*, not so much toward *her*, she was already down to the river.

"Then he went indoor, dressed himself, came out with his bags, walked *up* the lane toward St Giles, where they had his horse, I would think. Fifty feet up the lane, he stops, turns him round, sees me and

'Truda at the gate still, watching him: we had to, he looked so damn strange. Do I tell you what he did? He stooped to the ground, picked up one-two stones, and threw them, *threw*: at her and me. *Steinwerferpastor*: of course he could not hit us. One stone against a fence-post, the other into the mud. Splosch."

(x) Digressio Sine Excusatione: *Til Writes Of Til*
Steinwerferpastor. Steinwerfergott.

Yes, God (all Til's life) has hurled the most jagged, the most flint-splintering, and by God the best-aimed mountain-shards, at Til.

Esteemed *Herr Doktor* von G –, you are yourself a pastor, of your own independent conscience, in bonds to no corrupted Church, and therefore a soul (may Til hope?) to heal broken souls. This letter about Bale has been written – more or less against Til's will – with a pen full of clotted calumny, because such is and always has been the content of Til's ink-well. Our Luther once threw *his* against the Enemy: it seems as though the Enemy thereby got a taste for ink: searching for more of it, he found Til's. Til, in these pages, has but excavated his own guilt. He could tear them up this instant: but what would be the use? He has written them, he begins to know himself, such a beginning can *not* be farted away for a chorus of clowns' laughter. Bitter reaping of hopeful sowing, let Til's sickle continue to cut.

Do you ask, how this passionate student, this not-quite-graduate of Wittenberg when the Tongue of Fire was truly there in that city, ever came to be splitting his breeches among the muddy hovels of English Norfolkland?

Til was thirteen years old when Our Luther nailed his theses to the door, Til saw him do it, and entered his divinity-class only the week afterwards. To get there, Til had run from home. His father was an itinerant jester, a feral Rumpelstiltskin; while his mother was a coarse singer of funeral songs and marriage ditties to the deep-forest wood-cutters of the Siegenwald. They hunted Til down, fetched him abruptly from his beloved studies, enraged at their loss (not of their son, but of their savings which their son had stolen to pay his student-fee). Til's father gave him such a kicking he *unmanned* the boy for the rest of his life: no more about that . . .

He also did something with the blows of his boot to the lower pipe of Til's poor bowel. When he discovered, as a result, he had a son who was now able to pass wind like a thunderclap whenever he chose, he decided – perhaps repentantly – to give him real work upon the road instead of servant-toil, and to teach him the Eulenspiegel craft.

Then he died, and Til found *more* money, which ought to have gone to the widow, but bedamned if Til was giving it her: she'd enough other men to her bed to help her where she needed it. So until age of about twenty, though appearing no more than thirteen, Til was back at Wittenberg, there he stayed, there he all but graduated! He meant to become a pastor, presumptive eunuch though he might be (which could have been an obstacle, but he never had time to find out).

He had been in the habit of going upon the road when money ran short, to fill his student-purse with the proceeds of Eulenspiegel and Hanswurst from whatever audiences he could find. He was blowing his wind thus in some acrid little *Schnappshaus* the far side of Frankfurt when the Peasants' War came down on us: what could he do but take his part in it?

Not as soldier but as intellectual – for that is what Til was, clownery-boy or not. We lost.

A great officer, Adelbert von Weislingen, colonel-general to the Bishop of Bamberg, published Til's name in a list, upon a placard posted everywhere from Wuerttemberg to the Thueringer Wald:

> Konrad Spielmann, *Ideolog, Hochrevolutionskriminaldichter!*
> Price on his head! Fetch him! Dead or Alive!

Til's Wittenberg comrades, most of them, could not, would not, help him: for had not Our Luther branded all aid to the peasants as *Terrorismus* sheer and pure?

Even though hyena Weislingen was manifest papist, and his master the bishop a furious foe to all Lutherans.

So in haste, panic, determination, oversea into England, and to clowneries in England: and yet Til met with Christians there, and served his Bible-Christ as well as he could. And for a while, it was still *Luther's* Christ, for Til knew of none other that seemed equally decently fit for an honest man's prayer.

*

Til is having much to say to you, *Herr Doktor*, about love-longings, male and female, and the nauseous remorses to which they give rise. Til has been heating his own thoughts. Perhaps yours as well, but he doubts it. Til has hinted he had *tendencies*: you will be imagining God knows what, so let there now be a precise record.

It will no doubt one day be necessary for Til to choose a wife – complete abstinence from all woman-closeness (however severe one's incapacity) is unacceptably romish, or else damnably sodomite. If Til has no woman before he dies, he'll have lived more like a friar than Bale did, which would be mere feigned ascetic perversion. She must be a four-square widow-woman of inherited fortune and no desire for further child-bed. And no connection at all with stage-players or vagabond minstrels: not even were she a kinswoman of laurel-wreathed Hans Sachs, who admittedly was shoemaker before he was Master-Singer.

Til's thoughts on this are now absolutely *in order*.

It was not always so. The antinomian extravagancies of the Muenster Anabaptists exerted at one time a terrible python-eyed power upon sinful Til. Yes, and long before that sect infested Muenster; in Wittenberg in the 1520s, and then when their pastor Muenzer held a leadership in the Peasant's War, Til hung upon their fringes, drawn to them but repelled, recognising the strength of Luther's denunciation of them – 'infantile ecstaticism' was his *Kritik*, no? Their rejection of baptism save for fully-received believers was, arguably, a logical position: although by rigorous dialectic Til has come to detect its flaws.

Dialectic, however, was not – in this context – Til's only preoccupation.

In England, in constant company of the 'Birdcage' women and their sensualities, amid their mingling of religious harmony with an altogether other sort of song and dance, amid their half-German, half-English, half-natural, half-Sapphic affections, and above all amid their constant cruel ignoring of the *carnal needs of Til*, he spent hour upon hour trying to construct a doctrine that would accommodate his strange yearnings and his prurient observations, correctly, logically, within a tenable Christian perspective. Thus he came, in mind not body, to the walls of Muenster; whither the Anabaptists, as he heard, had migrated after all their tribulations.

That city in those years being metamorphosed (by the frenzy and fantasy of the anarchic Anabaptist pseudo-pope, Jan van Leyden) from a wholesome hard-working German town into – well, you remember what happened? – into the *Kingdom of the Saints!* They threatened the immediate slaughter of all who would not come in with them, declared hierarchical polygamy, blindly refused to countenance any moral law except van Leyden's hell-pit dictum: *"Sin greatly, brothers and sisters, because of sin is salvation made, and once elect to salvation there is no possibility of sin."*

In England Til hugged this doctrine to his secret heart.

Man was made in God's image, good: therefore all that man could do, every sin he could muster, was an image of Eternal God.

When Til, at age sixteen, walked lightly across a rope-hung bridge over a forest torrent in the Siegenwald, and noticed the rope frayed under his right hand, he saw that rope with the eyes of God. When he turned and watched his burly father swaying with drink down the path to the bridge behind him, Til saw *him* with the eyes of God. When the father's full weight was on the bridge and the rope began to break, Til's silence was the silence of God.

For Til's father was not *elected* to be recipient of Til's (God's) mercy.

It was the word of the Prophet of Muenster, years later, that must justify Til, for Luther's teaching gave him no such apparent clearness. Til's father in the image of God had neutered his own son: his boot had been God's boot, then his drowning was God's drowning.

Til was therefore God: and had drowned himself.

Til wrote several dissertations (in England) in support of Jan van Leyden, but was able to complete none of them. Flaws in logic, flaws in courage, interrupted his pen every time. In any case, publication would have been inconceivable, unless Til wished to be a martyr: his day in Diss – *pro tempore* – had sufficiently soothed his appetite. Was he to wave the blood-banner of Anabaptism in England, where papistry was scarcely bruised? No![1] Undeniably adventurist, immature, premature . . .

Til did make enquiries about how best to travel to Muenster: to roll there hog-like wanton in all that *sin-without-damnation*. Or rather, to watch them roll. That was all that Til wanted: to observe. The uncovering of the nakedness of the whoredoms of the land. But Til had no money. He held the purse of the minstrel-troupe, and Judas-wise considered embezzlement. But a Danziger ship-captain (doing business in London with Hansa merchants in the Steelyard) let him know he was too late.

The armies of the orthodox princes had taken Muenster. Van Leyden was dead, by such tortures as not even the cruellest Roman invented for Christian heroes in the days of Diocletian. Was deluded Jan a martyr? Or were we to rejoice that God's justice of Satan's Hades could so faithfully be made a model of, in a well-built German town, wholesome, hard-working, *heimatlich?*

This happened very shortly before Til (playing the role of Dutch Conrad) went with John Bale to Thorndon.

*

Most worshipful dear friend, von G – (if you are *not* to be Til's friend, all this paper from beginning to end will have been useless anyway): you are to understand this digression as a means to a better understanding, not only of Til, but of the man and woman whom he recommends to you. See them through Til's eyes, and then see them through your own, and then ask yourself: "Have these bewildered pilgrims not *deserved* a safe return to their own country, moreover has their country not deserved to have them back again, so to disorder its empirical disorders until at length God's good grace shall make all into good order at last?" She (Dorothea) used to talk of Paradise Garden. Consider how now she dwells in it, together with her Bale, the pair of them crouching so pudently beneath the bushes, grabbing at leaves to hide themselves, while their Maker stalks the glades in the cool of the day, demanding their presence, demanding they give account of their lives.

---

[1] Hence my calculated dissimulation in standing godfather to the infant baptism of La Haut-jambée's first child.

T. Eul.

Not for Til to do it for them: nor indeed, *Herr Doktor*, for you to do it either. Maybe, one day, they will *know themselves*.

Til has come to know himself.

Til now sets his feet toward John Calvin in Geneva: there indeed is the man to make a Kingdom of the Saints, and only through him shall Til, unworthy vessel, discover the True Path to Mount Sion: discipline, uncompromising, rigidly logical, the True Path to the True Hope of Til!

Calvin was three years in Strassburg. Did you ever meet him, attend his sermons, share his prayer? It may be, if you did, you took no great heed: he ministered largely to the French congregation, no? But it has been said he had conference with both Luther-men and Zwinglians, so you may possess a closer knowledge of him than Til has heretofore enjoyed. Dear friend, when Til goes to Geneva, join him if you can! The Emperor's politics must turn you out of Strassburg, you will have to make the choice. To be sure, Til has already in this treatise suggested England: but you should go to Geneva first. Same advice would have been given to Bale, except Til does not think him ready, not just yet, not for a long while, to offer up a testimony so vigorously purgative.

Geneva shall burn out the dross of both brain and heart, and thereafter our corrupted souls, born-again, new-washed in Jordan, must needs pervade all Christendom with Heaven-breath and Tongue of Fire.

(xi) Finis, *says Til*

One soul, and an English one, that can *never* have been born-again, was that of Thomas Cromwell. Let me complete my present writing with some note of a brief episode in his mordant and ominous career. John Bale is my informant, which is why it now comes to mind. It took place shortly before Cromwell was disgraced, prosecuted, executed.

I must tell you, that disgrace was largely because of his Lutheran-Germanic policy, which I had done so much to further. On the face of it, its most hopeful aspect was the marriage arranged for the King with Anna of Cleves. An alliance of uncomplicated foreign diplomacy quite free (for a change) from all sexual ingredients; only made possible because the nation at last had its male heir and Queen Jane had conveniently died of his birth (beyond all bounds of self-importance to imply that her sad fate *might* have been averted had she not chosen, immediately prior to the child's conception, to mock an overwrought

stage-player who was only *fulfilling his duty*? Divine Providence has
strange agents of cause-and-effect: unwise to disregard them). Even
so, I had nothing to do – overtly – with the *selection* of the new Queen.
She turned out a sort of *Huepfauf*-dancing aristocratic Rotraut, and
the King could not abide her. When I heard of this, I knew at once that
Cromwell would blame *me*: poor Til to be scapegoat again! I at once
broke connections with England, covered my traces, and turned
instead to earning money from the *Eulenspiegel* news-sheets, as you're
aware.

But Bale was still employed by Cromwell, still writing his plays for
him, and presenting them all over the southern parts. He had finally
been ejected by his bishop from the curacy. He was always absent
from the parish, anyway, carrying out his drama-projects. *I* would
have dismissed him, whatever his doctrine. A pastor's place is with his
people. He now could live adequately without his clergyman's
stipend: Cromwell gave him a sizeable subsidy. I understand he was at
last able to recommence keeping house again with Longlegs (I am not
sure exactly when: the entire Thorpe-le-Soken episode remains thoroughly enigmatical).

He was very glad to be no longer a practising cleric in 1539, when
the romanist faction in government made its first great gain against
Cromwell. The 'Whip-of-six-strings' was produced, a new set of
religious articles, half-a-dozen of them, far more old-guise than the
earlier ten, more or less compelling England to believe everything
believed before '33, except for the papal authority. Bale could never
have agreed to read it out in his church: he would infallibly have gone
to prison, and this time Cromwell would not have saved him.
Cromwell was already hard put to it to save himself.

All this by way of background to the extraordinary scene in Broad
Street, I imagine some time in the late spring of 1540.

Cromwell had just been created Earl of Essex: the requisite *hubris* to
turn his fall into true tragedy, so malevolently handed him on a velvet
cushion by the very prince-of-darkness who already had determined
his catastrophe! Overstatement? To think of Bale is to think of
theatre, to think of theatre is to swim in exaggerated rodomontade, to
fit the persons-of-the-play with the most violent motivations possible.
Though perhaps Henry was simply vacillating. He always looked so
very positive, but his vast body held a shrunken soul, he and
Wentworth were birds-of-a-feather.

*

Bale's arrival at Cromwell's house was ostensibly to offer congratulations upon his patron's earldom, and to submit a routine report from the acting-company. But of course Bale could never debase himself to formalities and matters-of-business. He had to bring everywhere his eruptions of clotted emotion with no respect for time or place. Can it be believed, he was set on a quarrel with Cromwell?

It was not that he had coldly decided to transfer his allegiance to the other side, as so many were doing at that time. The 'other side', in Bale's view, was the devil's side, Antichrist's: always had been, always would be. But at last, after four blind years, he had suddenly come to see that the Dissolution of the Monasteries had been little more than a fraud. You will remember how Cromwell jeered to me about Bale's plea to preserve libraries. Well, he must quite recently have taken the trouble to write an answer. 'If Cambridge can pay, Cambridge can have.' And Cambridge had been outbidden. Or had not even bothered to put in a bid at all.

After preliminary dutiful courtesies, Bale was unable to contain himself: he threw his distress bald-headed into a storm of expostulation. He roundly declared his integrity had been betrayed. And Cromwell sat and looked at him.

"My lord, I must regard my integrity as betrayed! Being your poetic and dramatic spokesman for your policy, your religious doctrine, I – I have no alternative but to – to tell you that – my lord, I have no words –!"

"You have come all this way to inform me, sir, you have no words? Where *are* the players at present? Devonshire, is it not? I have a note in my file, yes: Barnstaple, how were audiences in the west country?"

"My lord, I demand that I talk to you about –"

"About that for which you have no words, or if you have, they may be taken as uttered: I asked you a question."

Bale bridled. "Very well, my lord, I'll answer it, as I am not to be allowed my say. Much of the district is highly papist: we met with hostility, hostility toward the crown, not only for religion. Flanders corsairs with letters-of-marque from the Emperor are pillaging the sea-coast and French corsairs have been taking prizes, and then they have been fighting each other for the same prizes. They –".

"I know that, I have the file. The King's Ships in Plymouth are laid-up and dismasted, they cannot be recommissioned until I dissolve some Cambridge colleges and bring cash to the exchequer."

"Very well, my lord, if you know it, may I please be permitted to complete my point about these manuscripts –"

"Do you not hear what I say to you? Dr Bale, there will be no Cambridge, this country is undefended. Nor will there be an Oxford, colleges and monk-houses, two birds on the same branch, we have knocked only one of them down, I want your help to get them both, write me a play: yes, at once, I'd like it before August, explaining the uselessness of academic frivolities to the common weal of progressive citizens under rule of enlightened monarchy, and I want it at once; bring your company back from the west, commence rehearsals as soon as possible –"

Cromwell's voice that day was very swift, not loud, but on and on, and on, insistent rain upon a roof, a strange manner of expressing himself, quite out of his usual style of dropping abrupt disturbing phrases into his own brooding silence. Also that day, he spoke thickly, like a drunkard: he was not drunk. Bale was having trouble catching up with his train-of-meaning, and when he did, he was devastated. As vacuous as a gaping oyster.

"Why, my lord, I – I –"

"You have no words, you said so. August, maybe too late, better finish it by middle of June, in any case I must probably disband the acting-troupe, its expenses mount higher and higher, how can you justify these most monstrous charges for buskins? Cannot the players wear their every-day shoes? Whoever looks at an actor's feet? You do understand, it is vital our *intelligentsia* thoroughly understand this point, the Cleves wedding cannot be called-off, however much the King mislikes her, he is committed by solemn treaty: so he marries her and then divorce, I am trying to discover a pretext that will not malign the girl and anger her German kin, parties-to-treaty; shall we say: 'induced impotence in His Majesty's loins because of a prior anxiety that her father's people have no ships and cannot help him protect our sea-coasts'? I have drafted the whole thing in this file. And all that the massed intellect of this great nation can do, is to sit at its high-table wine and dispute syllogisms. You're as bad as any of them. Cambridge man, aren't you?"

"My lord: I must *tell* – I care little about Oxford – but Cambridge University is the cradle of the Reformed Faith! *I shall write for you no such a play*. And you yourself University Chancellor!"

It was almost inconceivably brave of Bale. He must have been the first man to refuse Cromwell to his face since Thomas More. He told me he could scarce comprehend he had done it. "Only the hand of God upon the root of my tongue could so have strengthened my utterance: and I knew that it *was* strong. I was not to be tempted – by anything – to withdraw it. No, nor put in fear. And we all know the fear that man could make. But astonishing, it was as though he had not heard. He dropped the matter altogether. He had never before dropped matters once his mind was set on them, he would work and work upon all persons till he bent them to his will."

*

Cromwell had gone on to talk of scholarship and his own life.

"I never went to a university. *I made myself*: abroad; work, self-education, marriage, a rich widow: did you know I was once a soldier? A mercenary band in Italy, fought for the Florentines against – I forget who, there was no great battle, our *Condottiere* sold his loyalty, sold *us*, so somebody shot him. Come here, over here, Bale, here, I've something to show you – what do you think of this?"

The room was his new study in his fine new widely-glazed oriel-turreted town-*palazzo*: the craftsmen were still at work upon part of the site, decorations not yet complete in any of the apartments. This chamber was hung with tapestry upon one wall-and-a-half where the oak panelling had yet to be fitted. Of the other two walls-and-a-half, one was all mullioned window, and the remainder already panelled: an exquisite carved work of the Italian taste. Cromwell pulled back the tapestry between the fireplace and a cupboard-alcove. The wall behind was rough stone, laid with batten for the panels: except a width of three feet of oak, already fixed.

"Why d'you suppose, Bale, they hung the arras over this piece of finished panelling? I told them, I don't like tapestry, I'll accept it as a makeshift rather than hurt my eyes with flint-rubble, but where you have it panelled already, let it be displayed. Display it now, I said, I want to look at it: but no, they covered this up."

Bale said something about the obtuseness of workmen, "congenital, inevitable": his remark was ignored. Cromwell was fiddling with a carving of a cupid's head.

"I discovered this myself: no-one had thought fit to show it me. Look." The panel came out from the wall into his hand, it was entirely upon hinges, a secret door.

"I followed it up, Bale, it leads through the thickness of the walls into the pantry. Convenient, you see, Bale, if I want a light supper at my desk-work, they don't have to fetch it down every corridor in the house."

He let the secret door swing silently shut again. He swithered across the room to a locked closet, opened it, with a crafty glance to-left-and-then-right as though enemies might be peeping, and took out a small book. Without a word he laid it on his desk, spread the pages, beckoned Bale. Spectacles adjusted, Bale bent over the desk beside him, and drew in his breath; astonished, indeed startled.

The volume had no text; it was a picture-book, each page a whole-page illuminated miniature, intricate, sumptuous, a jewelled dream of a book of dreams. At first sight Bale thought it was a calendar-sequence, twelve paintings of twelve months, with appropriate landscapes and typical activities. So, in a sense, it was: save that December showed a hell-scene, black pits, glowing flames, gaping monster-jaws; and June was apparently in heaven, golden stairways, silver thrones, stars and planets vivid in a violet firmament.

But the 'activities'? Every page swarmed with scores of tiny people, many of them full naked, all of them interwoven in lickerish debauch, red hot deep-delving amid each other's secret but laid-open declivities. Some were but partially clothed, their robes tucked up into girdles above their hips, or spilling from careless shoulders, or gaping in front from neck-band to hem. Bale took the naked figures for pagan divinities, Italian-wise, out of an Ovid-book perhaps, pursuing their animality in an antique world where they could not know they were *not* gods because they did not know the True God: he hoped, feverishly, that they were now *damned* for their usurping ignorance! A troubling thought, to desire the damnation of the ignorant, a most sinful theological perversion – ah! could it be that this book was damning *him*, after only the one short glance at it . . . ?

And then an observation, even more troubled: all of the men, ithyphallic, had tonsured heads; and the women were shorn, like nuns. Moreover, those partially clothed: they wore items of the garb of all orders of clergy, from popes to barefoot anchorites; a nun-habit (or at least a veil or wimple) on every woman. And there were whippings, mouthings, bindings, cuttings with knives.

Cromwell was talking. "The man that sent it me from Flanders said it might be the work of the notable Brabant limner, Jeronimo Bosch, d'you suppose? If not him, then a very considerable pupil. I think there is nothing like it in England?"

"But, my lord, do you mean to tell me, you have obtained this book for your *delight?*" Bale, at that moment, was totally the earnest clergyman, blinking his horror behind steamed spectacles.

"Delight?" Cromwell's puzzled repetition of the word suggested he found it foreign, from a language he did not know, and wanted a translation. "Delight? Oh surely not? But it is a craft-work, this, that dateth from before Luther, I should say thirty years old: conceived by one that surely had full experience of such enormity. It showeth so very plain the full truth of the popery-priesthood, their feigned vows, their hypocrite practice. I want an art-master who works in England to convert each picture into a woodcut, no less intricate than the original: and thereafter we print and publish, and let every young scholar, with his Bible and his Latin grammar, have such a book to his hand so he is warned all his schooldays of the enemy we confront. Give me a name? Would you think, Holbein? No, Holbein disappointed me by present-ing the Cleves lady so fair, and thereby he misled the King to all our confusions; but he does have the skill, and Bale, we do need skill, there are skilful men at court who undo all we have done, they *have* to be contra-manoeuvred."

"My lord, I – I have heard of this Bosch, and of sundry Flanders men who made pictures with him. They were not, my lord, concerned to refute the roman falsehoods, rather to affirm their own occult iniquity: these are no condemnation of the vices depicted, but a frenzy-pretence that they are not vices at all – you witness, my lord, the forerunners of the antinomians, of the Anabaptist secret heretics, at their orgiastic cult. The clerical garb was their favoured disguising. Observe this pope here, handling his yard as it might be an ale-keeper's spigot, why, he hath a veritable Christ-face, he is not Antichristus but Our Sorrowful Lord Himself, most shamefully placed in libel. Men knowing this will say openly, that this book is a Protestant creed. Alas, blasphemy."

"Oh, do you really think so? True? You do think so?"

Bale nodded: he hoped he thought so. He had hastily improvised. Perhaps it was a good guess (he knew nothing about Jeronimo Bosch): at any rate it seemed to avail.

"In that case we had best not publish, it would only discredit, we will keep the book for another time, perhaps *delight?* perhaps next year?" With uncharacteristic negligence, he left it open on the desk, and was at once across the room again, tapping his knuckles gently against the secret door.

★

"They can bring in my supper, you see, just creep with it through the narrow dark, and hope the soup isn't filled up with cobwebs. *Hope the assassin don't catch his dagger on a projecting bit of freestone*. What's odd about it, mark me, it wasn't on the plans I gave my approval to: and yet the master-mason has it on *his* plans, sharp as daybreak. Ask the question, who put it there?

"I'll tell you a story. About Italy. That *Condottiere*, he was shot, by an arrow, a sudden flying arrow, from just such a secret opening, in the garden of the castle where he made his headquarters. He had himself built that part of the castle himself: don't I know it, I was his clerk-of-works? Upon *his* plan, drawn up for him by his Chief of Engineers, no opening at all. And yet the hole was made, in the thickness of the wall. No trust, do you see, among his subordinates, and they were right. They *did* have need to murder him, or his treachery would have killed them all. And of course, had *they* been treacherous, and *he* been an honest man, they might equally have sought such a deadly opportunity. What d'you think of it?"

Bale thought, that if a curious little story of his own, which he remembered telling to Cromwell, should now have become Cromwell's story, it meant that Cromwell was no longer fit to exercise power of government. To be frank, he was ceasing to answer his helm: and the best thing Bale could do was to take flight to Germany without waiting for Cromwell's death.

At the same time, the Flemish book *might* have been a useful idea. He had argued against it instinctively, but only because his instinct told him that from Cromwell's state-of-mind no new project could be expected without some hideous hidden flaw. But he did wish it possible that he might privately own a cheap and neat Holbein version of those most terribly instructive pictures. He had, at home, he remembered, a jeweller's enlarging-glass: his spectacles were insufficient.

He left England, with Dorothea and the two young boys. Cromwell was arrested the following week.

*

The actors, on the shores of the Bristol Channel, heard of Bale's departure at least a fortnight before anyone told them what had happened to Cromwell. England is not a country of easy roads for messengers: Devonland and the Cornwelshland are more remote from

London than Our Luther in Wittenberg ever was from the Emperor's Austria.

The company got together, and addressed an urgent word to Cromwell (it arrived after he had been committed to the Tower), affirming their ill-timed loyalty, and repudiating Bale. The playwright, they said, had been "ever most contrarily-fashioned, inducing us against all propriety to bite the feeding hands and slight the reputations of great men, for no other reason than his own proud aggrandisement. That he hath now *defected* is matter for small wonder: though, mark you, my lord, we write from hindsight, we could never have foreseen. We greatly fear he seeketh refuge in the lairs of extreme sectarians, ex-Anabaptists, and worse. Forgive us our trespass, gracious my lord, that we did not watch him with a better attention."

This document did them no good. One by one they too all slipped under cover: a couple of them came to Germany, where they most respectfully sought out Bale, and asked him did he know of any work for them among the Almains? Understand me, they were men of some decency, and integrity in their trade: but frightened. They were no more than stage-players, when all is said.

Saith Til as he endeth: *Gott gruess Euch und Adies!*

CHILD AND GRANDCHILD

(4)

Old-Fashioned Judgement

Whenever Lydia came to London, she would find a comfortable inn and then spend two or three hours each day at a playhouse with Lucretia, thus conveniently avoiding lengthy sojourns in the East Cheap lodging, and the consequent awkward chance of meeting the sword-and-pistol man (or some other inauspicious shadow-of-a-nameless-stallion who had perhaps replaced him). Not necessary at all for her to butt herself up against the girl's wretched ecstasies, they would all be of the same forked and furnished shape, and none of them would be worthy: though it did appear she moved among gentlemen of a degree of good faith and honour.

So mother sat beside daughter in the second gallery of the Rose, or the Curtain or the Theatre in Shoreditch, or the new-built Swan, still all in her blacks, a dignified duenna-figure whom nobody tried to insult. Quite a number of people looked at her oddly: her public manners were not free, nor did she try to make them free, and her keen interest in the plays seemed all out of tune with her veiled face, her reserved deportment. It could only be detected from the tension of her hands, the odd glimpse of a breathless open mouth behind the veil, a quick leaning forward when the actors' rant fell suddenly silent for a startling new turn in the plot. But there were many who did detect it, and she began to be talked about. Of this she was quite unaware.

Her judgement of the plays was as old-fashioned as her appearance. She did her best to keep it separate from the unspoken and unwished-for workings of her private thought. For instance, one day, with great trepidation, she allowed Lucretia to take her to see a piece by Christopher Marlowe, whose very name still caused her conscience-cramps. At the end, gently but fervently, she whispered, "Why, Lucretia, this is not at all what I expected. The play is entirely moral. In the sorry death of this King Edward we see the sure reward for the poisonous vice of buggery, so vituperated against by my father, long

long before I knew what it meant. How therefore the poet's ill-repute?" And she clapped, and clapped, her black-gloved hands.

Lucretia looked at her in some surprise. "Is that what you thought you saw, mother? To my mind we have attended an altogether different play. One, rather, where a green young man of lively parts and vivid fantasy findeth the pillory-stocks of politic rule stop all the blood from his warm extremities, so at length he falleth prey to soldierly mudwits, sly contrivers, and by God it was not his fault! Foolish he was, and loose, but in no way evil-hearted."

Lydia sighed. "No," she said, "No: he married a clean lady and by his callous insulting conduct he made her a collusive murderess. Adulteress, to boot. Such men are a mortal danger, I say naught but thank heaven for a poet to point it out.

"However, you will still have your own opinion: let it be."

IV

(Tragical)

Letters of Loyalty

> And the kings of the earth, and the great men, and the rich men, and
> the chief captains, and the mighty men, and every bondman, and every
> free man, hid themselves in dens, and in rocks of the hills, and said to
> the hills, and rocks: fall on us, and hide us from the presence of him
> that sitteth on the seat.
>
> I know thy works and tribulation and poverty, but thou art rich: and
> I know the blasphemy of them which call themselves Jews and are not:
> but are the congregation of Satan.
>
> (Revelation of St John the Divine, Chapters 6 & 2)

In April 1541, nine months after the execution of Thomas Cromwell, Lord
Wentworth wrote in cipher to his old friend Sir Thomas Wyatt, the poet
who had been there, at Nettlestead, upon that first night of the garden-
maze. Wyatt's knighthood was reward for his loyal acceptance of the late
Anne Boleyn as Queen. A loyalty called in question when she went to the
block for adulteries. But he was pronounced innocent, and had to confirm
his innocence by several years' diligent work on behalf of Cromwell – so
diligent indeed that once again he discovered there was a question against
his loyalty: how could discredited Cromwell's knight be the King's true
knight? A murky corner. He was by no means, therefore, the safest man to
send letters to, even though they were in cipher. But he had written to
Wentworth: and Wentworth was afraid that if he were not answered, he
might write again, and less discreetly.

Anne of Cleves was now replaced as Queen by Catherine Howard, niece
to Duke Howard of Norfolk, factionally associated with Gardiner of
Winchester, the Old Guise scrambling back not only into the pulpit but
between the royal sheets: and the King was in love with her, insensate,
people said. The New Guise was in hard trouble.

Wyatt was suspected upon a report made by Bonner, Bishop of London
(and friend of Gardiner), a perspiratory fat man of a queasy political
conscience who had shared an embassy with Wyatt to the continental

powers a year or two before. Cromwell had briefed the pair of them: Bonner must now at once dissociate himself from any idea anywhere that he had been Cromwell's creature. He did this by accusing Wyatt and presenting himself as the King's honest watchdog upon their joint mission.

The obvious accusation was that Wyatt had intrigued with Lutherans. Bonner's thought was more contorted, as suited the arabesque of the time. He denounced Wyatt instead for intrigue with Cardinal Pole: leaving it to be understood that it was in fact Cromwell who had thus toyed with Rome (using his man Wyatt as a plausible double-agent to play Luther against the Pope, and Luther and the Pope together against the security of England), leaving it to be understood that the men of the Old Guise, Bonner, Gardiner, Norfolk, were stronger defences for the King's religious supremacy than any of the New. The tale was desperately vague, and so far from the truth that it was likely to be believed. Anything could now be believed about Cromwell. All loyal subjects were expected to believe such an 'anything' at all times, and to repeat it as loud as possible until the realm was thoroughly purged. Wyatt had been seen to weep when Cromwell's head was taken off. Great difficulty for the hapless Wyatt to repel Bonner's huge assertion: and yet, in a fashion, he had managed it.

Even so, Lord Wentworth must write to him with great care.

*

Dear friend,

This will, by God His Grace, reach you before you set sail for Calais to take your command there. I implore you not to slight the complexion of the said command: a lieutenant-generalship of light horse is no great office, but neither is it worthless. The defence of Calais is most crucial to the defence of the whole realm. Your promotion – I say 'promotion' because *you* say 'disgrace', a rash attribution craving instant correction, for the honour, and safety, of us all – is to be seen as a small stair-tread in a dark passage between the door of your last month's prison-cell and the sallyport that leads to the free fresh air of liberty and noble service. Break not your foot against it. Observe its rough edge, avoid its slippery surface, step boldly: you will ascend.

Despite all, I am persuaded that A···s[1] knows your quality.

---

[1] *Lord Wentworth's concealment of the already-ciphered names in his letter was highly elaborate, involving the Greek and Hebrew alphabets and a range of mythological pseudonyms. The process has been simplified in this transcript. Here, A···s = King Henry VIII, called Argus in Wentworth's system, no doubt because he saw danger from all directions. Other names have not necessarily been given with such allegorical fantasy: merely the initial letters (and sufficient other letters to make them clear to the reader), with the correct number of dots intervening, one for each letter omitted. Thus, B····r = Bonner. This should provide at least a flavour of Wentworth's characteristic timidity-of-state.*

B····r's charges against you were *not proven*, remember that. To be sure, you confessed. You confessed faults, because you have faults, and who has not? You did *not* confess treason. Ill-judgement, careless-ness, light-mindedness, lubricity, choler, vanity, poetry, and over-plus of liquor – all these combined in a confession paint the portrait of a human child, son of Adam, seeking redemption: they do not demean: they establish you, under God, as a very English gentleman, quite as fit for A···s's diplomacy as any other whom he might favour. That he chooses now to favour you with *military* rank of a class not quite grandiose is a sign only that he recognises all your other qualities that your confession could not (of its nature) include. I mean, your bold vigour, your bodily strength, your habit of abrupt command – parts more suited to the tented field than to cabinets of statesmen. They were exercised unwisely at the expense of your clerical col-league upon that ill-fated embassage: A···s now desires you to employ them where he needs them, against the French and stand no nonsense. Calais must remain ours: and you are the best for it. I write no more upon this topic. 'Promotion' is my word: see that it becomes yours.

Dear friend, why did you mention to me my late patronage of players? Long before T····s C······l's gross malfeasances became apparent I had ceased to have dealings with the sometime white-friar J··n B·le and his ignorant mimes. He is now in Germany and – please God – will stay there. I am not to be tripped into accepting any past responsibility for the extremities of his doctrine, either as priest or playwright.

And then your complaint that your paramour, Œ···e[1], was interrogated about your doings in oppressive and arbitrary fashion, whereas she that you call *my* paramour (you call her also J··n B·le's wife: I know nothing of his 'wife', he is a priest, he is not allowed one) was at one time, you allege, made safe from similar interrogators by my 'chivalrous intervention' – I quote your phrase expressly to refute it.

These two cases have nothing in common.

I admit it was cruelty to confront Œ···e with commissioners-of-enquiry (your word 'torturers' is not appropriate, no torture was employed either upon her or you – *my* voice, I said so, plainly, to my friends in the Council, 'no torture', and they accepted it): and I admit

---

[1] Œ···e = Oenone = Mrs Darrell, *Wyatt's mistress*.

that her ordeal was made worse by the circumstance that she is
expectant of your child. I hope and trust that she is none the worse for
it: and have sent to her to say so. It should not have happened. How
could she possibly have known what you were doing in France and
Spain in 1538?

On the other hand, you yourself made use of her evidence (in the
clearing of your name): should A · · · s be withheld from an equal
convenience? What she knew, she must declare, and somebody had to
ask her. None in the Council had any thought that she might be guilty,
not even B · · · · r thought she was guilty. If *I* were suspected, and *you*
were consulted by certain of the Council, you likewise would wonder
had I got a mistress, and how much might she know?

That I did have one, once, cannot be denied. But D · · · · · y
P · · · · · s[1] did not go to the Essex coast to keep her safe from questions
about *me*. She went because a rural brewer chose to wed her and
nurture her children. She went because by that time it had become
notorious that plays and minstrelsy in excess of A · · · s's requirements
were casting a factional slur upon the clarity of his government's
intentions in regard to the true light of reformed religion in England.
By which I mean – I know not what I mean, no choice but to be plain
with you, I thought you were a *diplomatist*, has all your career taught
you nothing of the virtues of silence and restraint? – you should *not*
have mentioned players! But you did, and in such terms that you leave
me no choice but to be plain, to set you right here and now upon the
entire matter. In the hope, nay the insistent confidence, that you will
never raise the subject again.

Fair warning, sir knight-provocative, another letter from you like
to the one I have just now read, and it goeth straight from my desk to
the Council. Moreover I set neither signature nor seal to these pages I
am writing, and if you play me false with them, I shall deny them
out-of-hand.

At the time when A · · · s was informed by his informed-conscience
that his marriage to Spanish C · · · · · · e was no marriage but incestuous sin (and furthermore that the papacy was collusive with such
sin, leaving the informed-conscience of his subjects with no remedy
but to agree that only A · · · s's informed-conscience could re-create
Christ's Church in such national shape and form as originally desired
by God's Will), in those days I spoke to you about the need to inform

---

[1] D · · · · · y P · · · · · s = Dorothy Parsons.

the awakening conscience of all the English of *what was to be done*. Some of us already, indeed long before, had made up our minds that the whole of Christendom had for centuries walked in error, and the proof of this error was now openly revealed to us by A · · ·s's marital cause – his consequent breach with Rome being thus no mere expedience but of a principle concomitant with the doctrines of St Paul as rediscovered for our generation by M · · · ·n L · · · ·r in Germany (not an obstacle that by that time L · · · ·r's own doctrine contained manifold errors of its own: we were subsequent to his eruption and therefore could control our insular earth-quakings here in a way perhaps not possible for him and his people oversea).

You will remember I said to you that the pulpits of our divines were not to be left to forge all this necessary work on their own: for here was to be disputation both vernacular and learned, and throughout all of England, lay, clerical, even of the distaff also: whereat you laughed and broke out coarsely that there was indeed "one distaff, she is D · · ·aë[1], she is Caesar's and already so deep into the disputation he hath fitted her his gold padlock to close off the scope of her spinning," and you preferred not to embroil yourself with your own heart thus hurtful wounded. Quiet loyalty and obedience would be your sacrificial portion, you said, but no exertion of initiative, you could not bear it, would not. I understood your lost love and refrained from further persuasion.

But we did speak in general of what might be ordered. I told you of Friar B · le, how his rage against the misuse of monastic rule had fetched out his spirit toward poetry, play-acting, the re-shaping of our English tongue for an enlightened generation of a new self-sufficient race: and I told you of the woman D · · · · ·y, the unwitting conturber of the mind and loins of B · le, in herself a singer and dancer of a notable invention, if her fantasy could be brought under a more sanguine influence than that of the King's Lynn minstrel-master who in those days held her in bond (he being papistical, and appertinent to the D · ke of N · · · · ·k).

"Bring them together," you said, "you have at once your vital voice to reach deep like an ivory backscratcher under the foul clothes of neglected England, clawing ruthless (from the naked skin) scabs, vermin, dead dried sweat – and also d'you not think the conjugation of the pair of 'em might at last free your white-friar from the guilty

[1] D · · ·aë = Danaë = Anne Boleyn.

sediment wherein he sticks at the bottom of his old-popery dung-basket?" You said you had often heard me lament B·le's stubbornness, his mulish reluctance to repudiate all-of-a-swoop his ingrained brainful of Carmelite doctrine.

But I told you how D · · · · ·y had become appalled by B · le, and how he, knowing this, was equal appalled by her. What to be done? Count Pandarus of Troy you were, upon that night in Nettlestead you conceived me your solution, it was adopted, it succeeded. At length: and to the wreck of my happiness.

God, how was I to have known that my wife would then have learned such grace of courtship to her husband so late in our married years?

You lost heart against your own wife sixteen years ago: will *she* even yet re-occupy your libertine fantasy and clap her sugared padlock on *your* spinning in such manner as *mine* did? By God's laws you should desire it. By human habit I can tell you it is far far from a smooth conclusion: avoid it if you can. No more of that now, I'll fill it out by way of *post scriptum*: I write this page on B · le and must not lose him, much as I might wish to, damn his blood.

"Bring them together," you said, and I did. But together meant the two embodiments, acting-company of men, minstrel-troupe of men and women. Horse and ass in the joint harness and I as coachman must discover my sorry void of ambidextrous skill. These artists were all my people, wherever they went my name gave them legitimacy: but some minstrels went north, some south and east, while the play-actors were to the west: and I was at court. No command over their work, I mean absolute *none*: I could see and hear them before they set out, I took every pain to ensure it, they made exact guarantee that what I had seen would be what they presented, no more and no less, in Poole and in Pomfret, and Ludlow Castle on the march of Wales: and then letter after letter comes squittering into London to let me know I was absurdly deceived! I became in six months a cuckold of cultural adultery. I said to B · le, "What meaneth this?"

He replied, "There are exigencies; greater length or lesser length, strong papists in the auditory or frenetic exceeders of M · · · ·n L · · · ·r, schooled gentlefolk or wordless churls: my lord," he averred, "it is not possible the same screed will do for all, and how can we know until we take our observances, of the playing-place (tavern-yard or house), of the people, of the words that have been given them heretofore from their parish pulpit, of the judgements of the local magistracy in regard to doctrinal dissidence? There is none can take such decision save he that ruleth the company, there and then upon their itinerary, *videlicet* myself, or the Dutch C · · · · d, or such other as hath the day-to-day business in hand. As for the minstrels, they as always must make at once their own rulings, each one for himself or herself between fingers on the lutestrings and voice in the open throat!

"Else you have correctitude but scant love for the living art: and where love leaveth your artists, so doth your auditory – my lord, English folk snuff dead dogma three mile away from their nostrils and close every vent against it!"

I did not understand. Surely a good dogma was the sole good that we purveyed? Surely he and I had agreed this before we started? And if he was so certain that to every cow its calf, so to each houseful of hearers their own playscreed (consoling some, provoking others, tickling these, smiting those), how did it happen that every audience he ever addressed seemed mortal offended by what he gave 'em?

He answered me straight enough: only those that were offended took trouble to write to me; the others were majority and had no need to write, being content with the work and therefore assuming that all went well everywhere and I myself in London must needs be content also, taking no news for good news, and peace-and-quiet for a merry kingdom. Perhaps so. Perhaps not so.

Perhaps also there was truth in his further assertion that *King John* was to be the chief play of the company and it was not yet complete (he took all ages to write that play, immense in length, amended daily as he wrote it, according to the news that came in upon every post: had God created world so, His seventh-day Sabbath would be still upon its way and His Sacred Hand failing arthritic!). Those works they presently offered were in part his own musings, to try this and to try that, to adapt an old popish piece ("inside-out, upside-down, my lord: the very irony of the contrivance shall strike them unexpected where they live!"), to translate some new Germanism, to put forward a sharp impromptu upon whatever sudden issue had arisen in every shire (aye, and then halt his *King John* yet again so that the impromptu may be laid within it as a new permanency): all these must be mere experiment, and experiment of its essence carried failure in its fardel upon an equal peradventure with success.

"Patience, my lord, patience," he shoved his nose into my face and threw his rheum all over my beard (oh but I waxed so qualmish at his self-flagellating bilious arrogance!), "Great A · · · s's proceedings are of necessity slow, being hemmed about by traitors in church and in state, let alone the inevitable retardations of law-making: we have all time in the world to perfect our well-salted variances upon his royal theme, and whenever we are not perfect, we return to Holy Scripture for fresh water from the divine well, for fresh salt from the divine *etcetera*," let me not run on, God's heart but the man was tedious. I demanded what did he mean – variance upon a theme? I thought we *were* the theme.

I said, "Unity above all, harmony in this kingdom, so that whatever lord A · · · s pronounceth, his loyal people shall be made ready to accept it upon stand of principle."

"L · · · · r's principle, Z · · · · li's, W · · · · · fe's,[1] or whose? I told you before we began, this company is to *search for truth*: searching meaneth probing, probing denoteth at all hazard a scarred heart. From the blood of their lacerations, they fill their pens and write to you: my lord, you should rejoice, you have made your mark upon England's apathy!"

As much as to say, he himself had not made up his mind what religion he desired to espouse. Oh I set myself to work upon him, laying his doubts, on my knees beside him in prayer, my brain entangling his in interminable dialectic, syllogism upon syllogism, capping all with great texts from the Scripture: and so, in good time, I brought him close enough to Switzer Z · · · · li to cause him cry, "At last at last, the arrow is flown, I am a new soul from the living water re-born and awash with love!" And then he must incontinent rewrite all his plays to accommodate his crystal vision. "Aye, rejoice!" he exhorted yet again.

Well: perhaps: rejoice . . . But rejoice when they wrote to A · · · s? I had never desired my players should be matter for contention in Council.

It now standeth against me as a tentative treason that I gave these same players to T · · · · s C · · · · · · l: that A · · · s has not yet thought of it, nor mine enemies put it into his mind, is more my good fortune than a well-contrived immunity. I do not thank you, sir poet, for raking it out in your ill-judged letter.

Because J · · n B · le was irresponsible, what could I be expected to do but deliver his daily danger to the one man in the land who held *all* responsibility?

[1] Z · · · · li = Zwingli: W · · · · · fe = Wycliffe.

Which phrase should mean A · · ·s: but you know and I know that C · · · · · l was *entrusted*: violation of his trust was dreamed of then by none of us, least of all by A · · ·s his royal self. Read your Tacitus; regard Sejanus the aspiring minister, regard Tiberius Caesar, their closeness, their sudden breach, the Procrustean agonies of all who had sought no more than to live loyal to imperial will. I had neither the ability, nor indeed the financial resource, to send intelligencers far and wide to report me the doings of my players: C · · · · · l had, and he did.

He reined in B · le like a rearing war-horse, and then put him out to grass at Thorndon, imposed his strictest orders upon that bloody-flux of a C · · · ·d, and finally took one look at D · · · · ·y P · · · · ·s the immeasurable long-legs, saying, "The bitch hath so sturdy a mind and limbs of her own, it were better she should swing them to her own destruction not ours." No wonder she was forced to fetch-in laundry to Drury Lane.

You see, C · · · · · l understood – which I, let me admit, had not – that the wildness of B · le (up to a point, and C · · · · · l knew the point, knew it exactly, at that time; though of course, in the upshot, not) had a certain advantage for him: such a poet let loose upon the unsuspecting auditories of England was a rattling stick thrust into a wasp's nest in a drain-pipe, all those who came out swarming to buzz and whirl and sting would otherwise have lain murderous silent, in close ambush awaiting their later more perilous hour.

But La Haut-jambée by contrast was no wild provoker, except of laughter and sensual love. La Haut-jambée made men *glow* toward the glowing future of reformed England: but if they laughed with her at the Pope they might shortly laugh at T · · · ·s C · · · · · l. They might even laugh at A · · ·s. They might even come to see that both Sejanus and his Caesar would soon be as dead and marbled as their precursors of marbled old Rome. While laughter, love, and her galliard red stockings, would continue to skip forward all unhindered by exact authority: and for C · · · · · l exact authority was *sine qua non*.

As for me, let me confess. A confession very much like unto yours – save you gave yours to all in Council, in public session assembled, and I give mine to you, individual and private, between the lines of a private cipher: well, sir, this Haut-jambée caused *me* to glow till I all but forgot my ulterior purpose.

There was another thing I quite forgot; I quite forgot the French pox (so they call it because France reeks with it, but to my thinking it cometh from Spain, whose sailormen found it in the Indies – as well they might, a place where bestial heathendom is now being 'perverted', rather than 'converted', to diabolic popery). When I came back from Paris, having seen such putrefaction (aye, and in some fair bodies I might otherwise have haply frequented), I found I could not conduct myself for an entire season toward venery, no, not even with my own dear wedded lady, however gently she besought me: and most gentle at that time were her new-rediscovered importunities. *Penis erectus non possibilis erat*, for the fear that had gone into him. At length, in regard to my wife, yes; as you know. You know also the great number of my dear children, already in excess of the blessed progeny of patriarch Jacob. *Grace à Dieu*.

You would think, in regard to Longlegs, bearing in mind the 'Birdcage' habitude, I would have been no less cautious than in my duties as diplomatist: *to take care*, meticulous, is indeed my very trade (it ought to be yours, and why *isn't* it?) But. Forgot the pox, forgot my wife, forgot my politic calculation, forgot even my religion. One week: it was the *glow*: I have confessed it to no-one but you.

I sinned: that's all it is, no more, and no less. Forgiveness is sure-promised me, upon confession to Our Lord Himself, His abounding mercy. No priest in between us: no equivocating instruction for ceremonies of specious penitence. Such is my doctrine.

Do you think I ought to tell my wife?

Answer me not. God alone maketh right answer. No equivocating instruction from any mortal fallible soul. I ask my God, do I do right to keep this a secret? She knoweth all other of my earlier defalcations. She knoweth and I am forgiven of her. God alone maketh right answer: I ask Him, He replieth not.

But sir, for your leering, for your gross scorning, I do have mine own answer! I had not sat at Cambridge among Doctors of Divinity with English text, Latin Text, Greek text, Hebrew, spread out before us, Word of God gripping our nerves to re-novate the corpse of Christendom, I say I had not sat there so many weeks, months, years, in order to dissolve myself into a lotus-eating ethnic, sprawled upon spread velvet, loose-gowned in the sunshine or no-gowned, surrounded by asphodel and a false warm dream of endlessness that inevitably must end in nothing, *nihil*, *nada*, *néant*, *niente*, *nichts*! No! For there was once a garden, it may have contained lotus, for sure it contained stark hoseless human shanks and no thought of shamefast fig-leaves: but now I was outside it, its gates were closed against me, the honest spade

of Christian Reformation was in my hand, bare furrows and flinty
ridges challenged, challenged, the sweat of my brow; the hope of their
harvest must ever be *ulterior*, and could never be forgotten.

So I had to forget her.

They tell me B · le did not. Or else *she* remembered him and chose to
forget her brewer.

They tell me they are together, still appalling one another, and
clutching their love-and-laughter and their bilious contumacity
beyond the bounds of this kingdom, beyond all possible bounds of *my*
comprehension. When I clipped them hip-to-hip for the furtherance
of my policy I tell you frankly I'd no notion what I did. "Father,
forgive him," do I hear them say? Am I to them an execution-squad
that has tramped 'em both uphill to their mutual conjoint Calvary?

All I know is, *she* had no doctrine, ever. She was the creature of her
human truth and believed only what came to her.

Whereas *he* could not believe unless first he had worried and snarled
and embrangled his brain to verge of madness with theoretical
justification; whereafter, like a stooping hawk, plunge claws into the
quarry and never mind at that short moment, was it the one he meant
to kill, or another one altogether! Whereafter, worry and snarling, and
embranglement all over again: for what he had done, for what he did,
for what he had yet to do.

And he and she to *live*, together? One of 'em must die first. Which?
And I tell you, no natural death.

And no place for a third betwixt the internecine two – neither a third
friend nor a third enemy. Yet, strange, there is always a third. It was
me; it was C · · · · d; failing either of us, it was that Easterling, the
pudgy Rotraut with her crop-head Sappho in the next-door 'Birdcage'
room; I think also (and inimically) it may have been the castanet
Spaniard in the opposite next-door – the one we cargoed out to
Santander in the bilboes, you remember, with her trim brown back so
scourged? No: B · le and Longlegs were never sufficient one to the
other; but oh, compared to either of them, all others have been
insufficient for each. *I* have, I know that. I tell you, at Cambridge, that
friar and myself: men called us David-and-Jonathan. I tried not to
probe what it meant. Our student-theology of the meetings at
the White Horse Inn necessarily lent itself to such very warm
companionships – what, when we reshaped all Christendom, how
could there *not* have been love?

But doctrine now is clear. My spade has marked its row for

consistent and continued delving. Wherever there is a great rock in
the soil before my feet, to turn the row, shift it edgeways, and so round
the obstacle. You damned O · · · · · s[1], there are boulders no man
should presume to heave! If he crush not himself with their weight,
then by Christ he crusheth others: I will not be responsible. Caesar's
duty is *my* duty, I will nevermore serve Sejanus, nor will I *be* Sejanus.
One man alone in England I now take for my pattern of life. I believe
you would say, Christian pattern? I hope you would. I refer to
A · · · · · · · p C · · · · · r:[2] you would not surely scorn *him*? Friend
O · · · · · s, he is *still in office*, and preacheth naught but an humble
virtue.

Which brings me, my friend, to A · · · s's magisterial insistence:
that you depart from your concubine and resume your lawful marriage. Understand but one thing: great A · · · s has heard you confess
that your love for Œ · · · e (and for other such, at home and abroad)
was part and parcel of all the carelessness, the ill-judgements, the
laches in duty, which aided the like of B · · · · r to indict you for
supposed treason. Part and parcel also of the vanity you confessed:
which therefore (to prove yourself) you must utterly relinquish.

Moreover, in that your wife's kinfolk are of the faction of D · ke
H · · · ·d of N · · · · · k, of B · · · · r himself, of the household of our
new C · · · e[3], her renewed cohabitation with you would be an overt
token that you are no longer a man of *any* faction. Except of that which
A · · · s has made inseparable from his full kingdom and from the
fullness of service he expects from all his subjects. You write to me –
and I quote from you – 'God damn it, how can I do it, am I to pull out
my very belly-conduits and reverse them inside-out like the fingers of
a too-tight glove?' My answer: of course not.

You are commanded no more than any public man may accomplish
and present: to demonstrate the outward and visible emblem of an
inward essential truth. Definition of a Sacrament, more or less. I do
not write thus to blaspheme but to show you the depth of my sincerity.

The essential inward truth of the Eucharist (as prescribed by the Six
Articles mandatory): chalice and paten contain the Blood and Body.
Outward emblem of the Eucharist: wine and bread, eaten and drunk.
In obedience to our faith we accept, as a Mystery, these apparent
incompatibles.

[1] O · · · · · s = Orpheus = Wyatt.
[2] A · · · · · · · p C · · · · r = Archbishop Cranmer.
[3] C · · e = Circe = Queen Catherine Howard.

Your essential inward truth: you and she are man and wife, one flesh, by law and religion. Outward emblem of your marriage: an antagonism between you, even in your secret longings. *You* drop your tears for your loss of illicit Œ···e. *She* (may I suppose?) hath her fantasy rasped continual by her dreams of the tautened thighs of her clandestine young men.

Query: how can I term these inward agonies an 'outward emblem'?

Answer: because you assert they are the sole reality of your marriage, by argument of 'common sense'. Good God, you need not me to tell you that brute-ignorant sectarians deny the Sacrament by 'common sense' – sole reality of bread-and-wine, they bawl, can be for naught but the good of the gut – I warn you, that is the *Fiend's* perception!

Dear O·····s, you have had your orders. Your outward emblem, your inward truth[1], incompatible, must yet come together in the Mystery of Obedience: delay it not.

Leave allegory. Approach practicality.

Let Lady Wyatt come to Calais, not with you, but a little while after. Furnish a chamber in the garrison with a noble double-bed. Have your own camp-cot made up for 'occasional use' in some appropriate guardroom to which your hours of command may call you whenever necessary. And then take expedient order that necessity rule *all* your hours. Your zeal of office will be noted by those upon your staff who must write reports to the Council (which effectively means to *me*: for my friends among those lords have handed me the charge of overseeing your behaviour when need be). The reports will convey that the Calais regiment has never had so devoted a leader. And then your lady's ladies will also be writing, to C··· e, and her uncle of N·····k: *they* will state that their mistress is now housed in caparison of such honour that all the Picardy Frenchmen believe her the one sole object of all your most amorous poems. She won't complain.

Ah, you say, but Œ··· e will. Ah, dear man, it will be hard for her.

Let me assure you I will assure myself that her child, when it is born, shall be decently looked-after by various of our good friends: and among them there will be one (but not me, I heave no such

---

[1] *written in the margin, not in cipher, but in Latin, a rapid afterthought:*
(You'll understand why I deprecate any possibility you should seek to *re-love* one another? Outward and Inward would become totally confused, between them your heart would break. Since the birth of my youngest child, my wife and I have scarce spoken. What it betokens, I know not. After so much pain – all that is left is *indifference?* Worst conceivable of all conclusions.)

boulder, not any more after this) to write to you and give you news upon every changing instant how they fare.

For God's sake have some sense: and send me no more letters.

*   *   *

The above came to Wyatt in the midst of a flurry of official despatches, as he stood on the foreshore at Deal: clatter and chaos of five-score remount horses for the Calais squadrons embarked in tossing luggers to be ferried out to the ships. He opened it impatiently, thinking at first it was yet another unnecessary routine schedule – lists of fodder-prices costed by Treasury for last week's stablings at Rochester Castle, or Tower of London inventories of the ordnance-stores shipped from Deptford (which ought to be in France by now, but God alone knew whether they'd even left the Thames). Then he recognised Wentworth's cipher and began to note down its substitutions onto the back of a bill-of-lading. When he saw what he decoded, he became so engorged with anger that he swung on his armoured heel and crunched furiously back over the shingle to the customs-house, to find himself some private room, immediately to compose his furious answer.

He had at once turned to Wentworth's final sentence, knowing well that the end of a political letter nine times out of ten was a Parthian marksman's treachery, and so it proved: of course it was to be ignored; such cowardice was insupportable, the bloody man must be told directly when, what, and why.

But even as he moved, he saw his quartermaster-clerk watching him. Not a functionary of his own appointment, but some lizard-eyed peculator hoisted upon him from the filing-closet of the King's secretary-at-war. Wyatt was a brave man, being a good poet: but recent experience had taught him at last some forethought. He stopped in his tracks, thrust the letter into the scarf that wrapped his helmet (white silk, from Mrs Darrell), and pretended to be looking about him for a farrier-serjeant on the skive.

Six hours later, in the ship-cabin, as his flotilla beat close-hauled to avoid the Goodwins, he had loneliness and calm enough to re-read Lord Wentworth's words, and to reply to them with cooler spirit. England was lost to sight in blustering wefts of rainy fog: it would be long before France was visible. It was as though he was suspended untouched, and for the hour untouchable, between danger of his King in London and danger of the foe abroad against his new garrison (he cared nothing for the danger of these contrary winds, being ignorant of sea-craft): he felt, therefore, he could

write dangerously and yet without danger. An illusion, he knew: but by
God he would not use cipher.

  Moreover, he would put his name.

*

To Lord Wentworth Spade-in-Hand, and of peasant-like ulterior
purpose: from Thomas Wyatt, Knight-at-arms, King's Commander
of his Calais Horse.
Sir,

  Do not presume ever to call me 'Orpheus' again.

  No, I mean to fix no quarrel on you, I have already my blood-
enemies, in court and in camp. I write only to establish myself as my
own man, to be sure of confessed ill-judgement, choler, vanity and the
rest, but my own man of my own errors, requiring no instruction as to
how to become another's.

  You serve not Sejanus? No, but you do serve Cicero, who spoke so
very well, shifting shifting with the times, always so hesitant-certain
he spoke always to the desired main chance, the preservation of a dead
republic: until that dead republic (its name then being Marcus
Antony) sent soldiers to sever his neck. Cicero, I still hear, is greatly
praised in our Latin schools. You, in your heedful cipher, take heed to
praise Canterbury. Sword for *his* neck, one day? Or fire for his whole
staked body? Or shall he sign himself free to the uttermost end,
repetitive recantation, reiterated reaffirmation? If any can do so, *he*
can. So praise him and be damned. We all uphold our own idols, of
gold or of trodden clay. After which words, no more from me upon
statecraft.

  And after these next words, no more upon marriage either.

  If you think I shall seek to re-love my lost-love wife, you are a fool,
and as great a fool as you were when you re-loved yours – or she you, as
you make it appear. Except positions were reversed, no? You were the
rambler and she took you back. After finding herself a chaplain who
suited *your* divinity rather than hers.

  You know well *my* position, indeed you express it: 'tautened thighs'
very true. Wentworth, I am commanded: and to save my life I obey
command (being a king's, it is no shame); I live with her and without
Darrell. But I offer her to the world as no more special than any other
high-born high-bought sluice-quim that should hang a cloved orange
above her stomacher to imply she knows no smell of smeared bed-
sheets as she paces the daylight. Let French Picards think what they

will, she lives where I am told to let her live, bed-furnishings are *her* business, her informant ladies-in-waiting may write as they choose about them, I shall not even see the room.

Thighs, yea, and tautened, let them strain as they list therein, I tell you I shall not see.

And as for the news of Darrell, if she herself cannot find means or heart to tell it me, then no-one shall: we have our own quiet bargain to which you (and various 'friends') are in no wise privy. Finish with that.

On the matter however of players and Wentworth-protected minstrels (which seem of their very name to startle you, as a gun-shot doth a grouse), I refuse to be put to silence. I am a poet and there was a time when poetry had hopes of you. Not king, duke, bishop, nor regimental quartermaster-clerk can prevent my expostulation theretoward, when thus compelled by the revealed ignorance of a man's comments who must know better.

I insist I repeat my argument about Bale, concerning which you slither and mistake my first strong point (deliberate? of course deliberate. You knew very well what I meant: and for chastisement of your evasion I must here and now say it again). I did not write to tell you that you did wrong to deliver him and his actors into the service of Cromwell. Nor to suggest that what you call his 'extremity' was in any way dishonourable to your reputation as *patronus musarum*. His moderation might have been, given the 'ulterior purpose' that in those days informed your patronage.

But, as it chanced, he was not moderate – a fact now made manifest by his High German *anabasis*, by the incomparable woman he carries with him in his sufferings, by the children he hath of her, by the very words you tell me he snarled to your beard. For integrity of his writing life he is a man I so greatly envy, despite his rebarbative manners, his horrid appearance, hard hot concealed carnality as hooked and twisted as a ram's-horn that must infallibly, cruelly, rend any sweet flesh it purports to condole. Yes, appalling, your own description: and all talk I ever had with him foundered upon incompatibles. I am glad he is out of my world. But, 'sblood, he is so rude English, we are all at a loss without him.

But none of that is germane. I object, and you know I object, to your incorrigible assumption that to gather-in to yourself (and faction) a poet to breathe forth your public recipes for the world's improvement is simultaneous to improve his poetry. Not only improve – but *create*!

Dust into Adam-shape, or rib-bone into Eve! Is not that your logic? For I had not heard that Bale was any sort of poet before you gave him his letter-of-marque. All you knew of him (all *we* knew of him, seeing you consulted me, as being of your faction also – though in politics, mark that, churchmanship, only: not poetry, never was): he was a student of other men's verse, an absorbent sponge for other men's plays, and he had given himself to the English language as St Lawrence gave his limbs to the gridiron.

I said, "Try him, he is an aspirant, an enthusiast, a devotee: but he would place a convolved matter within metre as blunt and raw as a ploughboy's February nose, and the twain will not cross-carry – the more so as his matter is always the first care of his creation. By my opinion such an outset will lead him straightway to sink in bogs of versified prose and scarce ever to win through to Parnassus' asphodel foothills."

My asphodel being a flower hard to be plucked and harsh to the hand (though it seemeth you think of it othergates?), Parnassus is to be flown upon, slantwise, rather than climbed as you'd storm a breach: if we top it at all it is only by fortunate hazard, however strong our dedication.

I then said, as you remind me, "Bring him together with Doll Longlegs." Not true that I counselled you to clip them into a two-backed beast for the better propagation of the cause. That was your thought and yours only, arrived at (may I guess?) when you found you could not discern where your 'glow' at her music and dance left off and your dialectic against popery began. You first used her as your lover to continue and fulfil the glow, and then you used her as your minstrel to fulfil your commitment to Christ: and your mind was so transported that you ran both actions together as though oil might be mixed with water – both are liquid, both will boil, but they never in fact *are* together: ask your cook. Perhaps you did ask your cook? At any rate, you saw your error, and slipped yourself, waterish, out from under the oil, letting it pour into the cauldron of Bale.

Whereas my poor recommendation had simply been in hope that Bale, as a learning playwright, might be taught by what *she* had learned, from those Olivers, their grace and stateliness, in a word their *Italianism* – oh as popish as it comes, after all they were Norfolk's people; but reformed England needs such beauty. To seek it from our Bales alone – why, we might as well go questing for Virgil's Venus in the hovels of Gropecunt Lane.

I asked Bale once, had he read any work of young Surrey's? I refrained from my own name, being as modest as I am vain.

He said, in brief, that the Earl of Surrey, as son to the Duke of Norfolk, must be so arrogant papist that his verse could have no service but bum-cleansing.

I repeated, had he read?

He said, yes, he thought he had: something fetched out of Petrarch, what had Petrarch to say to a stalwart English corn-factor much perplexed for his soul's salvation and no less for the decay of agriculture?

As for his command – which you say should have been your command – of his players upon circuit. Some little time before he went to Thorndon, but after Cromwell had taken charge of the acting-company, a time in fact when you claim Bale was held already under tight rein by his master, I was at a certain house – in Sussex, no matter whose – where our host had these players to his Whitsun.

The piece given was *A Comedy concerning Three Laws, of Nature, Moses, and Christ, corrupted by the Sodomites, Pharisees and Papists*, above two hours in length and as learned as Aristotle. As the play was writ for you, I will not give the plot; but to summarise the conclusion so you'll know that in truth I listened to it: the three laws corrupted had in our days been restored by valiant King Henry, as Josiah in the old Jews' kingdom restored such law as they then had – *id est*: of Nature and of Moses.

It was a grave house, and none there would have disputed the poet's contention. I did not dispute it. We nodded our heads and looked wise, saying, "how true these profound statements, how needful to have 'em made, lest in the heat of politic strife we forget our grounds of championship."

But then came in (the Third Act already afoot) a quiet fellow, a chaplain, I believe, from a nearby house of nuns, who was not quite of the same opinion. I take it he was no uttermost papist, or he would not have expected welcome that night: but he adhered perhaps less well-fixed than some of us to the sudden movements of government, a man (you might say) clinging on to the rail of a jerking cart-arse as the teamster whips forward his beasts, fearful at each moment he will be flung into the mire. I daresay too he was distressed by the intimate shocks imposed upon his nunnery-ladies as they heard of their imminent dissolution, although he maintained no stubbornness that in the cloister abode the best virtues of Christendom, nor the most needful.

He paid heed to the play for some twenty minutes or so, until the players came to a pause. Law-of-Moses as a blind cripple had been staggering about the acting-place, knocking his crutch against our knees to 'bring us within the action' – or so a smug dame beside me was simpering in high excitement. I wonder had she ever sat in a foremost bench at a play before? Every market-place clown will bang his slap-stick upon heads within reach, and they'll often go so far as to surge among the people and grapple with chits' paps: but no doubt this was the first time she had ever been mauled by a sacred personage out of Holy Writ.

The stage being clear of actors, and some music-and-song intervening from the gallery of the hall, this nuns'-priest suddenly speaks. "Dr Bale," says he, diffident, but with threat of the shrew, "Dr Bale, may we ask a question?"

It so befell, there was no Dr Bale.

He had been onstage at commencement, well enough, elocuting his prologue, but now he had gone, who knew where? Perhaps into the courtyard to cool his head, it was a hot night. (In fact, he was unwell: strain of play-touring without his Dorothy worked great danger upon his health, poor brute.)

But the pause was now complete, the music ended, on came an Evangelist to proceed with Act Four. The chaplain asks again, "Who among you will hear my question?" Evangelist takes no note of him, rides over him with some fourteen loud lines – "I am Christ's Gospel" – desperate solemn: then through a gap in the curtain the Vice, Infidelity, crying his devious greeting, clasping Evangelist from behind like a boisterous hearty ale-mate. No argument but your Bale knew how to rattle-up *quick* against *slow* and so keep his listeners alive; his watchers too, expert diversity of both dialogue and stage-movement.

But here is this chaplain importunate, he will *not* permit the play's progress: "If you please, a simple question: I would prefer it answered now, so your plot from henceforward will be clearer to my mind."

And this time his voice is not stinted, even brisk Infidelity had to cease. Our good host, ever mindful of the ease of his invited friends, called pleasantly, "You should answer him, sirs. We are happy to wait till his difficulty is made up: after all, you are here for our present enlightenment."

Thereupon the two players stand stupid, and the other three of the
company creep toward them to find what has chanced: five-in-a-row in
our midst; Evangelist (bride-white robe and an open book of Scripture), Infidelity (a sort of East Cheap cutpurse), False Doctrine (a
divinity-doctor with spectacles the size of saucers and a pyramidical
false nose), Hypocrisy (a friar's habit: grey-friar's, not white. I suspect
Bale even now maintains Carmel above Assisi: to perpetuate thus old
jealousy into a new reformed age might well be hypocrisy indeed?, and – at end of the line – God-the-Father, half-changed into
his next costume (God's-Vengeance), *videlicet* in his undershirt,
with gold-corded buskins to his knees, beard and sceptre in one hand
and a cup of hot wine in the other.

The nuns'-priest is quite abashed now, having so many to accost,
for truly – as he promised – his question is to be in essence quite
simple; though a good answer, I fear, far less so.

"By your favours, you have shown us Law-of-Moses despoiled and
hurt by the malice of Ambition and Covetousness, cognate with the
Pharisees, I understand. Good. But why do you contrive it that the
two wicked practisers lay a complot betwixt 'em to advocate popery,
before they assail the Old Testament Laws? Whatever we think of
popery – and notwithstanding its present corruption, it did once hold
out hope for Christendom against bloody-minded tyrants and heretics
– I say, whatever we think of it, it can *not* have been pre-ordained by
the powers of sin while the message-upon-earth of Lord Jesus was yet
unspoken.

"Your play, masters, would say to me that Christ's Ministry was all
but in vain, if its eventual papal abuse was held as a certainty as far
back into man's history as Sinai?

"I do not wish to dispute all your play-making out-of-hand, for
there is much worth in your speeches and much to trouble the
Christian conscience – which is as it should be. But unless I am made
to understand by your poetries that Gabriel Archangel to Our Lady
Mary brought such unprecedent tidings that the whole world was – for
a space – made utterly new, then I know not why I wear this tonsure.

"Pray you, sirs, resolve me my unclarity upon this point."

I cannot say the priest was offended by the play: I believe he was so
truly taken by its combative force that he felt in all conscience he must
niggle like an honest man where he believed he spied a fault. The
others in hall were sagely respectful, and accepted his right to do this.
At any rate, most of 'em: the soft woman to my left became incensed

and cried out for the actors to continue, the chaplain was a spoil-art breaking into the illusion with his theologic pedantry, what business had he to question the considered work of our notable poet? She having already praised the actors for themselves breaking in to their own illusion. I told her if Law-of-Moses was to hustle me with his crutch, then let him and his fellows justify their theatric pretences when called upon to do so – flaws of logic ought not to be violently covered-over by hectoring us unmerciful as an aid to their exposition: I think it was partly that which had so disturbed the nuns'-priest, he had had a sharp crack from the damned actor's ferrule on the lines –

> Have to your clergy a diligent respect,
> And see they do not corrupt the laws of God,
> For that doth require a terrible heavy rod.

– as though Bale's players had the right to assume good and bad thoughts among their audience and to punish for the latter even as they guessed at them.

Howbeit, now that the 'bad thoughts' of this one audience-member had been openly proclaimed, they did not know at all how to handle it.

God-the-Father, quaffing his tiring-room drink, began by ignoring the chief point at issue (a hard point, I will admit – to what extent *can* we say the Devil's work is predestinate? *I* know not the answer): and instead he latched on to the priest's side-remark about popery having been a shield against tyrants. Unavoidable historical truth, I'd have thought: what of Attila the Hun? What of all those savage cruel kings and dukes – alleged Christian – up and down all through Europe in the centuries immediate-after collapse of the Western Caesars? Who dare say the romish church did not in those days civilize? Who was it sent Augustine to Canterbury, but a pope, and a very great pope?

But no: the egregious actor, who had previous held the stage as Maker and Creator of All-thing, was not yet divorced from his face-paint glory; and incontinent he berated the unfortunate priest as having treasonably aspersed our Sovereign Lord the King, and all his Ministers, *and* all his Bishops, and what a wonder the Lords of Justice had not already haled such a stinkard-begrudger to Tyburn!

After that, another chimed in – Evangelist, as high and proud as the Gospels (in his hand) are meek and charitable – with a pseudo-courteous sneer, that unless one had the grace to comprehend the sophisticate devices of the stage-play at its highest reach of accomplished art, one should not presume to meddle with the meanings of such – for was there not allegory therein, poetic wisdom, far far beyond the chop-logic of schoolmen's sermons? He prated, then they *all* prated, of 'suspension of time as a stage-function not related to any time of actuality', of 'character-abstraction being employed for the drawing-forth of essential as opposed to superficial statement' – oh a dreadful barge-freight of undigested indigestible draff, which I could not think was Bale's. That tedious and arbitrary Teuton had been at them for certain: I always told you *he* was a mistake.

With no desire to prolong my 'oil-and-water' similitudes of personal hurtful application, I must at this point return to La Haut-jambée. Because the contrast between Bale's players and herself in their treatment of those to whom they played was conspicuous, and defies suppression.

In her room at the 'Birdcage' (unlike some of the other women – may I specify the Angelina[1]?) she was never contemptuous, she never immediately crammed us unconsulted with her artistry as though we were all great cuckoo-mouths demanding glut of provender, and too greedy to discriminate. She was never less than a hostess; if she rallied us, or even abused us, it was within that freedom a lady hath under the shadow of her own bed-canopy, where none shall enter save wished-for friends (no matter at all that we had paid her maid an entrance-money).

She sometimes would ask us what we desired to hear: not necess-arily would she give it us, if she preferred to present another thing, and yet it always chanced (or she always so conjured it) that the 'other thing', even as she offered it, seemed better that that which we called-for. Then again, we might not seem responsive, so perhaps she would make a feint of not wishing to perform at all. She'd commence one song or dance, and play some nervous trick with it, as a clever swordsman will seem only to feel the balance of his weapon, switching it tentative left and right, till all of a sudden you become aware he is already embarked full-bodied into thrust after thrust, lethal, hard, unstoppable; and then – just as suddenly – he stops, twinkles his hilt between fingers, and behold he is smiting with the edge: why, his

---

[1] Gross untruth, you insinuating machiavel, that *we* had her scourged and transported! For sure, we all consulted over the unacceptable connivance of 'castanet Spaniard' with daggermen and intelligencers: but – *if* you'll search your memory? – it was *I* that said "hurt her not, neither by chain nor whip-lash: she is beautiful and loveth God's Mother, moreover I have enjoyed her. Send her packing to her Emperor's ambassador, let *him* take order to have her out of the land!" Which he would have done: she embarrassed. No: you know yourself cruel, you'd share the burden? But not with *me*: by Christ I'll not have it!

Thos Wyatt, knt.

theme is quite changed. If La Haut-jambée did this, she would maintain it maybe an entire half-hour, talking and laughing between-times (and letting us talk and laugh with her), or then again she might curse herself, or make mock of *our* inconstancy. Or perhap she would so ignore us that we thought she hated our coming thither. Until she – by what secret intuitive? – upon a moment had grasped our mood, and found means to engrasp it with *her* mood: and at once she knew her art, knew what was to be performed, and how; and after that, neither pause nor falter till she came to the end of her turn.

Any doubts from her hearers about what they had heard – any flaws we might detect in her discourse (as the Sussex chaplain with his 'simple question') – she would always allow us the grace of a full objection, and if she could answer it, well: if not, we had liberty to knock the next week at any other door in the house, and seek *there* to be flattered for our prejudice.

I insulted her once, being bitter at heart. When she expelled me, I felt more shame than if I'd been thrown out of church for befouling God's font-water.

But nothing church-like at all about those rowdy 'Birdcage' galleries. It was a troubled and troubling young woman I had abused with mine own trouble, her damaged art was her own person, not any sacred mystery; and so she made me aware.

When she performed outside the 'Birdcage' – as several times I had her to my London lodging, for myself and friends (male and female) in religion and politics and poetry – she came as a guest and behaved as a guest, undertaking the spirit of the evening with a sort of work that should clarify our public cause as acutely as may be. She never deferred to the cause (nor to us), servile: rather she came *wearing* it like a well-fitted hood, accepted compliments upon its cut and fashion, was prepared to change it if any could prove it torn or moth-eaten; to all other criticism she responded with good reason and in no-wise en-angered.

She gave us song-ballads, for example, with verses wherein we must answer her back: if she or we knew no such verses, it was up to us to invent 'em. She once made an entire night's work of the singing and dancing of the trial of Thomas More – God, but that was wounding work, impregnate with agony and death which she dared us to mock at our peril. Her point being this: she sang the King's part, and those of Boleyn and Cromwell, while we must find the argument (all in impromptu stanzas with *ababbcc* rhyme – hers being the *abab*, ours *bcc*) to save Sir Thomas's life. I learned, I dare swear, more of the moral intricacies of that sad business from her one supper-time *pseudo-comedia quasi-satira* than from all the procedings in court, or from all the hortatory parliament-speeches that had dinned it into our nation's ears. The King came not out of it well (which would have made for much danger in a less private place), yet the romish case was all in ruin: and *yet* at the end our hearts broke for More's courage – even those of us that had roundly condemned him (and still would condemn, were his headstrongness repeated today). The whole thing most sharp and pitiful, and withal so harsh and bawdy, we knew not when we left off our laughter and began to weep.

For her singing of Cromwell alone, I am not surprised at all he gave your minstrel-troupe the go-by. Damnable nonsense for you to tell me she had 'no doctrine, ever'.

To connect her with the house in Sussex. Had La Haut-jambée been on that stage, all must have fallen out quite different. But she was not there, and quite apparent that her Bale had never regarded her as a wiser art-maker than himself (though I do not say a *better* one, am I better than Surrey? Or Virgil than Catullus?). As it was: half the audience commenced to hate their neighbouring priest, half hated the players and warmed towards the priest; all of them forgot why they were there in the first place – to listen to a play of controversy the better to inform themselves of all the dispute that divideth the land, and thus, being informed, to resolve it: into a new more perfect shape for the common weal, and so at length achieve their long-sought liberties, no? As *you* say, as *you* say too! 'Twas somewhere in the flow of your letter?

I tell you, by night's end, there was more lust for roasting heretics and whipping and racking poor dissident limbs than that manor-house had ever known in the worst days of old superstition. When John Bale came into them to help take the applause at what he thought would be the final line, he found 'em still a-wrangling, and two gentlemen from the next parish had in sooth loosed their daggers half-out. Well: there was some smoothing, and by degrees the party broke up.

I took Bale aside. "For God's sake, man, d'you *mean* to make a battle?"

"Against popery we are *all* in battle, and the sooner these easy ones can be roused up to enstomach it, the more quick and efficacious will be our ultimate victory. No quarter for complacence: Armageddon is at hand. My words are a poor weapon in the grasp of the righteous, but praise heaven the righteous are here, and they will wield it!''

"Wield it at whom? There has been no popery, sir, in *this* house, only misconception and artistic intransigence." By which he was clearly abashed.

"Oh. Oh I see . . . That may be so. And if so, it should not be. No . . . There are new men in the company, perhaps not fully schooled, I had hoped that young Conrad would have –"

"Young Conrad did: and they *are* schooled. I was told, when you and Wentworth first conceived this company, your purpose would be to convince all men equally of the rightness of the New Guise. If they were convinced already, to encourage them in their conviction. If this is no longer what Cromwell desires of you, you should either quit his service, or come openly out with it: that England is so divided, no playmaking can now minister to the nation *in toto*, and that therefore you have embraced a factional embitterment, and seek for enemies as fiercely as you do friends. It would be honest. How far it would be compatible with Christ Jesu Man-of-Sorrows is your concern, not mine: you are the clergyman."

"I am. I am a factionalist. Religion is split asunder: we are right and they are wrong. And yet, it is very odd . . ."

He shook his head as one thoroughly puzzled; and maybe a little ashamed – not of his partisanship (which made him proud), but rather that he did not quite know how he had arrived where he was. "At the start, the most of our actors were declared of no party. I spoke to them, to persuade them, as you have spoke to me: we were embarked together upon a quest, we must bring our hearers along with us, else surely we would lose them all. I was afraid that in my zeal I would seem to set a rabid chase-hound at government's heels by causing aroused audiences to make demands of reformation so urgent they could not be fulfilled. In a sense I have done just this, but willy-nilly, almost unwitting. I did not believe one should force people's hearts: that would be mere arrogance, as arrogant as any pope. And a pope rearing up from below is surely no better than that pontiff already enthroned: for both must intimidate to work their singular will. No, I would not have had that: nor would I have it now. Nonetheless, it does appear that this *is* the manner of the world now-a-days, for all these players are younger than I am, the children of the new age. They are fixed in their fury before I even recruit them for the work. Don't you see, they are chase-hounds at *my* heels?''

That had not been my impression. Having heard the braving actors,
having watched their features closely as they clamoured against the
chaplain for his rational dissection, I spied beneath their paintwork a
fluttering uncertainty. It rose up in my mind that, prior to their
engagement, they had been no more committed to Bale's advanced
doctrine than any of their predecessors in the company. Neither were
they now committed: most gut-yearning anxious to *appear so*, that was
all. They had not needed Bale's 'persuasion' to enfold them into his
quest. Somehow they had learned that to advance themselves in their
business, it was imperative they make instant and scandalous prot-
estation of an intellectual extremity passing far beyond any argument
in the play that they performed. They forgot they were mere vessels to
contain the author's words and sound them forth when precisely
tapped; they forgot they had no skill to write those words of their own
invention: his play had become *them*, and they must now embody it,
whether as his fiction-persons or (as now) their own selves. And not
being men of any great subtlety, they embodied it twice as crude as it
stood (by his pen) in their screeds.

From whom had they learned this? Conrad? Oh certainly Conrad:
but the 'manner of the world now-a-days' had infected Conrad too.
The 'manner of the world now-a-days' included Bale's plays. It
included me, and you, and even Bishop Bonner, when we took our
commands from Cromwell and vied for his favour, uncovering papish
plots, informing, denouncing, sitting upon trials, adding our signa-
tures to all those documents affirming our loyal service as though
no-one could believe it from our deeds.

Cromwell was not immune to it: neither (and I whisper) was His
Majesty himself. If Bale and Bale's wife were marched to the self-same
Calvary, so also were Sejanus and Caesar, and on the other side, Pole
and the Emperor; while Emperor, Pope, the shifting King of France,
and all the Lutherite German princes, played ring-a-ring-roses within
one twisted circlet of thorns. All this in the name of replenishing
Christ's Kingdom and (in our England) of national deliverance. I do
believe God laughed at us. Could I believe He had *planned* such a
drowning-down vortex?[1] Who should benefit, save only the valiant,

---

[1] No: but I might believe He *had* planned to send us the pox. Not for so bluntly punitive a reason
as some would maintain, to retribute our sins of lechery: He hath hell to do that with, and eternal,
if He be so minded. His Son told us Siloam Tower, that fell upon the people, fell not for that they
were exceptional wicked; which I take to be a parable-word against our making such disasters
specific. But the pox, being a part of the *manner-of-the-world-now-a-days*, is also part of God's
laughter thereat: when clowns laugh, the public laughs; when the public laughs, the clowns

but heathen, Turk? For I hear, and hear grimly, the Turk out of his whole-heartedness now maketh great gains in the eastward lands and the middle sea: hath England today a policy to take any account of it? (Our merchants and ship-masters would sure be blithe to hear of one)

I said naught of this to Bale. He is learned and most sharp of his invention but I would not say intelligent. He gabbled on at me about his players: "Chase-hounds," he repeated, "at *my* heels, and I must welcome their barking, because if they are not England in search for her deliverance, what are they?"

I *said*: "Bloody fools who need a strict reminder that they live to serve the public, not to order us about! We have enough jacks-in-office, and to spare, for that already."

I *could* have said, but did not (in response to a secret thought which was even then stitching sutures of sudden dread at my tongue's nerve): "Blame not the dogs but the huntsmen that whistle them on: if Ambition and Covetousness despoiled the Law of Moses and erected popes for their convenience, is it not possible that once again they have planned full cry (*and from within*) against the new-found Gospel-truth?" I myself had just that week been arranging with Cromwell my profits from dissolved monasteries: bad conscience as much as discretion caused me muffle the whisper of my fears. And yet Cromwell had been good to me, for space of years he was *my pillar*.

I did not know, and dared not directly ask, how much did Bale realise the expedient cynic worldliness of Smokey-faced Tom? Damn sure impoverished Bale drew no sort of profit beyond his immediate playmaker's fee. Why, I do not think he even drew his dissolution-pension, as made available by government to certain favoured priors of friar-houses: first, because he had wilfully left the Carmelites before the order was officially abolished; and, second, because Cromwell (after Bale's gaoling at Greenwich) advised him not to press for the money, "in case questions might be asked, politically-damaging, about the irregular Haute-jambée, her children, Lambeth Palace . . .?", the wink-and-the-nod. I presume that *you* knew this? I presume you in some way compensated him? *Did* you?

Entire and perfect irony, and the clue to all my doubts about poets

---

laugh, redoubled – who begins it? who ends? God, but *I* laughed when *you* wrote you'd had no woman-flesh for fear of pox. Exact the same reason, at the same season, for Haut-jambée's refusing me her bed. And then both of you forgot it, together? I think you *should* tell your wife. She is most godly: of a surety, she will *laugh*.

Thos. Wyatt, knt.

in factional service (which, in a divided state, can also mean state-service): the very villains of Bale's play were a true-pictured portrait of the man who had paid him to make it.

And he knew not that this was so.

Quem deus perdere vult, prius dementat. Second thoughts: there *is* a Plan.

As to why our own Maker should wish to destroy us by means of our own Free Will and thereunto createth our frenzy (to say naught of His concomitant laughter), ask a clergyman, ask Bale, ask the nun's-priest, ask Cranmer: but none of 'em will agree upon an answer. *My* work is to defend Calais.

> I am as I am and so will I be
> But how that I am none knoweth truly.
> Be it evil, be it well, be I bound, be I free,
> I am as I am and so will I be.
>
> > I remain,
> > WYATT.

★

Lord Wentworth did not show the letter to the Privy Council. He read it once, and then burnt it; and never wrote to Wyatt again.

(5)

Oil And Vinegar, Lemon And Brandywine

Lydia Lowlyheart arrived in London on one of her visits in the spring of 1595: she meant to stay for most of a week, or if need be, longer, chiefly to consult lawyers about the Canterbury house; but also of course to see Lucretia. She had not written to tell her she was coming, the journey was spur-of-the-moment, prompted by a sudden fear that briberies and litigious accommodations were taking place behind her back – her parish clergyman had been talking too widely and let things out he shouldn't.

She found a room at the Saracen's Head near Newgate. The people of the house knew her and knew her tastes. Her legal business might take her to the Inns of Court, to Doctors' Commons below St Paul's, or to Westminster Hall; the hostelry was well-enough placed for all of these. She had been straight to her lawyer before even going there: now she needed dinner, and after dinner – to visit Lucretia. The waiter in the eating-room immediately drew her attention to the playbills tacked up on the buttery-screens: "I expect, ma'am, you'll want to see the week's stage-fare, as is your usual?" The first bill she read drove dinner straight out of her mind: in a tremor of high excitement she pulled it from the screens and shot speechless into the street. It was absurd, so stately a woman, so sober-dressed, so Calvin-Geneva-like, rushing through London with the impetus of a royal post-runner, her cumbrous bumroll under piled skirts bouncing about on her rump. The waiter and her travelling-maid followed her to the yard-gate, dropped back, and watched her go, bewilderment all over their faces.

"We made a dooms early start from the Blackheath inn this morning," said the maid. "Had to see that lawyer afore even the sun got up, so she made out. My view of it, these litigators have untangled a part of her brains. Well . . ."

At East Cheap, Lucretia's landlady stood aside in consternation to let her unannounced up the stairs, she must have thought there was a death in the family.

Lucretia, for a wonder, was out of bed (St Magnus's clock was just striking noon). She sat at breakfast with a young man. It was immediately obvious he was not the unknown who had previously left sword and pistols in her room, but a much less formidable kind of creature, quick body and slight, dressed in a plain bottle-green, burnt-brown curls of hair receding from his forehead, big round intent brown eyes, a soft womanish mouth, a brief smear of a moustache. Not quite as young as he seemed at first sight: he might have been thirty; and Lucretia, flustered by her mother's delirious arrival, forgot to introduce him.

If Lydia herself had been the less flustered, she might have noticed a dark-faced biting tension between this man and her daughter. She might have noticed that the breakfast was on the table but no-one was eating.

She troubled herself for none of it, she flapped and flicked the playbill like a warrant of arrest into Lucretia's angry eyes. "Please, please," she urged, "this afternoon, only the one performance, you must come with me, at the Swan, we have just time, they won't blow the trumpet for another hour, you can dress yourself properly and still we have time – Lucretia, what are you staring at? Child, do you not realise, it's your *grandfather's play*!"

Lucretia, impatient: "I'm sorry, mother, no. I have seen it, it is not: not even the same title. You told me his play was called, in full, *King John of the English*: this one is *The Troublesome Reign of King John*, but six or seven years old at the most."

"Six or seven years *too* old: they wrote it the year of Spain's Armada, and all that that betokens." The soft-mouthed man was thrusting himself in, with what Lydia thought an impertinent knowingness. "The Swan company only mount it as a favour to Henslowe, who knows he'll lose money if he ventures it at the Rose: he needs it to be shown at once, before he concedes loss of right in it; to forestall us at the Theatre. But it will not serve. He hopes of course to glut the public with the tediousness of King John: but in fact it will entice 'em. They'll come running to see ours as soon as we can stage it, if only to make the comparison. They know that when *we* handle aged matter we always innovate with dexterity and fresh-minted wit: old favourite tales, by all means, but every time they must be new. Henslowe won't perceive it."

"Of course he perceives it," Lucretia snapped at him, "Why else has he been harassing you to improve *The Spanish Tragedy*?"

"Because Tony Munday told him that if he paid me enough for it, it would keep my larcenous fingers out of King John. But management being management, Henslowe refused the price. *Ergo*, I work for the Burbages, and very like for them only, if their payments continue fluent. So Munday's old cud is regurgitated unaltered, until all become weary of it. Which I hazard will be this very day before supper.

"Madam, I do beg your pardon, you must think me most rude: your daughter and I are accustomed to these jarrings and marrings, they would scarcely boil an egg. I will leave her to simmer in your cool company: I have a new stage-garb to wear this afternoon, fantastic armour cap-a-pie, I must to Shoreditch and attire myself in good time." He bowed and went out.

After a short silence: "Yes, I do think him rude," said Lydia. "Is he player or poet, or what? How is he called?" She was hurt the man had sneered at Armada-year patriotism. In Canterbury they had been so close to the intended Spanish beach-head that they would remember the great deliverance for ever.

Lucretia bit her lip. "Mother, he is something of each; every colour in his coat for every hue of woman (or of man) he might meet in the street: or elsewhere. Elsewhere today being *here*, I am vexed, as you have seen. He is one that thinks well of himself: he makes demands. Also, being ill-wed, and coercively – so he says – to a rural shrew, he fears the mothers of all young women, I'm glad he's gone. How is he called? His rivals in the business call him Oily Willy the Shakescene, a sight more rude than *my* name for him. For me, he has the title of a very pathetic song-ballad, Sweet William's Ghost, how about that? For I'm never quite sure if he's a true apparition of himself or a damnable illusion. I only like him because he dislikes Munday. And you should not trouble yourself, faith, to see this *Troublesome Reign*. Munday wrote most of it. I shall not go."

"But I shall, whether you come with me or not. Mr Munday confided me his great honour for the fame of Bale. Important I should discover how far he shows it in his own play-making. It is not a small matter that among these younger men at least one should remember the old. Too much, though, to have hoped that the old man's plays themselves would have marched into this altered age.

"I do bear in mind, when we came home from the Cantons, and all in England seemed alive again, Elizabeth queen, no more burnings, no more submission to *fiat* of Spain and the Empire, he took for granted they would seek him out, demand his work on every stage: and they did not. There was some invitation that *King John* be presented at Ipswich to greet Her Majesty upon her progress there, but no: in the end they let him know it was not suited (they so sagely thought) to their New Happy Dawn of Reconciliation . . . Not only that, but the Queen had proclaimed strict prohibition of all plays that should treat upon 'matters of religion or the governance of the estate of the common weal'. I was only a child when this was sent to my father by hand of a friend in Westminster. But how well I remember his reading of it."

*

Bale had stormed up stairs and down, the fatal paper in his hand.

"This is worse," he cried, "than Mary's time! At least popery plays were then permitted, they were true to their own beliefs. Witness this Udall, that I knew when he called himself Lutheran; and then when he sniffed the wind and went rome-wise into Gardiner's service, teaching – aye, and sodomising – the pretty youths of Eton College, he had his pardons, did he not, that he thereupon in Mary's time was made high-master of the Westminster School and all his vice forgotten. Why? Because he made plays for her, *Respublica* to welcome the horrid reversions of her reign, the very year I was flung out of Ireland! They did not prohibit *him* – of course, he was an Oxford man – and the Clerkenwell Christ-plays, they too found revival, for the obfuscation of people's souls.

"But now that those knaves are at last knocked out at door, we of the true party must not retort with our purified muse? It is intolerable! Did I waste myself abroad, first seven years and now again five, like Jacob in the tents of Laban, in order to return for *this!* Lydia, child Lydia, your father is a mouth-gagged man."

*

Lydia was for the moment so rapt into her memory that she did not see what she saw: a piece of paper in Lucretia's hands being torn and torn and then the fragments of it crumpled and let flutter to the floorboards.

She said only: "Today for me to hear just how disciple Munday shall reactivate the gospel of Bale. Today for me and I must not miss it."

Was it Bale's or was it Munday's, the face most in her mind when she called for her boat to the Bankside?

The Swan was half-empty, and the audience seemed unintelligent. She watched the play with the keenest attention, counting, as it were, each point of its argument from one glove-tip to the other, drawing in her breath, nipping her tongue between her teeth, angrily spitting 'hush!' over her shoulder if someone near her coughed, shuffled, or talked. When it was over, and the house cleared, she sat still in her seat with her face between her hands, as though she dared not move until the full two-hours-and-more was thoroughly settled in her mind.

Munday came quietly into the gallery behind her.

She had not seen him during the play, but he had seen her. She was not surprised to find him there. She would not admit to herself that she had waited upon the off-chance that he would appear. When he said, "Dear madam, I am most honoured, we must talk, have you the leisure?" she could have replied, "Alas, no." Why didn't she?

She had not been so pleased with *The Troublesome Reign* that she needed absolutely to shower praise upon one of its authors. Nor had she been so displeased that she felt compelled to pick crow-pie with him. But she allowed him to take her arm and lead her easily along the river-strand to the Bear at the Bridge-foot, a gentlefolk's tavern in what he said was the better part of Southwark, and sit her down before a platter of sweetbreads and a light salad. She noticed that the 'gentlefolk' seemed largely appropriate to the sign of the house, in that they had rolled in boisterously from the bear-baiting, and were clashing tankards and breaking earthenware and damning their own souls in the bar. But Munday found a secluded window-alcove where they could look out upon the bridge and the boats, in peace: he tipped the waiter to pull a curtain, shutting them off from the crowd.

He had little to say: he was waiting for her to speak her opinion. He ordered a halved lemon and squeezed it over the salad, he filled her glass with brandywine, he waited. All his life he had been filling glasses and waiting for others to commit themselves.

At length she was ready. She moved her veil slightly aside to let herself eat and drink.

"I think, sir, you have in your play too much of history. For your persons, King John, the King of France, the Pope's Legate, and so forth, live on your stage only in their own time. True, there is strong vehemence against popery, for example, where the English king cries defiance to the legate – have I the words aright?

> What hast thou, or the Pope thy master, to do, to demand of me how I employ mine own? Know, Sir Priest, as I honour the Church and holy churchmen, so I scorn to be subject to the greatest Prelate in the world!

Splendid fury and your public cheered it, in their sincere and foolish way. But any more than the faded fury of ten generations gone and past? In my father's play, which you say you have read, King John is also King Henry and he ruled my father's England as well as his own: forgive me, I am a faded woman – I am myself a generation past – it is probably not good sense I prefer their hot conflict to the colder backward look you poets now choose to offer us.

"Another thing, who was this 'Falconbridge' – I suppose you got him from the chronicles – routing out the corrupt friars, finding harlots hid in their furniture? Undeniably, most comical –

> Oh I am undone,
> Fair Alice the nun
> Hath took up her rest
> In the Abbot's chest –

and I laughed.

"But how many friars are now in England? Easy to mock what has ceased to exist. And easy to know it has ceased to exist when you call a prior of grey-friars an 'abbot'. Remember, Bale had been a white-friar, and a prior too, I was brought up knowing these things, though he rarely spoke of them as his *personal* history: I think much had happened in those friar-houses to make him unhappy and silent about his days there. But *he* would have laughed at your scene also, although, like me, he would have stuck into it his pins of precise knowledge.

"Yet I know he'd have invented no Falconbridge. Rather might he have put forward a type of stout virtue, England's Honesty, or Wise Discovery, or something of that sort of name, who could hale into daylight not only Pope Innocent's friars but also these Jesuit spies that today do so infest the kingdom. Such a personage might now and then put on a knight's helmet and call himself 'Falconbridge' for the nonce, just as he might in another scene, in peasant-dress, be 'Colin Clout', or even – changing his stage-platform as it were in the one speech from *anno* 1200 to 1588 – 'Sir Francis Walsingham' in a gown-of-state. Such was ever Bale's habit of writing; I must needs be a little grieved to find it fallen out of fashion.

"A different matter with the King Edward play I saw not long since at the Rose. There again it was all old history, but as I saw its meaning, it had less of politic allegory, of the governance of the estate of the common weal – it searched out one man and his sins, it was already allegory in that it made the man a 'king', as it were King Humanity, and beset him with virtues and vices. His designation as Plantagenet was all but accidental. Which was proven when his murderer came, at a sudden cry from him who employed him:

'Lightborn, come forth!'

– and he rose to a blast of music from a trap-door behind a swift-opened curtain, his face masked, his hands like hairy claws. Was not this the Prince of Darkness raised up almost by necromancy? I think the playwright made another piece on such a theme? I don't believe Lightborn is a name from any chronicle. To me it saith 'Lucifer', the conveyor of God's light in renegade shame to the kindling of the stoves of Dis. No sir, *King Edward* was a moral emblem, perfect applicable to the viciousness of our own time, as your play is not: for carnality continues, every young man hath his Gaveston-tempter, his sage counsellors for him to disregard, if he will; and woman-love for him to slight and spoil when his eyes are sufficient blinded.

"As I say, dynastic history was merely there to add a glamour. The Edward-man would have been no less true had they shown him as a – as a schoolmaster."

"Or even a player or play-maker. Yes: I have met such." There was a gliding hint of immediate knowledge in Munday's comment. He seemed to brood about it, slily, over his meat. Lydia had her own brooding, and did not notice. Then he smiled. "Two reasons, madam, for the decline of so brave a manner of play-making, except when the matter is – as you say – of private sin within one single soul.

"First, the Queen's censor will not have it. His decisions are beyond appeal. To harry Jesuits upon the stage is to provoke tumult in our audience. With a virgin Queen – no immediate heir to throne or policy – all tumult (for whatever just cause) must at all cost be avoided. But if we show the old friars, judicious people know we hint at Jesuits, and so we still hold to our truth.

"Second, since your father's day, and in great part from his example, there has arisen, even among the rudest, fervent lust for the splendour of history. An awakened nation that withstood Spain's fleet and sends her own armed ships not only to encompass Ireland but to extend our English power into islands and main of the new-found land, such a nation seeketh ever more and more news of her ancestors, what they did, what they thought, their very habit as they lived. Therefore Falconbridge, just such a man as did stalk through those times unfearing, our people need to know him, to look direct upon his face, and thereby renew their blood. Do you not see that?"

She nodded. "Of course I see it. There is loss in your play, and yet gain. Of course I see. And I do remember tumult. Kilkenny was a terrible time: and yet there we found a glory. All could see my father's plays there, like 'em or not, and no-one had to count pennies for a box-holder before he could enter his place. My father wrote openly, for enemies and friends, but never for this thing called 'management' – a thing of usury, I do believe? He managed his own players and I think they often starved: but *he* chose the theme of their enactments. And then he had the courage to stand alone upon stage and tell the world from his own mouth it was *his* theme and who dared challenge it? *Baleus Prolocutor*: the name is set four-square upon the first page of his every screed.

"When I found you that day among your fellows at the Rose, you were knives-out at them over who should write what and who should prevent it? And management overcame you. Deny it not, Mr Munday, I smelt vinegar in the noontide." She laughed. Very loud, almost strident. So did he, after a moment, but he was surprised, and (she thought) shamefaced.

"Henslowe," he said, "had called us to conference about a play of Sir Thomas More. Yes, I had to write – for my bread-and-gravy, write – even though More was romanist, because as a citizen he was so well-forward for the liberties of Londoners: just to handle the man's good English life, they said, and touch not the contumacity of his death? Impossible task, and censorship was encurdled against us. I think you heard them take from me the scene of the insurrection, wherein the London journeymen made mob against Flemishers who had swarmed into England and stolen their employment.

"Which is what I wrote. These starving English, justly enraged against the foreigners, and how it breaketh More's heart to have to bring severe law upon 'em, how he strove to secure their pardons, defending to the king their right to the good of their own country, and so, and so . . . But we have Flemings here in these days, and folk are enraged *now*: danger of tumult? Change the play: change the playwright for that portion of the play. In effect, my *own* employment, that very morning stolen, but not by any Fleming. Henslowe gave it to the Oily Willy who will now, I hear, usurp King John if he is not directly stopped.

"Retrospectively I did achieve a sort of half-triumph over him: his revised scene of riot had so long a speech of More *defending* the foreign interlopers, craving pity for 'em, I know not what, that he too was accused of most carelessly provoking tumult; and the whole tale of the insurrection was forbidden complete. The play was never shown. For the best: however handled, it must somehow give credence to popery. I would surely have been sick-hearted to have shared in its making, and surely not now able to lift mine eyes to the fair face of the daughter of John Bale."

*

Her veil, she discovered, at some time while they sat at table, had been folded up over her hat-brim, and she did not know when. Now she let it drop again: but gave no other sign she detected courtship in his modest words.

V

(*Historical-pastoral*)

Vocation of the New Guise

*And after that, I heard the voice of much people in heaven, saying:
Alleluia. Salvation and glory and honour, and power be ascribed to
the Lord our God, for true and righteous are his judgements, because he
hath judged the great whore (which did corrupt the earth with her
fornication) and hath avenged the blood of his servants of her hand.*
   One woe is past, and behold two woes come yet after this.
         (Revelation of St John the Divine, Chapters 19 & 9)

(i) '*Ware Of The Lizard*

When Bale returned from Germany to England, it was to discover that
the vengeful intrigues of the New Guise had regained the initiative
even before little Prince Edward became king. Henry VIII, swollen
and shrunken, went to his grave in the very midst of a fierce purge of
his principal old-guise statesmen – Norfolk sent to prison, Surrey
beheaded, Gardiner swept out of favour, Cranmer brought in again;
and no end of responsible men abruptly changing sides like panic-
stricken ferry-passengers ordered to steady the boat.

For some time Protestants and papists had been gaoled and killed in
approximately equal numbers. By this last jump of the see-saw, the
unchallenged reformed hands of Seymour Duke of Somerset clutched
and held the executive power. He was the young king's Lord Protector; Cranmer his co-adjutor: and only papists were to go to gaol.
Protestant England was at last to be a doctrinally-consistent state – no
more fudging: neither pope's rule nor popish dogma, and assuredly no
half-popish dogma; transubstantiate Mass would become a public
offence, and if the clergy had wives, let them keep them before the
world and welcome. 'Mrs Parson' should be a title to be proud of,
Martha in her own household combining her virtues with those of the
studious Mary. The very word 'Protestant', deriving from Germany,
and hitherto avoided as a felon-setting pejorative, was now to be sung
aloud from fully-Scriptural pulpits, to the music of Old Testament

psalms in English. Christ, to the same strong tune, pushed His Mother into the chill of the backyard (where her doubtful magics would have but small force) and sat His own pious family round His patriarchal board within-doors.

*

After a sickening two-week endurance of adverse North Sea tempest, Bale and Dorothy landed at Harwich in sparkling sunshine, he with his arm close around her, their two sons running down the gangplank ahead of them, hallooing like Scythians; and behind, a German nursemaid, engaged only for the voyage. She carried Lydia, seven days old, tiny, swaddled, and faintly chirruping, who had come into the world in the reeking tween-decks of the Bremen ship.

Bale had written letters ahead of him, and in Power's Quay Inn at Harwich, where he would stay until Dorothy recovered, he met by appointment a decent Protestant divine – one of his old Cambridge friends – not a *priest*, that was all gone, but a *minister*, just like St Paul. Unlike St Paul this good man wore no tonsure – for the first time in thirty years.

Bale was in a vile temper: just before disembarking he was accosted by the ship's purser demanding additional passage-money for the new baby, a species of extortion only too typical, he furiously informed his fellow-guests, of those infidel batteners and cozeners that hung upon the hems of men-of-God travelling the world in painful witness to His Holy Passion. He had been forced to pay something (not quite so much as was asked for) to be allowed to leave the ship at all, and his friend's excellent news – delivered in a rush of enthusiastic hand-shakes and embraces – did not at once flow through to his full understanding.

When it did – "A cure of souls? You *do* mean a *parish* cure, I *am* to be full Vicar? For if they offer me once again the humiliating subordination of Thorndon, I will not accept!"

"My dear Bale, it may be more than that! The Archbishop's chaplain was talking in terms of a *deanery*."

"Chaplain? Which one? Do I know him? Of course I know him! How else would my preferment be so hot in his mouth, hey? Hey, Dot, d'you hear the news, he said 'deanery', Cranmer's chaplain, before even you and I knew upon what ship we would travel! Oh *which* chaplain? I must write to him! – has this house pen-and-ink, d'you imagine? Hey, landlord, pen-and-ink: and God's blessing, do I smell devilled kidneys –?"

But then he heard the chaplain's name. "Dr Ponet? Lord above us, not *him*. Lord above us, a man of nothing. A flurrier-scurrier like Chaucer's Law-Serjeant that seemeth ever busier than he is, by the Lord I put no trust in any deanery from *Johnny Ponet*! Dear sir, you disappoint me. Nay I see myself waiting *years* for it. Oh why could you not have told me some firmer word than that? Why not a word, please God, from Cranmer –?"

There had been other exiled Protestants on the same ship, they were crowding into the inn, meeting their friends, rejoicing, singing praise, Israel returning from Babylon as recorded by Ezra the home-bringer: only Bale's voice was discordant.

Dorothy told him he was discordant: and he suddenly remembered to introduce her to his friend. To say in an English tavern, strong and confident, "Reverend sir, may I present to you Mrs Bale?" was so strange a thing for him, and so impossible to do without cheerfulness, that all his mood changed at once. He bustled the landlord about, ordering a bedroom for Dorothy, ordering food and drink (but his wary fingers in his purse as he did so, a furtive pre-reckoning), cajoling the nursemaid in German, slapping the table-top when the waiter was slow.

"Oh well, very well, if you tell me that Ponet has truly improved his abilities these last few years, if you tell me he's as well-seen at Lambeth and at court as you tell me he is, then very like I *shall* be beholden to him, very like I shall thrive upon his interest. I concede he and I have been always much at one in matters of doctrine: of course we have. No discouragement!"

His raucous laughter became infective, the inn rang with new Protestant jocularity and progressively-augmenting jibes against such of their enemies as Gardiner ("wanton wagtail Winchester, bawd-master of the Bankside"), or Bonner ("butcher buttock-face"), both of whom had been gaoled as soon as the new King came in; but now were out again and foaming over, unless they could speedily be stoppered.

Old-fashioned Christians in the landlord's service must have quailed for England's future. Jews coming back to Jerusalem, or Goths among the suburbs of Rome . . . ?

*

Then Bale recollected another matter, and anxiously put the question, to receive again a splendid answer: the late king's law against controversial religious drama was repealed; not only were Bale's plays still known, but one or more of them had been performed at the coronation festivities! Only for the fact that his informant had not seen these shows, Bale would have talked about them all night: but literary emotion brought him on to something else – had Dorothy ever heard of Power's Quay Inn before?

She said she had (and did not remind him that Thorpe-le-Soken was only a few miles away). He told her he'd be bound she never had been told that John Skelton Laureate had written his famous satire *The Bowge of Court* in this very house, nay more, in the very room with its dormer-window looking out over the harbour, which even now he had bespoke for him and her.

"By 'bowge' or 'rewards' of court, he had reference to the false hopes of sedulous career-seeking in the ante-chambers of great men, a degradation from which perhaps I am preserved by Johnny Ponet's welcome bounty. Skelton tells us in his poem that he chanced to board a ship here – no doubt a Bremen packet, so carnivorous the rabble that manned her! He makes implicit comparison with the Almain book *Narrenschiff, anglice* 'The Ship of Fools': though to my mind Skelton's work is the apter writing and more envigoured. Ah, sweetheart, do you know, this conjunction of dead poet and live poet all unexpected beneath this roof must be an intended omen! No less than a Sign from God. Presumptuous to suggest it should betoken my advancement: but at least it denotes all liberty, all justice so long-delayed, at last within the English shore!"

A general cheer from their fellow-drinkers. Dorothy did not disagree, but in a voice quieter than her usual (she was much weakened in health, and not only from the childbirth; though she did her best to conceal it), she quoted to her live poet two lines-and-a-half from the dead one:

> . . . that when ye think all danger for to pass,
> 'Ware of the lizard lieth lurking in the grass:
> Quoth Skelton Laureate.

Bale stared at her in amazement. He wanted to say, "Pooh, nonsense!" but then he understood she might be quite right. His own liberty would be no liberty without employment and somewhere to live. If Ponet did not come up to his apparent promises, who would?

'Sedulous career-seeking'? It was all very well for the like of Skelton (in his youth) to denounce such a business: but without it, might not a man parch to death at the fountain's brim?

*

In fact, chaplain Ponet was not totally a vain hope. Bale went straight to Lambeth, renewed his acquaintance with him, and was at once given some provisional work in the palace-library: also a house, Ponet's own property, near St George's in Southwark, at a low rent. Apprenticeships were found, under reliable masters, for the two boys (one at a scrivener's, the other with a notary-public). As for the benefice, it might be better he should not seek constant interviews with the Archbishop (which would only be self-defeating), but he was assured he would not have long to wait – Cranmer's patronage was generous. Also, of course, there were certain lay lords always eager to advance so firm a Protestant, men with the ear of the Protector. Bale thought Dorothy was culpably wrong-headed to forbid him to write to Wentworth.

It soon became obvious that some other lords held views upon Bale. He had caused far more offence than he knew of. Several of his books and pamphlets, published from Germany, had attacked King Henry's ministers for their destruction of Cromwell and associated old-guise policies: many of these ministers were nowadays King Edward's, wielding far too much influence even yet. "Iscariots, turncoats, leprous Gehazis" – but they *were* great men; and not even Cranmer was quite able to surmount their malice.

One other difficult matter. The Southwark house was Ponet's only by leasehold, the ground-landlord being Bishop Gardiner, and the building in Winchester diocese. True, Gardiner *was* having to bear himself humbly in this new reign: prison had frightened him. But also it had maddened him: toward his worst opponents his vindictive frenzy was unbridled. Bale alas was one of them: he was not yet back from Germany when Gardiner began to send reports about his writings to the Protector, demanding increased curbs upon the press, rigorous prosecution of the authors and printers of all such scurrility. Somerset had filed the letters and taken no further action; having carefully decided that even the most virulent Protestant polemic ought to be allowed its head, at least for a judicious interval: King Henry had *over*-curbed it and the censorship now stank in the public nose. Such an attitude drove Gardiner into dogged malevolence. He briefed lawyers, he had resort to ridiculous antique property-statutes, he started proceedings against Bale (as secondary tenant) for an extortionate and unprecedented ground-rent. On receiving notice that this claim would be contested in the *civil* courts, the Bishop immediately sent in *diocesan* officers to evict the Bale household from the property.

Dorothy stood (with Lydia at breast) watching the furniture, the books, the utensils and clothing, Lydia's cradle, dumped all over the road in the rain: "The bloody 'Birdcage', for the second time round: and where is Dr Ponet to play John Bale and rescue us?"

When Ponet at long last arrived, his news was none too good. He had applied to the courts for an injunction, unsuccessfully. The judge had ruled that the Bishop's case had a 'basis in law': Dr Bale's residency could not be upheld now that he was effectively (albeit illegally) unhoused. ("You didn't offer a big enough bribe," snapped Dorothy, and Ponet twitched his fingers against his nose with discomfiture.) At the same time, the judge added, cross-litigation might be open to Bale: a claim of damages against Winchester for deterioration of his moveables, disruption to his peace as a liege of his sovereign lord the king, possibly assault-and-battery. Expensive, interminable: Bale swore he would *do* it.

Meanwhile he and his family found temporary shelter in an empty coach-house at Lambeth Palace.

The first writ he ordered to be sent down to Winchester was refused as *ultra vires*; the second because it ought to have been addressed to the Archdeacon rather than to the Bishop. When a third came back rejected on the ground that the Archdeacon could only be sued (on behalf of the chapter *in toto et seriatim*) if the chapter-members were prepared individually to affix their names to a deed-of-acknowledgement, Ponet said: 'It won't do. This is a fox for all corners. Dr Bale, you yourself must go to his city and stay there until you prevail. Here in London we are too removed: he will out-catch us at every throw."

*

The next week, in the streets of Winchester, Bale paced anxiously outside the office of a local lawyer. His own lawyer was inside, 'taking soundings'.

Stephen Gardiner, white-faced, chewing his lower lip, came at a swift stride from the cathedral-close, followed hard at heel by a solicitous secretary with the episcopal writing-case under his arm. Bale saw who it was, asked himself for an instant should he risk a confrontation? – decided, "most decidedly *no*, I'm here to see lawyers, lawyers alas mean 'arm's-length', out of his way, sharp!" – and swung to avoid him. His foot caught on a loose stone, he fell sideways, landed right against Gardiner's shoulder. The preoccupied bishop gave his usual impatient snort, his notion of an apology, heaved Bale almost bodily away from his path: and, as he did so, recognised him.

Their eyes met, their eyes flashed, neither of them had a word to say. (Neither of them had *ever* spoken, one to the other: acrimonious 'arm's-length' upon very rare public occasions had been their sole mutual experience.) Out of Gardiner's tight mouth, a sudden deranged scream, loud as a trodden puppy, "He doth murder God's Church, he doth murder God's Church . . . !" over and over again; he seized his writing-case with such violence that the secretary staggered against the wall; he pulled a pen-knife the size of a dagger from a slot in the spine of it: and immediately with his other hand caught hold of Bale's beard.

Bale in his turn caught hold of the bishop's arm: they were fixed rigid against one another, straining muscles, bared teeth, and Gardiner's continued scream.

Astonishing tableau: the busy street stood stock-still to watch it. Somebody laughed. Then it seemed as though all Winchester was laughing.

The next move was the secretary's. He detached his master from his prey, he hurried him off into the nearby door of some diocesan building, the people could hear him screaming still as he was forcibly borne upstairs.

Bale's comment, when joined by his attorney: "I cannot believe it, a bedlamite ruffian footpad with lawn-sleeves! And when they laughed, they laughed at *him!*" He vaunted himself. Satan in a brass bucket had fallen backwards into his tub.

Nothing more was heard of the lawsuit after that.

It would no doubt have lapsed in any case: a month later the Bishop of Winchester was once more in prison, for refusing government doctrine regarding the Eucharist, and refusing the authority of the Privy Council over the Church.

Bale brought Dorothy and Lydia back into the Southwark house. He was invited to Canterbury (at his own cost) to preach in the Cathedral, a sermon against Gardiner's contumacy – a sort of act of restitution on the part of Cranmer, who was, however, unable to attend service there that Sunday. Nonetheless, Bale was altogether above himself with the occasion: and he *sang* his opening text. It was not even a biblical text, but a bit of a ballad he and Dorothy had made for a Winchester minstrel-friend who had also suffered under Gardiner:

> God hath put down the mighty men,
> Mad-raging He runneth them up and down!
> Oh see them grin their teeth and roar
> Like the wild-wood swine of Gadara town.

At the end of the sermon he sang all the other verses. Dorothy played the cittern, and joined her voice to his.

Ponet told Bale he had enjoyed it very much. The invitation was not repeated.

Dorothy said that she ought to have done *all* the singing: Bale could declaim but his music-voice was unendurable. He replied that minstrelcraft, from now on, must be a thing of the past for both of them. Conditions had changed. He did not even have an acting-company, although some of his plays were sometimes performed, commonly in colleges, commonly without anyone troubling to inform him, and of course without payment for the use of his work. He fervently wished he had never sent the scripts to the printer. But he *had* been in exile and no end to it in sight: what the devil else could he have done? He began to get very depressed.

*

His depression increased as the months, the years, wore on. Still no preferment, still the influential occult voices in Council warning the Protector and the Archbishop against him. He waited hopelessly in great men's ante-chambers, received smiles, congratulations upon all his noble work (ecclesiastical and poetic): and that was all he received. Dear heaven, but the lizard *lurked*.

And even the expected national liberty, the 'justice so long delayed', seemed as far away as ever. The commons in Devon and Cornwall rose in rebellion, demanding an end to enclosures, and restoration of the Mass. They associated their increased oppression with religious rather than economic innovation, driving Somerset to political despair. He had vainly but sincerely tried to abate the greed of landlords, feeling confident (like Bale) that a degree of social justice must grow from church-reformation: although he himself had had no scruples about gaining all he could from the heaped-up monastic spoils.

Ambition and *Covetousness*, their plans were well-laid.

To the Southwark house, one evening, came a travelling harpist from the west country. He had heard that Mrs Bale (and also her husband) had once lived among the minstrel-folk and so would never turn them away. He sang a song of the troubles of his district.

> Commons to close and keep,
> Poor folk for bread to cry and weep,
> Towns pulled down to pasture sheep:
> This is the *New Guise* –

was the imprudent first stanza.

Bale lost his temper and ordered him out of the house.

Dorothy was in two shakes of a broom-handle of declaring then and there that minstrel-craft was *her* craft, not Bale's; and that he nor no-one should close off music in her presence unless she called for it. But she had promised him in Germany that she understood the difference between clergyman's wife and poet's wife: and as long as he sought so wearily for clergy-preferment she must conduct herself in accordance. Lydia had to be fed.

Which did not stop her slipping out of the back door, running round the side-entry to catch up the minstrel, bringing him into the wash-house and giving him an improvised supper. She also gave him a lecture: let him never again, she said, for the very honour of the craft, confuse traditional religion with popular liberty. His trade was *her* trade, she told him, she and he were committed to TRUTH. She sang him a verse, John Ball's upon 'John the Miller', with some prose-patter appended:

> . . . the King's Son of Heaven shall pay for all.
> Be ware or ye be woe!
> Know your friend from your foe.

> Look that Piers Ploughman go to his work, and chastise well Hob the Robber, and take with you John Trueman and all his fellows, and no more.

"'Know your friend from your foe,'"she repeated: "John Ball began life as a mass-priest and ended as an honest Lollard. Mr Bale was a shave-pate friar, until he found that he lived among foes. *Your* foes, and the foes of Devon, the foes of Cornwall: dear friend, you should think upon it."

The man said he would remake his song for her: but she never heard whether he did.

She went back in to her husband, and gave *him* a lecture. Hospitality for *all* minstrels, and *then* argue about their songs; you cannot argue about what you have not let a man sing. All this being her rule from now on in his house, let him keep to it if he wanted her to keep his. He said nothing, but thrust out his lips and scratched at his beard. He was clearly a little ashamed.

The more so because he understood she had taken care to save his face, by calling the harpist into the wash-house in apparent secrecy, and not defying her husband in front of him. But Bale *knew* about the wash-house and knew that Dorothy knew he knew. He felt he had been *used*, like an old cuckold in a Laughable Farce; not to further her illicit pleasures but to confirm her strictest principles: which made him even more ashamed.

Then, and quite tentatively, she laid forward a notion. If this sort of misleading song-ballad (and it had been a *strong-made* ballad, with a fine quavering lamenting air to it, easily picked-up) was now going the professional circuits, was it not time for her to put herself once again upon the road, and counter it with her old repertory? "At least in London: if I do not travel much outside town, the care of Lydia would not obstruct, she will be weaned after a month or two. Your Lambeth library-work gives you sufficient to employ a dry-nurse to live-in: and did not Ponet promise to examine the whole matter of your dissolution-pension? If indeed you prove entitled, there are arrears in a mountain-size awaiting for you somewhere. Don't you see, I am afraid for all the work we did in Cromwell's time – what was it you said once? – to *rehabilitate* the craft; years of work, John Bale, and I see it all gone to waste. Would you have that?"

"If that's what's happening, your songs'll not mend it. The cause is deeper rooted, the aggrandising folly of the rulers of this land. Let you sing, if you think you must: not for *me* to prohibit you. But not as La Haute-jambée: because where are her free merry gentlemen we used to count upon our side? Crapulous, they are today, be-paunched and coagulate with the shameful spoil they have all been making. Be ruled by me and seek your audiences among the severer clergy, and among those that heed their testimony. There is still some conscience there. Mind you, it will be no frolic."

She thought: "Indeed not. But it will not make implausible all hope of John Bale's preferment. Whereas who'd advance a cleric with the old Longlegs to his bed? For sure, nobody; after poor Ponet's trouble."

'Ponet's trouble' was to have got himself married, very suddenly, and without telling any of his friends. At three-and-thirty he was young to be already so petitioned by needy divines; but surely a little too old for his first full flood of sexual excitement ("unless all these years he's been *whipping*," as Dorothy said, unkindly enough, to Bale). Mrs Ponet had at once, and by everyone, been regarded as a misjudgement. She was fashionable, pretentious, prejudiced, and more dismissive of her husband's middle-class intellectual circle than if she had been sib to a marquess. Unfortunately it transpired that in fact she was wife to a butcher: he was still alive, and in Nottingham. There seemed but one solution: Johnny Ponet must dissolve the bigamous marriage through the church courts, as quickly and quietly as possible; and subsidise the deprived butcher for the loss of his bed-property at the rate of God-knew-what *per annum*. The case was now proceeding, slowly, and much too conspicuously. It was all a great grief, and good reformers did their best not to mention it.

So Dorothy did not mention it, aloud. Instead she said, dutifully, "Sir, with the severer clergy I will try what I can do. I think I will not get very far. And certainly I will not sing in church: Canterbury was ill-advised. But you had to attempt it. We had to discover the true temper of these new-guise days."

"Oh God and Mary Gipsy," again she thought, concealing her thought, "God be with the merry gentlemen. Young men and young women were but seeking for Paradise Garden. Is it my fault they bloody *ransacked* it?"

*

She earned a small regular income, from then on, out of her music and (to some extent) her dancing: and she kept herself carefully within bounds, selecting her houses of call, dressing demurely, developing a much more pious repertory than the one she had used before their exile. She hoped she was increasing (rather than deadening) her talent. In Germany it had been over-long buried. She had observed there, and misliked, and determined not *quite* to emulate, the Lutheran pastor-wives' lymphatic submission, which she attributed to the Almain climate, too punctual and predictable in its seasonal

pattern. She would not even think of the 'lymphatic submission' of
Thorpe-le-Soken. But it did distress her sometimes to consider that
she might be losing all the gaiety, spontaneity, indeed all the wickedness, she believed she had once possessed. To regain it, she must lose
Bale. If she lost Bale she would almost certainly lose Lydia.

She had 'promised him in Germany?' Well, a sort of a promise, not
quite honest. She knew, and he did not, that with it went reservation:
if need be, she would be a pastor-wife, but if that was *all* she was to be,
she would die first, or run mad and kill him. On the other hand there
had been a promise, and much more precisely framed, not to Bale but
to God, in the belly of the ship. If she lived through her child-bearing,
she would make herself, for God, into a woman who would not
diminish her husband at a time when he was required to be large. (Her
present opinion: this was such a time. The commons of England, the
clergy of England, needed largeness as never before, and if they didn't
get it, they'd be *shrivelled*). Also in the ship, when she was distracted
with pain and fear, she had made another promise: to Lady Mary,
God's Mother, to whom in theory no prayers must now be offered. If
the child lived through the child-bearing (and if, as Dorothy hoped, it
was a girl) she would rear her as a truthful singer of Lady Mary's own
music:

> He hath put down the mighty men
> And from their seat hath brought them low,
> He chargeth them their backs to bend
> To dig and delve and reap and sow.
>
> From low degree he brings us up
> Exalting us with hearts made gay:
> Our hungry bellies now are full
> And the rich man's, empty, sent away.

– a version of the Virgin's song she had had years ago from the
Doncaster man: she sang it aloud in the belly of the ship, for as long as
she could, until her agony was over, her prayer answered.

All told, she concluded, a mask of sobriety was the easiest one she
could now wear. Underneath it she could be turbulent, at home with
Bale she could be turbulent: while her present style of professional
work prevented her from 'breaking out' within its professional boundaries, in public, to the hurt and discredit of husband and her own truth.
'Birdcage' eroticism, for example, if she employed it for audiences these

days, might very likely overpower her emotion, with God only knew what results.

Bale still had in mind to recommence his own old work, and form a strongly Protestant acting company: but this could not be done without patronage, and patronage for the Drama seemed as hard for him to find as patronage in the Church. In God's good time, he told himself, the New Guise would truly renew itself.

Meanwhile . . .

Meanwhile, he had an enormous plan, to rewrite altogether the complete traditional cycle of Bible plays, all the tales and more, that had been shown, for example, at Clerkenwell; from Creation to Last Judgement: and to persuade some wealthy city to establish them as its annual festival – totally Protestant, and dissociated from any papist saint's-day or Corpus Christi superstition. Oddly, he was encouraged by something he read of a man that even Protestants regarded as an arch-heretic: the priest Arius, in the days of Constantine, had taken his theology to the people of the Alexandrian slums by way of street-ballads; and then had attempted to metamorphose the Greco-Roman theatre into a house of Christian art by replacing its repertory of heathen god-legends with the true story of Christ, all to be written in the manner of Seneca, nay even of Terence or Plautus! Had Arius been orthodox, and not damnably in filthy error (as regards the nature of the Second Person of the Trinity), he would certainly have succeeded in so noble a scheme.

In England, reformed England, there was no doubt ideologically that it could be done. In due time. It would be an unshaken statement of the faith of the new-born English, to give artistic pride to their national fulfilled religion: but *now*, when folk were starving? How should such a project be paid for? A 'wealthy city'? If cities were rich, it was because villages all around them fell to ruin. Bale could not tolerate dramatic beauty built upon a needless and wanton charnel-house.

Nevertheless, he continued writing; and his house filled up slowly with ragged piles of manuscript, every inch of every page covered with close lines of his tetchy tight-penned handwriting, like a beetle's neurotic footprints.

He was also putting together his great history of the British writers (not only English, but Scots and Welsh as well), how from the very beginning they had girded against popish pretension.

*

The war in the south-west counties – it had indeed become a regular murderous war – was still raging, when London heard of another, and greater, insurrection in Norfolk. This time it was not papist. Nearly all the insurgents were country-folk of the reformed doctrine, and some came from Suffolk as well. Thorndon was mentioned in one report. Lord Wentworth was mentioned, as lieutenant-general to the Earl of Warwick, who commanded the King's eastern army (including in it a dreadful regiment of mercenary Almain-Swiss), and marched to drive the rebels out of Norwich. The cause of the rebellion was enclosures and the consequent starvation of the villagers: and thousands upon thousands of villagers took part in it, over seven times as many as Norfolk could have mustered in the regular conscriptions of a national war for the King.

Norwich, Wentworth, Thorndon, all these names struck at Dorothy's life. No chance, she thought, not yet, to make any sort of song out of *this*. If John Ball must live again (and she had so long believed he had to), why could he not have returned to a part of the land not quite so impregnate with her own past conturbations? Bale too was unable to cope with the tidings they heard, and for much the same reasons. He did manage a sermon – in St Saviour's, the Southwark church that had once been Mary Overy of the black-canons and was now cleansed by Act of Parliament of both idolatry and monkishness: Bale was sometimes asked to assist the Vicar, *locum tenens* when no stipendiary curate was available. He told the congregation that these peasants' mortal wrongs ought to have been recognised and remedied by the new-made English Church, and had not been. The Vicar advised him afterwards to keep terrorism out of the pulpit if he ever wanted to preach there again.

(ii) *Lord Wentworth Reports*

As soon as the Norfolk rebels were defeated, with much slaughter (over three thousand were killed, it was thought, though no-one troubled to make an accurate count), the Earl of Warwick returned to London with the greater part of his army. He left behind him the Lord Wentworth, who was to assist the Norwich authorities with the restoration of their city's normal life, and generally to oversee the law-and-order of the surrounding countryside. Wentworth wrote, from Norwich Castle, regularly to Warwick, with whom he had not previously been closely associated. His reports by right should have gone direct to his cousin Somerset, but that relationship had become strained: Somerset ought never to have allowed the rebellion (above all not in East Anglia, Wentworth's own country!); Devon and Cornwall must surely have been sufficient warning to him; his unwise expressions of sympathy for peasant grievances had developed into self-fulfilling prophecies; a strong feeling had built up among men of affairs that true statesmanship in government had sadly given way to a liberal weakness and that maybe it was time for a change.

One of Wentworth's letters did not deal solely with administrative matters.

*   *   *

My lord,

I have been considering the execution of the man Kett and his brother, late leaders of this notable sedition. When they have been tried in London and convicted, I suggest the court be requested to return them to Norfolk for death. It will be a more cogent exemplar to their sometime adherents here than to the multitudes of Tyburn or Tower Hill, where agrarian crime is but small temptation. It may be said that *all* treason is temptation to the disaffected in these tormented times, and that the foremost rebels should suffer in the foremost city: but London has seen so many hanged and headed and burned of recent years that her citizens must by now be either hardened incorrigible to the pains of justice or else so properly intimidated as to need no further example.

Whereas there are many in Norfolk who still believe that Kett's cause was an honest one, and that the King would e'en have supported it, had not your lordship been so arbitrary as to bring in the foreign Switzers over the Lord Protector's head: there is much talk to this day of 'Germanic military occupation', as though government were not entitled to secure its right by whatever means should fall to hand. It might be as well, however, to replace the remaining companies (I refer specific to Kellermann's Reiters-knechts and Schultz's Bombardiers, against whom are proven divers sad rapes and plunderings) with a like force of English levies, if such can be found who are not needed in Scotland, France, or the south-west parts. Alack, these augmenting wars come upon us from every side!

By Christ, my lord, but a sharp stop must be made, and that

shortly. Be assured of my fullest assistance, whatever stroke you may choose to pull.

The manner of the Ketts' executions should be carefully determined. One of them might be hanged from the Wymondham church-steeple, in the town of their saturnine births; the other (I suggest Robert, as being the elder and more maleficial) could conceivably be winched up, strangulating in a severe collar, to the full height of this Norwich Castle, to swing here in his chains until he should putrefy. The whole city, as you know, hath a view of the keep unobstructed, and those of the people who defended the King's Writ will thereby for months be gladdened at heart, while those who did not will proportionately abash their hopes of further mutiny. Wat Tyler and John Ball *redivivi* must not be allowed any second chance of a ghost-walk.

*

Should your lordship indeed find convenient occasion to supplant certain malpractisers in government (I name no names but well you know them), it is probable that you will wish to take order for the stronger promulgation of religious truth: there is still over-much foolery in too many parishes with masquing Masses and the rag-vestments of Babylon Antichrist. Pray consider how the virtuous Dr Parker, mine old Cantab comrade, was so courageous as to present himself, all unarmed save for Holy Writ, in the very camp of Kett's rabble: he exhorted them in the name of Christ Scriptural to desist from violent enterprise and let legal remedy make end to their grievance, as became lawful Englishmen of a free nation. But what did they call him but an hireling hedge-priest, procured by noxious gentlemen, to bring to the driven people 'words of sale and a tongue bound with rewards'! This has been said to be an evidence of their Protestant rectitude, that they expected not to be 'betrayed' by a minister of their own sort: an argument afforded colour by the preachments of Dr Latimer upon 'justice and restitution' (with him also was I schoolfellow, hearing oft his discourse at the White Horse Inn).

I fear, though, that Latimer is now thoroughly given over to a rancorous loving-kindness of levelling, which – however much it may seem to ground itself upon Our Lord's Beatitudes – sorteth not with an orderly commonwealth. It is well he was enforced by King Henry to resign his bishopric at the time of the Six Articles.

Nevertheless, I still hold that occult popery was far more at the back of the Norfolk rising than has heretofore been acknowledged. Or, at any rate, the occult workings of the agents of popery from abroad, who might easily have inflamed men to an ultra-Protestant extreme, both to discredit the Reformed Doctrine and to make unstable our English state. Pole, the pseudo-Cardinal, still playeth his romish pranks at all hazard between Italy and Spain and the Emperor's lowlands: we do ill to discount his power. I have, as you did advise me, taken measures to insert mine own agents into all parishes here and in especial at the seaports, to guard against these subverting attempts. For the which, I require more moneys: shall it be arranged?

*

Mention of Latimer bringeth to mind his examination, with others, in the last years of Henry's reign, when Gardiner and Norfolk had persuaded His late Majesty that Protestantism sought the crown's overthrow (being in fact their *own* overthrow they thus desperately hoped to forestall). Among those 'others' was Mrs Askew – or Mrs Kyme by her marital style – who was, you remember, in the upshot burned to death. Her martyrdom commenced with her having been compelled to marry a papist (or, as we must now say, a Roman Catholic: the consolidation of Protestant faith in late years having rendered the 'Old Guise' so separate from the living church that it is now clearly a sect upon its own, and – God willing – withering daily). This man would not tolerate his young wife's reformed spirit. So in 1539, at the age of eighteen, alone, against Kyme's tyrannical will, she came to London from her home in Lincolnshire to find could she obtain divorce from him upon ground of his religious coercion.

But the crisis of the Six Articles, and of Cromwell's fore-threatened fall, was already hard upon us. It was felt undesirable that so provocative a cause be admitted to the law-courts. Her husband's people came south hunting her to hale her back to her own county: for a while she was able to hide herself, though at last his malice prevailed.

A woman that gave her shelter was known to me, a Mrs Brewer, now Mrs Bale and wife to a distinguished (but disappointed) clergyman in the Archbishop's service at Lambeth.

I do not know how Anne Askew met Mrs Brewer, who was then

living in obscure circumstances in some untoward corner of the town. But it seems that she (Askew) had no other close friends in London, and that an attachment sprang between them from more than religious sympathy. Mrs Brewer, it must be said, was something like half-way into a criminal manner of life, and was able to enlist the help of some highly-blown-upon persons to conceal Mrs Askew from her husband. One in particular, a blackamoor wench from the whorehouses, was later hanged for gross cozenage of drunken sailors: but that is not to my purpose here.

The following year Mrs Brewer fled to the Germanies, where until the year of '47 she lived in (I am sure) Christian marriage with the Rev Dr John Bale, playwright and scholar. Through the secret passage of sundry documents, aided by the understanding of his wife, this Bale was enabled to publish an entire account of Anne Askew's subsequent unfortune. You are aware how she was, in '45, cast away by her papist husband and then – because he found he was legally unable to marry again until her death – denounced by him as an heretic. She was examined by Bonner and Gardiner, who thought it likely her evidence might lead to the exposure and ruin of that excellent circle of Protestant ladies presided over by our excellent Queen Catherine (Parr). Since her first visit to London, Anne Askew's acquaintance with learned and devout ladies had advanced far beyond Mrs Brewer's squalid by-lanes of unlicensed minstrel-craft.

To make a short end, she was tortured on the rack by Lord Chancellor Wriothesley in person and Solicitor-General Rich: an unheard-of outrage to a gentlewoman, and a turd-splash of unending shame upon the two high-placed time-servers that accomplished it. She spoke not, save to tell them: "That which you call your God is a piece of bread. For proof whereof, let it lie in a box three months and it will be mouldy." To incriminate the Queen, nor any other person, naught: and yet they had dragged her well-nigh full asunder into butcher's joints. Then they burned her, with other confessors.

But somehow, betwixt rack and stake, her own brave story of these barbarities was writ out in her own tormented shaking hand. 'Twas this pregnant paper, conveyed to the Bales in Germany, that returned thence to England and wrought so much to stir opinion to put down Bonners, Gardiners, Wriothesleys – although Rich is now Lord Chancellor – my lord, have a care of him, he professed friendship to More and Fisher and betrayed them to Cromwell and betrayed *him* to the Howard faction, and now, if all I am told should be true, he offereth himself unto your lordship for the furtherance of your future. Likewise Wriothesley puts out claim to be your lordship's good friend. My lord, let you use these men, but not trust them. Remember Mrs Askew. There *are* those about your lordship's person that may be trusted unto the death. *Experto crede*.

*

Which bringeth me to my chief point.

There is a duty owed to Bale and to Bale's wife (in especial to her). A duty of state: not of private men who might offer some passing patronage and then withdraw it under cover of a politic necessity (such gliding tergiversations demean us all, but are nonetheless sorely frequent, you need not me to tell your lordship). I find it mine own present honour and duty to take up the furtherance of this state-duty I speak of, and therefore make bold to refer it to your lordship e'en now, whenas I am made so gratulate by your lordship's smile of favour.

Perhaps a goodly parish (or an even better benefice) shall fall vacant for Dr Bale, at all events some small advancement for the two sons he and Mrs (*quondam*) Brewer are rearing as their own? They will be of her undoubted womb, though their paternity standeth perhaps open to question.

*

Concerning one of the sons, the older, she was placed once in a very grave danger, by coincidence in this very Norwich. I knew little of the affair until I came here in my present service and made requisite examination of all the chief citizens to discover the precise roots of rebellion and resistance to rebellion over the past few years, for which purpose I was furnished with the justice-archives of the town. In the records for the same year as Anne Askew her martyrdom I found the name of Bale: and thereupon, being driven by who knows what spurt of whimsical curiosity, I gave over my immediate business and set about to follow it up. Pray pardon me, my lord, that I tell it you at length, it is a tale well worthy of our stout English in those times, I feel need to clear it from my bosom.

Out of Germany Dr Bale had transmitted his son John to England to be bound prentice to a Norwich bookseller-and-printer. He was confident, you see, that the true faith would shortly prevail, and his days would be ended (as those of the patriarch Job) in his own land once again at peace with God. Therefore his children must not be metamorphosed foreign: whatever trade they were put to must be in England under an English master. He chose, as he thought, a good man of Protestant leaning, and sent the boy (no more than ten years of age) under care of a trusted messenger. By the same means he sent and received letters for nigh twelve months, and to all appearance the child was prospering.

But then, there was sudden reversal. His messenger, a Yarmouth merchant's travelling-man, came to him from his regular voyage and carried no letter. He could tell him no more but that the printer had fallen insolvent, *banca-rotta*, his press having been broke in punishment for his making of 'seditious books' – or what to some ignoramus constable had seemed to be books of an undue difficult thought. There had been no prosecution: the constable's action was peremptory 'in consequence of a reasoned suspicion' and the justices had supported it. But the master was now unable to keep his journeymen and prentices, and young John had been taken, in settlement of debt, by a paper-maker of the town.

The travelling-man, greatly concerned, had sought out the boy, but had not been able to speak with him. His new master averred that a child with no visible parents was in all likelihood a thief's-get and not fitted for the proper privileges of prenticehood, so he employed him behind his workshop upon lowest menial household work, as sweeping, privy-cleansing, cart-loading, digging the cabbage-patch. No stranger from outland parts, he swore, had the right to interfere, still less to penetrate his inner house and cross-question his people.

The travelling-man did not dare carry the tale to any law-officer, lest Dr Bale, as a Protestant exile, should be named and thus incriminate him. But he did survey the premises from the back-entry, and was just able to catch a sight of the child sharing a plate of scraps with a hound-in-kennel, it being a day of pouring rain and he had on no more than a brief shirt, his poor young shanks all naked and bestreaked with mud of the yard.

Now when he told this to Dr Bale in Wittenberg, of course the first question was, "How can I get to England and rescue him, how?" And of course the only answer: "If you dare show face in

Norwich, being so very well known there, of a surety they will have you in prison upon-the-chop and no remedy!"

Will you believe then that his Dorothy (*id est* Mrs Bale), from the strength of her own heart, without companion – the travelling-man had to pass onward to Prague – went at once by ship to Yarmouth, and thence to Norwich, and thence (with no money left save those few coins she could slip into her glove) straight to the knavish paper-maker!

She hurled her anger at his head and gave him no chance to answer it: he fell away from her against his shelving, pulling it down around him, quires of foolscap all over the shop. Therewithal she strode past him (did I tell you she is a big woman?) and routed through the house until she found her boy in a cellar-hole, she pulled him out, and out again through house and shop regardless, and God alone can say whither she would have taken him next; but the paper-maker had had time to call from his door for help, the watch came running down the street, bows-and-bills and hue-and-cry: and thus all of them to Guildhall for a hearing afore the bench.

Now, this ought to have been, in any honest and moderate age, opportunity for her case to be made and the paper-maker's oppression rebuked, if not chastised. But where was the bribe she should have had ready? And how was she to know which of the city-officials were friends with the paper-maker or rivals? And worst of all, should she be found out to be who she was, could she not be connected (by due enquiry) with Mrs Askew, who even then in London Tower lay waiting, with distorted limbs, to be drawn in her shift on a wattle-sledge over sharp stones through puddled horsedung to her burning-place at Smithfield? My lord, if I write with a passion, it is because these were terrible days, my heart faileth at them yet, so cruel cruel the tribulations then put upon Christ His saints. (Oh you, my lord, had the better part, defending the realm by sea and land: those of us at the king's court met no such simplicities of duty).

Do I say then that Dorothy was a saint? After all I have hinted of her already? No, she was not, nor is not: I would lie to you if I pretended it. Askew was a saint for certain, not Dorothy, no. But I did meet her, once, and cannot think of her now without thinking of the chains they fixed upon her, the smackings of their fists in her face, the greedy grabbings of their hands at her body, that day in the Norwich courthouse.

For here is how it fell out, my pen trembleth for what might have ensued, but praise the Lord, did not. Before the paper-maker could ope his lying mouth before the justices, she had already swept him and the court and all into the whirlwind of her full-heart complaint: she pleaded every form of exorbitant illegality in the treatment of her unhappy child. And why not? It could not be denied. She demanded no more than her due: a writ of release for him into her hand that she might thereupon take him with her and go her ways to find him a righteous master.

Of necessity, and with seeming correctitude, the justice must first make question, by what writ already did the paper-maker hold the boy? Some document was brought forward, of a most idle appearance, neither sealed nor stamped, and the witness of no notary upon it. It would have been cast out, as not at all to the purpose, save that at the bottom was the boy's name endited, and that in his own hand.

They said, "Child John, did you sign this name?"

He, always truthful, for such had ever been his parents' teaching, between his tears admitted, "Yea, verily." And behold, his case was lost.

My lord, a true magistrate would surely have made more question? God knoweth in these years when grown men and women have signed so much of public weight under terror of authority, and against their own conscience, indeed their eternal welfare, was it to be believed that a child of mere eleven might not be coerced by a paper-maker? At which of course Dorothy demanded her right for a proper appeal and to seek the aid of an advocate, thinking only that her soonest thing was to heave the case from out this corrupt and local court (where all seemed friends together, banded against the stranger) into the fair hearing of a royal judge upon Assize Circuit. How she would pay was not for that moment: Lord God would provide, even as His ravens brought meat unto Elijah.

But then the justice put to her, had she the proper papers for young John's first apprenticeship, to the printer, the *banca-rotta*? Now here was a hard point. Those papers she had indeed: but the name on them was that of the travelling-man aforesaid, who was, as we know, in Bohemia and could not avouch 'em. He was given as short-time guardian to his ward, Master John Bale, whereas Dorothy had come to England under the name of 'Brewer', for security against arrest when she landed at the port. In her haste and anger she had not thought of this disparity, and as 'Brewer' she had declared herself upon entry into Guildhall. Now then, the dreaded question: who was Bale? Dare she admit him, or must she save herself and pronounce her child bastard, a plausible escape from the dilemma, but one that should not entitle her to any sovereignty over his prenticehood.

For an instant she stood dumbfoundered: and the Mayor of Norwich filled up her silence with the rudest interjection. This mayor was upon the bench, and till now he had not spoken but had gazed main hard upon Dorothy as a man that would have known her had she appeared there othergates clad. And now, with a frantic and most popish oath he cried out: "Nose-rag of Holy Mary, I have it! She is the one they called Doll Longlegs, she danced stark before rutting serjeants in Toddy Hamstring's ale-cellar, yea and she displayed herself even to the small red hairs that grew around her curlicue!"

His fellow-justice, at this, did not laugh with the general mirth, but lowered over her strict and dragonish: "Woman, is it the truth? The rogue Hamstring is still in business, he will swear anything to save his naughty trade, take heed lest we now summon him to testify to your discomfiture."

And the Mayor again: "Is it not so, that after those years, you did enwed yourself illegal to a whoremaster priest, Friar Bale of this city, whom all knew as Bale-zebub for his horrid debauchery? And did he not turn heretic, and fly abroad from the Church's wrath?"

"She wedded a priest?" – the other justice – "But that by the King's Six Articles is immediate imprisonment, nay death if it can be proven. Where and when this outrageous marriage, speak, mistress, you are commanded: this court would hear your sacrilege!"

My lord, I have the record. The court-clerk, at all events, was faithful to his trust and did not mince her words. No less constant than Mrs Askew, she held herself bolt upright, and (as I read her reported utterances) she spoke in a quiet strong voice, as decent as Bethany Martha, for all her past salacity – which I hazard she could not have helped: she had been in want and without friends, naught but her fair flesh for livelihood.

"Sirs, I am Bale's wife by Christian matrimony in a chapel consecrate. You must ask of Lambeth Palace, where our sacrament was made."

At this such a great to-do. Did she mean that Cranmer himself had married them? If she did, was that good to hear? (leading to great favour from the King for uncovering the Archbishop's misdoings), or bad? (if he *had* married them, perhaps he was authorised to do so, and then what would be said of the Norwich justices for backslighting him?) Best thought, they would not believe her – after all she was only a twat-dancer – or, better still, they would not hear her: so they all began to talk aloud as though she had naught to say.

But she had, and she continued with it: "Let me urge you," she pleaded, and the court-clerk wrote it down, "before you accuse me further, to seek in your own church-history of this your noble Norwich. Where you shall find a certain saint (as so described in the olden time, for to tell truth his reputation hath of late generations somewhat failed), Saint William, called 'murdered martyr', to whose shrine in Christ Church Abbey pious offerings were longtime brought."

They sniffed and snorted. William of Norwich being a fair young lad in Stephen's reign that fell to a strange death by torture, by some man or men a-lust for boy-slaughter, after no doubt a sodomy-rape: such was ever, I've heard said, the most notable English vice. But it was apportioned to the Jews, by the ignorant people who held all Jews as human-sacrificers (vicious error, arising from there being no Scripture then Englished, so how could they know of the Great Reprieve of Isaac, branding ritual murder for all time an abominable thing to Jewry?). Very like they craved a Jew-hunt in Norwich, all the better to grip some usurers' money-chests. Therefore, and without proof, this William became martyr and saint: until a pope wiser than most of his order took steps to put a stop to it. Which occasioned the justices' snorts. As bigots and papists they could not decide whether to affirm William's sanctity or despise it: queer predicament.

However that was not the argument that Dorothy wished to give 'em.

She said, "Who was St William's mother?", which of course they knew not, so she answered her own question: "Elwina, a priest's daughter. And his aunt was Lavina, certified in the chronicles, without censure, as a priest's wife. Why, the memory of these two women was kept by your monks almost as holy as William's. Either must this legend be a wicked thing and all unworthy of Norwich prayers, or else mine own marriage to Dr Bale is a good one. It cannot be both ways."

Aghast then they gazed. Little they knew, truly; but they did know the papal deprecation of the William tale had naught to do with his parentage – only the motives of his murder. And whence had she this obscure intelligence? (She had had it from Bale long since: thank Jesu for her minstrel's memory that thus preserved it in her brain!)

As for her dancing naked, she confessed it with utmost meekness: yes, she said, she was once an harlot, and now she was a married wife, did they not recognise atonement when they saw it? "Or do you rather find atonement more criminal than sin? For if you do, I espy your doctrine to be as strong an heresy as any you allege against my husband, and I think there is no church-teacher that would not agree with me." In which she spoke somewhat wild: she had no great theology, but neither had those on the bench. She went on to tell them that Bale was never in no wise seditious but spake and wrote always in defence of the King's proceedings: but this they would not hear. Without any clear mandate of law they committed her forthwith to prison and hustled themselves out of the courtroom with unconscionable banging of books and swirling of gowns through the doorway.

Of her immediate ill-treatment I cannot bring myself to speak, I have writ but a portion of it above: just to say now that her warders had heard the Mayor describe her 'curlicue' and were of course disposed to make their filthy sport about it. Her child was also confined, most horrible for one so young, but here was a ground for hope. He had not been restored to the paper-maker, and – even in gaol – was permitted his mother's care. This more by default than design: the magistrates had been so en-angered they quite forgot to make order for him.

What followed is not all upon record, but I made use of my powers here to interrogate the sometime mayor, and did not stint the full terrors of mine office, I assure your lordship. This man, being suspected papist, and thus liable to be named as one of Kett's late provokers and occult abettors, told at once what he knew and I needed no thumbscrew (though it lay on my desk as I questioned him). It emerged that in the prison-house was a warder of the name of Hogg – or Hogg-shite, though perhaps this latter was more nick-name than paternal inheritance – and he in time past had pursued his function at the old bishop's gaol. He had once conceived a tenderness for the youthful Dolly in Hamstring's cellar: which ancient subversion of his commonly brutal urges now stood her in most marvellous good stead. He secured her a private room and demanded no payment, no not even her carnal favours, which I account an astonishing thing, and true evidence – refuting Calvin – that all men may yet be saved by their own amendment (to which be added Grace), how deep soever they may have sunk themselves into slough of their prior foulness.

Of his own good heart the man Hogg sought out an honest attorney for her, who went straightway with a law-serjeant to a judge-in-chambers, this being by lucky hap the very time of the Assizes. Both attorney and barrister were strongly of the reformed party, and no doubt also the judge, with the result (to speak it bluntly) their efforts were no more precisely legal than had been the magistrates'. It is apparent from the record that a deal of juggling took place, but a juggling in favour of liberty and equity on behalf of the oppressed, which no man can easily condemn. In short, the cause of Dorothy need thrust no further through the tangles of law, a warrant for her release was sent down to the prison, and she and her loved John walked freely into the streets of freedom.

'Twas no more than a week of confinement, neither mother nor child had contracted the gaol-fever, and the ill food had not had time to destroy their stomachs beyond the few days' bloody flux inevitable for all prisoners ere they custom themselves again to Christian diet. For her costs: gaol-fees, law-fees, the passage-money back to Wittenberg for herself and her son – what happened but her attorney convened together his Protestant friends (to the number of nigh a score, and all of them living then in great peril of the Six Articles), to whom he made prayer for a generous contribution: and they stinted not. And so, in the end, a prosperous deliverance, but oh by how narrow an hair's-breadth!

*

What hurts my heart, my lord, is this: had some magnate of the realm been advertised sufficient soon of all the circumstance that threatened her, she might have been saved her ordeal, and her sweet boy would not have seen his mother the hapless prey of wicked turnkeys in abuse of their moral trust. As for the good turnkey, Hogg: I have ascertained he is dead of the gaol-fever, but hath left behind him a wife and children, whose necessities are now, by mine own action, relieved. I regard this as *my* salvation-deed, akin to his when he succoured his one-time pretty Longlegs, and I beg heaven it may likewise go down to me at Day of Judgement.

Similarly, I sought out attorney and serjeant-at-law. The latter too is now dead: but the attorney, of all things, was held here in a castle dungeon, awaiting trial for collusion with Kett. No doubt about his guilt, far more heinous in a learned man than in any silly rustic clown: he admitted it with pride, being infected by poor Latimer's ravings. I trust your lordship will not find it an unacceptable leniency that I have given him free pardon, upon condition that he laud it not to all and sundry in the despite of His Majesty's right justice upon other rebels.

Against the sometime mayor, and the other false magistrate, is nothing grave proven that I can find, nor against the paper-maker. But I was able to fault them on certain city ordinances: the pavement, for example, before the paper-maker's shop, being marred with an irregular dung-heap. I took measure to ensure that they were harshly fined for these delinquencies, add to which the loss of valued civic privileges, to their sorrow and my joyful vindication.

*

To turn to a matter of state, which I had not thought of until today, when a post reached me from Ireland. My correspondent there informs me that it is surely high time for our Protestant faith to be at last fully promulgated among the loyal English of that island. Bootless to offer it to wild Ersemen, they know not even correct doctrine of their own popery: how can they, until made civil by enforcement of English law, and abolition of their own old law, bardic, traditionary, barbaric, fit only for the red men of Peru. But even in that is progress carried forward. King Henry's sage policy of receiving the chieftains' submission upon proviso they accept earldoms in the English manner (to turn lawless democratical tribes into an obedient tenantry) has shown itself a high success. Among furthest parts of the land there is already established subordinate social degree and a needful dependence upon the Crown.

At the same time all this is useless unless the Mass once and for all be cast out of the churches in our Pale. Dublin Parliament did give

passage for King Henry's laws for his own Supremacy, and did hail
him King of Ireland instead of, as formerly, 'Lord': the essential
foundation. But now, I am told, much romanism has come back in,
and our latest Lord Deputy no stirrer against it. He himself hath
knelt at Mass in the Dublin Christ Church: upon challenge from an
English divine, he did reply that reformed service had not been said
to his knowledge in any Irish church, so where was he to worship
save in such house of God as was handy to his use, whatever the
form of prayer within it?

It so chanceth, under God, that in England our form is the seemly
Common Prayer Book of King Edward, as read in every parish by
unassailable decree. What ails us we have not enforced it into
Ireland? Little purpose to harry the Deputy, he is no clergyman but
a soldier, who will always (while he hath wars to fight) put divine
matters on the hinder hook. I think not one bishop in Ireland is a
convinced man for reform, wherefore all goeth so damnable mud-
dily. True, they are chiefly English, but English of an outworn sort:
new men are urgently required.

Your lordship no doubt will hear more of this from others. But in
the guess that my letters are less equivocal in their informings than
some you will receive (or rather, at this present, the Lord Protector
will receive) from alleged more authoritative persons, I make bold
to slide forward my small hint.

*

If there should come a time when your lordship may justly hold
your deserved state toward both realm and monarch, I do pray that
any patronage you think fit to bestow upon Dr Bale and his brave
lady will appear as your lordship's alone. I would not be seen in it.
Count it my humility, if you will: I am a man that liketh not right
hand to witness the good deeds of left. In all, be assured I suggest
naught save for the good of England.

*   *   *

Wentworth signed the letter and then sat for a while, chewing his
nails, and stabbing his pen upon the table-top, until a splash or two of
black ink hit the paper across his name. It was hard to decide whether
to refrain from adding a post-script.

At last he did write one, quickly and messily, the quill-point having
been spoiled by his stabbing: he could not find it in him to pause and

call for another. So the last page of his letter looked all over sick with the smallpox.

* * *

Anne Askew, before her torture, was urged by Shaxton, deposed Bishop of Salisbury, to recant (even as he had done), and thereby avoid the fire. Shaxton had frequented the Cambridge White Horse, I remember him nigh as well as Parker or Latimer, or Bale. As bishop he fetched more of Luther into his diocese than any of 'em, Latimer excepted. Yet his arrest for heresy made him a coward, and hers brought her close to godhood. Do you know what she said when he spread out his weakness before her, showing as it were his recantation on her cell-floor as a babe might display its voided *faeces*?

She told him first it had been better had he never been born, and then: "I will not sing a new song of the Lord in a strange land." Which was a comment more painful deep than many of our Protestants could ever dream of. For surely this ancient England has been in truth a 'strange land', and all our well-loved homes and churches no more than exile-camps, many years beyond our own births and the births of our parents, and so back again through history until when? Dr Bale has well-studied it, he knoweth the commencement of popery, the generation that stole us to Babylon. Our 'New Guise' is in truth most old, and Mrs Askew knew it too.

Before she burned, Shaxton stood over above her in Smithfield, placed there by church and government, to preach against her 'contumacy' the last sermon she should ever hear. And do you know, she listened – yea, my lord, and with charity – to his apostate terrified words, as though there was e'en yet some instruction to be had of 'em. But then she curled her lip in scorn and closed off his noise, saying: "There he misseth and speaketh without book."

So they put fire to the faggots.

Oh yes, and she was a poet. In prison she wrote this:

> I saw a royal throne
> Where justice should have sit,
> But in her stead was one
> Of moody cruel wit.
> Then thought I, 'Jesus Lord,
> When thou shalt judge us all,

> Hard is it to record
> On these men what will fall.
> Yet, Lord, I thee desire,
> For that they do to me,
> Let them not taste the hire
> Of their iniquity.
>
> God save the King.

Let us not taste it. Oh God, let us not.

*   *   *

He superscribed his letter and sent it, to the forthcoming Sejanus. He was not afraid of government agents intercepting the packet: those agents worked now for Warwick, it was the Protector's mail they were ordered to open.

(iii) *Oh God Let Us Not*

Before long, Somerset had fallen, and Warwick controlled the kingdom.

Not long again, and Somerset was executed upon charges of attempting to regain his power by *coup d'état*: the Earl of Warwick became a Duke, of Northumberland.

Lord Wentworth had been made Lord Chamberlain for his help in Northumberland's schemes: in less than two years he was dead.

He was only fifty and to all appearance his health was as bold as ever. He fell down with a stroke while at prayer in Nettlestead house-chapel, a plain whitewashed tabernacle, most austerely furnished. When his people came running to assist him, they found he could still speak, in a frightening side-mouthed manner: the only words he made, from then on until his life left him, were, "Let us not taste it, oh God let us not taste it."

He gave frantic half-aborted signs that something should be brought him from his cabinet. At last his wife found the right thing. It was a small round German picture she had not seen before – Venus and Cupid. When she held it up to him he made more of his desperate signs. He seemed to mean her to turn it round, so that he could only see the back of it.

There was an inscription on the back: *Memento Mater* (grammatically incompetent: perhaps 'Remember, O mother', or 'Remember the mother', or even, 'The mother remembers'). So she showed this to him, wondering, and he lay down more easily onto the pillows. He stared hard at the bad Latin. He said, once again, "Oh God let us not," and that was all. He left behind him sixteen legitimate children. His wife's womb had served him well. She was a steadfast gentle lady: and if she suffered for her marriage she let no-one ever know of it. Except perhaps her closest clergymen.

(iv) *Women-of-Christ*

Wentworth had not been quite correct in his story of Anne Askew. Her first visit to London was not to obtain a divorce by legal means, but simply a wild and uninformed attempt to escape her marriage, which had already produced one child and put another into her body. She was not at that time a convinced Protestant: all she knew was that her husband was a horror, his old-guise bigotry being but a part of it. She was a great reader, and knew too many books (not all of them on religious matters) for Kyme's country-squire comfort. Whenever he caught her studying he would hit out at her with his fist or his riding-crop, and once he had his grooms beat her and lock her overnight into a harness-room. He also complained of her to the village priest, who took his side and harangued her about the wickedness of women who set themselves up as teachers (from Saint Paul).

When she argued she was no teacher but only a learner, she was told she could learn all that was necessary from the priest, any further instruction was a vanity.

She arrived in London disguised as a peasant-girl, having stolen some household money and bribed a Lincolnshire carrier to give her passage in his wagon. She knew nothing about the city; the carrier, a man of good heart but not much sense, put her in the hands of the hostess of the tavern where he unloaded his consignments. This woman dealt in country-girls either for maid-service or prostitution: but she recognised Anne as being something very different, and was at a loss.

Fortunately she knew Dorothy, who was living just then neither with Bale nor without him, having left the children for a while in Thorpe-le-Soken (under the care of Joe Brewer's sister) until the political situation became clearer. Dorothy had a little room in a lodging-house in Thames Street, which she shared with her old maid, Belle-Savage, and a number of shifty transients: a fairly dangerous habitation, but she did not mean to stay there very long. Bale came often to see her: a degree of reassurance. He was however heavily involved with his actors and intermittently out-of-town on tour.

From this place she arranged for Anne to stay in various similar locations – moving her from one to another in the hope of throwing off Mr Kyme and his friends who were looking for her all over the city. She could not quite see how the affair was going to end: her style of life was quite unsuitable for a refined young gentlewoman like Anne, and certainly Anne had been startled and disgusted at first. There was talk of shipping her abroad: but although that might have suited a heretic clergyman on-the-run, it was not at all the sort of thing for a pregnant woman with no companions.

Nothing had been decided when Kyme at last caught up with the runaway. He came raging to the house where she was, and it was only by good luck that Bale happened to be there that day with one or two of his players. These were able to prevent an immediate physical attack upon Anne, and they went so far as to get a magistrate to bind Kyme over to keep the peace: but they could not stop him bringing his wife home to Lincolnshire.

It had, altogether, been a useless attempt at assisting her, and might well have made things worse.

*

Some very long conversations took place during those few weeks, between Dorothy and Anne, and also between Anne and Bale. With Dorothy she talked endlessly about marriage, and women's intellect, and the cruelty of Saint Paul as interpreted by her husband's priests. But with Bale she was enforced to listen, it was never easy to talk to *him* at any emotional length, however kind his intentions – you were always interrupted, whether you were male or female. Bale gave her another aspect of Saint Paul, and earnestly listed all those names of woman-gospellers that are mentioned in the *Acts of the Apostles* and the various *Epistles*. He also explained to her the principles of reformed religion, and she took them in very seriously indeed.

This worried Dorothy, who detected certain signs of fanaticism in Anne's character. She could not openly say these were undesirable: a young woman, she thought, had a right to her convictions, and to argue against them would only be to do Kyme's work for him. But when Anne, with white set face and no tears in her eyes, finally bid good-bye to her and walked off down the street, wrist firmly grasped by her husband's raw red hand, spine as straight as a flagpole, growing womb inescapably bulged out in front, Dorothy could not avoid a cold and fearful presentiment. Death as well as birth was being marched back to Lincolnshire. She said as much to Bale, and received in return an offended homily.

She and he were both finding it hard to accommodate themselves one to the other. Thorpe-le-Soken had created some rift between them, although they never willingly mentioned that place or its people in any of their talk together. At this time his sexual demands upon her were insatiable. She thought it must be because of the stimulation of all his rehearsals, and she wished that she too could take part as a woman-player and so meet him in what he needed with a fuller knowledge.

Her stimulation from her renewed minstrel-work (not so much of it as when she lived in the 'Birdcage', but nonetheless it was considerable) was affecting her desires, in her own way, which was not Bale's way, nor at Bale's times, which were never quite her times. She needed warmth, of caresses and companionship, and close talk with an intimate friend. She did not want his constant satyr-prod jabbing between her legs: and that, it seemed, was all he could think of.

Anne Askew was to her a great practical difficulty (and she suffered from her impotence to help her): but also an assuagement of longing, something she thought Anne might not understand, so she never dared to hint it. 'Assuagement'? Not entirely. If Anne's company to an extent calmed her, so – in another way – it disturbed her, frustrated her, brought tremblings into her body quite out of tune with the superficial meaning of the friendship between the pair of them. Dorothy knew what this meant: this was no fit situation for Gillian or Rotraut repetitions and she would not let it happen. But if Anne did not weep when Kyme took her home, Dorothy did, an hour or so later, and Bale heard her, and disliked it.

*

Not for the first time, she wondered what ill spirit had entered her that she had ever allowed this man his damned marriage? Nothing had been made easier by it, it was no more than a hasty solution to a suddenly-sprung problem that carried with it all these new problems tenfold. But honestly she did not know what else she could have done. She and he had their mutual loyalty, and through all the reversals of their lives it must surely be far better never to reverse *that*.

But now he told her he could not bear her to contradict his teachings to another child-of-Christ – he had marked with sorrow some of her sidelong remarks to Mrs Askew – true salvation, he pronounced heavily, came only from what Laodiceans (luke-warm, to be spat from the mouth) called, in their apathy, 'fanaticism'.

She said, "If you think that of me, why the devil am I your wife?" She shivered. Some things ought never to be said. But he was not taken aback: a little perplexed, perhaps, that was all.

"Why, Dorothy, for your art-making. God told me. And thereafter, *I* have told *you* often." As indeed he had. "It is not strange?" he asked, pathetically.

"No," she murmured, "no, not strange at all. And as for art, you do always survey my work and tell me this of it or that, correcting me, encouraging; and you let me do the same for you. Why then must your priest-work be shut from me? Is it fair?" This was a very odd thing for her to say, as she knew as soon as she said it, his 'priest-work' had been something she had always tried her best to avoid, indeed forget about. Now she suddenly realised, with fear, that she was deadly jealous of Anne Askew: a woman whom she loved had sat at Bale's feet and accepted his perilous thoughts so wide-open that when, but an hour afterwards, he would take hold of *her*, Dorothy, and swive her the length of her bed, was he not in his fantasy thrusting himself into Anne?

She had rather, therefore, that Bale should not answer her, not now, oh no, let the subject at once be changed. But to what? Her mind could not leave Anne alone. So she broached to Bale another issue upon which Anne had been quite unresponsive, while to Dorothy it seemed of drastic importance. "What of her children, John? Have you not thought of them? I do, all the time. She left one, only a babe, in the den of that ogre-husband, and ran from him with the other inside her: and yet in all our talk of what should be done for her, she never mentioned them, even once. Does she want them to die, so she might gain eternal life? Because they are Kyme's and therefore not really hers, and they only inhibit her quest? Don't you see, in regard to *our* children . . ." Not a sentence she wished to finish: it would have led to Thorpe-le-Soken.

She waited one second to see would Bale take it up, but no. She went on swiftly, "Of course, she should have been a man, but if she had been, she'd have grown up like you: and that would have been unchancy enough."

All he said in reply was: "I daresay Mrs Askew is the first religious woman – I mean *religious*, not superstitious – whom you ever will have met. Or at least, met to talk to at any length. True religion must always disturb. Mary and Martha: read your Gospel, it's all there."

He paused and clawed at his groin (they were dressed only in their nightwear for breakfast, their short spaces of life together had become very unkempt and careless). She told him to pull his shirt down. Shamefacedly he obeyed, ate some porridge, and then spoke again.

"Maybe I should have been a woman. That way your love would have been smoother?"

Dorothy added more water to the wine-jug, pouring it through a handkerchief because there was dirt in it (Thames Street water-carriers were an idle gang of heed-naughts). Undiluted wine first thing in the day would only make her drunk and sometimes now she felt she was getting drunk a little too often. The well at Brewer's inn had given very sweet water. She said, "Oh God but it is hard. I have not known my life so hard, no, not since Toddy Hamstring's cellar." He dressed himself, embraced her fiercely, and went out upon his business: the players were in Kent, he must find a horse from the livery-stables and join them, whereas she had to go to Esher to sing.

(v) *Graven Images*

No sooner had Somerset lost his power than Bale's fortune began to change.

For a start, his mentor Ponet was made Bishop of Rochester. He would have found Bale a parish in that diocese, or a stall in the cathedral, except that none was immediately vacant. At the same time there came a discreet whisper down the Lambeth corridors that Rochester was but a stepping-stone. A far greater thing was in prospect – what might Dr Ponet think of *Winchester*? For it had been decided that Gardiner, confined in the Tower, would very shortly be deprived of his mitre – they had to do that soon, or else release him – and Ponet, as theological theorist, was exactly what the nation required for his replacement. Winchester See being traditionally reserved for a man of intellectual note, whereas mere simple piety was thought more than sufficient for Rochester. Ponet was a prodigious theorist, his personal fecklessness notwithstanding.

He counselled Bale to wait, just a little while, just a little more patience: and this time he spoke with authority. The obstructive men in Council, who had spited Bale for so long, had quite lost their advantage with the fall of the Protector. Cranmer and the Earl of Warwick (he was not yet Northumberland) were hand-in-hand upon church-preferments. All would indeed be very well.

Bale in Southwark began to receive, by weekly post from Rochester, large budgets of documentary research, ecclesiastical studies; to be worked upon for Dr Ponet's various theses. He was paid for this labour as befitted the amanuensis of a scholarly brand-new bishop. He felt briskly in tune with the vigorous world. And not even jealous of Ponet. That is to say, not *very* jealous.

Even more was he in tune, when, in March 1551, Ponet was translated to Winchester. At once an appointment for Bale, Episcopal Chaplain, and – better still – a cure of souls: Vicar of the Parish of Bishopstoke near Southampton, within easy ride of the cathedral-city; a verdant agreeable village on the bank of an idyllic river, no hostile resident squire, a congregation well-disposed to reformed ideas. Not that the people knew much about such things. But Bishop Gardiner's late parson there had been a man after his master's character, harsh and peremptory: any doctrine that *he* used to denounce was perceived as beneficial.

Bale (and Bale's wife) had a warm and generous welcome, not completely undermined by the subsequent progressive revelation of their eccentricities.

*

Bale's first and most obvious oddity was the plays. His furniture was scarcely over the vicarage threshold when he started straight in to organise the village for his *Comedy concerning Three Laws*. For the first time for years he had a potential cast ready to his hand, and he was not going to waste a day before rehearsing them. The people, of course, were used to the traditional plays, old-guise-religious and secular, that had been presented time-out-of-mind in Southampton. Their previous haughty clergyman had also put on Nativities and Passions and so forth in the church, compelling tongue-tied parishioners to learn very difficult lines, usually written in Latin. Bale's lines were not nearly so difficult (although lengthy), but the *content* of the plays was truly startling. A few local conservatives spread the word he was heretical, but Bishop Ponet was ready for them. The detractors were officially rebuked, the plays continued.

Far stranger than the plays, however, was Dorothy and her music.

She very soon saw that Bishopstoke was not Canterbury, and as a parson's legal wife was so grotesque an innovation anyway, she might just as well sing what she wanted where she wanted. She sometimes consulted Bale, sometimes not: she made her own personal effort not to embarrass him, but . . .

She did think, if he *had* to be embarrassed, why the devil wasn't he embarrassed at himself? When she first knew him – Friar Bale-zebub – he was able to observe himself much more acutely than he could nowadays. His long-awaited arrival at a regular clerical status, in a long-awaited Protestant Church, was making him very conceited. She would brood about this.

*

They were in truth a strange couple to represent Christ among the Hampshire fields: but then no doubt the fields of Galilee had been even more surprised. Could it have been, as Dorothy argued when she was at her most contrary, that Jesus Himself was a minstrel, singing parables as song-ballads, while St John played the hurdy-gurdy and St Matthew carried round the hat? A neighbouring vicar, who was supping with the Bales when she put forward this theory, snapped back irritably that were such a frivolous idea conceivable, then it must have been *Judas* that took the money, he being the purse-holder – *vide* John's *Gospel*.

"Quite right," he said, "to think of minstrel-profit going straight into the hands of an embezzler: has not all this so-called art been a theft of the people's spirit?" Bale handled him nearly as savagely as he did the Devon harpist, and he never came to supper again. And yet both he and Bale had been helping one another, not very long before, in the onerous and almost hysterical work of destroying all images, painted and carved, from within their churches. Neither of them could afford the charges of Southampton building-contractors, and the local men had all refused the job – it was 'unchancy', a 'widder-shins work', 'not fitten to be done, save under darkness, Sir John, and'll cost you more nor ordinary, seeing as how my poor lads'll need priming with good liquor afore any of 'em dare put hand to it', and so forth.

The day Bale dragged down the great rood from above the screen, there was a fearful thunderstorm that smote an oak-tree in the churchyard and nearly killed an old man who had been sheltering under it. By sheer chance Dorothy called him in to the porch at the crucial moment and so saved his life. Later, Bale preached that all must think only of how life had been *saved*: *that* was the Sign – for no-one disputed God had given a Sign of some sort – let them not brood upon the endangering of Daddy Hodge (grouchy old devil). But the tree was a 'fairy-tree': its destruction was also a Sign. Opinions differed as to its being toward good, or evil, omen. Dorothy made no songs about this. She fell ill for a week and took to her bed, condemning herself for her feeble-mindedness. In truth it was not the fall of the rood that chiefly upset her. The desecration of the little lady-chapel at the east end of the south aisle preyed on her mind far worse. She had lit the bonfire where the Virgin's statue had been burned, she had lit it with her own hand, just to prove she was *not* feeble-minded: every night of that hideous week she dreamed that the staring thin-faced wooden figure had waved at her out of the flames and cried pitifully in an unknown language. Every day, however, she made a point of remembering the silver collar from the Virgin's neck sold by Bale in Southampton, the money all gone into the poorbox: could this benefit have been achieved *without* burning the image? Simply to rob it would have seemed, well, robbery. One had to be consistent about such things.

And Bale had to say so, often. His sermons upon 'graven images' occurred with augmenting frequency throughout this period. He could never be sure that the people had thoroughly grasped the point. He was not always sure he had grasped it himself. He knew full well that idols in Christian churches fell foul of the Second Commandment; and that the priests of popery, by concealing the Commandment all these centuries in the Latin tongue, had conspired to keep the knowledge of it from the misled laity, the better to accrue their shrine-offerings and feed their guts therewith. Now that the Scripture was available to all in honest English, there was no excuse for perpetuating the superstition. But did the Commandment mean that no graven images at all were ever to be made? Because, if so, what about his illustrated books, upon which he spent so much of his stipend, and which he so loved? And what about – for example – the village inn, with its new loyal signboard of King Edward's head, surmounting two royal hands holding open a vast Bible? Or did it only mean that no images were to be made expressly for bowing-down-to? He recollected that that had been the official popery explanation in the old days anyway, even though it was so often disregarded in practice. The Jews, he understood, made no images whatsoever, and the

Commandment had been first addressed to *them*. But then it was a serious error to determine Christian conduct from the erroneous deeds of Jewry: it only led to Anabaptism or worse. He would worry all this out from his pulpit, concluding, with a great smack of his hands on the rail, that the "puppets and doll-toys torn out of this church were most certainly bowed-down-to and therefore most certainly idols: the huge golden pagod of Nebuchadnezzar (virtuously despised by Shadrach, Meshach, and Abednego, when they heard the band of music) was their father and their mother, and praise Jesu we have no more of 'em!" Then, the next Sunday, he would recollect that the Ark of the Jewish Temple was decorated with cherubim. Was a winged cherub a graven image, he would earnestly ask his congregation? "No, of course not," he would reply, "for it was in the likeness of nothing on earth or in heaven or under the earth, it was no more than the presentation of an idea, an ideal, of a brilliant abstracted glory: and then again it is a serious error to expect complete consistency from the erroneous deeds of Jewry . . ."

A contentious churchwarden asked him once was it not also idolatry to represent God in an acted play? He had the answer for that one, had had it indeed, well-prepared, for several years. An actor does not 'represent'. An actor is already created in God's image – *vide Genesis* – and if he is described by a play-screed as God Himself, then he offers to the public (and to God) no more than a brief and necessarily imperfect fulfilment of the said image: he is in no wise man-created, like a statue of the Virgin Mary. "But his screed is man-created," persisted the church-warden, "Bale-created, sir, one might say, with due respect?"

"So are my *sermons* Bale-created!" The Vicar was annoyed, but felt it had to be dealt with. "Yet you listen to them: or so I hope. And agree with 'em or not, you would not call 'em idols?" Hard to know what he would have done, had the churchwarden said they *were* idols. There were fools enough in England to make such an assertion those days, Anabaptists or worse. But Bishopstoke was a simple village, the man had asked his question not to provoke Bale but to confound a romanist farmer across the valley who had sneered at the whole idea of Protestant drama: and so the matter rested. But 'Bale-created' became a local catch-phrase and was used to describe anything out of the ordinary that took place in the district. It was flattering, perhaps.

Bale then felt he had to preach about stage-plays. Dorothy told him afterwards he over-passed his meaning ridiculously when he said that folk did not bow-down-to or worship actors. She knew better, having been very clearly 'worshipped' by one or two incandescent young men at the 'Birdcage', and having had her own experiences of carnal arousement when watching certain players in London, and elsewhere. And certain minstrels.

Gillian's face there and then in her mind: and the words died on her lips . . . So she let her husband snort her objections away in his most dismissive manner: because she foresaw that if she kept to the point he would wander into his old bypaths of digits and gutters and such, splayed mares, the use of willow-switches, and yet again distress himself over and over at his own inconsistencies. There was no doubt he was trying his best and there was no purpose to be served in playing tricks of argument on this particular issue. She *liked* the sexuality of the stage, but this was no time to say so, nor even to insist that it had to be taken into account. She wished she had not mentioned it. It was possible he might all of a sudden renounce plays altogether, and then where would be her life? And yet her dancing naked in Norwich had disgusted her. Why condemn poor Bale for inconsistency, when she herself . . . ? Enough of it!

The entire business of image-breaking and its associated unhingement of everyone's emotions was causing him great turmoil. Dorothy had not quite expected it: she knew well that he had not expected it at all. And the last thing he expected was that squires and even parsons would strip their churches not only of images but of all other fittings and furniture of any value and then pocket the proceeds-of-sale for their own advantage. Of course he preached furiously against it: but how should his denunciations affect what went on in other men's parishes? It was idolatry compounded, he swore, deserving worse hell-pains, far far worse, than graven images themselves. But those whom he reviled, when they heard of it, laughed. They had the money, they had been defeating popery, what more could this mad vicar want?

Legally-speaking they had right on their side. Just as Cromwell, legally-speaking, would have been perfectly entitled to proceed with his plans to dissolve the universities if all had gone his way. Bale preached, and they laughed, and he preached yet again, against Mammon: and his poor folk in their threadbare clothes on the cold flagstones of the nave listened to him, approving, but wishing just a little that Mammon might tempt *them* for a while. He rolled his eyes around them, swung his beard over against their serried heads, and frantically groaned that Mammon ruled this middle-earth, and how can Reform prevent it? He endeavoured to explain how: but after dark, alone with Dorothy, in their tangled consolatory bed, he groaned again and repeated the question. His answer now seemed no answer, Lord Jesus was a long way off, and then he groaned even more because the bed *did* console him and he feared it was a sin (or at least a worldly illusion, blinding him to the things of the spirit). In his heart he was turning over the terrible possibility of re-affirming his celibate vow. If he did, would it be possible to clutch himself just that much closer to his duty and Protestant truth? He thought of this, and fled from it, he feared it too would be a sin. It would certainly not be consistent.

He allowed the consolation, and never asked her was *she* consoled? His sleep was heavy and without dreams, once his loins achieved their surfeit. So of course he did not know how she lay awake beside him and pondered upon his death-like slumber. He had talked to her once about a heathen goddess, Kali, and then, another time, he had read to her from Malory's Arthur-book the tale of how a witch-woman enticed the potent Merlin into the cleft of a rock and deprived him of all his power, so 'that he came never out for all the craft he could do, and so she departed and left him . . . for he might never be holpen but by her that put him there.' "Kali again," Bale had said, "although our English poets call her Nymue, sharpened teeth in a sweet mouth, oh a crocodile to gobble all up." When he said it, his own teeth were gobbling at her nipple and both of them were gripped with laughter. She too was biting, at his neck. But she thought of it otherwise when she lay awake and he snored, and at those times she never felt any sort of merriment. He had believed he would be happy in Bishop-stoke.

*

Dorothy had not believed that *she* would be happy, she had known from the beginning that life with Bale could not ever be that, that parish-life with him might well prove an utter misery. In fact, it did not; because – despite all his confusions – Bale was a vigorous vicar, and imaginative. He had had little chance in Thorndon to show his quality, but in Bishopstoke he was never idle, and for the most part his activities were full of good sense.

Dorothy, after all, had never seen him as a white-friar administer-ing his priories according to their rule, smothering all his doubts about the correctness of Carmelite principles. At Bishopstoke the principles gave him no doubts at all: they were those of the primitive church, their enforcement was a travail of love determined by Scripture. Where Scripture was clear, Bale's life became very clear. (It was just a pity that 'graven images' were cause for dispute everywhere: *no-one* had that much clarity.) He was particularly good at visiting the cottages, and reading the Bible to the ignorant inhabitants who had never heard God's Word in English but sought only Christ's comfort for their heavily-burdened lives. When he was a friar he would have listened to their confessions and begged them for money. Now he gave them money (his own, as a rule), and tried to make his readings an adequate substitute for the intimacy of the discredited confessional. He said it was the *only* substitute, and it is possible they found it adequate. For certain he reached their hearts far more closely than at Thorndon: he had learned a lot from that experience.

(vi) *Grasped By A Giant Hand*

It was a sort of relief to Dorothy at Bishopstoke, that Bale's continued intermittent illnesses began to abate his old lechery. Relief, and disappointment, she had grown awkwardly used to him. But she had had six pregnancies (her first one, aborted by Nelly; and in recent years in Germany one still-born child, and then one miscarriage, before Lydia was safely delivered). She had always been hardy, not likely she would otherwise have survived her time with the Lowestoft Rover: but now, when she came to Hampshire at the age of thirty-seven, she was beginning to be tired, unseasonably, inwards and outwards, already a grizzled streak in her red hair.

He was fifty-six, and not young with it. Their marriage could not fairly be called 'January-and-May'; but 'November-and-August' might have been near to the mark. Moreover his friary years had given him irradicable bachelor habits: to live easily with a woman and a young child was even yet far from natural to him, his quick temper was often out of control. In the 'Birdcage' Dorothy had been at times a petulant princess, where such self-absorbed vanity was not only tolerated but essential to the business. To bring her temperament into a parsonage was a delicate consideration: and provoked many (who did not know her in any depth but had heard the strength of her tongue) to call her 'Elijah's own Jezebel'. She was aware of this and tried hard to moderate herself, but only with a limited success.

Now and then, in their narrow over-frequented house (for both of them refused to shut themselves away from the people behind a barrier of sacred pretension), they could find space and time to pretend they were fresh young lovers: something of course that they had never been, either with each other or with earlier partners. Unless, in the case of Dorothy, one was to include Gillian – but was it Gillian she had loved, or the beauty of the art she had shared with her at Oliver's house? She had never been able to unravel all the strands of that memory completely: it was a wound that would not heal. So the pretence was not easy; and yet she needed it, and yet she was not sure just what it was she *did* need.

*

She was anxious to have no more pregnancies, indeed the apothecary (they could not afford a physician) strictly warned her against it. She recollected all she could of Nelly's old precepts: because despite herself, and despite all her dark twisted history of men and of women – not excluding Bale himself, whose nakedness she had uncovered to no conclusive 'happy ending' – she still felt herself at unpredictable seasons invisibly grasped all over by what seemed a giant hand of caressing desire, and she had to do something to free herself of its weight. If this meant Bale and his threshing bed-violence, then so it had to be: he was anyway no longer quite so barbarous as he used to be.

'Bull-in-the-bush' had ungracefully aged into a spikey inconvenient hedgehog: she sometimes thought his mentality was altogether more trouble than his body was worth, and then she would sit in her house-place (while he was at large on parish duties) spinning or sewing, or telling herself she span and sewed, and talking unwisely and for hours to his young clerk, Richard Foster.

Richard was always in and out of the vicarage upon his tasks, he would always seek any reason to leave work aside for twenty minutes – or thirty – or, not uncommonly, for most of the afternoon . . . Richard loved to hear about the 'Birdcage', and he loved to disapprove of it on the best religious principles, and Dorothy loved to condemn him for his cold-nosed intolerance, and all in an atmosphere of collusive private jokes: so between the pair of them they were very much at their hearts'-ease. If there was more to it than that, then she kept it successfully private, even as private as Wentworth's fort or Thorpe-le-Soken.

At the same time – or rather at different times of the same days, the mornings, after service in the church – Richard would be enclosed with Bale in Bale's tiny study: and he was an adaptable young man. He reached as near an intimacy with the Vicar as he did with the Vicar's lady, though it was not so personal: more academic, theological, historical, poetic, as far as a rural parish clerk could manage to approach the high learning of a Cambridge doctor. Richard did manage, very well, and Bale delighted to teach him. They read together, in English and Latin, and the inferior Southampton grammar school that Richard had attended would have been astonished at his new attainments. Once Dorothy overheard them mastering Ovid together, and Ovid on the *Art of Love*, what was more. The giant hand curled around her as she listened. She did not, of course, follow the Latin itself, but Bale's English comments on it, and Richard's breathy responses, made the nature of the conversation very clear to her. The giant hand had sharp nails: but she did not let Richard know, that afternoon, how she had been scratched, and she was careful not to eavesdrop again. Each to each, a separate privacy: keep the home harmonious, keep secrets, spin and sew. If, upon some other day, Bale introduced his pupil to Martial or Catullus on the subject of young slave-boys dressing their masters' dinner, or waiting upon them in the baths, she made sure she heard nothing of it.

After her afternoons with Richard when the giant hand was rougher and closer to her and her immediate privacy with Bale became restless, all-at-edges, jagged, like the hour before thunder, she brooded how she should introduce an awkward thing she had to put to him. There was a recommendation of Nelly's which she had always avoided because she could not make up her mind about God's mind on these matters (she had no trust in Bale's certain knowledge of God's mind). At last, one night, half-an-hour after they had climbed into their bed, and neither of them were sleeping, and she had refused him her body – to his muttering, nigh-weeping discomfiture – and the bed-clothes seemed very hot and prickly, she whispered it in his ear, whispering also what the apothecary had said.

Bale sprang sideways from her, smartly – in moral horror? physical repulsion? or merely parsonical disapprobation? – she could not be sure: but the sheets and blankets fell off the bed, Bale's feet banged against the partition, Lydia and the nurse-girl in their sleeping-closet behind it might well have been awoken. "*Contra naturam?*" With her maddening half-laugh Dorothy repeated Bale's instinctive cry. "I cannot think so" she told him. "For how can Nature, against herself, put it into our minds to desire a certain thing unless it is of itself natural? Question surely ought to be, how far is Nature against God? Oh, but Bale, this is your boyhood heresy, and you'll need your books-of-reference, you'll need your pretty Richard to check down the index-pages, and by God you shall not have them, not now, not in my bedchamber. Either you want what I have offered you, to conquer my little Zion as did King David his great one, or you don't. It's not as though *I* wanted it, damn you . . ."

She turned her head from him, buried her face in the pillow, and argued as it were *sotto voce* with its goose-feathers: "And don't tell me you abhor it: I know that you long for it and I know what you *do* abhor, that when a child you were *forced*, by men whose subsequent conduct half-killed you with terror of hell. And of that too we read in *Genesis*, the Sodomites buried in brimstone because Lot's guest-friends were to have been similarly *forced* by them, so do we not deduce their sin to be breach-of-hospitality surrounding the act of venery, rather than the exact type of the venery itself? Not so long afterward, Lot's daughters bestrode their own father's loins, which I'd say was as much 'against Nature' as any of the other: but *they* were not brimstoned, they gave birth all unhindered to their own little brothers. Only their unfortunate mother became a pillar of salt, and what had *she* done? Nothing, but to wish she had once again her ruined home, and to look at it in tears as it burned."

Bale heard her, but he would not answer. He whimpered. He crouched away from her in the corner of the bed, absurd, with his nightshirt dragged up to his armpits, his hairy thighs pressed tight together as though to command his tool to smallness. After a while, she lifted her head, and said to him, in a dead voice: "Look, if you prefer Richard, I'll say nothing. He's a boy of such warm heart, he'd do neither of us any harm. There, you see, I've said it. What more in this world can I say?" Upon her last few words her voice fell away completely. Still Bale would not answer. Neither did he move. She pulled the sheet over them, and they lay all night in silence, back to back, not touching, very still in their hot summer sweat. Neither of them spoke of the incident again.

Not even a few days later, when they took their evening stroll through fields and coppices beside the river: Bale had gone down to the water's edge to watch some shipmen bringing a coasting-vessel (laden with timber for his church-repairs) upstream from Southampton under oars. They were singing as they pulled, and he waved his cap at them, merrily. When he turned round, he saw Dorothy standing against a willow-trunk, half-concealed. She held a lithe branch of the willow, and proffered it, with her half-laugh, half-shrinking of herself, as if but half of her wanted to do it. The boat disappeared round the bend of the stream: no-one else was in sight. He looked hard into her eyes and her glance did not waver. His did. He laid his hand upon the switch, and it stirred between both their hands like a dowser's divining-rod.

Then all in the one sharp movement, he pulled it from her, clutched it in both of *his* hands, and snapped it. He stepped swiftly back to the water, his thick shoes squelched among the bullrushes, he hurled the broken twigs as far as he could. They landed on the water and floated away. Then he strode, not looking to see if she followed him, until he came to a ditch filled with nettles and brambles: into which he plunged his hands, his arms up to the elbow, and wrung them about there, tearing the skin, blistering it with the hostile plants.

On his knees at this mad work, he turned his head: she was behind him, her face averted. She said: "You tried to ask me, many times these last years, but never succeeded, what about Joe Brewer? Was he husband in deed as well as word, ever? Well, he was a virtuous man, and virtue is its own reward, they say. *I* was not virtuous: but my friends have always held me to be a free-hearted gift-giver. One gift, just the once, was sufficient: he told me, 'Maiden, I have my own reward, virtue's, like in the proverb. I'm an old man, and was lonely, so I thank you. But not again. A second time would not be freedom but more like, you'd say, captivity. But my thanks.' You hear that, he called me 'maiden'. As you did once, I think. Nor did he break me in three and throw me away."

*

Tithes were a serious difficulty for Bale. His stipend as Bishop's Chaplain was insufficient to keep a family and maintain the Bishop-stoke household, even though the parsonage was very small (little more than a cottage), and his pretensions to a clerical gentry-life were smaller still. His vicar's-tenth was therefore essential – or at least *some* of it was. But he could not get away from that contentious preaching he had made at Southwark: a reformed clergy must speak for the people *against* bloodsuckers, not i'th'name of God dip teeth in the vein for itself!

In one of his Bishopstoke 'Mammon'-sermons he took courage, and confronted the crux. He would set an example: he would start that very year with a public redistribution of the greater part of his tithes.

But even here, he discovered, he contradicted his own good intentions, because those farmers who paid the largest tithe took immediate and growling offence. If Parson was so determined he'd have none of their moneys, they argued, then they ought to be given back to those that had paid 'em, shilling for shilling. To thrust 'em into the poorbox to be handed out as an equal dole to the entire parish, or as an *un*equal dole to those most in want, was no better than a highway purse-taking. And how could such a daft-headed trick serve to prevent enclosures? All knew that the Lord of the Manor (until lately the Bishop; but now, for heaven's sake, the *Crown*!) was the only one that fenced off the common.

The complainants got together and threatened recourse to the courts. At which point Bale fell ill with another ague, and Dorothy took advantage to spend much of the tithe-fund on overdue carpenters' bills for the church. The removal of the images had weakened the struts of the music-gallery (which had been buttressed by some sturdy oaken saints): and when Bale set up ladders to whitewash the painted Bethlehem scenes on the ceiling panels, dry-rot had been discovered in the roof-beams. The money for the repairs was notoriously outstanding and had to come from *somewhere*. She hated herself for doing it. But craftsmen who had carried out work needed their just wage no less than dispossessed cottagers required relief. She thought God's plan was as wretchedly inconsistent here as it was in regard to venery: who in His whole Creation could ever know which good to choose and which ill to eschew first?

One day, as she sat with Richard, she alarmed and distressed him by weeping from dinner until suppertime, and could give him no reason for it except 'Norwich, and Anne Askew', which he did not understand.

About this time she resumed her old habit of bathing. She had limited herself in Bishopstoke to one bath a month, as being the maximum compatible with vicarage proprieties, and even then too likely to remind folk of London profligacy. Now she boiled water for her submersion at least upon every Saturday and sometimes on Tuesdays as well. This caused a great deal of talk, and there were those who went so far as to hint that she painted her face (which in fact she never did). But it fitted the Jezebel-notion, and it also fitted another one – that she was a supposedly reformed Magdalene, brought out of a life of shame and devil-possession by Bale in imitation of Christ, but as Bale was not Christ his efforts had been less successful, and certainly not miraculous. 'Dame Maudlin *Bale-created*' was the exact word of scandal, and she soon came to hear it. She had no choice but to hear it, because several village mothers refused to allow their children to play any more with Lydia. Both John and Paul were apprenticed away from home, and the little girl was very lonely in the vicarage now: her father consoled her by telling her of lonely Ruth new in the land of Judah from the people of heathen Moab, and her mother consoled her by teaching her music, but she grew up quite strange and inward-looking, until some of the parishioners began to whisper that she might be a changeling-child. Bale himself never discovered the grounds for all these whisperings: his own view of Dorothy's baths was that her skin was her own to keep clean or dirty as she wished, God would surely know if a washed woman was a whited sepulchre, it was not for her husband or anyone else to interfere. But he did hope she would avoid the agues: they were bred out of the River Itchen water-meadows, and continual stripping and sluicing could only increase their danger.

(vii) *King Winter At Southampton*

Northumberland had done nothing about Wentworth's recommendation of Bale, except to tell his secretary to enquire into the matter quietly – it would be unwise to snub Wentworth just when he most needed his support: but on the other hand there were other allies involved in the imminent destruction of Protector Somerset, and *their* views had to be taken into account. Bale was too awkward a character for promotion at an awkward hour. The secretary's assessment was that John Ponet had Bale's future in hand; Northumberland could trust Ponet: a more personal patronage might well be a good idea later.

'Later' was 1552, when two bishoprics fell vacant in Ireland. The Duke searched his files for guidance, checking all those confidential opinions upon Irish affairs which from time to time had been offered to him. Wentworth's letter was re-examined: conclusions were drawn.

"This Bale, Hampshire vicar . . . ? Has a very odd wife. Will they notice it in Ireland?"

"Probably not, your grace: their native clergy are promiscuous.

But Mrs Bale has not pranced as a robeless bacchanal for many a long year: or if she has, we have no news of it."

"There was something about a sermon in Southwark. Gave aid-and-comfort to the Norfolk terrorists."

"Not quite, your grace. He asked the congregation, if report is correct, to pray that your grace, as trusted war-leader of a Protestant people, might bring our distressed Israel into proper order by proper justice, by your mercy as much as your wrath, remembering how David reproached Joab for the needless death of Absalom, how Christ upon the Cross accepted the penitence of the dying malefactor, nor did He rail upon the other one who railed against *Him*. Bale himself is from the east parts. His affections were stirred. No harm, I'd suggest, in his hope that a great man might be merciful."

"It well accordeth with the reputation we seek, provided our wrath be not *condemned*. Did he condemn?"

"He condemned those enclosing landlords whose ill-timed imbecility made the rebellion."

"I all but condemned them myself. Good God if I'd had 'em under command in the Channel Fleet, I'd have mast-headed the lot of them . . . Something else about John Bale? Ah: yes; he wanted his dissolution-pension. A monumental pile of letters in somebody's file. Did he get it?"

"I think, your grace, he draws it as current. It is the arrears he cannot obtain. Dr Ponet is still writing to Treasury on his behalf."

"If we make him a bishop he won't need his arrears. I'd be glad to do a good turn to Treasury."

"Indeed, your grace: a judicious thought . . ."

"Sound it out then."

Sounding out, however, brought the news that Bale had fallen very ill. The Duke shrugged his shoulders and began to look for another candidate.

*

Bale knew nothing of this: all he understood, on his sickbed in the vicarage, where he lay day and night shivering, sweating under a pile of blankets, was that he was unable to perform even the simplest parish duty, and that the King (on a progress of the south parts) was about to visit Southampton.

Bale and Edward had never met: but the Vicar of Bishopstoke

strongly believed an almost mystical relationship existed, or ought to
exist, between himself and this solemnly Protestant heir to his old
hero, his old terror, King Henry from whom he fled. For he insisted
these days that Henry *was* a hero, at times cruelly misled by malicious
renegade faction, but nonetheless heart-of-oak: his own exile was
Gardiner's doing, Bonner's doing, anyone's doing whose name came
to mind, so long as it was not the King's. For had Henry not died in
Cranmer's arms, and did not Bale himself wear his now formidable
beard as a token to the nation's loss? He tore at the beard in delirious
frustration that young Edward should come and go, Southampton but
six miles away, and he not be there to bid him welcome. Six miles, nay
only five, he *must* go, it was August weather, hot and glittering, rain
had passed, the Itchen valley was shining green and silver and the
hills behind Bishopstoke were thick with foliage, alive with singing
birds: Richard could ride pillion to hold him firm in the saddle.

He almost struck Dorothy when she attempted to push him back
among the bedclothes.

At last, swathed in cloaks and riding-coats, hooded cape enclosing
head and beard beneath his crammed-down beret, and reinforced by
several scarves, he took horse toward the town like King Winter in an
emblematic play riding out to lay waste King Summer's landscape.
He had once been stout and jowly, now he was bent and lean: he
nodded forward in the saddle with his shoulders as high as his
head.

Up the slope toward the Bar-gate, in under the portcullis, and
English Street was a crush of people all arrived to see the King. They
were pushing and heaving and defiling past each other's angry elbows,
most of them not clear where to go or when. Some said the King was in
the castle, others that he was staying at the Dolphin further down the
street, others thought he was not yet in town at all but would enter in
two hours' time from a boat at the West Quay. These were country-
people, just come in, many of them had passed Bale and Richard on
the road, none of them knew anything; and the watchmen at the gate,
who probably *did* know, were very rude to all enquirers. Bale felt he
ought to go to the Dolphin to put up his horse, whether the King was
there or not: it was the noblest inn, the most fitting for a man of his
station. But then what was his station? Cambridge doctor? Learned
poet? Ideologue of the new England? Friend of Cranmer? Yes, but
. . . Southampton knew him chiefly as a parson out-at-pocket and the
Dolphin would never accept his IOU, not even for a pint of cider and a

slab of cheese. Richard, holding his purse, aware of how little was in it, said gently, "Johnson's Beerhouse, sir, I think," and Bale, with an angry growl, turned his horse into the West Street.

To reach Johnson's they must pass St Michael's Church: and they found it was impossible. The little square in front of the church doors was packed to overflowing with a crowd that so jammed against the market-building there that it threatened to drive it off its penthouse-posts and collapse it onto the cobblestones. A cordon of yeomen was the cause of all this pressure, they were swaying between the crowd and the top of Bull Street, struggling to keep Bull Street clear, extending their halberds horizontally like a continuous fence-rail, and banging them hard into breastbones and adam's-apples.

If they could not get through this crowd they could not get down to Johnson's. But why was the crowd here: and who were the people that comprised it? Bale blinked his reddened eyes around him under the peak of his hood; yes, his guess was right, these were men of Southampton, he knew several faces (owed them money, indeed), and of course those straining yeomen were not the civic watch but royal men of the royal guard – "Dear Richard, we have achieved! His Majesty is in that house!" At the far side of Bull Street was a fine rich merchant-house with a balcony over the porch: and it was true, the guards were there to hold the people clear of it. Bale's horse trod on a citizen and he and Richard nearly fell off. They scrambled out of the saddle before they were pulled out. "Look, Richard, take the horse, back you go, the way we came, and so down French Street, attain the beerhouse from behind: sharp, boy, make it sharp, and return to me here!"

He flung himself into the press, keeping his eyes fixed on the embroidered royal arms draped over the balcony rail. A servant was adjusting it, smoothing its folds. Elbows and fists and knees – when he wanted to, Bale could be an intensely sturdy shover, even when fresh from sickbed – and here he was in less than a minute, clutching up against a halberd-staff, bristling his beard into the eyes of an angry serjeant, telling him all in a rush who he was, what he had suffered, who were his friends, who had been his patrons, and what were the titles of all the books he had written. The serjeant was intelligent enough to understand that Protestant ministers with a history of persecution were not the sort to be discouraged: many of them *did* have patrons, although their manners and appearance were often very odd. He relaxed his halberd a foot-and-a-half and allowed Bale inside the cordon. Nor did he put out his hand for money. Perhaps (as Bale told Dorothy later) he was a 'true confessor' himself.

They let him stand a few paces in front of the rabble, a lonely prophet-like witness to the glory that was within the house: Elijah, as it were, waiting to take post in front of Ahab's penitent chariot on the road to Jezreel. But in fact, save for the royal arms and the yeomen, one might have thought there was nothing within the house, for all the evidence to be seen from outside. The gate into the yard was closed and guarded, and all the windows appeared to be shuttered or curtained. A word went through the crowd that the King was ill and might have to cancel all public appearance. Bale's heart sank.

But he stayed there. Who knew what might yet transpire? He was aware of Richard, standing near him, behind the halberds, without the horse. He shivered in the hot sun; the grey hairs of his beard nevertheless ran with rivulets of sweat, although a griping chill had caught his loins and his throat was so sore he felt he'd swallowed iron filings. Seagulls from down at the harbour came swinging and shrieking overhead, confused, for this was the fish-market and today there were only people and not a fish-scale to be seen. Bale stayed: for at least an hour.

A splendid gentleman came out onto the balcony, and glanced casually up and down the street. Bale's heart gave a leap: he knew him! "Mr Fillpot!" he cried in excitement, "Richard, do you not see, it is the kinsman of our Archdeacon, it is Mr Fillpot, once of the Revels Office, the man who in King Henry's time made the arrangements for my acting-company – Mr Fillpot, it is I, John Bale!"

The gentleman looked at him, obviously not recognising him, wondering had he to do with yet another crankish madman, so frequent an occurrence when the court made a progress. "Mr Fillpot," shouted Bale, "Behold, sir, I have grown a beard!" The crowd began to laugh, even Richard laughed, and the serjeant regretted he had allowed Bale his little privilege. He moved officiously to hustle him away. But by now Fillpot had been joined by two more gentlemen, and suddenly between them they understood the truth.

"Why, Doctor Bale, of course, sir, yes!" Fillpot was immediately suffused with apologetic cordiality. "Serjeant, all is right, all is quite right, Dr Bale is well-known. Though to tell truth we had all thought he was dead!"

"No sir, not dead yet," Bale's voice began to resound, and then collapsed into a dismal croaking. "Like Simeon that holy father, how can I die before I have seen my King?"

"Stay there, sir, stay there." And the three gentlemen went back into the upper room.

A few minutes later, a thin pale boy, in elaborate brocaded clothes, but dragging a great fur gown around them as though he felt as poorly as Bale, came out onto the balcony. He cast his wan smile upon the people with an obvious painful effort. The people of course cheered and waved their caps in the air. Perhaps it was the King, perhaps not: but he looked as like his pictures as anyone could hope for. Bale went straight down upon one knee (not caring at all whether he would be able to rise again) and then found himself in a difficulty. His beret-strings were so tightly-knotted round his hood and throat that he could not get them off. He was still struggling with them when the boy spoke to him – no question but it *must* be the King.

"My dear Dr Bale," he said, and his voice was very sweet, if too faint to be easily heard out-of-doors, and also extremely shaky: his long white fingers were trembling, too. "My dear Dr Bale, we are mighty enmoven you should have took such heavy care and labour to be with us here today. Now get you home at once, good doctor, to your bed and recover yourself. We too have been invalid, we well know the imprudence of exposure to the open air. And pray, sir, have with you our warmest greeting to all our loyal and religious people in Bishop-thorpe: had it been the Lord's will we would e'en have made journey there also, but alas, our own health . . ."

Richard was terrified that Bale might correct the King over the name of the parish, it was just the sort of thing he would do: but fortunately there was no time, an elderly man in black gown (a doctor? a tutor?) came out on the balcony behind the boy, helped him wrap himself anew in his slipping furs, and solicitously led him back into the house. Bale saw him shudder violently. The pretty speech was left unfinished.

Bale said: "He will die soon. He is a saint of the true faith and God calleth him." But he said it to himself: aloud, such words were probably treason, however compassionately intended.

*

As vicar and clerk finished their brief refreshment and emerged into the beerhouse yard to reclaim their horse (the ostler's fee emptied their purse), one of the royal yeomen came running in under the arch and called on Bale by name. He had been sent, he told him, to enquire most sincerely just how much improved *was* the doctor's health? Bale could hardly speak for coughing and spitting, but he managed to answer: "Yestreen I was a man with no life in me. Today I ride ten miles, and tomorrow I shall preach like Isaiah! Sir, the King's Majesty hath restored me immeasurable! How old shall he be? Fourteen? Why, he addressed me as though he were my father. Oh sir, he is an infant Samuel." And unusually, at such mention, he thought only of the infant Samuel: the buggering friars of Norwich did not come into his mind at all.

(viii) *God's Vocation*

Mr Fillpot, the other courtiers, and no doubt the King himself, would have assumed that Bale's visit to Southampton, under such circumstances, had been a calculated (and perfectly reasonable) attempt to put himself forward for preferment. Oddly enough, they would have been wrong: and Dorothy – even in her angriest mood against Bale – had she heard of such a suggestion, would have known they were wrong and declared it forcibly. His surprise, therefore, the following day, when the letter arrived at Bishopstoke from the Clerk of the Council, was not at all feigned. He had neither expected nor desired to be appointed a bishop, still less to the Diocese of Ossory. Of course, he was gratified, how could he help being gratified? But he was also disconcerted and depressed.

"Had it been an English bishopric, oh a huge responsibility, but there is so much work to be done in England in consolidation of reform that I could not think to refuse, I would conceive that God commanded me. But, to Ireland? I know nothing of Ireland, the realm is full of good men that have experience there already and can surely be sent thither again to secure the Lord's business with expedient knowledge, informed wisdom: what can *I* make of the frowardness of that land? Moreover, I can't afford it. Why, the cost of the sea-passage alone – and what of my state of health? – oh Dorothy, do you not think I am too old?"

"If commandment to a bishopric is indeed God's vocation when the bishopric is English, do you tell me – to an Irish diocese – the call comes from elsewhere? I had thought divine summons would be more-of-a-piece. It is either God's voice in both cases, or else in both cases mere politic working. Belike your friends at court believe you to be honoured by this, belike it is not your friends but jealous enemies that wish it upon you? You alone can decide which."

"Enemies? It could be possible.

"When the late Lord Wentworth had Cromwell put me into Thorndon, young Conrad told me straight, 'Banishment', he said, and I would not hear him. But for years I have known I am too direct for some of these time-servers, even in Bishopstoke there are those who gird against me from the neighbouring gentry, from among my own cloth. It could be they would well wish me far out of the land lest I uncover their sluggishness for reform. Their refusal to bring right justice along with the new prayer-book. Their cormorant greed and Mammon-worship, yea. Knowing in their hearts that Ireland is irreformable, so there all my zeal must perish. It could be possible. But Dorothy, I must hear it from *you*: would you have me accept, or no?"

"You will go your own way, whatever I tell you. But first you ought to ask, not should you accept this bishopric, but how far is *any* bishopric a thing you can accommodate? How far is such an office necessary? I heard you say, once, had it not been for bishops, there could have been no pope. An institution, you said, conducive only to pride and tyranny."

"You well know I said that in regard to Bishop Gardiner and no-one else."

"What then of Bishop Latimer? When he left off his see at Worcester because he could not sign the Six Articles, he swore he would never return to it, and he has not. He preaches the Word now freely out of his own conscience, unobstructed by pomp or title, a simple shepherd of no politics save only the truth of Christian life: you agree with me, I have heard you say so, since he reverted to his plain state his sermons have gained one hundredfold in the surety of their moral strength."

"Latimer never laid claim that there is no need for bishops. That is the claim of Calvin: and I cannot hold with Calvin." He expounded to her for a quarter-of-an-hour the scriptural justifications for episcopal office, how it might avoid the blasphemies of papist corruption and lead the church into correct gospel-working, how it better suited a Protestant bishop to be poor, old, sick, incompetent even, if thereby he could re-approach the primitive apostolic condition, as Clement of Rome, for example (wrongly called Peter's successor as pope), a slave and yet a bishop, converting senators and imperial courtiers to Christ, and never clad othergates than in a slave's humble homespun. "No arrogant prince but a suffering servant," he said, several times.

"Very well," she sighed, "I understand. Because you are quite unsuited, you are therefore most suitable, so of course you must go to Ossory."

He slitted his eyes at her, suspicious, fearful of mockery. Was it so, if he refused he'd be denying his own logic; while if he accepted, his logic's flaw would be exposed – the suffering servant might suffer so much he'd prove unable to fulfil his function at all? He saw clearly his wife did not wish him to be bishop. But suppose he'd been offered Winchester? She had of late complained about the hard condition of their life, surely she'd not object to preferment to Winchester? "Would you?"

"Yes I would. You could not possibly cope with Winchester."

This angered him. She demeaned his abilities. He had spent hours denouncing the ill-administration of Winchester diocese, even under the obliging Ponet, and he had worked out, theoretically, a host of schemes for its improvement: if he *were* to be appointed there, he would show himself a marvellous bishop!

"Called by God?" she said.

"Of course called by God. In fact of course by the King, but the King worketh only through advice of his bishops, and the bishops are instructed through prayer."

"Then through prayer they are instructed to call the King to call *you* into Ireland. It cannot be had both ways: except on this one point, why should the church in Ireland be under rule of the English king?"

"Because –" he was exasperated by her ignorance – "because the Parliament of Ireland, and all the wild chieftains (except those still in rebellion) have proclaimed him their legitimate sovereign. Wherever he rules, he is head of the church. The Irish cannot have his secular rule without the religious: if I am to be bishop, it will be my task to ensure the latter."

"To enforce it upon them? Against their will?"

"You know nothing about their will. Neither do I. If I go thither, I shall discover it. But let me tell you, ma'am, I opine already that if the Irish have not yet taken hold of the principles of reform, it can only be that no reformer has been so well-concerned as to explain them."

He was determined he could do no other than act upon God's call, but he had to be quite sure that he recognised it correctly. He believed he had been called to his marriage, to his parish, to his poetry-work if it came to that: but these in comparison were minor vocations. His first great vocation should have been into the Carmelites: but he had never been able to see it so. He was a child then, and compelled, by family; and then later, into priest's orders, by an inevitable friarish process of career. Now, however, God had the chance for an unequivocal bellow in his lug: and he was not going to miss it.

*

And when he went to London, after an interval of indecisive correspondence to and fro the court and Lambeth Palace, he found that the Duke of Northumberland re-echoed all his thoughts. In a brief private interview the Duke made very clear just why he wanted Bale appointed.

"At present our state-officers there have hung divinity *on the hinder hook*: pull it down, sir, and flourish it, as though it were a battle-flag!"

Northumberland had a fine record as general and admiral, he was a spiteful inspiriting swart-faced camp-and-quarterdeck man, he banged his fist convincingly upon his desk till the documents flew about him. "The trouble has been," he growled, "even their popery was damnable idle, they took what they were given by all those ancient saints of theirs, Patrick, Columba, Bridget, Kevin, Brendan, Moling, you know the names, and they have never changed anything since. The great part of 'em do not go to church at all, not even to the Mass, because their saints did it all for 'em eight hundred years ago. The same with their politics. Every tribe, every chieftain, even of our English-Irish, conduct themselves equally freely: Butlers and Fitzgeralds ignore the Crown altogether except when it suits 'em; and as for the English-made towns, Galway, Limerick, Kilkenny, they might just as well be your old Italian city-states for all the co-operation we get. D'you know Galway and Limerick, not so many years ago, went so far as to declare war, one upon the other?"

"But, your grace, what of Dublin?"

"Oh Dublin is nothing but a beach-head for our new-landed troops. I say 'new-landed': God, they've been there since Second Henry, but you'd think they came but yesterday and have not yet unloaded their ships. Which is why it is so important you make Kilkenny a trustable town. It belongs to the Butlers, but the chief Butler, Earl of Ormond, is in England, a young man, being brought to some sense of governmental responsibility at the King's court. When he is permitted to return and take up his local rule, I want Kilkenny and all its region to be ready for him, a safe extension of our Pale, so that it will not be possible he should shift it from obedience: the Butlers are to be brought to heel, and we start in their own town by catching the souls of the citizens."

As he talked, he looked hard into Bale's face. He saw that all this story of an all-but-anarchic colony might alarm the man more than persuade him. He had a comprehensive dossier upon Bale: Lord Wentworth had provided much of it. Northumberland was a sharp dossier-user; when he moved to gain his power he had carefully found out which men who might support him could be tempted by a promise of a quick return to popery, and which would prefer him to lead England toward Calvin's Geneva, so in the upshot both Old Guise and extremist New had been stirring most vigorously on his subterranean behalf. Now this conversation must be swiftly worked round to a touch-to-the-quick upon what he knew of John Bale.

"I want Ireland totally England's – *your* function, if you go there; and I know you can do it. Because if not, what will happen? The Emperor, or the French, will fill the island full of papist soldiery, and jump thence into England by the unguarded rear-entry – sodomitical rape, Bale, like David into Jerusalem, hah! Except this time it is the Jebusites to re-conquer their old high-place!"

Bale too said, "Hah!" and nodded his head, then "hah" again, a grunt behind his beard. But his lips twitched, and Northumberland thought that the expression in his worried eyes had shifted significantly.

*

So the Duke went on to add a few more significant facts: in particular the circumstance that the Pope was now appointing his own rival Irish bishops, seditiously to challenge those already put there by the Crown. The Primate of Armagh, for instance, was forced to abide in Dublin, because the irreconcilable northern tribes had accepted the papal nominee and would not allow the true Archbishop to return to his diocese. "It's not even as though Rome had given 'em an Englishman, still less one of their own Irish. The pretender to Armagh is a damn Scotchman, what d'you think of that? *I'll* tell you what to think of it, Bale, next thing we'll have the papist Queen-mother of Scotland – who is a *Frenchwoman*, let me remind you – laying claim to all of Ireland: and half the Irish will receive her with music-and-dancing in the streets! Tell me, have you heard of the Society of Jesus?"

"The Pope's new priest-agents, no?"

"Correct: and in a secret conclave sworn to stop at nothing till disguised and ubiquitous they restore his power!"

"God save us, your grace, they're in England already?"

"Pray heaven, not yet. But in Ireland it is rumoured this Scotchman is one of them . . . Dr Bale, let me give you a final persuasion: confidential, not a word outside these walls."

He lowered his voice and leant across the desk. Bale squatted forward on his chair to hear him, like an old tom-cat, staring eyes and twitching whisker.

"I am by no means certain that our beloved King is as recovered from his ailment as was hoped. Indeed some of us doubt he will ever recover. It *ought* to be possible to ensure a Protestant succession." Now Bale had no idea how this was to be done: the romanist Lady Mary – being as far as he knew – the obvious heir to the throne, and it must surely be high treason to suggest otherwise? Certainly the King's ill health was making many honest people very frightened for the future. He kept silence and waited. The Duke spoke most slowly: his eyes were opaque.

"But if not, then we must be clear that a – a non-Protestant monarch shall not find the kingdom – Bale, I mean the entire kingdom – in such condition that its faith may be easily reverted. In England there is this assurance, even the most papistical magnates have enriched themselves under Cromwell with the proceeds of the monk-houses, they will not quickly give them up, though for sure the Pope would insist on it. But in Ireland that is scarcely the case, there have been no widespread expropriations, the land is too poor anyway, and the magnates too discoordinate. Thus for such a monarch, in that island, great support must needs accrue, an immediate lever to repapalise England. So therefore, time is short. You take my meaning?"

Bale had taken it. And then, he took the bishopric.

*

And, at once, home to Hampshire. He told Dorothy: she drew away from his arms almost as though he carried lice. "Northumberland? You saw Northumberland, he told you that? I thought it was Cranmer you went up to London to see."

"I did, and all that he said to me cohered with the words of the Duke. Except, being Archbishop, he spoke more of the necessity to bring into Ireland daily use of the *Common Prayer Book*, ensure that the English Scriptures are at all places available to –"

"Do not the Irish have their own language?"

"For those that rule the island the English tongue is of course current, even if they be not English by birth, and –"

"– and therefore it behoves a bishop to first feed the wolves before he can succour the flock?"

"Good heaven, what do you mean? That is not the way of it at all!"

"Three years ago your keen Northumberland sent in his Germans with blade and partisan among the peasants outside of Norwich and whether those unhappy creatures sought quarter or not, three thousand of them dead before nightfall. As you say, a courageous ruler, a curt-minded soldier indeed. Shall he do this to the Irish if they do not heed your episcopal Word?"

"If they do heed the Word, there will be no need even to think of doing it. Madam, I am despatched to carry mercy to that rancorous people. Why, you talk as though the swordsmen were murdering there already, and they wish me to preach upon a field of slaughtered folk. Which would truly be a mockery of God: but be assured it is altogether the other way about."

"Are the swordsmen *not* there? I have heard of wars in Ireland ever since I heard of Ireland. Very like it is *because of* the wars the Word has not taken root. Very like they seek their freedom before they would hear how free is the religion of those that keep freedom from them."

"You mouth yet again from no knowledge and not to the purpose at all. All these matters are close-ravelled and crave counsel of some sublety to unwind them. So let me provide it you. First, I will not accept that the Irish are oppressed. To understand their condition it boots we look back to the time of King Henry the Second, who laid no claim to Ireland until certain Irish chiefs sought the help, unofficial, of his captains in their wars – wars against each other, *native* wars unstoppable, congenital, hereditary, *unwinnable* indeed without Henry's Norman-English to bring them to an order. Which they did, and made great status there as successful mercenary officers; nay more than that, they grew already into the substance of Irish chiefs. He, being a severe king, saw that shortly they would rule all that land for their own, and withhold their due obedience from *him*. So of course he must declare himself Lord of Ireland and enforce it."

"Ah that was the Lordship that was given him by Papal Bull?"

"As ever you have chattered much and understood too little!" Her introduction of the Vatican into his argument was, in Bale's eyes, most underhand. "Second Henry, killer of Becket, was *no sort* of papalist! He was met with a deadly ignorance, both in England and Ireland, and had no choice but to address it in the terms it could take hold of. As I do to you: I must *simplify* the history!

"Every year since Henry's time those same Norman-English-Irish have attempted unceasing to break from our nation's rule.

"The close adjacence of the islands will not allow it; even were some Butler or Fitzgerald to be elected King of the Irish, by every voice in Ireland, we could not tolerate it. No more than could we tolerate a great magnate of the north parts, as it might be the Earl of Cumberland, setting his own petty crown on his own head: he owes a sworn duty to central authority, and is susceptible to authority's law. You can not call that oppression. Besides, if there *be* oppression, it is Butlers, Fitzgeralds, and the rest, that do perpetrate it. King's government must needs free the people from their tyranny, as happened already in England. Do you think that we here should return ourselves in the name of liberty to the mutilations of the Barons' Wars?"

"I was not alive at the time of the Barons' Wars, so how can I say how they mutilated?"

"You are aware of my play *King John*, I do suppose you are, Mrs Bale? God knoweth, you had enough to do with its making. But over above my small poor works, you may read in the chronicles, first of the Anglo-Saxons, and then Matthew Paris, how he describes expressly the –"

"It seems to me, John Bale, you can read anything in the chronicles, and yet derive no wisdom. From my very little wisdom I observe one thing you have not mentioned. Out-of-the-realm English should follow the king's rule: good. Because they were sworn his men before they went oversea. But those to whom they went, and I mean the Irish-Irish, what had they ever sworn? By what right are *they* accounted the King of England's men?"

"To begin with, I understand they do not inhabit Kilkenny, except as peasant-serfs under oppression from the Butlers. For the rest of them, in their own areas, some *have* sworn, sworn handclasp strongly, and then renegued upon their oaths. They dwell scattered amid moor and mountain, they have no consistent rulers, they live largely by rapine, and in short are no more civil than the many-armed voracious kraken-fish that batten beneath the deepsea weed. Oh they talk about

freedom indeed, but a freedom to burn and kill. Only through
Christian monarchy can they be brought into Christendom, and that,
with God's help, we shall accomplish."

She sighed. Was she convinced? Well, she knew that when he said
she mouthed from no knowledge, he was not wrong. But was he right,
to assume she must be more ignorant than he, even though he had read
all the chronicles?

"With God's help," she said mournfully, "when we get there we
shall see; see what we *can* accomplish, find out in Kilkenny the
smallness of our subtle unravelling." And then she went on to ask how
much time they had to make their arrangements before the journey. It
seemed there was no hurry, probably not until after Christmas.
Government would tell him when they needed him to assume his see.

Somehow, after her words to him, he lost much of the new
enthusiasm he had worked-up on the ride from London. But he did
feel he was well-shed of his ague-fevers, he did feel a good bodily
energy, he did feel that God's Vocation might be speaking to him
through his bones and veins: if so, then his mind would accommodate
it, very shortly.

(ix) *Magics*

She spent time, a few weeks later, talking to Clerk Richard about
Ireland. He had been asked by Bale to come to Kilkenny with them,
he was *full* of enthusiasm, thoroughly uncritical: although he did not
try to argue very strongly against Dorothy. He agreed with her, 'when
we get there, we shall see', without any implication they might be
taken aback by what they saw and would have to adjust their attitudes.
Richard felt, very simply, that England was entrusted with the welfare
of less-fortunate peoples, for England's reformation was such a
singular mark of God's favour that it brought with it multitudinous
(and often tiresome) duties: also in other directions had the English
been vouchsafed a special place under God's Providence.

"Our parliament-commons," he instanced, "granted to restrain
our kings from enormities, just as kings restrain the noblemen, and
the people restrain parliament. Our reformed church-doctrine,
neither popish nor insensate new-guise (I mean, insensate as Anabaptism, or – as some would say – Calvin). I think it must be because
we are an island and thereby protected from the foreigners' contagion." He could now and then be as pompous as Bale: perhaps he

learned it from him. Dorothy wished him to learn somewhat from her too.

"Silly Richard, dear youth, the Irish are an island, and filled coast-to-coast with contagion of foreigners."

"Nay verily, Mrs Bale, the French and Spaniards are kept very strictly away, by the Lord Deputy his garrison there."

"Not quite what I meant," she said: but she did not want to quarrel with him. She moved to another aspect of the case. "I have not told Dr Bale, but I have often wondered, am I not half an Irishwoman? My mother, whom I scarcely remember, was a sort of tinker, I suppose, her people followed the roads in a gang, sometimes settling here, or settling there, by ones and by twos. She fell out with her own kin: I know not what she did to offend 'em, but then she fell in with a Cambridge priest, to his ultimate sorrow, not for any love of him. He was no more than a port in storm to her, I think. But from what I saw myself, when I was on the roads, such gangs are often Irish. Not necessarily born in Ireland: they have wandered here a long number of inconstant generations, coming and going, back to Ireland again, into Wales, also Scotland.

"What I do recollect of her would not contradict this thought I have had. She used, when sober, to tell me stories, and I have not heard such stories since, or not quite in the same way. Tales of giants and magic, great water-horses in stagnant meres, soldiers in foredoomed battles for the sake of a bull, a man who being dead lives on in a wild boar's body and thus seeks out and slays his killer on top of a mountain. I call them to mind but vaguely: they were all of them very strange. She had one of an angry poet who murdered another poet and was turned into a mad bird for punishment."

"Oh I have heard that one: it is a legend of British Merlin."

"Even so? It is not in the Malory-book . . . But there *would* be some relation with the magics of King Arthur's age. She told also of an island in a deep dark cold lake, where upon a time lived dragons: until a holy saint came and drove them all out. Having ridded the place of them, he discovered that the pit they had infested in midst of the isle was now opened all the way down into the spleen, liver and bowels of the earth: and at the bottom thereof lay Purgatory. So let a devout man – or woman, there have been many women at it – watch, pray, and fast upon that island for sufficient long time, they shall be granted a true vision of all that betides us after our death. Whereby there hath ever been incomparable holiness from the place: greater far than in any other shrine in the land. I did not know, being so small when she told me this, that the land was not our own land. But in late years I have heard of an Irish shrine, much the same, called Purgatory of Patrick. I daresay – for its superstition – my husband will put it down, if he find it within his diocese?"

"I think it is not there, ma'am, but to the far north-west, among the unreconciled tribes. But if it is still frequented, it must needs be put down. There is no such a thing as Purgatory."

"You are right, my flower, quite right: if what is meant is a hole in the ground. I think we live our Purgatory before our death, not after it. God, but I *know* we do.

"However, that is not the intention of my tale. I merely remind myself of it now for the chance that my mother was Irish. It was a legend of her people, so perhaps they were *my* people also. And yet, do you not see, I cannot go over there with my John and then tell them so: I do not *know* it for certain, nor ever will know. To them I shall be the wife of the English Bishop and that is all. For scorn or for welcome? We shall see when we get there.

"Let me tell you, if he is right, and we do in truth travel thither to steer the people clear of the military chastisement of Duke Northumberland, then we go for a good purpose: anything to keep that man out of anybody's land! Oh anything, my gentle boy, even to the blocking-off of their holy dens of Purgatory: I wonder do they know this Duke and what he will threaten against them, if they submit not to his angry power? I shall try my best to tell them. But listen, Richard, listen, you must promise me here and now, not a word to John Bale of what I have said."

He promised. He found her confidences often foolish, though always sweet, and it did not disturb him that his betrothed in Southampton was not a party to them. Dorothy, whenever she met the girl, was as kind to her as to him, and surely there was no harm?

*

For a minister's house, Bishopstoke Parsonage had a great deal of highly secular music going on at all times in it. So it was nothing out-of-the-way for Dorothy to take down her cittern and sing and play with Richard, even when Bale was not there. Lydia would often come in to clap her hands and sing as well: they were teaching her to dance. This particular afternoon, Dorothy taught both daughter and clerk an old English ditty which she had half-forgotten for years, and they worked upon some dance-steps to go with it.

It expressed, she said, the respect which the English of the minstrel-trade had ever held for the Irish, for their religious and poetic grace. When they came to Kilkenny, they must bear it in mind always.

A most plaintive air, perhaps in itself Irish.

> I am of Ireland
> And of the holy land
> Of Ireland.
> Good sir, pray I thee,
> For of saint charity,
> Come and dance with me
> In Ireland.

Lydia danced the role of the Irishwoman, leading her mother and Richard (as foreigners) over the seas to dance with her: which they did, in a tender and companionable fashion, while the music went round and round. Dorothy felt quite cheered up.

*

They took ship at Bristol, from the city-quay opposite St Stephen's Church. Mid-January, storming with snow: the last portion of cargo for Waterford was slung up from the yardarm. Dorothy, Richard and Lydia watched upon the deck, hooded, cloaked, gloved and booted like stuffed dolls as broad as they were tall; while Bale, flying scarf-ends and trailing hems, skidded up and down beside the hatch-way, shouting to the cranemen in the name of God to take care!

The over-full cargo-net contained the two wagon-loads of precious books that had so tediously lumbered along with them through the winter from Bishopstoke: he saw a swaying packing-case had lost its lid, he shouted again and ran to be beneath it if anything fell out. *He* fell, scattering his limbs under the seamen's feet; he slithered away into the scuppers, and raised his head just in time to see all his library after all safely lowered into the hold.

"God thank you for your good care, my good men," he gasped.

"Will you Christ-sake get yourself out of it," snarled the boatswain, and then remembered, just remembered, to add, "Bishop". Bale did not think he ought to demand to be called 'My lord'. He knew they would not have spoken thus to Gardiner, and he angrily rejoiced at it, more or less.

As the ship edged down-river through the Avon gorge, Dorothy, still on deck, despite the knifing cold, asked him one final sour question, a farewell as it were to England: "If the King had offered you a choice, Bale, to be Bishop of Ossory, or his Laureate Orator Royal (as was your John Skelton), which would you have accepted?"

He gazed upon her bleakly, then looked again at the cliffs of the gorge. His answer was historical, brought to his mind, no doubt, by his studies in the history of Ireland: "When Second Henry, Plantagenet, kept his paramour Fair Rosamund at Woodstock, jealous Queen Eleanor came to her privily and offered her in one hand a dagger, in the other a poison-cup. So which should *she* have chosen? Oh the service of a virtuous prince is most beautiful: yet oft it destroyeth the servant."

After that Dorothy uttered no more reproaches.

Their voyage was hard, but not delayed, a violent wind from east-north-east catching hold of their starboard quarter and whirling them to Ireland through the snows.

More Brandywine

Having paid Lydia his glancing erotic compliment, Anthony Munday dropped his eyes, poured out another glass of brandywine, turned the talk rapidly back again to plays and playwrights: he spoke with intensity.

"Of course, no shame to tell you of my present occupation. As it were in recompense for being inveigled towards subversive More, I plan a new play of Sir John Oldcastle, Lollard under Henry the Fifth. I have not yet begun to write: but your father's account of Sir John's martyrdom is my source-chronicle, that and Holinshed, I study them daily. A problem: the king that burned him being *England's Hal*, how do we praise Oldcastle and yet not too greatly dispraise the king? Was Agincourt contemptible because Oldcastle burned? Henry-the-Fifth plays have long been favourite: I must not offend their audience. Rather, to turn them gently to a more comprehensive historical view. When I commence writing, you might perhaps be interested to look over my tentative screeds?"

"I think your problem is no problem." Lydia spoke judicially, almost censoriously. "My father lived and suffered under another *England's Hal*. And he said, as many said, that his cruel Hal was 'a great king'. But was he? No denying, in his reign there were great things accomplished. Did he do them himself, or was he drave by the storms of circumstance? As an anointed king, therefore God's Chosen, he of course has kept his name upon every deed of government, and yet we cannot know what he in his heart thought of any of 'em. God's solemn choice of him made marble-stone of his humanity, glazed and glittering with the oil consecrate. Our common praise and *dis*praise of him as an Adam-stark man are surely beside the question. We must leave such specious judgement to God.

"But his people could not so leave it. The deeds of his sovereignty, stamped with his name, were carried out by *them*, and endured by *them*, and *they* were the ones who hated or loved what was done. They themselves were the 'storms-of-circumstance': the people stirred, the king must move, they drave and they were driven. So where will *they* be in your screed?

"I have seen a Henry-the-Fifth play, what did they call it? *The Famous Victories*. Well, it would have been better to have made it about one of his soldiers, not him. Now I think of it, in that play, there was indeed an 'Oldcastle', a ruffian-companion of the king's boyhood: which was not so, he should in truth have been the king's soldier, and then he became God's soldier, no? He may not have judged the king, but he judged the king's actions: so why not show your Hal at all points through the eyes of the *true* Oldcastle? Or, if you carry your tale later, even to glorious Agincourt, set forward some bold bowman to be both chorus and actor, and let *him* in his turn give a judgement upon Oldcastle. Thereby from a doubled viewing-place your public will observe the entire reign, the contradictions of its consequence.

"Which is not how Bale would have writ it. I only try to shape *my* mind to the manner of things now-a-days, as you tell me they are. Would your Henslowe understand?"

"No; oh no, no no not at all. He wants a roarer for Alleyn to play. Maybe Oldcastle might roar: but a common bowman – he's for the clown, or we throw the whole company into discord one with the other. If kings must lose humanity, in God's name, what about players? To cast a man just once as a monarch with colours-and-drum is to anoint him for all time beyond the reach of meagre playwrights. He can never be brought down. That's what's wrong with Willy Shake-scene. He devises these clever tricks, and he does it so insidiously, some of the players will e'en accept it. Yes, *he* would be capable of bringing bewildered conscript ruffians, or Irish mercenaries even, into the battles of France, and killing the king's glory with their words, and they would not be clowns neither. Yet somehow the king's role would still seem to remain heroical. He divides his plays this way and that till no-one knows what they mean. I believe he destroys our trade: we are at root but simple folk and our public is simple too. Good and bad, black and white, your father would have known."

"I think I have met this 'Willy' you speak of. He was not agreeable."

"Met him? You mean, he coiled against you and you knew not what you had met until he rippled his way out of the room, and then you distasted him?"

Lydia smiled. His jealousy was so overt she had to despise it: but she warmed to it too. The poet in Lucretia's lodging had been both oily and spiney, more eel-like than serpentine perhaps. At least Anthony Munday talked to her as though she existed. If he was devious, he was honestly devious, and much more handsome than the other. She knew exactly what he wanted. To court her, and to denigrate his rival. Somehow the two intentions were one: she was not yet quite sure how. She would have another glass of brandywine and see could she not penetrate his driftings.

He sat with a frown, clicked tongue against teeth, about to make up his mind to say something, wondering if she was ready for it. She was, she settled back upon her stool and smiled her small encouragement. The veil was up again, she had forgotten how, maybe she had put it up without thinking, to give more urgency to her 'bold bowman' speech.

"Mrs Lowlyheart," he began again with a new precise formality, conversation as though from scratch between two just come together for the first time. "Mrs Lowlyheart, I make no mistake to suggest you met him at your daughter's place? Is it possible you have had cause to think that Lucretia conceals things?"

This was not what she had expected. Her reaction was sharp, alarmed. "Things, conceal? What sort of things?"

"If I knew, it would be easy. I could so easily – ah – arrange matters: keep Lucretia out of trouble and yet ensure that those embroiling her received the full reward of their perilous intrigue. I would have to know how far, how deep, she was involved, and . . ."

"He's the only one of her friends you have met?"

"Some singers, and musicians, at a masque in Highgate; her music-master: that's all."

"No harm from any of those. I know them all myself."

"No harm? Good God, you frighten me. Mr Munday, what *is* the harm? Sir, you must tell me, I am her mother, tell me, tell me –!"

His eyes shot from left to right and then from right to left, checking who was near them in the inn-parlour through the gap that he pulled in the alcove-curtains, a crafty narrow gap, no more than six inches; a furtive swiftness was one of his skills, like a soft-footed animal hunting by night.

"Not here," he breathed. "Come to my house."

VI

(Tragical-comical)

I Am Of Ireland

And I saw in the right hand of him, that sat in the throne, a book written within and on the backside, sealed with seven seals. And I saw a strong angel preaching with a loud voice: Who is worthy to open the book, and to loose the seals thereof? And no man in heaven, nor in earth, neither under the earth, was able to open the book, neither to look thereon. And I wept much, because no man was found worthy to open and to read the book, neither to look thereon.

(Revelation of St John the Divine, Chapter 5)

Bale wrote his own account of his time in Kilkenny. He published it from his place of second exile, when Catholic Mary was Queen. He called it *The Vocation of John Bale to the Bishopric of Ossory, etc.*, and shaped it like a sermon, full of comparisons between himself and Saint Paul, and many justifications of all that he did and hoped for, with analagous scriptural texts to prove him right.

He had a frontispiece engraved. This picture, made exactly to his orders, showed the 'English Christian' confronted, very dangerously, by the threatening 'Irish Papist'. It was like a scene from the sort of stage-play he had witnessed, indeed written and acted, so many times: all argument compressed into two opposed characters, protagonist and antagonist, King Summer and King Winter, John Baptist and Herod, Christ and Antichrist. The 'English Christian' is shown with a pious sorrowful face, head devoutly on one side, hands meekly folded in pacifistic supplication. A gentle little lamb rubbing itself softly against his leg, confident of protection. On his head is a soft bonnet. The 'Irish Papist', on the other hand, comes striding forward drawing a falchion, his face tilted angrily upwards, aggressive moustachios, a fierce *banditto* hat; and at his command a savage dog hungering to tear the tripes of both the lamb and its kind guardian.

The drawing gives little hope that the Englishman will be able to save himself, short of a miracle. For at the time it was made, *Bale* had not saved himself: or at least, not as an Englishman with a country of his own to be safe in. As far as he could tell, all was back as it had been before, back even to the days when he stood in Norwich market-place, a terrified child held hideously in thrall to sight and stench of a burning Lollard.

The only hope for England was the Lady Elizabeth, and word came she was in the Tower. Lady Jane (who was, he must bitterly admit, no more than a strung puppet for Northumberland's intriguing knuckle-joints) had lost her head; Northumberland had lost his head, relapsing into sheer popery in his very last shameful moments: and nearly all those Lords who had supported Jane had changed their coats again and given allegiance to Queen Mary.

And yet, had he thought about it, he might have found ground for hope: Queen Mary's Irish policy was as coercive as any Protestant's, she laid hold of Gaelic clan-territories, and with a thoroughly non-sectarian free hand she planted them full of English. It was as though she had read Bale's mind and telepathically adopted the logical kill-or-cure for the contradictions of statecraft he diagnosed. Religious contradictions would also have been abolished, had she only been Protestant, and followed the same plan. No government before hers had so overtly made a colony there as a deliberate political choice. All previous settlements had been almost accidental, regretted by the English Crown for the effort and expense required to maintain their security. Mary's colony *was* the security, a hard determined company of defensive and offensive property-owners who would truly make the land their own. She was sure, as Bale would have been sure, (had his thought progressed so ruthlessly devoid of emotion) that to eliminate all the Irish was the only possible means of bringing all Irish warfare to an end for ever.

But, Mary being Queen, it was not to be a Protestant end. Bale became confused about how he should take this. Did he hate the Irish primarily because of their religion, or because they were not English? Probably in his own mind the distinction was unclear. Catholic English were his own people, though abominably misled. Catholic Irish were an enemy. Protestant Irish (had there been any) would likewise have been an enemy, their religion would have been hypocritical and would only have made them worse. For that was the way he found Ireland, the short time he lived amongst its people: and he never looked beyond it.

★

An Irish opinion upon John Bale as bishop is hard to discover. So many wars, so much destruction, both of manuscripts and people with memories. But Anthony Munday heard a story.

In his spare time, and for a useful remittance, Munday acted as a cunning operative for Queen Elizabeth's intelligence service, defending the commonwealth from Jesuits, Spaniards, Irish. His own manner of life was scarcely devout: but at the bottom of his rakish ways lay a profound sump of murky hatred for anything to do with the Old Religion. Family traditions, perhaps: he was born in frightened London at the start of Mary's reign, when Bonner was again Bishop and faggots were lit in Smithfield. He found it no dishonour to be an *agent-provocateur*.

He went to Rome, once, in 1579, to gather evidence against Catholics in England: while there, he met an informative Irishman.

Munday's assumed identity for this conversation was 'Mr Oaktree', idealist papist, helping to bring the exiled Irish into contact with Vatican officials, English Jesuits, and Italian mercenary captains, for the furtherance of a new rebellion in Ireland. An expedition was being planned to land Spanish, Italian and Irish troops upon the sea-coast of south-west Munster. An English priest was already commissioned by the Holy Father to accompany it as Papal Nuncio. There seemed reason to believe it would succeed, having the virtues of complete surprise. Except that Munday had found out: and was determined to find out more.

As 'Mr Oaktree' he was unsuspected: even the Irish whom he met were sure of his loyalty. He let them know he was a poet, and went so far as to confect a few passionately Catholic verses to consolidate his reputation with them. In this way he fell in with a colleague in the art, Proinsias Dubh[1] Ó Dálaigh, from the seaboard of Clare, a member of a famous family of Gaelic poets, currently in the service of one of the chieftains of the proposed expedition. Years before, he had served the Butlers in Kilkenny. He remembered a great deal from those days.

Ó Dálaigh was as much a soldier as a poet: he was about fifty years old, a leathery sardonic wanderer, embittered by his life, but nonetheless flashing out with a kind of irrelevant gaiety at the most unexpected moments. When he talked to Munday he brought with him a friend, a small fat Ulster friar, who was ready to interpret. His narrative, in a *trattoria* looking out onto the Piazza Campo de'Fiori from behind a

---

[1] Black Francis.

breastwork of Chianti bottles and a steaming mound of *cannelloni*, was not strictly to Munday's purpose, as it involved no incrimination of modern-day suspects. But in itself it was interesting. Munday already knew something of John Bale and already he revered his memory: he was glad to find out more. This is what he was told. Or rather, what he would have been told if Brother Declan's laborious translation into a mixture of Latin and ungainly English had not here and there obscured the detailed meaning.

* * *

(i) *Poet Would Meet Poet*

> Great delight to the ragged-arsed Ó Dálaigh
> That a Saxon unsolicited should purchase his dinner for him.
> But greater delight that this same young Saxon is a galliard lover
> Of blessed Muire[1], sweet milk-giving Cow of the Ocean.

Two couplets, alliterative, assonantal, as my share for the feast's reckoning!

Tell this poet – if he can remember them and repeat them to himself and his friends – they are worth a deal more than brass money: Ó Dálaigh does not make his verses for everyone.

So he asks me about a poet: *Bale*, he says, an English poet . . . Hard to answer. Oh indeed, I knew the man, I was in Cianneach's-church[2] when he came there, in Cianneach's-church when he *went*: but I knew him as a bishop, or *supposed* bishop anyway, I knew him as a beastly governor, I knew him as a roaring fool. Poet? Sure, somebody told me so: and do you know, I took a notion to enquire. Would your young man here, Brother Deaglán, find the circumstance of interest? God knows who'd find anything at all of any interest in that lamentable piece of history: but there, isn't it the English history as well as our own, so perhaps it deserves his hearing.

There was a trouble in Cianneach's-church, trouble of bloodshed, trouble of hatred, I had exulted in it – being an unruly young soldier – for a little bit too long. My bowels rose against it at last; I had to consider, as a good Christian, maybe it was time for a peace-making? Now I knew, we all knew, that this bishop was the one cause of the trouble. And as far as I could tell, he had not talked with a Gaelic

---

[1] Mary (the Virgin).
[2] *Cill Chainnigh* (Kilkenny).

Irishman all the time he had been on our island. Language, of course;
it was not easy for him: but some of us had a little English, some of us
were otherwise very adequately learned. While he was most *dreadfully*
learned (after the English fashion), and also they called him poet. So
maybe there was a chance myself and himself could find a few words
between us, upon that ground if no other. If you like, the same class of
words you and I are now having, young man: except that you and I
share the religion, and he did not . . . Which was a difficulty; but if
need be, I was happy (for perhaps an hour) to accept him as a
lord-bishop.

So I put on my best embroidered soldier's long-shirt, my red-and-
gold jacket, a pair of speckled trews newly-washed, very carefully I
combed my hair, and I brought no weapons with me but only sword
and a sling of pistols – I did not want him thinking I was come to him
to quarrel. I was sure he was persuaded all we gentlemen of the
kern-band lived for nothing but hard quarrelling.

I should tell you, a day or two previously there had been proclamation of the new Queen of the English, a woman that *did* share the
religion. Which laid open the Bishop of the late King to heavy peril,
you would suppose. However, he had turned it around upon all of us,
to our angry surprise, with a monstrous great zest of bravery; crying at
the cross for obedience to the Queen, praying at the high-church for
the safety of the Queen, and then – to complete his boast with a
topmost brag, quite lunatic – he made an acted play out of his own
surly poetry and the English-Irish bloody gentry-boys performed it in
the street! In passing, let me tell you, he seems to have argued,
through the course of its rhetoric, that Holy Father the Pope is
Unholiness the Devil-of-Hell and any that think different are born fools
from their very font-water . . . Fools or blackguards. He had his say.

Seems to have argued. I speak carefully, because the play was all in
English and I myself saw no more than the start of it. For all I know it
may have been made of a strong-boned decisive poetry to take hold of
the beard's hair and lift it straight away from the face. But there was
none in Cainneach's-church to judge it. They either hated it or (if they
were inside-outside dodgers, of the English-Irish town-people) they
clenched teeth and endured it. I took one look at the posturings, said,
"God run away with this coarse English culture," and went down with
my own poems (my satires upon this bishop's doings) to some friends
in a shebeen, with music.

I could have done the man more justice: I wonder would *I* have the courage to give *my* poems out aloud in a foemen's town? The occasion has never arisen. And besides, to sing poems – maybe only to a few – is always an easier matter, and a sight less courageous, then setting yourself on a scaffold with a host of queer-dressed actors, any one of them able and ready to mis-speak, mis-sing, mis-walk, and toss all your year's work to the wind. Acted plays are no kind of a Gaelic custom, at all events. We are better off without them. Whoever has a gift for performance, they should tell their own tales and make their own jokes, and not try to pretend they are other persons than they are. That way they won't get *taken* by the spirits of the long-dead, and I mean it sincerely: we are altogether too close to the dead as it is, let them not come into our skin.

Which is to say, this Saxon poet was brave that day in several directions, and I thought it over afterwards, and went up to his bishop-house to speak with him from that understanding.

Of course they'd not let me in at the front. As I told you, there'd been bloodshed, he had a guard on his gate – a sorry pair of dogface matchlock-men from the city train-band, English-Irish, very low. But it was no game of mine to argue with them just then. I knew a fine barefoot girl of the Ó Braonáin people who helped keep the bishop-house kitchen, and I knew how to get her to fetch me in at window: which she did, around sunset. I spent a moment or two – or an hour or two – with her (I had to justify my employment of her), until, it being dark night, I judged it time for her to lead me without candle up some steps, along some hallways, till I stood before a certain door. Through the keyhole I could see there was light in the room. So I kissed her and she slipped away then.

I went in: very deftly. It was his writing-room, he sat at a table with his back turned, he did not know I was there before I put hand round his mouth. He was in fear of course, so I encouraged him, laying my sword on a stool, unslinging my pistols. He did not call out.

I was always well able to keep, and command, silence.

*

Once he understood that all I wanted to do was to talk to him, poet-to-poet, he sat quiet and made no disturbance. Gael-poet to Saxon-poet? I preferred to think of it as Queen's-poet to King's-poet. My own work, as I used to put it, was for the "Queen of Heaven Herself and for the Queen of Ó Dálaigh's heart" (whoever *she* might be at any given time). As far as I could see, he composed for a

King-God only, and for the god-claiming blasphemy of the little King
of England – or rather, the King's *keepers* – who had sent him amongst
us to bishop himself so proudly.

I was enraged with my lack of forethought that I had brought no
interpreter. I had a fair comprehension of the English tongue when I
heard it, if not spoken too fast, and if the speaker were born in Ireland
(the English noise from England is greatly distracting to listen to). But
as for speaking it myself: well, I had some facility – more than I have
now, after Spain and Italy all these lost years (you'll notice I am so
discourteous as not to try talking English to *you*). Some facility, but
not enough; no, not for that occasion – serious business, *that* occasion;
men's lives, men's souls, were dependent on it very likely. And
women's moreover: which I'll come to later.

Oh I'll tell you, but Jesus knows I must have sounded like God's
own idiot in that bishop's enclosed little room, airless and damp.

He questioned me, very loud, very slow, making his English as one
would to a sick child – and I'll give it you in English so you'll see:

> "*You are a poet. In your own tongue? Because you say so? Can you prove? Of
> the Old Guise, no doubt?*"

I said, not *quite* understanding, but having nonetheless my own
notion what he meant by the 'Old Guise':

> "*I will not be making my verses of any guise, whatever. Ó Dálaigh does be his
> own poet, and that is truth. Ó Dálaigh does be telling the chief poets they are
> dead men, so: old-guise, not making new verses for my people. Sir: it is in my
> mind you yourself are making new. Making free, so: wouldn't you say? Oh this
> nation does be a war-camp, darts and axes all around us bloody bugger-up and
> fucking bollox. Sir, the people are after roaring for a fucking gate-open and a
> clear field and only for your damn Saxon words and prayers and books you're the
> man might give it us, so. But Mary-help, Christ-help! the way it is, we get from
> you your bloody wall-fence, more axes, goddam darts, swords, bows, guns,
> outside of ours to threat us inward: you go wrong, you go wide altogether, we will
> be thinking, so we will: Ó Dálaigh tells you truth whatever!*"

I could have orated like a chieftain's praise-poet (which I am not) all
the night to him, until sunrise: only I could see he had deaf ears. And
by God I knew the reason. Could I be blamed that my tottering
English had been learned from the English soldiermen, there were
words in it (had I but known them) that were out of all decorum for a
serious discourse? Fair play, you are laughing yourself. But *he* was

not. He thought surely I spoke to insult him, or the brain that I uttered from was as broken as the words, and as barbarous. How *should* he believe me a poet?

Had he chosen to *listen*, though, he might have detected in my speech some rudimentary sense, and even a poet's concept: if I'd been using the Gaelic I could have sung it to an air, if I'd had an air to sing it to. In short, all I wished to tell him was that Ó Dálaigh was not at all the sort of man to spurn any 'new guise', whether of poet's art, or priest's mystery, or lordship of the nations – *provided always* there was a decency about its intentions and its means of arrival. In his case, there had not been: but I did desire to tell him it was not too late to amend it; and if *he* so desired, I could help him. For let you know, I was heart-cramped with the arrogant foolishness of so many of our people at that time, the way they laid themselves open to every insidious class of criminal stroke and trickery, only because the man that practised it would be 'one of our own', and spewed his mouth against the English always. (By God, but to get yourself a reputation, it needs no more than the *mouth*. For the rest of a man's life-dealings, we the Irish are oblivious entirely).

I stumbled on, broken words, tottering English, saying a few more things. He grew impatient. Interrupted me.

"Poet? Don't lie to me, boy. You are a kern-soldier: look at your gear, hear your foul threatenings!"

Because I said the *goddam* twice or thrice too often, I suppose he concluded I was ferocious against him. Bad mistake, but mine entirely, not his. And I did not quite see it, there and then. I tried to explain:

"I am Proinsias Dubh Ó Dálaigh, kern-soldier, and why not? Will you come here till I tell you – I think the new guise may not be altogether crossroads from Blessed Saint Patrick, Saint Bridget, and all the old ones whatever – holy prayer on the mountains and in the glens and in the –"

I wanted him to understand that the first Christian word in Ireland had been a 'new guise' in those days; and if the High King's druids had fought against it, didn't we now know them to have been mistaken, narrow and padlock-souled? So exactly the same error very possibly with *ourselves*? But thinking me no more than what his prejudice saw in front of him, he could not hear me. Mind you, I was endeavouring to soften my manner, as I saw I had made a fault in courtesy: and so much he *did* hear. He said, not quite so sourly:

"You are a papist, my poor fellow, and shut up in your dark language. If a learned man were to teach you king's English, you could then read the Scriptures and comprehend. For in this book is all God's Truth: and it is my Truth that hath brought it to you. I must speak to the master of the college on your behalf. Are there others of your sort among the soldiery here?"

He held up a great book, which made me mad. I told him, very abruptly, that I had the Latin: I *knew* the book. And if I wanted it in another tongue, then 'king's English' would not be my choice:

"Are Christ and Saints so fuck-stupid they have never laid hold on the Gaelic? By God, if not them fuck-stupid, then you!"

He was so shocked, he just sat there gaping. At last:

"You are outrageous! Why did you come here?"

I said, because I admired him; because of his play, if nothing else.

I said also, because I had heard he was about to be called-out heretic by that new Queen of his (and it *was* well-proven later that she was fonder of heresy-trials than a vixen of poultry); but rather than fall frantic with terror for his predicament, he had put all of *us* into sudden danger by showing us up as seditious traitors and himself springing clear as the only loyal one in Cainneach's-church! Which was, I said, a powerful stroke and worthy of a cunning poet. As for his Truth, though . . . Well, we all would have preferred he had not tried to *force* it upon us. That way unhappily we'd only come to hate it, whereas, being such a cunning man, he might have given it us a little more *gradually*, with more *courtesy* perhaps, in our own language if that could have been possible, because how could he know we would not be glad in the end to welcome it? He would not take offence, then, if a sincere fellow-poet was thus to hint at his small fault in cunning? It was well-known, in our common calling, that a neat fraternal criticism could be accepted easily without dishonour, and it would not surely be another '*outrageous*' if I suggested a glass of usquebaugh, one poet to another as – as a pair of –

I was about to say 'friends', believe me I was indeed about to say so, I had gone so far; being more careful than before with my words – I don't think I'd included so much of the *foul*, no, not this time around. And I do think he caught my intent, oh to be sure I think he did.

He said, half to himself, with a bark of an angry laugh:

"Begging for drink, are we? Hah, I thought it'd come to that before long."

He said too, precise and chill, but his eyes were very hot:

> *"Young man, you are badly mistaken if you believe for one short minute that I am to be wheedled and whinged at in pursuit of this fantasy of yours. The Ersemen's language is a savage language, quite unfit for our nowadays Truth. God knows you'll take it hard that I say so: but I tell you I speak advisedly, I speak with scholarship. For we in England had our own savage tongues: the likes of Langland and Chaucer made them civil for us, the like of Wycliffe brought divinity into them."*

It's a fact, I did not know the names of these, his Saxon poets: but I'm convinced he did not invoke them falsely. He spoke with scholarship. And went on so speaking, but angrier and angrier at every biting phrase. To be brief (for he was *not* brief, and much of his hard English ran away from my understanding), he informed me that the progress of intellect was more advanced in his language than in any other, even the Latin. And that the progress of intellect, the renewal of the True Gospel, and the general well-being of the human race throughout this world, all journeyed together inseparable like Christ-Risen and Disciples on the road to Emmaus. It was, he said, arrogant and atavistic nonsense for me to pretend my nation could have any part in this, so long as we rejected the plain reality of the case: no New Guise in Ireland without England to nurture it. For unless we enjoyed that nurture all our dreams must dissolve into sloth and confusion. How could they not, if we insisted upon living as our fathers had lived ten hundred years before?

> *"'All the old ones whatever – holy prayer on the mountains and in the glens . . .!' And the same, I make no doubt, goeth for your poets in equal case with your saints. God's mercy, boy, d'you tell me of Tradition? Traditional Caedmon, Traditional Taliesin the Welshman, would devour you and spit you out! Traditional King Alfred of poems and chronicle would make you his washpot like Moab!'*

He had quoted my own words back at me with such contemptuous malice I could have heaved up my sword and taken his great calf's-head off: indeed, I had my hand out for it.

But I saw at that moment he had no mind to insult me. His thoughts were far beyond my insignificant presence in his room. His face upturned toward the ceiling, his Bible-book waved up along with it – the man was crying to his God. And Ó Dálaigh caught most of his cry: and Ó Dálaigh was long to remember it:

"Lord, Lord, Thou knowest, Lord Christ, that in Thy service I have given all and they cast it backward against me as a stubborn she-ass that lifteth her tail and staleth along the wind! No, never for this generation of ignoramous aliens, never for these Irish Thy handfasted Eternal Truth: I preached not for their heedless ears, nor did I show my plays for the enlightenment of their scab-shotten minds. But only as a Sign; to pluck me-ward their rancid malignance into yet further outbreaks of fury, so that when they drive me out it shall never be said, never, by envious detractors, that Bale's own weakness in Kilkenny was his ruin. O God, didst Thou not strive to harden Pharaoh's heart against Thy Chosen, that his chastisement by Thy vengeance be therefore all the greater, and for Moses Thy servant the greater glory therewithal? So be it, Lord, with me and these . . ."

So you see how it was. He had *intended* the trouble – he had *intended* the shed blood: for his own 'greater glory' and our unfortunate hurt. It took me a small while to gather the full drift of his speech. While I rolled it, incredulous, in and out of my understanding, it was slowly borne in on me we were no longer alone.

His red-haired woman was standing behind us, in her pleated white English-made night-gown, like a vision of the chalk-faced Morrígan[1]. He and I were both turned from the door, the shades upon his reading-candles cast a darkness away from the table; so how long she had stood there, I don't know. I guessed from the set of her tight painful lips she'd heard all the last part of what we'd said. Oh and he guessed it too. He shovelled his book under his oxter and whipped himself out at door as though the devil had come in to sweep him. You'd have thought he'd have had more shame than to leave his daughter's mother alone near midnight with a *wild Irisher* and sword-and-pistols, and her hair all abroad upon her bosom, shoulders, round bare arms. But I suspect he was too perturbed to do otherwise. I cannot think such behaviour would be usual for him.

Of her and me, and what we said then, and what I thought of it – better I should defer narrating it, until I've told you a number of matters germane to the whole business. You'll understand it better, so . . . Yes, and *he'd* have understood it better, had I only had the wit to talk to him in *Latin*. My torture, I was as stupid as I believed *he* was!

(ii) *Justification Of A Poet-Soldier*

Begin with what I said to the King's-poet about *my* poetry: "telling the chief poets they are dead men." Since I was twelve years old I'd had

---

[1] An ancient Irish Death-Goddess.

enough and more than enough of chief poets. Because that was the age when they put me to the Poets' School, on the Hill of the White Brow[1], and I'm as angry at them all as though it were yesterday. This School was an inheritance of the Ó Dálaighs: the master-poet was my father's brother; it was held an appropriate course to have me into it as a boy, to learn the art and take my status as so many of my kin had done throughout time without memory. Although *my* memory, half-trained, was never able to assimilate the needful genealogy, nor can it now, if you bought me three dinners. Besides, the kin of the Gael is of no interest to the English, so I will not weary you.

Poet's description of the Poets' School; I give it you in the approved style. Which means I have to chant it, though I happen not have my harp:

The student poets convened under the presidency of my uncle in a rough, scrubby, leaky-thatch enclosure, well-planted outside the cabins with the bunched and grasping whitethorn, overlooking a muddy tidewater inlet where seals swam, between two townlands – the Place of Behan's People,[2] the Head of the Sea[3] – themselves half-thrust into the sea by the spreading knees of the hill-table we called Stoney[4], lovely summit broad-cast with flowers, swarming with song-birds, flowing with watersprings no less musical than the birds, and all a-frown among its corrugations of sharp rock like my uncle's censorious brow. Behind our enclosure on its promontory was huge extent of a wide bay, sunset-shimmering, fish-teeming, ship-sail-freckled; but English-haunted upon its northern strand, where they mis-title their cold city as 'Galway' (coarse corruption of its true name, name of a lovely woman who drowned in the river there once when none but Irish lived in the land).[5] We were all taught to hate that city.

For if we walked but a few paces from the narrow doorways (voiding rheumy turfsmoke) of the huts of our labour, we could see its turret walls where the bright light broke jewels of infinite refraction from the carved stonework, after rain the distant town gleamed white as ivory in our sight, and my uncle would be telling me, "Sister's son, in that wasp-nest, as it clings to the armpit of ocean, neither O nor Mac of the noble Irish is permitted to walk: no poet receives gold rings, no master craftsman of an ancient race gains welcome for his skill."

That will do, for description. Now for a judgement.

*

[1] *Finnabhair* (Finnavarra).
[2] *Baile Uí Bheacháin* (Ballyvaughan).
[3] *Cinn Mhara* (Kinvara).
[4] *an Boirinn* (the Burren).
[5] *Gaillimh*.

My uncle's judgement upon the English colony-city was in fact the only judgement ever given to us to bestow upon any of the rulers of our island, be they Saxon or Gael: either they had-in poets to praise them and receive reward, or they did not.

If they did, then we praised, and my uncle taught us how.

If not, then we reviled, and again we were taught the technique: in either case, as hard to the brain and memory as the whole duty of mankind under God's law. But once it was learned: to what purpose?

The sole cause, content, reason and expediency of our woven verses was to tell a good man he was better than good: to tell a bad man (provided he gave wage and status to poets) he was a good man: to tell a mean man (provided only that his purse was not empty to poets, however else it might be to the poor and pleading of his chieftainship), to tell *him* he was more generous than the generosity of Fionn, of whom it was said that if the trees' leaves were of silver and the sea's waves of gold, Fionn would have given them all away. To seek public dignity by creative *in*dignity: and I found myself too proud for it.

A specific occasion: at the age of sixteen. I took boat, upon a holy-day, across the bay, and made entry into Gaillimh. To test, for my own boyish adventure and curiosity, how strongly kept was this English rule about 'neither O nor Mac'. Be damned if it was kept at all: the town was full of country Irish, buying and selling and talking the language all up and down like jaybirds. I could clearly see, if our people were consistently to be expelled, the citizens there'd have no trade whatever. Though mind you, there was a grossness, a contempt, in the town's-people's dealing with us; and that too I could see, no less quickly. At all events, I prowled around, and by the evening I had found a young woman, a gaudy Blake she was; *Mistress-Maiden* Philadelphia Blake, English-Irish of very good family, exciting herself beyond all measure by taking drink with long-haired Gaels of good family or of none, and then taking them brisk to her bed: which she did indeed with me (and thereby saved me from the curfew – for that part of the colony's rules was certainly most strictly adhered to).

Before I left her I had made her a song, one of my best, because *she* had been the very best (and little in my life after has contradicted my inexperienced amorous estimate). I sang the song, back at the White Brow, for our preceptors to mark to my account. Like a young apprentice-fool I left her name in it unaltered (and oh Jesus such a *known* name!), shouting itself aloud in the very first line –

Silver-ear-lobed Philadelphia Blake! for whom,
(As for the new moon in a March-tide storm-night's surgings and
    black-dark)
The hurling clouds make way at command of the pride of your
    brightness –
Do not forget Ó Dálaigh! Think how his homeward skiff
Shall swim south from you, rocking, quaking, like his heart –

And so forth. They did *not* share my good opinion of the song. Nor
could they find fault with it, in metre or metaphor. But by Christ's
wine they *rejected* it: and condemned me, moreover, to six months'
penalty of bread-and water – for daring to make verses of such a lovely
skill for 'a woman of bad character and she half-English'. . .

So there it was.

So I left the Poets' School, being no more than half a poet, and took
up the sword-and-dart of the short-contract kern, being no more than
half a fighter; earned my bread and meat by warfare, and made poems
for my own happiness – 'Queen's-poems', yes?

No shame to Ó Dálaigh to kill men for my chieftain's gifts, for the
sword is honest: he that wields it can as easily be killed himself. And if
the cause of the warfare should turn out to be unjust, why then, did I
not always specify in my contract that its terms would be thereby
broken, and I should hold myself free to transfer my widow-making
hand-strength to whomever offered a fairer reason for it?

It was thus that I found myself one of a band of free gentlemen-
fighters in the service of the de Buitléar kin – in origin, their name is
English, Butler – of Cainneach's-church, the town called for that saint
who went with Colmcille to bring Christ across the northern water to
Iona to the Pict-peoples, where they honour him still by the name of
Kenneth. (These disparities of language have to be explained: understand them, you understand my nation as your Bale never did, did
he?)

So how came I here so low as to cadge from a scholarly youth who
cares nothing for my degradation nor my aching distance from my
home? although he swears (and I believe him) that the lively hope now
bred in me out of my very poverty will also be *his* hope entirely:
restoration of ancient grace – whether of church or of freedom of life
for the land-inheriting Gael, not important – our cause is the same and
I love him. So tell him so, Brother Deaglán, in his own tongue . . .

*

You say, in the English that 'Bale' means 'harm'? No better signification: great pity I did not know it at the time, oh conceive what a
poem was thus lost to Ó Dálaigh through ignorance. Perhaps not too
late, I can make one even yet, a poem of memory to call tears from the
eyes of the wild geese in their wanderings, tears of laughter that such a
blockhead should have lost them their own sweet land and walled up
against them the gate of their homestead enclosure.

For we called him *Balla*, which, tell him, Brother, tell him, is the
Irish word for a *wall*: hard, blind, unyielding, to keep men out, to
keep men in, until determined as to their ownership by clerks' pens in
fearsome books, and the heart's death of death's head judges.

Seánín an Balla . . . oh, Johnny the Wall . . .

When I say I served the de Buitléars, let him not understand that I
did so in despite of the liberty of my own people: true, these Ormond
lords were three parts English, arguing always with the MacGearoid
chiefs – Fitzgeralds, you understand, the 'Geraldines' of Kildare – as
to which of their foreign name should in the end be kings of all
Ireland. But they had also the good Gaelic tongue; and their women as
often as not were reared among the grass-heaped beds of the clans-
men, not from slated English box-houses where all love would be shut
in and the snow-breasted truth of beauty did not dare to spring forth to
the spring moonrise.

It was honourable service. The more so as I was no galloglass to
march and drill under day-wage orders. I'll agree that the galloglass
are in our day for the most part true Irish (though the name does
denote they were once all recruited foreign): but of a very coarse
culture, slavery and labourage like as not among their ancestors, while
the de Builtléar kern-companies were all listed from free gentlemen,
or have I said so already?

Oh and I'll agree that there were Englishmen in the de Buitléar
service: but who took any heed of *them*? It was only to satisfy the King
of England they were there at all. In a well-conducted war they would
all of them have run away surely, to leave the honour of the de Buitléar
house in the hands of the true people. No, I'll not deny my service:
though I do not think today so easy an accommodation would be
possible for an Irish sword-hirer; today we must look far more nearly
to the inner reasons behind the mustering and marching of men. As I
have learned to my cost: or else why am I here?

*

But, at that time were we fools? Did we not see what the English were up to? How could we, when we never thought it would ever be possible they should make such effort to conquer all Ireland?

For a chieftain of the west to submit to the English king had never been a deed of consequence: they all did it and all forgot it. For a MacGearoid or a de Buitléar to take an earldom from that king and then pretend to control the land on his behalf was a poet's fiction, no more. If it was de Buitléar land or MacGearoid, well enough, they had a right to it: if they could impose themselves on other chieftains, well enough too, they had the power for it – but that they did it for the King of England; fair play, they believed it in England, but we knew better.

And the same tale with the church. From time to time the English bishops put their monks into Ireland when they saw that our Irish monks took no notice of their orders, and they had a need to be obeyed by *somebody*. But who gave a damn for any bishop? Every clan had its monks and friars, their priors and abbots were chiefs' kinsmen, with their sons to sustain the monasteries after their death: no harm for a monk to have sons, no harm for a chieftain to have his subordinate bed-women, it was custom of the people and neither God nor the clan's wealth took damage from it. How should they, when the strength of kinship was thus continually increased?

But at the time when I went to Cainneach's-church there was a great cloud of change came over the nations, hiding the hilltops little by little: until suddenly not even the white cabins on the lower slopes could be spied through the folds of mist.

In Cainnech's-church there was no great de Buitléar: he was in London learning Englishness from the King, and with him his young kinsman Mac Giolla Pádraig. Therefore we of the contract-soldiers served a hole in the mist instead of a chief: the only man to give us command was a lesser de Buitléar, Lord Mountgarret, and by God he was a simple soul.

He would sooner have his kerns into his hall to dance and pipe than to draw cattle from an enemy forest to make himself rich. If we asked him 'when do we take booty?', he would reply, 'wait for the Earl', by which he meant his chief: these English titles were the death of us.

All this while the Cainneach's-church townsmen were lifting themselves higher and higher and talking their English louder and louder: you would think it was Londonmen they were, the clip of their short haircuts and their legs in woven stockings and little swords sticking out behind them no weightier than a botcher's needle.

(iii) *Johnny-the-Wall Makes Things Regular*

Until, upon no warning, in the weeping thaw at the end of black winter, comes this Wall out of the thickened fog. A chunk of stone and limed mortar heaved into the town on a litter, God save us he was a sick man, and yet from his swaying bed as they lifted him up the slope to the bishop's house we saw him thrust out his head all tangled beard and bloodshot eyes, and his first words, oh the Virgin! (I won't trouble you again with his English): "This cannot be the cathedral close, it is a worse hovel-warren than Drury Lane."

One said to him then, he was in the Irish-town, had he reached Cainneach's-church by the other bridge he would have passed through the English-town, and so seen the city's splendour. To which he answered: "Why was I not told the King's rebels had their own town, and God's high church inside it? In Southampton I was used to the English Street and the French Street, but there in the olden time the French had been permitted, as an alien suppliant cluster, to make their own quarter for their own trade. But here it seems rule is reversed, we the English are made suppliant; intolerable: in the King's Ireland His Majesty cannot hold his own cathedral? but must leave it encompassed by these – these naked creatures from whose tongue such a flow of gibberish? I would have thought, without the walls was their own proper place!" – there being those thronging round him that did indeed put shame on the Gaelic race with outstretched hands of base mendicity.

I was approaching beside him with some two or three of my troop, I thought it courteous to drive the scruff of the country away and to lead him myself to his gate, but all he said to me was, "No no, not a penny just yet, have patience, rogue, distribution of alms at the fitting time and not before: let our pastoral responsibilities first be clearly regulated." From that instant I was done with him: but God help me I thought it was only his Englishness.

*

Then it was we began to hear tales of his behaviour on his way thither. Do you know they were as the stories of the drunken man from the fair through seven townlands, each with its dramshop to halt him, who cried out 'Good-night to you, so,' to a pillar-stone on a mound, and meeting a lively woman he untrussed himself to piss on her skirt? I have often heard such foolishness told of the Irish by the English when breaking their contemptuous humour – you'll have heard it yourself –

"Ho, Teague, come here a minute, will you listen to a new Irish joke, damn-your-eyes?" Well, the things they narrated of the Wall were an *English* joke the proportions of a stud-bull, and by God we knew them true, for there he was amongst us. With only this distinction, I do not think he was ever drunk. It was himself, in all sobriety, and twenty-four baronies laughed at him. Since then, there has been less laughter.

We had no notion at all he was first of a multitude.

Common knowledge, I won't deny it, that the English had changed their religion, though none could make out why. Some said it was to enable their king to change his wife: a good enough excuse for *him* surely? but no call to compel it upon others. Nor did they try, to begin with: or if they tried, they made damn certain to hide their efforts from devout people. Of course none of those English soldiers they sent over to call themselves Lord Deputy (why would they not simply cast lots every five years between de Buitléar and MacGearoid for the office: that's much how it always was, and what harm?) would have been so irresponsible to the needs of his work as to meddle between our priests and their prayers – although some of them, I have to say it, were great hands at the messing and meddling.

They had enough to do to get the people, even those that conceived themselves English, to obey the smallest rule out of London on such matters as taxes and landlordship, you'd have thought in all this world they'd not want to *add* to their problem. But they did, and more by token that during much of the year in question there was in the Hurdle-ford[1] no Lord Deputy: I'd say he'd been appointed but had not yet had the leisure to assemble his gear for the journey. Which left, I suppose, a fair crowd of clerks and officers hanging fire and in want of employment, a few bishops in warm lodgings on the banks of the Black Pool[2] hoping and trusting they'd not be disturbed: that was the King's Irish government and good luck to it, we all said.

By and large it was a quiet time, only for some rural rapine, a little augmented by the last year's bad harvest. Most days myself and my fellows would be out on patrol, hunting marauders and absorbing their prey; I remember a gold chain and two brace of new pistols that came to my kitbag out of that winter's work.

*

[1] *Baile Átha Cliath* (Dublin).
[2] *Dubhlinn* (Dublin – an alternative name).

To begin with, the Wall landed at the Bank of the Haunch[1], to take his way straight to the Hurdle-ford, to be bishoped by such bishops as were there: one bishop makes another, as you know; and however bad the bishop, the blessed virtue is in his hands regardless, having come down from Christ's own hands. Apart from that, it seems to me, the best part of a bishop's duty should be to keep himself out of the world until his hands are in requisition: that way we'd have small trouble upon doctrine. Bishops' hands to continue the bishops and priests, priests' hands to continue the mass, and the Pope over all to ensure that the hands are laid always according to the proper prohibitions and spoken words. Beyond that, every gentleman to his own deeds: if they are idle deeds his enemies will let him know of it in short order.

Brother Deaglán shakes his head: but in truth, 'to love God and love your neighbour' is very little different from the thoughts I am after pronouncing. A gentleman that loves his neighbour finds his enemies become friends – some of them. A gentleman that loves God needs now and then a schooled cleric of appropriate lineage to put his love upon the right road of observance, which is to say, into the care of the Saints: who I take to be God's clan-captains with a keen eye to the laws of His hunting-forest and arable acreage: you would not, for example, go after the deer on Ó Súilleabháin land without a sure ghillie of the Ó Súilleabháins to guide you: and you would be less than prudent if the ghillie you chose was in ill-favour with his clan-captains. Any other course than that would be desperate discourtesy: why, it would put you in peril of feud, to the embarrassment of your own chief – who would surely have your blood even if the Ó Súilleabháins failed.

At the Bank of the Haunch there was trouble already. The Wall met in the street with a funeral of the Gael, and decided that the customary keening of the mourners that followed after was in some way an offence to his status. He made an outlandish ruction, and left them all with the idea that the Saints they invoked were blood-enemies of his own Saints; which they rightly thought no less offensive, whose town was he in anyway, that his English Saints wanted to conquer it?

After that he travelled north, and stopped a night at Causeway Hill[2]. The priest was hospitable, and the priest's wife cooked a great dinner for him. Would you believe the bloody man, now, cross-questioning the poor woman upon when and where the wedding had been held? Sure everyone knows a priest's wife can not be married in

[1] *Port Láirge* (Waterford).
[2] *Cnoc na Tóchair* (Knocktopher).

the normal form of the thing: and when the priest – to prove his lineage, as would any decent Irishman – explained he was the son of the prior of the white-friars in that place, this Wall almost split in sunder. Old Jericho town by comparison fluttered down like a last-year's rook's-nest. It turned out he had been himself some class of a white-friar: and moreover, it turned out that, desirous of a wife, he had thrown away his friar's gown! But not his priesthood, the virtues of his hands at Mass, because all know that that's unthrowable. And yet he had his bed-woman with him. He stood her up before the hearth and said to the Causeway Hill priest, "A married wife before God's altar, and so ought yours to be, and so had ought your mother! Now that I am Bishop, we will see these things made regular."

(iv) Non-Bishop-Making

The next stage of his journey should have brought him into Cainneach's-church. But he chose to ride right through the town without stopping, even to look at the place. He slept at an English garrison-tower a few miles beyond in the country. His reason? He had no 'authority' until he had been made bishop at the Black Pool: and he was sure he'd be so disgusted by what he'd see, he would not be able to brook it if he could not at once amend it.

And then, when he got to the Black Pool . . . you could call it discourtesy there, you could certainly call it desperate: I am not at all sure it did not discredit entirely any pretensions he later made to be a regular bishop at all. And he so stout a man for regularity at every turn!

For a bishop must be made in accordance with traditional form, the hands, the spoken words, or not at all. Just as a chief poet is made by his submission to other chief poets of certain verses in prescribed metres, upon traditional matter, with prescribed references, similes, ancestral allusions. I have said I do not hold with our chief poets and their instruction, which I know – being a free poet – will do nothing but cripple the soul. So therefore it would not surprise me there should be those that say the same of bishops. But if they do, they should call themselves *free* Christians and avoid all use of bishops or churches or priests or anything else that coheres to what has been always done. Brother Deaglán, dear man, hold your peace, I'm not finished.

For then comes the question: *can* a Christian be 'free'? Is not that the serpent's question to Adam and Eve? On such a business I am ignorant: and also I do not dare. I am a soldier but I do not dare. Whereas no-one went to hell for the making of irregular verses. There is *that* much of a difference between bishops and chief poets. The power of our old druids has been divided, do you see. They were poets and they were bishops (at least, a class of pagan bishop) at one and the same time. Thanks be to God, not any more. Some of them, by the early Saints, were made bishops and saints themselves. Others remained simply poets. And the strongest powers did not go with the poets.

But leaving poets out of this: the Wall, more like a Bastion, or a Buttress – no, a Blockhouse – stood himself forward amongst his fellow-bishops as refractory as could be, and *refused* the traditional form!

He had come into Ireland with a new King's Book of English Prayer, by which alone he'd be bishop or die. And in it all the words were changed. And changed a deal further than mere bringing them out of the Latin.

He also refused the crozier, and demanded instead to be handed another book, God's Bible, in English again. There was argument in the Christ Church for the whole morning until evening, and still he stood his ground. At last, in despair, they gabbled out his words of English and gave him his book, and slapped on their hands, and told him he was bishop indeed.

Now I know he was not: and *they* must have known it, and – let me tell you what I think – I think that *he* knew it. A sacred rite of God's own ordering? I have seen cattle on a fair-green haggled over with more ceremony . . .

*

And yet, after all that, back to his diocese upon the roar, maintaining, complaining, proclaiming his hoarse orders: *of course* he was no 'free Christian' because (according to his own account) he was as bishoped a bishop as any between Constantinople and Rome. My opinion: he knew well he was no bishop-of-God but bishop-of-the-King, which meant the English soldiers if the Irish did not obey him. My opinion, he preferred it that way.

One strange thing from this bishop-making (or non-bishop-making), which I tell you for your English thought: I know Brother Deaglán's already. There were two in the Christ Church to have the hands laid on them that day, the Wall himself, and a man that did claim to be Bishop of Lady Macha's Height[1] – I should say Archbishop, for Macha's Height is the head-church of all Ireland as ordained by holy Pádraig[2]. Now to Macha's Height already the Pope had given us a good man, a Gael of Albain[3] over the water, but the English despited him, and sent forward this false claimant. So however sure his hand-laying, such a one would never be bishop, or never in Macha's Height: perhaps in spirit he would have the powers, but not in any *place*, until a fit see was found for him, which must be done by the Pope of course.

And he knew that, and they all knew it: and he was afraid to his heart of this English book the Wall put before him. For under terms of that book the Pope would never accept him bishop, nor would any heedful priest: and if no priest, then no layman either. But in the end, after all the hours of contention and malfunction and crimination and deprecation in chapter-house, nave and chancel (which he sat through in a soft silence, daring neither black word nor pale), he shook his lips, he twisted his back, as though without speech to tell them, "This Wall is too high for the likes of myself to clamber, I will do as he desires and hold still where he stands." And he took that same book and said to them, low-voiced, wearily: "With this book make me a bishop," so they did.

He went home to his house and he died.

His house at the Hurdle-ford, of course, not upon Macha's Height: by God the Gaels of Ulaidh[4] had no hardship in keeping him out. More power to them, says Brother Deaglán, they're uncomfortable men entirely.

*

Do we say that his death was God's Judgement? Many in Ireland would agree: and in Rome they would agree. Good. But how came it that the Wall did not die?

When he passed toward Cainneach's-church such a sickness was upon him that every inch of his skin was one blotch and where there were two boils on the Macha's Height man there were three upon this Wall, where the Macha's Height man had five shudders this Wall had

---

[1] *Árd Macha* (Armagh).
[2] Patrick.
[3] Scotland.
[4] Ulster.

five-and-twenty, for every drop of red sweat from the pores of the
Macha's Height man this Wall oozed a jugful-and-a-half. And yet he
lived. And yet, after one night in his Cainneach's-church bishop-
house, he announced himself cured, as by miracle: and went straight
into his high chancel to preach.

The first thing he preached was that he and the dead Macha's
Height man had eaten poison from the hands of the priests of the
Hurdle-ford: and God had preserved *him* for having shown not a
tremor of cowardice, whereas the Macha's Height man had agreed to
the King's book out of cowardice alone, and so died from it.

That was his tale. Brother Deaglán will explain it: he will say that
Macha's Height, being the soul and heart of Éire (and also an
unconquered stronghold of the Gael) hides in the very stones of its
holy hill God's Judgement to be always unleashed upon those who
insult it. He will remind you how, in pagan days, the woman Macha
(whom they called Goddess, being ignorant: or rather, being better
poets than any alive today) was insulted in that place and spread her
curse over it so strongly that only the hero CúChulainn was able to
withstand the creep of its debilitation. By the same token, says
Brother Deaglán, Cainneach's-church is a town that has yielded itself
to the 'Butlers', half-English: and is therefore a place deserving of all
forms of that oppression which the men of the north have rejected by
the force of their own valour. And he *would* say that, wouldn't he,
himself being a northern man? By his view, to Cainneach's-church
was the Wall sent as a sharp thorn – after justly receiving a sharp thorn
in his own flesh (through his illness) – it is a matter for God's wager,
which will surrender first, under pressure of the thorns: the corrupted
town, or the bawling bishop? When God sees the result, then He
knows where His Judgement has been cast.

Well, Brother, fair play. If you are right, then I am paid for it.
Maybe in the heel of the hunt, you *are* right, for look at me now . . .

But there is, too, another opinion. I think the Macha's Height man
was indeed given poison, not by any of our priests, but by the Wall, in
order to show the other bishops, and through them the King in
London, that it was high time they sent over a Lord Deputy with
sufficient soldiers to keep Cainneach's-church safe for his bishoping
until all his work there should be done. He himself was after taking a
small portion of the same poison, to enhance his plausibility.

What's wrong with that? I'll tell you what's right about it: it lifts
away from the Cainneach's-church kern-bands any hint of imputed

scorn that their service under de Buitléar was improper, and it fits easily the English habit of persuading the Irish by hidden terror. Because already the Wall had the hidden terror of the English troops clasped into his Bible-book: why would he not let it out in terms of deadly-nightshade crushed between a handful of cress – or whatever was the exact means of putting death into a bowl of broth? Make your choice.

(v) Work Of The Wall

But if you do take my opinion, then you will ask yourself this: what should have been this 'work' that the Wall must fulfil in Cainneach's-church? Easy to say, he must assert more strongly the rule of the English King. That might have been done, and a damn sight better done, by accommodating all his business to the desires of the Irish people, and making himself a lovely man, as holy Padráig (also from over the water) once did ten hundred years ago.

If he saw such a course before him, he refused it of set purpose. So, the purpose of his purpose, on assumption he was not stark mad? I have thought about it these twenty-six years, since that night I crept into his house: and the sum of my mind-harrowing I have compressed into a short verse. Let you hear it now and turn it over.

> For the English, as for the Irish, their own freedom is the jewel of life.
> But who can be free that are bound to the wishes of others?
> And who can be free that have others fast-bound to their wish?
> Therefore, for the Irish, no freedom with the English amongst us.
> Therefore, for the English, no freedom until the Irish are free.
> If the English, knowing this, say to the Irish: 'Be free,'
> And then say further, 'Your freedom shall be a free gift from my hand',
> What do they do but bind Irish even closer into English rope?
> Freedom given from the one place becomes slavery in the other
> Enforcing a gratitude, enforcing a subservience,
> Enforcing the low bow, the hand to the forehead, the lordship-acceptance
> And so must return as a new slavery to those that gave it.
> Freedom can not be given: only taken, because the taking
> Is in itself freedom, without which no freedom
> (Neither of choice, nor of self-contentment,
> Nor of ability from strength experienced).
> Jewel of life being your own life:
> Give it away, you must needs be dead.

Why, yes, I do believe he came to Ireland *to do us good*.

Therefore he *was* good: and all that he saw that he did not understand must be bad of course and fit to be changed. And if bad, then of the Devil.

So to threaten us with English soldiers was to the Wall no more of a cruelty than to threaten the Devil with pains of hell, and what else did God do when He kicked him out of heaven? So the Wall's purpose was to make himself God. All he forgot was, we might not permit it.

Now, never before had any Englishmen come to Ireland with so purposeful a purpose. All they wanted, in past time, was a thirty-two-teethbite of Irish land, they were robbers and we met them as robbers, having among our own clans the same class of experience: and we understood them and they understood us, so in consequence we fought as equals. Sometimes as equal soldiers, always equal for crude intention: snatch or clutch, no difference in spirit at all. And before them, sea-rovers of the Lochlannach[1]; and before them, some vain attempt by the Romans; and before them all the tribes of the Gael (which is to say, the sons of Mileadh of Spain): and before them, Lady Danu's Nations[2] and the Men of the Womb-bags[3] – ever the same, snatch-and-clutch, clutch-and-snatch, and fight battles a short space: and then once again peace. The invader in your daughter's bed and your grandchildren half-his and half-yours. Which is hard, but I'd say natural. Look at the English, you've had it too: what about Uilliam Concaire[4]?

                    *   *   *

At this point Proinsias Dubh digressed into a lengthy analysis of racial origins, Jewish, Trojan, Greek, Spanish, North African and British; as well as Irish. Despite his reservations toward the curriculum of the Poets' School in his youth, he had clearly remembered a vast amount of what he had been told concerning his ancestors and everyone else's. Munday was interested, from a personal point of view (he himself would have much appreciated having reputable ancestors to boast about, and some of the Irishman's excursus seemed to offer him clues as to how to find them), but it had very little to do with Bale: and at last he ventured to hint as much. Brother Declan was all apologies, explaining that a poet's kin-listings were a terrible hard thing to interrupt. But he smoothed the implied discourtesy, passing the hint in Irish to Proinsias Dubh, who immediately changed his tack.

[1] Scandinavians.
[2] *Tuatha Dé Danaan.*
[3] *FirBolg.*
[4] William the Conqueror.

(vi) *More About The Work Of The Wall*
Brother Deaglán tips me the wink. Young sir, my full regrets: no
propriety in thus displaying curious lineage to a fatigued Londonman,
when all those in his island of the true old British blood are beyond
now in An Bhreatain Bheag[1] and a different nation entirely. Let us
return to this hod-handed Wall and his overpowering self-
construction. We spoke of invaders and fighting against invaders?

But to fight against a robber who comes for your own advantage,
most *un*natural and harder than hard.

And since the Wall, that's how they *all* come: since the Wall we
must find a way of repelling them that is not the old way. Since the
Wall I have determined I shall not return to my people until that way is
made clear to me. Would you say that Spain and the Pope are a fit pair
of marking-posts to lead my feet onto it? For if not, I am a finished
man.

*

No difficulty for the Wall to find means to his purpose: we'll leave
aside the poisoning, for that is not proved. His tactic was four-fold.

First, by means of preaching. This did not trouble me for I never
went to hear preaching and certainly not in the English. At times the
grey-friars would come amongst us in our billets with a bottle of
usquebaugh and some good Gaelic words for our comfort: they would
hope to get a confession, and I daresay they did, for some of the kern
were not always very easy in their mind about manslaughters. You can
face a man's vengeance-feud far better if you know God has already
forgiven you. But whatever the Wall said from his pulpit to the
English-ears was sour enough and bitter for anyone. Sometimes the
church was empty – they refused to hear him – and then again it would
be fleabag-full – for they could not bear not to know what new
bristle-scalp sacrilege would be spewed from his mouth. He assailed
the Mass, the Mother of God, the Holy Pope, the priests' characters,
the Saints of Ireland, the true Archbishop of Macha's Height, and
every shape-and-form of devotion that was practised all over the land.

Second: his own devotions. Every prayer in his high church was out
of his English book, and every meaning of every prayer was of
England, not Christendom. No Mass but a sort of drinking-party and
the stuffing of throats with soft lumps of meaningless bread. No

[1] Wales

confessions. No prayers for the dead. He also had the Englished Bible-book chained up to the wall of the nave, and begged and blustered day-in day-out for the people to turn the pages and read it themselves. But because the priests told them the Devil lived in that book (so he did: for who translated it, if not another English Wall?), I think very few of them dared. I think to give people a falsified book is more terrible than false preaching. At least with a preacher you can take note of his voice; his working features; the ups and downs, the windmill-wavings, the diggings, the hackings and splittings of his hands and fingers: you know by those, can he be trusted. But in a book you see wisdom, as it appears, collected long since: the very sight of it creates some belief. No foolishness of our chief poets that they do not write their verses but compel them to memory, compel their pupils' memory likewise. You can credit what you remember, for you remember whence it came.

Third: his secret dealings with stone-masons, carpenters, tailors, whom he must have paid far more than is common, for they went against their own best wishes and pulled down for him the saints' statues, tore out the altar of God, put into the church a sordid table (as it might have been a dramshop bar), hung all the church with scrawled cloths of written English (texts out of his Bible mis-versions, and arrogance from the King's book) as though people went up into the House of God to read, rather than to tell beads to the Saints. He wore no proper vestments (being a bishop, so he claimed, but no priest): only a long black gown like a lawyer-man scheming how best to get at your fortune. So what was all this work but the one huge discourtesy to those put by the King under his charge? Think now: when an honest gentleman receives an insult, all uncalled-for, from where he should least expect it, what does he do? Go for his sword? Smite with his fist? Call back a return insult? Not at all: or not at first. Later, perhaps, very likely. But there and then he is thrown down upon himself, silent, unable to know north from south, for the startlement that is in it. And so with Cainneach's-church. The entire town was huddled against tree-trunks as though whipped there by unbeatable wind. You've seen birds on a day of storm that could make not an inch of headway. God knows that was just us.

And that being so, his fourth tactic came very neatly in for him. To cause, in Cainneach's-church, a new division of the people where already there was division enough. We had Gaelic against English, town against castle, streets against fields, young against old, rich against poor. Now he threw amongst us King's-Christ against God's-Christ, and – strange though it seems to speak it – he was not without friends for his King's-Christ. At first I could not see where he found them, his preachings and all the rest being so blatant.

It was all most distressing to the kern-band: we foresaw violence and were by no means clear which side of it we would be expected to espouse. Our chief was on the whole well-disposed to the English royal house (why else was he in England?), but we had had no message from him, nor had we heard he had abandoned his religion there (except perhaps as a strategical matter of form). We were enlisted to keep good order in his territories: surely that did not mean protecting disturbers of the peace, such as the Wall?

I was delegated by my comrades to speak for them, as their unofficial poet, to the chief's kinsman, Lord Mountgarret. This involved a certain delicacy: Mountgarret had his own poet, an Ó Heóghusa of the northern school, from above the Black Pig's Dyke, a pomposity of a man who thought he ought also to be praise-singer to the kern-band, and utterly refused recognition of *my* status – 'irregular', 'unqualified', 'without professional mandate', were the only sort of words he had for Ó Dálaigh. But by good luck this dreary speaking-trumpet was away in the Geraldine lands, spreading eulogies among the chiefs there, in pursuit of some doubtful de Buitléar policy of clan-alliance. So I found myself obstructed by no damfool protocol-quarrel.

(vii) *Lord Mountgarret Suggests*

Mountgarret – as always – was free-mannered, jocular, warm, friendly, confiding, a well-shaped handsome gentleman who shook my hand and then put drink into it, and I observed he had taken care to wear the Irish clothes for our talk together. We walked, by appointment, through the woods of the castle demesne, this being the proper thing for a Gaelic captain greeting his people: there should of course have been gorse and bracken upon a hillside, and red deer running the slopes above, but Cainneach's-church was a soft country, tilled arable among hedges, as they tell me it is in England: these woods were the next best thing. At least, we could rejoice in the birdsong, and the river running full was just below us.

I said to him, "Mountgarret, is there nothing to be done? Only yesterday I heard from a galloglass that this Wall had made a bargain with seven devils beyond the water: they gave him a long-legged woman upon condition he came into Ireland to catch every Irish soul into the slack of her placket and so bring us all down to hell. Now I am not so foolish as to believe these fellows' fears, there is no-one more scattered in his wits than a drunken galloglass: but if that's the class of talk, then surely something must be done?"

He kicked his toe against a tree-root and stubbed a mushroom into pulp. By which I knew there was a difficulty.

"Son of Art son of Colm son of Donal," says he (he was always exact in deploying the names of our lineage), "there is a difficulty. My kinsman the Earl is absent. Therefore there are some in the town who look more than at other times toward the English for all their favours – favour of trade, favour of law, favour of taxes, you well understand the creeping tendency of merchantmen? Now I suspect that those among them whose names bear the greatest weight –" he meant Ó Séa, the City-sovereign, he was too delicate to say so direct "– have in mind that an English bishop straight from the King will advance their hopes more strongly than an earl who is not here and a lord deputy who is not here. I doubt they have no other thought upon church-doctrine than you have or I have: their intention is to their ledgers, to their strong-boxes, that is all."

"At expense of all else?" I cried out. "Why, surely, Mountgarret, we can at once prove them wrong, so degraded a calculation! Let me go with the men of the kern-band and break open their shops and strong-boxes, tear every ledger, ransack every storehouse: make such rapine in Cainneach's-church that they will know for ever-after this bishop brings only grief to them and no increase of riches at all!"

He was working with a small dagger at the bark of a white birchtree, graving into it a black draft of the de Buitléar shield-badge (which is drinking-cups portrayed, they were cup-bearers – 'butlers' – to the English king when the English religion was still Christ's). I took this as a sign that he needed to assert his blood, but yet was not sure how: he reminded himself, you see, of the greatness of his birth, thereby hoping to enkindle his wisdom. But – as I have said – for all his good manners, he was a simple soul, a hole in the mist, and I looked for but little decision from him.

"Ah no," says he. "No . . . we have at present peace and quiet, and our chieftain in England is by way of a surety for it, a hostage there, if you take my meaning. Most desperate discourtesy to endanger him by ravage and ransack through the streets of his own town. You remember Tomás of the Geraldine?" I did indeed: that brave young chief, all

in his silk, his father being gaoled in London, made rebellion in
Ireland to sustain his name and honour and so concluded with such
butchery and blood. Nor did the old father survive. Ormond could be
dealt with no less curtly than a MacGearoid of Kildare: if that's what
king's government demanded. I began to see the difficulty.

"Do you see the difficulty?" says he. "Now in my opinion," says
he, "and clearing our mind always to the best interests of our absent
Earl my nephew." As he spoke (his voice down to a murmur, almost
he spoke to himself), we found it commenced to rain. As a free-
hearted Gaelic gentleman he did not at once move away to his castle,
but pulled his rug-mantle over his head and sat down in the lee of a
tree: I did likewise. Discourtesy to me, had he gone in-door, for it
would have seemed he thought me unfit for the weather and therefore
no use to the kern-band. Discourtesy to him, had I suggested shelter,
for I was his guest and as such it was not proper to make his
dispositions for him. Ah, in this Rome of exile we have none of these
pretty touches. And I do believe two Englishmen would have run
straight for the porch.

"The best interests of the Earl . . ." he says. "Let us say that at this
present the Earl has no knowledge, either in person or by trusted
deputy, of what goes on. Therefore he must be given it, and that is the
first thing. If indeed he is provided reason to believe that there is an
insult to himself and to his people from the behaviour of the Bishop,
then to be sure he will expect his people upon the place to make what
arrangements they think best, at the same time he can take his choice
of what, when, and how much, to put into the ear of the King: and so –
as it were – pre-empt any hard consequence? Would it not be a good
notion, now, for myself and one or two others, of plausible state and
maturity, to make a direct request to the Bishop, in all innocence, that
he offer a special Mass, at our expense, for – for what, do you
suppose?"

"Oh I cannot tell you that, Mountgarret, you'll have a Mass for your
own intention whatever, not my business to direct your worship."

"True for you, Proinsias Dubh: but it should not be just *any*
intention. Something upon which the Bishop will be bound surely to
fix his principles, or neglect them altogether. If you see a dart is after
fired at you, you move either to the east or the west: to stand upon your
own middle is to be sure of a hole in your pelt, always assuming your
enemy is a good shot. I think he is."

He meant, you see, to remind me of his own prowess with the

dart-hurling: at which no man of the kern-band could best him, we all knew that. He'd either make the Wall skip or fall down, but he had to be certain of his weapon. He flew the thought about in his brain for a few moments, while we both grew very wet: and then, with a grin, "The intention shall be, the good health of the King of the English! You'll have heard, Proinsias Dubh, that the unfortunate little fellow is none the better since his sickness last year? Now, there is no way the Bishop can deny some class of orison for him: by God but he'll be making his own, fearfully enough, I daresay, for what'll happen him if the King dies?

"Now the nature of *our* orison: the day of Naomh Anna[1] is upon us very shortly. Herself as Our Lady's Mother, Immaculate Conception and all the rest of it, we know already to be an abhorrence to this Wall. So we ask for a Mass, for the King, upon Anna's Day, and in honour of Anna. And we ask for it in all formality. And after that, each man's opinion as to whatever ought to follow . . ."

Ah, he seemed to think it was a fine intricate decisive plot. Well, it was not so: but it had to serve until time should show us a better.

*

The request to the Wall was made a few days later by Mountgarret and a King's Judge, a man of the name of Howth, English-Irish kin, and close acquaintance of the Cainneach's-church merchantmen. If the Wall refused Howth, then the merchantman-tribe might be split: but Howth was not so sharp as to see this. To him there was no reason why the King's Bishop should not be easy with him, the King's health was his first thought. For his second thought he had scarce a thought of what you might call the *theology*. Took it for granted, in the long run the Wall *must* believe in the same God that he did. I suppose he had been sleeping through the great part of the sermons. At all events he slept always upon the justice-bench, it was a notable joke.

The two of them rode to the bishop's-house in all full state, gold chains and gowns, and we of the kern ran beside them as escort. They were in with the Bishop the best part of an hour, while we threw dice and sang songs in the forecourt, and did our best to handle the handmaids on the laundry green. (I think the Wall was a strict husband of his episcopal revenue, he could have hired thrice the servants he did, maybe he was not used to lord's privilege, a base

---

[1] Saint Anne.

class of a man whatever, meagre). And when they came out – oh, Mountgarret had a laugh on him you could roast a blood-sausage at; while as for Howth, I have never seen a red-faced man turned so black and purple in so small a short time.

"I am accused of idolatry, accused of idolatry, that goat-beard canting bastard in there called me 'wicked' to my very face for my duty to the poor young boy in London and my duty to the Saints of Heaven." He was on his horse and away, clattering down the twisted lane without another word to any of us.

Mountgarret said: "Why, gentlemen, it is even worse than we thought. For now the word is come that the King is perhaps dead. So a Mass for his health must be changed to a Requiem, and where is the priest that will conduct it? Our Bishop has forbidden them all: but Mr Howth rides straightway to discharge them of their obedience. Oh God I do surely fear this must lead to ransack and ravage . . ."

(viii) *Ransack And Ravage*

To think back upon it now, the King's death, so soon thereafter, ought at once to have given us pause. We did not at first believe that any but Máire na nDólás[1] (or more bluntly, as we now call her, An Gadaí Máire[2]) could succeed him, and she being always religious, we looked of course for immediate Masses and the rebuilding of the holy altars. So no more talk of ransack but great drinking and fine hopeful poetry and priests so full of wine they danced to the whistle-and-bones at every street-corner.

But then came in more stories: that this Northumberland man that had guided the King was in train to make a different Queen, he was after marrying his small son to a girleen of the English the very minute they had hair on their groins; and she, it appeared, was more entitled to the Crown than Máire, though I cannot tell you how. But at the same time we heard also that in order to get acceptance from some English lords for this match, the Cailín Léannte[3] (as we called her: Sinéad or Jane was her christened name) should promise the Mass in all churches just as earnestly as Máire, so thereby the loss of Máire would be no loss to her religious friends.

[1] Mary of the Sorrows.
[2] The Thief Mary.
[3] The Learned Girl.

Soon it was brought to us, as true as if it had come to Fionn's thumb from the Salmon of Knowledge, that Sinéad was now Queen indeed: and all were to proclaim her and all were to make merry with every possible church-rejoicing, which was done, and the angry Bishop must endure it as best he could. His best was to scuttle off out of it, to his farmstead, north up the river: but more about that later. Because then came in a very different news – a very great lie indeed, but none knew how to receive it: all these shifts and strokes beyond in England had bred of course a weed-field of treacheries, and somehow between them all – so we were told – the Earl of Ormond was killed dead, and his young kinsman Mac Giolla Pádraig was likewise killed dead. If the new Queen knew the murderers she was not able to hang them, for her promises made to their kin.

At once, then, an end to the harps and dancing: time now for nothing but ransack, in which surely we of the kern-band were not to be the hindmost. I had out of it a silver helmet, a belt-knife with a boar's-tusk handle, and enough embroidered silk to make me a bright new long-shirt for parade. And never a thought as I wore it of unlucky Tomás MacGearoid. And never a word against it from Mountgarret or any other: I tell you there was bloody outrage among the loyal men of the de Buitléars in Cainneach's-church and in all the baronies there-about. In particular, you may imagine, the kern and galloglass of Mac Giolla Pádraig, who had their occupation in a wide range of the rural parts, and went so far as to set fire under a number of thatches, not so much for any feud against the people who dwelt there, but by token of 'a great smoke from the murdered chief's country that will pepper their nostrils in London', as one of them said to me.

This same man, a galloglass-bagpiper as stupid-happy with his doings as a pig in its own dung, told also how an Englishwoman had run down ordering his troop for help as they rode among the cabins at the foot of her husband's tower. She was wife to Matthew King, contract-captain of the Mac Giolla Pádraig service, gone to England some time before, to confer with his chief. He was of course of the English-Irish. And when in Ireland he would rule his farm and carry his own person as though his rank were the same as his name. And now his wife was after assault by a whole host of his farm-servants, who had broken into her tower and wrecked her gear, which she attempted all in terror to load onto carts, for Cainneach's-church, for safety. And in truth, those damned galloglass ought well to have protected her: her man's service was the same as their own. And they ought to have considered, if their chief was indeed dead in England, Captain King also must be in grave danger there.

But all they saw was, she was an Englishwoman: they pulled off the clothes from her back, and emptied her carts, and drove their axes into four of her house-servants, and so left her stripped to her shift and roaring between the cabins of the townland with the corpses around her feet. Which was neither good sense nor decency, and far more than Mountgarret or anyone else intended.

There was also a tale that the Geraldine were in process of making one of their clan a new King of all Ireland, and that this was supported from Ó Néill and Ó Domhnaill in the north: which, if true, had been a marvellous thing (but dangerous too, a MacGearoid was never likely to have continued obedience given him by the de Buitléar men, so we might look for mortal war). But at once, upon the hearing of it, an obnoxious tower of the Lord Deputy's direct command was encircled by the de Buitléar kern: and when the Englishmen inside it came out to say what they thought of us, nine of them were killed dead. I had some part in that myself, being altogether so youthful-foolish as to believe what I was told. Mind you, now, I do not apologise: a tower of the King's English is not at all the same thing as one held for Mac Giolla Pádraig, and I give oath there was no abuse of women there.

*

On the chance you are deciding that such affairs are mere Irish, and there can never be remission from them – had we not had the Wall as Bishop in Cainneach's-church, none of it need have happened at all. A good bishop would first not have offended us; second, he would have taken care to be in good odour with Mountgarret (and not only with the chief cheaters from among the city ledgermen); third, he would have called a council of Mountgarret and Ó Séa and Howth and his own elder priests the moment all these tales came slipping and sneaking through the fair-day crowds. There had been nothing but peace and quiet until he refused the Anna Mass.

True, if Mountgarret had had more wit than cleverness, there would have been no perilous words of 'each man's opinion as to whatever ought to follow'. But none should come to Ireland without he first knows how to understand the likes of Mountgarret: no easy lesson to learn.

It was strange to me that in those days of ransack none of the

kern-bands or other went for the Wall. He was saving his hay, or
attempting it (in the end he gave it over for the constant teem of rain),
and they did say he had a good guard of English upon his hayfields,
though I never heard of anyone travelling out there to see. Fact of the
matter, I daresay, he was known to all and sundry as a squalid man for
his house-arrangements, nothing but books and papers, and who'd
want to take booty of those? Which is proof that our distaste of him
still fell short of blood-anger, proof even that we did not know to our
own selves just why we were so angry. Ever the way with a troubled
people, so hurt that they cannot think straight. Only in Rome have I
been able to think.

But then, a new circumstance: and this time there *was* blood-anger.
Máire na nDólás in England turned all round on her supplanters,
Northumberland and the Cailín Léannta were tossed into dungeons,
those who had thrown their caps for them were on the run and
terrified. Mountgarret and all Cainneach's-church, Ó Séa as well, had
thrown caps: only the Wall was clear of it. He took advantage there
and then to walk on our heads.

Call him stupid, call him sour-hearted, call him wilfully ignorant:
but at core of the man, he had found a devil, and given it *our* name.
Which, at core of the man, gave him his bravery, so it did.

There are some that will die before they deny their God. These
churches of Rome are full of their monuments, and we all know the
marble ring-fort they call *Il Colosseo*.

But *I* say, to some men, denying a devil is as hard as to deny God:
and the Wall was one such. He *needed* his martyrdom, for his own
pride: he said so. I hope he didn't get it. I never heard . . .

(ix) *The Red-Headed Morrígan*

At the end of his plays, they say, his long-legged woman took the
scaffold and danced like a witch-demon.

Up till then, in the city, she had kept herself remarkably quiet: we
thought, for an English one, she had a sort of sensitivity. The
kitchen-girl I told you of – Gráinne, her name was – *she* said the Wall
himself was lordly, abrupt and cross-grained (though at times conde-
scending-avuncular) with his household: whereas his woman had no
pride at all. Except when it came to her music, which was of quality,
undeniable. Even though she spoke no Irish she would sing with the
servants and get the servants to sing to her. She would also get them to

speak to her, attempting to *learn* our language: a noteworthy circumstance, but doubtful to hear. Was she endeavouring to *inveigle* us?

And then, she went and danced. Incomprehensible altogether. Very few saw her do it, but the word ran quickly around. I heard it that evening in the shebeen.

I was savage with myself in there, and with my poetry, that I could make no better satire against the Wall than the one I was struggling to compose. I had wrecked myself keel-and-rudder on what to say about his child-breeding. He had a whole litter in England, we were told, but the maiden he brought to Ireland was so queer a little person, between six years and ten, impossible to say exactly, with a face on her like an old woman of sixty – and then again at other moments she would seem so young-unformed she had never been in the world at all. Had she walked out on us from a green hill of the Síde[1], we would have taken it as only natural. Far too easy (and so no poet-skill at all) just to mock at her as 'clodlet clod's-daughter', which for most of these English gets would be the fairest term of disfavour. No, to tell truth the Wall did procreate as a poet ought to procreate, and had I had such a girleen myself I would have wept for joy. And yet for sorrow also: she would not be a happy one.

It was thinking of her, and so of her mother, and so of her father when he was not being King's-bishop but was naked with his woman and loving her – thinking of that drove me up to his house direct that very night: and so I saw him and her together.

*

When I was left by him alone with her, I could think of no words. I picked up my weapons, trying to look as though I had no idea in the world of how they were used, trying to slide out of the room without scaring her. *She* was not my quarrel . To my surprise, she blocked my way. She had a smile on her face, a smile of a friend, I was face-to-face with a red-headed friend.

"*Grace Brennan let you in, I suppose*." She said that in English, and gave Gráinne's name in English. But then at once she was talking my own language, even worse than I could handle hers.

"You are Proinsias Dubh. Gráinne has said. Gráinne was in wrong. To allow you. Gráinne did not have ought. You are her lover. She loves. I do not rebuke her, so. You are a poet. To see *him*. You have

---

[1] Supernatural Otherworld.

seen. I am sorry. Now you are enemy of him. Enemy-poet, enemy-
Irish, enemy-religion. I am sorry. We had not wanted it."

I was puzzled about that smile of hers, d'you see? It was a friend's
smile, I had thought, but it never moved: nor did her eyes move. I had
thought they were looking into mine. In a sense, they were, but I
wondered did they see me? She was shocked altogether of course. But
she'd said, 'we'. Stumbling in her Gaelic, or . . . ?

I spoke to her, slowly, so she could understand me easily. I felt it
was more courteous to appear to have no difficulty with her version of
my language, so I did not try English.

"We . . . ?" I went straight past my own question unanswered:
"But you have the right of it, so; *he* is my enemy now. But not you.
You are *not* my quarrel, never shall be."

I was to a degree dazzled by her. She was by no means young, in
no way apparently amorous, other men's middle-aged bed-women
were not commonly my love-prey; indeed, having just parted from
Gráinne, I had no need at all of any such thing. It was a dazzlement, it
was not desire. I was rooted there, will you credit me? all but swearing
never to leave her service. We have a phrase, 'under bonds', a sort of
sacred enchantment, women in our old poems often put men under
these strange bonds. So Derdriu with Noisiu in the great tale of *The
Cattle-Raid*. But he did take her to wife: and in my case, with this one,
such a notion was for laughter entirely.

Good Sense said to me, "Go away from here. The King's-bishop has
knocked over the chess-board: nothing *she* can do to pick it up again."

And silly No-sense said, aloud to her out of my mouth, and in her
own tongue:

"Why did you dance?"

She answered me, dream-like, still staring straight through me:

*"I've heard already it's been taken as an insult to the people here, Grace told me
– I mean, Gráinne. She did not think it insult, but she knows me better than
most. I'd be glad if you'd not think so, neither. I danced for Jesus Saviour,
self-starved and devil-haunted, as He came out of that desert place. I danced
because John Bale through his art had brought Him out even as Bale, even as
Bale, even as John Bale had once brought me from devils and from privation
into a life of – into a life of – why, there was love when I most needed it, there was
safety when I most needed it, although devils were not dead, any more than terror
was dead. Tonight I am in terror, John Bale cannot deliver me, for he is the
cause of it."*

So he was, I had heard and seen how. She had taken up her life with one man, I daresay: now she found herself with another. To her horror and perplexity, they both had the same name, at least that's how Ó Dálaigh regarded it.

Also, to *my* horror, she was beginning to laugh, and it looked as though she'd not know how to stop.

"Dubh," she spluttered wildly, in her distressful Gaelic again, "O small man Dubh. Small man raven-hair. Small tom-cat of our Gráinne. That you are his enemy, so it must be, you are mine. Also so of all the English. His Bible-Christ no good here. I do not want it. I will not help it. I am sorry. He was poet and is not. He is finish. My dance, mine for him, finish of me: blacked me, darked me – how – ?" She lost her words and shot into English, still choking with that sob of a laugh:

"I tell you my last dance, danced for you, though you'll not believe me, it tainted me, insulted me with the insult it held for you. Now I can never know you. What shall I do?"

I said, "Lady, you should leave this country. Find your own again and live there happily in your beauty where none of us will need to hate you."

Then at last she was in control of herself: her voice took on a quiet formality, more or less.

"He came here because he said God had called him. I knew, I bloody knew, he'd mis-heard. We had hoped, and it wasn't possible. Never be possible, never again."

" 'We'? You'd say, him, and you? You say, he did be hoping?"

"Oh God, sir, his hope, whatever it might have been, over all those long years back, is no more to me now than one great question and no more trust."

She looked hard at me, truly *at* me this time, into my heart, she was trying to persuade *me*, if nobody else:

"I told his deacon, you know, it was the last dance: but could give no better reason than one I had – had dreamed. Tonight, though, I experienced, from his own mouth, the complete reason, exact. I am afraid my good song is quite dead."

Upon which, she sang, in English, about Ireland, to what I knew to be an Irish air. I did not know who had made the words. I was astonished that an English poet should have thought that way about us. If there are any such alive today, why do we not hear you? Or has your cold cruel *Madonna* Eilís[1], virgin-goddess of no religion, stifled your voices entirely? I remember so clearly the last brief lines of the song:

> *Good sir, pray I thee,*
> *For of saint charity,*
> *Come and dance with me*
> *In Ireland.*

She concluded with a queer little lovely dance-movement turning into a slow curtsey: she shook her head most mournfully, bidding me farewell, and her eyes bright with tears. I kissed her hand the way I'd seen a Frenchman that came once to visit Mountgarret and his lady. Oh God it was sad, and I did a damage to the poetry of it – my torture, but I hurt the poetry, catching my pistol-sling against a bench-end and all but falling higgledy-piggledy as I went out into the dark passage-way; looking back at her, I was, where she stood sharp upright on her long straight legs in the candle-lit room. I thought how the bastards had yelled and clawed at King's wife, and how that must not happen to this one.

'Friend' had been the wrong word, though. Perhaps not, had things been otherwise. But my first word was the right word.

Our old poets have informed us that the Morrígan would be seen hanging, hovering, spreading her bone-white arms and laughing with all her teeth, at nightfall above that field where on the morrow was doomed a great slaughter.

*

The first talk of death was the very next day, in Ruairi Óg's shebeen.

I went along with it, and why not? I had done what I could to avert it: to tell them the Wall had provoked them *in order* to have them drive him out was no sort of argument against it; rather the reverse. His behaviour gave us this choice: let him have his desire and return to England to tell them that the Irish were congenitally incorrigible, or let the English understand we were worse than incorrigible – *formidable*: yes!

Two of the galloglass-band informed me that some of the lads would be hearing a few words from some very holy priests in Ruairi Óg's, if I cared to bring a choice party of gentlemen-kern. We would all find it

---

[1] Elizabeth.

much to the purpose. As a rule I'd not have paid attention to any galloglass, on any matter out of the usual run of soldiers' business: they were meddlers and messers and best left alone. But on this occasion, when I knew what I now knew . . .

The priests were English-Irish, from the high-church above – all very high and devout, much accusation of Luther. I knew nothing about Luther, and I dared wager he too had never heard of the Irish. But the priests had him stuck in their throat and wanted only to stick him in ours: not appropriate. Then they gave us a new word, 'protestant', and told us that we were now 'catholic', where before we had always been Christian. Why in God's name should the name of His people be changed?

But at last came into the dramshop another sort of priest altogether, Brother Iarlaith of the Franciscans, a good fiery grey old man of the Connacht islands whom we loved, and he had the right of it for our fellows. I have always a warmth for these friars anyway, Brother Deaglán here is my chief friend in Rome, and my own saint-name of course is in honour of their founder. Brother Iarlaith did not trouble our head with Luther: but said it out, loud and clear, the Wall's purpose was none other than to pervert the English-Irish into turning their religion against the religion of the Gael, the better to lay hold on the little that was left of the clan-lands in the east and then in consequence all the lands of the north and west where till that day there were no English. But once, he said, the English-Irish had ridded themselves of the Mass then nothing would prevent them ridding the whole island of Gaelic life and making of it a new blank England, deserted of all its people, "to be filled up with thousands of English – all in hatred of the Gael (for they'll be taught we are devil-worshippers) – and as hungry as the freshwater pike. And do not tell me they are not hungry: such famishment in England that their ignorant rural people are suspended from church-towers like scarecrows for daring to demand bread from their lords!"

Which was a new thing to me: and persuasive beyond anything. I had always thought the English at home to be fat and juice-dripping as spitted goose. But in those days I was half-educated, and that's the truth. I did not even know that in England the Wall himself was a noted man for the defence of the poor against their oppressors; chieftains, ledger-men, prelates. Against prelates – or certain prelates

– upon the poignant ground that such men had often been foreigners, or appointed by foreigners for the benefit of foreign strong-boxes (one *big* strong-box of course, the Roman Pope's. I live in Rome. My religion is not so blind as to be totally unaware that there *are* certain greeds in this city). Well, as they say, keep a loyal hound-dog to guard your house and children, he'll merit all you give him by way of love and good-treatment; but never trust him not to run at night if your neighbour has sheep on his land. It was not only that a commonly-humane man such as the Wall was *allowed* out of doors by moonrise: he was damn well *let loose* there; the hidden snarl inside his blood leapt up at the chance! I blame his keepers more than him: but he was old enough and well-enough schooled to know better. Even the most favourite hound must be slain if he grows into a sheep-worrier. And very well Brother Iarlaith understood it.

"Don't leave this Wall alive," says he. "Murder," says he, "is a wicked sin to be sure: but self-preservation is a duty, not for ourselves but all our people. Naomh Peadair[1] of the Keys found Ananias and Sapphira with their fingers in the church strong-box all those years since in Jerusalem, and is it not the same tale here? Think of the death he put upon that bad couple out of his holy power!"

"Ah well now," says a doubtful galloglass, after all the strong cries for fierce action: "Isn't the bloody man too well-guarded? We don't want to go running ourselves into an ambush, d'you see what I mean?" (I stayed silent on the matter of Gráinne and the kitchen-window. I have my honour. Add to which, furious killers in a dark house will throw their murder into all whom they meet. I was young enough to think that it need not be so, if it happened in the open air). "After the affair of Captain King," went on the galloglass, "his wife and his castle, d'you know? these English will take good care to protect themselves with long guns, and devil a bit of ordnance do we have, by God they never let us near the gunpowder." (All nonsense, of course: most of them owned their own matchlocks. I suppose he meant cannon. But when was his like ever capable of handling a breaching-piece?) "Axes and darts and swords are all that's fit for *us poor hoors*, d'you see what I mean?"

We all despised him for his weakness: but nonetheless the de Buitléars' English soldier-troop *was* the better-armed, and I would not trust Mountgarret not to order them to fire upon us, if it came to so sharp an hour.

But at the cold end of the room, where he sat all this while with his hat over his eyes and a cup of buttermilk in his hand rather than usquebaugh, was a white-faced tight-mouthed pale-haired garnet-eyed English-Irish dwarf of a man with shoulders the breadth of a bucket-yoke and a neck you couldn't span with a waist-belt. A rancorous farming skinflint, with enough land to be called *squireen*, but he had it gripped from his own English-Irish in the neighbour-hood, and the Gaelic people had nothing against him: or not much. Even so, it was strange he was there, and now we found out why.

"I haven't too many words of your language," says he, going far to prove it with his brute pronunciations, "but for those that don't know me, I am Barnaby Bolger of the Field of the Waters." His Saxon blood had not prevented his owning a good Gaelic name, Ó Bolguidhir, which translates as *yellow belly*, let's excuse him for not boasting of it. He went on, "This damned Bishop has land tilled which he calls the church land, but by right it ought to be *my* land: and by God, boys, it *is* mine, and by God and by Christ I'm having it back, so I am. Is there a priest here can tell me, what right has a heretic to lay claim to *any* land even if they do call it the patrimony of the church?

"And if they do so call it," he roared, "doesn't it make his claim sheer blasphemy, what? what d'you say to it? holy fathers, what? Anyway, that's *my* view. So whatever you choose to do, boys, my hand on it: good help! And to start with already, this heretic's sent word he'll be at his farm above there, saving the hay – in *my* rightful meadow – that any fool could have saved before the rains came down, had he only thought it decent to ask me as his neighbour for my experience of wind and cloud.

"He'll have all his dirty house-people, and his bitch and his she-puppy and that English bloody deacon of his, out daily with the forks and rakes, all in terror of more rain by the end of the week. And damn the soldier-man in it. The English captains gave him nothing, not even a camp-cook. But you have to catch him in the field. His farm is a walled-yard and a tower, and the man here is right, you'd never take it lacking the gunpowder."

The same doubtful galloglass asked cautiously, what would Montgarret say?

Another man, of Mac Giolla Pádraig's band, came in on top of him with scorn: "Have none of you heard the priesteens? Máire of England will put down Luther and if we put down the Wall what else will we get but her thanks and Mountgarret knows it! What will *he* get but the *credit*, mind you: not a portion of blame in the world! And that without soil of his fingers in the grease: so that's him!"

Brother Iarlaith takes him up on that. "Don't you be so certain of Máire na nDólás, I am warning you! She has indeed called her clergy to re-establish the Mass, but how long for, and how strongly such a course will outmaster the Saxon greed is not known, and I for one will put no trust in it. Do you suppose she is able to order all the booty from monks and friars to be returned whence it came? The very shift on the woman's hips was paid for out of the nuns' dowries."

"House-people, bitch, she-puppy . . ." Those were the words that should have clapped me across the throat and sprung my mouth open there and then to say NO.

To an extent of course I *did* say no – by way of a question to Brother Iarlaith: "There's no self-preservation in attacking the man's family, it'll fetch us only into disrepute, and not at all upon a parallel with the death of Sapphira – you brought up the Holy Book, Brother: confirm me I have the sense of it correct?"

To which he answered me: "True for you, son of Art: for we read Ananias's wife was as deep into the embezzlement as he himself: I've no reason to believe that *this* fellow's woman is. You men are to commit no massacre! or if you do, by Holy Mary, you'll not get away with it on any absolution from *me!*"

I did believe they all shared the same respect for him that I had. I took their grunts of agreement as a genuine oath-binding. (I heard afterwards that even while the grey-friar was declaring himself, one of those damnable high-church clergy was winking from behind his back, and in the upshot *he* was the one to absolve them from what happened. He absolved *me*, I won't deny it. Oh a malignant contriver, he was, but an authentic priest; with the *power*. I had to confess to *someone*).

So thereupon, and reassured, I told them a piece of news: "Mount-garret gave me, only this evening, a most curious sideways word. He was hinting that if any of the kern-band should think it needful for their expenses to adopt a second service, it would not count against them in regard to their contracts with him. Can anyone tell me what they think he might have meant?"

"*I* can, I do believe," offers this priest (the one that was after winking. Of course it was the town-priests most directly under threat from English bishopings: itinerant Gaelic friars being largely outside such control): "Mr Bolger and ourselves have a few silver pieces put together, upon the odd chance that you gentlemen were light-sporraned. There need be no contract in writing, a good fair-day hand-clap between honest men, that is all."

I suppose that sort of sliding business from a certain class of clergy might well be a reason for honest men beyond (in England, Germany, or wherever) to turn Luther and damn the Pope. But for us, you see, turning Luther meant not only discourteous breach of all the vows we'd have given to the Saints, but by now it had come to signify a man's acceptance of English rule, *even though* the new Queen appeared – for the time – to be good Christian. The life of the people being put in peril, all along with a man's *eternal* life. Two very strong reasons against but one, odds doubled, d'you see? and besides, I'd never delude myself that Luther's priests were any straighter than ours. Not after what the Wall had said, with his Bible-book held high in his hand! New Guise being no better, then, than the worst corners of Old Guise, best stick to what you know: and so I have . . . As I told you, druids and poets are damn well separated for hundreds of years.

(x) *Death In The Hayfield*

Our ambush being thus commissioned, and paid for in sincere advance, we determined the day and the hour and left it to Barney Two-and-a-half-cubits (which was Bolger's name among his work-servants) to scout out the circumstance. As it happened, the plan was betrayed, by the galloglass-captain's drunken horseboy, who went careering on a stolen steed, two days too early, through the Wall's farmyard just as the haywains were rolling in; and called aloud that a bishop's head was a great dinner in any man's kettle and every horse in the place would be Mountgarret's.

They did not quite know what to make of his blundering threats, but they did know there was something to be feared. So half of the bishop's-farm men were kept at home to guard the buildings, and the Wall and his wife and daughter made certain to stay within doors. Thereby, and God be thanked for it, I kept my honour in regard to *her*. God be cursed for it: in no other way did I keep it at all . . .

Viewed solely as a soldier's work, and to use a word for it of soldiers'–English, the whole proceeding was a *fuck-stupid-bollox* entirely.

Our famous Barney Two-and-a-half was so distracted by a gratuitous burglary at his *own* house (perpetrated, to all appearance, by broken men of the Ó Cléirighs' country who knew nothing of our intentions), that he quite forgot his scouting.

So the day appointed found no-one in the hayfield save a few harmless labourers. The Bishop of course had never a thought of *their* danger: he believed it was himself alone under threat.

I could wish that it had been. I could wish I had no part of it. Ananias and Sapphira be damned: this was blood-guilt, and for five years it killed my poetry as stone-dead as we killed them. Four men, one girl. Oh yes, one of them was certainly English, the Wall's young deacon: as it turned out, a Saxon savage who thrust wounds of red vengeance into a galloglass with his pitchfork and then into a pair of kern and would have done so to me too, had not a well-thrown dart cleft his kidneys from behind. His was an honest man-slaughter. But the others?

I suppose the girl was no more than sixteen, she ran and a galloglass sprang after her, chopping with his axe at her backbone as you'd commence to fell a sapling-tree.

I'll tell you a thing: she was not my Gráinne, but she screeched in Irish. She screeches even yet in my sleep.

*

Little importance to my mind afterward, that only the week earlier the Wall had been compelled to hear his high-church bells rung for hours by archbishop's order from the Hurdle-ford, to signal the restoration of God's true altar and the Holy Mass.

Little importance that the next Sunday he himself had from the Archbishop a most personal order to celebrate Mass with his own hands and voice. Rather than do so, he rode straight out of town, north. Some people said it was his conscience that drove him: he truly thought the Mass was damnable. *I* knew he had another motive. Perhaps it was by now his *only* motive. But I would not be unjust, even to *him* . . .

And even less importance, that after the hayfield the City-sovereign Ó Séa found for him a close guard of four hundred Englishmen from the Lord Deputy's garrisons as well as from the town-levies, and it was they brought him safe to the Pale.

Oh we had no stomach to kill him again, and indeed we did not try.

I drank all the priests' money in one night. No sooner had I finished, I put fingers in my throat and tried to spew up against the castle-cornerstones to void every drop of it. But my guts held it down, my bladder held it in, I seemed unable to vomit or piss. Why, that liquor lives inside me still. And Mother of God, in my sleep she still screeches.

*   *   *

At the end of his long discourse, Proinsias Dubh fell suddenly silent, a dark glowering silence. When Munday cautiously prompted him to say a little more, he shook his head, rose heavily to his feet like a man about to sleep-walk, and was half-way out of the room before he recollected his courtesy. His words of thanks and leave-taking were correct but laconic, his bow was abrupt.

Munday and the friar, without speech to each other, watched him through the bead-curtain as he crossed over the *piazza*, a strong bog-soldier's lope; and then he suddenly slipped sideways into the mouth of a dark alleyway as though taking cover in underbrush. It was incongruous to see him thus, in his vainglorious but threadbare Italian clothes, with his close-cropped head and the Toledo rapier propping up his short cloak – "Yes, of course," Munday thought, "so very much like a botcher's needle, upon so untownly a man."

"He will go to make a song," said Brother Declan. "A song first for his mistress: sure I cannot tell you whether indeed he has one, but that will be the choice of his song-making. And then he will make another, calling his mistress the Lady Éire and giving her a torn green cloak to be mended and restored by the valour of the foster-brothers. And the second song will be known and sung by all the Irish of the contingent before this expedition sets sail. Jesus bless him, he's a valued man."

"I am sorry he could not say more about the play in Kilkenny: I would have wished he had seen it in full, and could give me a full poet's criticism."

"Matter-a-damn for that," the friar snorted, "It was a rude insulting carry-on, by all accounts, and the people knew their minds on it when they hurled the bigoted blackguard out-of-town."

"And yet he found men to act in it. There must have been some sense of – of art-making?"

"God, boy, the Irish will always find people to destroy their own country altogether. 'Art-making'? Traitor-making: but we'll soon have an end to it, so we will.

"'Tis great pity, though, I do detect upon good Proinsias Dubh a class of a black despair. Amn't I always telling the man surely, if his poetry says one thing and his heart says another, he is neither poet nor happy soldier? He should forget that poor colleen: and remember only the bright youth and the grey beauty of old age that's laid in the grave by thousands at the hand of the foreigner's malice. Ah God the lovely white feet of 'em when we danced to the harp in Donegal."

The jolly little man was now unpleasantly maudlin. Munday thought it was time to leave. The more so as Brother Declan was edging himself into a series of objurgations upon the Catholics of England and Anglo-Ireland, whose alleged faith, he dribbled out, was only by way of bewildering the foolish Irish into giving up their vaunted struggle. "Small help from your damned Londonmen, let them kill their cruel Queen or keep her, but sorra the pity of any amongst ye for the misfortunes of the Gael . . ."

*

Munday went then to his lodgings, to write a secret report to his spy-master, Sir Francis Walsingham. But before he began it, he made a few notes in his common-place book upon the subject of John Bale; being a little nonplussed by an aspect of Ó Dálaigh's story. It was of keen professional interest to him (both as intelligencer and student of statecraft), and he thought he ought to clarify it. So he wrote:

Quaere:
If J.B. so great a fool in Ireland as this Irishman says he was, why then did D. of North'l'd send him thither? For D. of N. no fool, tho' assuredly a false knave, and labyrinth-souled.

Responsa (sed non satis):
D. of N. had need of an Irish rebellion to turn men's hearts from English troubles, as enclosures, *etcetera*?
or:
D. of N. cared naught for Irish trouble, but only desirous such as J.B. be well out of England – over-many strong Protestants were stiffening Cranmer (and the King) unduly, D. of N. must have his Church *pliable*, to bend it even Rome-ward if need be. Knew no God himself, but sought ever the advantage to his power from every complexion of faith?
or:
D. of N. had design to stir Ireland to war through *foolishness of underlings:* thereafter to cut off tallest heads of broken rebels: thereafter, *in his own person*, to make generous peace, and pardon all others, achieving thus a great name there for wisdom and kindness, and – by allowing a specious freedom for Irish popery – he'd keep 'em loyal (to him only), so offer Pope, Spain, France, Jesuits, no further hope of nourishment from superfluity of Irish grievance?

Any, or all, of these.
D. of N.'s plots on Monday were never his schemes for Tuesday, and by Wednesday he'd reconstitute the full admixture all over again. But poor J.B., scapegoat every good day o'th'week. No less of a dandled doll than J. Grey herself. I'd have thought Black F. might ha'seen it? But Irish subtlety only sees a *selection* of English ditto. In the end, I think, our treachery must always o'er-master theirs. Why? Because we *are* masters. All they can ever do is *aspire*. As is proven.

Munday wished to prove it again; writing at once to Walsingham, laying out for him in well-balanced argument how the Catholic force bound for Ireland contained ravaged fanatics urgent to make an exterminating war-of-religion: but how also at the same time it contained the seeds of its own collapse, in that religion was not its sole criterion, and even its most intelligent members had not yet decided what the primary objective ought to be. England, he concluded, would have no great difficulty in resisting the 'foreigners' malice', provided that the Queen's security-forces showed sufficient resolution and hardness of purpose.

Soon afterwards, the contingents set sail, and were no longer within Munday's terms of reference. He returned to his principal duty, to infiltrate the English Catholics, where – so long as his cover remained unpenetrated – he was at least not assailed at random by reflections on his nationality, and language. It was a relief to him. He enjoyed espionage, but preferred it not too unpredictable.

The allied landings in south-west Ireland proved in fact an appalling disaster. In the end the troops were cut off, and besieged at Smerwick in the 'Golden Fort'. Their Italian *condottiere* surrendered, upon what he believed to be terms, to the Queen's Lord Deputy, who immediately broke his word and had every prisoner put to death, approximately six hundred of them. Also the Irish women who had come in to live with the soldiers.

One of the murdered men was Proinsias Dubh Ó Dálaigh. Munday thought it not probable he would have been aware, in the frenzy of massacre, how two English poets were immediately responsible for it – Edmund Spenser, the Lord Deputy's secretary, who drafted the orders; and Captain Walter Ralegh, in charge of the execution-squad. Nor were *they* likely to know who Ó Dálaigh was. Had they known, they would no doubt have segregated him with the garrison's papist priests for torture as well as death. Irish poets were held to be worse than the Queen's worst enemies, because of their skill in firing-up courage.

The atrocity in itself only escalated the rebellion, even though it deterred Pope and Spaniards from sending any more help. And as the fighting went on and on, so the cruelties became more frequent, and more poets – English and Irish – denounced them and justified them in their partisan outpourings.

*

More than thirteen years after his dinner in Rome, Munday heard of Ó Dálaigh again: of all places, in Wapping. He and Lucretia were newly-embarked upon a tide-rapid of unthinking lubricity, much as the watermen at roaring ebb would shoot the arches of London Bridge. He took her to a sailormen's boozing-ken to carouse among bawdy company and clear her conscience of any remaining dregs of Lowlyheart that might hinder their mutual wantonness.

It turned out there was but little in the place to excite desire. It was dirty, noisy, full of tobacco-smoke, and several of the customers (who might or might not have been smugglers – he told her they were) had a tendency to resent strangers. He had to keep Lucretia carefully in a dark corner in case some ruffian demanded her company and tried to force a quarrel upon him. In point of fact, nobody did: they were mostly playing cards and yelping dispersedly about the malefactions of ships' officers.

Now and then one of them started a song, usually without finishing it. The women in the place were no doubt of abandoned character, but not very free with it. They each seemed to know their man and stayed beside him: it was obviously a house of habit and valued as such by its clients. But a small group at the next table, men who had come in together (at a guess they were all newly paid-off from the same ship), became rather more continuous in their music than the others had been.

Among them was an Irish mariner, whom they addressed as 'Kinsale'. He was a slight youth of a shy nervous temperament, probably much stronger than he looked, being neatly-built and wiry, and his accent was soft and remote. He had little to say, but when he said it, he seemed to sing.

His English friends indeed wanted him to sing in real earnest: "Go on with you, Kinsale, give us *The Long-Legged Queen*, o'course you bloody can, mate, there's nothing to stop you in here, nobody's bloody listening, o'course you can sing it in here –" and so on. It was not apparent whether Kinsale wished nobody to listen or was refusing because he feared that nobody would.

One of the group insisted that he sang the song in his own language: "Never mind these daft buggers that say they can't follow the story, it's the tune as tells the story, mate, that tune and your Irish words sit into one another like a cat and new-born kittens . . ." At length a degree of local silence was achieved, and young Kinsale bashfully responded.

He pulled his bonnet down over his eyes and then looked up at the sooty rafters, tapping two fingers on the table, very gentle, to bring himself into a rhythm. He muttered, scarcely audibly, "*Amhrán bhanríon na gcos fada*[1]", and went on tapping. Lucretia watched him, fascinated. She herself was just beginning her own professional music, and all performances were of interest. This man, however, seemed to be about to sing only for himself: his friends and the wider company in the room were vanishing from his awareness entirely.

His song *was* in Irish, of a very strange desolate resonance, it sounded like a grief-filled lament, but then upon certain phrases its nature changed without warning to a screaming hectoring ferocity, and then again to a sensual lilt. He completed perhaps three stanzas, and gave every indication of going on all night – Lucretia could have listened all night – but he sharply broke off as though something in the room disquieted him, and he had done wrong to start singing there at all. He sat back on the bench and held his face sideways, still half-hidden by his bonnet-brim, affecting not to be affected by the plaudits of his friends, or indeed by the general banging of mugs on table-tops all round, no mistake as to the genuine delight he had aroused.

"Od's foreskin," said Lucretia to Munday's ear in a sort of hungry gasp (she was at that time grossly given to swearing, an oblique declaration that London was not Canterbury), "I've never heard in all my life so woundily beautiful a song-ballad. Tony-love, it came straight in under my farthingale, a hot torch to light a brace of candles, one in each of my tetins, for God's mercy ask him to teach it me!"

"He never will: it's his own song. And besides, you can't speak Erse." But she persisted against his evasions, until it occurred to him that her bodily longing for the song might easily enough be trans-

---

[1] The song of the long-legged queen.

muted into more longing for himself, so he went over to speak to the sailor. Kinsale was even shyer with Munday than with his own companions, but they encouraged him ("Go on, mate, he's a gentleman, gentleman-poet like as not, don't hold back from fame-an'-fortune!"): and at last he admitted that he knew some English words for part of the song, though by no means as deep-meaning as the Irish, and he would attempt them for the young lady, if she'd first grant him pardon for commencing the song without asking would she care to hear it.

She came at once and sat beside him, her eyes fixed on his unshaven face and the sweet-natured mouth from which such uncanny sublimity had emerged.

He said: "I should tell you, ma'am, this song was first made by Proinsias Dubh Ó Dálaigh – you might know him as Francey Daly? – a great poet of my people who is after dying these twelve years in the southern war. I should tell you he was in Rome the time he put it together, and 'tis said it was a Roman lady he had in his thought. But there are those that say, no: she was in Ireland the woman he sang of, and he made both words and air as a memory of her, so. Here's how it goes to start with.

> "O she walked all in sunshine
>   and she danced in the rain
> And her face in the sunshine
>   was covered with a veil
> A veil of fine muslin
>   and linen and pale silk
> She shook it like the rowan-tree
>   does be blowing on the hill.
>
> "But when the rain fell
>   and her dancing began
> She lifted it off from her face
>   and was fully to be seen
> And who was there to see it?
>   there is no-one to tell
> For the long-leggéd woman
>   danced all by herself.
>
> "She danced to encapture me
>   and to tie my heart to those hearts
> Who led me to the fighting,
>   put the blade into my belt,

And forbade me to pull it
   till I came to the tawny field
Where the long-leggéd woman
   would bring my foe to me.

"O who did she bring
   but herself and all alone?
So sorrowful a long-leggéd woman
   was never to this day seen.
'You must kill me, pretty soldier'
   was all that she could say:
Like wine of Bordeaux
   the blood ran from her bent white nape.

"O Rome of the priests
   and Spain of the silver
And Burren-slope of flowers
   that scarcely know hard winter,
Not all of your lovely beauties
   can ever make up for me
The long-leggéd woman
   whom I espied but never did see.

"I daresay, ma'am, being put into the English, and all disorderly at that – my own words, d'ye see, for the English focsle-boys when we do be having a brief space in the dog-watches – it'll not be altogether the class of song you'd understand, I mean to say the tale-and-story of it in a manner of speaking is a hidden one, but that was always the way with Ó Dálaigh, so it was . . . The Burren-hill lies over from Galway, I thought I should tell you that. Ó Dálaigh lived there."

                        *

She learned the song very quickly, but never managed his way of delivering it.

Munday's love-making that night was lacking in tenderness: he said the song had mis-humoured him.

"Scalp-o-thorn-holes, Tony, that's no reason why *you* should mis-humour *me*." Lucretia was growing irritated, discordant with him. It was not long before they parted.

Roast Beef

Lydia was quite sure that the house in the busy little Westminster cul-de-sac to which Munday brought her was not really 'his house' in the sense that he lived there with his wife and family. She had a vague idea that his regular home was near Threadneedle Street, among aldermen and such-like, or had someone told her Cornhill? Not that she had ever been so openly interested as to make direct enquiry . . .

But this was no more than a dark pair of rooms above-stairs, furnished more like a counting-house than a dwelling: she did deduce a bed in the small inner chamber. On the ground floor was a printing-office, booksellers' shops on either side. "Yes," he said, watching her eyes behind her veil, and guessing the course of her thought, "Convenient for a writer and a reader, and I am both: I apply myself to more than the ephemera of the playhouse. Here, in these streets and courts, is government, church, royalty: all our new reformed England and the recordings thereof. Across the laneway William Caxton first began to print, the man in the workshop below still has drawers full of Caxton's old type. In that church –" he pointed out through the window: a buttress of St Margaret's blocked the view across to the Palace Yard, "– John Skelton, laureate poet, is buried: much acclaimed, I think, by your father. And it was in the garret next door, to the left, that Skelton hid for years, in sanctuary from the anger of Cardinal Wolsey.

"I have another reason to live in Westminster. If I were a papist I would say it was a 'special devotion' to a particular martyred saint. But I am so far from being a papist that to put it in such terms would be a blasphemy. I do not *pray* to this saint, only to the Lord God for Whose Good Name he died, and Who may (in response to my prayers) infuse my spirit with the spirit of that man's most gorgeous death. His name was William Flower.

"Of course, not here, but Smithfield, is where most of our London martyrs burned, Anne Askew, for example. Oldcastle died at St Giles, the top end of Drury Lane. There was a very wide dispersal of glory, providential, manure of seething blood scattered all about the city to feed the roots of our true religion. See –!" he pointed again, with such abruptness that she bent her head against the casement to catch a view of what he meant her to look at, his finger was thrusting sideways, "– see, beyond the buttress, between the east-chapel of the Abbey and the Queen's Palace, do you see three square yards of pavement? In Mary's time, the lonely Golgotha of Mr Flower upon those three square yards. His Gethsemane: just behind the very gables we stand under, in the nave of Margaret's church. Before he burned, they cut his hand off. He had been a black-monk; now he was a Protestant, he had taken a wife. And I think of your father.

"Upon an Easter Day, in St Margaret's, to William Flower, at parish worship, it came suddenly that what he heard was not the Lord's Supper, as prescribed in the Upper Room, but idolatrous mockery Mass, Antichrist in His Father's House, as prescribed by Mary of Blood: and the blood came behind his eyes. He carried at his belt a chopping-knife, having just trimmed some faggots for his wife's kitchen fire. The rage of the Holy Spirit flung up his hand there and then for him – there and then for the Cleansing of the Temple. Mrs Lowlyheart, his morning faggots were as his own faggots for his own fire – he ran at the deceiving priest, struck with his knife the priest's blood into the chalice, so the wine it contained was indeed transubstantiate: for once, a true miracle, blood was announced, blood was observed, what else could they do but burn him?

"He was murderous? sacrilegious? who's to judge? Stark mad, you might say, but very very brave. And I think of your father, making his brave brave plays in the very face of the wild Irish.

"I tell you what *I* do: I crouch, in *my* Upper Room, at this window, just here, twist my neck toward the open space, and I think of the lovely ghost of brave Mr William Flower lifting itself up from the ash-heap in shimmering spirals of blue-grey smoke. On a summer's afternoon I even think I can see it. And then I must turn to my desk and scribble foolishness for Henslowe's ranters.

"It craves exorbitant courage to go to death for a belief. And not only for a true belief. Papists die brave. Condemned Jesuits write poems. Many of them better poems than *I* could conceive. Their treasons are something more than a mere naughtiness and malice. Which is why they have to die. On the other hand, irresponsible mischief merits not the sumptuosity of the black-hung scaffold."

For the first time she was aware of the sinister nature of the man: she suddenly felt she was brought here for some perfectly dreadful purpose. The bed-post she could see through the door ajar to the next room was not just of a pleasure-bed, though none the less voluptuous. She began to lose command of herself.

With difficulty she forced the words. "To speak to me of Lucretia . . . ?"

"Did she tell you I seduced her?"

"Yes."

"Not true. Not *quite* true. But no excuse: it should not have happened. She was in grief, I allowed myself to be taken advantage of thereby, so that I took advantage. And then it ended. But my interest did not end. We said to one another, not lovers any more, but friends, we shall stay friends. And so I would have, but she didn't. And I tried to find why. She said to me once, 'When my love swears that he is made of truth, I do believe him, though I know he lies, therefore I lie with him and he with me, that in our faults by lies we flattered be.'"

"Lucretia said that? She talks in verse?"

"Oh yes, and it took me a moment longer than it took you to realise it. But it was none of *my* verse, and I did not think she herself would be quite so succinct a poet: so whose . . . ?

"When I spoke to her, here, of the dead men and women of Smithfield, of martyred Flower, I saw her face cloud: I saw pain and recollection of all that she had fled from in Canterbury, I saw Foxe's noble martyr-book as it were with her own hand shoved into a blazing rubbish-heap. And I saw her skip, with scorched fingers, from one bonfire to the next, so eager was she to clear herself from all fires, yet unable to see any path of avoidance except that which she was trained to follow, smoke to smoke, flame to flame, she could not get out of the cinder-field.

"Now she haunts papists, whereas heretofore the reformed Christ in shape of her father haunted her. Her Shake-scene poet of lies is one of them. He never says so, but I *know* it, as I'd know from an aching bone-joint that the wind lies north-east. I'll wager his *King John* will fail even to mention the papal quarrel – or, if it does, he'll so balance the plot with dynastic crime that the whole noble story's no more help to England's liberties than an Agincourt bow-stave strung with a tassel of wool!"

"You – you are telling me – Lucretia's lover is a Rome-agent? A *Jesuit*? No."

"No. He has not the courage. Mischief, I said. I said, irresponsible. He is one that cannot bear an enforced stability in the state. Half of him longs for it, the other half is terrified of the means of its enforcement. Or disgusted thereby. Challenge him, he'd tell you his stomach so heaves against punishment, he will swoon upon Fleet Street to hear the mere wheels of the whipping-cart, let alone the roped harlots screaming behind it."

Lydia thought to herself, "So will I." She did not want to argue, only prayed to endure suspense until this wedge-faced grey wolf brought together the teeth of his purpose. She was caught inside his lair, perhaps she was mad to have allowed herself: but she would not, could not now, take flight.

For a few wild minutes he ran on, white bubbles of rage flecking the ends of his mouth, about the 'Shake-scene' and the threat he posed – not exactly to Munday himself, nor indeed to true religion itself, but rather to the *honest showing* of true religion, true patriotism, true morality, on the once so stalwart English stage, now falling (or was it fallen?) into ambiguous decay. Munday's feud – she had no doubt it was a raw-corrosive feud – seemed based upon his rival's knack of asserting in his work all the nation's needful virtues, and speciously, acceptably, to players and unthinking public: while no more than a few – including Munday, "*c'la va sans dire*" – (for he broke into divers languages in the haste of his malignity) – "no more than a lonely few have the urgent insight to espy how counterfeit the fellow is, *diavolo!* not one word of what he writes but turns about within itself to savage its own plain meaning: and who will gain from such quick trickery? Management? So long as there is blood enough spilt by his mephitic heroes, yes, so long as there is hint enough of the amorous catamite in his love-passages; but to feed the greed of management, to starve the livelihood of colleague-poets, these alone are not his *raisons d'être*.

"Only one chief beneficiary of the spiritual confusion he doth propagate, only one force in the kingdom that could have set him to engender it – and pay for it moreover with their indulgences for his vice – the Jesuitic hydra-coils, they are swarming all around us, coils, we have to hack them and chop them, ah lady, we must *hack!*"

Then he took a great deep breath and his smoothness was re-established.

"Ah lady, let me show you."

He grasped her gently (but most firmly) by the wrist and so led her, to a bookshelf in the inner room.

It was hard by the head of his bed, an insomniac's remedy, she assumed. He touched one or two volumes with the back of a knuckle, without speaking, and then stepped back to let her look at their titles. The first she picked out was poetry. *"Rape of Lucrece . . . ?"*

"Printed last year," he said, "Subject and title, I suspect, not accidental. Mind you, I do not believe he achieved her body by violation. But he thinks – with some guilt – of her spirit, and he writes in emblems. It is a fine intertwined elaborated work, if all you know of Lucrece comes from the Roman authors and no nearer home . . . Try the next one."

A devotional volume: *St Mary Magdalene's Tears*.

"Robert Southwell? Who is he?"

"Jesuit. And they hanged him, cut open his entrails, heart out, yard-and-ballocks off, all his chitterlings on the bonfire, Tyburn, six weeks ago. He wrote his poems. Good ones: if all you know of Christ is from Scripture and you never heard of Philip of Spain or the Pope that guides his working.

> "As I in hoary winter's night
> Stood shivering in the snow,
> Surprised I was with sudden heat
> Which made my heart to glow –"

He quoted the lines with no great expression, he might have been murmuring a list of grocery-purchases.

> "And lifting up a fearful eye
> To view what fire was near,
> A pretty babe all burning bright
> Did in the air appear –"

She nearly said the poem was beautiful: but instead she clenched her mouth shut. She knew that he knew that she thought so, she knew that he thought so himself.

> "He vanished out of sight
> And swiftly shrunk away,
> And straight I callèd unto mind
> That it was Christmas Day."

She was a pinnace with too large a sail-spread caught unawares by a squall. She ought to have downed canvas and put her head towards it, instead she thought only to do her frantic best to heel away – no use – her back was against the bed-post: no, she could retreat no further, and Munday stood between her and the door. He waved his knuckle, still crooked, toward the books.

"I call that shelf my witness-box. Everything in it incriminates, or is writ by those already elsewhere incriminated. Madam, we can make no compromise between loving-kindness and the realm's safety. That Southwell man walked in disguise, not as a priest but as an honest Englishman that made poems and heard plays and seemed, had you met him, the very heart of the stalwart oak-tree. Well, I met him. I found who he was and I told my neighbour. I would like you to meet my neighbour."

"I do not want to meet your neighbour."

"Please? For Lucretia's sake?"

He spoke like a good-natured physician, offering an unsavoury draught to a patient made childish by illness. He brought Lydia out of his rooms, through a small door onto a rickety covered gallery. It led over a dog-leg-shaped and sordid back-yard to the first floor of a nearby house. Here he tapped, with the back of his knuckle, on a curtained window.

*

The top panel opened, cautiously, and a round stupid moon-face peered through the gap.

"Oooh . . ." said the face, a noise like a cow lowing. Lydia saw the boy's mouth had no more than three teeth in it: but was it a boy's? A sort of idiot face, perhaps he was fifty, impossible to tell.

"Mester Munday, oooh aye. Mester Topcliffe, he's down cellarage: he'll come up if I gie un a call. Am I to gie un a call?"

"What does he do down there, Thad? Working, is he?"

"Nay, mester, not working. We don't have no guests just now. Like, greasing the wheels an' that. Sent me up to fill his grease-pot, see? We gotten us good dripping off'n yesterday's roast beef. Thad had roast beef an' all. Thad likes it right fat, he does."

"Never mind your roast beef, boy. Tell your master I want to see him: I've brought a lady, let us in."

Thad opened the lower half of the window, pulled back the curtain, and they stepped inside. He left them alone in a room which seemed to be a kitchen, unwashed plates, pans part-full of old soups and burnt porridge, stale ends of loaves, fish-bones on trenchers. A cat was on the floor dragging a herring's head and part of a backbone.

They heard Thad's feet going downstairs, voices, then other feet coming up. Mr Topcliffe, in his grubby shirt-sleeves, his stained encrusted leather apron, seemed an elderly artisan, skilled at his work, untrustworthy as regards his bill: heavy-set, yellow-jowled, grey-haired, with a beard like a mildewed scrubbing-brush, a very false genial voice from somewhere in the north parts.

"I'll not shake hands, lady, they're all over muck. The boy and I are cleansing machines, waiting on the lull to end. Mr Munday tell you my trade, did he?"

Munday shook his head. "No sir, not yet. Mrs Lowlyheart, Mr Topcliffe is Member of Parliament for Old Sarum, where nobody lives except sheep. Sheep, thank God, by definition, have no religion, so their orthodox loyalty may be taken for granted. He did use to be Member for Beverley in Yorkshire, you perhaps know there was once a most flourishing minstrels' guild there? Not any more."

"Not any more." Topcliffe chuckled reminiscently. "And that lot weren't sheep, not by no means. Goats. And they stank putrid. But we ousted 'em, bagpipe and baggage, on account of intransigent popery. That were afore my time there. Poor little lad King Edward, his chaps scoured out their Beverley chantry for 'em: altars and candles in Mary's kirk there right through King Henry's years, all parliament-acts flat defied, you'd not believe it, shocking. None o' that these days, praise the Lord. Aye, these days we've got 'em right sorted."

"Mr Topcliffe is the Queen's Detector, Mrs Lowlyheart. Finds priests, finds their treasons, and when they come to his house, they are his guests, and then they tell him everything. So he gives them to government."

"That's right, lady, private guests. Paying-guests, mind you; if they've nowt to tell, they can bide here till they pass the cash. I've to make ends meet somehow. But most whiles they confess. Queen's Detector's not an office, it's a job. And a job that can't be done in the Tower, or anywhere else official; all manner of legal quirks to cramp the hand of government, you'd not believe. As far as government goes in public, what we do here's not known about. Of course there's a scale of fees, so much a head from Treasury (covert budget, you understand), *if* the head confesses, but that's no more nor speculative: no confession, no queen's fee. So I've to be smart, smarter nor they are, and some of 'em are damn smart. They train 'em up to it, you know, Spanish and Italian training, smart. That Southwell, now, he were a fox, doubling and turning, and as cunning as they come."

"I told you he'd be difficult: he was a poet, he would shuffle and shift his words three times as fast as your run-of-the-mill equivocator."

Topcliffe laughed, or Lydia supposed he laughed: it was like any other man clearing nose and throat of catarrh. He and Munday exchanged glances, Munday jerked his head slightly toward the staircase.

"Poet and Jesuit all in one," said Topcliffe, "You know what I'd call that? I'd call it cheese on top of cream. Over-rich for right nourishment. Will the lady see machines? Some ladies like to, even in working-hours. It's a queer taste, but I'd not deprive 'em, though I do have to make a small charge."

"Mrs Lowlyheart should view them *gratis*. To oblige a friend, yes?"

"Of course, of course, Mr Munday, any friend o' yourn, of course, of course, this way."

"No, no, no, no – " Lydia tried to refuse, but Munday's eyes said 'Lucretia', and she followed Topcliffe in helpless silence.

*

The stairs were dark and slimy, the whole house seemed to be darkened by curtains, there were doors on the ground floor with felt nailed over them: and in the cellarage was one candle, and Thad rubbing grease onto some ratchets. The stone vault was impregnated with ancient rotten smells, the secretions of bodily fear long soaked into the masonry, impossible to scrape away. The cat had come down after them and sniffed about on the puddled floor, delicately finding dry places for her feet.

"Light another glim, Thad, we want the lady to see proper and not get her shoes mired. Damn expenses, light two. Beg pardon for the wet, ma'am, but Thad and me was slopping out just afore you come in. We've to keep the place cleanly, up to a point, any road: nobody's workshop's improved by letting it get all clarted-up."

The two extra candles showed her everything, or almost everything. She knew what a rack was: she had seen the engravings in Foxe.

Some of the other appliances did not make immediate sense. There were hooks and staples in the ceiling, walls, and floor. A couple of pulley-arrangements projecting high up from the cove of the vault. Ropes, chains, and straps. A brazier, with variously-headed iron bars propped against it. Some pincers. A row of pegs with five whips and three canes hanging from them. One of the canes had small pins driven through it at two-inch intervals, just an eighth-of-an-inch projecting from the surface of the rod. Another one was bound with varnished strips of cloth. There were other, smaller, items as well, lying on a bench beside a large screw-vice.

Thad went on with his greasing.

Munday said, "She don't want to know what all this is for. Well able to imagine it; shall we go?"

He took Lydia's elbow and steered her to the stair-foot. As they climbed, something ran over her foot. She thought it was the cat, then looked and saw a rat. She did not scream: she was for years a housekeeping woman well-used to such creatures in cellars or store-rooms.

Topcliffe followed them up, and opened a door on the ground floor for them. It led out into a side street, right under the walls of the Abbey. He shook hands with Munday, saying, "I hope the lady appreciated? It's always good business to let good religious folk know they're safe and sound in London. If she should hear of anyone that's any way in my line, she can tip me the word, right? Through you, that's most tactful: usual commission?"

He closed his door and left them in the street, upon cobblestones where grass grew, and dank young weeds. It was a gentle warm evening, with the beginnings of a gentle light rain. There was no-one in sight in this narrow gloomy corner, although the noise of the main Westminster thoroughfares came to their ears from behind the buildings. Munday gave his right hand a prolonged vigorous wipe against the hem of his cloak, and kept his eyes upon Lydia.

"Very well, very well," said Lydia, so quiet he could hardly hear her, "Very well, you are damnable cruel, and you want me for your bed or you give my daughter to *him*." Her voice tailed away: he had to ask her, with his easy courtesy, to repeat her last few words. When she did so, he seemed astonished. His dark eyes opened wide at her.

She bowed her head and continued, speech muffled by her veil. "I have no choice, what can I do? Where's your house? I've lost my direction? Where?" She turned about and about.

He caught her hand and steadied her. "Lydia, Lydia, what do you take me for? You surely cannot think I am so debased a rogue? This place is a pit of hell: and I, a poet, led you through it, as Virgil did Dante: did Dante call Virgil cruel? Your father's God made this –" his hand, now fully wiped, indicated the blind facade of Topcliffe's house, swinging the fingers up and down – "and some of us who serve that God must now and then serve in the cellarage: or else who will view the stars? Above and below are clipped together, it is a beast with two backs.

"There is nothing you need do, but tell Lucretia to be very careful: and then tell her to tell her Shake-scene friend what *he* must do, and do it *now*. First, he is holding papers (or she is, on his behalf), which I believe to contain names. Those names should be with government, properly by way of Topcliffe: let her bring them to me, and neither she nor her friend will hear further of the matter. If they are not brought, they will be looked-for. Mr Topcliffe employs keen searchers: whatever they find, they fetch here, be it of paper or flesh-and-blood.

"And then, second, there is to be no more of any *King John* at the Shoreditch Theatre. In view of what I have forewarned you of the likely nature of that play, you should be glad to present such a condition. And if it is not abided by, then his name goes to Topcliffe, inevitably with those of his paramours, male or female. That's all; and quick to accomplish: so surely there's no offence?"

She opened her mouth to answer, but the words refused emergence. He lightly lifted her veil, and no less lightly kissed her upon the mouth with his own wide-open mouth. Their tongues met before she could close her teeth. An hour ago she would have held herself there, tongue into tongue, deploring it, delighting in it. Lowlyheart had taught her nothing of such tingling juxtapositions. Now she started back and snatched the veil into its proper place.

"You are a damnable cruel young man."

She turned, and turned, and went wildly: he did not try to stop her. He broke out a slow smile, his thin top lip creeping up his pink gums, to hear her say 'young man'. She could not be more than a half-dozen years the elder; and ripe with it, that tongue had trembled, he felt its warmth even yet under his palate. "Tortoise wins," he told himself. "Had the daughter, had *her*. The kiss counts, no need for more. Tony, go home."

He made his way in good heart, to the river, to his boat, through the city to Threadneedle Street, to a defeated wife, to the clamorous children who called him 'dadda'.

VII

(Comical-historical-tragical-pastoral)

Narrenschiff

And the merchants of the earth shall weep and wail in themselves, because no man will buy their ware any more, the ware of gold, and silver, and of precious stones, of pearl, and silk, and purple, and all thynen wood, and all manner vessels of most precious wood, and of brass, and of iron, cinnamon, and odours, and ointments, and frankincense, and wine, and oil, and fine flour, and wheat, and cattle, and sheep, and horses, and chariots, and bodies and souls of men.

For at one hour so great riches is come to nought. And every ship governor, and all they that occupy ships, and shipmen that work in the sea, stood afar off and cried.

(Revelation of St John the Divine, Chapter 18)

(i) *The Bishop's* Congé

Mid-September, 1553: and with a hundred bows and bills of the Kilkenny train-bands and a hundred horse-troopers of the Lord Deputy's flying-column, Bale, Dorothy and Lydia were escorted out of the city at a very early hour, not quite dark, not quite sunrise, a miserable streak of yellow-grey coming up over the eastern trees, and a promise of more rain. Mr Shea had hauled himself up from his bed to see them off. He was genuinely upset. He did not exactly like Bale: but Dorothy had taken his fancy, and Lydia was a little sweetheart. Also, he had in a manner committed himself to this unchancy bishop, and God alone knew what his enemies in the place would be making of it: a more calculating man might well have stayed in bed. But the reputation of his office depended upon a safe departure, and – as far as possible – a dignified one for Bale.

"Mind you," he said boldly, "I have nothing to say, sir, on the question of your doctrine. You had a right to put it forward, and Kilkenny, as I take it, had a right to say no. But when all's told, you're the Bishop, and there ought to have been respect. The way you said it, at the market-cross, the Queen is the Queen, and God put her there. What troubles me now, sir, is where she's going to put *you*."

"For that," muttered Bale, "Christ in mercy will dispose."

"Ah, but I admire your courage, no man'll take that from you. I hear the new Lord Deputy will be arriving any day now, in Dublin by the end of the week, they say. He's a man we've had before, he was always very accommodating in any cross-crackle of dispute. Which is why he lost the job the last time. I make no doubt he'll put you right, you'll be back here safe and hearty before the Christmas."

It did not sound as though the City-sovereign looked forward to such an outcome, despite his reassuring smile.

"No, Mr Shea, I shall not. Not if I must offer the Mass. Not if I must plead the cause of Antichrist in Christ's own temple." Shea winced at the uncompromising tone, and remembered a more practical matter.

"These soldier-lads that travel with you. My train-band can only bring you to the boundary-stone at edge of the town liberties. But after that the Lord Deputy's men will see you guarded as far as Leighlin Bridge. That's a good twenty miles, but they've no orders to go any further. You'll have to make your own arrangements with the captain of the castle there. He's a good man, young Nick Hern, I make no doubt he'll see you right all the way into Dublin . . . Mrs Bale, it's been an honour. Begod, ma'am, it's been a pleasure. Mrs Shea asked me to tell you, any time you're back in town again, bread and broth will be on the table, and maybe one of your fine songs after it? And you too, me little darling, my lovely doat, oh isn't she the world's princess!"

*

They rattled off in column down the hill and across the upper bridge. This route out of Kilkenny brought them clear of the houses very speedily, there was little chance of an ambush, the bridge being already secured by a picket of hackbut-men. Beyond the river they must make detour by way of the Gallows Hill to rejoin the Dublin road, a steep muddy climb up a rutted track where the wagon with Bale's books bogged down for the first time. It was to stick fast again and again before they got to Leighlin Bridge. As it was, not all his books were on it, he had had to leave the heaviest cases behind. He never saw them again.

"Make haste," he urged, "make haste! Broad day will be upon us and our enemies will discern us here, our journey will be prevented, already they must have heard us in the houses of the Irish-town, every galloglass will be about our ears!" The soldiers strained at the wheels, swearing to themselves: they did not need his exhortations.

A crapulous old man in a filthy black clerical gown came swaying out of a hovel. He cackled with delight at what he saw. "So now the heretic bishop receives his *congé* from the orthodox! Oh he too now knows the wormwood. Be damned to you, John Bale, as you journey with the hosts of hell. Ho, soldiers – any one of ye want an instant confirmation? These hands still hold the glory, these hands still hold the power. And Friar Bale knows now what it's like to have the hands laid on and taken off, Friar Bale is as dispossessed as Nangle, hah!"

He was flourishing ten palsied fingers in the air under the nose of the corporal-major of the flying-column, who struck them away with a grunt of derision. Bale stared contemptuously at the drunkard, did not trouble to answer his taunts, he had heard them all before. For this seedy swollen-faced blear-eyed relic was also, so he claimed, a bishop: he had been appointed years ago to the Diocese of Clonfert in the west, only to be expelled by the local clan-chief in favour of a kinsman. He had never regained his see, and now wandered the country earning a beggarman's livelihood from occasional confirmations of children at twopence a head and as much as he could drink. In the tumult along the Coal Market just before the plays were acted, Bale had heard a priest calling out, "No Bale for Ossory Bishop: choose Nangle, choose Nangle!" And the crowd around him had roared approval.

Dr Richard Nangle, ex-bishop, vomited suddenly onto the ground right between the corporal-major's feet, and was angrily hustled away.

The corporal-major stepped back in disgust. "D'you know, sir, that nasty old bugger was brought a dog wrapped up in a sheet with tuppence hanging round its neck, one of them damned Butler galloglass-bastards fetched it into him for a joke; and, Jesus, he confirmed it before he knew what he was doing! Right then, we've got your wheels unstuck: all right, lads, back in the saddle, let's be having you . . . !"

Just beyond Gallows Hill was the boundary-stone. Bale called a halt, despite the surly protest of the Lord Deputy's troop-commander. "You will halt, Mr Cornet: I have religious duties. Be so good as to require your men to uncover their heads."

He himself dismounted, knelt, and prayed aloud, in formal com-mination of the wicked city of Kilkenny. Then he stood and cocked up his right foot. "I am commanded of my Lord to shake off the dust from my shoes against this place as a godly token that they received me not: so that it will, at Day of Judgement, be a byword and a shooting-of-lips. Let you all bear witness." As the dust on his soles was wet clotted sludge, he found himself unable to shake it: it held fast, he had to force a pellet loose with his thumb-nail. He flicked it scornfully backwards, it fell flat to the ground.   He had hoped it would have flown. Nonetheless the gesture was made, the train-band turned back home; the march resumed.

*

Captain Nicholas Hern of the Queen's castle at Leighlin Bridge was a brusque and competent young officer. He had served five years in Ireland and knew what had to be done. Evidence that he also went regardless and did it: the seven ghastly marauders' heads impaled above the arch of his gate-house. Two of them were old and disintegrated, but among the other five could still be seen the occasional eyeball gleaming: his task of pacification had very recently increased.

He was not pleased when the horse-troopers brought in the Bales and their wagon hours after the expected time. It was already well past midnight: the weary cavalcade wound untidily into the cresset-lit courtyard, grumbling, groaning, sagging in their saddles, a disgrace to the profession of arms.

Lydia, all the way, had been astride Dorothy's horse in front of her mother. When she was lifted down, she fainted and fell. Dorothy spoke to Bale for the first time since they left Kilkenny: "This child will be deathly ill: for heaven's sake get her to bed, get her to bed!"

Bale, no less exhausted, was not quite sure about the arrangements. "It may be we must go straight onward, chuck, at least after meat and drink, I do not know the Captain's wishes . . ."

"*I* will tell you the Captain's wishes." Hern disliked all clergymen, whatever their doctrine. "You have no escort until the morning. These men will return to Kilkenny, they are urgently needed back there. I can spare you another five-and-twenty (at your own expense) to be with you until Dublin. Under so small an escort you will all be riding fast. You cannot take that wagon."

Bale began to clamour angrily about his books, but to no avail.

"If you hadn't had those wheels today you'd have been here long before sunset. You're lucky to have got here at all. Any marauders would have assumed from them you were carrying a pay-chest: why they didn't, I can't imagine. Where's that damfool Cornet? What possessed you, boy, to let him bring this ridiculous ark?"

Bale kept on arguing: why must the escort be so small, if thereby his books were abandoned? Surely the Captain must know the value to a churchman of the materials of his scholarship – ?

"If you want them, you must pay for them. Fifty men, at your own expense, double day-wages for all the time you're on the road."

"Sir, I do not have that sort of sum about my person. But a letter-of-credit upon Lombard Street, I am sure that Archbishop Cranmer would guarantee payment –"

"Archbishop who? Are you sure he's still there? The last I heard, he was arrested; or about to be arrested. Can't you find me a better name than that?"

*

The wagon remained at Leighlin Bridge. Hern agreed, reluctantly (and at a price adapted to Bale's purse), to take all good care of its contents until the Bishop came to claim them again – *if* such a normal activity was going to be possible, which he took good leave to doubt.

During the night Bale lay awake on a straw palliasse in the great hall listening to the drip-drip-drip of water running down the inside of the walls, and he trembled for his fragile volumes in such storage. Dorothy and Lydia were put to sleep in Mrs Hern's bed. She was probably not a wife but a native camp-woman 'for duration of posting only': she spoke hardly any English. However, she was kind. She made soothing Gaelic noises to them both and hugged and kissed Lydia. She was a very dirty trollopy creature and her bed smelled, but Dorothy was long past caring about that.

Before dawn next morning, as the escort assembled, the Captain gave Bale a sort of scrawled receipt for the books. All it said was:

> Recvd, fr. Mr Bile, Bysspe, moche payper & parchemyn, in box and bagge, to be wardid untyl pled for.
>
> N. Hern, Ryall Seneschall.

He refused to make it more precise.

When Bale persisted, he said, "Two or three weeks ago this road would have been safe for six wagons with an escort of twelve troopers. Until *you* came to Kilkenny, the whole countryside was thoroughly cowed." And he tramped off to his breakfast, leaving them to take the trail.

As he had promised, they took it at great speed. Bale had loaded his saddle-bags with as many books as could be crammed into them. They slowed him down and the soldiers kept threatening to toss them out by the wayside. It was a terrible journey and lasted nearly a week.

Despite the receipt, he never again saw the books he left at Leighlin Bridge.

(ii) *Fevers*

When they reached Dublin, the books in the saddlebags, and some others which the pack-horses had been carrying along with the Bales' more portable luggage, were handed over to the Rev. Mr Williams, an English cleric of genuine Protestant belief. He had been friendly to Bale earlier in the year, and still held some official position in Dublin Castle, ecclesiastical liaison between the Lord Deputy's office and the Archbishop. Mr Williams was not sanguine about the future. "My dear Lord Bishop," he said to Bale, "I cannot say what will be the outcome. The news from London is very bad. I don't think they have begun proceedings against Cranmer, not yet, at any rate not yet. But poor Latimer is certainly to be arraigned. Perhaps for treason, perhaps heresy, perhaps both. The Queen will never forgive any churchman that connived at her mother's divorce and her own proclamation as bastard. Never. Both Bonner and Gardiner are out of gaol and riding a very high horse. They need to: they both connived. Unequivocal popery is now their sole preservation.

"Already there is talk that Pole is being fetched from Europe back to England to cardinalise amongst us, Papal Legate perhaps, perhaps even Archbishop, in Cranmer's place; I don't know. National Act of Repentance by way of the *Auto-da-fé*, absolute Spanish hysteria, by which token did you hear she may one of these days wed herself to young Philip the emperor's son? It beareth not contemplation.

"Nevertheless, my dear sir, I will personally ensure that these books are preserved in clean dry storage free from rats, I will personally place them among the Castle Muniments here, the Lord Deputy's people will not object to that, they never go into their own archives at all if they can help it, might discover far too much about how they should be governing the country. At least *books* may be made safe.

"Which is more than can be said for us. If things get any worse I might have to go to the Germanies; I won't be able personally to keep an eye on your books alas, no not at all. What will you do?"

Bale never saw the books again, he never saw Dublin again, but at this stage he was desperately attempting not to look so far into the future. He must see the Archbishop of Dublin, he must see the Lord Deputy, he must officially discover the exact shape of his position: and then – well, perhaps then he could begin to make some plans. The fact is, he was exhausted, Lydia was very ill, Dorothy seemed to be ill, as much in her mind (he feared) as her body: he would probably be ill himself.

Where *was* the Lord Deputy?

"The latest word is that he won't be here till next month, or even the month after that – new government in London, he has a great deal to discuss with them before he comes over, no doubt."

"The month after that? I cannot afford to lodge in Dublin until November! As it is, I trespass sorely upon your Christian hospitality."

"The Archbishop on his own initiative will not be able to help you at all: he is far too busy making his own peace with the Queen. He has thoroughly restored the Mass: but that consecration-service of yours is a very black bar across his hopes, *and* he has a wife to be shuffled somewhere if he still has any thought of keeping himself sweet with government. I think he means to marry her to one of his clerks and so pretend she was never his. Would you do a thing like that?"

"By heaven, sir, I would sooner burn!" Bale's voice was forthright, strenuous: but his thoughts were of Thorpe-le-Soken. He did not really listen to the rest of Mr Williams's apprehensive flow of gossip.

"No, dear Lord Bishop, if I were you I would not so much as *try* to have personal word with the Archbishop: only last evening as he sate at his ale-bench – even in midst of trouble he is always as ever an epicure – his cup in his hand, and swaying it up and down till the liquor spilled everywhere, 'By the Lord Christ's Five Wounds,' he swore, 'this Ossory ass shall preach no more in my archdiocese: if he cometh hither, Mr Williams, you shall tell him so incontinent. More trouble into Ireland with that one rampaging Ponet's-prentice than any we have ever had from the Ersemen-priests themselves.' It may be the Lord Deputy will make all smooth between you: but who can know what they say to him in London before he setteth forward his voyage . . . ?"

"I cannot understand –" Bale's mind was progressing independently of Williams – "I cannot understand how all could fall down so quickly. In King Edward's fifth year it seemed certain the whole of England was impregnate with secure reform. And yet all it needeth is the crown on Mary's head, and at once holus-bolus reversed. Have our great men not one single principle of faith and conduct left amongst them?"

"My lord, it is the fault of Duke Northumberland more than any: to pretend full-hearted Protestantism as a mere cloak for his politic working was surely to cast doubt, of complexion the very ugliest, upon all men's revived religion. And then, being forsworn on the scaffold itself, how can any after that have trust in lords and princes?"

Bale offered no comment: he had himself dedicated one of his polemical books to Northumberland, hailing him as a new Moses who could fetch England-Israel into the Promised Land; the book was in print and it incriminated. Oh God, his runagate rashness, he was no more heedful of the necessary serpent's wisdom than had been young Almain Conrad upon the fair-green of Diss all those years since, all those years . . . ! He began to shudder. He was falling ill.

"It crosseth my mind, dear sir," the fool Williams would *not* keep quiet, "that neither have we been sage as serpents *nor* meek as the turtle-dove, and therewithal our discomfitures. In this Ireland in particular: where popery was ever sluggish, high superstition but not fanatic; now it might be we have *aroused* a fanatic spirit that shall never be put down here. The backwards people for the first time are craving a militant church to hang out the Pope's banner, to elevate Antichrist as their one and only emblem, nay it will be their slavery in years to come, but as they see it today it is their main hope of *liberty*! Ah, God, sir, so heavy a consequence, and yet all that we did was for their souls' saving, our intent was never ill, bear witness your own letters that so well inveighed from Kilkenny about the cruelty of the Butlers' soldiery and their oppression of the rural folk!"

He understood, as he perorated, that he spoke to little purpose: Bale's attempt to demolish his argument foundered into an ague-fuddle of incoherent exclaimings. Mr Williams became immediately concerned for him; and also not a little for himself. His house in the Fish-shambles Street was very small for three new occupants, and if all of them were to take to their sickbeds . . . ?

"I must see what my housekeeper has to say about the health of your wife and your little girl, very hard for us to know what to do, as we do not know for how long you are here . . . Perhaps a good hot cordial drink, and should I not find a physician?"

"No, no," grunted Bale, "no: they are money-sucking scoundrels. In your Dublin, I have experience. For sake of purse they extend sickness, they will alleviate but never cure. An honest apothecary might be of some service, if he come not too dear. But I think, with rest and quiet, we shall all be very well."

*

For several days they stayed with Williams, the three of them, in their beds, high fever and vomiting: they had been soaked and chilled upon the road, as well as exhausted, and they each had their own variety of terror to worsen the physical stress. An apothecary did come, and his medicines made some improvement. Bale was the first to get up: he did not dress but sat beside Dorothy, stroking her head and trying to get her to talk to him.

He was not certain whether her words were from reasoned thought or delirious fantasy. He would probably have done better to have left her alone to sleep as Lydia, thank heaven, was sleeping. But he itched and prickled for her opinion: apart from pessimistic Williams, he had no-one else to turn to, never before had he felt so desperately driven.

"It is essential," he kept saying, "we show government we have no fear. We are honest Christians, we did our duty according to our King's commandment. In obedience to Saint Paul's precept. I have therefore writ a letter in very strong terms for the Lord Deputy when he gets here, to complain against the incompetence of his officers in his absence. Why were no security-forces sent to Kilkenny until the day before I left? Why did the man Hern endeavour to extract profit from our tribulation? Why did –"

"Why did they burn Joan Bocher?" Dorothy was tossing herself from side to side upon her pillow, her voice a gathering moan, almost like the funeral-keen Bale had hated so in Waterford. "Why did they burn her, why did they burn her, why did they burn . . . ? You burnt; you did: *you!*" She suddenly pulled herself up, and stabbed out a shaking finger into his face.

Bale knew what she meant. Mrs Bocher's case had been queer and distressing: he had never been able to account to himself properly the rights and wrongs of it and he knew that for the past three years Dorothy had held it bitterly and painfully in her mind, now and then bringing it out when annoyed by his more blatant dogmatisms.

For Joan Bocher had been burned by Protestants – by Cranmer, by King Edward's government – for the extremity of her Protestantism, called 'heresy' no less: she had alleged that the Incarnation of Christ was no such thing, that the Holy Ghost had passed through the Virgin Mary as light through glass and delivered the Blessed Child onto the stable-floor in front of His mother's knees somehow without any flesh-contact of human motherhood. Dorothy had admitted such a view must be nonsense: an eating walking man cannot be made of nothing but pure light.

But she also said: "Is it not poetry? My first son, at any rate, was born very like that: or seemed to be born so. They cannot go to burn Mrs Bocher for poetry: John, you must prevent it!" How could he prevent it? They were in Hereford at the time. Bale was hunting manuscripts for Ponet, and local clergy had asked Dorothy to sing at the Dean's birthday-feast: the news was old before it reached them. And ought he to want to prevent it? Joan Bocher had been called an Anabaptist: Anabaptism was devil-worship, look at Muenster!

But Mrs Bocher, while the Bales were in Germany, had become very close friends with Anne Askew. Bale told himself that was it: his wife loved the lovers of her love, and was anyway filled with guilt concerning the death of Anne. These were deeply-mired waters, he had better not probe with his toe.

But now, shrunken-cheeked and glaring, she thrust Joan at him again: "You saw that boy burnt in Norwich and 'no more of it, no more of it' you said; and then they burnt *her* because *she* said, 'no more of it, the Word of God has been made free for the people's soul of poetry' – when you heard she was to die you did not complain, so you burnt her yourself and now you have a queen that is seeking to burn *you*! And when I was in Thorpe-le-Soken –"

"Oh hush, sweetheart, hush, no more of that, I pray you –"

"When I was in Thorpe-le-Soken you went to another burning: do not tell me you did not, for the verses were writ in your hand, I found once the draft of it huddled among your foul-papers and I never said a word, but I never forgot it – even now I can rehearse it you!

> David Darvel Gatheren
> As said the Welsh men
> Fetched outlaws out of hell
> Now he is come with spear and shield
> In flames to burn at Smithfield
> For in Wales he may not dwell
> And Forest the friar
> That obstinate liar
> That wilfully shall be dead
> In his contumacy
> The gospel doth deny
> The King to be Supreme Head!"

As she rattled through the poem, her gabbling words reached higher and higher, she ended almost on a scream, and fell back into the pillow, burying her face in it, moaning and rolling. Bale saw that her ropes of sweated hair were now grey all over and her neck was as scrawny as a beanstalk in winter.

He said, "Why did you not tell me you had uncovered those words? It is true I did write them. Friar Forest was a malignant papist, he plotted against church and state, what else could Cromwell do but prosecute him to the uttermost? I was Cromwell's own poet, I could not refuse the commission, *King John* was just then about to be rehearsed for Canterbury, the acting-company's finances needed urgent replenishment. I did not seek the task, for God's sake I took no joy in it. Nor do I suppose that Latimer took joy in it when he preached at Forest's burning. They put the verses on a placard above the stake. When I heard about that I had stomach-cramp three days: I had refused to be there when it happened.

"Oh Dot, Dot, why did you not tell me you found them?"

"Upon a placard, John Bale? In Hebrew, Greek, and Latin, INRI?" She rolled over onto her back and lay staring up at him.

He could not meet her eyes. "Why did you not tell me?"

"Why did *you* not tell *me*, ever, that you had written them? Fifteen years you kept it secret. INRI. *Quod scripsi scripsi.* Mr Williams's housekeeper will bring you water to wash your hands." Foot and elbow out of her bed as though to go to the stairhead and call for the woman. Bale held her upon the mattress, almost by main force: she was very weak and did not resist him.

"There is another consideration, Dot, will you please listen? I have reason to believe Cromwell inveigled me on-a-purpose. When he first asked for the poem he gave me to understand they were only to burn Darvel Gatheren. So I wrote him six lines and then – as it were by accident – he asked for six more, and then –"

"You were his poet and so you wrote. Tell me, who was Darvel Gatheren, that you hymned his destruction so easily?"

"But you know who he was, chuck, you speak too disingenuous. He was a vast image, a huge horseman with a spear, an idol of painted wood, from a Welsh church where the ignorant made superstitious offering. No remorse at burning *him*. He was not even a Christian saint, but an ancient pagan god that the Christians had misapplied. Masculine counterpart of that same preserved heathenism we saw in the church near Kilkenny." He referred to a weird stone-carving right above the altar in one of the chancels of his diocese: he had discovered it on a visitation, and the parish priest had only laughed when he pointed it out. Later on Dorothy had insisted upon seeing it herself. A grotesque naked woman with long dugs like wineskins and claw-like hands pulling open the great gape of her cunt. The priest had called it 'the Shee-woman with the hole', meaning to say she was a witch-fairy of the *Síde*, and had said something (half in Irish) about the womb-blessings of St Bridget, to which Bale had made angry rejoinder. He demanded she be chiselled out of the wall, but the orders were given too late. Before they could take effect, Bale's own chiselling from Kilkenny was already hard upon him.

Dorothy's violent emotion seemed for a while to be stilled. She spoke quietly, with downcast eyes, as though to herself. "Richard said the hole-woman was an image of the Whore of Babylon, he was going to tell John Bale it ought to be left there as an evidence of true Protestants having lived one time in Ireland. I wonder John Bale hadn't thought of that himself? They danced with me and we dance no more. Chisel her (and she is stone). Burn him (and he is wood). Burn her and her and him (who are flesh). And poor Richard dies with a spear.

"Wood and stone are only poetry, Joan Bocher was poetry, Friar Forest of course was malignant, being a man of strong opinion almost as strong as Friar Bale's, Richard and Anne were two flowers from a garland of true-love: and nothing burns easier than paper.

"Bale, do you keep hold like an old wing-broken jackdaw of everything you ever write? Beware beware, if I can find: so can others, and they carry hot fire . . ." She drifted off into her fever-speech, and he went away to his own bed, still feverish himself.

*

"Stone," he muttered, "stone, wood, stone, fire. Into which of them — or all of them? — has transubstantiated her woman's-heart? For if it were not so, how *could* she be ignorant that I too loved sweet Richard Foster? She sees nothing and she dances not. John Bale, a forsaken man: Paul of Tarsus, a forsaken man."

He consoled himself with the *Acts of the Apostles* (amended, 'she' for 'ye'): "'What doeth she, weeping and tormenting mine heart? Soothly I am ready, not only for to be bounden, but and to die in Jerusalem for the name of the Lord Jesu.'" He did not quite pervert his text so far as to say 'London' instead of 'Jerusalem': there might be somewhere else more expedient for the Lord to call him to. He had to wait. He could not yet decide.

(iii) *Embarkation*

Another week, their healths were restored, but they did not dare go out of the house. Mr Williams had heard at the Castle that, firstly, the Lord Deputy was still making no haste to travel; second, Bale's letter to him had been read by subordinate officials and was very much resented, so that no-one in the Castle would now raise a finger to help him: and third, some informants had passed on the word that assassins had been paid by the Pope's Dublin agents to 'put Bale off the walk' (in the Irish phrase). If they were indeed the Pope's agents, presumably these days they must also be government-agents? No, there was no proof, but Mr Williams was quite sure such a warning was to be heeded. Bale must leave Ireland, without delay, in secret. How could it be arranged?

Without asking Bale's permission, Mr Williams did his best to arrange it. He spent all day down upon the quays in private conference with ship-masters, supercargoes, and sailors' boarding-house keepers, and returned rather gloomily. He had been looking, he said, for a vessel for the Hansa ports, or, failing that, Flanders.

"Flanders is no good," said Bale. "Flanders is the Emperor's land and altogether choleric papist! Good God, they burned Tyndale in Flanders!"

"No: but there are Protestant Netherland-Dutch at large upon the sea who could carry you secretly to brethren in Amsterdam or Rotterdam, and thence to Luther's Germany by land. But alas there are none such in the bay at this present, nor expected. Every ship here is for Portugal, Spain, or England: except one. What say you to Scotland?"

"Scotland! Why, man, their Queen-mother is another Romish Mary! She sweepeth the saints of Christ into her fire-breathing maw, a very dragon!"

Dorothy said, "Do you believe that? What then of the letter you had three months ago from David Lindsay about his play?" Lindsay, who had written so fulsomely to Bale in praise of *King John* had since kept up a desultory correspondence with him, chiefly on matters theatrical. As a royal official, Lindsay had to be careful about anything bearing upon religion or politics in letters to foreign parts; but it was true that his *Satire of the Three Estates* had been performed the previous year, at Cupar, with great success, and was now commissioned by the Queen-mother for a new presentation in Edinburgh. Moreover, Lindsay wrote, he had adapted certain notions from *King John*, notably the idea that his 'King' and the 'Three Estates' should not be seen simply as allegorical emblems, but –

> – the black verity of puir Scotland her complaint anent justice and reformatioun lang syne sleipand: bot now maist dreidfully arousit. Tak tent, John, for we sall ding for Her Graicis solace mickle straiks upon hurdies and craigs of fause ecclesiasts!

If Lindsay was not a Protestant, he was certainly no strong papist, and yet it seemed that his work was approved.

"Is it possible he would give me harbourage? I have no time to send a letter before me."

"Oh he'll give you harbourage if you hold your tongue. Put him in danger and he won't. John, you have little choice."

*

The ship in question was the *Rosebud-Picard* of Gravesend, arrived in Dublin bay with a cargo of tin from Cornwall and now chartered to bring herrings to Glasgow. A picard was a very small two-masted vessel of sprit-sail rig, not adapted at all for the comfort of passengers: which was all to the good, she would not be closely watched. The charterers' supercargo was a Dublin-resident Englishman, from Maldon in Essex (Bale's ears pricked up hopefully), of no great religion but well-experienced in shipping doubtful freights. He had in the past, thought Mr Williams, helped persecuted confessors into the realm; and, if properly paid, might now help them out of it.

Bale counted the coins in his purse.

The *Rosebud* was now loaded and lay, not in the river, but at moorings off Ringsend, awaiting the weather. The supercargo (to be known as 'Thomas': his surname best kept out of it until they were at sea) would expect the Bales that night in the Wild Rapparee tavern just beside Ringsend church. For obvious reasons, Mr Williams could not escort them there, but they could not miss the house: it had a signboard showing a breechless kern brandishing a dart (Bale drew his breath in sharply). Thomas insisted Bale came dressed as a common seaman, and Mrs Bale should look like a seaman's wife. Crews of coasting vessels often had their families on board with them, it would not appear strange.

The clothing presented no problem: Mr Williams sent his house-boy round a number of slop-sellers, and he returned with a pair of loose trousers, a knitted gansey, a tarpaulin jacket, shapeless boots, and a sealskin cap. The housekeeper provided a coarse woollen gown and an Irish rug-mantle for Dorothy, while Lydia's own garments had been so badly travel-worn on the ride from Kilkenny they would do very well as they were, once some embroidered borders were unstitched.

*

The road to Ringsend village helped their disguise: a two-mile tramp, heavy-laden with luggage, along the south shore of Liffey estuary with an unseasonable east wind blowing sleety rain into their faces all the way. They had to ford the sandbar mouth of the little River Dodder, which meant they arrived at the Wild Rapparee befouled, wet, and disordered: when they entered the bar they steamed.

Lydia was placed on her mother's lap, wrapped to the eyes in a blanket, while Bale looked around for a man called Thomas. Among the damp maritime customers was one in almost a gentleman's costume, and he had seen them come in. He was a fresh-faced young fellow with an engaging grin and an irresponsible appearance of enjoying the adventure for its own sake. He left his drinking-companions at the end of the bar and swaggered carelessly across the room. "Hello there," he called, "you'll be the new cooper to help keep my herring-casks caulked? Have a cup of Irish ruin. And get some into that kidling, she looks half-perished."

He compelled them to accept hot usquebaugh (against Bale's better judgement, though Dorothy swallowed it down fiercely enough), and then crouched for a confidential whisper. "Fear not, we have a cooper, but you're shipped as his mate just in case of any jack-in-office jolts from the port authorities. Talk like a churl Suffolk-man – that's where you're from, right? – and none o'these damn paddies'll understand a word you say. Nay, until you're in the cockboat, don't say anything at all. Just drink and be jovial. The old man knows you're coming but he don't know who you are. Let him think what he thinks already, you're a ne'er-do-well debtor on the run, plenty of *them* from port to port, let your good lady swear and curse at you for your feckless drunken ways, right? Oh –"

He broke off, glancing quickly over his shoulder as a big raw-boned man, in an unbuttoned sea-jerkin and his shirt open to the waist, pushed in through the door. "I don't like the looks of that. Watty Cosgrave is *not* a good friend. Avoid his eye."

"Who is he?"

"He's the sort of deep-water malcontent that shows himself the better man by opening his naked breast on a night like this, that's who he is. To speak serious, though, he's pilot of *French Maggie*: she dropped anchor a couple of hours ago. My opinion, he's here for no good. They've had a damned empty cruise so far and he's going to want his profit somehow."

This was highly enigmatical, but he condescended to explain. *French Maggie* was a Flanders man-of-war, under privateer's commission from the Emperor, looking to prey upon French shipping (the Holy Roman Empire being at war with France). Properly known as the *Marguerite-Debonaire-Carrack-of-France*, she had been built in La Rochelle as long ago as Henry VII's English reign, she had served as a French king's-ship, was then sold, as obsolete, to Walter Cosgrave. Cosgrave fitted her out for whaling, and sailed from Dalkey (in Dublin Bay) upon a number of voyages to Greenland waters and the Banks of the New-found Land: but he fell foul of the Bristol skippers when he tried to poach their catch, he had sea-battles with their ships, and was eventually driven out of his enterprise. After that, he made a deal with a dubious Flushing company, who wanted the vessel on the cheap for both war and commerce: they bought three-fourths of her at a third of her value, leaving him with one-quarter ownership, and installing him as master. But then they decided they would prefer an experienced fighting-man in command, and Cosgrave found himself degraded to pilot.

"He sold all his other bottoms to buy her in the first place, so he had to accept the berth. But it's made him mad jealous and he hates the world. Now I suppose he brings the old tub to Ireland to show off his local knowledge: but there's not one Frenchman here today in bay or river, and he's going to look a bloody fool. He'll tell his captain anything to get hold of a prey: that's why we've to be careful. He knows my face and he don't like it. He don't like any English-born Dubliner in the shipping-trade. I wish to God our boat was here."

They sat talking as unobtrusively as they could, with heads averted, for another ten minutes or so. Then Lydia began to whimper, and the noise caught Cosgrave's attention.

He looked searchingly in their direction, but did not move away from his seat. Every time Bale glanced round at him he saw the same unwavering stare, two watery-blue malevolent eyes in a harsh wind-scoured face, a few flags of whitey-brown hair falling across a knobby forehead, a row of teeth like those in a horse-skull. Dorothy kicked her husband abruptly: "Godsake stop looking round!"

At last the door burst open: a seaman with a lantern stuck his face in and called, "*Rosebud*'s boat's at the jetty! Let's not lose no time, then: it's blowing up vicious out there."

They grabbed at their baggage-rolls and scrambled to their feet. Lydia, startled from her half-sleep, gave a wail of distress. "Quiet, little precious, not a sound, trust in Jesus, we'll soon be home." Concerned not to frighten her further, Bale forgot his Suffolk accent. Add scholar's voice to landsman's gait, his appearance going out of the bar-room could scarcely have been that of a sea-cooper: they could only hope they moved so swiftly that Cosgrave (or anyone else) would not have noticed.

*

Later, in his *Vocation* book, Bale was to write of Saint Paul, how –

– in the city of Damascon, being laid wait for by the lieutenant of King Aretha, he was let down at a window in a basket, and so escaped his hands (*Acts* ix). I, in the city of Dublin, being assaulted of Papists, was conveyed away in the night in mariner's apparel, and so escaped that danger by God's help.

Had he not had this pious similitude to frame in his mind during the switchback see-saw sink-and-swerve plunging of the boat to the ship through more than a mile of dark toppling ridges of surf, he would no doubt have been even sicker than he was. Lydia and Dorothy found no such intellectual distraction: they simply threw up and wished for death.

*

The motion of the barge-shaped *Rosebud* at anchor was not quite so drastic: but it wrenched at their inwards badly enough. The master, a small crisp-whiskered Londoner, neat and respectable in his tarpaulin as any aproned haberdasher behind a shop-counter, gave them no great welcome. Legs astride on his bucketing deck, he looked them over with a frown and turned to Thomas: "They have paid you the passage-money, I hope, sir?"

"Better than that from 'em, skipper, half-share in the charter: your commission of course as percentage agreed."

"Most business-like; glad to hear it. Show 'em to the cabin, please . . . Hello though: what the devil d'you leave behind you on the Ringsend jetty?"

Ashore, through the blackness, gleamed a few dim lights from cottage windows: and also a far brighter light, waving in an obvious but inexplicable rhythm. "Why, I don't know," said Thomas slowly, "I cannot think it is meant for us . . ." But he sounded worried, and communicated worry to Bale and Dorothy.

(iv) French Maggie *Takes A Prey*

The mate, coming aft at a run, interrupted; calling attention to another light, only a few cables'-lengths to seaward, waved in a similar fashion between two lanterns, no doubt on the poop of another anchored ship.

"*French Maggie*," said the master, "talking to her shore-boat: but why such fuss? They'll not get lost." The moon at that moment slipped clear of the swift clouds, outlining against her radiance the awkward bulk of the carrack, a great black fort-wall on the tossing combers. Something white and in motion seemed to show against the silhouette, and then the moon was in again; nothing to be seen but night, all the lantern-sparks were quenched.

The mate was puzzled. "She's not unfurling sail?" he said, "Surely he can't be so daft as to try for an offing in this? Why, he'll pile hisself on Sandymount!"

"That's his business, mister. Ours is to keep all snug. Have you checked out that anchor-cable?"

"So you do not sail directly, sir?" put in Bale unnecessarily.

The master bristled at him. "Wrong wind, wrong tide: God'll send what He sends in the morning. Just now we're in some danger and I'll thank you not to flap your mouth. I said, show 'em the cabin."

It took some time for them to get themselves and their packets of luggage down the steep hatchway: Dorothy, holding Lydia, was helping to pass items to Bale at the bottom of the ladder, while Thomas carried them along into the tiny cabin under the poop, where it seemed they were all to be stowed together with the ship's officers, when, very suddenly, very scaringly, came a new interruption – or rather, a most violent alarm.

The picard's crew were all running and shouting, and there was also a strange shouting from the sea. Thomas and the Bales left off what they were doing and hastened to the taffrail to see what it was. A big longboat, rowed by at least a dozen, was pitching strongly toward them from the shore, already it was almost under their quarter: and at the same time another shaft of moonlight showed the carrack's high looming fore-castle outrageously close above the starboard bow.

The master bellowed something about keeping boarders off the deck, but too late; the longboat had hooked on: Walter Cosgrave, all cutlass and pistol and teeth, led a rush of men into the *Rosebud's* waist. There was no fighting: no-one was ready, and anyway it was not that kind of a crew. Those below decks were made to come up, and Cosgrave swore filthily at them. He was hailed from the carrack in Flemish and he hailed back impatiently: he was not yet ready to re-embark, they should drop another anchor over there and wait, he hoped to Christ they'd put a buoy on the cable they'd already cut. Bale could understand a fair amount of Flemish: enough to make clear to him that *Marguerite*'s pilot had the connivance but by no means the fullest approval of his captain.

"I want youse fucking French," roared Cosgrave, now in English, to the people of the *Rosebud*: "Youse French fucking bowsies that drank your lucky in the Rapparee, two men and a mot and a chiseler: get 'em tied." He identified the Bales and Thomas, and slapped the picard's mate about the face until he told him what they had done with their baggage. Then, with wrists bound, and their baggage thrown after them, they were pushed to the ship's side and – "into the boat, sharp, while I see what this hooker's got hid for me!" Holding a cutlass against the mate's throat, he secured the master's full purse without argument. It held his 'commission percentage' handed him by Thomas only fifteen minutes before. Another, and more urgent, hail prevented him from further search. Frustrated, he jumped for the boat, landing heavily on Dorothy and Lydia where his men had flung them down.

"Out oars and away with it," he ordered, "Twenty-to-one the sodding louser forgot to buoy my cable . . . !" Two of his men were in *Rosebud*'s cockboat and rowing to the carrack alongside them: no chance now for the picard to send to the shore for help.

★

Ropes were dropped from *Marguerite*'s mainyard and made fast round Dorothy and Lydia. They were hauled to the deck like cargo-sacks, screaming and twisting. Lydia's cries were pain and terror, Dorothy's pain and rage: it was horrifying for Bale to see it, he had never felt such humiliating impotence. He and Thomas had their bonds cut, they could make their own climb up the ship's side. Thomas kept a sullen silence. Bale shouted all the way up, averring his episcopal status, insisting he was no Frenchman, demanding his rights as a Queen's subject in the Queen's own tidewaters. He felt he was probably imprudent to make such protests – he saw how the foreign sailors were laughing – but his fury would not permit him any appearance of submission.

Upon the deck he attempted to go to his wife and daughter. Dorothy's face was all over blood, and Lydia with a hurt leg had collapsed onto the planks. The privateersmen held him back. Walter Cosgrave swore continuously in English, Irish and Flemish.

A man, perhaps the captain, was calling down from the twelve-foot-high poop, in Flemish: "Walter, we are too close to this lee shore, I have warned you, tide is flooding still, I gave orders to wait for the ebb! Bring the ship to safe mooring and then we can see your prey."

"Master-at-arms," shouted Cosgrave, "you know what to do with them." And then, in English: "I've to teach this sodger's-sutler how to sail a bastard cruise." He scrambled up, to con the vessel, nimbly scaling a series of battens fixed across the face of the poop.

The master-at-arms, lantern in one hand, belaying-pin in the other, cleared the prisoners down a hatchway, into a pitch-black low-ceiled compartment hard in the stern, loud with the creak and groan of the archaic steering-gear on the deck below: they could hear the constant orders that Cosgrave had to yell absurdly down through four tiers of hatches and then repeated up again by the men at the tiller – "Hard a-larboard!" "Hard a-starboard, *mijnheer*." "I said larboard, make it *larboard* – Jasus, *godverdoemen*, get a son-of-a-whore boy there to pass the fucking word so they can poxy hear it, ye handless *amadhauns* . . . !"

The master-at-arms wasted no time. "All clothes off," he barked, "Bare-arse naked!" Bale's continued expostulations were instantly cut short: the belaying-pin struck into his stomach and doubled him up. As he retched, he saw Thomas was already undressing.

"Lord Christ, not my wife," he groaned, "For His mercy, not my wife and child!" Thomas, pulling arms from jacket-sleeves, was more discreet: "*Mijnheer*, surely your religious Emperor gives no orders to despoil gentlewomen?" The master-at-arms took no notice but put a grip upon Dorothy's gown-top as though to drag it loose from its laces. She had for a moment stopped screaming: now she redoubled her outcry. "One hand," she shrieked, "one hand between my body and my clothes, I'll tear your throat from your damned neck-bone! Off!" she shouted, "off . . .!" The man backed off: perhaps he did have no orders. Dorothy's wrists were no longer fastened, she swept Lydia into her arms, and stood her ground defying him, stooped under the low deck-beams.

He turned again to Bale and Thomas. "Not yet clothes-off? Another strike?" He swung the belaying-pin. "Meanwhile is perhaps no trouble to keep woman-breast under cover just yet. You: hold cow-and-calf." His two mates pushed Dorothy against the bulkheads, while Thomas and Bale dropped their last garments on the deck. "Now then," said the master-at-arms, "Just to wait please for *Mijnheer* Walter." He squatted down and rummaged the clothes, finding nothing, it seemed, of interest to him. Then he bundled them up in his arms and took them out of the cabin, followed by his men, who bolted the door behind them.

*

Dorothy said nothing, except to whisper a hopeless encouragement to Lydia, trying to laugh, trying to pretend it was only a game that had got too rough. Bale, his hands absurdly clasped together across his privities in the dark, thought of the apostle and said what he would later write: "As Paul, against his will, was put into a ship of Adramitium, coupled with other prisoners of Jewry, conveyed forth to Italy, and there safely delivered, as in the *Acts*, twenty-seven and twenty-eight, so was I and my companions . . ." and then he stopped because Thomas was laughing.

"You laugh, sir, I suppose, being certain of our rescue?"

"Oh we're not going to get rescued, they stole *Rosebud*'s cockboat, and even if they hadn't, who could come and help us? Government keeps no more than the one cruiser in this bay, she lies in Bullock Harbour armed only with falconets and hailshot-pieces. No, Bishop, no: but it's comical they call us French. Maybe we *should* be French. Maybe a damn sight safer than to let 'em know you're a Luther bishop?"

"They must find out the truth. I have books in my baggage, papers."

"I don't suppose they'll look at those till they pull out of this damfool anchorage. Our best chance is they should run aground: they nearly did ten minutes ago, or did you not notice? But Walter's an able man, they won't. This wind is due to shift. He'll have us clear of Head-of-Howth by mid-morning. God-a-mercy but it's cold to be childbirth-stark in an east wind midnight, brrr!"

After that there was silence among them for a long time. Lydia fell fast asleep, the tears sticky-wet on her face. The chill of the damp cabin forced the two naked men close to one another: Thomas grinned to himself at the incongruity, he was an amorous young fellow among the women, and to put his arms round Bale and hug him tight to his bosom struck him shrewdly for its contrast with previous naked couplings he had enjoyed. The more so as Bale held himself both aloof and very near, a strange feeling. Another man, less spontaneous in his physical responses than Thomas, might have been disturbed by it.

Bale said to himself: "Can it be possible this lusty youth knoweth not Original Sin? Would God I were so innocent: and yet such innocence in our fallen world is but a token of essential guilt. This is not Eden, it is a pirate's prison, and corrupteth all if we permit it. Let us pray." He prayed (silently, afraid of Thomas's laughter) and cuddled as close as he dared: it really was excessively cold.

Overhead, the shouts, the thumps, the running of feet, the dragging of ropes on the deck, re-echoed through the hull, with dire intervals of slamming and splashing as the carrack surged among the waves in first one direction then another.

(v) 'For Which Of Them Will They Give Us The Mostest Money?'

Their misery lasted for hours, until a pale grey dawn light began to creep through the port-holes, and they could see in what sort of den they had been put. It was unfurnished, save for cannon: two large culverins inside padlocked stern-ports, and smaller swivel-guns fixed into openings which were permanently uncovered, too narrow to escape through, but large enough to let in on them the wind and spray. There was a tub of dirty drinking-water and an unscoured latrine-bucket. It was clearly a space reserved for captives, and they were the first to receive its welcome.

A crucifix, nailed to the stern-post, left no doubt as to the ship's doctrine. Bale muttered about 'graven images', glowered at the thing, his fingers itching. Thomas saw him and hastened to avert a disastrous outburst of zeal. "You toss that ornament overboard, you'll get us hanged before they're ready to do it," he said wearily: he was no longer in any state to laugh. Bale restrained himself, and looked instead at the waste of waters foaming up along the leeside gunports.

Thomas had been right. The wind was abated and now blew from the south. *Marguerite* was tacking to weather Howth Head, a slow process; bits of rocky shore with a bracken-topped hill above them kept coming and going up-and-down in their field of vision. They were very near.

"She's no easier athwart the breeze than a bloody barn-door," commented Thomas. On a promontory was a neat stone house with battlements and a gun-platform: from its flagstaff a crowned harp on a blue field, the Irish government colours.

Dorothy stared at it, her bruised lips, caked with blood, drawn back from her teeth like a hound's: "Who lives there, Mr Thomas? No way we could signal them? Fly a scarf out of window or something? Or something, man, damn your eyes, we *must* –! Oh it *is* a Queen's building –?"

"Customs-office," said Thomas. "They keep a pinnace there to inspect vessels at anchor in the roads. Fair guess, they never bothered to inspect aboard this one. No tangling with the Emperor, that'll be their watchword. If you try and fly a signal they'll only tell each other you're drying laundry. Even so, we *could* make a demand of the old man: he's not Watty Cosgrave, and we haven't had a sight of him yet. Come on, let's get another gut-full of belaying-pin, are you with me?"

He jerked at Bale's elbow, seeing the bishop for the moment fallen into a dullness of despair; and then began banging on the door and shouting in bad Flemish for the captain. Bale saw Dorothy looking at Thomas, not at *him*. The horrid intimacy of their situation oppressed him, was she as conscious of the men's nakedness as he was? It angered his very soul to think she might not be, to imagine that she had her mind solely upon their ill-treatment, while his own ran in so many unexpected directions: Eden? Parnassus? Why could he not keep Cromwell's nasty Bosch-book out of his fantasy?

He staggered to his feet alongside Thomas and began banging on the door as well.

Lydia, waking, said, "Why is dadda so silly, hitting the door with his fists and all bare?"

Dorothy laid the child's head against her breast, talking as much to herself as to Lydia: "When they made him a bishop, God told him he was silly, but he wouldn't believe. So now you see God makes him into nothing but a cloutless fool because nothing can be sillier than that. Go to sleep and wake up again and you'll find him your dadda once more. It could happen."

What did happen was the master-at-arms angrily opening the door. "Be silent, arse-holes, you are heard. He will see you. Two men. Come topside."

"Topside" meant having to go up to the open waist-deck and from there onto the poop by clambering the slippery battens, an unpleasant business in their nakedness, and the crew did not spare them ridicule. Cosgrave, still at con, showed his teeth and spat. They were hurried past him down a ladder, and so into the captain's great cabin. As they went, Thomas took note of the state of the ship: he saw crude tarred clapboard nailed in and among the remains of old enrichment, fragments of carved ogival-work crocketted and once gilded, scrollery, three-quarters of a sculpted Arethusa-with-mermaids across the taffrail. The stern-castle now resembled a huge two-storey dog-kennel covering a third of the ship's length: and yet *Marguerite-Debonaire* had been long ago a resplendent vessel, as sumptuous as the French princess from whom she had her name. But her design had never embodied the intellectual grace that made Margaret of Navarre, poet and reformer, respected even among such as Bale. All her life this ship was bitch and brute in every weather. Walter Cosgrave's bad bargain: you could read it in his face.

*

The captain, behind his cabin-table with his purser, was a stout blond moustachioed military-looking man; cunning-stupid eyes, green as gooseberries, half-buried under folds of flesh. All the papers, books, money, from Bale's luggage spread out in front of him. "Give them their clothes," he said, without looking up.

The clothes were in a heap on the deck. Not dignified, dressing in such circumstances, but better than remaining nude.

"You are French," stated the captain, in Flemish. The two captives both started talking at once, Bale shouting, "No no no!", Thomas more precisely refuting the assertion: "If we are, why do your officers all swear at us in English?"

"Enough." The captain cut their uproar short: "I cannot understand. If I cannot understand it is French for all I care. Pilot Walter calls you French."

"Pilot Walter is a bloody liar, and that house beyond the rocks there is the customs-house: we think you should put us ashore to sort out who we really are. The Queen's Searcher is Mr Parker, he knows me well enough." Thomas spoke to the point, but Bale was too disturbed to support him with equal reason. He had one leg into his trousers and one leg out, he staggered about the cabin and called down God's wrath upon ship and crew for their abuse of Christ's chosen, he lunged fruitlessly for his open wallet on the table to find his bishop's seal and prove himself, he commanded the captain at once to reveal the name of the Pope's agent who had paid for this man-snatching, he referred to his wife and daughter as Prisca and Valeria, Christian martyrs under Diocletian, indeed Diocletian's wife and daughter, such their nobility, such their fortitude . . . The master-at-arms hit him hard under the jaw: he subsided half-stunned.

The purser was sifting the documents with some show of intelligence. He said, in a sort of English: "It says here you are divinity-doctor, says 'bishop', do I read 'bishop'? How can you be *bisschop*? Look at your trouser, *matros-kleding*, shipman-trousers, *neen*?"

"Look at his shirt," retorted Thomas, "Fine linen with white embroidery." It was true, Bale had not changed his shirt for his disguise.

"Very good. He has doctor-shirt. So which he steal: shirt or trousers? Let us say at some time some gull-fools have thought him bishop: but on Scotland ship, with *woman*, running? To hide himself, we are still to think so: why? I tell you what I tell to Captain Cornelis; he is either criminal-imposter in Ireland, or Frenchman on the sea. Captain says, for which of them will they give us the mostest money? All right: very good: we will consider."

The captain spoke again. "If you are French we take you to Vlissingen, for imperial government to arrange ransom. If you are English we hand you over to the government of your own queen. We expect a good bounty, you are fugitives, with forged papers: the old one afraid of justice, the young one helping him flee. But we don't give you up in Dublin, they will pretend we did wrong to take you without a warrant and so they will devise excuses to withhold our money. So probably Waterford, if the weather is suitable. If not, then perhaps England. *Mijnheer*, do they understand?"

The purser nodded, and finished the interview with some more of his English. "Captain Cornelis has to say, your woman and small girl will be not ill-treat. But room for them, separate, is not possible, we are a ship to fight, not *plezier-boot*, no *luxus-jacht*, yes? Master-at-arms will bring you mattress, so you sleep and we give food. Make trouble, we chain you, take clothes again, woman too. Watch for trouble. Go!"

Thomas helped Bale to his feet and was leading him to the companionway, when the wide feet of Walter Cosgrave came bouncing down it in their sea-boots. The pilot pushed straight past and announced to the captain: "Wind swinging westerly, I'd say from the sky she'll be more north than west any hour now, fair for Carnsore, if that's what you want, though God knows when you get there if you'll be able to reach round to Waterford. Did you find these gobshites Frenchmen or what are they?"

"Keep those prisoners here a moment," ordered Cornelis. "I want to talk to you, Walter. No more French than you or I. What made you think they were?"

Cosgrave was not abashed. "They played it that quare in the Rapparee they must have been something. I knew for certain, whatever it was, there'd be profit in it, hook it or drag it."

Thomas was bold: "You knew for certain my face and it was no French face. Oh admit it, dammit, Watty, you've hooked and dragged this captain into war between Queen and Emperor if government should take it up. You don't think they'll make him a duke for it in Flushing when he gets home?" A pause while the purser translated. The captain pulled his drooping lip and hooded his eyes at the pilot. He was obviously becoming worried.

Cosgrave laughed. "Oh right for you, so; I fucking knew your face. I fucking knew the class o'business you like to ship along of your herrings. Look here now, Cornelis –" he was into Flemish again – "old Dangle-tool here calls himself a bishop, right? So what sort of sodding bishop's on the run out of Queen's Ireland these days, will you tell me that? It's not just a rogue-bounty you'll hope for in return for him, but church-cash for digging-out heresy, and if the English don't stump up with it, you can for sure find a pope's-inquisitor in Zeeland or wherever else? Matter-a-damn what they say about war: Queen and Emperor both are a pair of damn good Catholics."

"Ah, yes," said the captain, looking most carefully at Bale. "Thank you, Walter, yes: much to be thought about . . . Prisoners to quarters, take them."

The master-at-arms hurried them down again and locked them up.

There were palliasses now in their cabin, spilling over with lice. They sat down on them regardless. They too had much to think about.

*

It is to be supposed that Bale had never known from his wife such sheer coldness as now fell between them on this voyage. He would not acknowledge he was in any way at fault: she would not acknowledge his very existence, except obliquely by the occasional taunt she would make about him to Lydia – poor child, little Lydia was still in a babyish dream: the 'sturdy girl, stout trouper' that had marched by the portative-organ through the angry streets of Kilkenny had slid right back into the nursery, even the cradle. She would not eat the ship's food, which was wholesome, though vilely prepared, and Dorothy must hold her for hours against her unbuttoned breast in a mad hope that God might send milk to her through the nipple. Or if not God, then *Someone*: in her secret heart-root, Protestant Dorothy knew that she had not killed the Blessed Virgin upon the Bishopstoke bonfire, in her heart-root she knew the Virgin forgave *all* women, only provided She was remembered. So Dorothy remembered Her: and Lydia did seem to derive some comfort from the suckling; and, for short intervals, sleep.

In return, Bale ignored his wife, talked incessantly to Thomas about Saint Paul, pressing his hand involuntarily, once even stroking his cheek, desperate for some human warmth.

But Thomas was tired of Bale, and his youthful resilience had been badly undermined by the threat of inquisitors. He was quite without strong doctrine, but that was no mitigation: he had thoughtlessly helped a proscribed heretic, his very thoughtlessness would be counted against him. And had he not heard that the Low Countries were now trending Spanish-wise rather than Austrian in the flavour of their imperial government? Treachery, however, was no part of his nature. It never struck him he could save himself by a timely denunciation of Bale. Instead, he watched events, particularly the tension between Cosgrave and Cornelis, and tried to think, tried in vain to discuss it with Bale, how to work it to their advantage. He had little to do with Dorothy. Perhaps she held him to blame for their predicament. Perhaps he reminded her of Richard Foster. She only spoke to him when absolutely necessary.

*

When Lydia grew discontented with the dry dug, she whinged and squirmed and vomited and wet her breechings, finally bursting out into heart-rending sobs. Dorothy tried to sing to her. She herself was so dull-spirited, she could only think of one song: the Saint Paul ballad of the ex-friar from Doncaster, years and years ago. Probably Bale's apostolic *exempla* had put it in her mind; but it had its own appropriateness, quite apart from *his* incorrigible self-importance. She would never have admitted she had taken note of what he had been saying.

> Across the sea and across the sea
> Far over the sea in the ship of Rome,
> For Christ His sake I must leave my love
> And never more come sailing home.
>
> On Macedon strand my love doth dwell
> Where she weaves the robes of the purple red
> And the beams of love over Macedon strand
> Shine gently gently on Lydia's head.
>
> O shall I ever see her more?
> And shall I hold her in my arm?
> From Rome I shall fly in the Arms of Christ
> To fetch her safe from hurt and harm.

But Lydia began to whinge again: "Please, mamma, not to sing, not to sing, mamma, *please* –" and Dorothy had to give up.

"Oh my darling, why is it you cannot bear mamma's music these days, you used so to love to hear it?"

Bale said, to Thomas: "The poor maid was frighted by mischief-tales of a witch-woman's ghost in Kilkenny. I thought she had forgot it weeks since. But it still daunts her worse than the blood-thirst of these Flushinger villains. Notwithstanding I have told her Mrs Alice was no likely witch but a primitive Lollard, such as lived, I have always held, in the years prior to Wycliffe, firming him a basis for his own developed doctrine. Which is what I believed last month. Now I am not so sure. Malory's romance of the endless end of Merlin mayhap hath very truth to it. There *could* have been a Nymue in Kilkenny; drawing exemplar for her *succuba* life from one or other of the noxious images she'd have seen in the chancels thereabout. And doubtless she would have sung: aye, a cracked voice on a rocking deck, making seasick a man's ears."

He spat these last words with such wickedness that Thomas stared at him in amazement. Otherwise the young fellow had made little of his remarks: he was not a reader of books.

*

In the event, *Marguerite* did not put in to Waterford. From scraps of information from the master-at-arms (who had become slightly more communicative, though no less vindictive, than at first) Thomas deduced Cosgrave's advice to the captain: that Ireland was too disaffected, government's chief interest was to get dissidents out of the country, not back in; and the Waterford authorities would probably refuse to accept Bale even as a gift. Bale thereupon made furious demands to be handed over to the Mayor of Waterford: he was ready, he said, to face trial with clear conscience; he was ready to confront the justice of Nero Caesar himself! But the demands got no further than the master-at-arms, who hit him yet again as one might hit an importunate schoolboy, bolting the door on his roarings.

Dorothy laughed: and told Lydia a story.

"Upon a time there was a shrewd rabbit who found dead meat for an old lion, and made himself so useful none of the lion's friends ever ate him. One day the huntsmen caught many lions and put them into the king's cages. The old lion was one of them, and he begged could the rabbit come too. This was agreed, and they were all fed by the royal beast-keeper: mutton for the lions, lettuce for the rabbit. The King's courtiers would come and wonder at the rabbit in the lion's cage, and the rabbit was very proud of himself, to be admired by so many fine people. But the lions were not happy, they yearned for the freedom of their wide hot grassland home. Some of the younger ones began to talk of hunting the poor rabbit round and round inside the cage, the nearest they could reach to their old manner of life. So the rabbit, hearing this, and becoming alarmed, said, 'You want to be free? I'll help you to be free!' and he burrowed and burrowed for them under the walls that held the cage-bars, till a whole length of the bars fell down and all the lions escaped. They ran straight out into a field just beside the king's castle where lived the sheep that the royal beast-keeper used to kill for the lions' food. At once they started leaping at the sheep and killing them for themselves: but the old lion was too old to leap. The rabbit said, 'Never mind, I'll kill you a fine fat sheep!' After all this time in the cage, he had forgotten he was no lion, and that freedom for lions and freedom for rabbits are not quite the same. He also forgot that even sheep have their own freedom, to eat their greenstuff just like rabbits. He showed his buck-teeth and snarled (if you've ever heard a rabbit snarl?): and he sprang at a wise mother-sheep who was protecting her little ones from the lions behind a bush. She was so heavy with all her wool that she trampled him into a dry ditch. The old lion got no dinner, and the rabbit had his mouth so cruel-choked with green stinging-neetles that he never from that day forward made another boastful word."

"What was the rabbit called, mamma?"

"Oh, sometimes they called him 'Bale-zebub', but that only made him idle and proud."

Lydia nestled her head and went to sleep. Dorothy finished the tale for herself: "'Dangle-tool' would have been more suitable, perhaps they called him that as well." She had been listening with half-an-ear to the jibes of the master-at-arms.

Bale wept, for the fate of his remaining few books; as he had last seen them, sodden with seawater, scattered like so many lettuce-leaves all over the captain's table.

(vi) *The Perilous Beach*

As Paul's ship was caught betwixt Candia and Melita, and could not resist the winds; so was ours betwixt Milford Haven and Waterford. As they had an exceeding tempest upon the sea; so had we likewise. As they were without hope of safeguard; so were we also. As they were almost famished and drowned, so were we. As God comforted them, so did he us. As they were in conclusion cast into an island, so were we into St Ives in Cornwall.

No more than two days of storm, but Bale wrote the truth: they all nearly died. *Marguerite* was quite incapable of answering to her helm in such huge seas, and the gale from the north-west drove her sideways and bare-poled across the mouth of the Bristol Channel like a man trying to carry a plank along the edge of a mountain. In the prisoners' quarters the water came in through the swivel-ports and washed out again from the scupper-holes at deck-level: there were times when it was thigh-deep, upon particularly heavy rolls. No need for sea experience to know so tall a carrack was bound to be top-heavy: which ought to have made for despair. The crew were despairing; but for the prisoners, more complicated emotions.

Two alternative hopes, and which was the worse to cling to: hope of drowning or of escape-from-drowning and thereafter the inquisitors' fire?

Dorothy said once, as she pulled Lydia clear of yet another galloping flood, "This child was born of water, between two waves, on the Bremen ship. I think those waves have heard of her trouble and so return here to fetch her home. Ah, but a question, who called them?" If she talked like an oracle, she was not able to behave with concomitant solemnity: they were tumbled from one side of the deck to the other, yelping and spewing, and the ship's noise was incessant – a city in riot could have been no louder.

*

On the third morning, they ran in tatters round Bamaluz Point and dropped anchor in the bay of St Ives. Lydia's waves, for good reason or bad, had decided they did not want her just yet. Also, some credit to the pilot. Were he ever to leave the ship, Captain Cornelis would be much at a loss.

Bale, peering through a gunport, saw grey stone houses clawing the slope of a wind-shaven hill, and concluded it was an Irish haven: then Thomas recognised the little fishers' chapel on the headland, and the granite church built so close to highwater-line that it seemed to set its feet in the sea. "Cornwall," he said, "Papist country, they rebelled against King Edward, so no doubt Mary is their darling girl."

But Cornelis had a different view. His pilot *had* left him, grabbing the cockboat and sculling himself ashore the minute the anchor was down. As he went, he shouted out a few words about replacements for the damaged rigging, and shipwrights' services: but the captain suspected he was out to scout the land for a reward for Bale and party, with himself to gain the largest portion. Cornelis sent down his purser to talk to the prisoners, reminding him that Bale's baggage held more money than they had a right to expect (for his foreseeable length of journeying, Bale had thought it insufficient; but from all his years of poverty he always underestimated): and that as they had it safe in the great cabin above, it might be better to keep hold of it – bird in the hand – than to trust to Walter Cosgrave and his speculative schemes of innumerable fowl upon branches out of reach.

The purser, a wide-mouthed frog-faced Dordrechter, surveyed the wreck and ruin of the prison-cabin and licked his lips with a big wet tongue. "This is not good. We had flying tempest: why did we not perish? Man-of-God amongst us, likely, thinks Captain Cornelis. Not Jonah, stern-chase from Jonah: he thinks your prayers like Holy Paul have preserved us every man."

This was a line of argument that would have deceived Bale into believing anything: he immediately puffed himself out, nearly as froggish as the little Dutchman. "I did, sir, as you say, commend ourselves – captives and captors – to our Maker, and –"

"Very good. So how are you heretic? Heretic prayers would have sunken the ship . . . How, *mijnheer*: difficulty. This man Walter is no good. He has said, before he went, said to mates upon our deck, that he takes the skiff ashore here to meet a so-great gratitude: for to his nation is accorded the commencement of the Cornwelsh fishing, two of the Irish three-lifetimes-since brought new shape of fishnet to Cornwall, since when all from Ireland is marvellous thing for Cornwelsh prosperity – in St Ives they will believe all that Irish Walter tells them.

"But Captain Cornelis asks himself: what is this feud and hatred from Walter against *you*? Religion alone? Here at sea we have one religion: either God helps or He destroys, and today we have been helped. No, it is not religion, but Irish against English!"

The purser laboriously showed (what Thomas had already shown) how English competition had ruined Walter's whaling-ventures: how an English bishop at the pilot's mercy might be as glaring an object of vengeance as even a Bristol skipper.

"But no good, you see: this is profit-cruise, communal, we can not use our time upon one fool man his vengeances."

So Cornelis was proposing – and he hoped they would agree – to bring all of them openly ashore with him, as passengers not prisoners; and, if they were arrested upon Walter's information, to defend and protect them in the name of the Emperor.

"Passenger upon empire-ship is sacred man to English Queen, *ja*? *Soja*, you are happy: *so neen*, compensation in long-length is paid for your blood."

Bale thought hard upon the ambiguities and intricacies of all this. He looked at Thomas, who shrugged his shoulders. He looked at Dorothy who turned her head away. He must speak upon his own: "If you mean to protect me, why bring me ashore at all? You could refuse to give me up, and then take me to some further port, some German port, you have my money, you know you will be paid?"

Dorothy, looking out at a port-hole, said quietly, "If the reward-money is greater than *your* money then his protection is withdrawn. And he needs to show St Ives that you are *his* property and the captain's, not that damned pilot's."

"Clever *vrouw*," leered the purser. "She is clever clever *vrouw*, but not wise. We do not yet know who is most power in this town."

It might, as the pilot hoped, be friends of the Irish; it might (and very likely) be Mary's Catholics: but also, bearing in mind how recent was the change of rulers, it might still be King Edward's Protestants left to clear up the detritus of rebellion. If the latter, they would be Bale's good friends.

Would they be the Dutchmen's?

For Cornelis was a trifle afraid. St Ives was no great port: but he had seen a pair of gun-platforms in range of the anchorage, and several ships at moorings, individually smaller than *French Maggie*, but able to combine against her with menace. It was essential that Walter should not be allowed to let the authorities think there were English people hidden from them aboard the carrack – "belligerent ship of Empire with storm-damage, most woundable in English port because England not being at war." The purser talked of "neutrality-protocols, law-dangers, they could seize us or sink, you see what I say, *neen*?" Cornelis had little choice but to exhibit his prisoners. How long they would really *be* prisoners could only depend upon political conditions in St Ives.

"We will give you your good clothes: in your bags I see you have them, *bysschop-kleding* like Holy Paul. And all shall know how well we have treat you."

Bale twisted his beard, doubtfully. "Are all of us to come ashore?"

"But of course, for clever *vrouw*, for pretty maiden, for strong young man, clean fresh air, a dry street, and *goddank*!" The purser emphasised that if they did exactly what Cornelis told them in the town, it was not at all impossible he would bring them at last into Germany among Protestants. But if they made trouble . . . The purser shot out his thick lips and blew through them like a foghorn, indicative, they supposed, of some sort of maritime last-rites.

"One quarter-hour together alone," he concluded, "You will think now how you answer."

They all three argued back and forward for ten minutes of the quarter-hour. None of them really knew what they ought to do. The only thing they were all agreed on was that the captain could not be trusted. At last Thomas said, "*Rosebud* on her last voyage was at the port of Hayle, just round the bay from here. Her master told me something I've just this minute thought about: it could be of use. That rebellion they had in Cornwall was only in part for religion: the people cried for old popery because government forbade it, not so much because they wanted it. They're like the Irish here, different language, different customs. Seems the Protestant clergy gave them English in their churches, English Bible, English instruction, paid no heed when they were asked for the Cornwelsh tongue instead. The old-guise priests, though they prayed in Latin, were happy enough to preach in Cornwelsh, all their Christ-plays were in Cornwelsh too. This bishop, you see, that King Edward sent 'em, had made his own English Bible, and that was the thing fixed him so intolerant positive no Cornwelsh ought to be used."

"It would," said Dorothy, "yes. Is it not just what that poor harper told you, in Southwark four years ago, except you would not listen and drove him pitiless from your door? So who was this positive bishop? Not hard to find him a bedfellow."

Her sneer was misfired: Bale grinned with malice from ear to ear. "Wrong!" he shouted, "Wrong! Spleen, woman, brings forth your ill-judgement as cold winter doth engender the chilblain. Miles Coverdale was not made bishop till after rebellion was over, and by the Lord he wrought mightily here! Blame not that well-ordered man! He was mine honest friend at Cambridge and I love every word from his pen. I hear now this Queen hath had him dispossessed. Well: but there is yet hope. You remind me of cause for great hope! For Coverdale in Exeter diocese bred such godly devotion among the heretofore-benighted that even in this wild place there must surely be men that have heard his word, who will not be put down by old papistry revivified, who will know me for what I am and take my part against all comers!"

As he spoke, the captain entered. Bale swung round to him. "Good captain, we receive your offer. We will step upon this perilous beach."

"So, child, let us go cleanse ourselves," whispered Dorothy to Lydia. "Rabbit is once again lion. God keep him out of nettle-ditches."

*

Captain Cornelis in a small west-country harbour-town was something of an embarrassment. Before he took to the sea, he had held ancient's rank among the landsknechts in the German wars, and for his shore-going best he chose to clothe himself in his old outlandish gear – huge breeches slashed and beribboned with a codpiece half the size of his head, puffed sleeves like a brace of bomb-mortars, a great hat overflowing with plumes (tightly tied against the storm-wind), and a frantic two-handed sword. None the less, he was impressive, in a dunghill-cock sort of way, and it seemed the local magnates would need to be impressed. For Cosgrave had done his work: town-bailiff and constables were waiting for the captain's boat on the little pier that ran out from the Wharf, not far from the Shallop Inn.

The bailiff politely explained there had been an information lodged concerning the English folk aboard the *Marguerite*. "Quite exact," answered the purser, "Very good, they are here, you see them one two three and child."

"Prisoners?" asked the bailiff.

"No, no: but full-paid passengers."

"Passengers for where?"

Cornelis twirled his moustachio; stuck out his padded chest; exerted leverage on the hilt of his sword, causing the point to rear behind him. "Captain Cornelis would ask you, *mijnheer*, by what right you put question, *of hij komt, dan of hij gaat* – if he comes, if he goes – to ship-captain of the Emperor?"

The bailiff was a little intimidated, and looked round nervously at the crowd. Despite continuous irruption of gale-gusts down the narrow streets, nearly everyone in St Ives had come to the Wharf to see the strangers, any mistakes that were made would be most disagreeably public. He swallowed and coughed for a moment, caught his bonnet that was blowing away, then stated stolidly that the magistrate in receipt of the information-received was at present in the Shallop parlour; and therefore, if the foreign gentleman would care to accompany him there, together with his passengers . . . ?

The purser looked at the captain and interpreted his prolonged growl: "He says yes: so we come."

Thomas said to Bale, "If they're seeing us under the ale-stake, they can't have made up their minds. There's a courthouse and lockup in this place, you know: I was afraid we'd be taken there. They can be damnable strict if they want to be. Pirates, fish-poachers, and so forth. Hang 'em out of hand on the promontory."

(vii) *At The Shallop Inn*

When they entered the Shallop, the bailiff made sure they were not followed in by the crowd: this would be no open trial but a private examination. The parlour had been arranged, a ring of stools for a few leading townsmen and a table for the magistrate. He was a gnarled meagre iron-eyed elderly man in muddy riding-clothes. He said immediately, "Sit them down, sit them down," so they all found places. "Now then," he said, "Which is the one that pretends to be bishop?"

Bale stood up. "Sir, I do not pretend. I am consecrate Bishop of Ossory in Ireland, and I have not yet been deprived."

"Oh? You have some reason to think you *ought* to be deprived?"

"Between me and my Saviour, sir, no: but between me and the Queen, that might be different."

"By God, and it *might*!" The old man became suddenly venomous. "Because I already took occasion to find out who you were. I was sent for this morning from my farm, express, emergency, great urgency so they said, as being the one man in these parts with good ear for all church matters. My name, sir, is Downings: I am proud, I tell you, proud, that I drew sword – yes, with these chalk-stone finger-joints – for the sake of Our Blessed Lady and the late holy monks of Bodmin when King Edward's heretic Protector imposed perversion through the land! And you, sir, Bale or Boil, were one of his vicious sectarians. Oh yes I have found you out."

"Mr Downings –": the magistrate's clerk, a smooth man with a smooth voice. "By your favour, sir: he may be heretic, but no word that he is deprived, no warrant for his arrest, we are not able to prosecute, nor yet remand in custody, nor even impose bail. There is no charge against him."

"Not *yet* there isn't. Where's that pilot?"

Walter Cosgrave was brought in from the adjacent bar-room. He had not just been idling there. In fact, as Bale wrote later, the pilot was 'as drunk as an ape'. The smooth clerk smiled to himself. Perhaps the liquor had been paid for by a furtive and helpful hand. At all events, it was a development that baffled Mr Downings.

For the drunkenness was of a sort that could only be immediately obvious to those who had already met Cosgrave, and the magistrate had not. Walter moved very slowly and carefully into the parlour, and very carefully sat down on a beer-keg in the corner, with his back half-turned to the company. He belched quietly into his hand, several long belches, one after the other, and suddenly leaned over so far sideways that it seemed he must topple to the floor: but he just balanced. Then he rolled his head slowly, and mumbled, no less slowly: "A good witness is well-sworn, fucking-well sworn, your man in there did the swearing, from a blackjack of aquavit. Wheresthedep'sitions?"

"Stand up, sir, *stand up!*" Downing's eyes were like gimlets, and Walter countered them with all his teeth.

He did stand, like *French Maggie* righting herself after a violent beam-seas wave. He laid one hand to a post that held up the ceiling-joists, and smiled all round, ghastly white. He was sworn: or rather, he smiled and belched across the book, and they took it for an oath.

"You accuse the man John Bale of heresy and treason. Upon what ground?"

"Ground. Scotchman's ground."

"What?"

"Amn't I after telling youse, Scotchman's. Come here till I tell youse: he was for the Scotchmen last thing at night. Now I don't call that honest. I don't fucking call it honest! Now I ask youse all, I fucking ask, would youse call it *fucking honest*?" He was now holding with both hands to the ceiling-post and roaring as though he hailed from the masthead.

The clerk, folded hands and downcast eyes, made a gentle intervention: "I think he means to say, sir, that Bishop Bale was taking passage upon a ship for a Scottish port, after dark, that being the state of the tide. In itself it is not unlawful: a criminal purpose would have to be adduced." And then, looking up fiercely: "You had cause, Mr Pilot, to suspect criminal purpose? Well?"

"*Answer!*" thundered Downings.

With a thump Walter sat on his beer-keg, shook his head, belched. Several of the leading citizens laughed. The magistrate rose furiously to his feet: "You're his captain – you – !", pointing a quivering finger at Cornelis: "What the devil have you to say to it?"

Cornelis spoke in Flemish, a great truculent flow of Flemish, and the purser stemmed it to translate. "He says, please, this drunken pilot is a man of no good conduct. He says, please, to send him to ship: we will travel him out of England, and out at once of all your nuisance, stand no nonsense, *geen aardigheden dulden!*"

"God's soul, sir, you had better: by the Mass, you abuse justice. Good God, what do I here?" The magistrate snatched up his riding-crop and adjourned proceedings *sine die*. Cosgrave went lurching after him crying out that he owned three-quarters of *French Maggie* if he only had his rights but the Netherland-Dutch had sodding cheated him and the Bristow men deserved keel-hauling. The bailiff tried to soothe him, and led him into the bar again as though stalling an unruly bullock.

"*Dank u*," said Cornelis.

(viii) *At The Golden Lion*

Outside the Shallop the wind leapt and screamed among the roof-ridges, the anchored craft in the bay danced like goblins at their taut cables. Word was spreading, in Cornish and English, of what had happened at the inn; Bale and Cornelis were both hissed and cheered, there was a good deal of disorderly laughter, and some noisy quarrelling, throughout the crowd: it might have been Kilkenny. Public opinion was clearly volatile and not at all easy to analyse.

The *Marguerite's* boats were now discharging gangs of boisterous privateersmen onto the beach. It appeared that Cornelis had given most of his people a day's shore-leave while carpenter and sailmaker and their crews put the ship back into trim. One group, led by the chantyman with his doodlesack, went dancing and prancing heavy-booted into the Shallop, bellowing for *schnapps*.

The bailiff caught Bale by the elbow: "That purser of yours says you'd best bide ashore for tonight, he don't want no trouble seemingly betwixt you and the pilot on board: captain's abiding likewise, maybe wants to keep an eye on you. But don't ask a bed in the Shallop: that's where he'll be sleeping, but it's full of sailormen and St Ives fishers, there'll likely be knives out before dark. Justices'-clerk told me to tell you, the Golden Lion, abaft the church there, a much better house for the likes of you. Come, I'll walk you there."

"But the captain has my money."

"Don't you fret for that, sir. Justices'-clerk says he'll make all easy. Just for the one night, no trouble, this great wind'll never last, no. The captain knows that's where you'll be . . . Oh, and the clerk says, he'd be glad to take supper with you at the Lion, him and a few gentlemen, if so be as you'd oblige him. Mr Downings, he's back to his farmstead."

As they walked, the bailiff chattered very frankly about the state of feeling in St Ives. It seemed to be most complicated. The local Cornish were for Bale and against Downings, because Downings represented England's authority. But they were also against Bale because they yearned for the Old Religion and had a sympathy with the Irish. They were in favour of the Flemish sailors because they saw them as challenging the Bristol and Plymouth vested interests at sea. But they were also against them because foreigners were a threat to their fishing. Bale, unable to speak Cornish, would be a marked man for a quarrel anywhere in the town, except at the Golden Lion, where the landlord kept a strict rule, a Cornish room and an English room: you spoke the wrong tongue in either and you were barred.

It was an enormous relief to find clean dry beds in a stationary house. They all slept for several hours. Bale was awakened by a church bell, very loud, just outside the window of the sleeping-loft. He had forgotten it was Sunday, a most shameful neglect, he must immediately attend Evensong. He stirred up Dorothy, she rolled over, and growled, "Evensong? Evensong in a dog's turd. If they're calling it that you can call me bloody Longlegs." She went back to sleep again, pressing Lydia close to her bosom.

*

Of course she was quite right: the little granite church was thick with incense, lit from end to end with flaring devotional candles, the white-and-gold saints and angels against the curved beams of its roof gleamed in their light like candles themselves, glowering down at scandalised Bale with an angry contempt. The service was Vespers, in an odd muddle of ill-remembered Latin, only half of the rubric properly observed, but abundance of genuflexion and bell-ringing more appropriate to a High Mass. It was as though every possible ceremonial had all been jammed in together to prove the Old Guise still alive. A few demagogic words of Cornish made up the short homily. The priest was old and weatherbeaten, he bobbed and tramped roughly about in front of his gaudy altar like a fisherman checking his nets: perhaps in his spare time he *was* a fisherman.

He gave out a Litany in English, which he could scarcely pronounce. The responses from the people were reluctant, although their continuous bead-telling was fervent enough. Bale was on the point of leaving when he was accosted by the justices'-clerk. "Ah, you see how it is, sir, old-guise being now new-guise and that lubber must now talk his gibberish to Lord God for all of us. Shall we sup?"

The supper-party was comfortable: the clerk had brought three or four of the men who had been at the Shallop, and they were all high in praise of Bishop Coverdale, now deprived. There was an awkward incident when the priest suddenly erupted amongst them from the

'Cornwelsh room', apparently a trifle in liquor, and incoherently denunciatory. He was very angry with government that Coverdale had been allowed to leave the country with his wife and children: why wasn't he in gaol, hey? like many a better man in the previous reign? (Bale was heartened by this: maybe the Queen preferred her Protestants to escape rather than that she should go through the political difficulties of a heresy-hunt). As for that wife, well: children were one thing, he (the priest) had had two, and conceived in the one night moreover – ah, he remembered that night! – but their mothers were honest women married to good husbands by Sacrament of Holy Church, while a wife for a bishop was not just impossible, by the Mass it was a miracle!

The justices'-clerk led him on to talk more about miracles. The old fellow, it seemed, had himself worked a famous one: a wonderful draught of fishes in time of dearth, near as good as on Lake Galilee. Jesus alive had been in *that* boat, but at St Ives the priest fetched out to sea a consecrated Host and let it float upon the tide till all the fishes came in singing. "So in *my* boat, what's the odds, I too had sweet Lord Jesus Himself: so you tell me are those good folk here not blessed?"

Some fishermen, in the doorway behind the priest, applauded him heartily. The church bell was ringing again. "Compline," said the priest, "I've to go give 'em Compline: there'll be these Dutch into church tonight, if they be whoreson drunken, they'll feel my whoreson boot."

Dorothy had not been at the supper-party. She said she would beg some broth from the inn kitchen and feed Lydia and herself in the loft. Thomas as well was attending to his own affairs, spending the evening with a pilchard-salter whom he knew of by way of trade. He had already half-decided not to return on board the privateer, even though he, like Bale, had had to leave his luggage and money there. The pilchard-salter would, he was sure, advance him enough cash to get him back to Dublin, or at least to Bristol, where his employer had connections. His jolly adventure, assisting comical fugitives, had been far less amusing than he had looked for, and he was damned if he'd ever do anything so stupid again.

*

Dorothy slept very heavily, impervious to the convivial noise that rose up into the loft from the bars downstairs, impervious to the Compline bell, impervious to the everlasting howl of the wind through chinks of the gable between wall and thatch. But then something did rouse her: a different sort of sound altogether. Sudden harsh shouts, running feet, the clash of steel in the narrow street outside. By the time she was fully awake, its immediacy was gone, the running feet were now running away, and finally died away; and the shouts had receded uphill toward the north part of the town.

She made up her mind that the *Marguerite's* crew were making a rovers' night of it, and she turned her face back onto the pillow. This time, however, she found sleep impossible. The lice from the filthy ship were all over her: now that her utter exhaustion was partly relieved, she was unable to ignore them. She tossed about in the dark, scratching herself everywhere, dragging her nails through her hair, but it was useless. Somehow she would have to get water and wash.

It was, she thought, a good thing that her washing in Ireland had so declined. She had become almost as dirty as when she was a young girl: but if it had been otherwise, she could not have survived even one day upon *French Maggie*. She wondered that the sousing of the storm had not cleansed her. But these were no doubt sea-vermin and lived through all such hazards. Would the inn's water be of any use? She would have to try. She did not care to ask the people of the house: they would be disgusted for their beds, and would only want to know why she had not spoken of it before.

She was sleeping fully-clothed, not having had the strength to undress. Well, she would undress now, and tomorrow she would insist that Bale borrowed a clean gown for her from the wife of that justices'-clerk, or from someone. Also tomorrow she must deal with Lydia's lice and garments. Bale could find a way of reclothing his child as well before they all had to set sail again. But at present Lydia was asleep, so *let* her sleep, poor darling. Bale had come to bed and lay flat on his back snoring. No lice would trouble *him*, with his new cronies' mulled ale awash in his gut. The other loft-room beds were vacant: except for one bespoke by Thomas, and he was out on the town.

She crept down to the back-yard by the outside stair. There was no-one about, and the place was bright with moonshine: the storm-clouds were blown away, maybe before long the wind would blow itself out.

*

In the corner of the yard was a well. She lowered the bucket and started to wind it up. Immediately opposite her was a wicket-gate that

led into a back alley. As she turned the handle, slowly, it was a large
heavy bucket, she saw this gate swing half-open, then shut again, then
open again once more. At first she thought the wind was swaying it.

Then she saw Walter Cosgrave, his jerkin off, his shirt hanging
down from his belt in shreds over the rump of his trousers, a bloody
gash across his forehead, and a wide-bladed knife in his hand.

He was standing in the alley, pushing at the wicket in a tentative
sort of way, as though not quite sure whether it was a gate or a draped
curtain. His eyes were lurid in the moonlight: and they looked full into
hers.

He grinned. "Ssh," he said, "ssh . . . would you believe there's
been ructions? I'd best not make a noise. Some o'them Cornwall
lousers are out for Watty's blood. And why not, din'I take theirs?
D'you know what they sodding did? Our chantyman went to church,
and why wouldn't he go to church, damn good Cat'lic, just like the
Emperor. I'd best not make a noise: nor had you, if you don't want
this."

He had softly stepped up close to her and the knife glittered as
bright as his eyes. She held to the well-handle with both hands, rigid.

"Be the time the priest was finished, poor wee Claus had gone to
sleep. Any man'd go to sleep the way that bitch of a *Maggie's* after
hurling us these last days, wha'? And then when the bastard priest had
his church cleared and empty, what does he do but find Claus spread
out snorting against steps-o'-th'-font? Does he wake him with all
decency and put him on the road, he does not. First he slits his
bagpipe an'then he outs his dirty cock – sav'n-yr-presnce ma'am, y're
a priest's lady – he outs his cock from under his cassock and pishes a
quart-an-a-quarter splash into poor Claus's mouth. Wha'd'ya think
o'that, woman, wha'? I say he outs with his dirty –"

Dorothy collected herself and hitched the well-ratchet so that the
bucket would not slip. She had dealt with drunken men often enough.
It could have been worse. "So that's how the fighting started? Have
you hurt yourself? That's a bad cut."

"Bad cut," he gurgled, "Yeh. Ah y're a decent woman, and not an
ounce of ton's burthen in *French-fuckin'-Maggie* but belongs to Watty
Ó Cosgraigh if the poor Watser was allowed his rights. But Ó
Cosgraigh is a Teague name, yeh? An'that mag'strate lowered the
boom on it. Ssh, I said no noise . . . !"

He was whirling the knife between their faces, most expert, drink
or no drink. "D'ye see this boy here?" She turned her head. There

was another man, silently come into the yard. The snake-like young Spaniard who helped *Marguerite's* master-at-arms with his duties. He too had a knife. He stood frighteningly still.

"Him an' me have a prop'sition to put, missus, put to you. We din'look to find you here, but now we do, all th'easier, wha'? We've come to get oul' Dangle-tool, and run him straightaway to Spain for the cash-money that's mine by rights, little Pancho knows the place, Ferrol-port or else the Corunya, we can easy reach either of 'em in the longboat with mast-an'-sail, don't think we've not been able to nick hould of Corney-whiskers' sodding longboat, I don'like to be told I'm a liar!"

She forced her eyes away from his knife and looked instead at the silver medallion that hung on his bare tattooed chest: St Christopher or Iago of Compostella? She could not make it out.

"Now I've guessed, an' little Pancho's fuckin' *seen*, the class-o'-manners between you an'oul'Dangle-tool: we'd say you'd be willing-an'-aisy to have him sold away south in Spain where they're all of 'em damn-good-Cat'lics and know well what they should do with him? From Ferrol an' the Corunya only a few miles mule-back, take or leave, to Compostell'-of-Saint-James, an' Saint James's priesteens are great men for damn-good-Cat'lics an' terrible bloody men for your nun-fucking Luthers, yeh? Y'know wha' I mean? So he's above there, this minute, isn'he, sleeping off his supper, yeh? An 'th'chiselur, yeh? Fair enough. An'you, missus, wha'? come below for a rinse?

"An'bechrist but the bucket's too heavy for her, she's not able for the power o'th'handle. So wha'd'ya do, missus, but go softly aloft, *softly*: tell Dangle-tool you need his help to revolve it, bring him down, and we'll do the rest. That way no need for disturbance, that way you an'th'girleen go free: the Watser don't hold wi'the burning of females, only for witches, and you'd never be a witch? Would you, wha'? Would you?"

It *was* Compostella: the man had been pilgrim to Spain. Not only Pancho would know first-hand what went on there.

After a pause, she answered him, hard and sincere: "Spain would be good," she said. "Grill the bastard, roast him. But you're not going to get him. Lay a hand on him, he'll roar like a bull. There's a whole supper-party of friends of the court-clerk lying asleep inside there now, they have swords, you're bound to rouse 'em." Would they believe her? Her hands gripped the well-handle tight, tight: Lady Mary, let them not see how she trembled.

Cosgrave looked at Pancho, and Pancho shook his head: "Ah no no *señora*, no: I am quieter than fishes in stream, *I* go up ladder with you, when he wake I take child also. Any noise, knife under her ear: she is hostage all the way to seashore, perhaps also in boat to El Ferrol. No, we are not cruel: in Compostella we baptise her Catholic. But it is her life for his silence: his silence by your persuasion."

"That's it," concluded Cosgrave: his mouth shut upon the words like the lid of a box.

She shook her head, sad for the two men's foolishness. "But you don't even know whether Spain will pay anything for him. This is politics, English politics: English heretics are not Spain's business. But you do know that all his own money is still in your captain's cabin, and did he ever tell how much?"

Cosgrave looked at Pancho: Pancho looked at Cosgrave. She had hit upon something.

"That's what you want to plan for; and if I help you, you can give me a share, which is more than *he* ever gave, let him call me his wife or not."

The pilot scowled. "Only way to banjax that bastard Corney-whiskers is to get outa th'ship an'go. His cabin-chest's imp-im-fuckin'pregnable, so."

"Not for me." She set her head on one side and narrowed her eyes. "Because of the storm, there's been no time, but I never yet found an ungelded male creature impregnable to *me*." She remembered a moral play she had once seen in King's Lynn: Lady Sensuality had used just such a slow hoarse voice. She and Gillian, she remembered, had imitated it often, it had aroused them together quite contrary to the author's didactic intention.

Cosgrave was taken aback. "*You?* An oul'slag, lofty and grey, the likes o' you? Ha! any port in a storm. But if that's so, what made you take up with a badger of a bishop, you could ha'had the Lord Deputy, wha'?"

"Bishop to begin with, that's all. Not my fault if you chose to raid the *Rosebud*. I had my own plans for Scotland, the first of them being I should arrive there in full possession of the Bishop of Ossory's purse."

"Prove it," says he.

Her widening smile, most ominous-dreadful: but Cosgrave's taste in women's hilarity was none too fastidious. He saw a tongue between lips drawn back; he drew back his own lips as Dorothy began to whisper to him. Perhaps also he took her slow closure of dark-rimmed eyelids as a personal heraldic sign of appetite about to advance its banners. He listened to her wishes, to her proposals, to what he took to be her desire, he sucked hissingly through the gaps of his teeth.

"Any port in a storm." Harsh response: from his contempt, from his confidence, that she was no more than his due. "And Pancho?"

"If he wants. I'd have supposed he'd have thought me old meat. Just like you did. I'm not the judge."

Pancho slid his knife back into its sheath and smoothed his belt above his codpiece.

(ix) *The Fodder-Barn*

Thomas was very angry. His friend the pilchard-salter turned out to be no friend at all. After entertaining him all evening he flatly refused him the money: asserting (from the very middle of carefree wine-drinking and songs) that Irish herring-boats had moved in among the pilchards, and not one penny would he give to help a Dubliner home to ruin the good trade of St Ives.

Thomas blundered cursing all the way down to the Golden Lion. There were no lights in the house. It was far too late to disturb the landlord. Could he get in by the yard-gate? To his surprise it was open. He entered with great precaution, lest he be taken for a burglar. He pulled off his shoes and tip-toed with pain over gravel-stones to the outside stair. He was ragingly resigned now to Cornelis and his horrible ship, and that pained him far worse than sharp granite.

He heard an unaccountable human noise from a fodder-barn beside the gate: he stopped in his tracks. No, he *could* account for it.

He was not normally a salacious peeper, but for some young strap from the inn-kitchen to be moaning her copulative ecstasy, while he was tied, it seemed for life, to a ridiculous rutterkin pirate, angered him so much that he swore he must either break up this damned derry-down or have part of it.

He was drunk enough for any misdoings, and his rowdy prentice-years were not very far behind him. His intentions at that moment were quite as ugly as the state of his clothes, and *they* were all befouled with the malodorous overplus of his false friend's hospitality.

He peered round the doorpost: and stood still in complete amazement. The woman upon her knees in the straw with skirts thrown forward over her shoulders was only too well known to him. Her straight upturned profile, her long strong frame, her tangles of greying hair: no, he made no mistake under the dappled moonlight (holes in the barn-roof, not dark in there at all).

And no mistake about the men, one stooping over her, the other watching and dripping his mouthwater through too many teeth.

Thomas felt himself shocked: distressed, filled with abhorrence, unexpectedly hurt within himself. He crept away and up the stair, into the loft, into his bed: and lay awake for a long time. He thought at one stage he heard a queer high-pitched singing and a clapping of hands. And then he thought he must have slept after all, it must have been in his dream. And then he dreamed, or thought he dreamed, a rattling bird-like cry; or two cries, one upon the other.

But he was certainly not asleep when Dorothy came up. He lay very still and watched her between his eyelids. The moon was dropping low, and shone into the loft, almost horizontal, through one narrow gable-window. The Bales' bed was in the shadow-black corner of the room away from the shaft of light. So what he saw was not precise, lit only by reflection from the whitewashed wall, but at moments her body moved into the moonbeam and then out again: she revealed herself in curious jerks of vision. What he could not discern, he guessed-at.

She was not wearing her clothes but had them wrapped loosely around her. She dropped them off: he thought they were soaking wet from the noise they made flopping on the floor. She was nodding her head violently, and seemed to be talking: but no sound came to his ears. He watched her as she dragged down her stockings, preparing herself to go naked into the bed alongside her sleeping child: she bent over Lydia as if to make quite sure she *was* asleep. He had not imagined there would be such a tautness to the muscularity of her limbs. Several times she wiped her hand through her hair: she shook the hand as though it itched and stung. Her hair was wet. She was wet all over. The stockings on the floor in a silver pool of moonlight appeared to be thick with mud. Her husband snored on and on, his big nose prodding up like a tombstone, his beard straggled all over the blanket. With a sudden sideslip she went into the bed, keeping Lydia between herself and the old man. As she went, the moon caught her all down her back in an instant glimpse of silver: and then she was out of his sight.

*

An hour or so later, when the moon shifted along its full course to the west and downward, the inn-loft lost its light-pool: but to Thomas's inner vision the whitewashed wall was still staring white, the corner of the floor still shone, the muddy stockings and the soaked heap of garments there still assaulted his sleepless eyeballs. He had seen, he knew he had seen, even though he was so drunk: he had not understood. He lay stone-still in his bed, ignoring the *Marguerite's* lice that he carried most vilely all over him, and he puzzled his sottish brains.

He had thought Dorothy sour, inimical, twisted; had put it down to her uncomely age and the stress of the kidnap. After all, he himself had scarcely shown at his best since they were forced aboard the carrack. Now, a whole new conception of her: and how to make sense of it? This cantankerous concealed matron had a quality he could not possibly have guessed: but, having surprised it, he began to see in it the only logical comprehension of her unreadable character. She was nothing more nor less than Lechery full-length on a church wall-painting in St Audeon's of Dublin. He had studied it often, for there was as yet no Bale-vicar there to quench it with a coat of distemper: he used to wonder how the artist found a model for such an idea; a stark skinny bramble-haired wife with hot hard breasts like olives in brine, she rode furiously on a bucking goat; erotic, malevolent, haggard, exciting, deterrent, and all at once. The other six Deadly Sins, rampant cavalcade alongside her, were jolly jesters by comparison. She bore no obvious relation to his own amorous escapades; all the girls he knew were very ordinary young women and nothing of what they did with him could so contort their fresh young selves: nor *him*-self – or so he had told his intermittent conscience more times than he cared to reckon. But then they were *young* girls. This Bale woman must be – fifty? Of course, she had to suffer her husband, which would have excused almost anything. But then, did not *he* suffer *her*? How else to explain his yearning clutch at Thomas's body when they lay together, teeth chattering, in the dark night of the ship's tween-decks? Whose lonely lusts had been conjured up in bitter reaction to whose?

He came to no clear conclusion. He was very profoundly troubled: and remained so for as long as he knew her.

*

The following afternoon *Marguerite-Debonaire* cleared the headland for an undetermined destination, all four 'prisoner-passengers' aboard her. But not the ship's pilot, nor the master-at-arms' mate. Cornelis made no effort to find them. The Spanish boy was never

worth his salt: and Cosgrave's important services were more than
suspect after the business at the Shallop Inn. Quite capable out of
sheer malice of running the ship aground. Also, of course, by
desertion he must surely forfeit his share of the vessel. With luck, it
might revert to the captain.

A week later, the ostler at the Golden Lion was forking horse-dung
onto the midden, when something caught his eye – the toe of a
sea-boot sticking out of the muck. A little careful delving and the two
corpses were uncovered. Both of them had been killed with repeated
gliding knife-blows in front, back, and sides; almost (as the bailiff
said) "as though the murderer had been a-dancing of fandangos all
around 'em." It was concluded they had died in one of the many
brawls that disfigured the brief visit of the great carrack. Strange,
though, that no-one in the inn had heard anything. "Like a witchcraft," said the bailiff, "First to compel their mouths to make no
outcry, and then to have 'em bide there to suffer all this jerking with
the knife-blades an' that. Beats me how it was done. Certainly weren't
no fisherman. One o'their own, most likely: uncanny ways, these
foreign mariners, Turks an' allsorts they had aboard of her."

(x) *Journeys' Endings*

As the captain Julius courteously entreated Paul, and gave him liberty to go
unto his friends at Sidon, and to refresh him, so did our captain Cornelis
use us very gently with all favour and liberty at St Ives; what though he had
so currishly and cruelly intreated us afore. As Paul was stung of a biting
viper and not hurt, so was I of that viperous Walter.

Bale never knew how nearly lethal the viper's bite had been.
Dorothy told him nothing, and Thomas told him nothing. Dorothy's
demeanour, indeed, was so ill toward him that he omitted all reference
to her (and consequently to Lydia) in his published account, written
very shortly afterwards, still in the heat of his emotion. Saint Paul,
upon *his* journey, had had no family with him: Bale's spoiled the
analogy.

As great disputations were among the Jews at Rome concerning Paul, so
were there afterwards among the shippers in our return to their ship
concerning us. As the soldiers gave counsel to kill the prisoners, so were
there some of our men that gave counsel to have drowned us for our money,
and of some to have delivered us up to the Council of England, in hope of
great rewards.

This happened at Dover, where Cornelis thought to go back on his bargain, after he had clearly given Bale to understand he would bring him and his companions (for a reasonable fee) to Germany. Already there had been a contretemps at St Ives, the morning of the day of their departure: *Marguerite* had at first sailed without them, and they had to beg a fishing-boat to scurry after her as she tacked about to fetch herself out of the bay – the wind still being north-westerly, though very much abated. Cornelis had been all apologies, claiming (a) that he thought they were aboard, and (b) that their having stayed in the Golden Lion instead of the Shallop had confused his messenger when he sent them the word of departure. Of course he had been hoping to keep their money and belongings for himself without the trouble and inconvenience of their persons.

After that, he sailed a lengthy zig-zag rover's cruise, taking prizes all up and down the Channel, some of them genuinely French. But the specifics of his letter-of-marque were not to be taken seriously: he even captured vessels of his own Imperial Flanders. One English craft he plundered proved only to be carrying apples, which made him so vexed he sent the Bales and Thomas back into the prisoners' deck among a miserable crowd of new French captives (after St Ives he had allowed them the freedom of the officers' wardroom).

Cornelis put into Dover for news, and to replenish his water-casks. While there he got incautiously drunk with some carousing English soldiers, and boasted about Bale. Then he feared they would fetch Bale ashore and arrest him, and take all his money for themselves, so he retracted the statement and insisted that Bale had been landed at Southampton. Then he told his crew that he and the purser would ride direct to London and deal man-to-man with government. Then at last he was persuaded that Bale's money would so easily be his if he only kept his word and brought him to Germany.

All these arguments bred mutiny in the crew: there was Bale, there was the money; let Cornelis sort it out without further waste of time, it was encumbering the entire cruise. So he kept his word: up to a point.

Germany at the last moment proved not to be convenient, so instead he sailed home to Flushing in Zeeland, where Bale and Thomas paid their ransoms: and were finally, with Lydia and Dorothy, discharged from the Ship of Fools.

Into a town ruled by Catholics, who immediately put them under house-arrest; their custodian, an apologetic co-owner of the *Marguerite*.

But it chanced, by great good luck, that the local inquisitor was too ill to examine them. They had to wait until he got better: and the interval saved their liberties, perhaps their lives. Bale and Thomas between them employed it to good use, with such arguments, such importunities, such hortatory English arrogance toward the magistrates that the latter grew thoroughly scared of an international incident: Flushing had great trade with England. So, no charge; unconditional release; safe-conduct to the frontier for the Bales: and a swift ship to Ireland for the good supercargo, who had befriended them so casually to his own drastic cost and the probable loss of his employers' herring-profits.

> Thus hath my Lord God miraculously delivered me from all those danger-ous perils, and from the greedy mouths of devouring lions, into the worthy land of Germany once again; I hope to the glory of His most holy name; everlasting praise be to Him for it. Amen.

*

Dorothy was an old woman. She was not quite forty: but she was finished, and she knew she was finished. Her heroic secret crime in the Golden Lion's fodder-barn (if it *was* a crime: she herself thought it was, and there was no-one to give a contrary opinion) had used up the last of her heavy lifetime's reserve of strength. In Germany she began to drink, and the accumulated liquor by degrees put her reason to sleep. Nor did she wake when they moved on to the Swiss Cantons. Nor did she wake when Bale began his ferocious quarrelling with at least half of the other English refugees they came up against.

He stood for King Edward's prayer-book and apostolic episcopal succession against the men of Calvin, and the men of Calvin were the larger party. The despotic Scot, John Knox, accused him of intrigue with the Emperor, of bringing in papists to persecute true Protestant saints. Bale wrote, and he wrote, and he wrote, refuting all these calumnies, burning out the angry marrow from the depth of his aching bones.

When Mary Tudor died, and Elizabeth attained the throne, and Bale and his co-exiles could make their Passover and come thankfully for the second time to the waters of Jordan, Dorothy still slept. She was carried aboard the ship like the Palladium of Troy aboard the galley of refugee Aeneas, a sign-talisman of life recovering, but not quite life itself.

Bloody-Full-Of-Blame

Lydia, returned in bewildered haste to East Cheap, found Lucretia both insolent and devil-may-care: she was singing to her virginals, a foul angry ditty of love scorned and scorning back. When her mother came in, she did not stop, but sang louder, and drank from a bottle between stanzas, rapid swallows and the odd hiccup. Lydia sat down and waited for her to finish.

The torn paper on the floor caught her eye, she picked it up and mechanically began to put the pieces together. Some of them were already smoothed-out, as though Lucretia had tried to reassemble the writing herself and then thought better of it. Suddenly something about Lydia's posture caught the girl's attention: perhaps the fearfully shaking fingers, unable to handle the bits of paper, perhaps the draggled hair that had come down at one side under her hat behind her veil and hung loose over her collar, perhaps simply the intake of breath like an asthma between clenched teeth.

The music stopped: Lucretia stared. "Lord God, mother, where have you been? Plays ended three hours ago. Dark: and it's raining. God, you did not meet with footpads? Oh, tell me I should have gone with you: but I didn't, and I wouldn't, and I won't. Not to *his* plays. Can you not *think*?"

"Oh yes, I can think. Oh yes I met a footpad. Oh yes he has despoiled me. Oh Cretia, do you run frantic? Because if you don't, I do: and what is to be done?"

In Lydia's mind – and immediately out at her mouth all tumbling like stones from a shovel – not only Munday and Topcliffe and the 'boy' Thad: but young Marlowe and the way he died; or rather, the way no-one in Canterbury or in London seemed to know of the way he died, every tale was told quite differently, but whatever the truth, it must have begun like this – first foolishness, then threats, then the blackmail coercive, then the snapping of the trap! So she blurted all her terrors, and screamed at her daughter, contradicted herself, muddled her story, ended finally with nothing more definite to say beyond, "The papers, he said papers, Lucretia, I saw papers, I saw them in your room here, oh what is to be done . . . ?"

Lucretia's face was all crooked and set there, as it were a plaster-cast after death by apoplexy. She sprawled her elbows on the lid of the virginals, chin on her hands, her eyes looking out somewhere irrelevantly to the left over her mother's shoulder. When Lydia had finished, she said, "I've no papers. Nor did have, except for two days. And although he did know about it, it wasn't him that left them here but the other. And in good time I passed them safely to those for whom they were meant."

"What other?"

"Someone too big for Munday. Perhaps even too big for Topcliffe. Very like there were names on 'em which even now could incriminate. But not me. I don't have 'em. What I don't have, they can't find. Of course, they can plant. And they would, if they needed to. Point is, do they need? And who are they wanting to catch?"

"He spoke only of that – that man, that was in here this morning. He spoke of his play, at the Theatre."

"As far as I know, not yet written. And Tony Munday wants to stop it. So let him: why should I care?"

Lydia was strangely horrified by Lucretia's tone: not so much that it was callous towards her last night's fornicator, but downright vindictive. She had not thought she had a vindictive girl. She forced her memory upon the morning's talk. Had there been signs in it she had missed? An edge to it, yes, discordant jangling: but surely not spite?

"Cretia, you dribble, you have your lips but half-open, they are dribbling a bitter spite. This man has been your lover, he was only last night abed here, he has betrayed you, and you hate him? If that's it, then very well: not for the first time, is it? You lie upon a dung-heap, the blow-flies will bite, child. And so you must endure it. But this evening I saw worse, I saw worse, I saw worse than any blow-fly, my God they were greasing the wheels, and all the whip-handles were new-polished! Does your spite force you so far as to have him snatched and set down amongst *that*?"

Lucretia shook her head, slowly, as though tired with no wish to make the effort, but must because it was after all her mother, and somebody had to be told. She gave one muted hiccup and began, still staring over Lydia's shoulder.

"To put first things first, I am not betrayed: he is. And by me. Do you suppose that my mood is remorse? Perhaps, relief? One or the other, or both, and it hurts: but I don't think it's hate. Deepest love, and all to-broken. My fault? For once, yes: very probably, yes. But I have to say it's his, or else I might eat ratsbane. No no: that is a *joke*.

"Because for too long I had the two of them, don't you see? To begin with, the player-poet, and then, to vex him, his patron. Do I really mean, 'to vex him'? No, I don't mean. I am *not* a mere creature of spite. 'To vex *myself*, with contending pleasures': there, that puts it better. Oh you know about the patron, you saw his sword and pistols: I ought not to tell you his name. H.W., Mr H.W., perhaps will suffice. Except he's not a mister, he's bigger than that. But *I* call him 'W.H.', because when I got him to lie with me he had to turn himself right round about: an array of desirous gentlemen had bestowed on him a quite different posture. But he's *beautiful*, white body, red-gold hair, hardly older than I am, brave as Achilles – ah, maybe not quite Achilles, but Paris-Alexander of Troy, queen-taker, saucy challenger of thick-necked kings.

"As for his poet, nine years the elder, dark as a prune (didn't you think so?), he *was* thin and supple about his loins like a leatherwork marionette and by God that *stirred* me: but now he grows a belly, the pride of his spleen fills his head, his bad digestion talks in his sleep, three at least of his white teeth have gone black with bad diet, we never couple but we quarrel.

"The two of them: for too long, and I told such lies to both.

"And all that time they had each other, man-and-boy, poet-and-patron, tradesman's son and son of an earl. And they both told such lies to *me*.

"Oh yes, I knew all about them, buttock-games and flickering mouths, I knew and I didn't care, didn't even care about the transparency of their lies. For neither of 'em knew what *I* did when I gave myself to the other one: but now they've found out and they rage. Or I should say, poet rages, patron smiles and licks his cream. Last night was the poet's last night. Dear Jesus, the night before that, I had told him I was his for ever.

"Patron comes back tomorrow. Those papers, you see, were his: he was (I think) baptised papist, was Mr W.H., and still shifts his loyalty, it's very true that one day they *will* take his head off.

"But not just yet, not now, at court he is a golden god and he kisses the old Queen's tetins. Oh yes, mother, I am *lifted up* by his godlike desire toward me, his princely favour to my humble beauty: I am

sulky Venus carved in marble taking her ease upon a temple-porch. If
the Goths come marching in, they'll fire their gunstones at my womb
and crack me down onto the pavement.

"Before that happens, I'll find a husband. That's what I'll do. Live
quiet in virtue as a grocer's goody: a solid man with a country farm or a
high seat in a city guild. So long as he loves music, is not hostile to the
'business', will let me work when I need to work – I daresay there are
such, I met one at that house upon the Muswell Hill, no older than
thirty-five, he still buys me the odd dinner. But until then, no more
poets: just the one nobleman, and I'll last near as long as he does. Or at
least, until *he* marries, to a chit of his own station: no word of that yet.
And when he does, *if* he does, I'm sure he'll still use me. If only to have
my room, to leave all his nonsense in. Sometimes, papers. Sometimes,
his weapons and his swaggerer's raiment, for when he goes upon town
disguised to ruffle in bawdy-houses with decayed captains (but he's
not a Munday, he don't take me). Sometimes other things: like this
jewel. This is what my poet found, the token of my falsehood, yes?
First thing this early morning, put his hand on it when he groped for
his shirt."

She swept some stray stockings from the top of a chest: there was a
small leather case lying there unfastened. Inside it, a great bracelet of
arabesque gold-wire openwork set with emeralds and sapphires, a
miniature portrait upon the clasp, a motto: *Cette Lucrèce ne se tue point,
à moy la blessure, grace à Dieu.* Lydia looked at the tiny picture: "He
has very blue eyes," she said, "Very cold eyes, like his own sapphires.
Or is that the whim of the painter?"

"Veracious painter, mother, as truthful as God's Gospel. Tony
Munday told me once, this lovely face here had a grandfather: that fell
Wriothesley who shed his gown to put tender hand to the torture of
Anne Askew. You read the tale to me yourself in my own grandad's
book when I was seven. Think of it, and then tell yourself that you
need not tell *me* about Topcliffe and his cellarage. We live in such
times and suck them in with every spoon of peppered broth. What
harm, then, to forget them, in the honey-sweat of a generous bed?"

*

"Jesus Saviour, girl, I will tell you what harm!" Lydia was on her feet
and blazing. "You·and I have a duty to this poet, whom you so scorn
for his belly and his three bad teeth and his random naughty yard that
knoweth not the difference between your sore-abused quim and a

nobleman's buttocks – I will *not* let you sit here, twang your music, hiccup with drink, and dribble down your chin for hopelessness! I never told you that my mother in her last years was so soused with the Dutchland schnapps that even her bread-and-milk had to be adulterate with strong waters, they were so much become part of her blood! Oh God, let it not happen to you.

"Fulfil your duty, and it won't. Whether he's papist or not, he must be warned. You took it upon yourself to flee the cruel practices of your father's god, God curse his soul, and thereby caused me to flee them in alliance with you, so now you have mapped your road and you or I or both of us must walk it for very shame. If no-one else commands me, John Bale stands at my back. All he did and wrote-of was in hatred of the great cruelties: very like he mistook his purpose, very like by his whole life he made more cruelty than he quelled, so some-one must atone for him, and if not you, then me. Where is your poet?"

"At this hour of the night, I can't say. I can tell you two beds where he won't be . . . Tomorrow, is it Wednesday? he takes his break-fast at the Boar's Head, just round the corner: a thieves'-kitchen, they serve pork chops, he always gobbles them alone and without talking to anyone; habit of his work, unbreakable, so he says, he hears rogues' words and fixes them into his pen, God knows what raucous stage-scenes he'll bring out of that dirty house.

"But not being Tony Munday, he never offered to take *me*. Nor will he want to see *you* there. In the morning, first thing, I'll leave a note with Francis the pot-boy, he'll find out what else he does, besides his fried pork. And then you can make your arrangements. Mother, I'll do that much for you, and for him; and thereafter, on this business, I'm finished . . .

"Yes, you well might try to read it, he wrote that today, sitting in his shirt, on this very stool at my poor virginals."

Lydia was still fiddling with the torn paper, for the first time since she had picked it up she was making out the scribbled lines: it was a poem of sorts, all hasty, abrupt, diagonal across the sheet (which already had a stave of music written on it), not at all easy to decipher.

Lucretia seemed to know it by heart (or at least the start of it):

> "Th'expense of spirit in a waste of shame
> Is lust in action and till action lust
> Is perjur'd murd'rous bloody full of blame –

"That's as much as is legible, I'd say. The rest of it'll be all in the same sour old whine. 'Bloody-full-of-blame' is me, you know, not lust. He means me, so he calls me lust. He said to me as he began to write it, 'Here's a new key for your lock-hole, girl.' But why now? *I* told him all of it years since, told him about Munday, *my* thought, *my* experience, mine, of me and Munday, and now he makes it his and calls it new. Mind you, I didn't rhyme it. That's *his* skill, that's all he added: though God knows (though *he* don't), if I'd felt inclined, I could have done it myself.

"D'you remember what I wrote for hobbledehoy young Sam Tenterden? And the birch-twigs? Oh *we* remember: hit so hard they cracked and split and cut like knives, oh yes, you were too late to save me. But you'll save *him*, from the greased wheels? Why? So he'll write more of *these* . . . ?

"I'm going to sleep, mother: share my bed, it's a woundy long dark walk to the Saracen, dangerous. And wet: hear the rain."

It was true, there was a downpour, it swilled across the roof-tiles with noise unending like a mill-race.

VIII

(Scene indivdable, poem unlimited)

Lo, I have done the deed!

And I saw the dead, both great and small stand before God: and the books were opened, and another book was opened, which is the book of life, and the dead were judged of those things which were written in the books according to their deeds.
If any man have an ear, let him hear. He that leadeth into captivity, shall go in to captivity.
(Revelation of St John the Divine, chapters 20 & 13)

Bale did not even consider asking for his bishopric back again. Nor was it offered. A prebendary's sinecure in the nation's first metro-politan cathedral was more than sufficient. He was older than his old wife, in continuous ill-health, but not yet finished. He had all his books to write and to revise and to send round the country to any clergyman, nobleman or scholar that he thought might accord him glory.

He also wrote endlessly to Ireland, to the Lord Deputy, trying in vain to recover his library abandoned there in 1553.

He survived through five years of England's most famous reign, and then, one morning, apoplexy.

The same death as Lord Wentworth: although Bale had forewarn-ing of it, a preliminary seizure, apparently not severe. But the physician who bled him had been very grave as well as expensive. Sanguinity and choler were misplaced somehow among the patient's humours, and each strove for the mastery, with inevitable fatal consequence, or words to that effect. He understood, after the consultation, that he had not long to wait.

He lived with this knowledge in silence for a few days, but it had so greatly dumbfounded him that at last he had to do something. He suddenly sent for Lydia, commanding her to find out if her mother would see him, "– at once, daughter, at once, I wait below-stairs for her answer!" As a rule he and Dorothy had rather less connection than a pair of mutually-accusatory adulterers who must pretend to the world that their secret parts have shared no secret. She kept her semi-conscious bed and never said anything to her children, or to anyone else, that might suggest she knew there was a husband in the house. When he had visited her, she ignored him. For a while he used to sit and read the Bible aloud at her bedside: but in the end he gave up this practice, it was absurd giving out God's Word to such chillingly deaf ears.

Lydia (fifteen years old, withdrawn, hopeless, reading too many books, remembering too many terrors) went timidly into the sickly-pungent curtain-closed bedroom and gave the message. Dorothy smiled vaguely at her. "Your father?" she asked, faint and puzzled, and then answered her own question with a sudden access of assurance: "But dearest child, your father is a German sea-wave, how can he be here? He goeth quieter than fishes in stream: but notwithstanding he sweeps forward with weight, and so he shall meet with that other wave. When? Today? Yes, it could be today. If I must swim against him again, then I must . . ."

She waited in slumber until Bale crept to the bedpost and peeped cautiously round it, hoping she would look at him. He cleared his throat. No response. He growled, snarled, and spoke her name. He began unrestrainedly to splutter: how God was good, he knew that, but bitterly he resented having to die before he was seventy: he did not think it fully scriptural, such a confessor as himself should be permitted his natural span. Perhaps, though, it was a test of his faith: through faith (and not popish works) sinful man alone was justified. So he burst into agitated coherent voice and said so, to Dorothy, quite unsuitably, and at some length. Her slumber made him mad, though he was not so inhumane as to shout at her, having found long ago in Germany that it had no effect. Moreover, the doctor's warning . . .

Moreover, apart from the doctor, there was a matter that preyed on his mind. For quite a time, before his seizure, he experienced dreams. Bale had never taken much account of dreams: he knew that the Lord, or an angel perhaps, occasionally made use of them to communicate information: Joseph in Egypt, the Infant Samuel, the other Joseph and the three Wise Men, and so forth – all examples useful for writings and preachings, but he personally had not been vouchsafed anything of the sort.

And these dreams he was having – or rather *had* been having, the doctor's bleeding and subsequent purges had so weakened him he drifted now into bleary somnolence like a dead man already, but such blank nights, he feared, would not last – these dreams, he repeated to Dorothy, and twisted her counterpane between his hands in his great disturbance of mind – these dreams, he reiterated, could not by stretch of fantasy be directly attributed to God. It was in fact only the one dream: but it had come to him night after night. He had not told the doctor, he dared not tell the doctor; and then without his telling, the doctor had confirmed his apprehension. Demons? Could demons send dreams? Bale had been praying, incessantly, before sleep, to have "an end of it, O Lord, an end!" but still the dream returned, and when there was an end it was his seizure that brought it, and now he knew what *that* meant: the doctor had told him, "next time", next time would be last time, science spoke of approaching death. Did the dream also speak? Of approaching damnation? And both of them came on him together? Damnation of his marriage? Being fornication unrepented, vow-breach unrepented, if (after all) the Old Guise had been God's guise and the New Guise was of hell? And *if* this was the case, there was nothing he could do about it, no-one to tell about it, for he had forsworn priests and confession (certain beyond all backsliding that *they* were damnation), only himself now between his sins and God: if God did not tell him, *before* he came to die, that his righteous-ness was wickedness and his wickedness righteous, then *he* could not know it till his soul was fetched out yonder, to be set down trembling face-to-face with – with whomever had been sending him his dream?

He told all this to Dorothy: and when she seemed to sleep instead of hearing his terrible mutterings, he could not prevent himself telling her the dream.

*

"I was walking among mountains: the goat-herd's daughter said to me, 'Transylvania. Go to the castle and see him shoot.' So I climbed that high place, and no-one forbade me entrance. And there in a secret gallery I beheld an English bowman. He was all in green like Robin Hood to whom our memories revert so frequent when we are wearied of this tortured world and lie an-hungered for the free green forest and good fellowship of lawless rogues that knew not the politic corruption.

"He turned to me sharply and hissed.

"'Still!' quotha, 'Stand still! They will be here upon the instant.' He bent forward and peered through the window-hole, and I behind him, my wanton hands clasped his hinder-parts and he did not seem to note it, but peered again and clicked his tongue. Then through the further window I saw the enclosed garden, and the sunshine bright upon it, gold in a black box, gold and green in a frowsty rat-hole.

"'I am waiting all these hours,' he said, 'and still they have not come. Will she deprive me of my only chance? Ah but she is cunning: God knows but I am already outwitted.'

"He then told me his name was Bull. Yeoman John Bull of the castle guard: his sinewy haunches in his tight green hose were as graceful as the poplar-trees of Bishopstoke all along by the brimming river: but that was not to the purpose of this meeting, I must hear what he had to tell me. There was a priest here, he said, a man now of nothing, but who aforetime had been renowned for simple holiness, and then had made cause with new gospellers. All had thought him ready to free the Church in that land and restore the Truth of Scripture: but fie alas, he had slidden back! It was rumoured it was love of a woman that had slackened his zeal. And no doubt he did love her, before all else she was most loveable; and had the good priest with his utmost courage given over his tonsure and taken her in a sacrament-marriage, all would surely have rejoiced. Some said yet he meant to do it, and others said, 'Then why delay?'

"But one explanation, adjudged this archer: she was of greater account to the priest's fantasy as harlot than as wife, and by the same token she intended it thus, for she was none other than that Babylon whore of whom Saint John doth most lively endite, Baal-child she was, Baal-wife, Baal-mother.

"Wherefore she must die: and John Bull was executioner.

"I saw his face so curling vicious at the pleasure he had in his task, I near fainted upon the flagstone. And then again, I heard him hiss; and I spied through the hole: there she was, there was the silly priest. She sate among the greenery straight as a bollard upon her neat white hams, ankles crossed, knees wide; and he knelt betwixt her knees, his face not a hand-span from hers, a speckled shadowed hairy man, all lines in his skin and dry folds. His hands were pressed together, and she enclosed hers over them: and then she did stroke him, exceeding tender, countenance, trunk, and loins. All I could see of her, save for her caressing fingers, was the turn of her chin and right ear with its ear-ring, her cool straight lovely back, and a braid of red hair hanging down even to her breech.

"The bowman thrust me sideways, catching his breath in an agony,

teeth snapped at frightened Lydia as he went, for her clumsiness in taking his arm.

*

His death came the following morning after a night of no sleep, no dreams, but continual praying and pacing and scribbling in his notebooks. The last thing he wrote was this:

> She forgives? Forgives what? That all did *not* improve? How could it? Only provided that all was not made worse. If not made worse, no need for forgiveness. If need for forgiveness because all *has* been made worse, then forgive God, not Bale. For God put the bow into the hand of the archer, the archer's mark was the one small thing he could see through his narrow space, he must shoot at it or lie dead idle. Can we believe God created, for naught but a scandalous idleness? If that was His intent, if that the dream's meaning, then all world and all word is naught but a naughty deed, *His* deed, unforgiveable.

The final sentence was scored out and rewritten several times. Upon the last rewriting, upon the word 'unforgiveable', the stroke hit his brain and felled him across his inkwell.

On his desk beside his notes lay a poem lately sent him by a young lawyer, a Mr Googe, as a token of admiration for his plays, his literary research, his theology, his battle:

> Good agéd Bale that with thy hoary hairs
> Dost yet persist to turn the painful book,
> O happy man that hast attained such years
> And leav'st not yet on papers pale to look,
> Give over now to beat thy wearied brain
> And rest thy pen that long hath laboured sore.
> For agéd men unfit sure is such pain,
> And thee beseems to labour now no more.
>
> But thou I think Don Plato's part will play
> With book in hand to have thy dying day.

A few years later, Barnaby Googe was sent to Ireland as a civilian official upon the Lord Deputy's staff. Most of his poems were pastoral. His work for colonial government was always conscientious, exact to the point of pedantry. It had to be: such confusion of rebellion was unabating throughout his time there.

The Dry-Rot Scaffold

Crook-legged whey-faced Francis from the Boar's Head came to
Lucretia's with a message, mid-morning on the Wednesday: if the
lady her mother had real need to see the poet, let her be at the
Theatre's tiring-house an hour before the play-trumpet, he would not
have much time, she must excuse him: but to be frank the said poet
did not *wish* to have much time upon such a conversation, no doubt
Mrs Lydia knew why.

"What else did he say when you told him?" asked Lucretia.

"He gave over his chops, ma'am, and called for some gruel, and
then didn't eat that, but drank down a blackjack of sack and went
cursing, hit hisself on the doorpost going out. Not like him, you
know: he never exceeds before night. If that'll be his state on stage this
afternoon, there'll be cues dropped like plumstones all over the
boards. *Titus* today, innit? Well, it's his own lines, and they're old
enough; I dessay he thinks it won't signify."

The stage-doorkeeper would not let Lydia into the tiring-house
itself, it was forbidden to all women while the men and boys were
dressing: but there had been an arrangement made, she could talk to
the poet in the prompt-closet, a tiny space belonging to the book-
keeper/stage-manager, full of scripts, bits of costume, odds and ends
of properties mislaid from their rightful place. She sat on a hamper
and waited. She had a headache. This pokey room was increasing it
every minute. Her hands stuck with heat to the inside of her gloves.
She pulled the gloves off. She pulled her veil up, pulled off her hot
hat.

He came in to her, with a lurch. He was half-clothed in scarlet hose
and a silk shirt with puffed sleeves, trying to buckle a Roman cuirass
over it, and botching the job. A toga hung from his arm and trailed on
the floor and he did not seem to have noticed it. His swarthy face was
streaked with massive lines of white and blue make-up in conventional
(and shakily-painted) indication of great age.

"'Marcus Andronicus'," he sourly announced, "Antique straight-man, *tribunus plebis*, if that's the Latin, nothing to do but spout out pomposity and stand statue, today I am dead-centre maypole – that is, if I can keep myself upright – for everyone else's maniac shambles-dance. Hope you'll like it . . .

"Apologies, madam, for the squalor of this waiting-room, but –

> Why should Burbage build so foul a den
> Unless the gods delight in tragedies?

"Well?" He sat heavily, sweatily, crashing down closely beside her, nearly thrusting her off the hamper.

"You come to tell me I wrong your daughter. So I do. Did you ask her why? And if she told you, can you excuse her? Oh by God I'm sure you can't. You have a decency in your puritan black."

He had a definite indecency in his Senecan accoutrements, portions of which were straying about his legs. He fumbled ineptly with a gilded wreath which ought to have been on his brow but had caught in the top of his buskin.

She decided not to make the comment, and instead answered gently: "Sir, this is widow's black. My religion is in no wise relevant."

"Good: because neither is mine.

> Though Venus govern her desires,
> Saturn is dominator over – someone's –

but to neither abhorrent divinity today shall *I* burn any damned incense: perhaps you think, Bacchus? Already he has left me. When I get out on that stage, not a word mispositioned, you shall see."

And indeed he did seem to be catching a professional hold of himself. He firmly gripped on to the wreath and settled it, quite straight, above his eyes. He swayed to his feet and bunched up the toga to a shoulder-brooch. His movements were mechanical, but, at last, correct. He shook his head fiercely to banish his nonsense: and then smiled. "Apologies, madam," he said again, but this time without satire, "You've seen me at my worst. I've seen your daughter at her worst. Though in truth neither of us are devils. You'll know that of her already. I would be glad if you'd know it of me."

Lydia was perplexed. She had been so tormented-full of what she had come to tell him – full too of her own religious treachery, her apostasy even, in warning a supposed papist, a Jesuits' lackey, a – oh she knew not what he was, but heaven knew she should not be here –

his enemies were England's lieges, the man Topcliffe was the Queen's servant, Anthony Munday spoke with fervour of the 'awakened nation', and no-one had done more to wake it than Bale – no, she should not be here, and still less ought she to be here to defend Lucretia's vagaries, which is what it now appeared he was expecting her to do.

How could she begin? And with so little time. She could hear the other players in the tiring-house behind the wainscot clattering among their costumes, arguing, joking; and a murmur and bang of stage-hands outside on the platform hooking up curtains, dragging out and assembling the big set-pieces, 'City of Rome', 'Tomb of the Andronici', 'Woodland Glade' – she had seen this play at the Rose – a year ago? – and remembered it. Perhaps she should talk about that? At least, if she did, she need not start right in with her puritan reflections on the Poisonous Vice of Buggery, which, for some reason, were all she could immediately think of when she looked at his painted face and from there fell back into barbed fish-hook memories of Low-lyheart roaring in his schoolroom for some miserable child's breeches to be torn down for correction, so blind-souled ignorant he'd been (and she also) of what it was he'd really sought . . .

This was ridiculous: the man was impatient. She must say something: now.

"I saw this play at the Rose. I did not know you had written it. To what purpose the 'maniac shambles'? Sir, to what purpose? – severed hands, severed tongue, violation of rape, and devouring of man-flesh – oh sir, do you love cruelty? – for if you do, you must fear it, I mean in yourself: and if you fear it *in* yourself, then no doubt you fear it *for* yourself, and therefore my coming here . . ." She paused, out of breath, not at all certain of what she'd said.

His proximity was no less distressing than Munday's had been, except she felt no carnal temptation – thank heaven she did not: she was already beginning to wonder was she now quite as lewd as Cretia, her widow's weeds a black hypocrisy? Beginning to wonder? She had long known it. Yes, hypocrisy and she was damned. Old migraine of Calvin-Geneva clutched at her temple till she all but screamed with it. And yet she did this for the honour of Bale?

*

The Marcus-mask in front of her had gone suddenly grim, rigid mouth like a wound-scar cut across the strokes of face-paint.

"Why surely, it's an old play, madam, I would not write it today. We only present it to proclaim our contract-rights after a deed-of-exchange with Henslowe. By the same token he next week puts on a piece of ours. And thereby we clear the ledgers for our rewriting of *The Troublesome Reign*, as I think I mentioned yesterday, I don't know *what* I mentioned yesterday, my mind was a hurricane. Yet it is *my* play and I hold by it. 'Maniac shambles' is a cold-water well, where naked Truth shall sit and shudder.

"Not an hour ago in the Boar's Head, a discharged soldier from the Irish wars – or so he said: my own opinion, he had run from his colours to turn cutpurse – he caused half the idiot taproom to buy him drink upon drink as he bawled to us of death upon death, immeasurable mutilations, now, even now, in Enniskillen of Fermanagh, and how many in London had heard of it? I assure you *I* had not, yet it did not surprise me neither: did they know in Milan or Naples, or even in the suburbs of Rome, just exact what gallonage of blood the Andronicus scullions had to swab away down their masters' drain-channels?"

She had her cue and took it, asked him directly how much did *he* know of the close-windowed house in Westminster, of the fellow-poet that was its pimp, of the terror of religion that made all these matters possible, of his own peril, of her abasement that it should be her religion and her father's that now laid out its nets to catch him?

He heard her in a wild astonishment: waited while she sobbed dry-eyed. And then he laughed. She was sure he was not laughing out of amusement.

"And you are the daughter of Bale, that lived his life against the papists and lived his life against corrupt flesh, and would have forced with his bilious pen all this England into rectitude, considering never whether we wanted it or not? And now, in your fulfilled years, when you find that we don't want it, and you find that you yourself no longer want it either – but you do not truly know what you *do* want – you come to me to tell me I am a papist and in danger.

"And because I whored your daughter and have corrupted – or am corrupted by – a sweet young whore of mine own sex (and high station of nobility) – I say 'because' and not 'although' – because of this, you are my partisan, my only informed protector? I had thought you were Volumnia, whose random son was Coriolanus, whereas she remained imperdurable, bronze and porphyry of the Capitol . . . But now I think rather you are that high Egyptian that inveigled Antony into ruin and thereafter in luxurious joy made her ruin out of his. Why, madam, you are glorious.''

He laughed again, and his three bad teeth seemed to strike at her from out of his mouth like rusty bird-shot. She felt herself blush hot red, face, neck, and all down herself underneath her seemly busks.

'Very well, sir, if you mock me. I have told you my message. Good day.''

"No – !'' He caught her sleeve – "I don't mock, and you must not go. But I have to be short with you. The play is about to begin.

"First, I am no papist. My mother was, and she taught me so, *her* church, and I warm to it still. Beauty-of holiness, the sure enclosure of her Great Mother's arms which will never fail. But they failed. And all we find in the garden where she sang her songs are little twitching men like grasshoppers, they jerk in dismay among a litter of crumbled bones, they are impotently bleeding at nostril-hole and ear. With horror, with admiration, with most monstrous incomprehension, I went to Tyburn against my nature to – to *observe* – the death of Southwell. All I knew when I had seen it was that God did not desire it: not desire them to kill him, nor yet that he should will himself to suffer himself to be killed. He died like valiant Hector: he died for a dogmatical whirr of equivocating black-gowned grasshoppers.

"Then next, this wolf's-head Munday. He believes out of his jealousy that I am another Marlowe – another Munday, you could also say – winding myself in plot and counterplot till head-to-foot I'm a roll of spiderweb. Not so: and if he gropes at me through his brandywine the same way he groped at you, to catch at a loose end and unravel me like a rotten rag, he'll discover he has hold of nothing but a damned slippery gliding lizard-shape that runs into the running stream and can neither be seen nor touched.

"Mrs Lowlyheart, you're a slippery woman, though you will not admit it, you belong to this age, not your father's: and you swim with the best of us. Look at me: a poet with patrons, two of them. My personal red-haired boy with his white flanks and his treachery, he was for my private muse – and *into* her, moreover, he stole her away and I'm done with him. But not lost, I have the other. The men of this Theatre are the Lord Chamberlain's, his name is on the playbill, his protection unbreakable, unless we are so foolish as to throw it in his beard. As his servants we have servants' access to his knowledgeable backstairs. Do you know what fluttered out to us, from the bottom of those stairs, a little leaf of waste paper that missed its place in milord's rubbish-fire?"

He paused, and she could hear the Theatre's music tuning-up in the gallery above. His voice had dropped, his next few words were as though spoken to his own thoughts, clipped, quiet, exulting: "Wolf Topcliffe is a dead wolf, nail his head over the sheepfold gate. Very shortly, I don't know how shortly, but short and certain he goes to gaol. Exceeding his powers, extortion, false witness, it will all be proved. But between ourselves, for our own security, for security of your careless daughter – not a word of it outside. Wolves can glide as well as lizards, and we'll lose him if it's breathed."

"And Munday? Will he too –?"

"Oh I hope not: most discomfortable for the business if makers of plays once again were to be seen as rolls of spiderweb, we had enough of that with Marlowe. But it'll mean he's lost King John and lost him for ever – but of course he has anyway. I daresay he could always re-use his notions in some other disguise, as for instance the by-plot for a merry tale of Robin Hood, or something o'that; but his history-play *per se* is ours: Henslowe sold it over his head. Prompt-screed and rough-draft, they're on that shelf there: and look at this – we bought this too –"

*

He twisted his body round to fumble among papers that were piled all higgledy-piggledy. He pulled this one out and then that, and stopped, suddenly transfixed: Lydia thought for a moment he had pierced his finger on a nail, so sharply he drew in his breath.

· He yelped, "Yah!' – and then, more easily, "Madam, d'you believe in omens? *There's* a paperweight." He shot his elbow inward to let her see past the flounces of his shirt. He was grasping the corner of a stained and dog-eared sheaf of manuscript, for which he had had to burrow.

Sitting on top of it, previously obscured by three or four other scripts, was a tallow-coloured human hand. Plastered with blood, its truncated wrist ending in a hash of bloody fibres and bone-ends.

If he had expected to terrify Lydia he was mistaken: she knew where she was, she knew what was papier-maché and what was flesh, and only yesterday she had met Topcliffe. Between the real horror and the stage-pretence, no point of similarity. But of course she was momentarily startled: so was he, and that pleased her. He was still, quite observably, twitching. She gulped, smiled – a condescending smile, which she thought he resented – and asked him, "You said you bought? You bought what?"

"This."

He slid the manuscript out from under the severed hand and held it toward her. She read the thick-nibbed title.

PRO JOANNE ANGLORUM REGE: tragicall-hystorycall enterludes, compyled by Johan Bale, new-wryt in myne owne hand for my lord Privy Seal hys players.

She caught a glimpse of the first speech, headed 'Baleus Prolocutor'.

He slammed it down on an empty shelf. If *he* believed in omens, it might account for the way he spoke, a man with a cold grue running the length of his spine.

"For where did Henslowe find it? I think it was never printed. Munday and his colleagues used it. I shan't: I'll use *them*, and I'll use the chronicles, but your father is a dead wolf." His gratuitous malice was abrupt, no doubt involuntary, shockingly hurtful nonetheless.

Lydia hit him, hard across his face, with wide-open palm: she saw the smeared grease-paint on it, rubbed it off with the other palm, stood panting blue-handed like a druid-woman out of Julius Caesar's book.

He said: "Hit me and hit me again: but plays that would prove history to be more than a maniac shambles are plumed untruth cocking and crowing on a dry-rot scaffold, every line of 'em brings a new murder." He too was gasping and he spoke in violent haste, too strongly perhaps, perhaps what he said was not his maturely-considered view. If so, he had no chance to consider it, because the book-keeper hot-and-bothered pushed in between them, calling him out for his work, processional-entry, Act One, Scene One – "Why, you've not even made your face yet; or if you've made it, it needs mending. And for God's sake don't forget, you've to carry the emperor's crown, I've laid it out on the prop-table, you should ha' thought of it yourself . . . Name o' Mary, how did *that* get in here! They've been hunting it all over the tiring-house, I told Titus, if it couldn't be found he'd have to amputate himself in all verity."

*

He snatched up the red hand and hurried off, leaving Lydia with her pair of blue ones. Marcus Andronicus too was going out at the door: she could never remember afterwards just how she decided to do what she did next. It could be thought a small felony, but in such a cause she would gladly put 'thief' to her name. She seized hold of the manuscript, the ill-stitched title-page came asunder in her grip, but she stuffed the whole crumpled packet into her bodice. No Lord Chamberlain's knave should nail up her father's *dead wolf's head* here as a damned trophy of superannuated oblivion.

She trudged back towards Bishopsgate, did not look round behind her at the Shoreditch fields with their flooded ponds, half-starved suburban cattle knee-deep in the mud-plashes; nor, amongst them, at the two thronged playhouses, Theatre and Curtain, flags flying, money chinking-in at the doors.

She felt her skin thicken with the muggy heat of the afternoon, she felt the signs of a coming plague-summer, she must wash and wash again: and Lucretia must wash. If she wouldn't, she would scrub her herself. God knows, they both needed it, and oh God! how her head was aching. She made up her mind that Munday had been right about his rival – "He divides his plays this way and that, until no-one knows what they mean' – quite impossible to say so of Bale: whatever the faults of her father's truth, he had seen it most firmly and held to it: and this Shoreditch Ambidexter could never have lived without him. Self-tortured cruel small Munday, with his love for his torture-house and his dry lust for her own dried body, had to that degree been *right*: but if she were to try to explain it in such a season of gliding lizards, would anyone ever agree with her?